the greatest thing

Sarah Winifred Searle

:01

First Second

New York

First Second

Published by First Second
First Second is an imprint of Roaring Brook Press,
a division of Holtzbrinck Publishing Holdings Limited Partnership
120 Broadway, New York, NY 10271
firstsecondbooks.com

No references in this book to real organizations are intended to suggest any authorization, endorsement, or sponsorship by such organizations.

Library of Congress Control Number: 2021909951

Our books may be purchased in bulk for promotional, educational, or business use. Please contact your local bookseller or the Macmillan Corporate and Premium Sales Department at (800) 221-7945 ext. 5442 or by email at MacmillanSpecialMarkets@macmillan.com.

First edition, 2022
Edited by Robyn Chapman and Hazel Newlevant
Cover and interior book design by Molly Johanson
Authenticity readers: Gia Drew, Melanie Gillman, and Mey Rude
With special thanks to Janina Scarlet, PhD

Drawn and colored in Clip Studio Paint on an iPad.

Printed in China

ISBN 978-1-250-29723-5 (paperback)
10 9 8 7 6 5 4 3 2 1

ISBN 978-1-250-29722-8 (hardcover)
10 9 8 7 6 5 4 3 2 1

Don't miss your next favorite book from First Second! For the latest updates go to firstsecondnewsletter.com and sign up for our enewsletter.

*For Adam
and Matthew*

Content Note:
This book contains depictions
of self-harm and disordered eating.

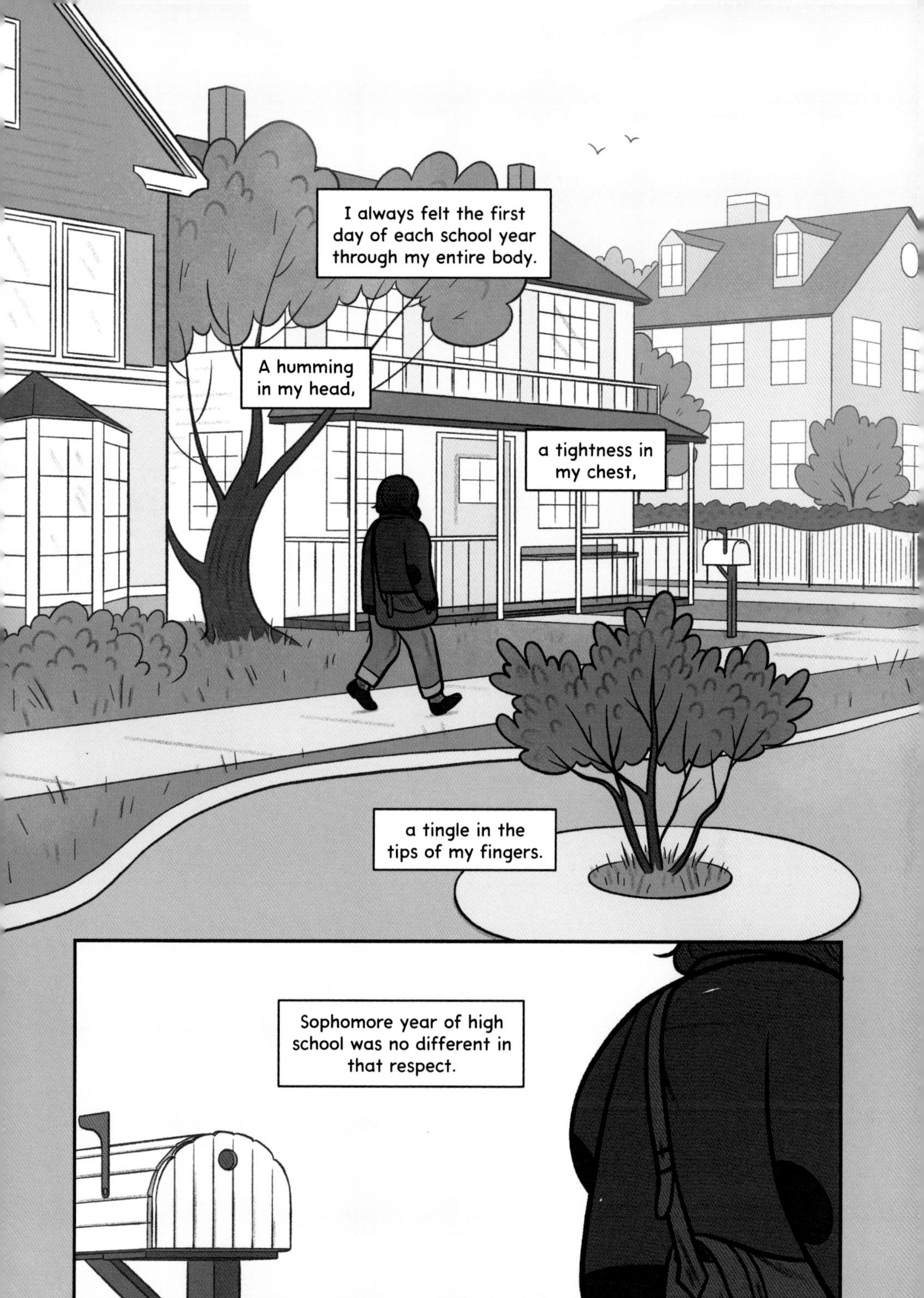
I always felt the first day of each school year through my entire body.
A humming in my head,
a tightness in my chest,
a tingle in the tips of my fingers.
Sophomore year of high school was no different in that respect.

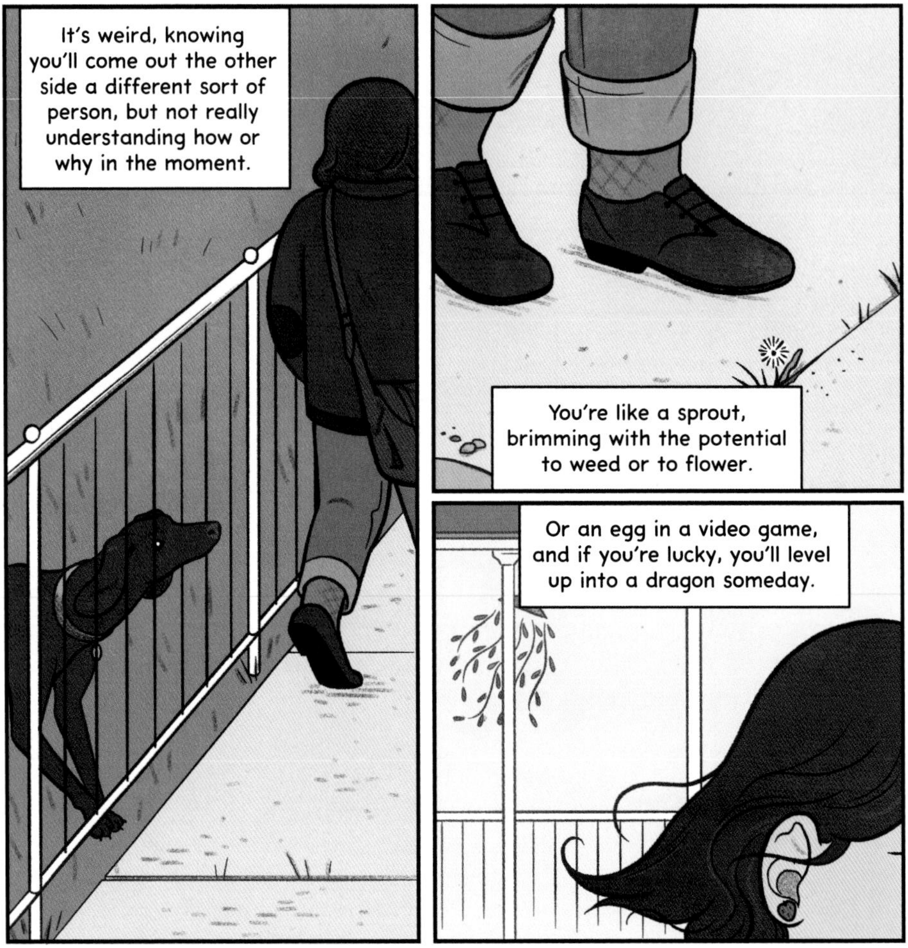
It's weird, knowing you'll come out the other side a different sort of person, but not really understanding how or why in the moment.
You're like a sprout, brimming with the potential to weed or to flower.
Or an egg in a video game, and if you're lucky, you'll level up into a dragon someday.

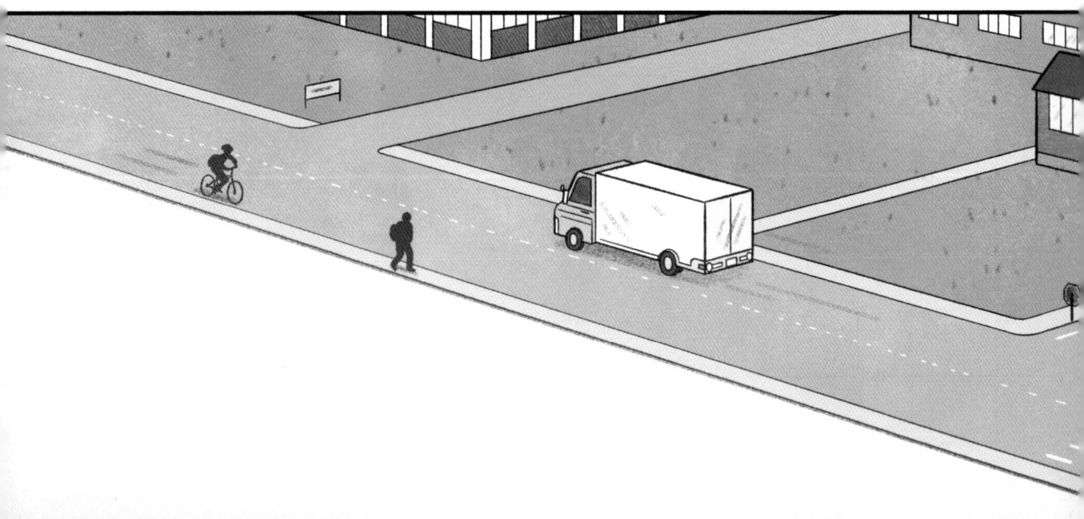

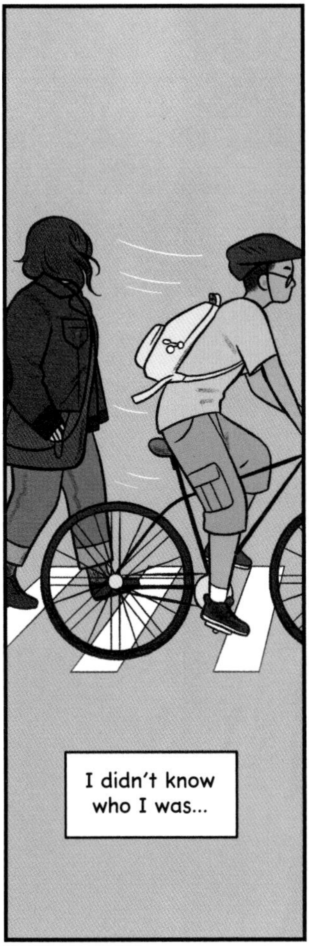
I didn't know
who I was...

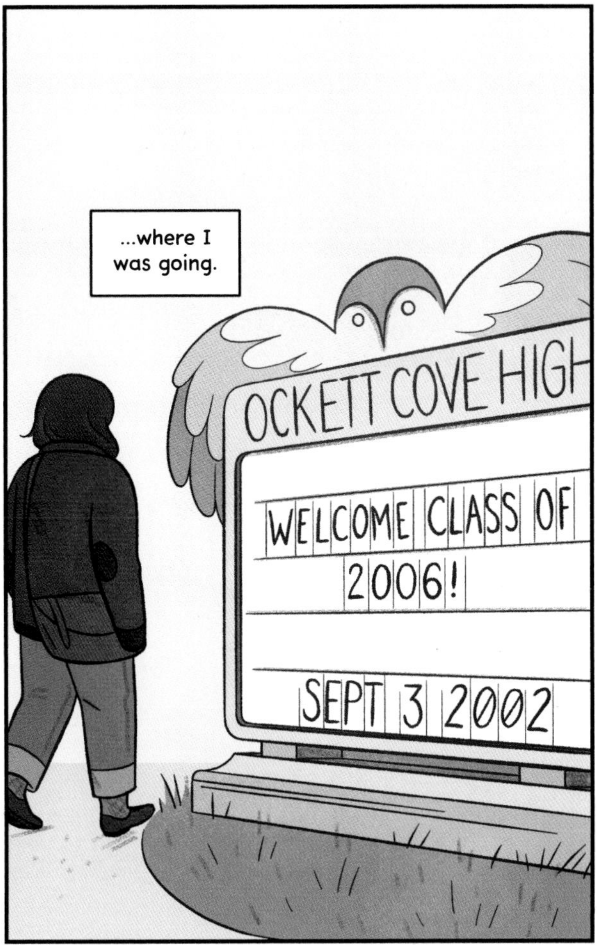
...where I
was going.
OCKETT COVE HIGH
WELCOME CLASS OF
2006!
SEPT 3 2002

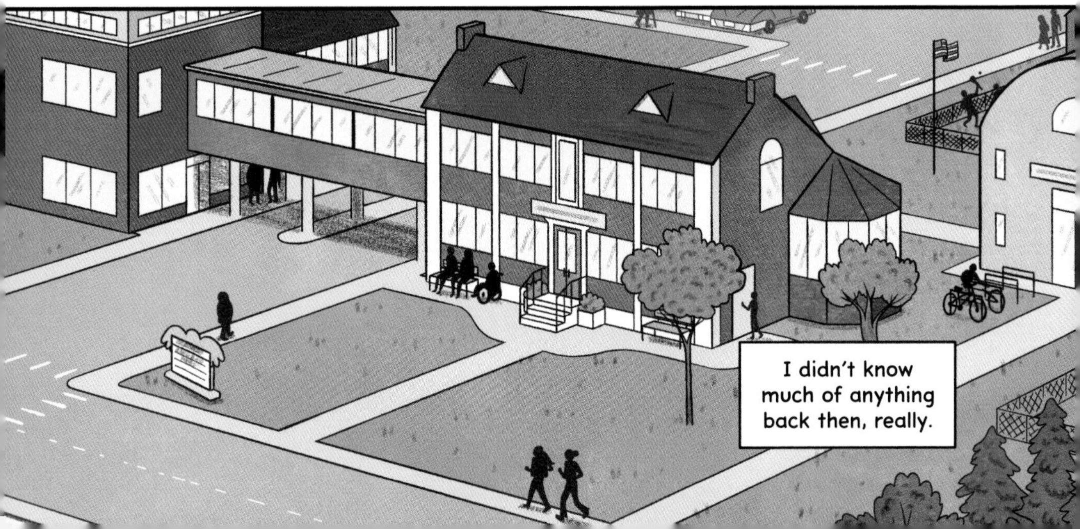
I didn't know
much of anything
back then, really.

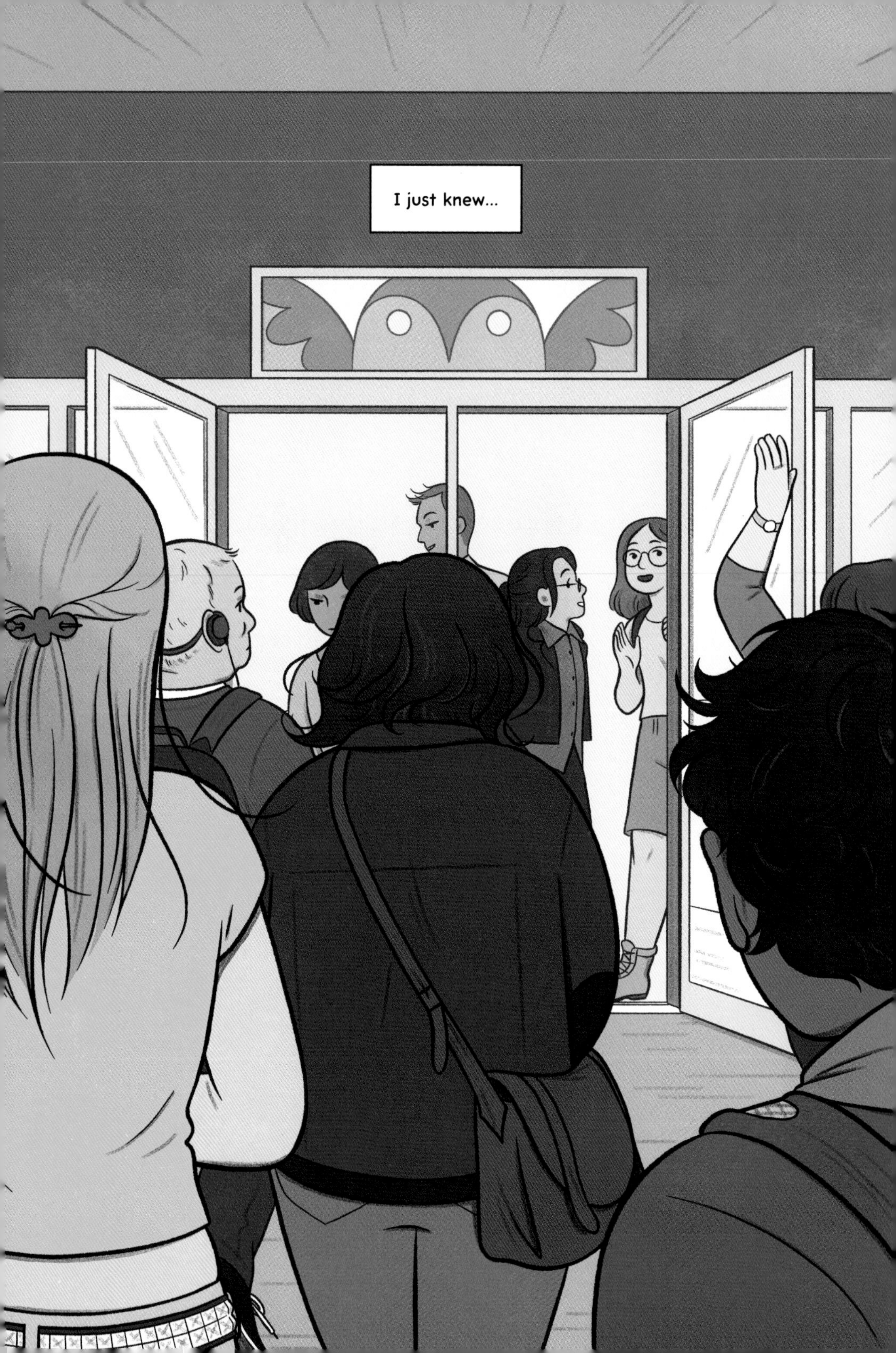
I just knew...

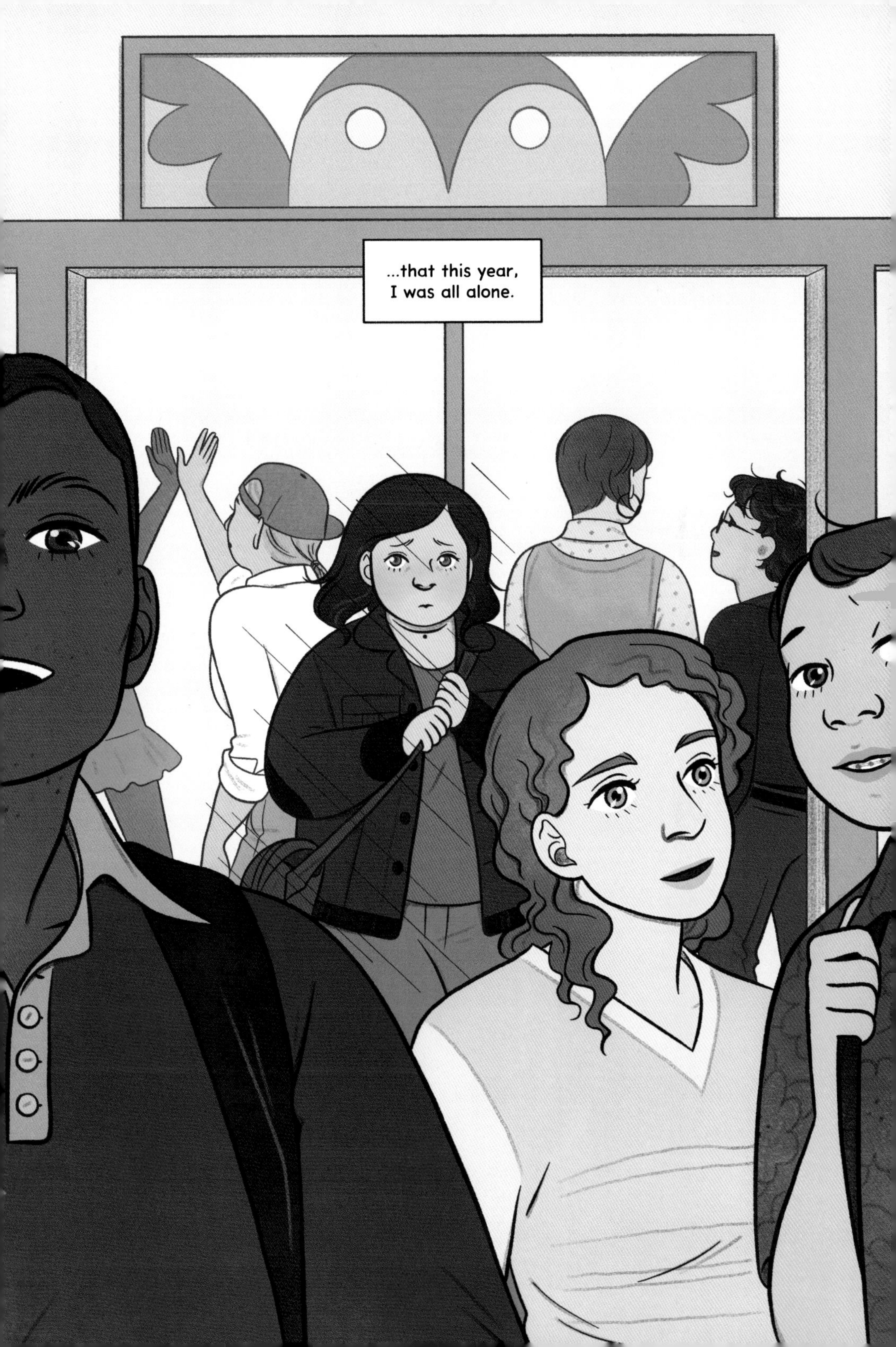
...that this year,
I was all alone.

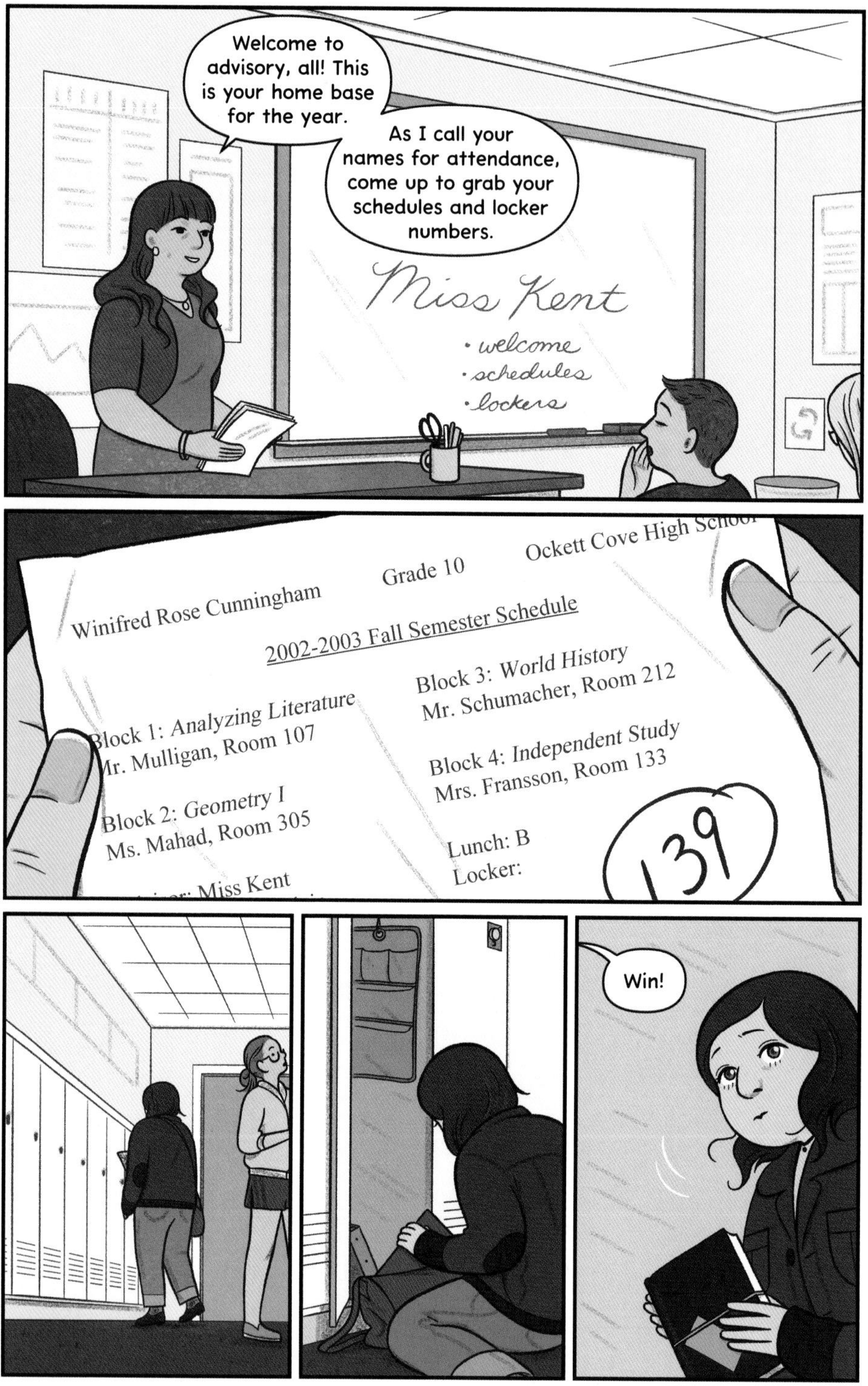
Welcome to advisory, all! This is your home base for the year.
As I call your names for attendance, come up to grab your schedules and locker numbers.
Miss Kent
• welcome
• schedules
• lockers
Winifred Rose Cunningham
Grade 10
Ockett Cove High Sch
2002-2003 Fall Semester Schedule
lock 1: Analyzing Literature
r. Mulligan, Room 107
Block 2: Geometry I
Ms. Mahad, Room 305
Miss Kent
Block 3: World History
Mr. Schumacher, Room 212
Block 4: Independent Study
Mrs. Fransson, Room 133
Lunch: B
Locker:
139
Win!

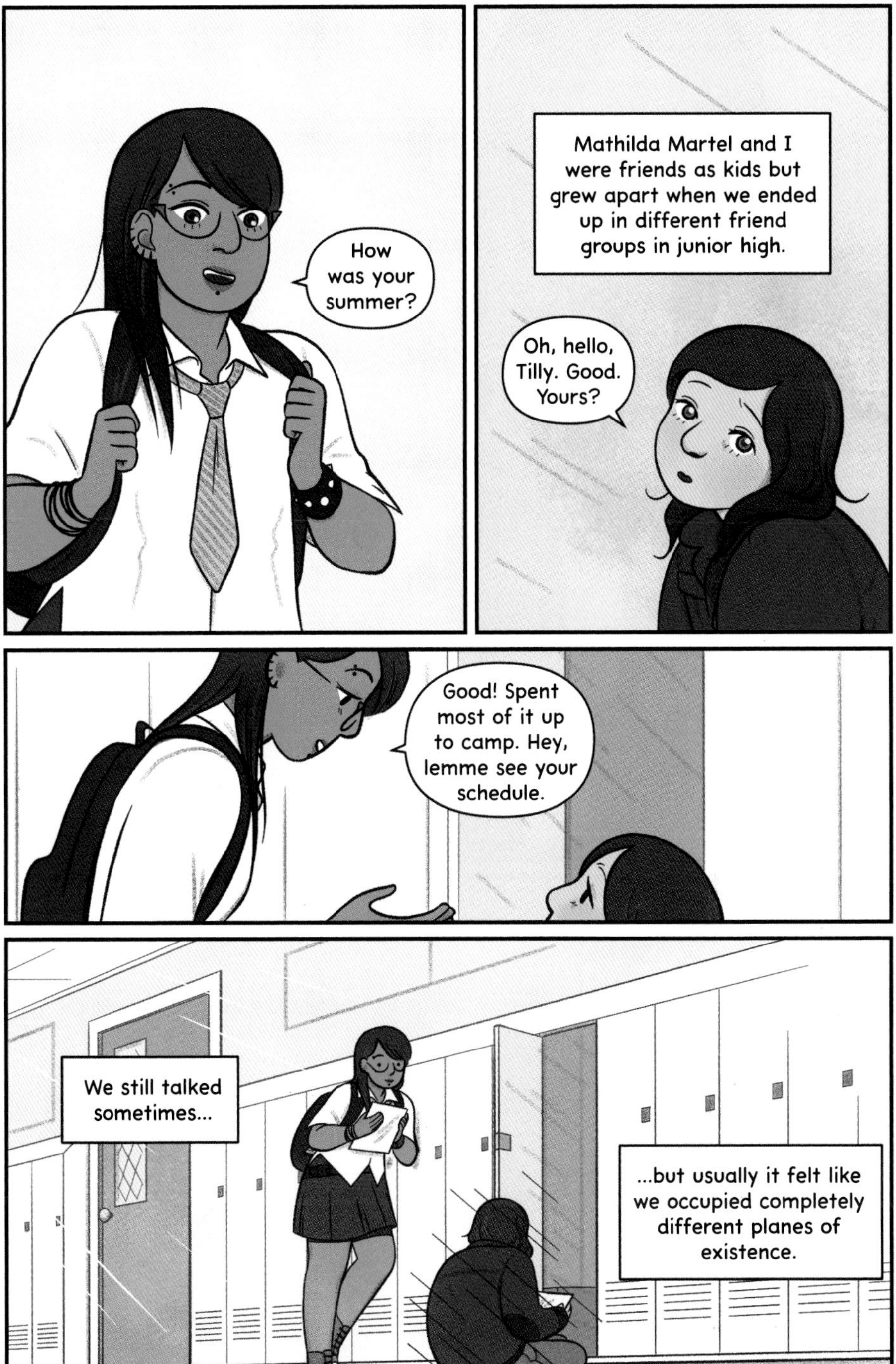
How was your summer?
Mathilda Martel and I were friends as kids but grew apart when we ended up in different friend groups in junior high.
Oh, hello, Tilly. Good. Yours?
Good! Spent most of it up to camp. Hey, lemme see your schedule.
We still talked sometimes...
...but usually it felt like we occupied completely different planes of existence.

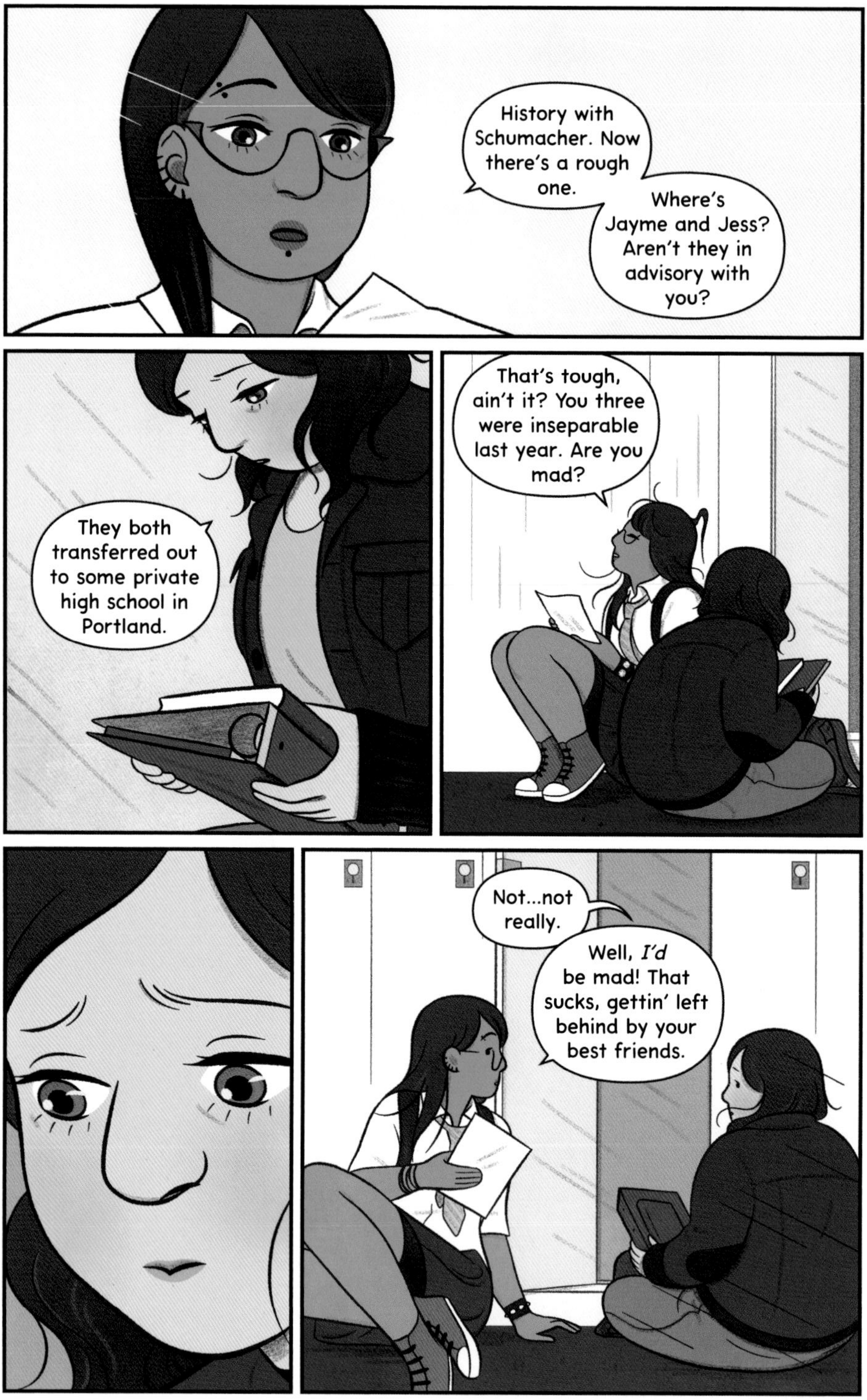
History with Schumacher. Now there's a rough one.
Where's Jayme and Jess? Aren't they in advisory with you?
They both transferred out to some private high school in Portland.
That's tough, ain't it? You three were inseparable last year. Are you mad?
Not...not really.
Well, *I'd* be mad! That sucks, gettin' left behind by your best friends.

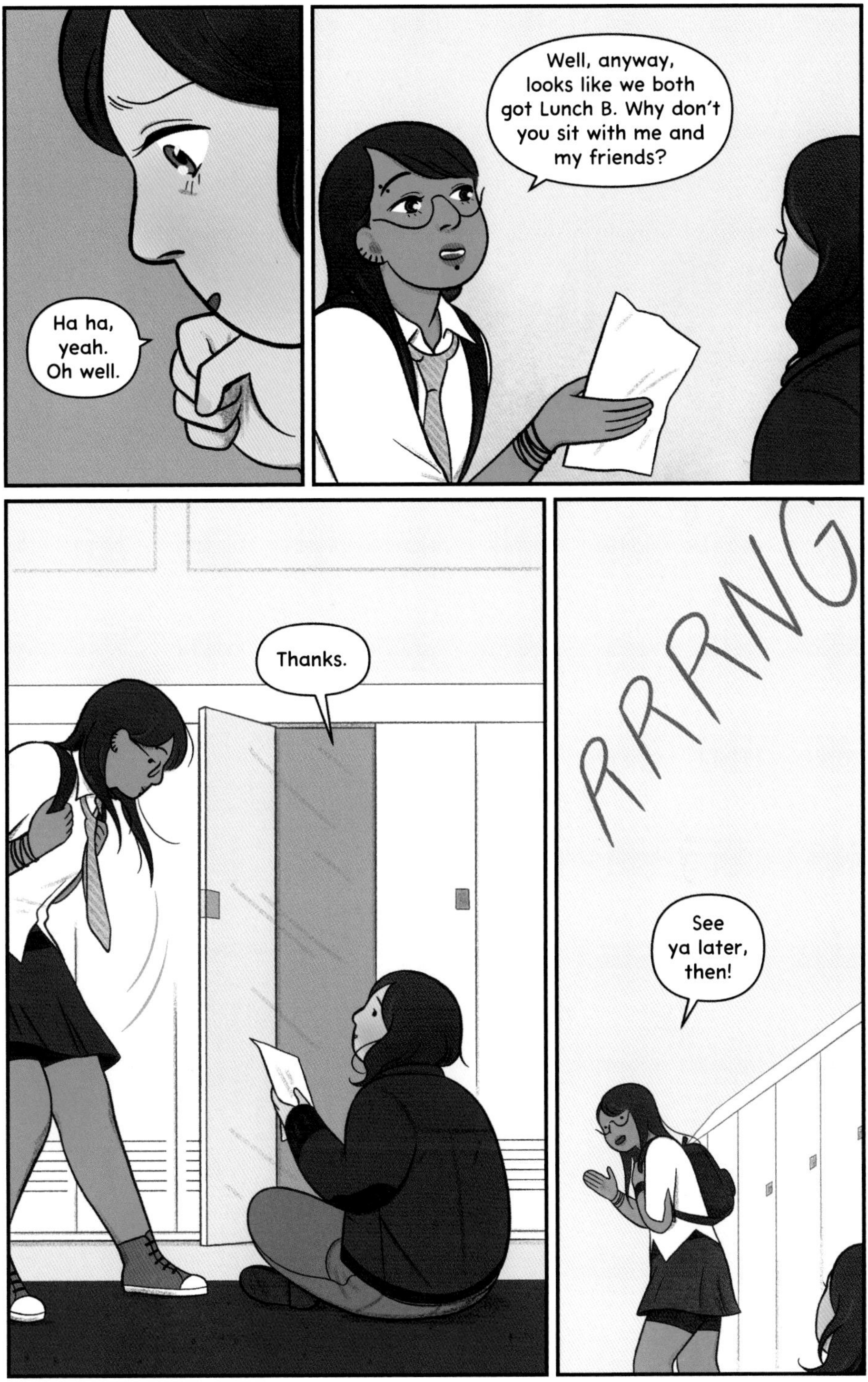
Ha ha, yeah. Oh well.
Well, anyway, looks like we both got Lunch B. Why don't you sit with me and my friends?
Thanks.
RRRNG
See ya later, then!

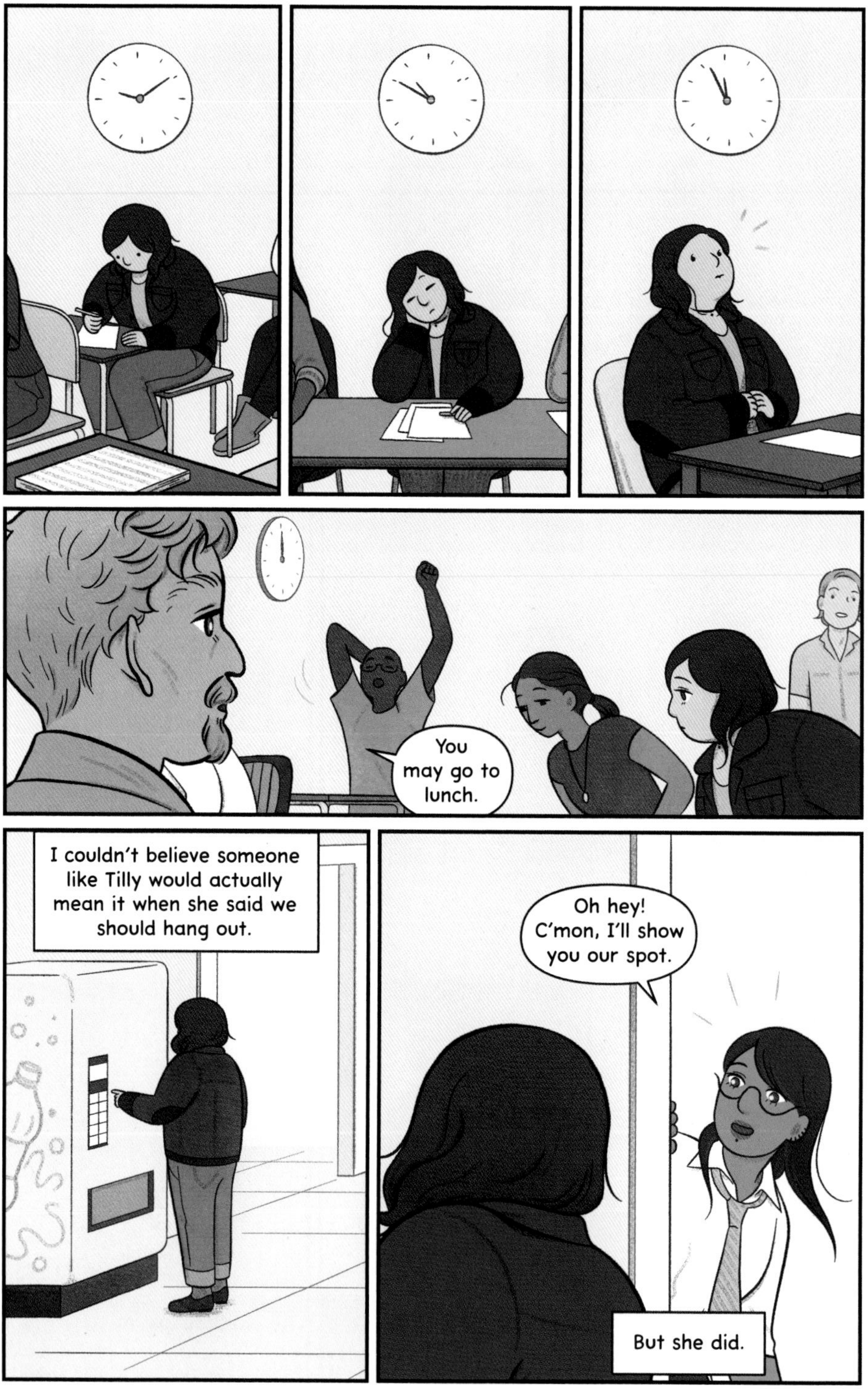
You may go to lunch.
I couldn't believe someone like Tilly would actually mean it when she said we should hang out.
Oh hey! C'mon, I'll show you our spot.
But she did.

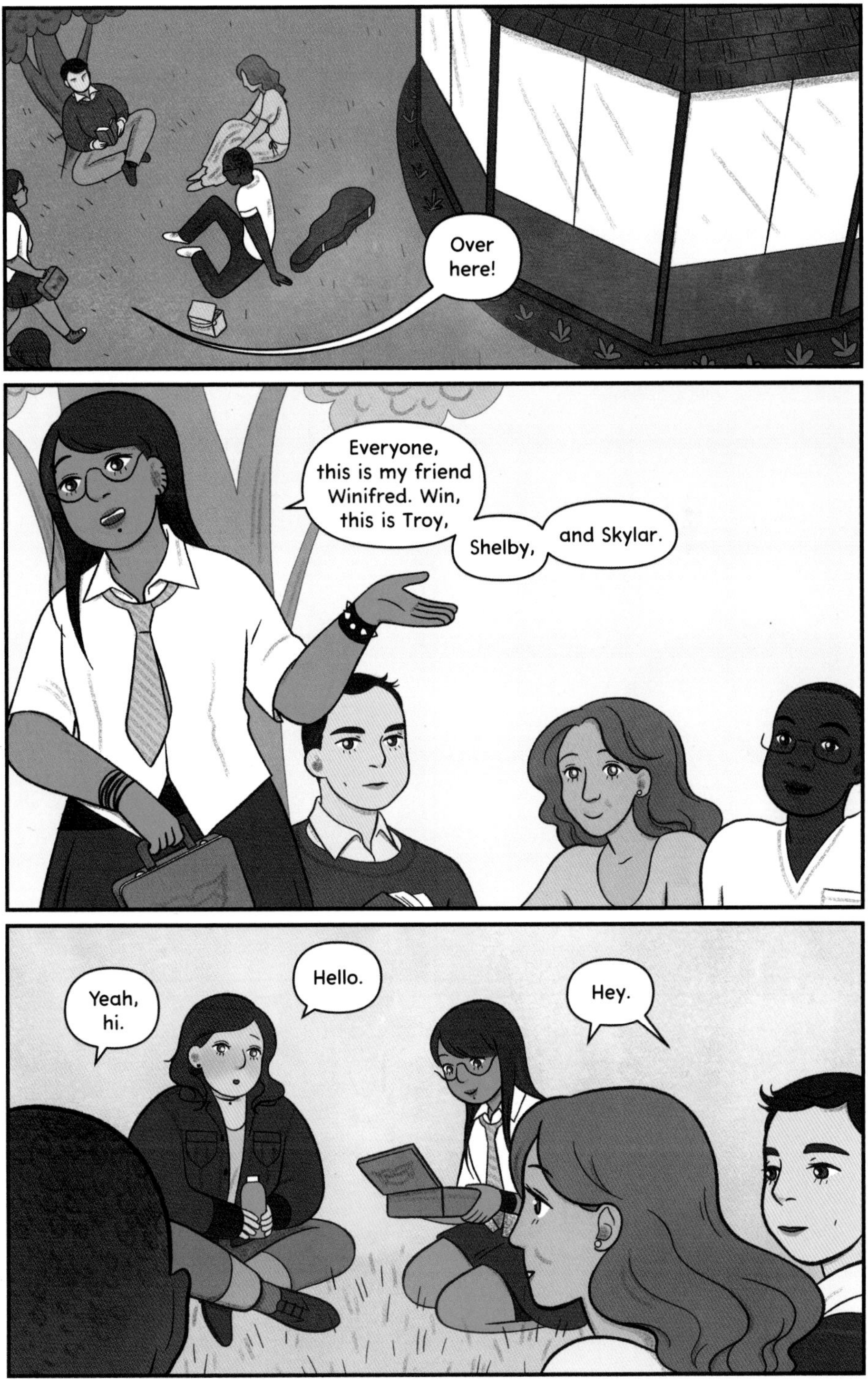
Over here!
Everyone, this is my friend Winifred. Win, this is Troy,
Shelby,
and Skylar.
Yeah, hi.
Hello.
Hey.

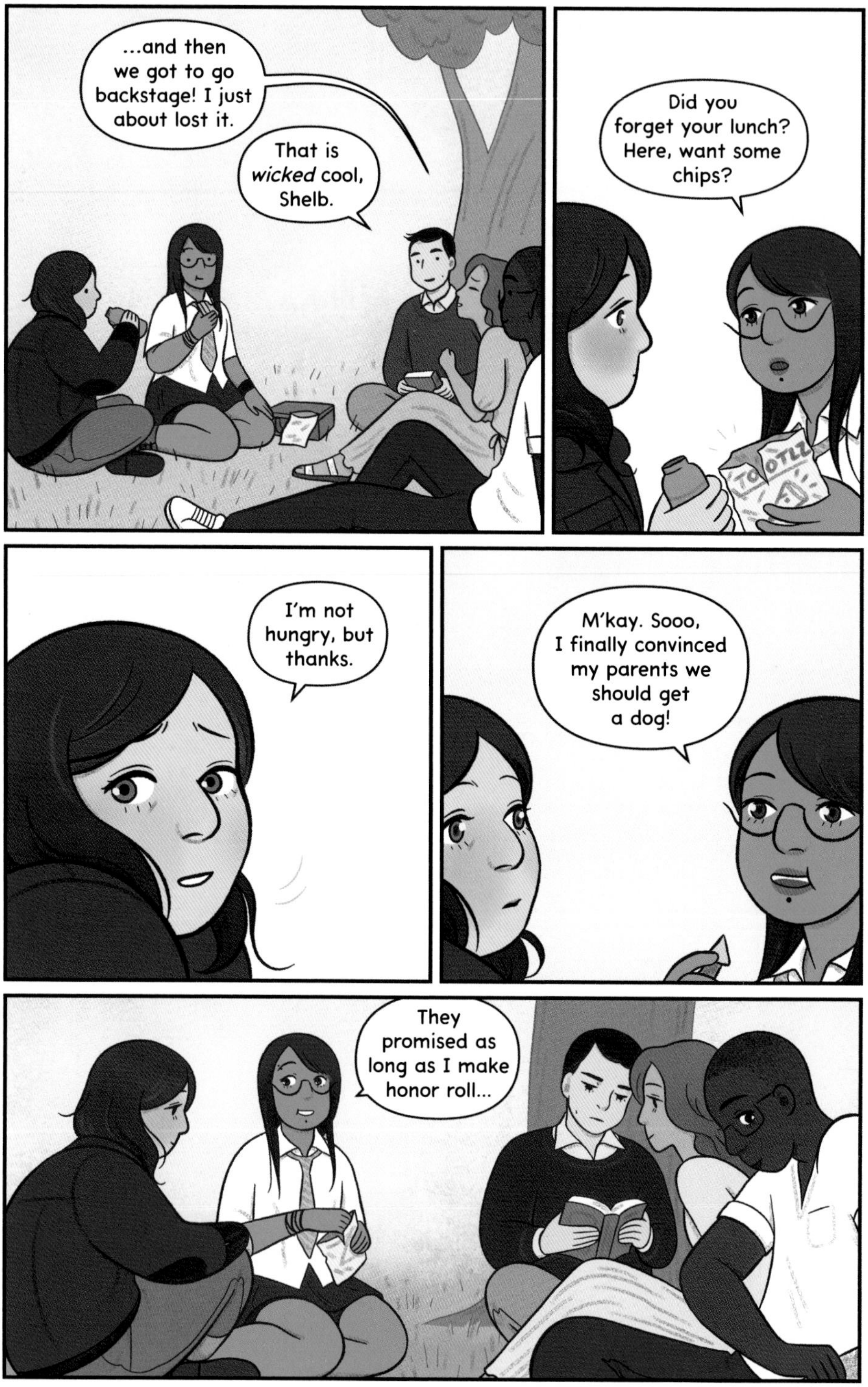
...and then we got to go backstage! I just about lost it.
That is wicked cool, Shelb.
Did you forget your lunch? Here, want some chips?
I'm not hungry, but thanks.
M'kay. Sooo, I finally convinced my parents we should get a dog!
They promised as long as I make honor roll...

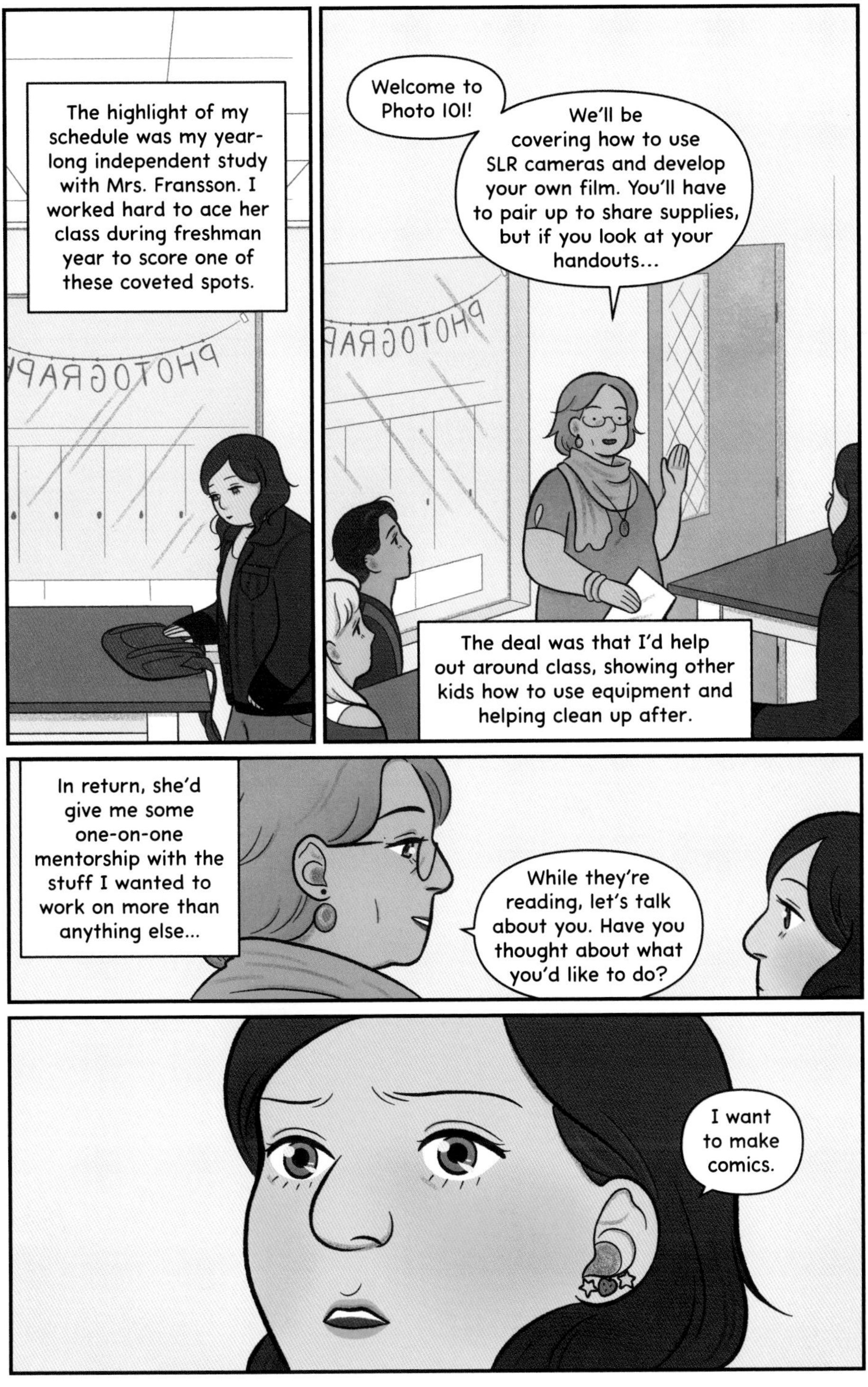

The highlight of my schedule was my year-long independent study with Mrs. Fransson. I worked hard to ace her class during freshman year to score one of these coveted spots.
Welcome to Photo 101!
We'll be covering how to use SLR cameras and develop your own film. You'll have to pair up to share supplies, but if you look at your handouts...
The deal was that I'd help out around class, showing other kids how to use equipment and helping clean up after.
In return, she'd give me some one-on-one mentorship with the stuff I wanted to work on more than anything else...
While they're reading, let's talk about you. Have you thought about what you'd like to do?
I want to make comics.

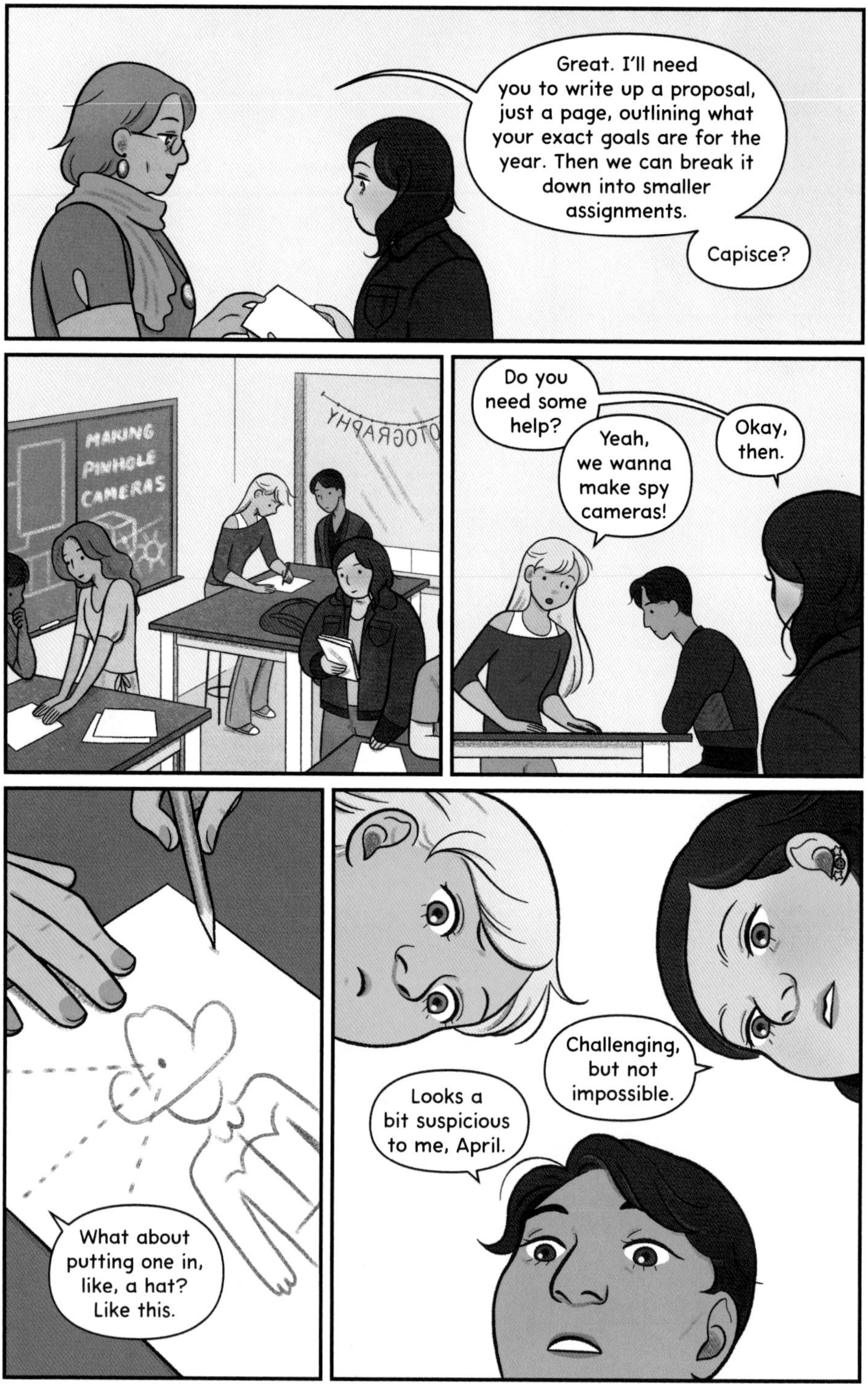
Great. I'll need you to write up a proposal, just a page, outlining what your exact goals are for the year. Then we can break it down into smaller assignments.
Capisce?
MAKING PINHOLE CAMERAS
Do you need some help?
Yeah, we wanna make spy cameras!
Okay, then.
What about putting one in, like, a hat? Like this.
Challenging, but not impossible.
Looks a bit suspicious to me, April.

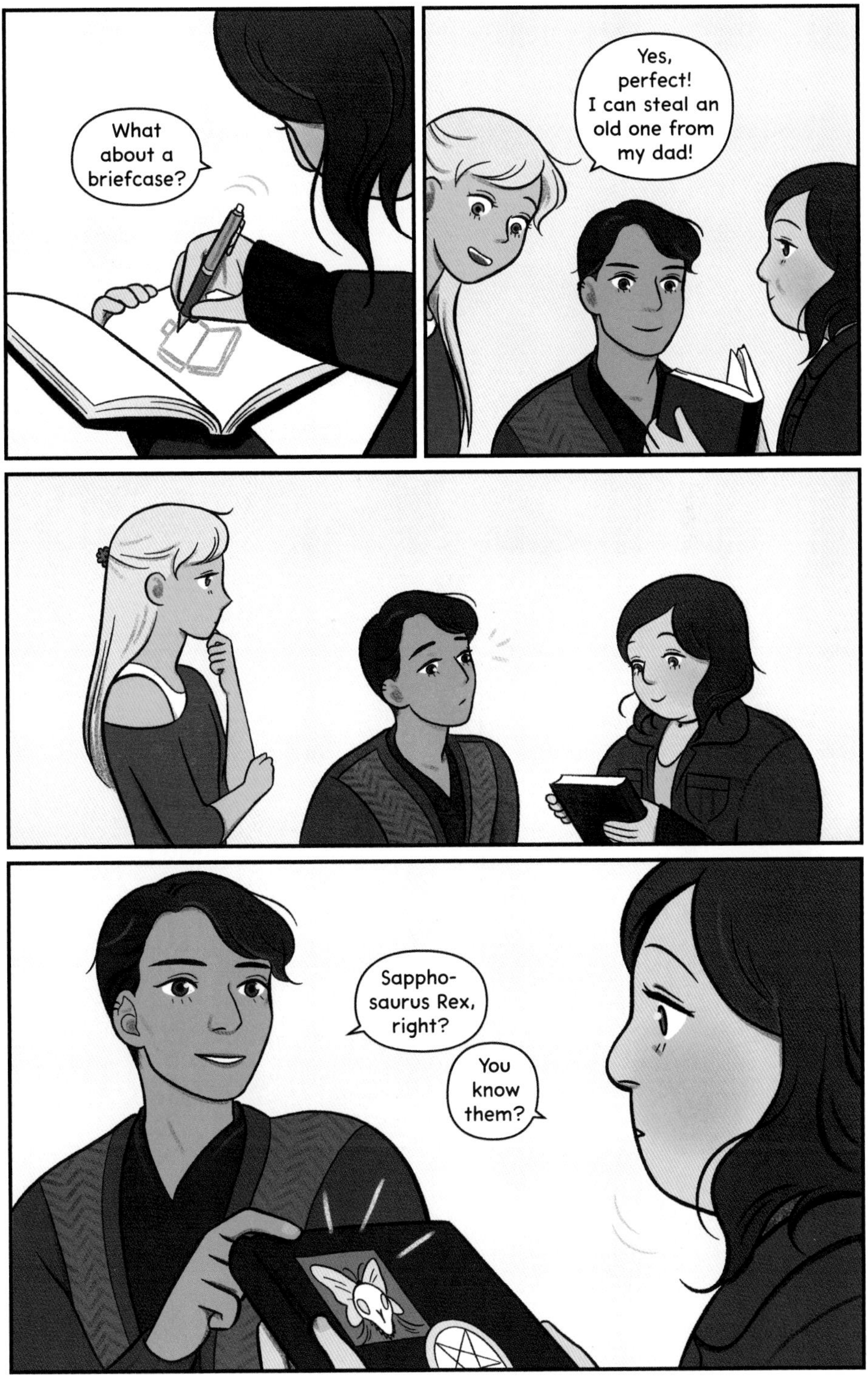
What about a briefcase?
Yes, perfect! I can steal an old one from my dad!
Sappho-saurus Rex, right?
You know them?

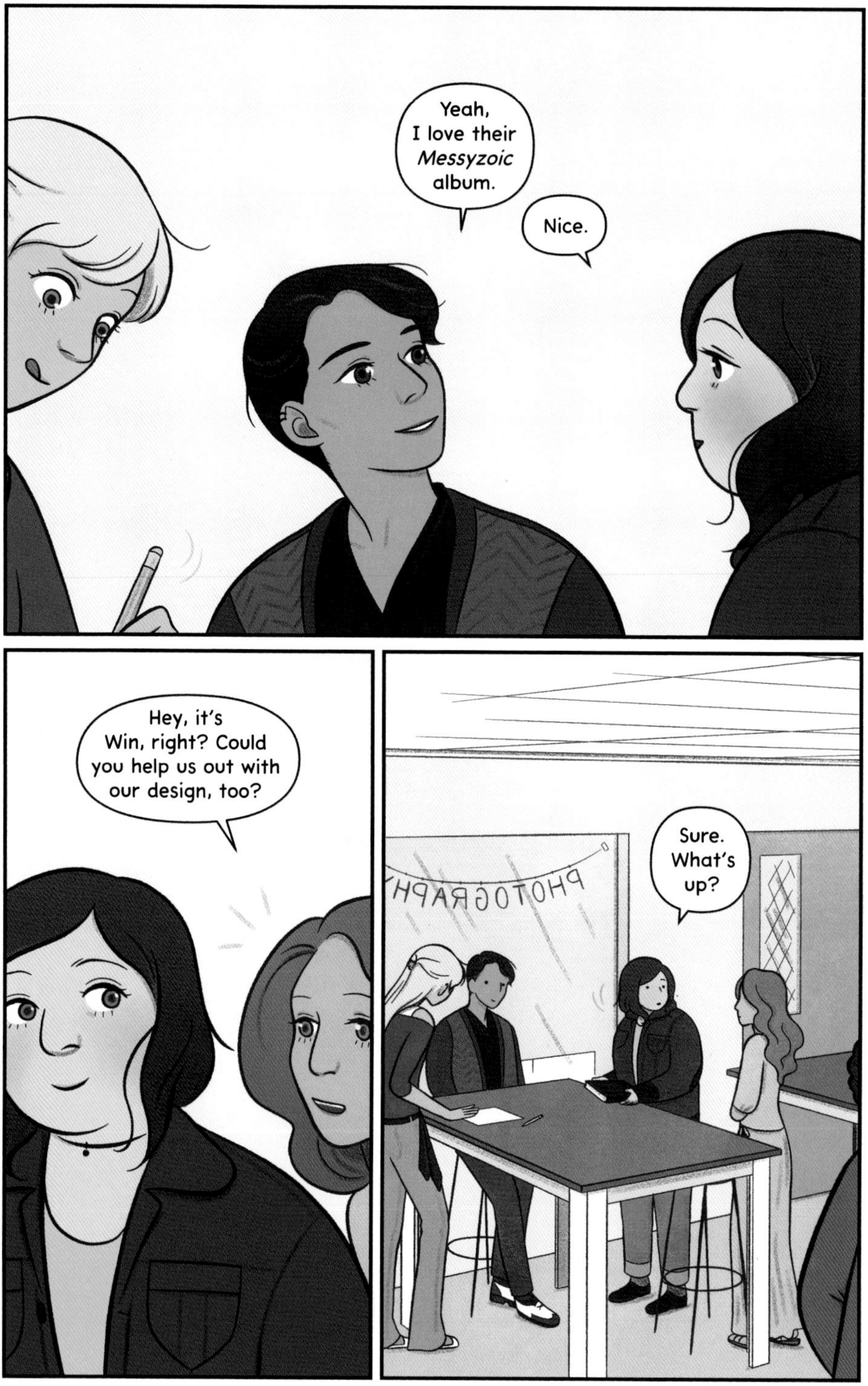
Yeah, I love their *Messyzoic* album.
Nice.
Hey, it's Win, right? Could you help us out with our design, too?
PHOTOGRAPHY
Sure. What's up?

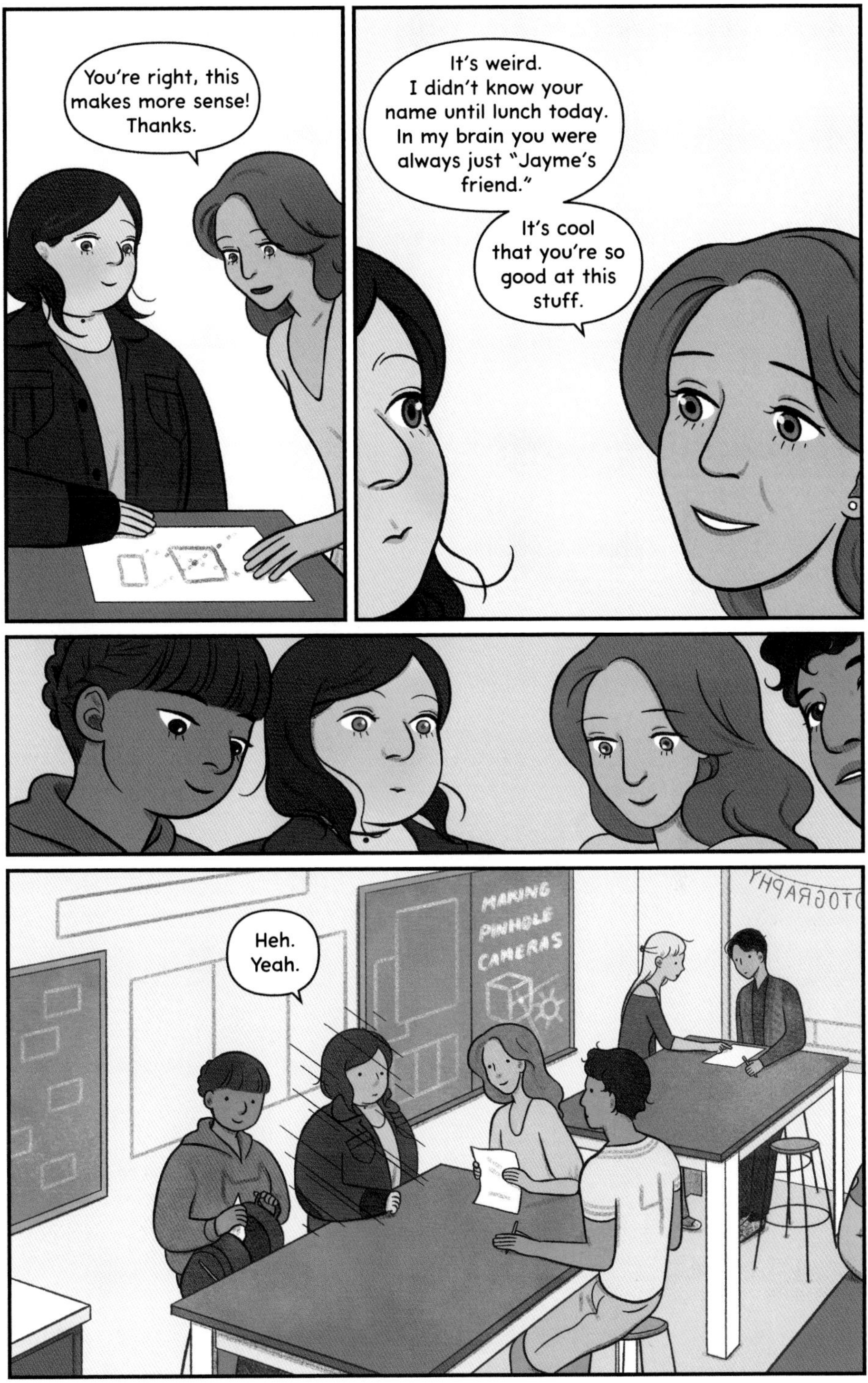
You're right, this makes more sense! Thanks.
It's weird. I didn't know your name until lunch today. In my brain you were always just "Jayme's friend."
It's cool that you're so good at this stuff.
MAKING PINHOLE CAMERAS
Heh. Yeah.

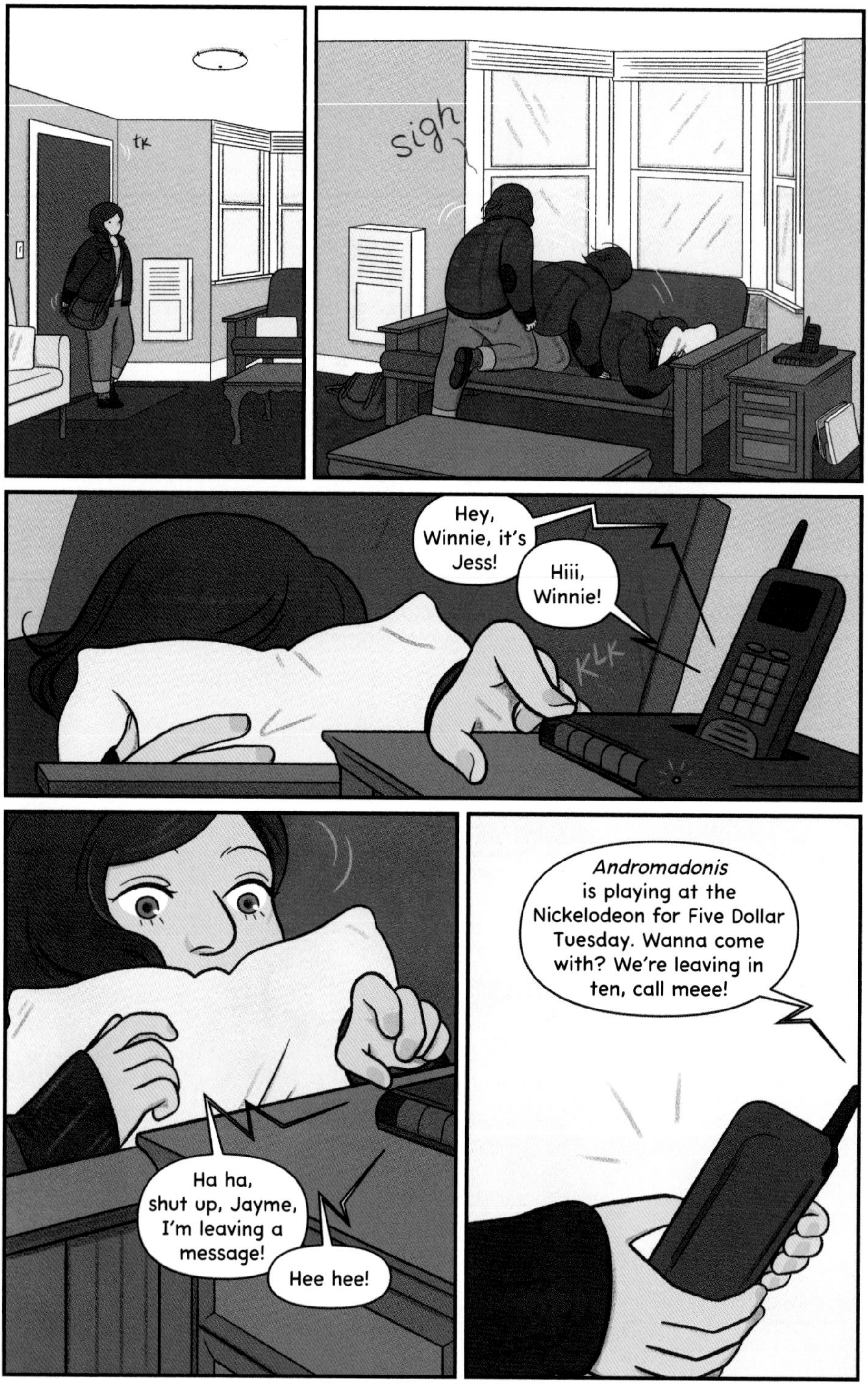
tk
sigh
Hey, Winnie, it's Jess!
Hiii, Winnie!
KLK
Ha ha, shut up, Jayme, I'm leaving a message!
Hee hee!
Andromadonis is playing at the Nickelodeon for Five Dollar Tuesday. Wanna come with? We're leaving in ten, call meee!

RNGG

RNGGG
RNGG

KLK

You've reached the Reed residence. We can't come to the phone right now, but—

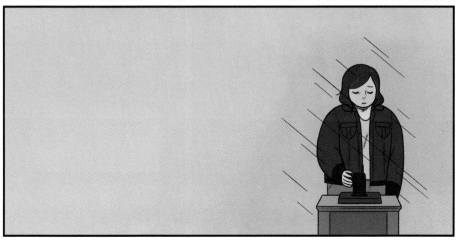

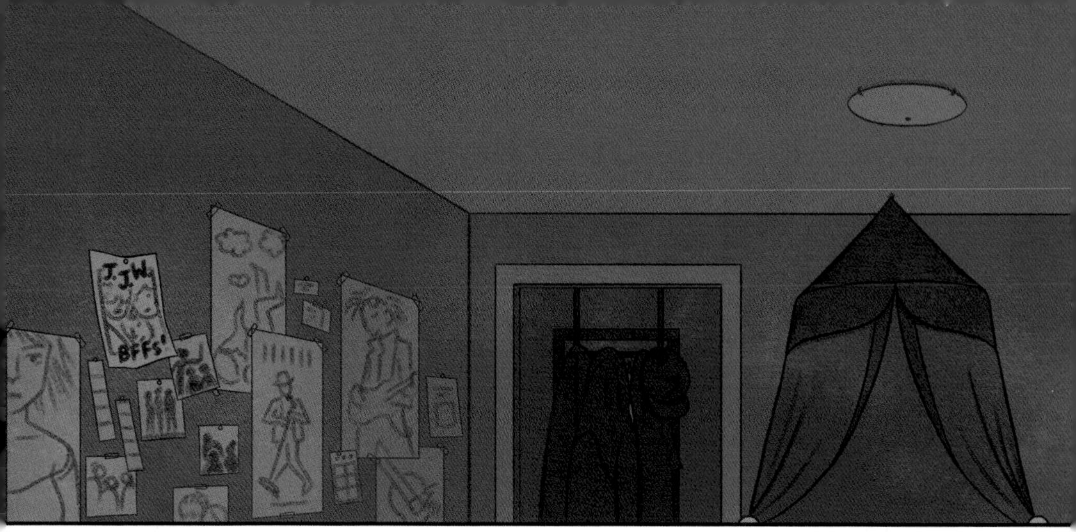

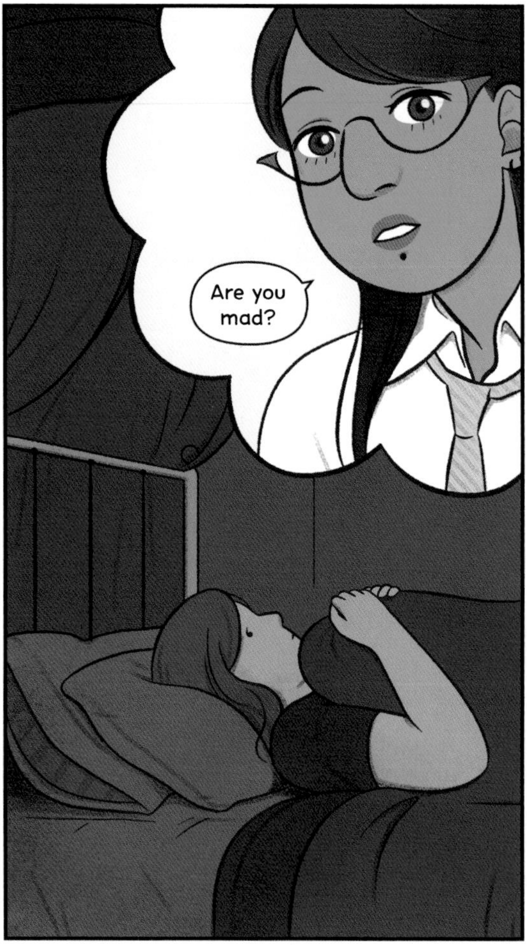
Are you mad?

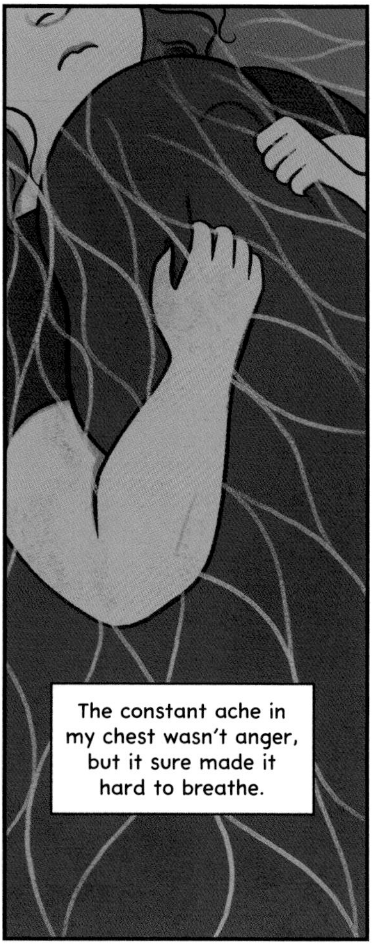
The constant ache in my chest wasn't anger, but it sure made it hard to breathe.

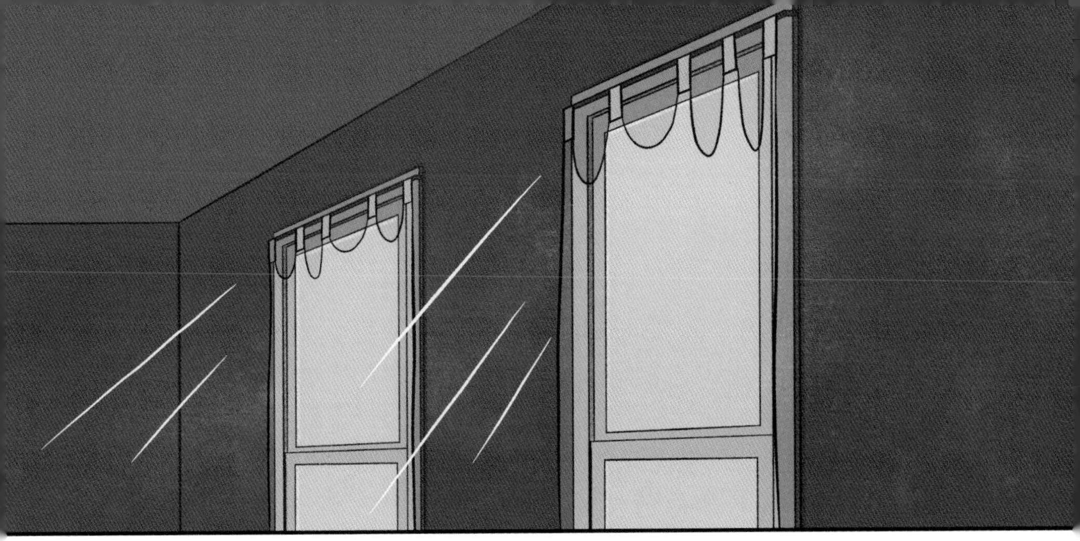

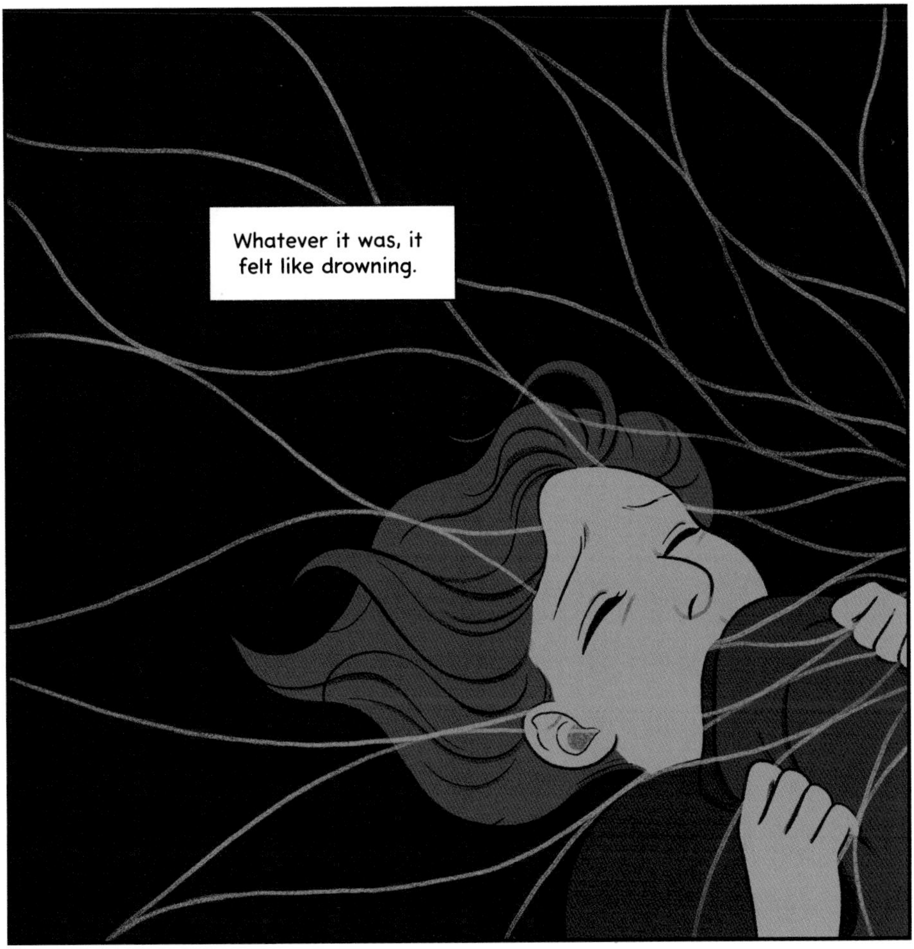
Whatever it was, it
felt like drowning.

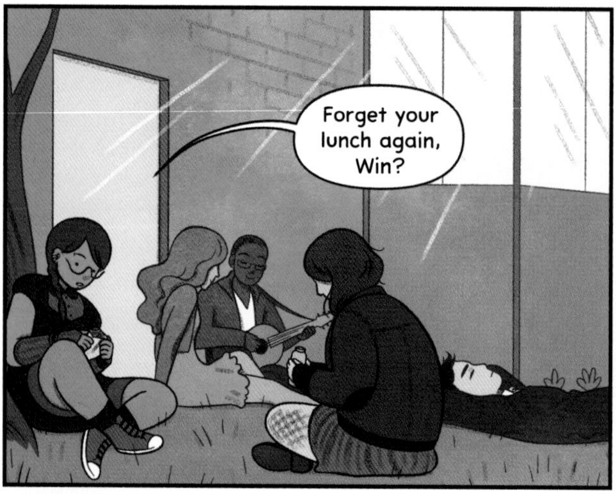
Forget your lunch again, Win?

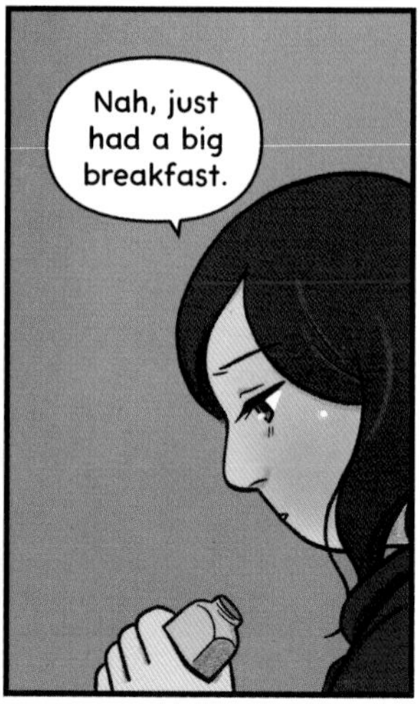
Nah, just had a big breakfast.

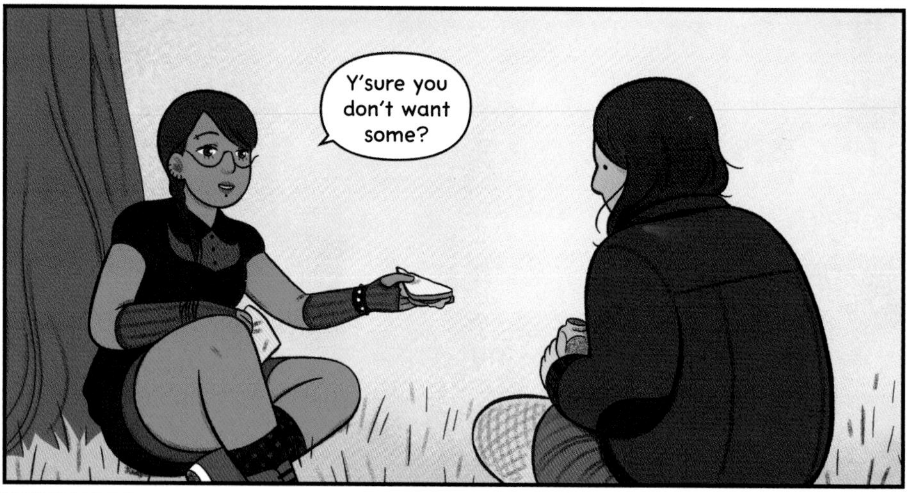
Y'sure you don't want some?

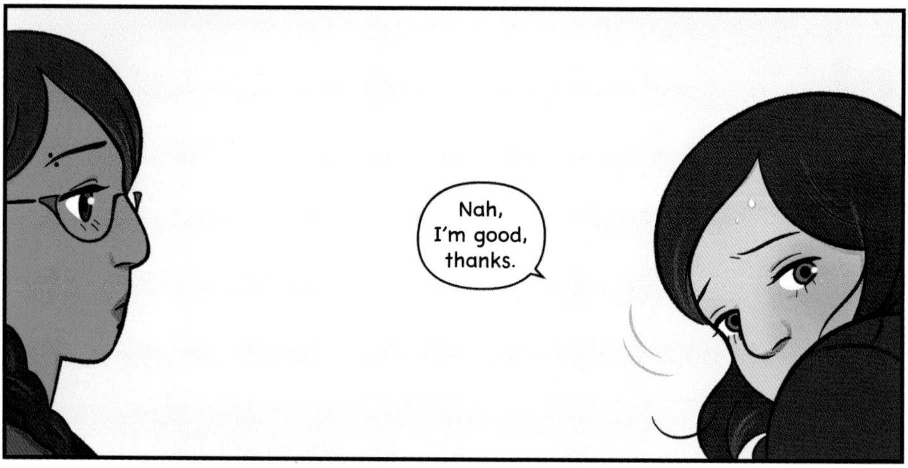
Nah, I'm good, thanks.

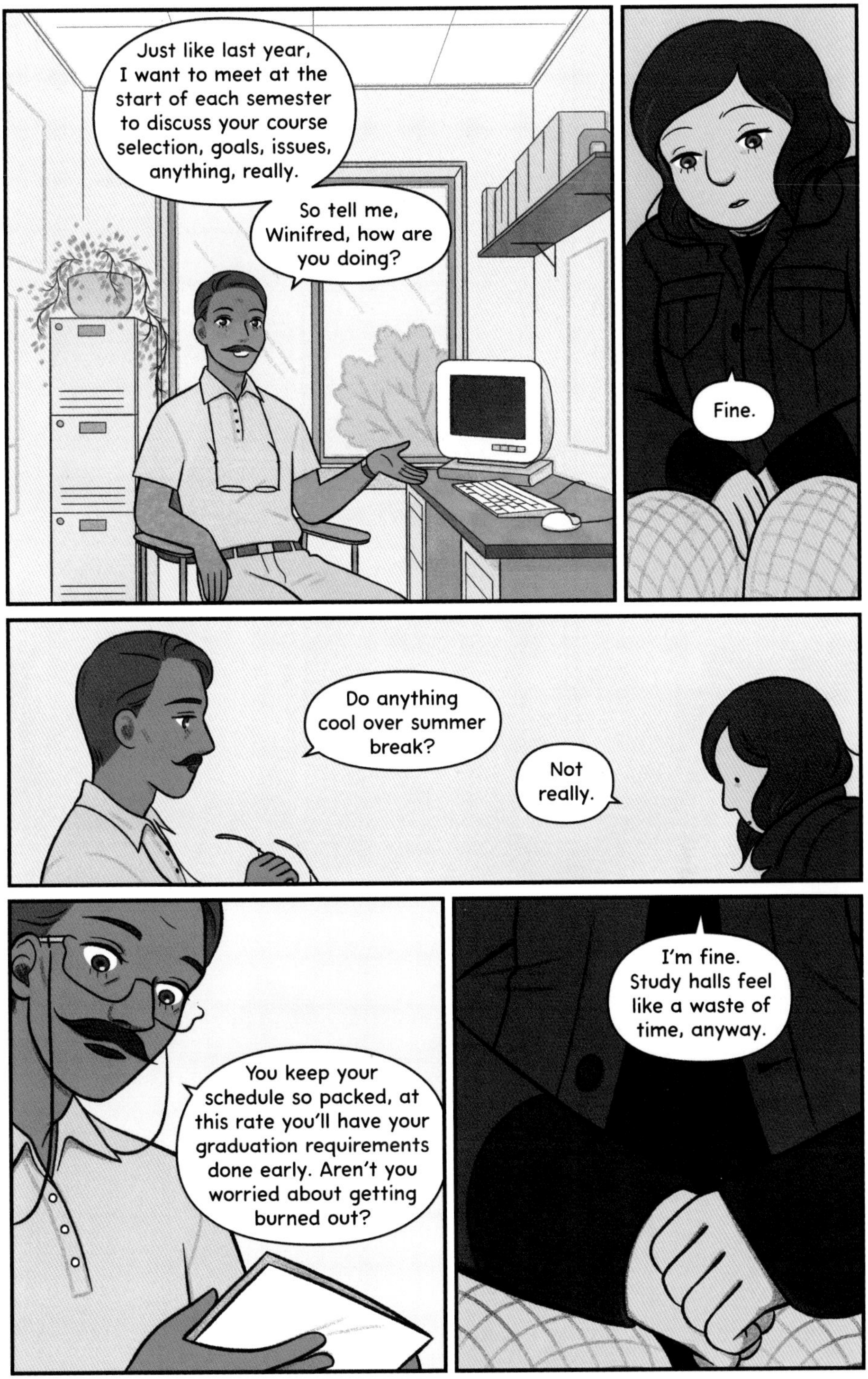
Just like last year, I want to meet at the start of each semester to discuss your course selection, goals, issues, anything, really.
So tell me, Winifred, how are you doing?
Fine.
Do anything cool over summer break?
Not really.
You keep your schedule so packed, at this rate you'll have your graduation requirements done early. Aren't you worried about getting burned out?
I'm fine. Study halls feel like a waste of time, anyway.

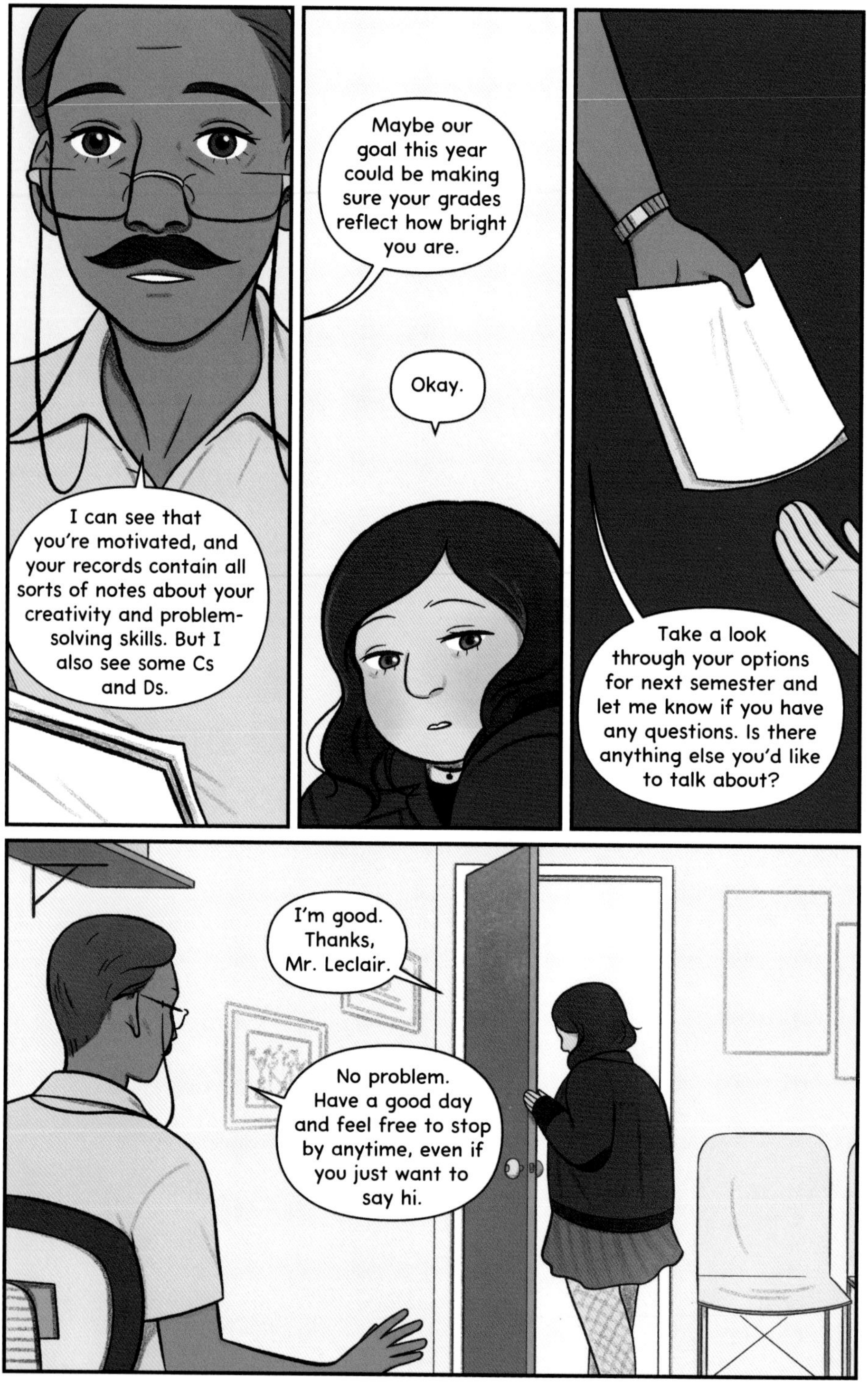
I can see that you're motivated, and your records contain all sorts of notes about your creativity and problem-solving skills. But I also see some Cs and Ds.
Maybe our goal this year could be making sure your grades reflect how bright you are.
Okay.
Take a look through your options for next semester and let me know if you have any questions. Is there anything else you'd like to talk about?
I'm good. Thanks, Mr. Leclair.
No problem. Have a good day and feel free to stop by anytime, even if you just want to say hi.

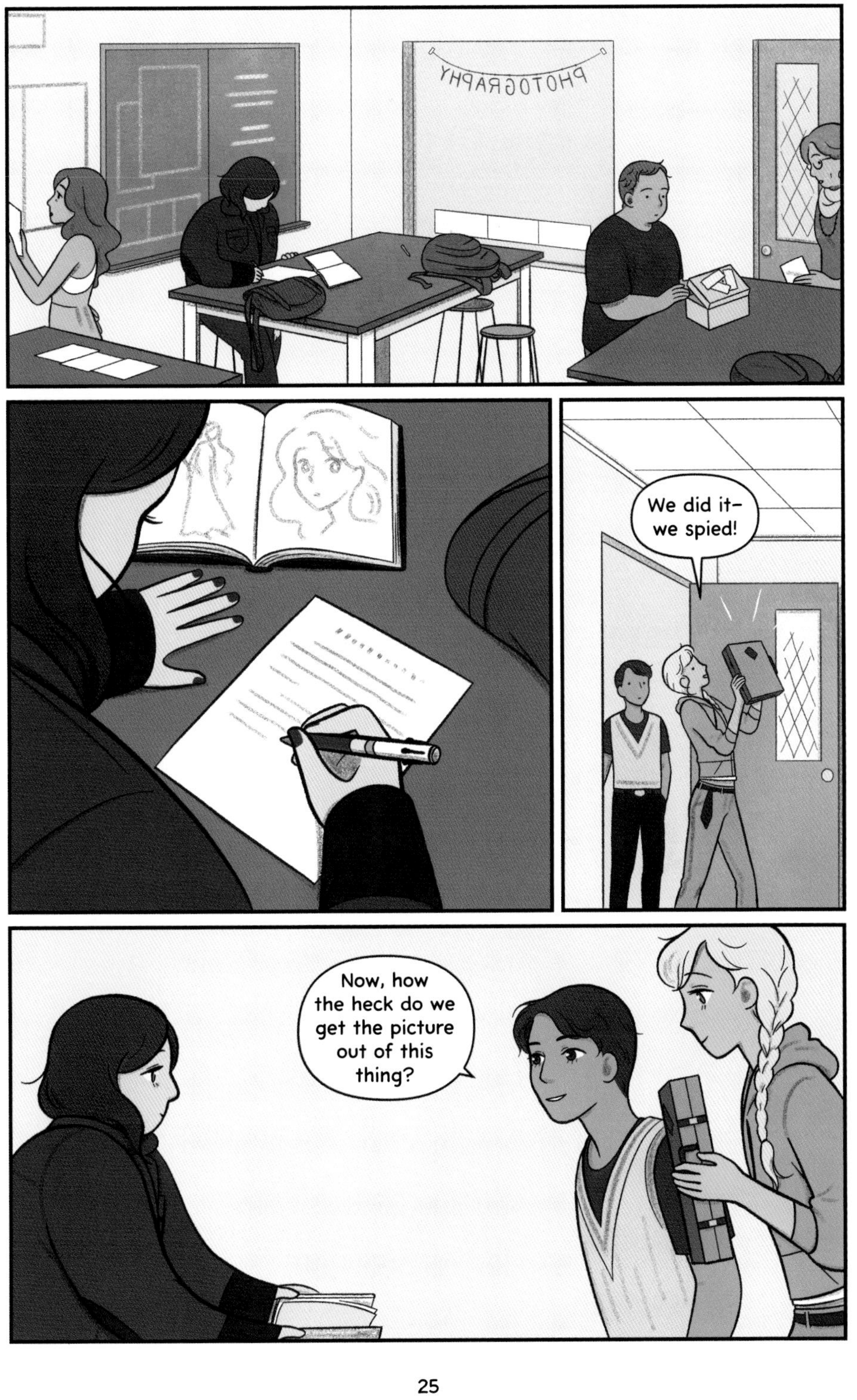
PHOTOGRAPHY
We did it— we spied!
Now, how the heck do we get the picture out of this thing?

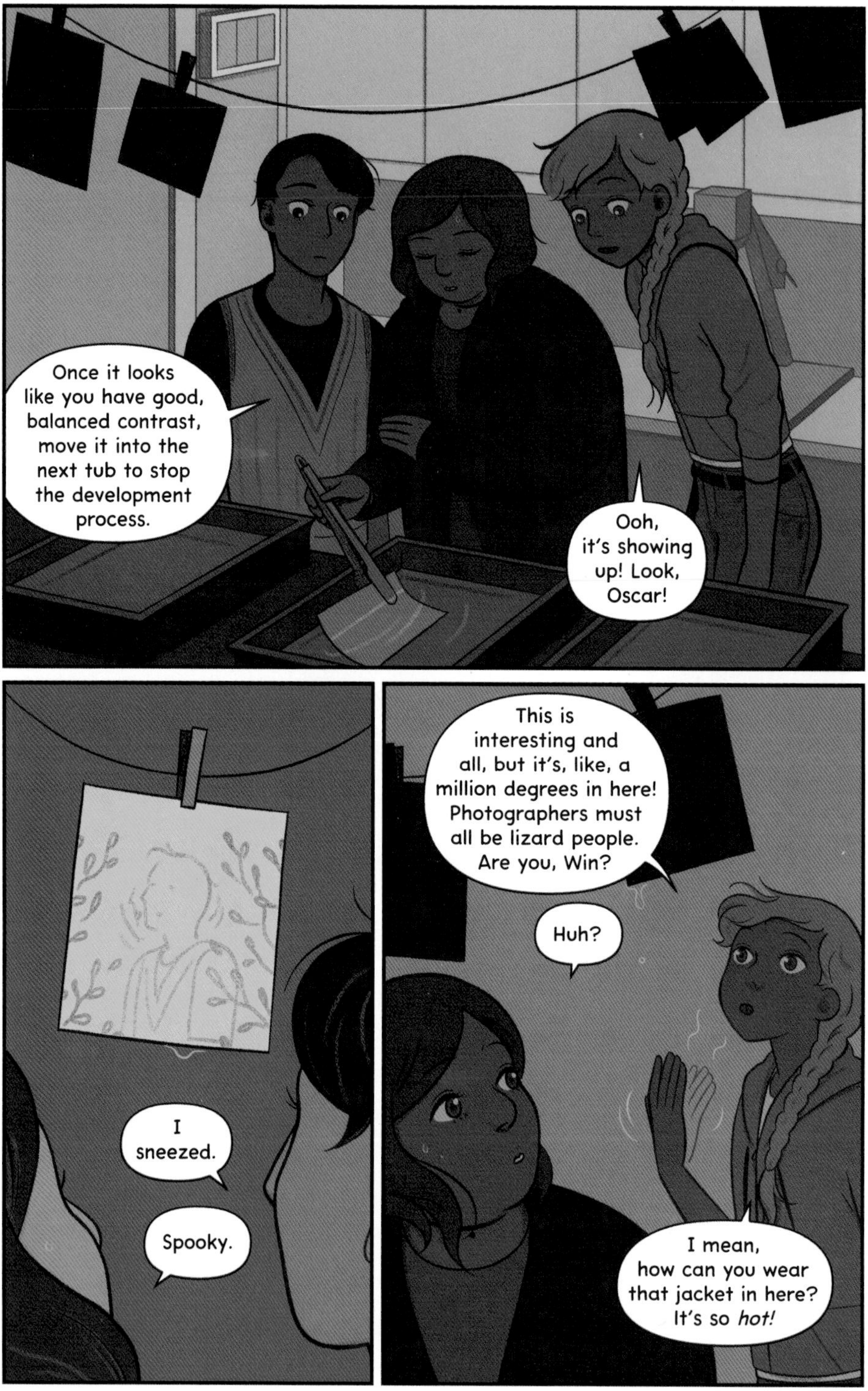
Once it looks like you have good, balanced contrast, move it into the next tub to stop the development process.
Ooh, it's showing up! Look, Oscar!
I sneezed.
Spooky.
This is interesting and all, but it's, like, a million degrees in here! Photographers must all be lizard people. Are you, Win?
Huh?
I mean, how can you wear that jacket in here? It's so *hot!*

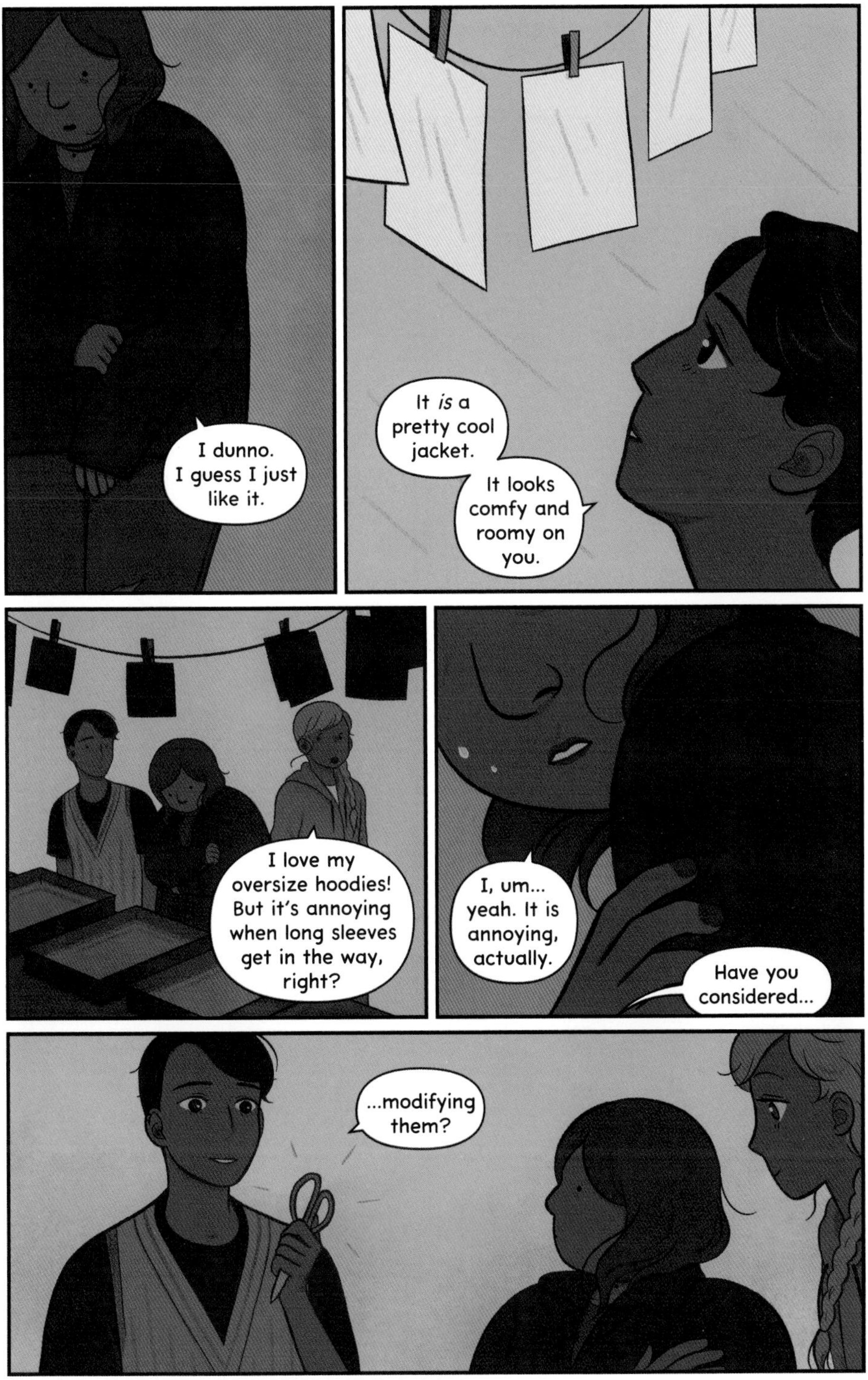
I dunno. I guess I just like it.
It *is* a pretty cool jacket.
It looks comfy and roomy on you.
I love my oversize hoodies! But it's annoying when long sleeves get in the way, right?
I, um... yeah. It is annoying, actually.
Have you considered...
...modifying them?

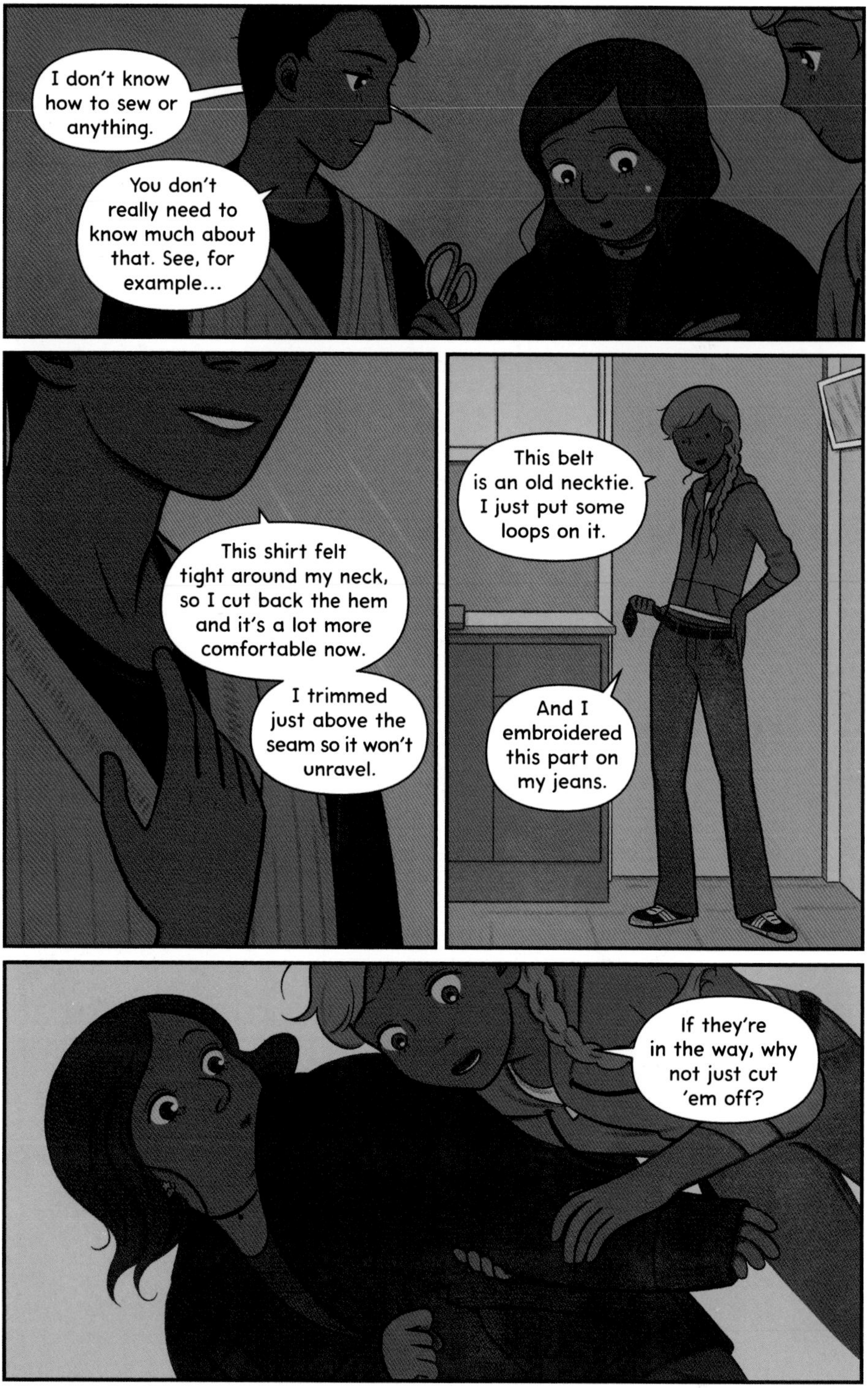
I don't know how to sew or anything.
You don't really need to know much about that. See, for example...
This shirt felt tight around my neck, so I cut back the hem and it's a lot more comfortable now.
I trimmed just above the seam so it won't unravel.
This belt is an old necktie. I just put some loops on it.
And I embroidered this part on my jeans.
If they're in the way, why not just cut 'em off?

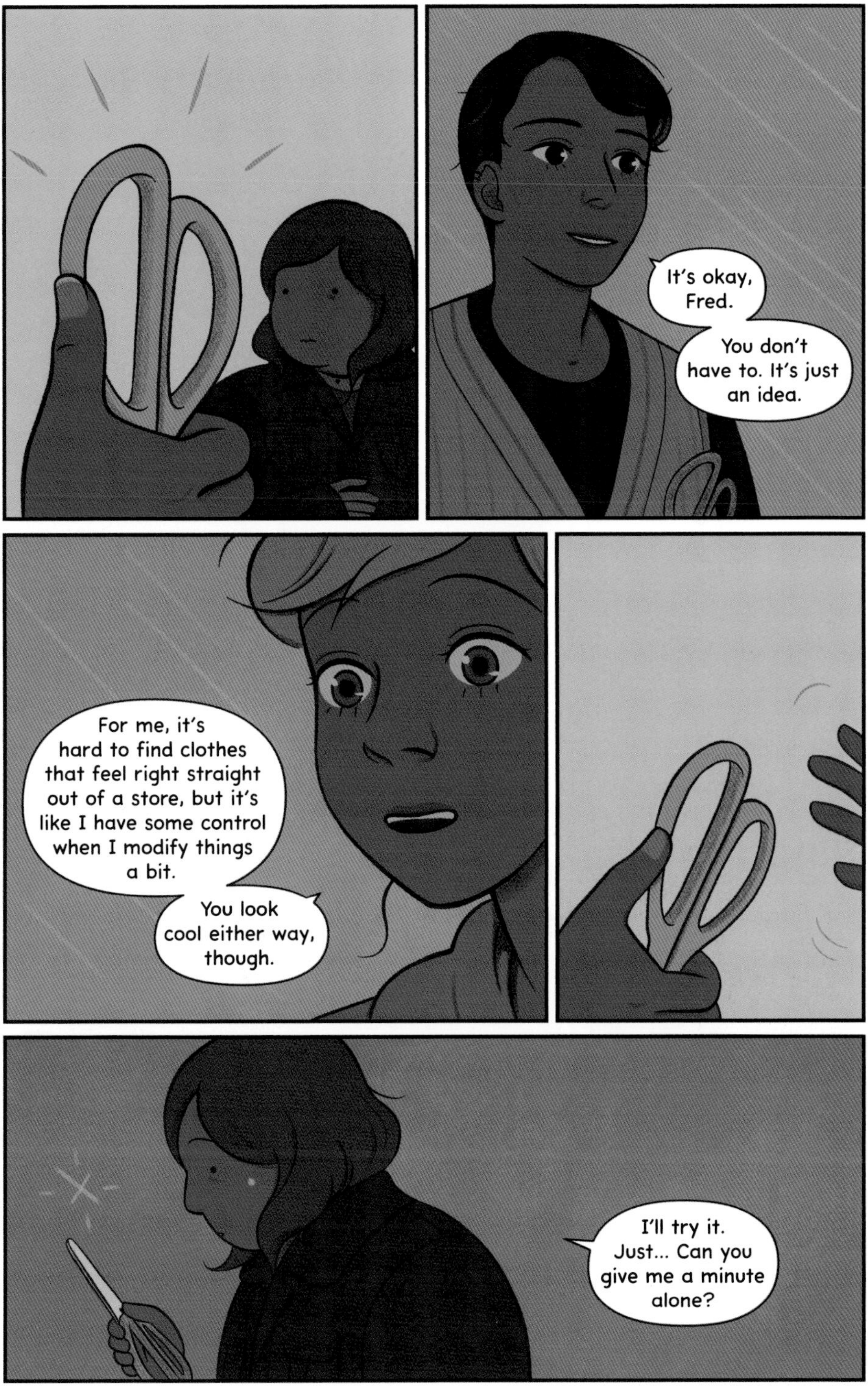
It's okay, Fred.
You don't have to. It's just an idea.
For me, it's hard to find clothes that feel right straight out of a store, but it's like I have some control when I modify things a bit.
You look cool either way, though.
I'll try it. Just... Can you give me a minute alone?

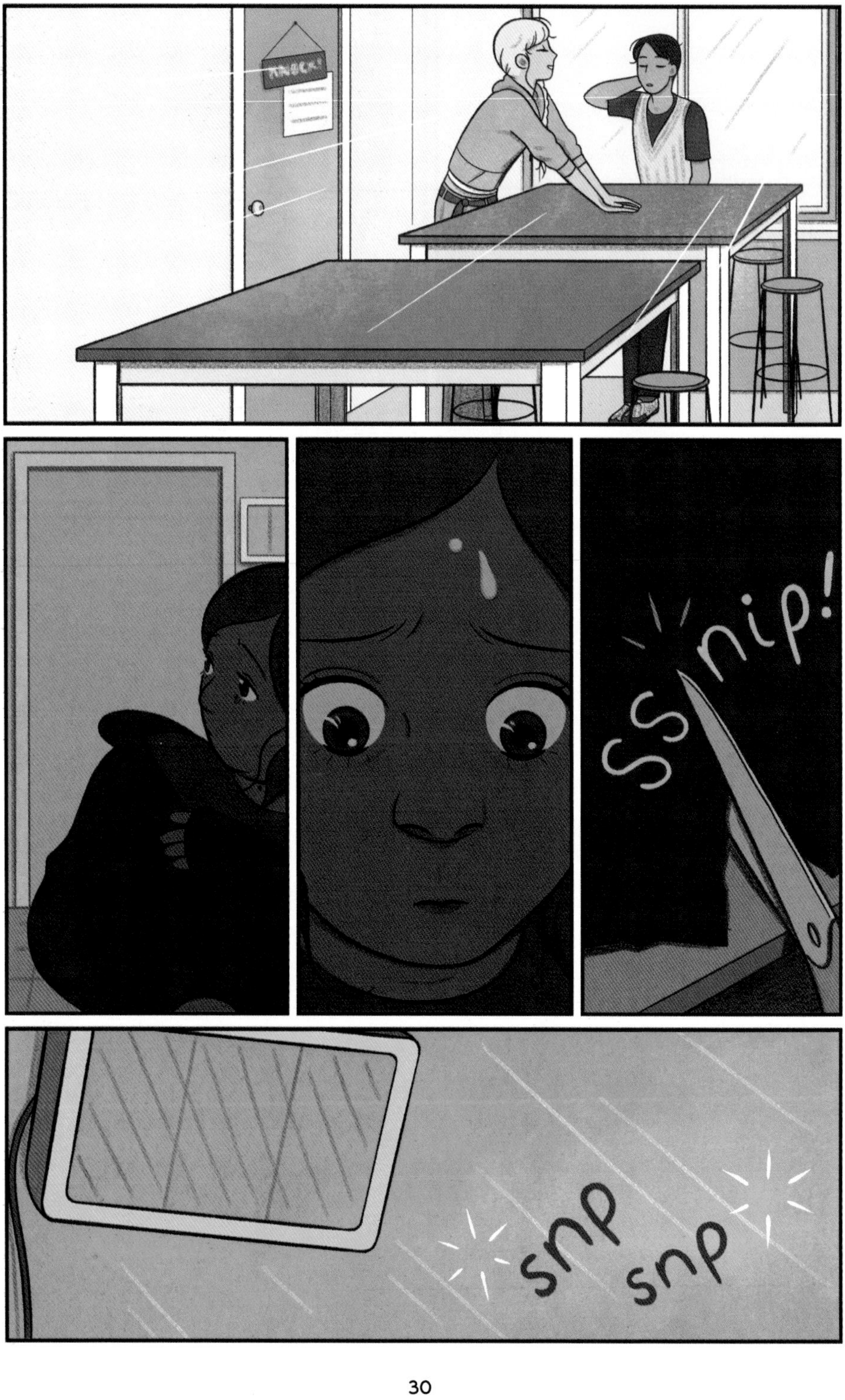
SSnip!
snp
snp

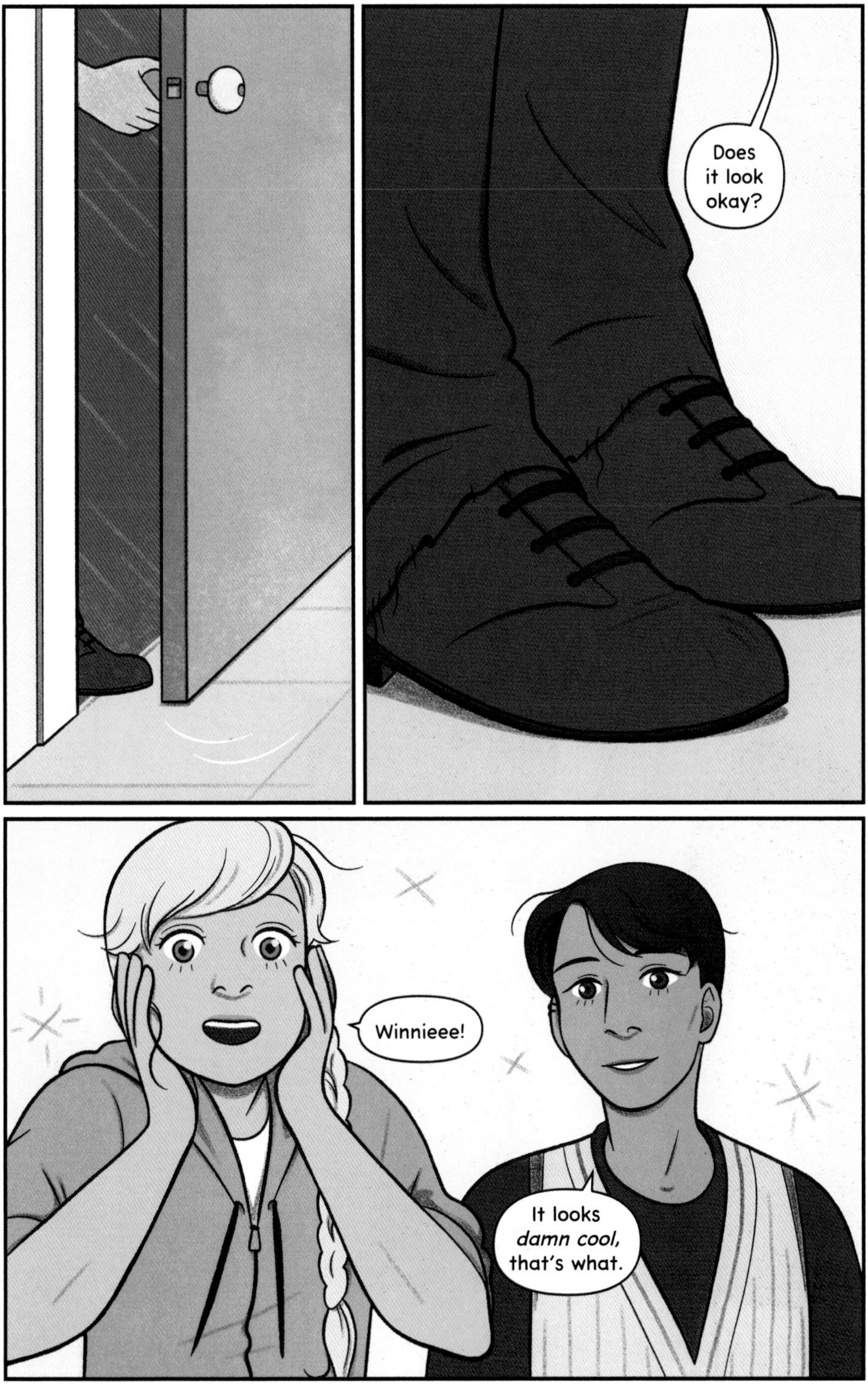
Does it look okay?
Winnieee!
It looks *damn cool,* that's what.

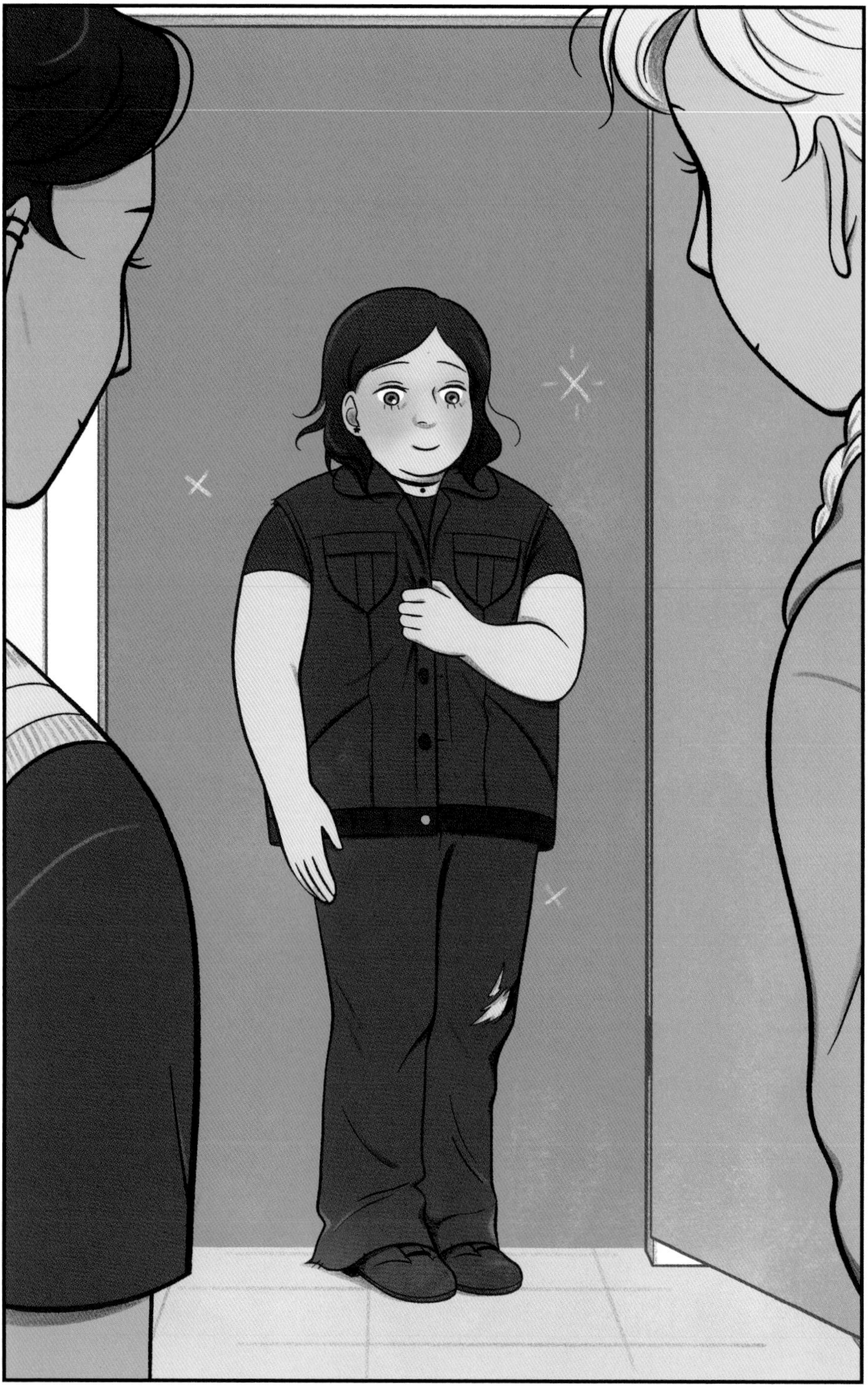

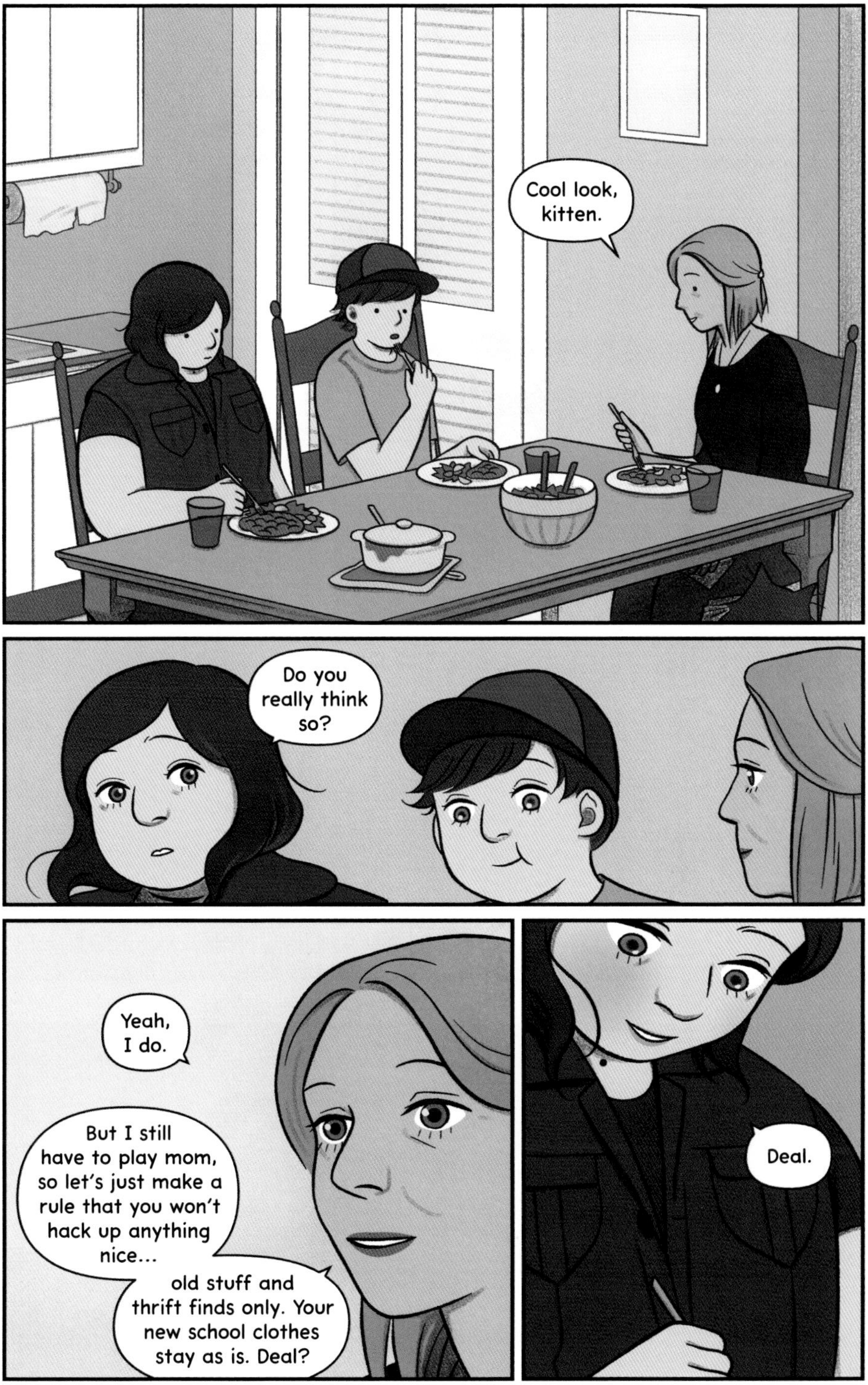
Cool look, kitten.
Do you really think so?
Yeah, I do.
But I still have to play mom, so let's just make a rule that you won't hack up anything nice...
old stuff and thrift finds only. Your new school clothes stay as is. Deal?
Deal.

I was so anxious about eating at school that skipping lunch always seemed like a good idea at the time, even if making up for it at dinner left me with a reliable bloat of regret.

But it didn't matter if a stomachache kept me up because I never slept much, anyway.

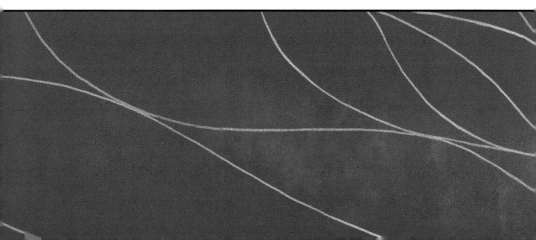

I didn't think I deserved to enjoy food. And I didn't think I deserved friends, either.

It was like they'd *seen* me. I was hiding under that jacket.

And it was eating me alive that this meant they'd seen me for who and what I really was:

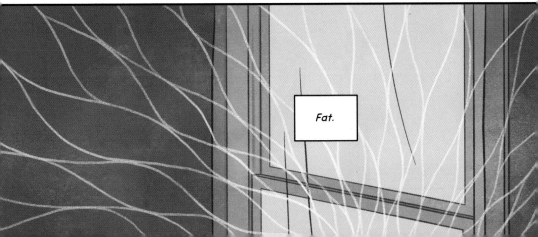

Fat.

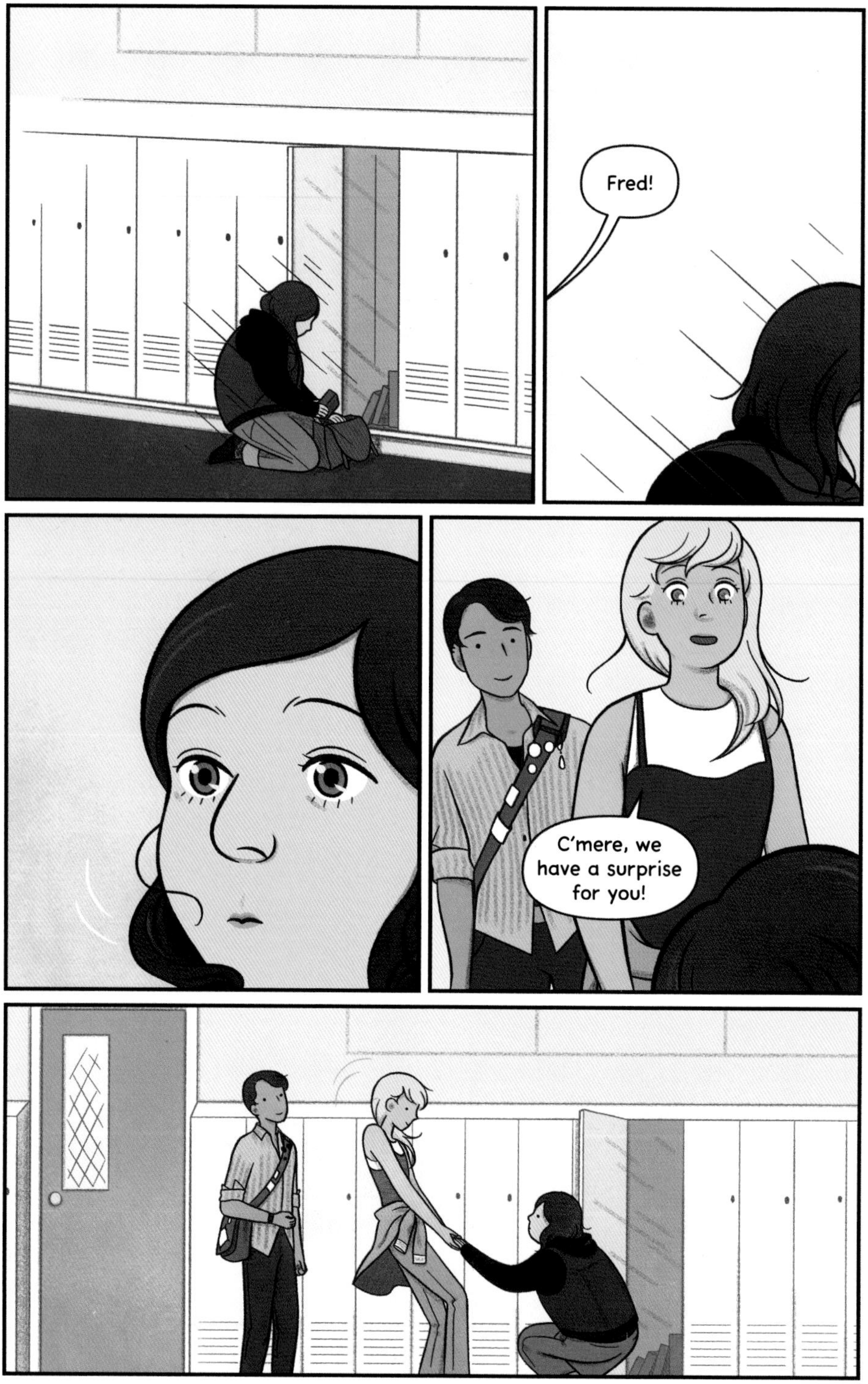
Fred!
C'mere, we have a surprise for you!

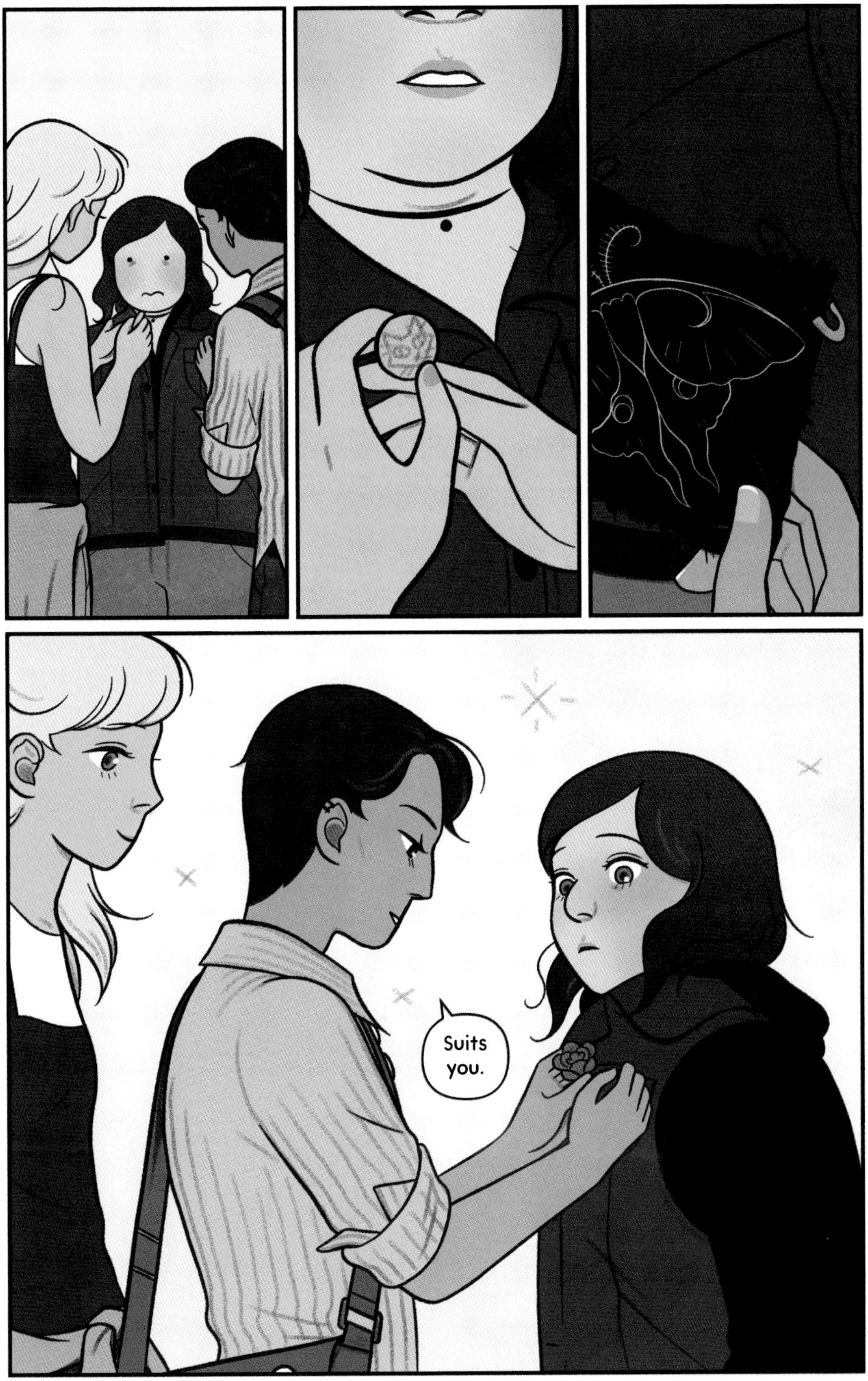
Suits you.

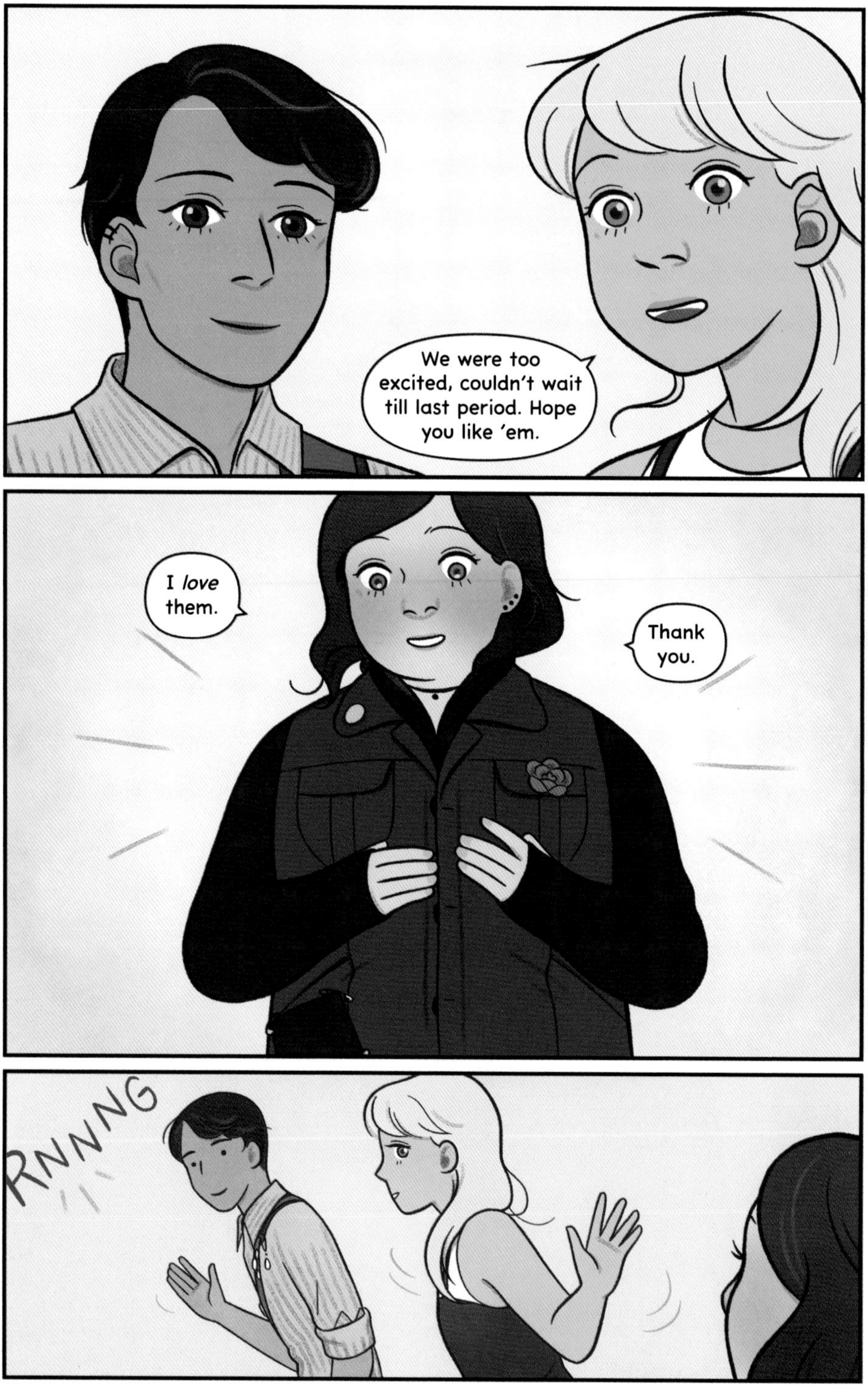
We were too excited, couldn't wait till last period. Hope you like 'em.
I *love* them.
Thank you.
RNNG

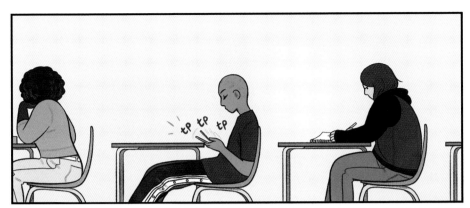

I like what you did with your jacket. You've got a great sense of style.

Thanks.

April and Oscar's gift of this vest gave me strength...

...and I'd wear it like armor for years to come.

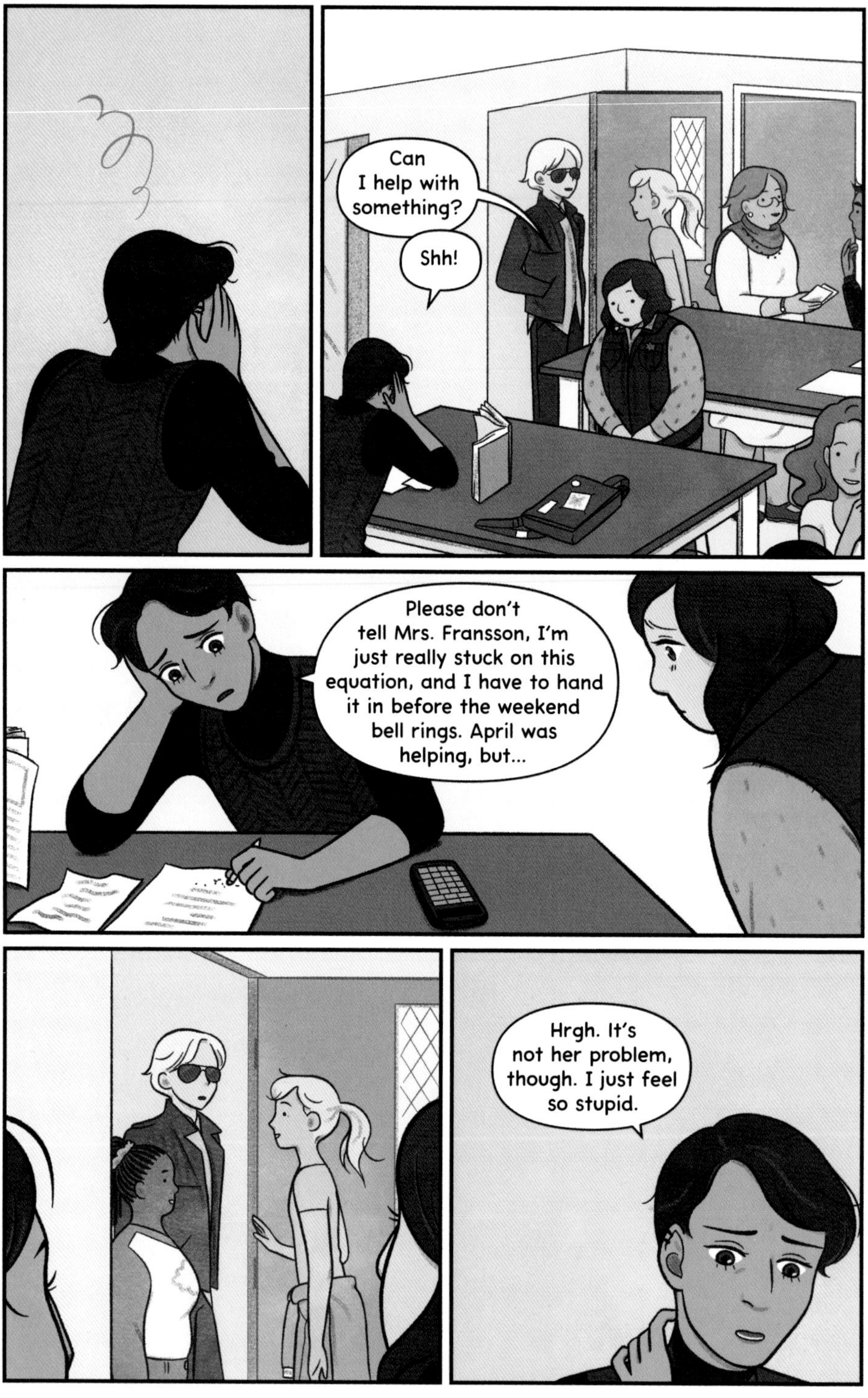
Can I help with something?
Shh!
Please don't tell Mrs. Fransson, I'm just really stuck on this equation, and I have to hand it in before the weekend bell rings. April was helping, but...
Hrgh. It's not her problem, though. I just feel so stupid.

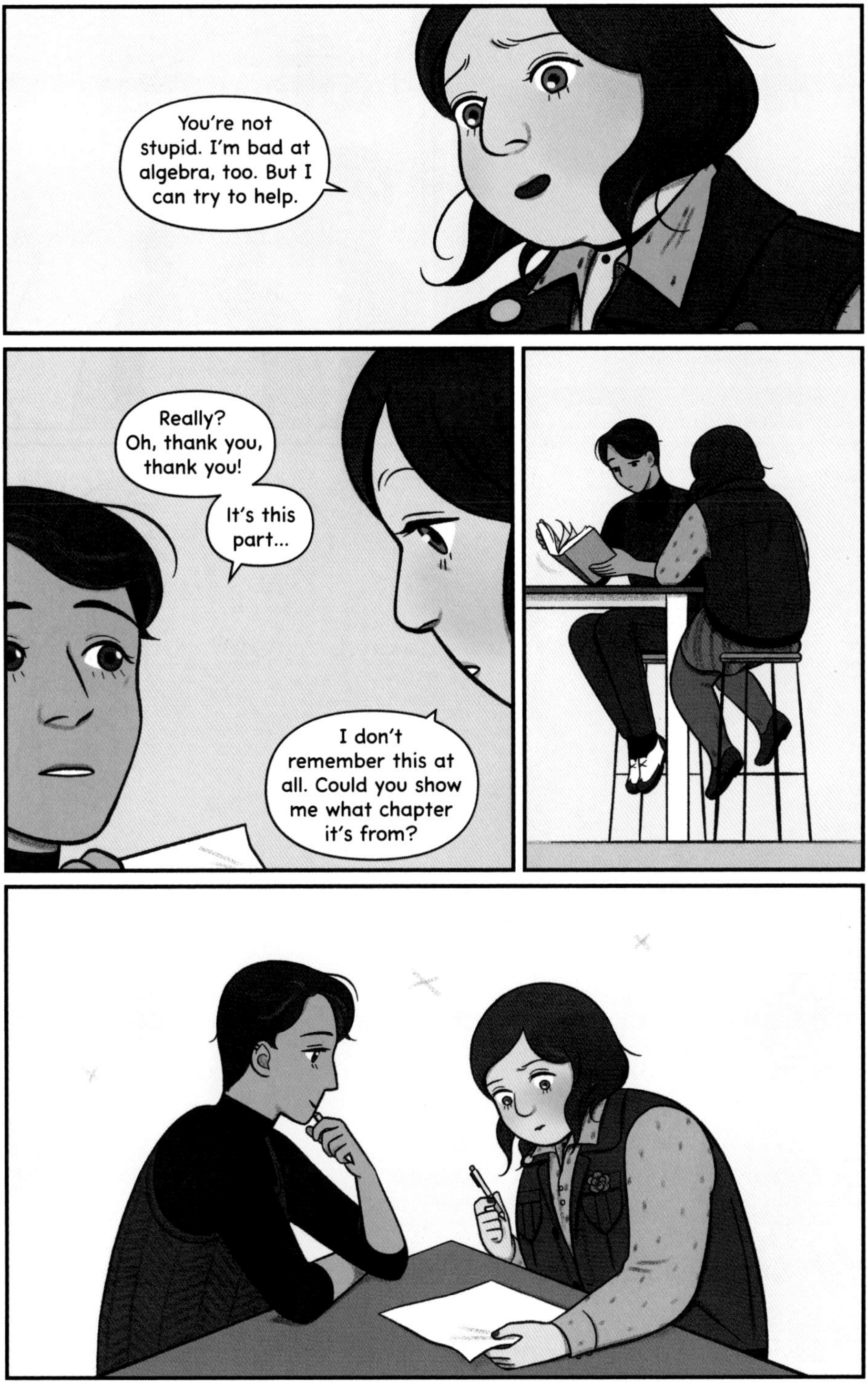
You're not stupid. I'm bad at algebra, too. But I can try to help.
Really? Oh, thank you, thank you!
It's this part...
I don't remember this at all. Could you show me what chapter it's from?

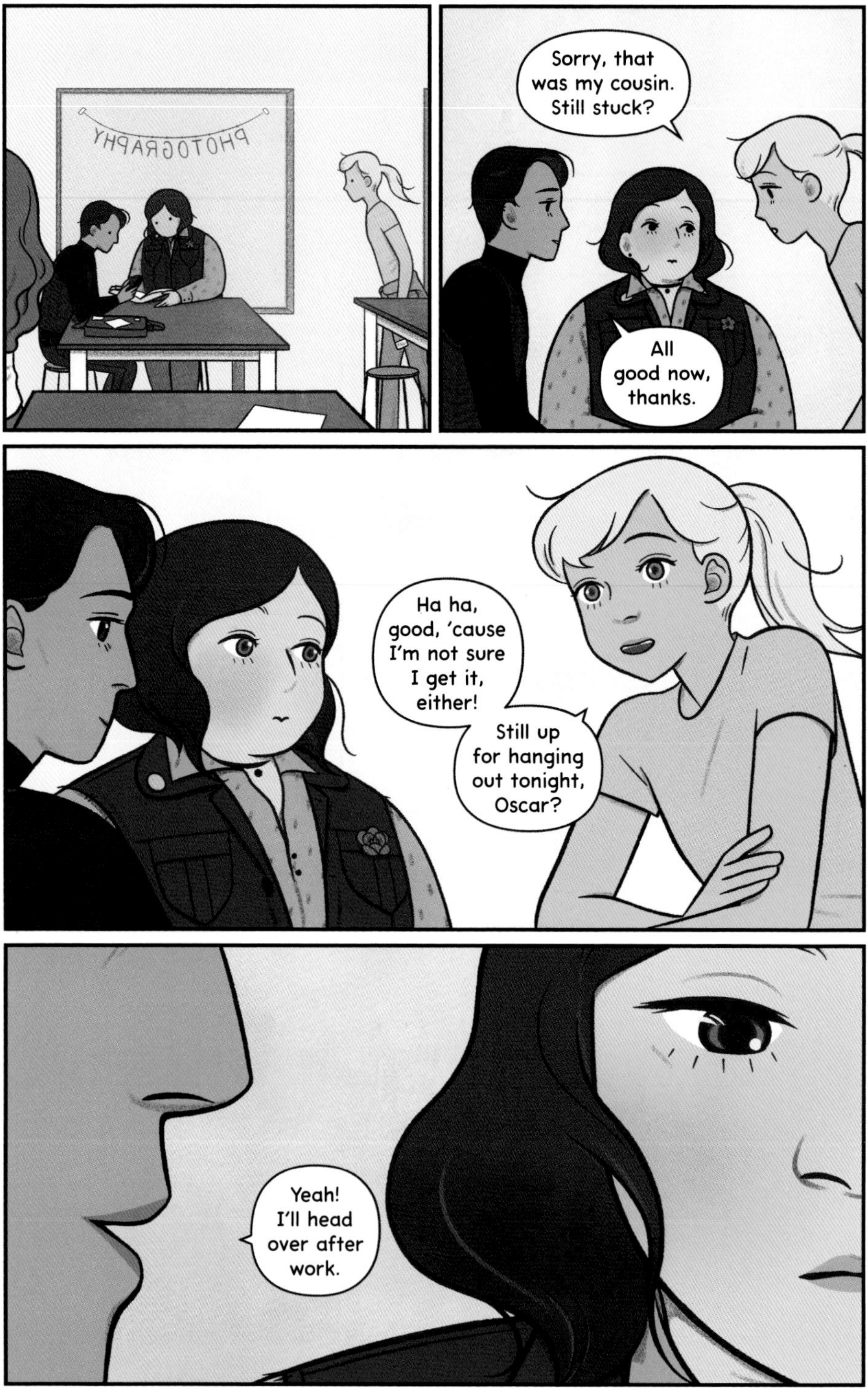
PHOTOGRAPHY
Sorry, that was my cousin. Still stuck?
All good now, thanks.
Ha ha, good, 'cause I'm not sure I get it, either!
Still up for hanging out tonight, Oscar?
Yeah! I'll head over after work.

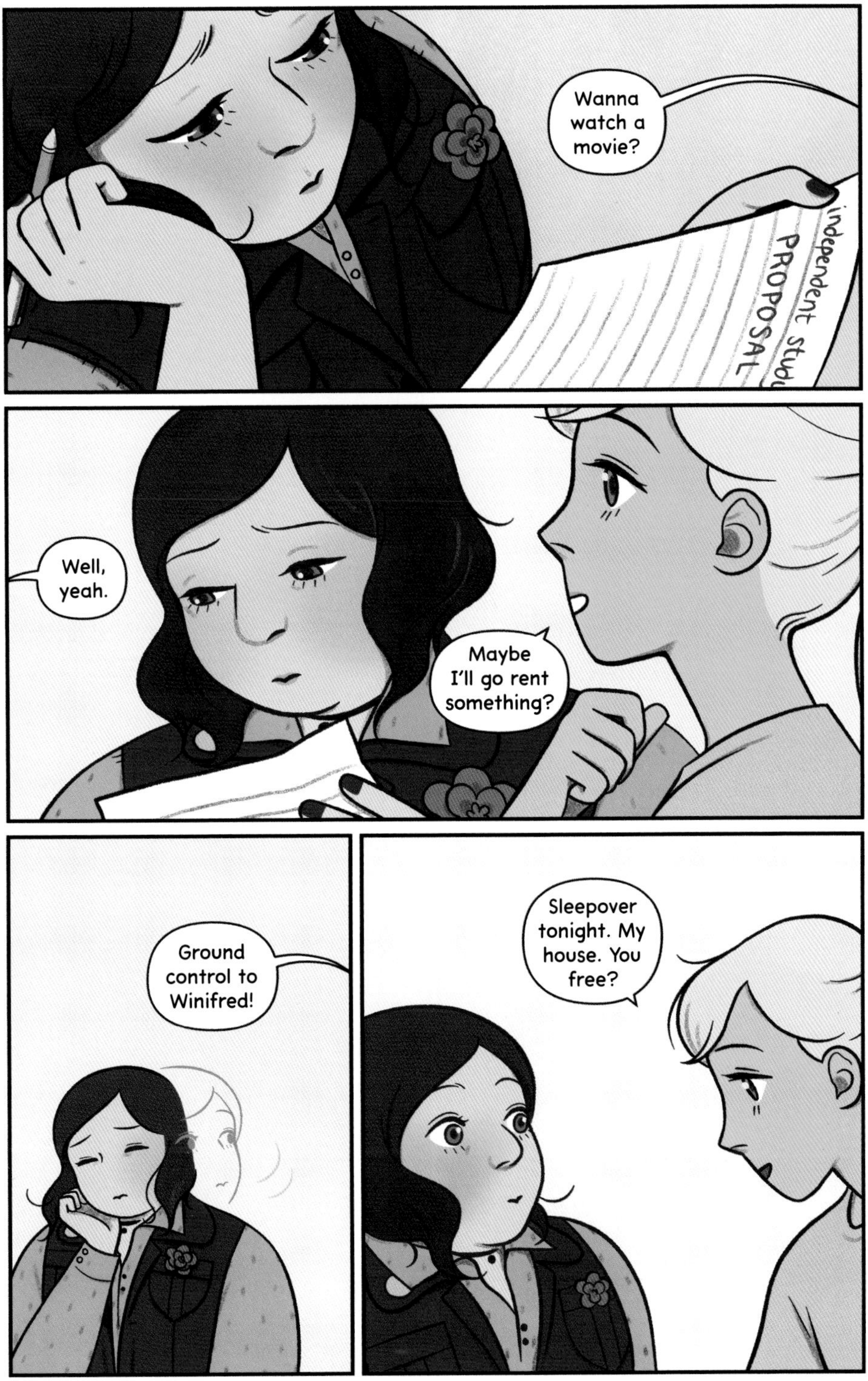
Wanna watch a movie?
independent
PROPOSAL
Well, yeah.
Maybe I'll go rent something?
Ground control to Winifred!
Sleepover tonight. My house. You free?

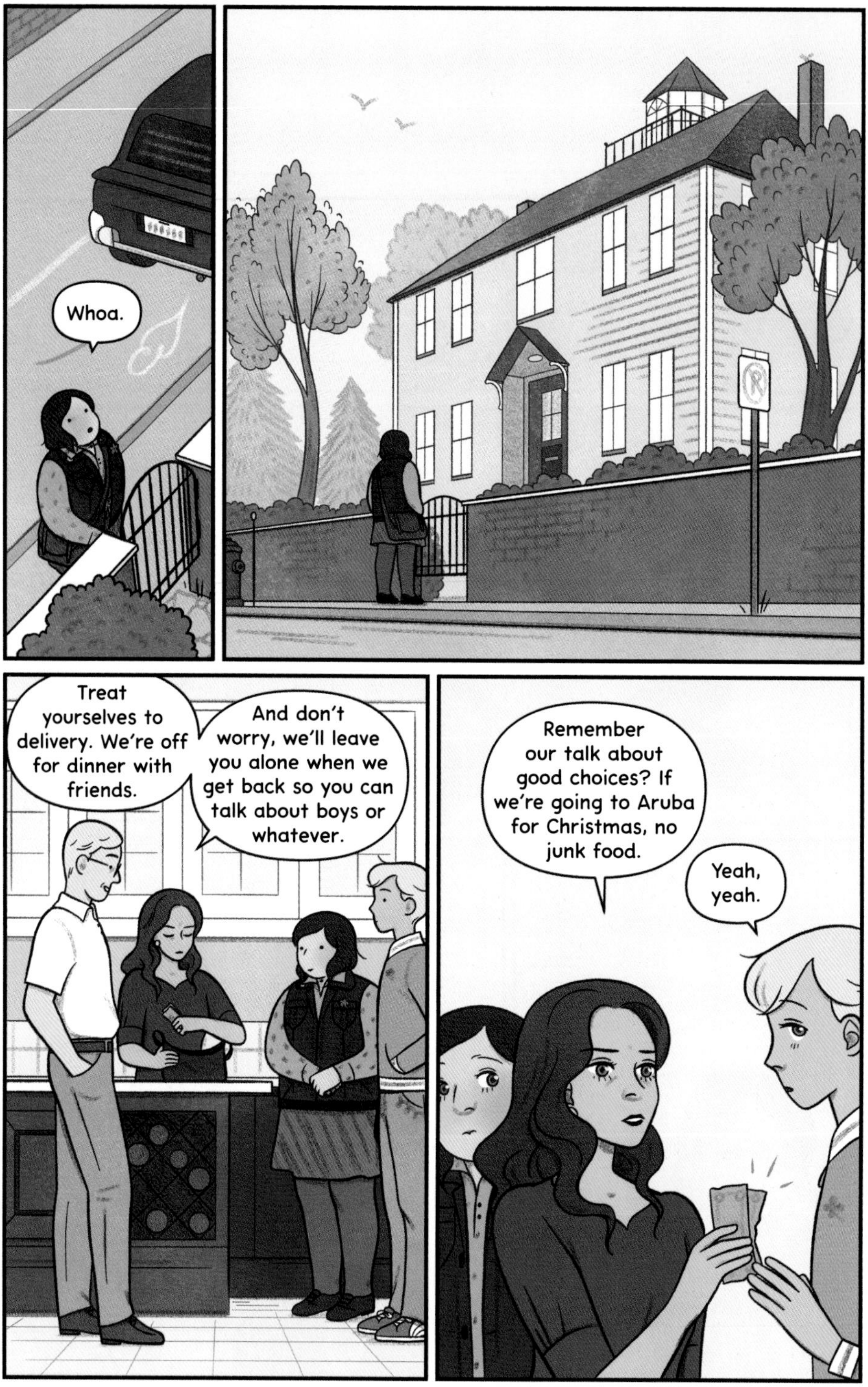
Whoa.
Treat yourselves to delivery. We're off for dinner with friends.
And don't worry, we'll leave you alone when we get back so you can talk about boys or whatever.
Remember our talk about good choices? If we're going to Aruba for Christmas, no junk food.
Yeah, yeah.

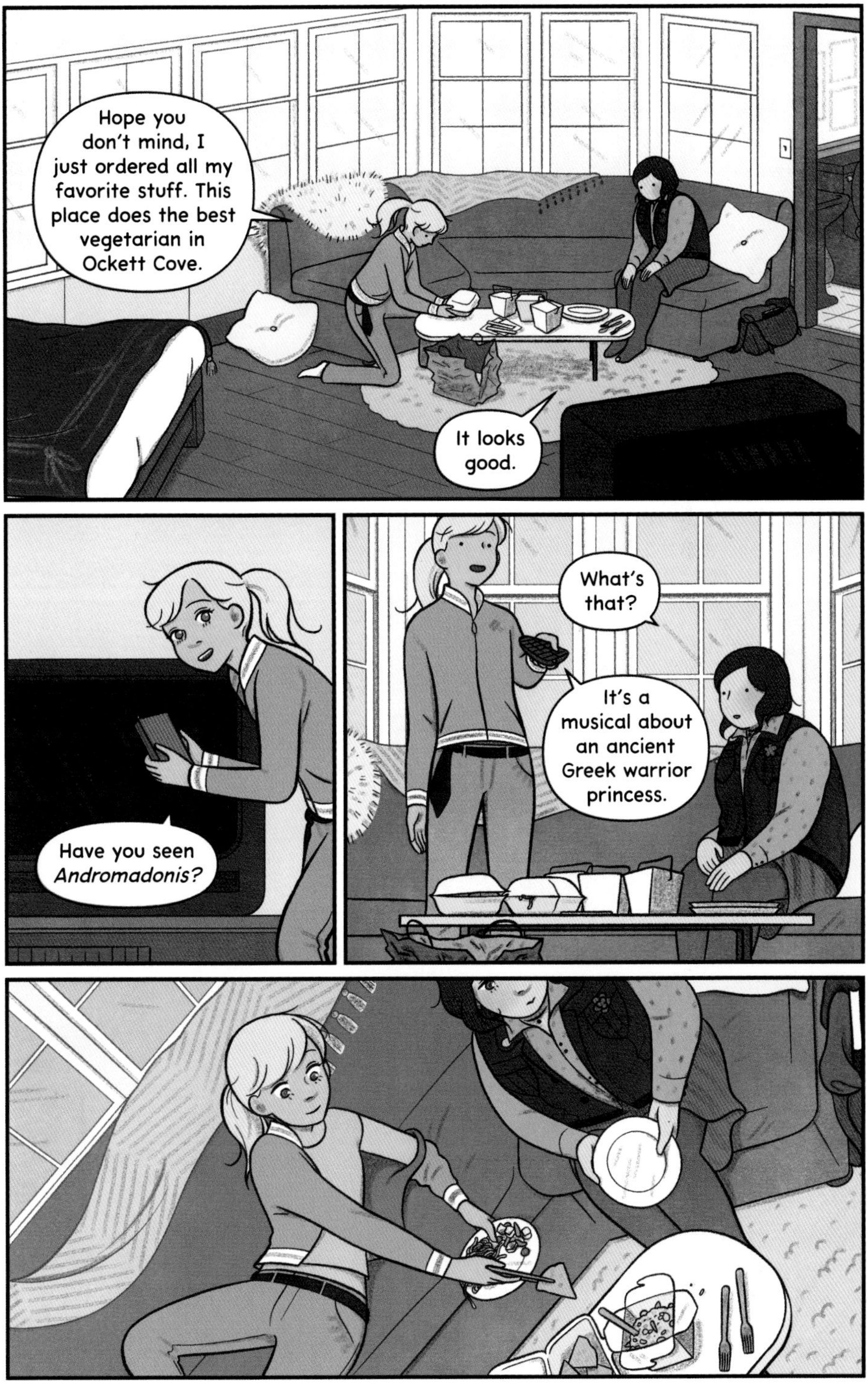
Hope you don't mind, I just ordered all my favorite stuff. This place does the best vegetarian in Ockett Cove.
It looks good.
Have you seen *Andromadonis?*
What's that?
It's a musical about an ancient Greek warrior princess.

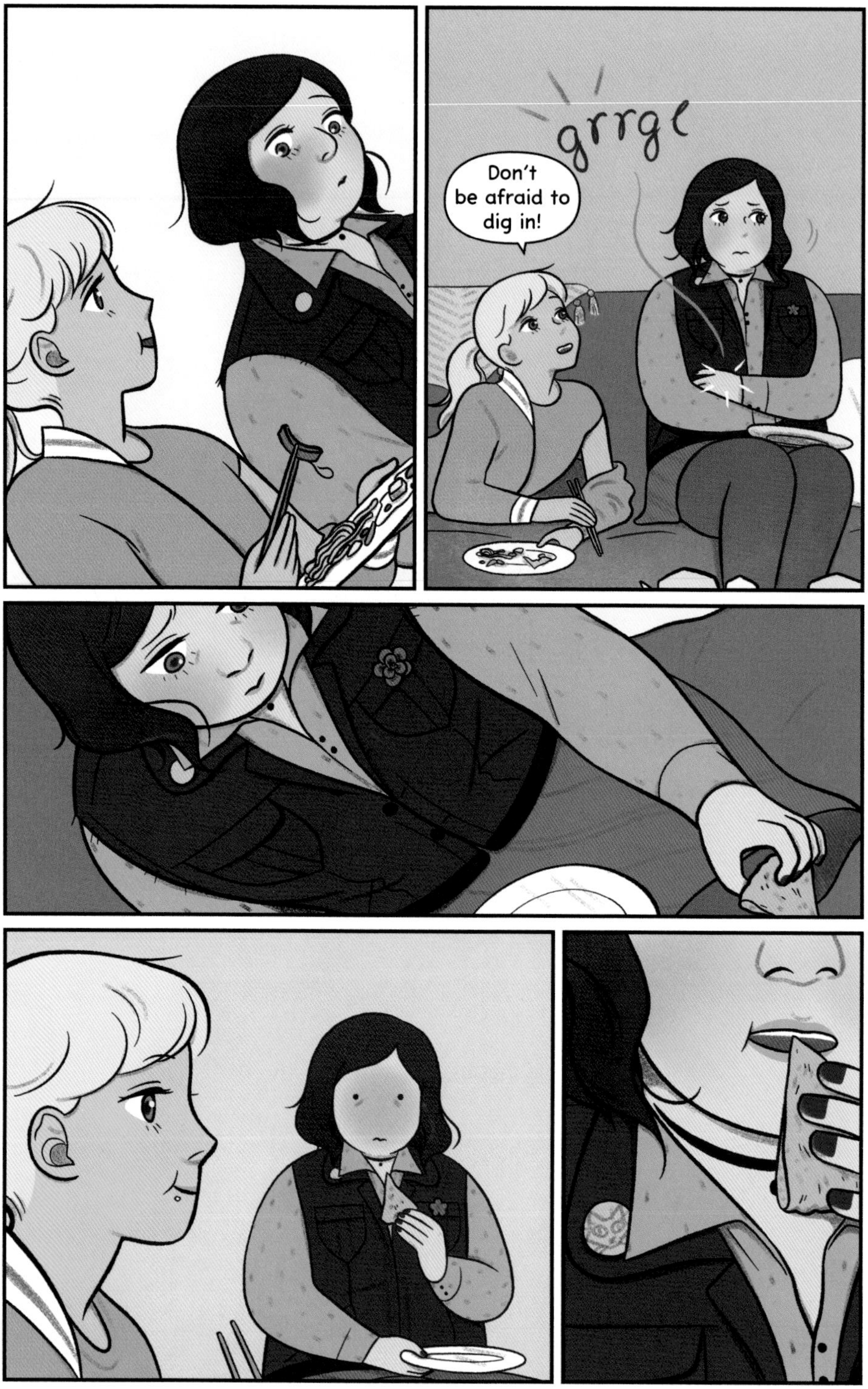
grrgl
Don't be afraid to dig in!

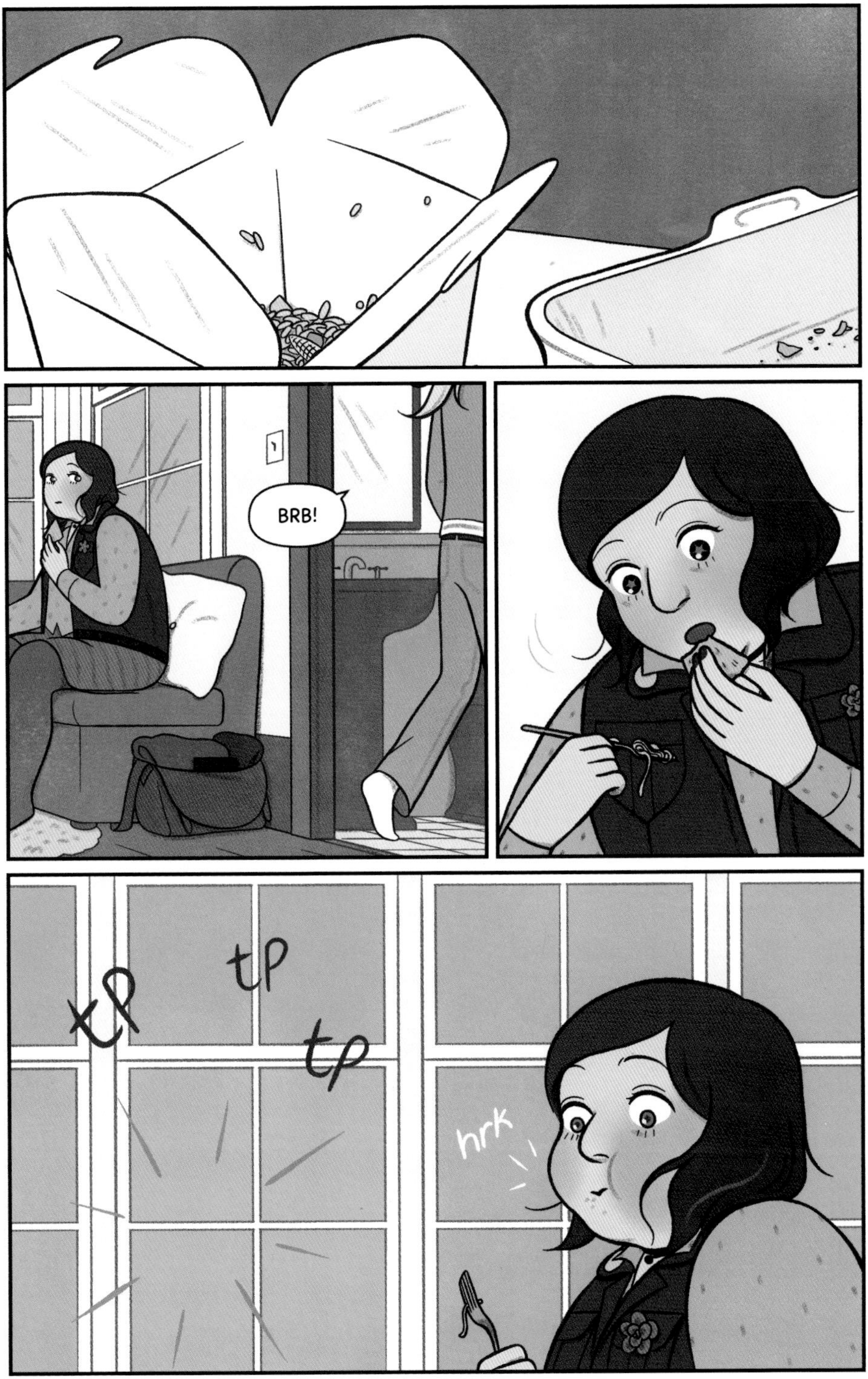
BRB!
tp
tp
tp
hrk

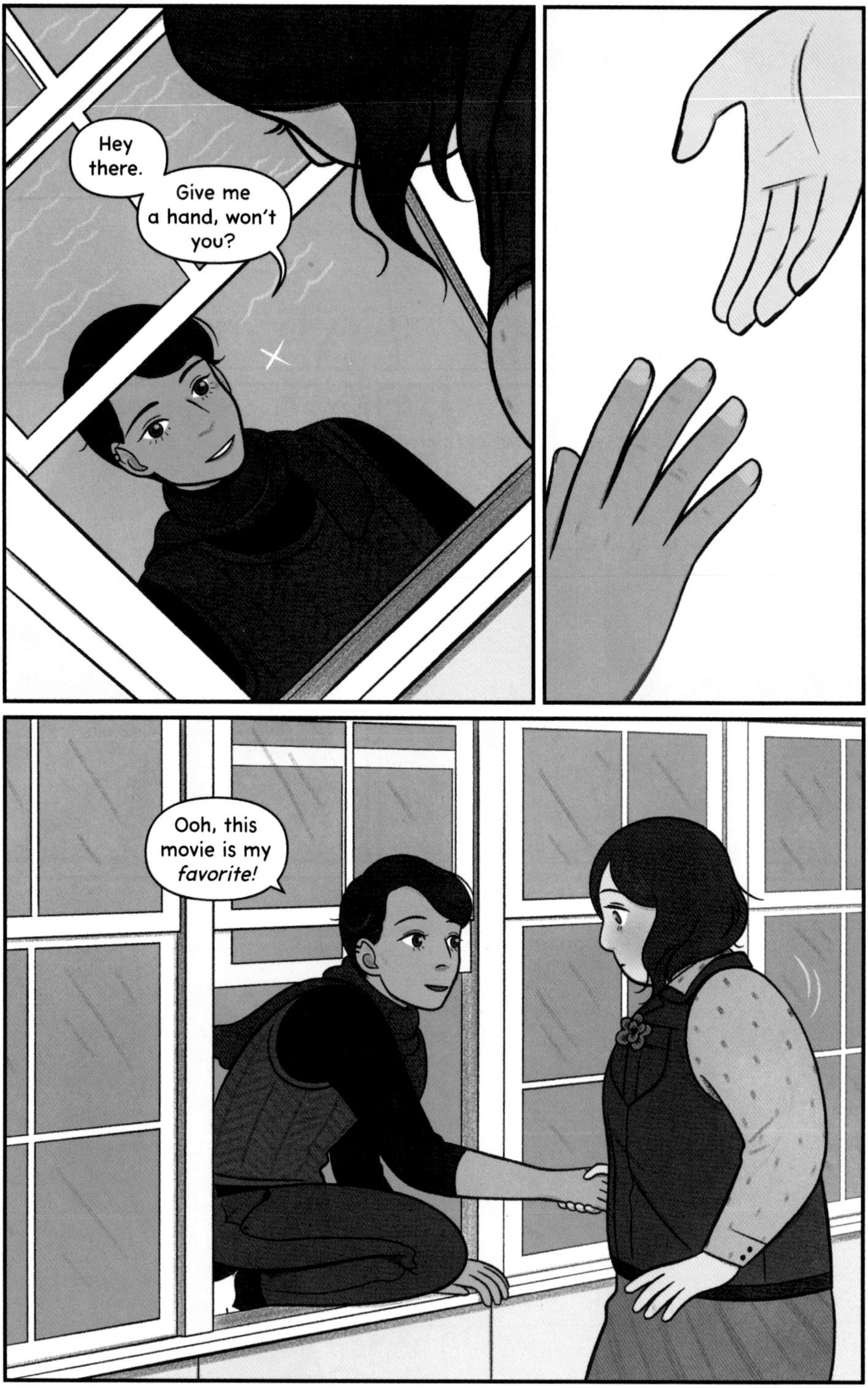
Hey there.
Give me a hand, won't you?
Ooh, this movie is my *favorite!*

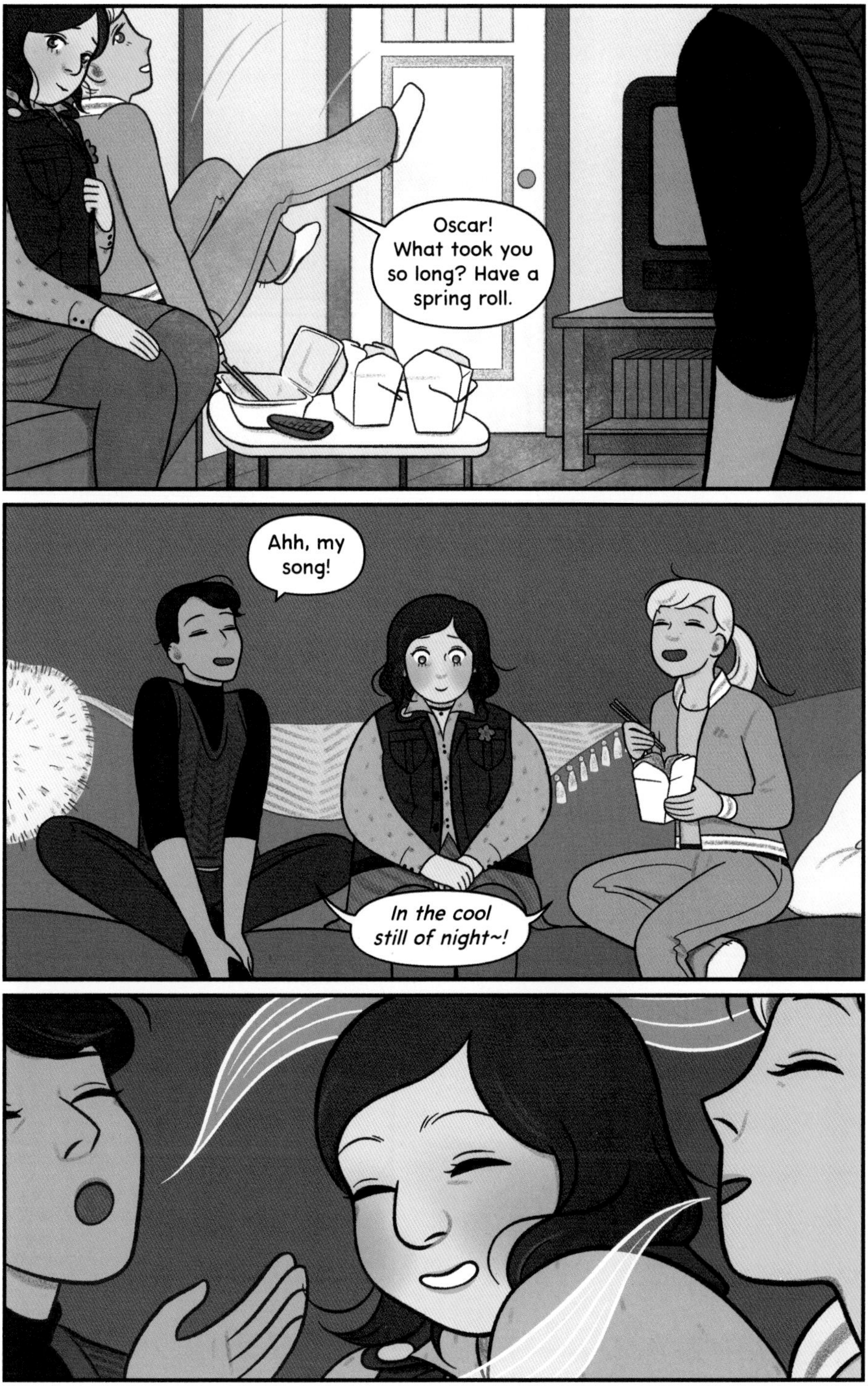
Oscar! What took you so long? Have a spring roll.
Ahh, my song!
In the cool still of night~!

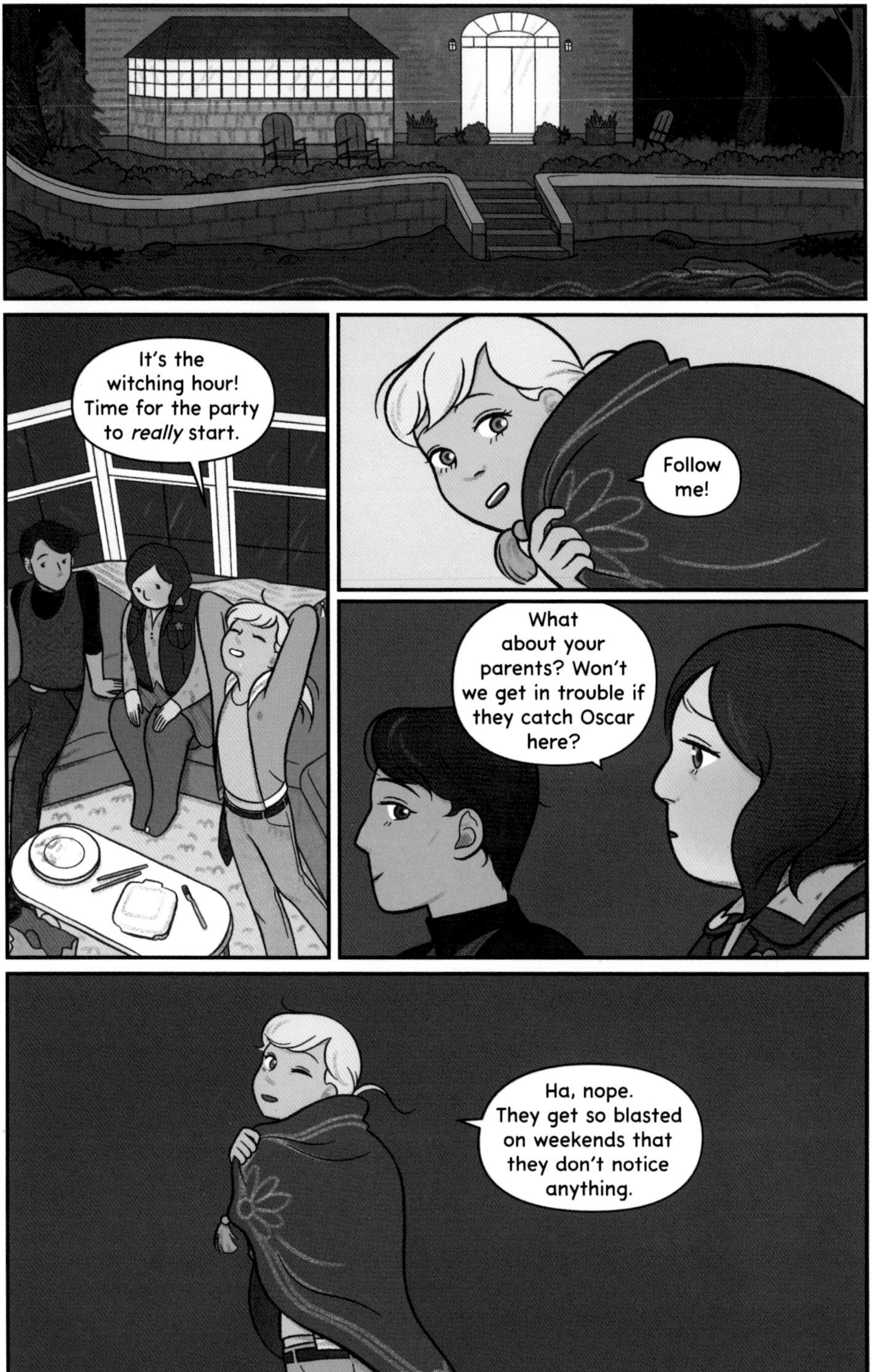
It's the witching hour! Time for the party to *really* start.
Follow me!
What about your parents? Won't we get in trouble if they catch Oscar here?
Ha, nope. They get so blasted on weekends that they don't notice anything.

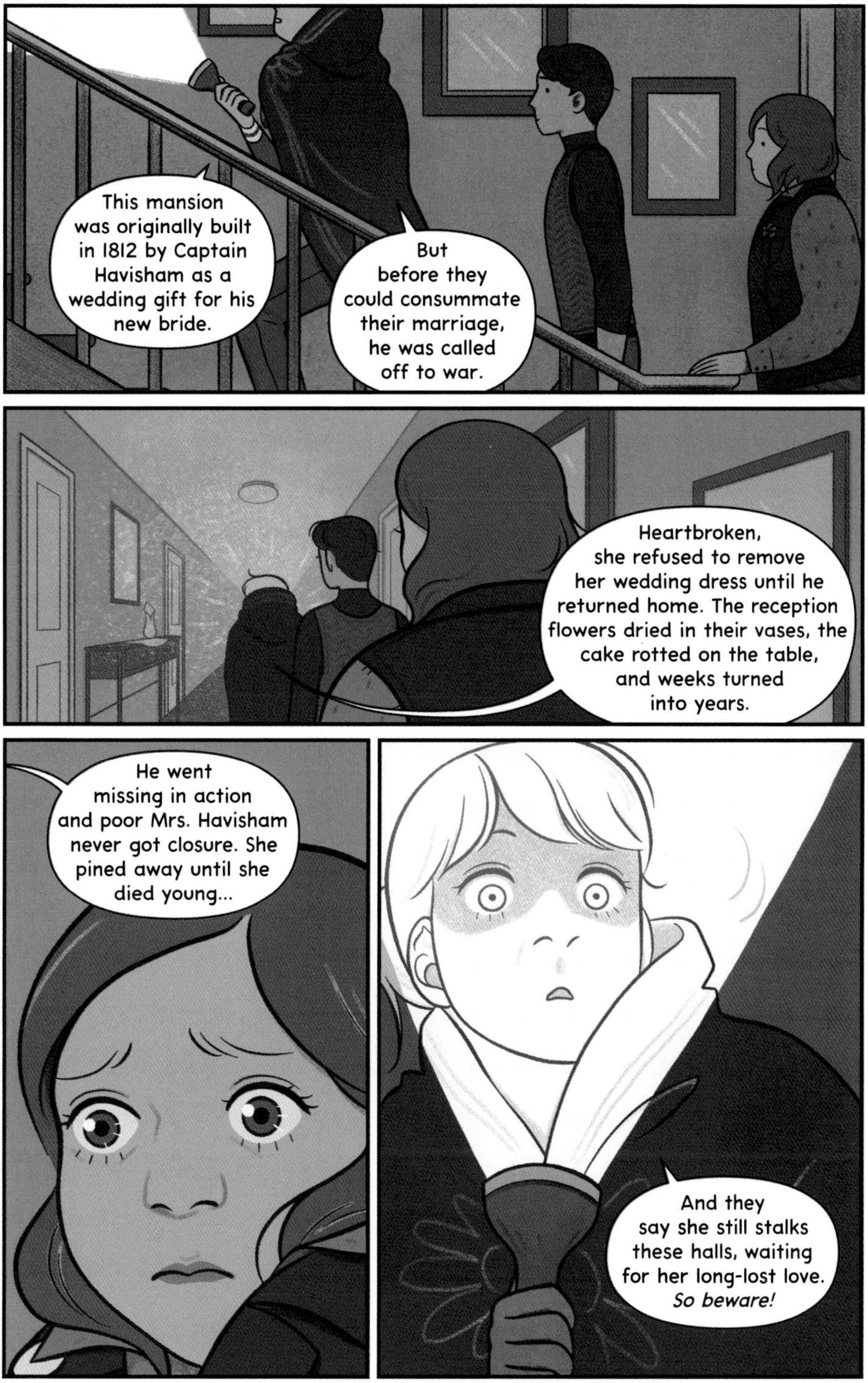
This mansion was originally built in 1812 by Captain Havisham as a wedding gift for his new bride.
But before they could consummate their marriage, he was called off to war.
Heartbroken, she refused to remove her wedding dress until he returned home. The reception flowers dried in their vases, the cake rotted on the table, and weeks turned into years.
He went missing in action and poor Mrs. Havisham never got closure. She pined away until she died young...
And they say she still stalks these halls, waiting for her long-lost love. *So beware!*

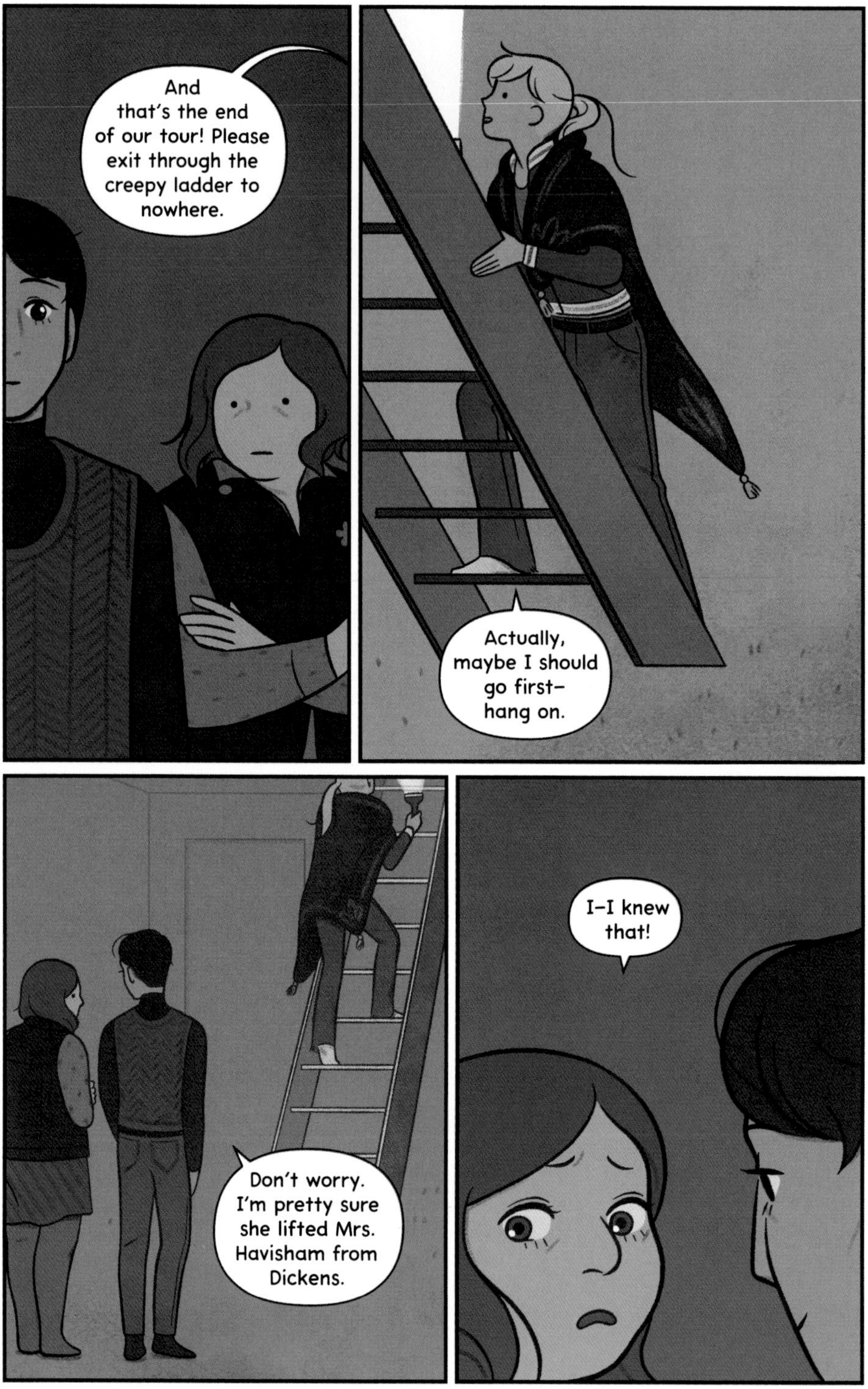
And that's the end of our tour! Please exit through the creepy ladder to nowhere.
Actually, maybe I should go first— hang on.
Don't worry. I'm pretty sure she lifted Mrs. Havisham from Dickens.
I—I knew that!

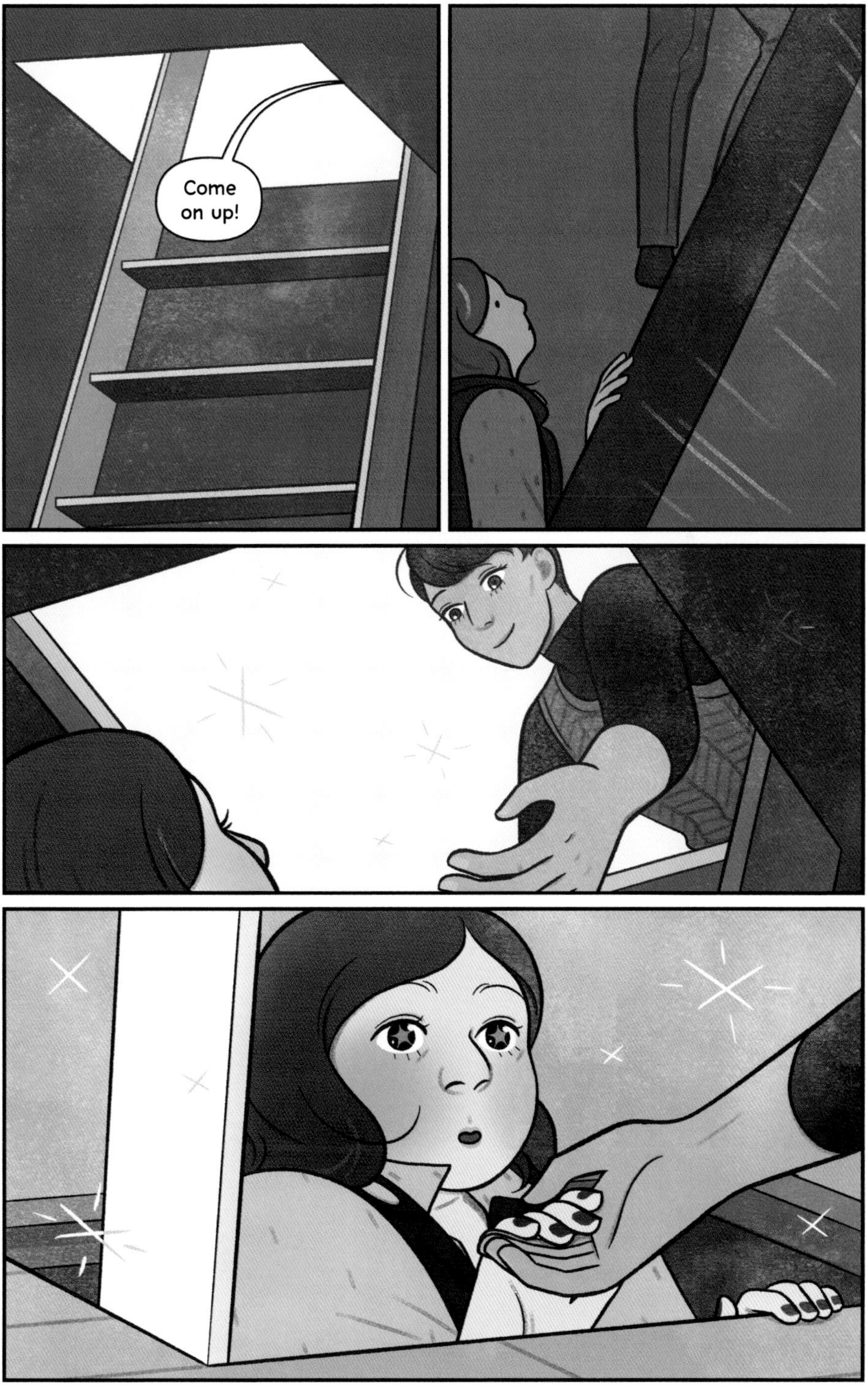
Come on up!

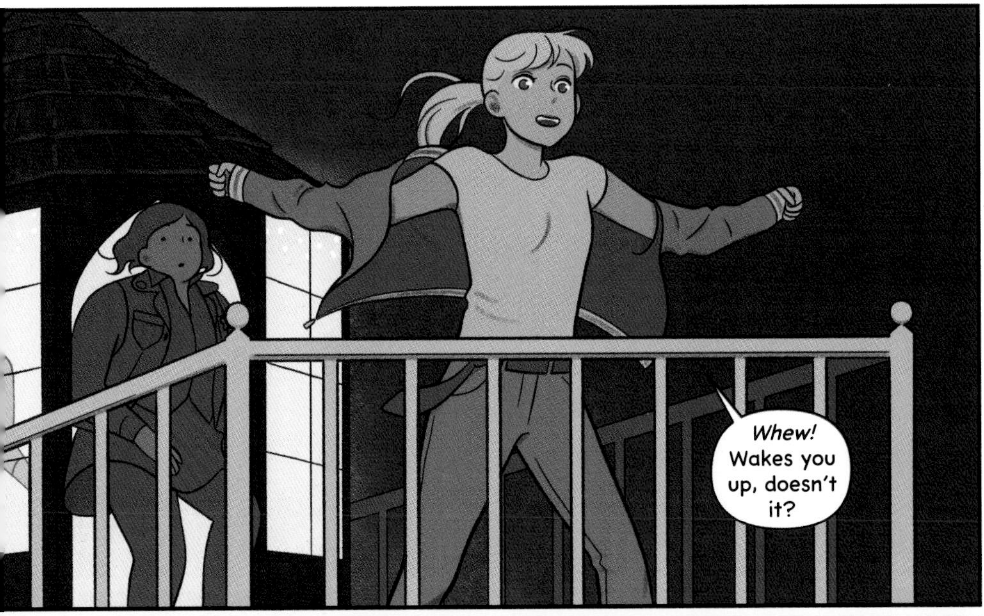
Whew! Wakes you up, doesn't it?
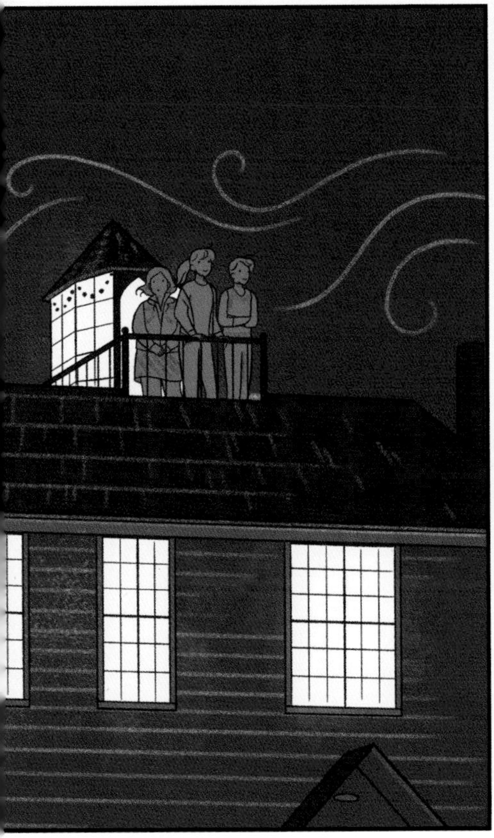
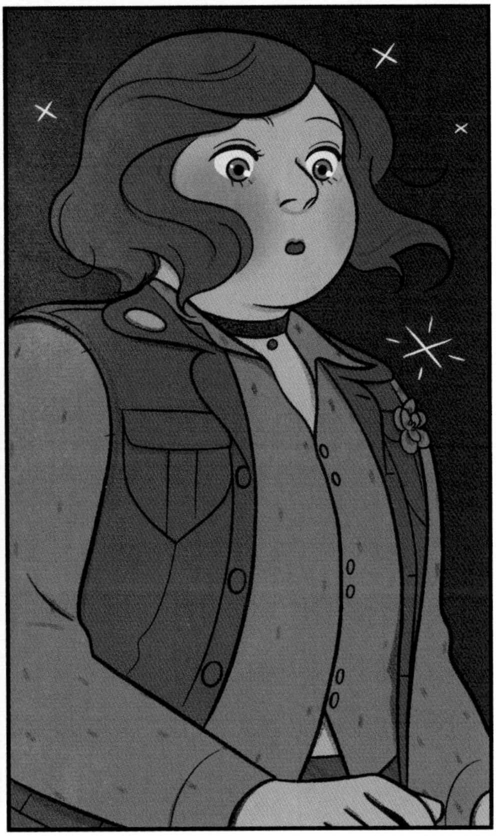

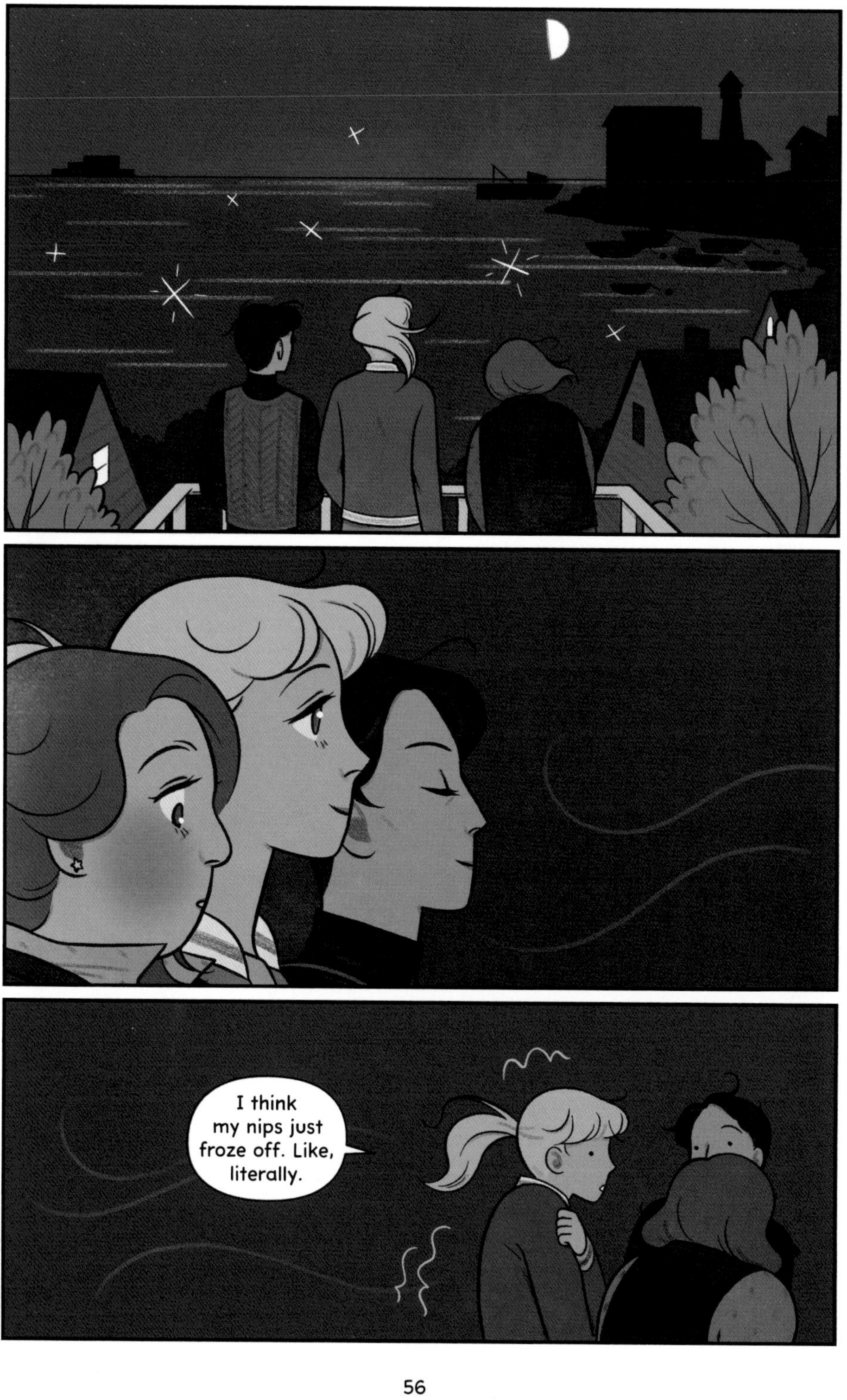
I think my nips just froze off. Like, literally.

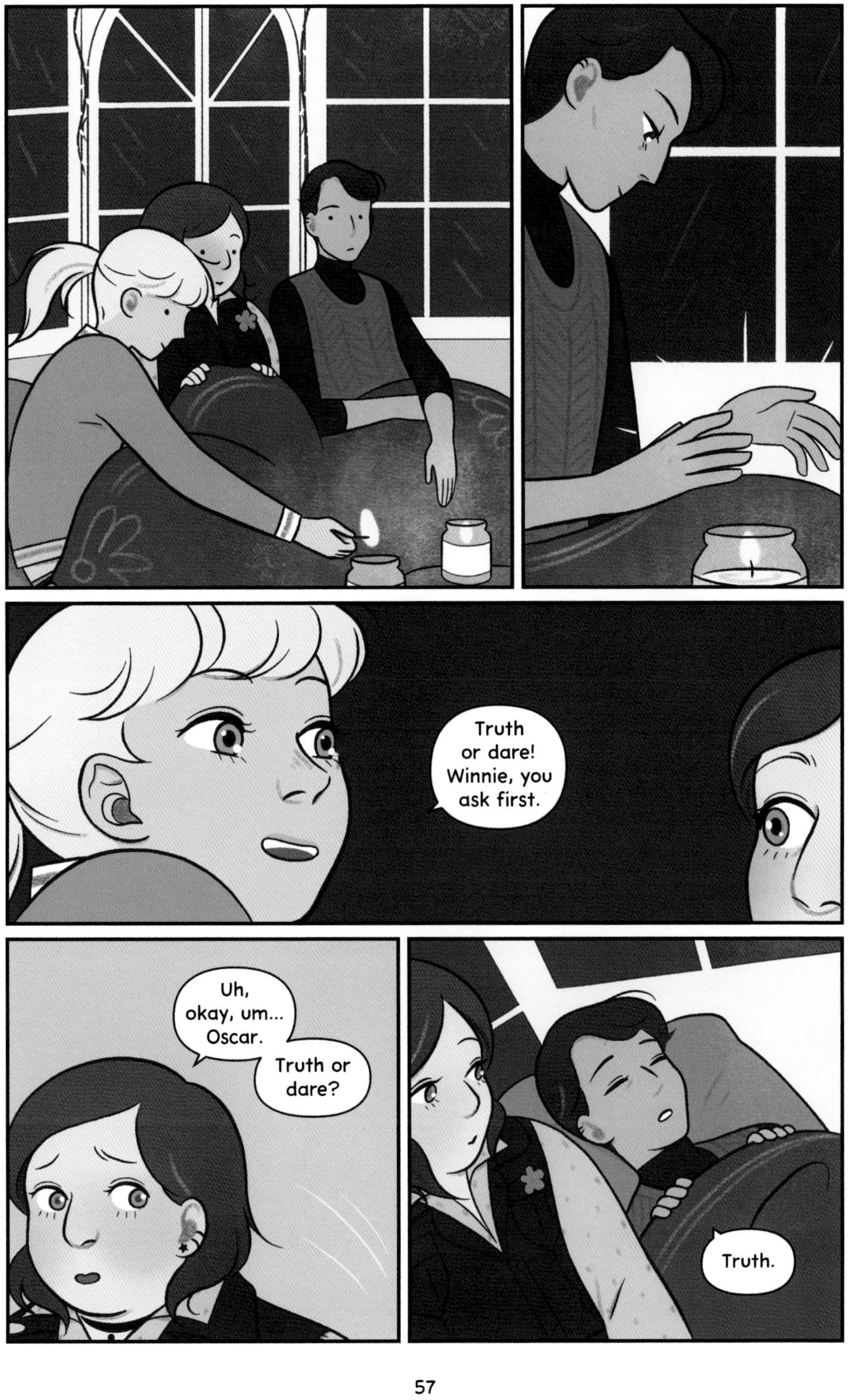
Truth or dare! Winnie, you ask first.
Uh, okay, um... Oscar.
Truth or dare?
Truth.

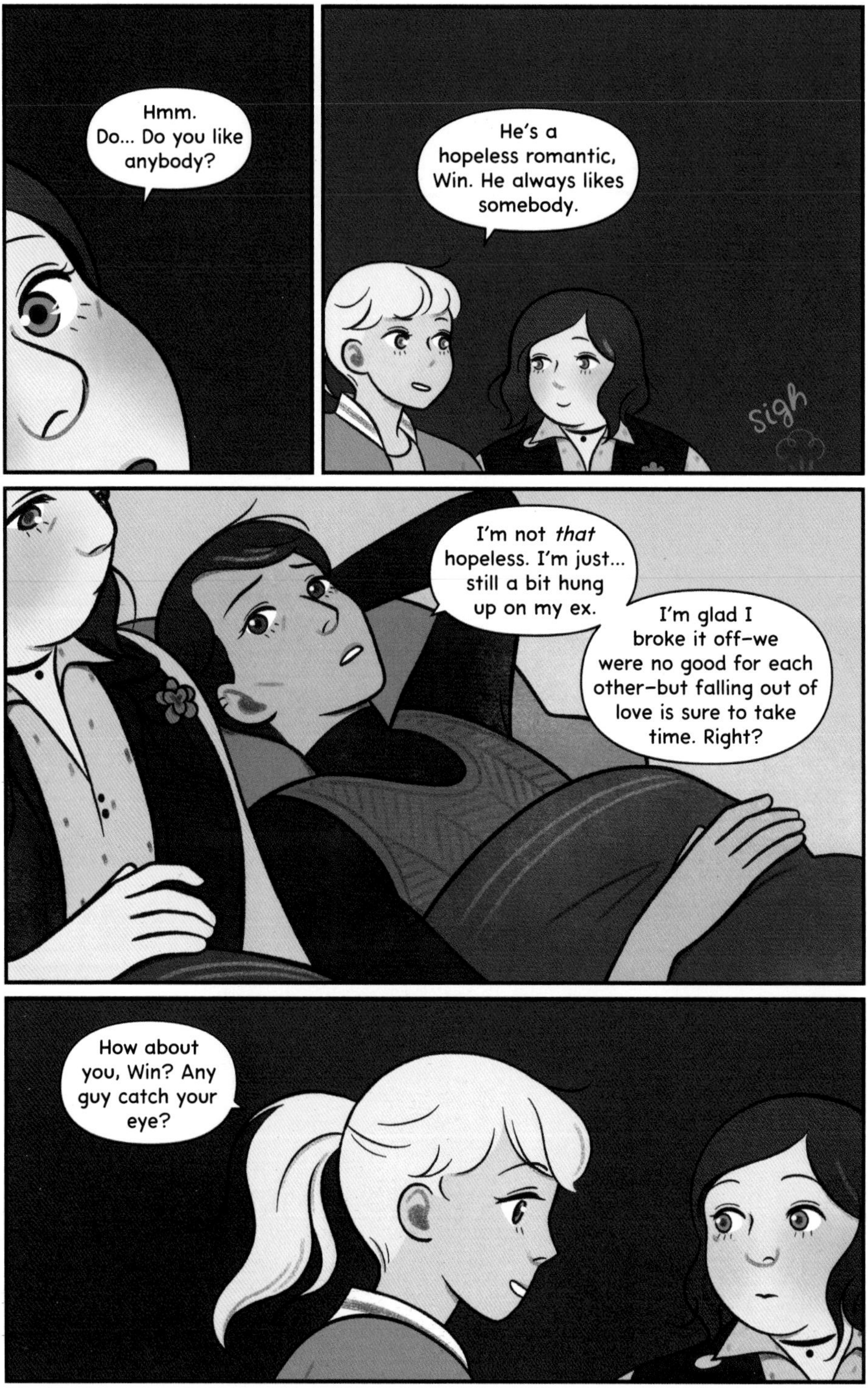
Hmm.
Do... Do you like anybody?
He's a hopeless romantic, Win. He always likes somebody.
sigh
I'm not *that* hopeless. I'm just... still a bit hung up on my ex.
I'm glad I broke it off—we were no good for each other—but falling out of love is sure to take time. Right?
How about you, Win? Any guy catch your eye?

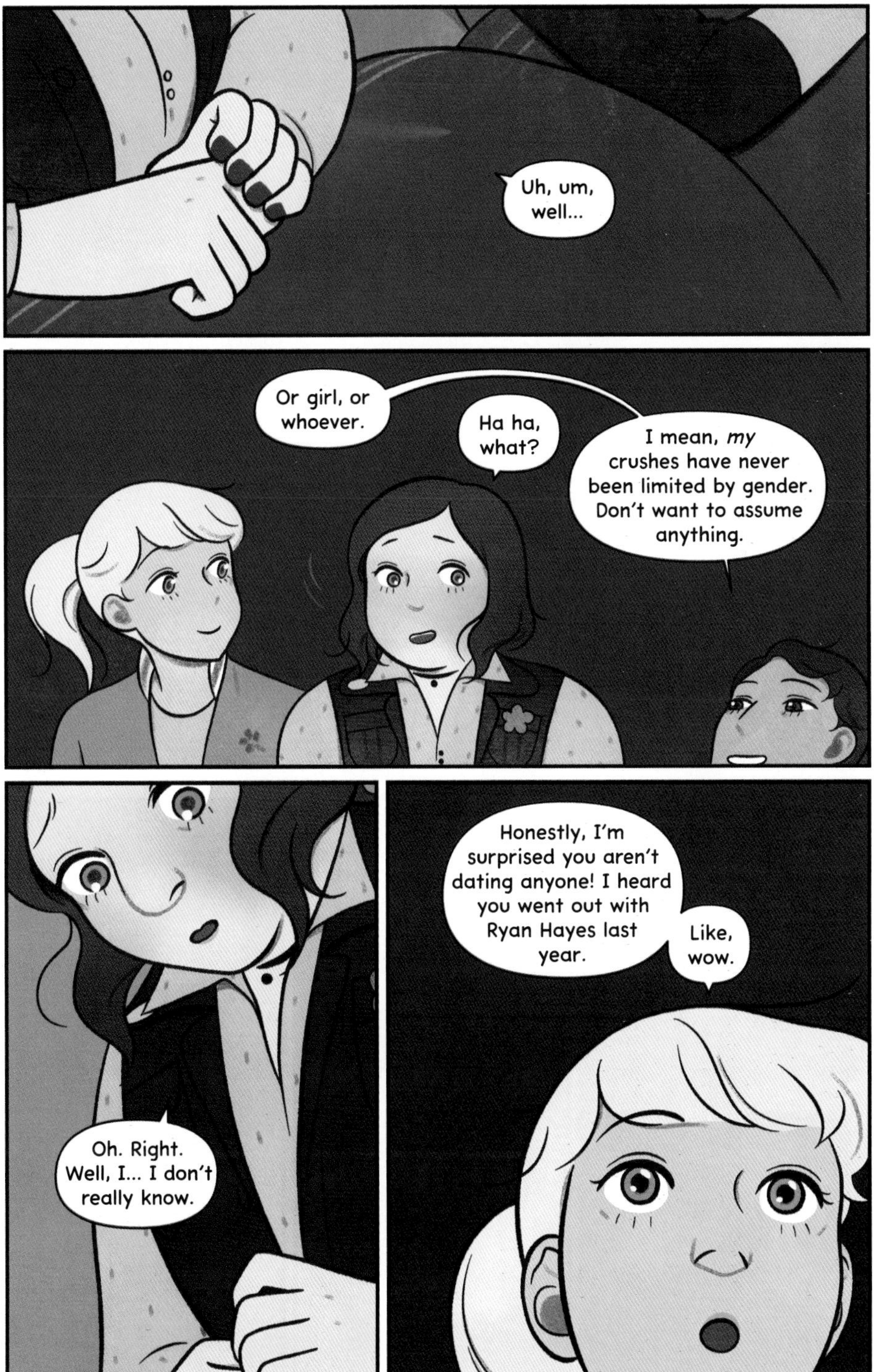
Uh, um, well...
Or girl, or whoever.
Ha ha, what?
I mean, *my* crushes have never been limited by gender. Don't want to assume anything.
Oh. Right. Well, I... I don't really know.
Honestly, I'm surprised you aren't dating anyone! I heard you went out with Ryan Hayes last year.
Like, wow.

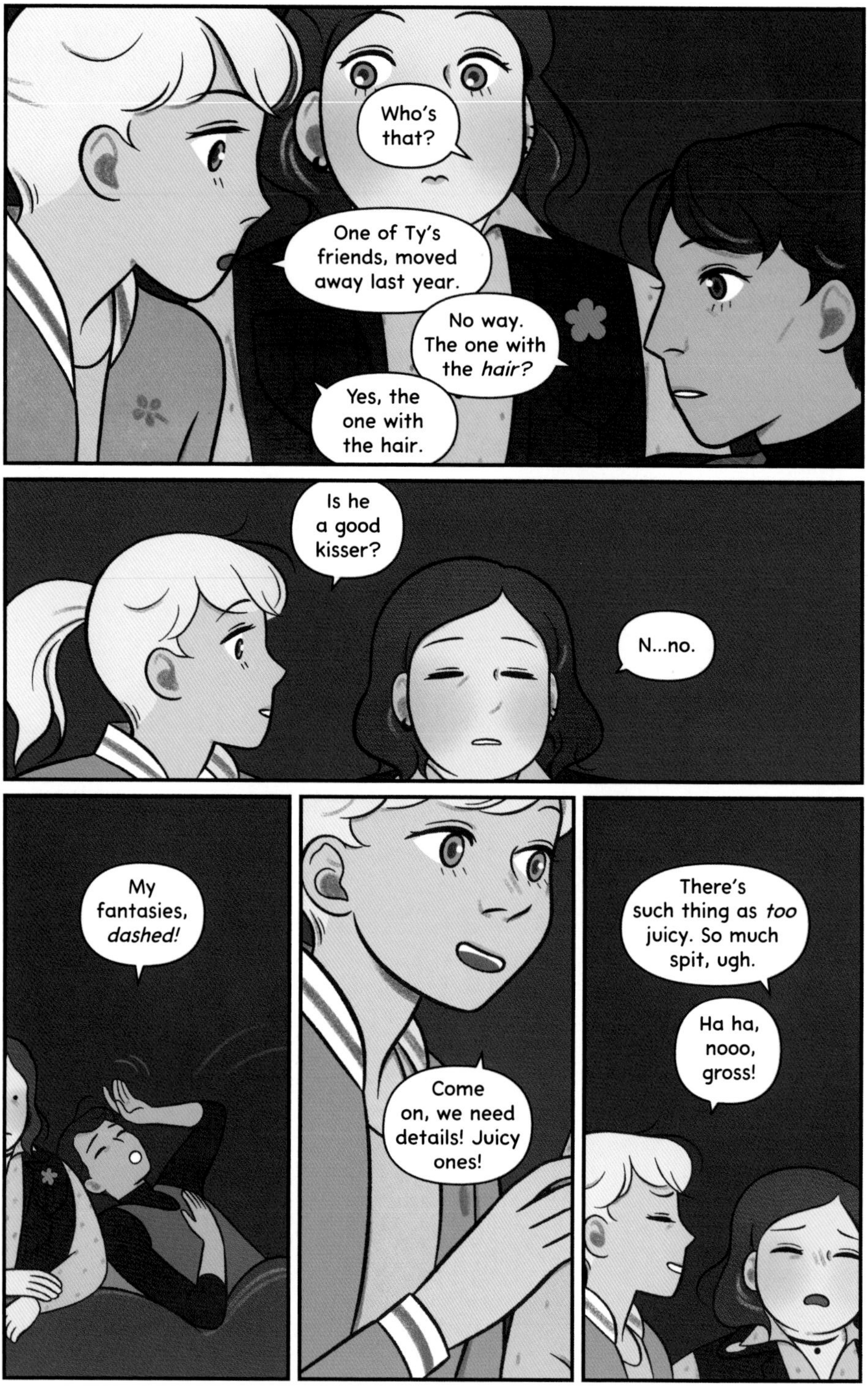
Who's that?
One of Ty's friends, moved away last year.
No way. The one with the *hair?*
Yes, the one with the hair.
Is he a good kisser?
N...no.
My fantasies, *dashed!*
Come on, we need details! Juicy ones!
There's such thing as *too* juicy. So much spit, ugh.
Ha ha, nooo, gross!

the C SHANTY

We'd met during a patio show at the record shop.

Hey. Winifred, right?

I'm Ryan.

I felt so lucky that he even knew I existed.

Can I give you a ride home?

Um, sure. Thanks.

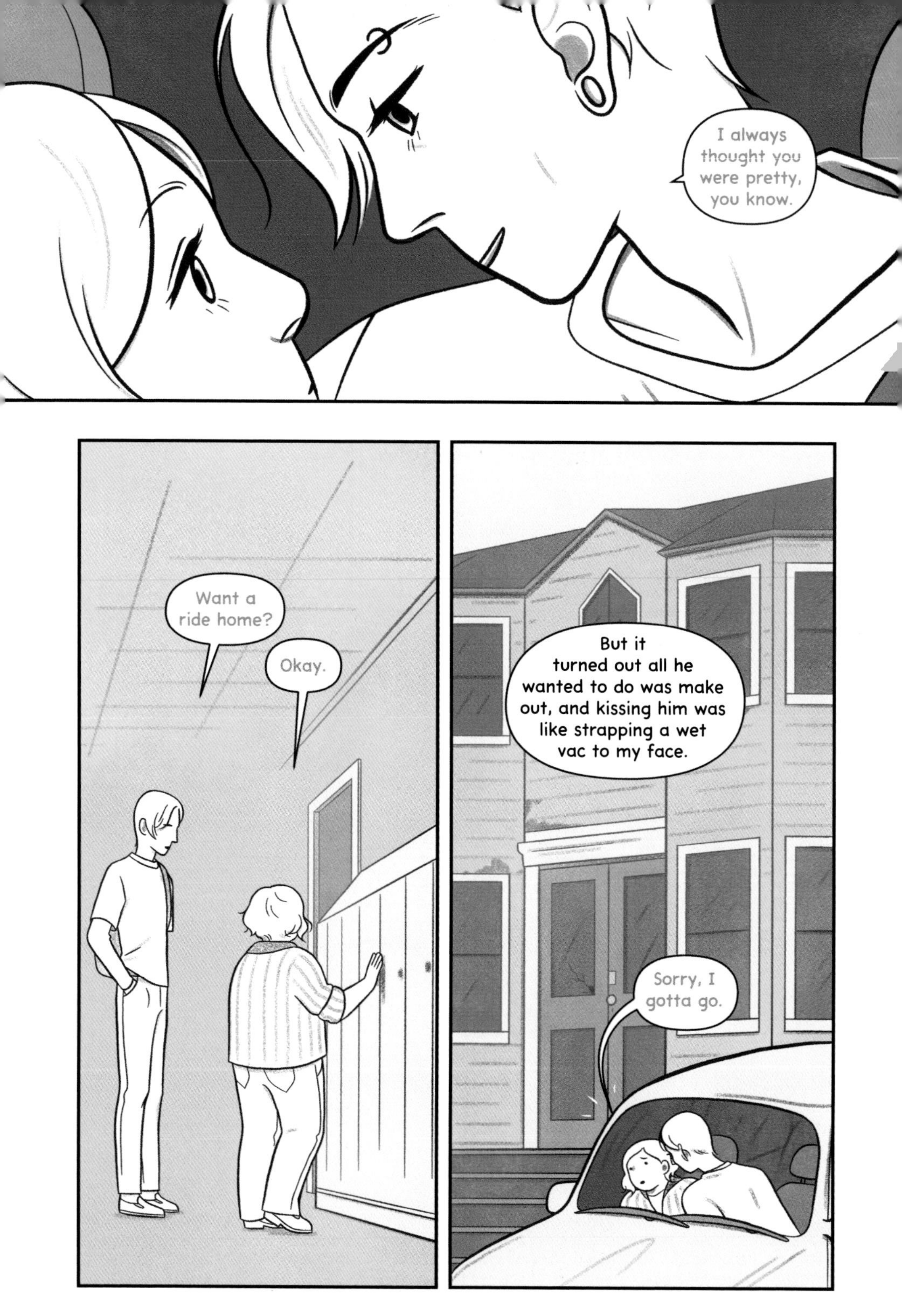
I always thought you were pretty, you know.
Want a ride home?
Okay.
But it turned out all he wanted to do was make out, and kissing him was like strapping a wet vac to my face.
Sorry, I gotta go.

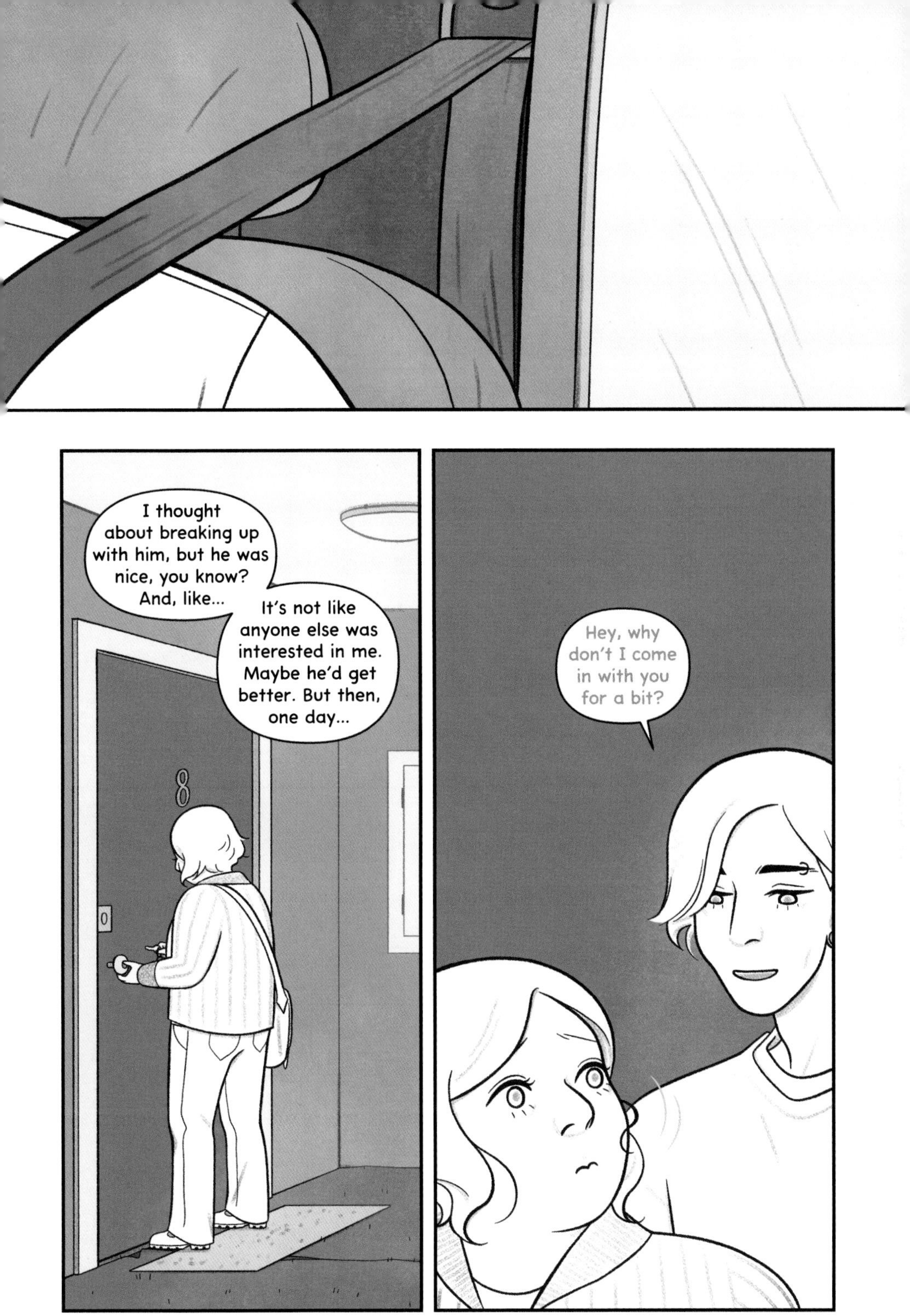
I thought about breaking up with him, but he was nice, you know? And, like...
It's not like anyone else was interested in me. Maybe he'd get better. But then, one day...
Hey, why don't I come in with you for a bit?

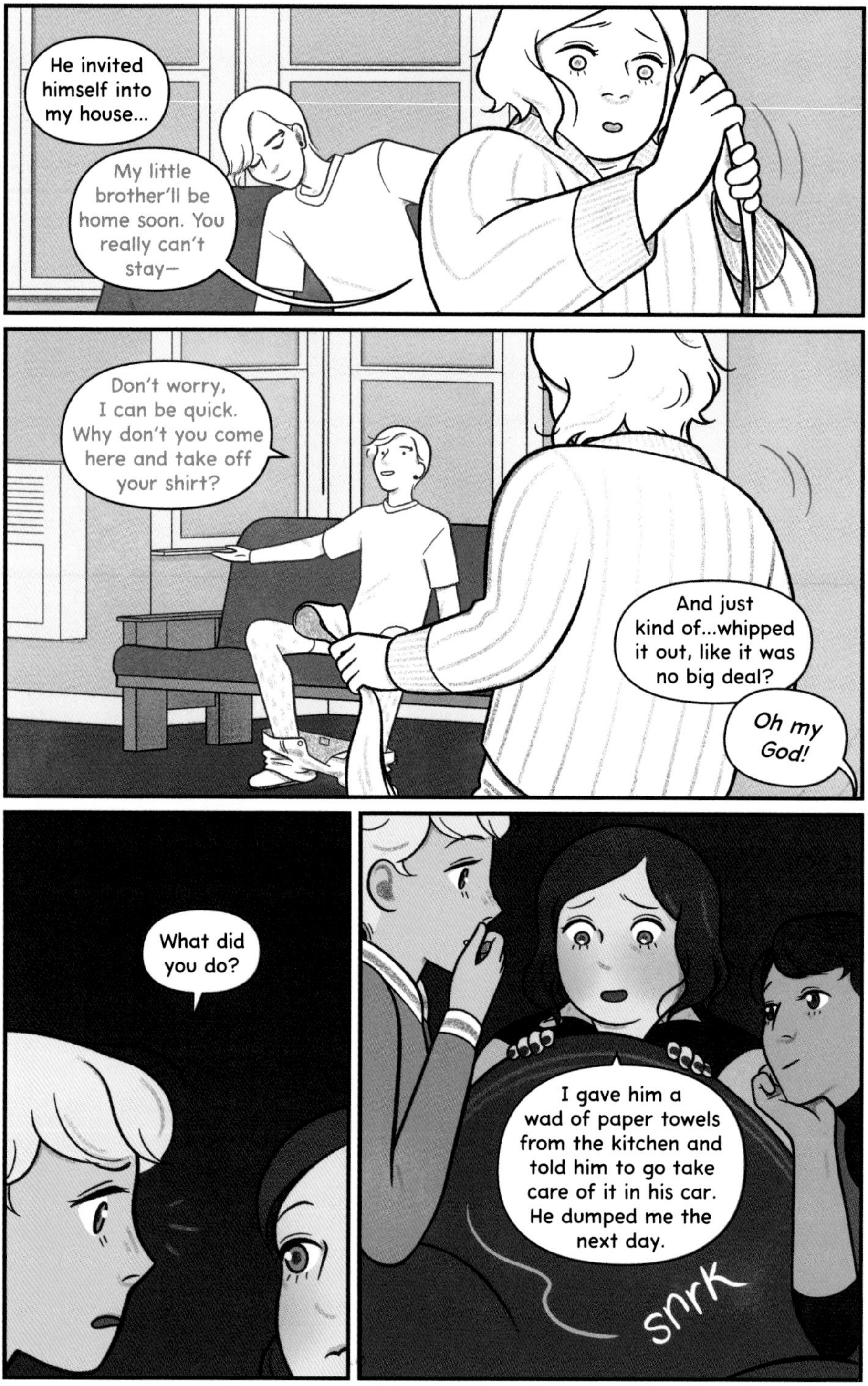
He invited himself into my house...
My little brother'll be home soon. You really can't stay—
Don't worry, I can be quick. Why don't you come here and take off your shirt?
And just kind of...whipped it out, like it was no big deal?
Oh my God!
What did you do?
I gave him a wad of paper towels from the kitchen and told him to go take care of it in his car. He dumped me the next day.
snrk

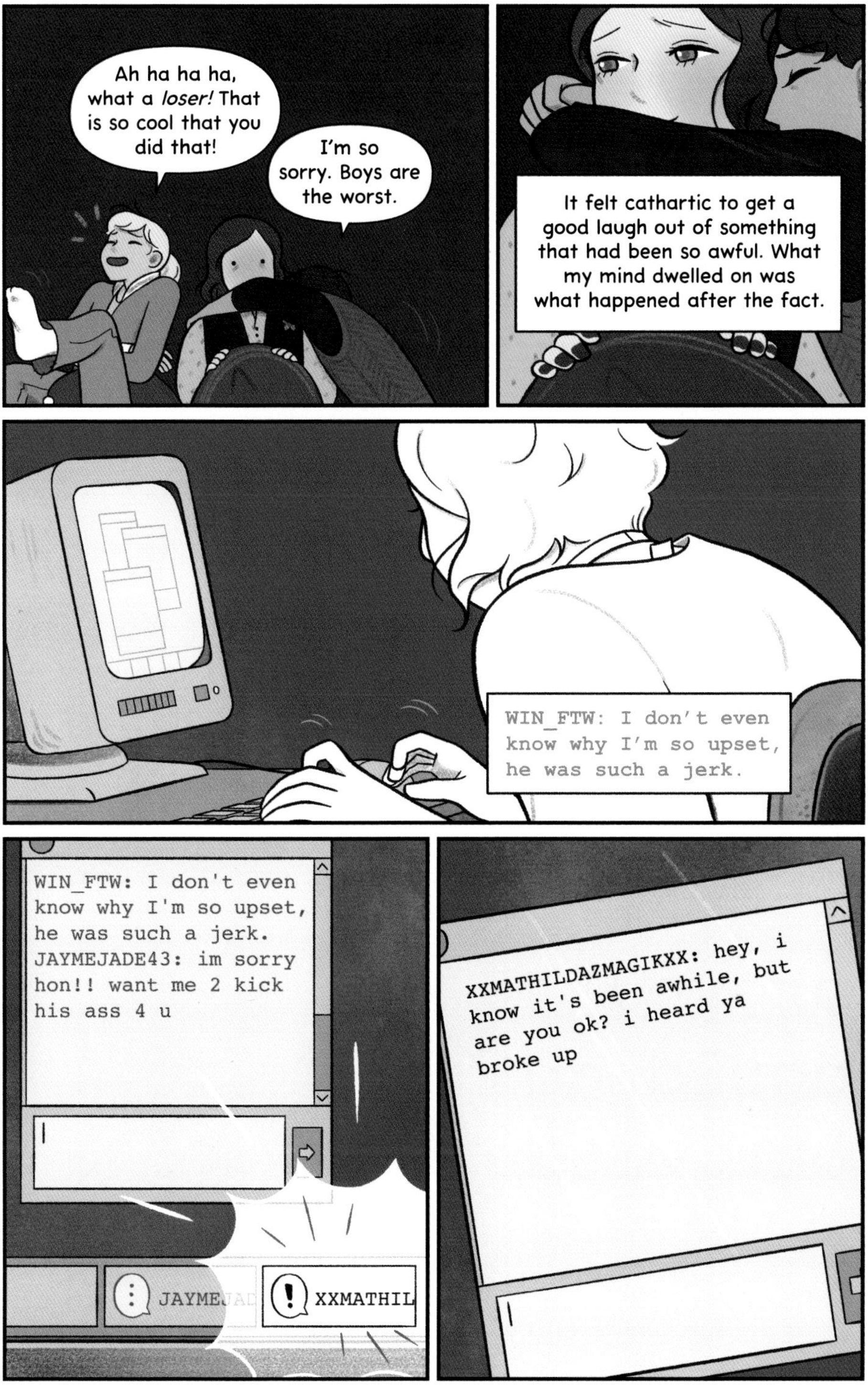
Ah ha ha ha, what a *loser!* That is so cool that you did that!
I'm so sorry. Boys are the worst.
It felt cathartic to get a good laugh out of something that had been so awful. What my mind dwelled on was what happened after the fact.
WIN_FTW: I don't even know why I'm so upset, he was such a jerk.
WIN_FTW: I don't even know why I'm so upset, he was such a jerk.
JAYMEJADE43: im sorry hon!! want me 2 kick his ass 4 u
JAYMEJAD
XXMATHIL
XXMATHILDAZMAGIKXX: hey, i know it's been awhile, but are you ok? i heard ya broke up

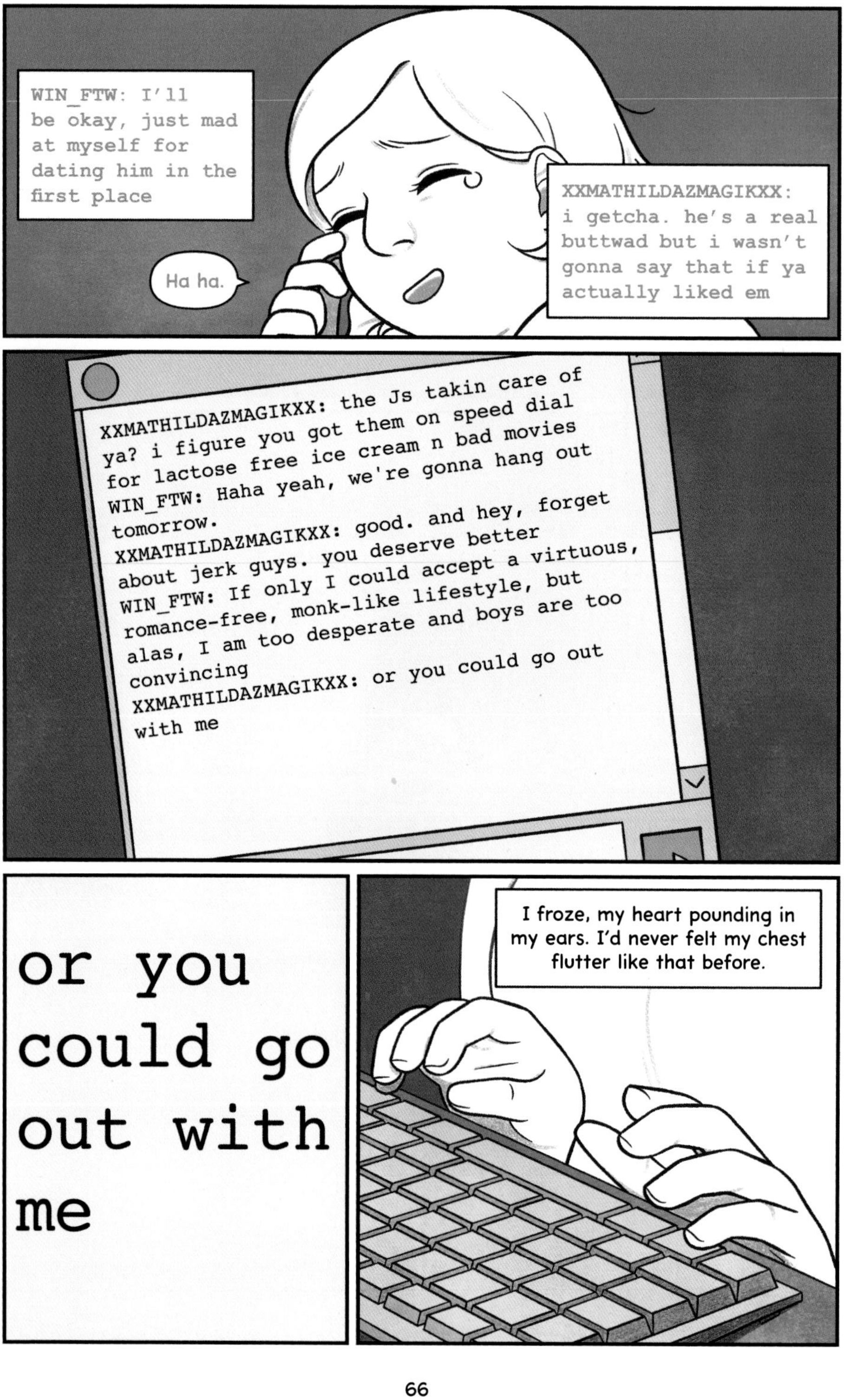
WIN_FTW: I'll be okay, just mad at myself for dating him in the first place
Ha ha.
XXMATHILDAZMAGIKXX: i getcha. he's a real buttwad but i wasn't gonna say that if ya actually liked em
XXMATHILDAZMAGIKXX: the Js takin care of ya? i figure you got them on speed dial for lactose free ice cream n bad movies
WIN_FTW: Haha yeah, we're gonna hang out tomorrow.
XXMATHILDAZMAGIKXX: good. and hey, forget about jerk guys. you deserve better
WIN_FTW: If only I could accept a virtuous, romance-free, monk-like lifestyle, but alas, I am too desperate and boys are too convincing
XXMATHILDAZMAGIKXX: or you could go out with me
or you could go out with me
I froze, my heart pounding in my ears. I'd never felt my chest flutter like that before.

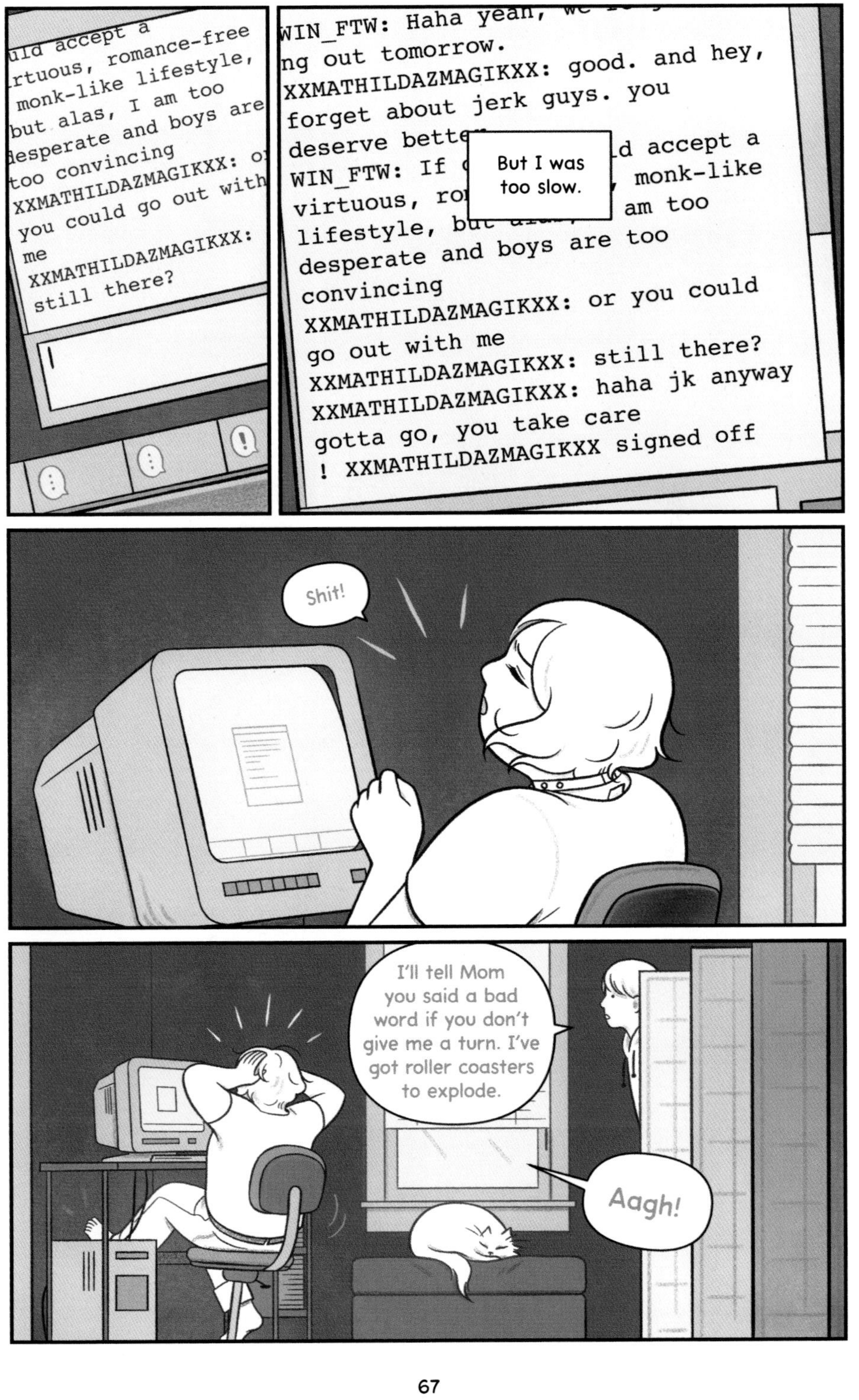
uld accept a
rtuous, romance-free
monk-like lifestyle,
but alas, I am too
desperate and boys are
too convincing
XXMATHILDAZMAGIKXX: o
you could go out with
me
XXMATHILDAZMAGIKXX:
still there?
WIN_FTW: Haha yeah,
ng out tomorrow.
XXMATHILDAZMAGIKXX: good. and hey,
forget about jerk guys. you
deserve bette
WIN_FTW: If
d accept a
virtuous, ro
, monk-like
lifestyle, bu
am too
desperate and boys are too
convincing
XXMATHILDAZMAGIKXX: or you could
go out with me
XXMATHILDAZMAGIKXX: still there?
XXMATHILDAZMAGIKXX: haha jk anyway
gotta go, you take care
! XXMATHILDAZMAGIKXX signed off
But I was too slow.
Shit!
I'll tell Mom you said a bad word if you don't give me a turn. I've got roller coasters to explode.
Aagh!

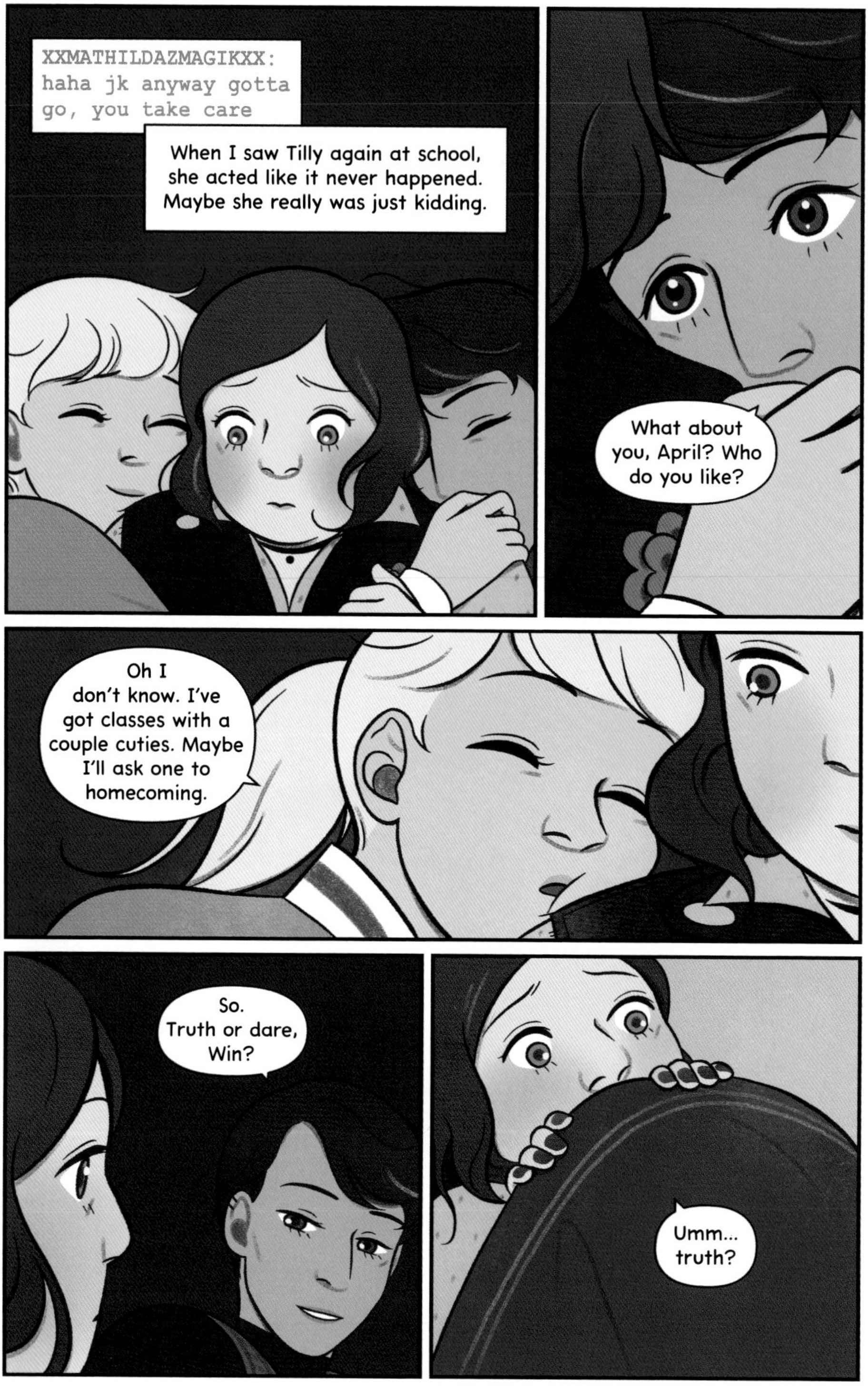
XXMATHILDAZMAGIKXX: haha jk anyway gotta go, you take care
When I saw Tilly again at school, she acted like it never happened. Maybe she really was just kidding.
What about you, April? Who do you like?
Oh I don't know. I've got classes with a couple cuties. Maybe I'll ask one to homecoming.
So. Truth or dare, Win?
Umm... truth?

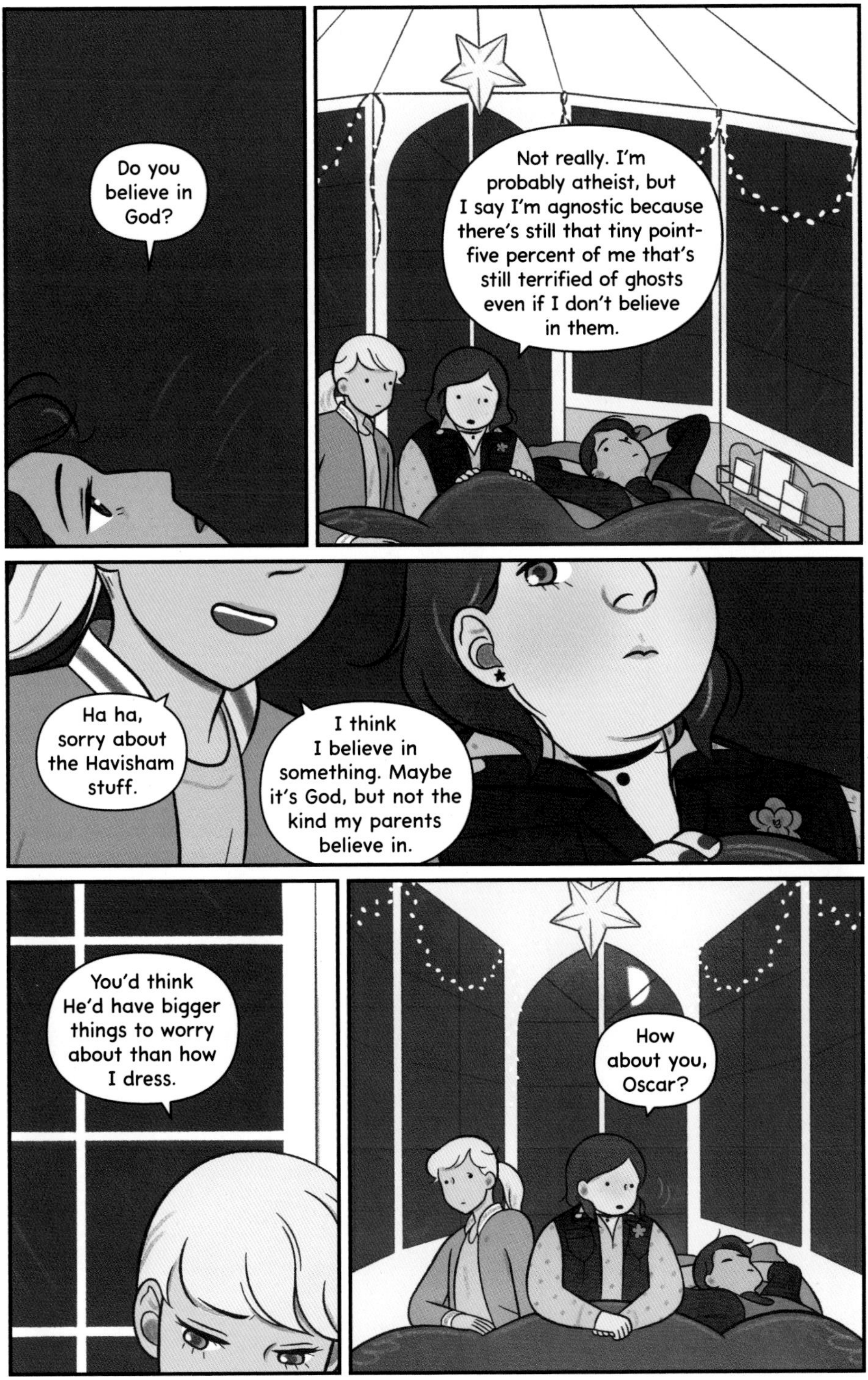
Do you believe in God?
Not really. I'm probably atheist, but I say I'm agnostic because there's still that tiny point-five percent of me that's still terrified of ghosts even if I don't believe in them.
Ha ha, sorry about the Havisham stuff.
I think I believe in something. Maybe it's God, but not the kind my parents believe in.
You'd think He'd have bigger things to worry about than how I dress.
How about you, Oscar?

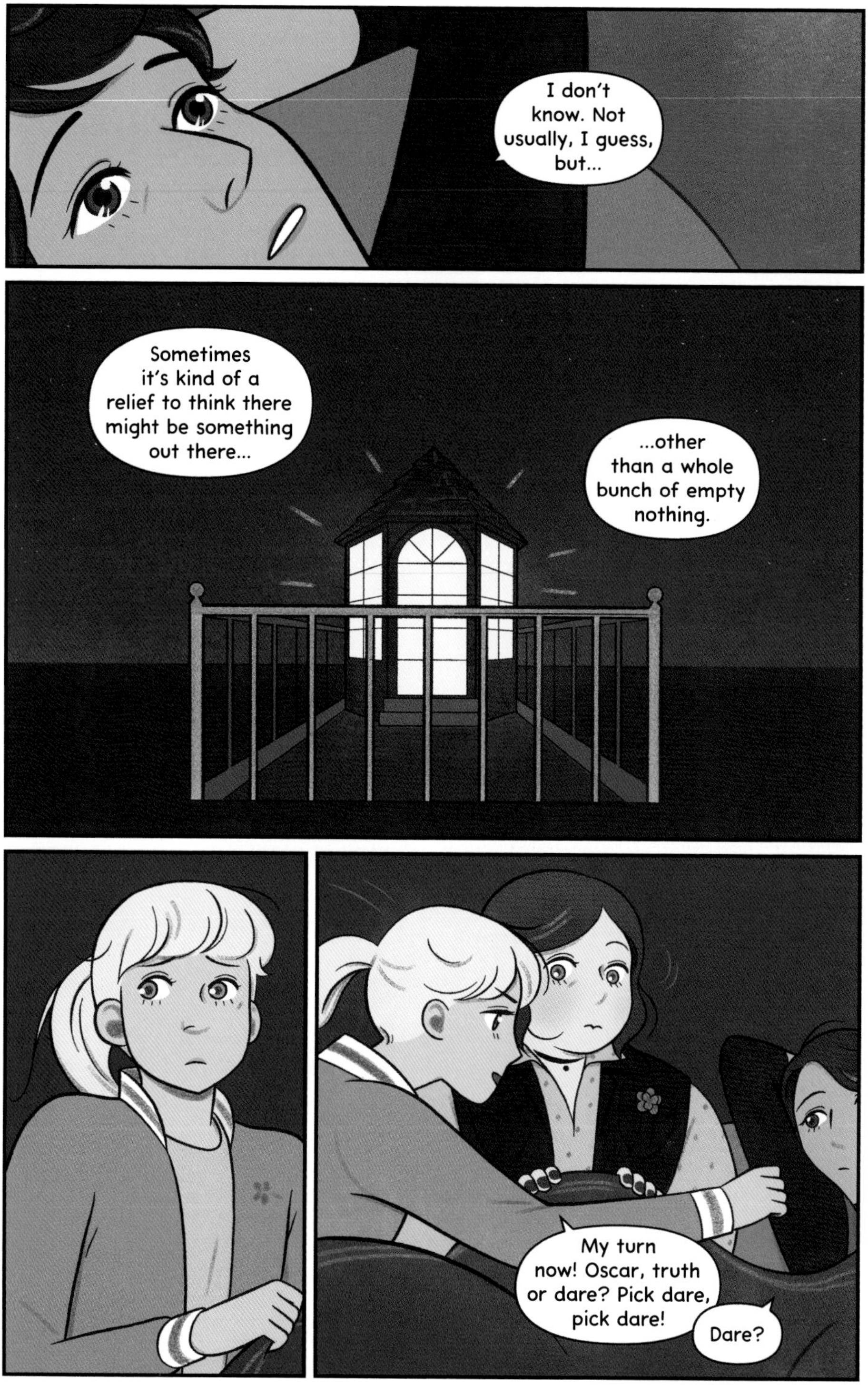
I don't know. Not usually, I guess, but...
Sometimes it's kind of a relief to think there might be something out there...
...other than a whole bunch of empty nothing.
My turn now! Oscar, truth or dare? Pick dare, pick dare!
Dare?

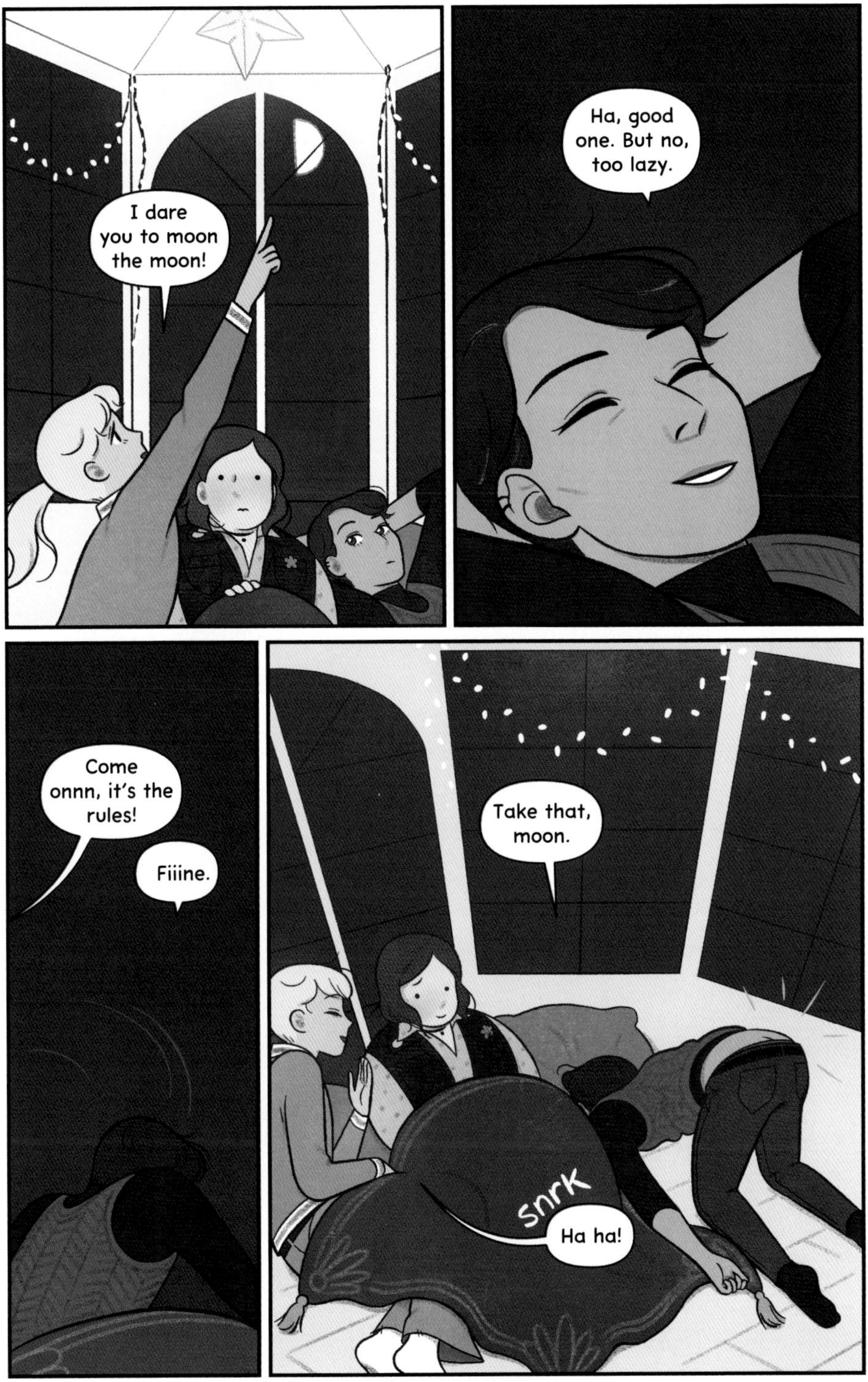
I dare you to moon the moon!
Ha, good one. But no, too lazy.
Come onnn, it's the rules!
Fiiine.
Take that, moon.
snrk
Ha ha!

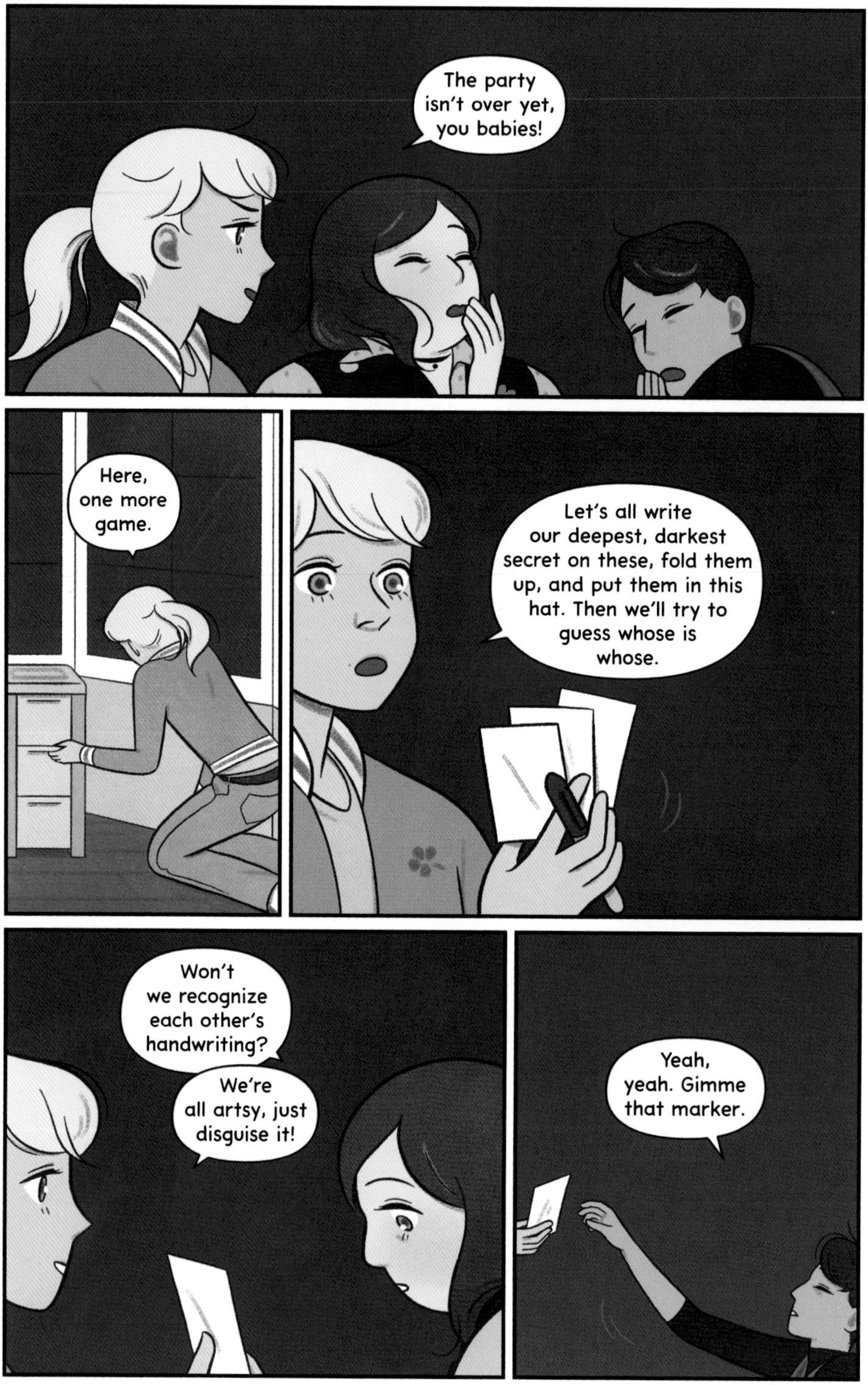
The party isn't over yet, you babies!
Here, one more game.
Let's all write our deepest, darkest secret on these, fold them up, and put them in this hat. Then we'll try to guess whose is whose.
Won't we recognize each other's handwriting?
We're all artsy, just disguise it!
Yeah, yeah. Gimme that marker.

Now, for the moment of truth!

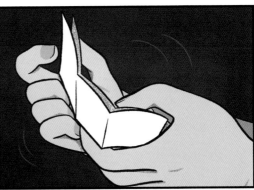

I hate myself

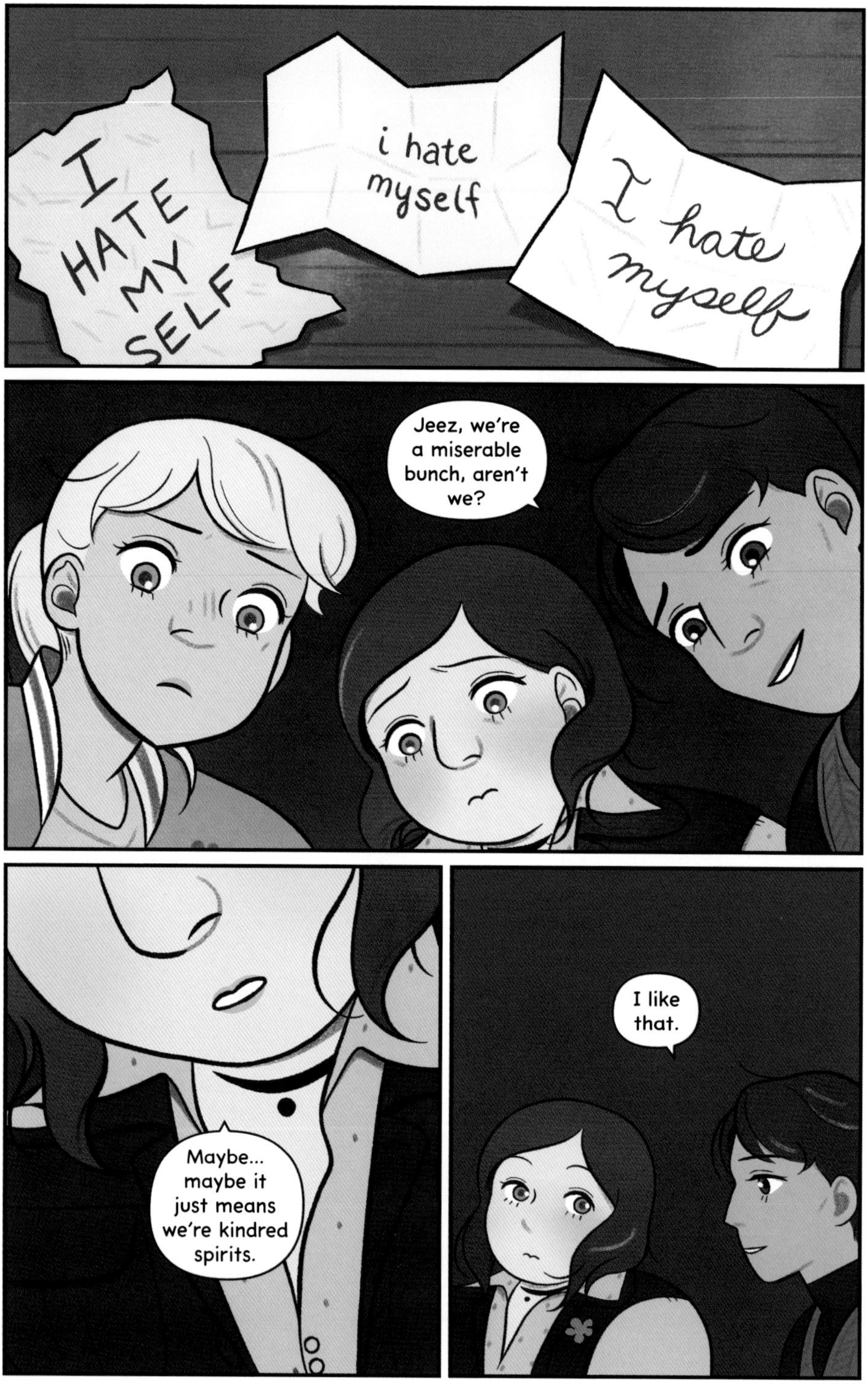
I HATE MY SELF
i hate myself
I hate myself
Jeez, we're a miserable bunch, aren't we?
Maybe... maybe it just means we're kindred spirits.
I like that.

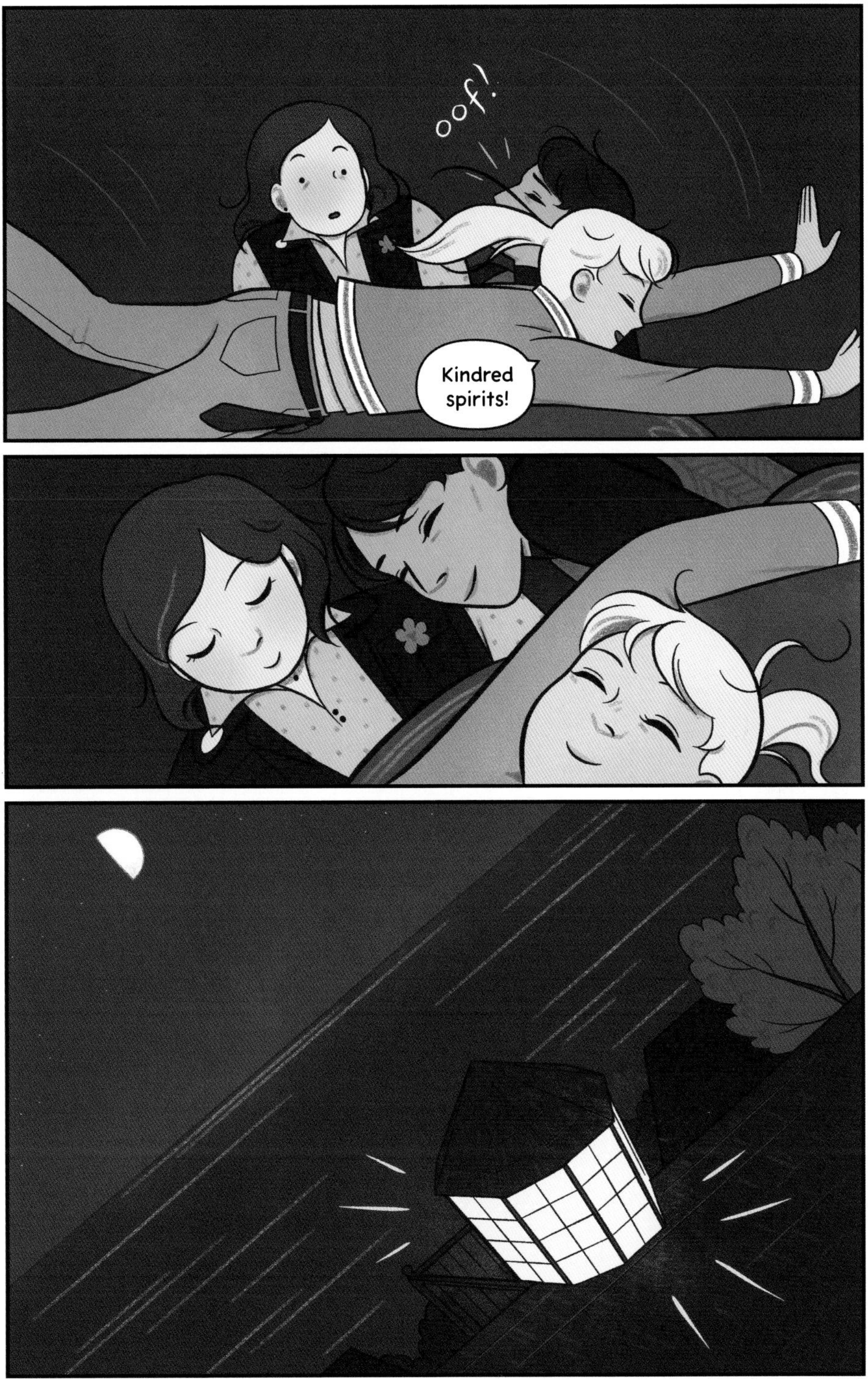
oof!
Kindred spirits!

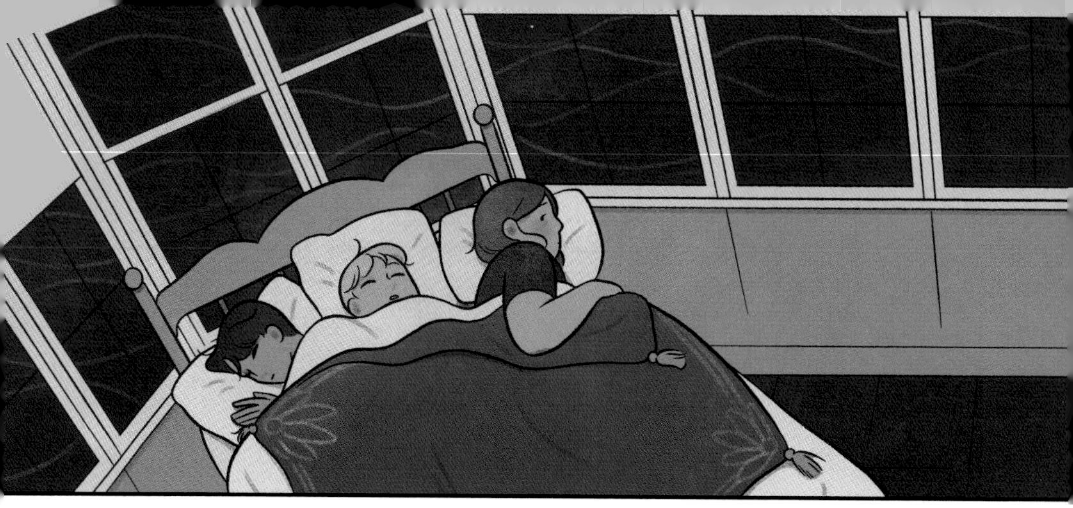

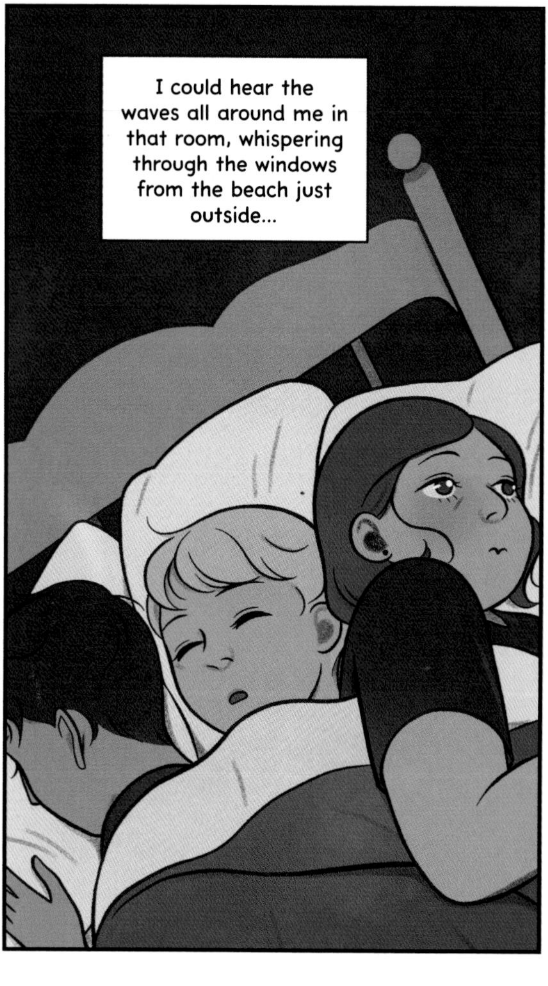
I could hear the waves all around me in that room, whispering through the windows from the beach just outside...

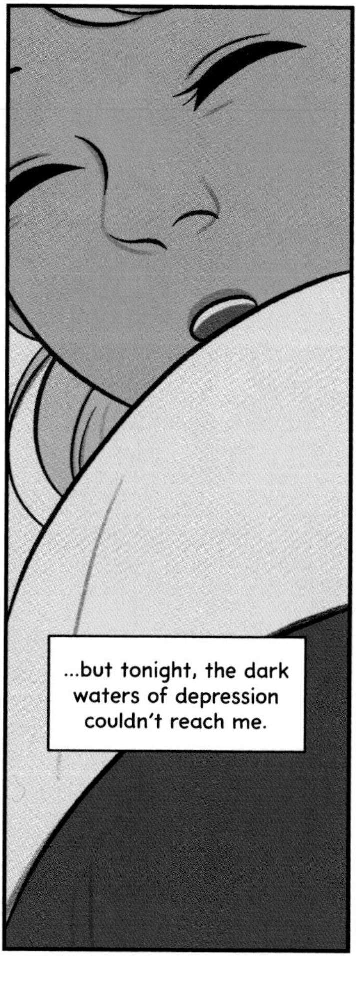
...but tonight, the dark waters of depression couldn't reach me.

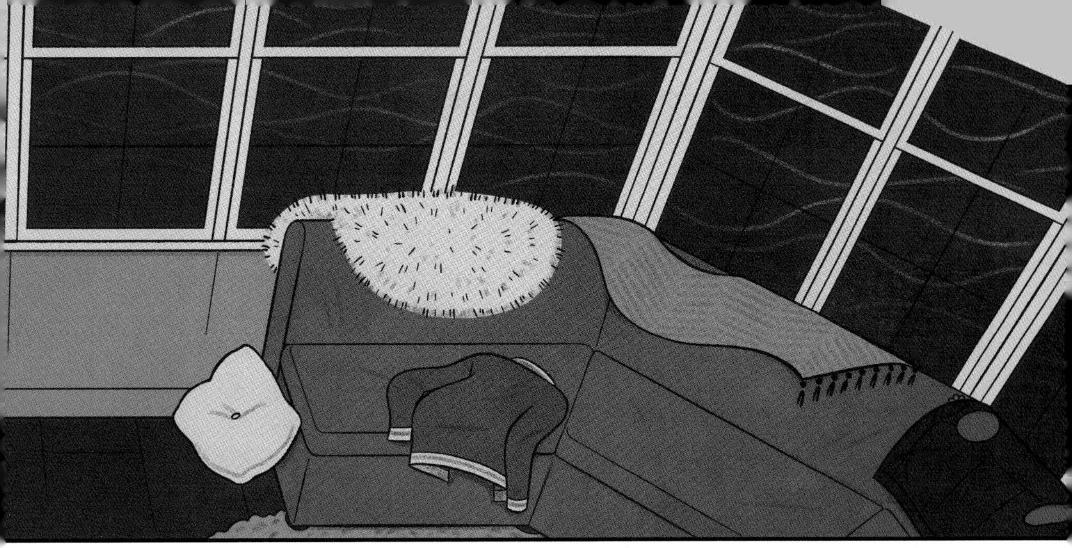

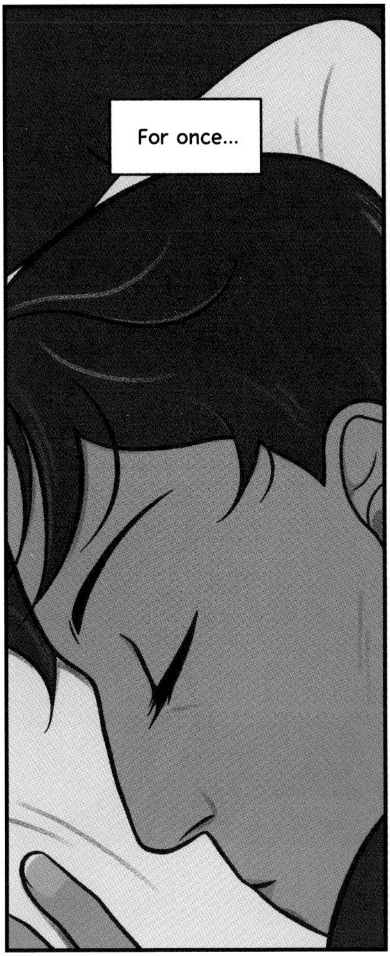
For once...

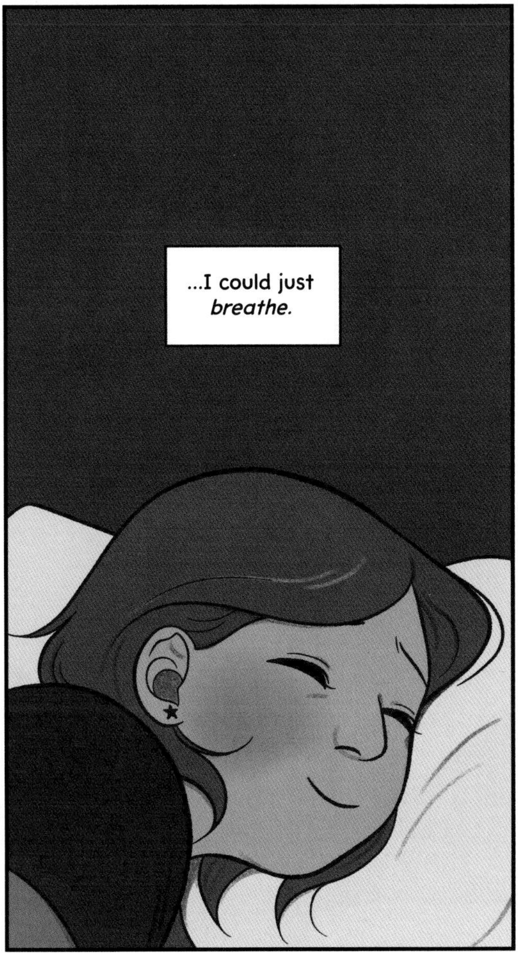
...I could just *breathe.*

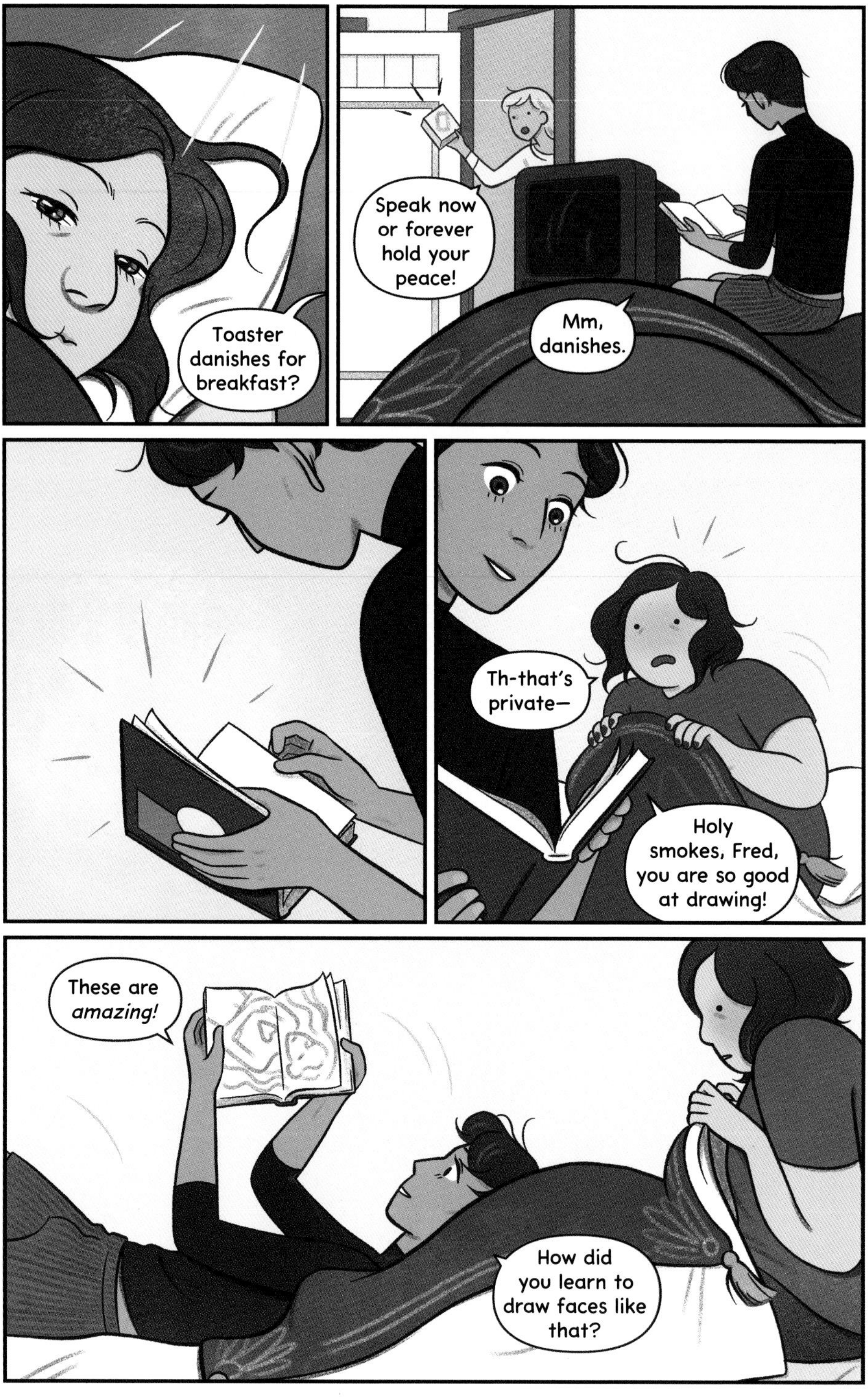
Toaster danishes for breakfast?
Speak now or forever hold your peace!
Mm, danishes.
Th-that's private—
Holy smokes, Fred, you are so good at drawing!
These are *amazing!*
How did you learn to draw faces like that?

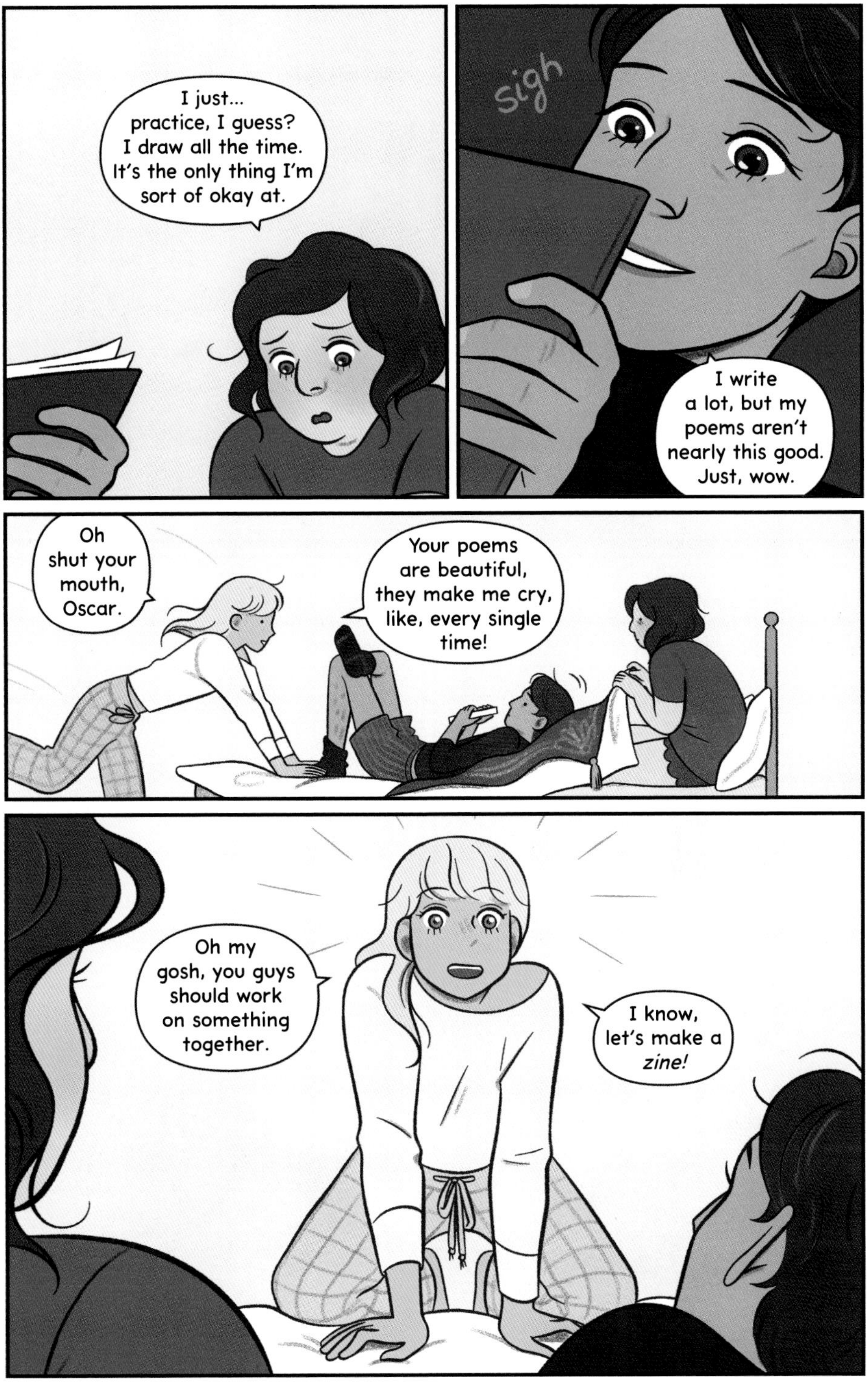

I just... practice, I guess? I draw all the time. It's the only thing I'm sort of okay at.
sigh
I write a lot, but my poems aren't nearly this good. Just, wow.
Oh shut your mouth, Oscar.
Your poems are beautiful, they make me cry, like, every single time!
Oh my gosh, you guys should work on something together.
I know, let's make a *zine!*

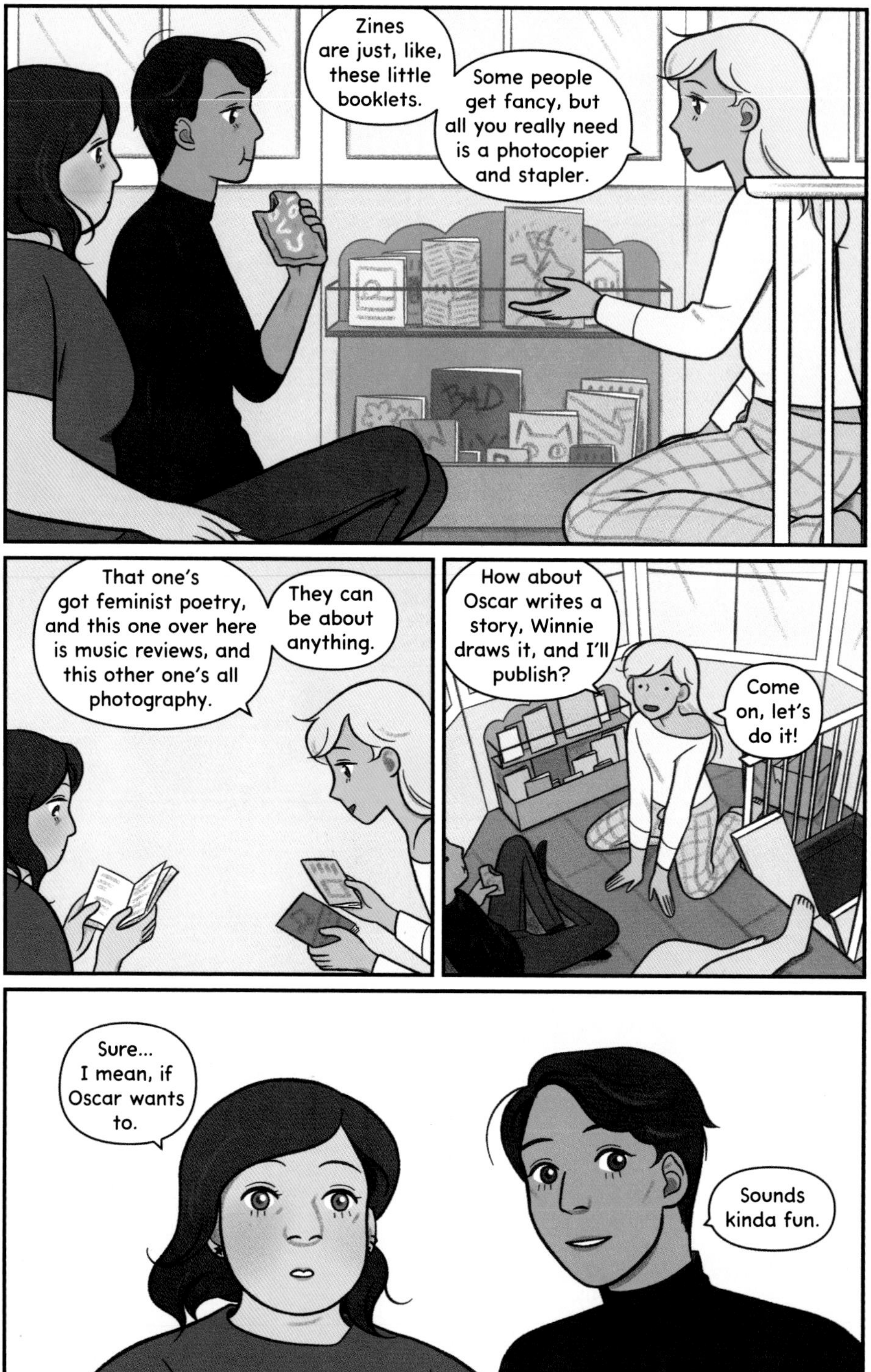
Zines are just, like, these little booklets.
Some people get fancy, but all you really need is a photocopier and stapler.
That one's got feminist poetry, and this one over here is music reviews, and this other one's all photography.
They can be about anything.
How about Oscar writes a story, Winnie draws it, and I'll publish?
Come on, let's do it!
Sure... I mean, if Oscar wants to.
Sounds kinda fun.

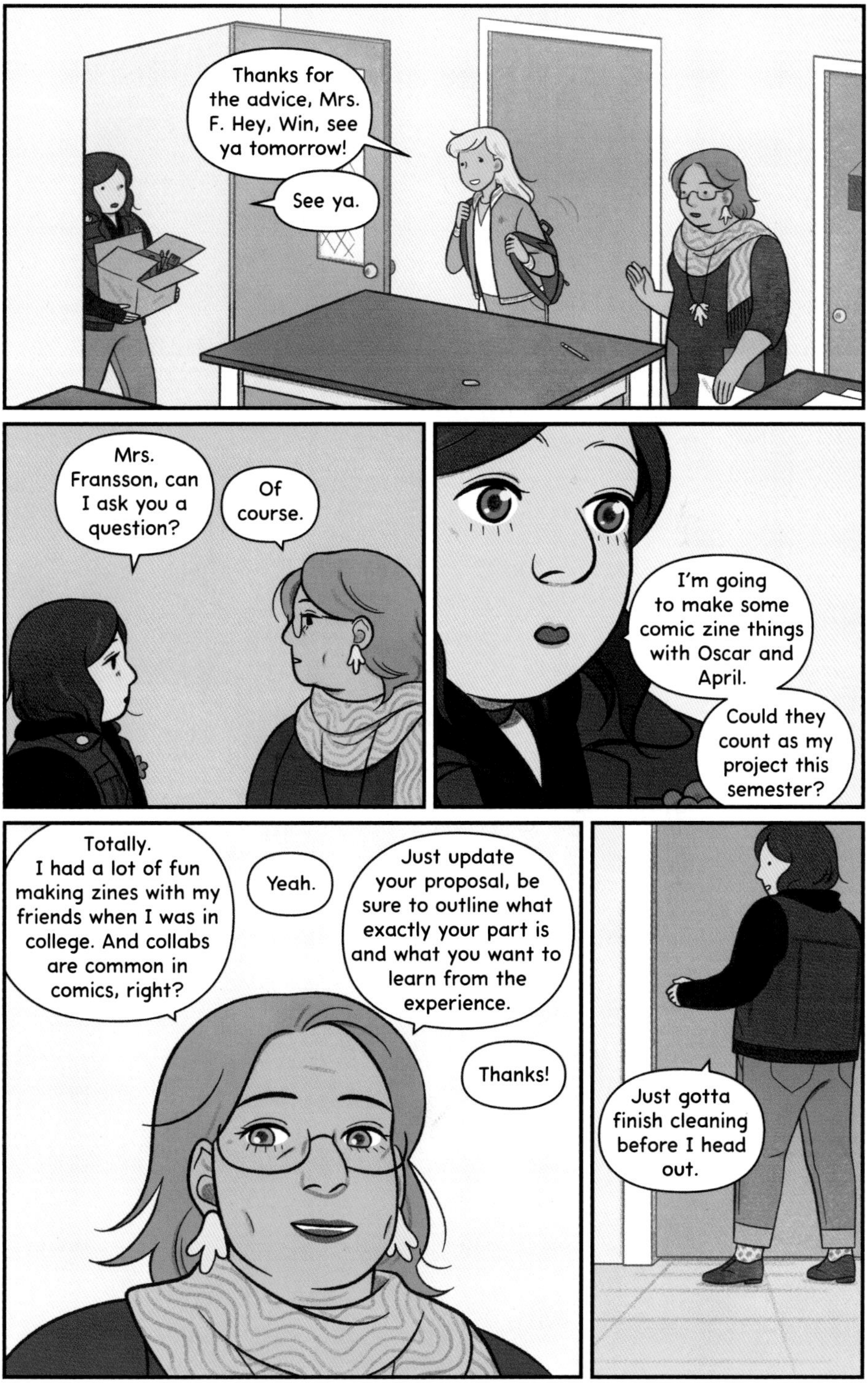
Thanks for the advice, Mrs. F. Hey, Win, see ya tomorrow!
See ya.
Mrs. Fransson, can I ask you a question?
Of course.
I'm going to make some comic zine things with Oscar and April.
Could they count as my project this semester?
Totally. I had a lot of fun making zines with my friends when I was in college. And collabs are common in comics, right?
Yeah.
Just update your proposal, be sure to outline what exactly your part is and what you want to learn from the experience.
Thanks!
Just gotta finish cleaning before I head out.

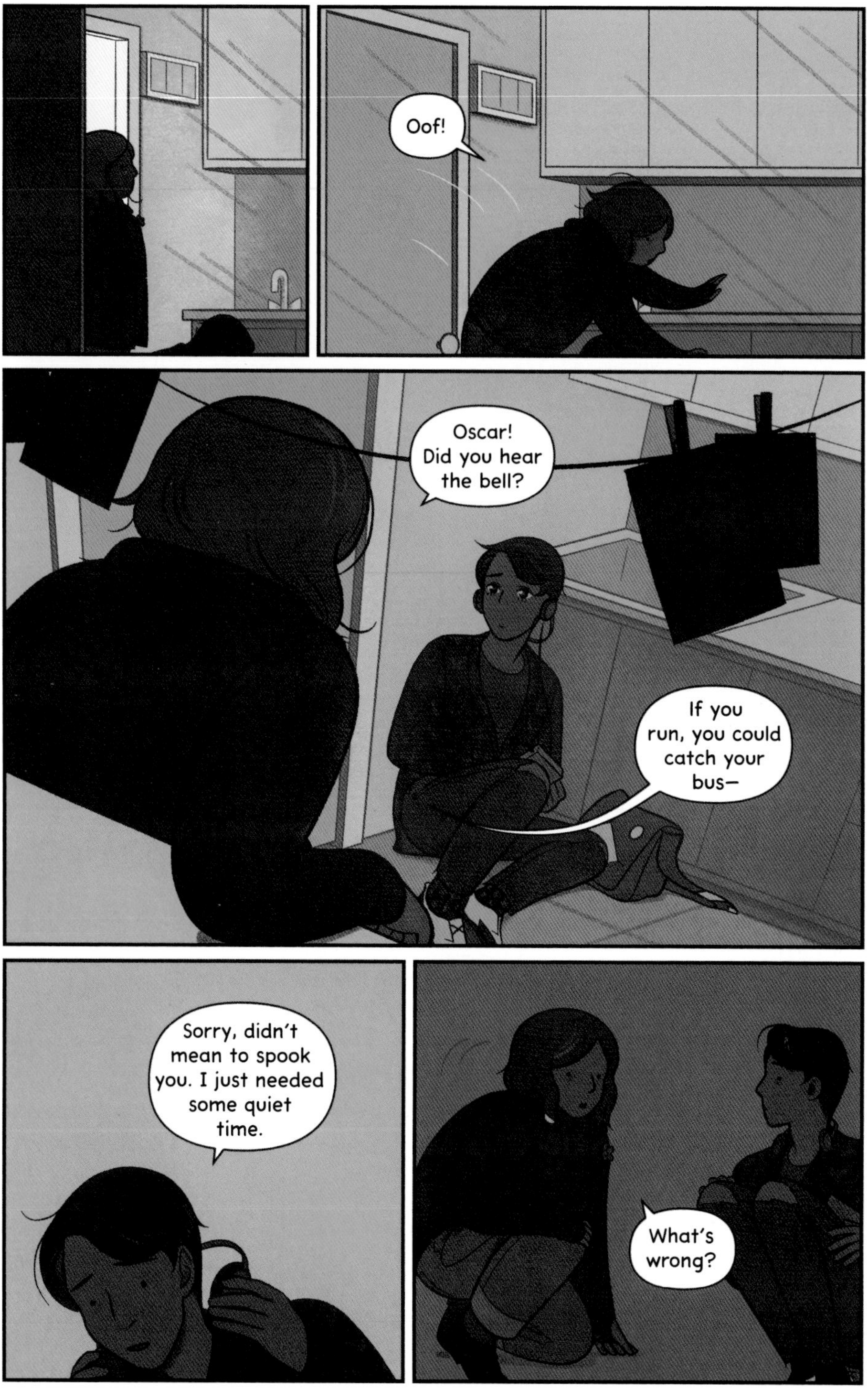
Oof!
Oscar! Did you hear the bell?
If you run, you could catch your bus—
Sorry, didn't mean to spook you. I just needed some quiet time.
What's wrong?

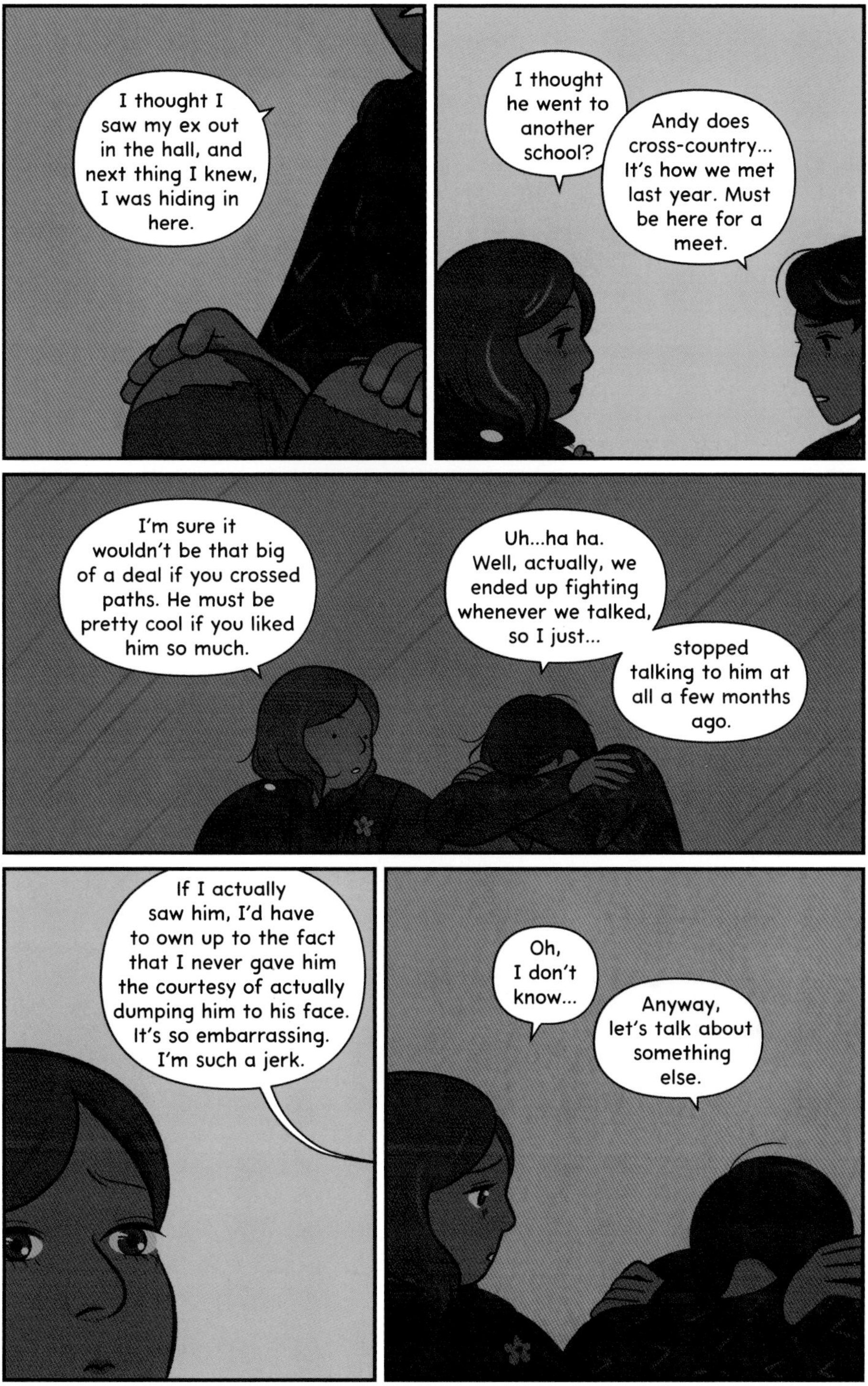
I thought I saw my ex out in the hall, and next thing I knew, I was hiding in here.
I thought he went to another school?
Andy does cross-country... It's how we met last year. Must be here for a meet.
I'm sure it wouldn't be that big of a deal if you crossed paths. He must be pretty cool if you liked him so much.
Uh...ha ha. Well, actually, we ended up fighting whenever we talked, so I just...
stopped talking to him at all a few months ago.
If I actually saw him, I'd have to own up to the fact that I never gave him the courtesy of actually dumping him to his face. It's so embarrassing. I'm such a jerk.
Oh, I don't know...
Anyway, let's talk about something else.

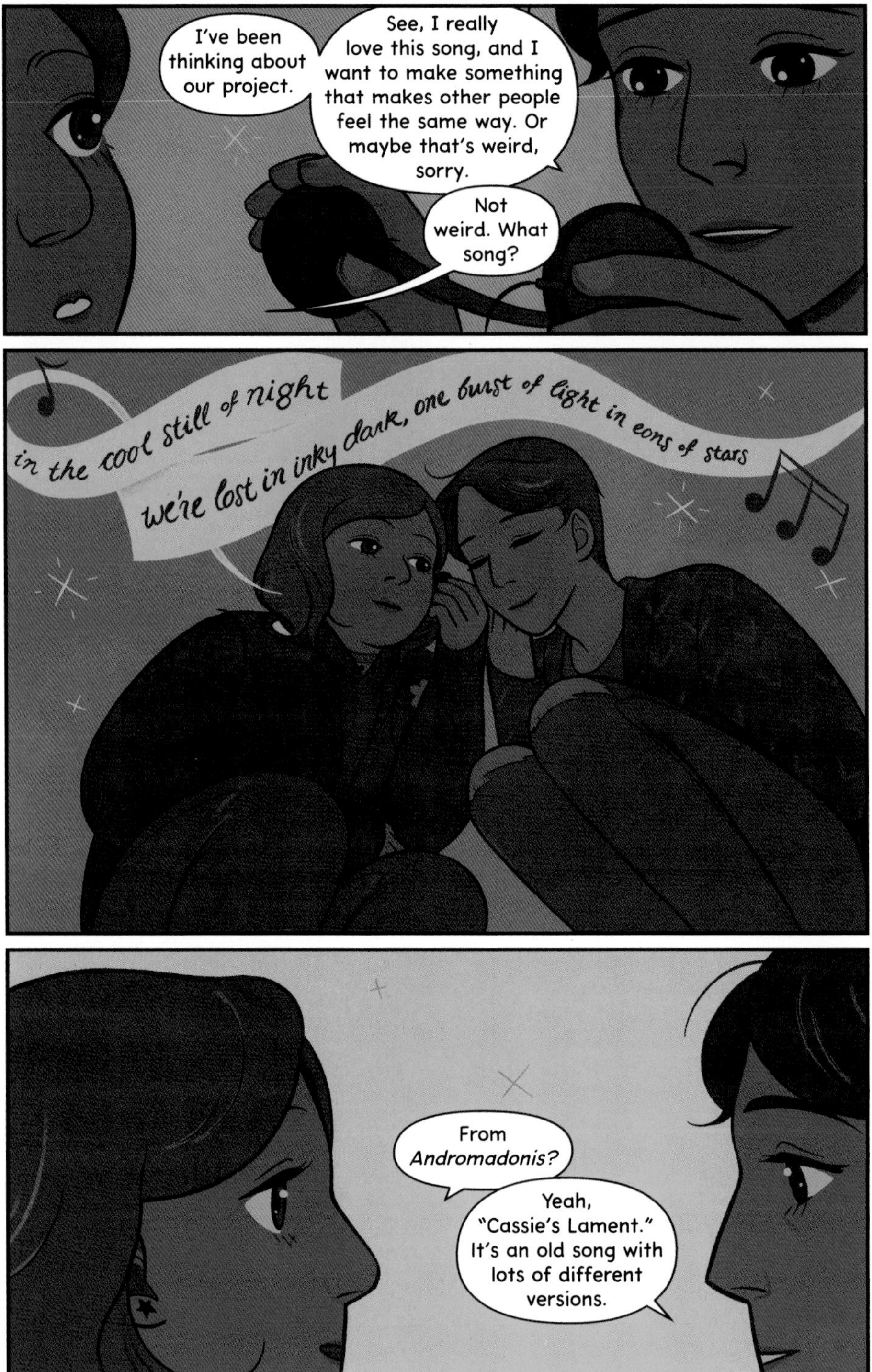
I've been thinking about our project.
See, I really love this song, and I want to make something that makes other people feel the same way. Or maybe that's weird, sorry.
Not weird. What song?
in the cool still of night
we're lost in inky dark, one burst of light in eons of stars
From *Andromadonis?*
Yeah, "Cassie's Lament." It's an old song with lots of different versions.

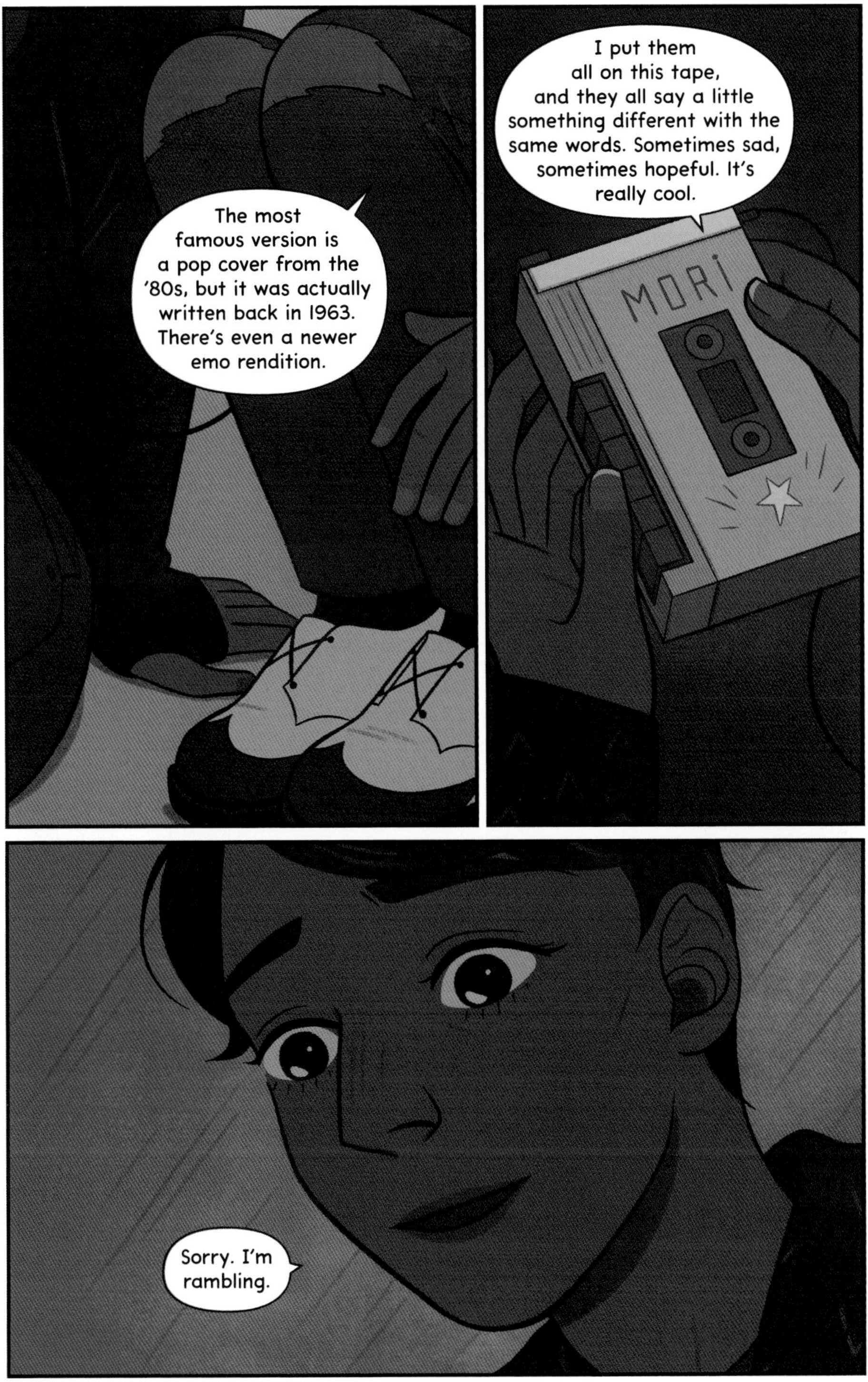
The most famous version is a pop cover from the '80s, but it was actually written back in 1963. There's even a newer emo rendition.
I put them all on this tape, and they all say a little something different with the same words. Sometimes sad, sometimes hopeful. It's really cool.
MORI
Sorry. I'm rambling.

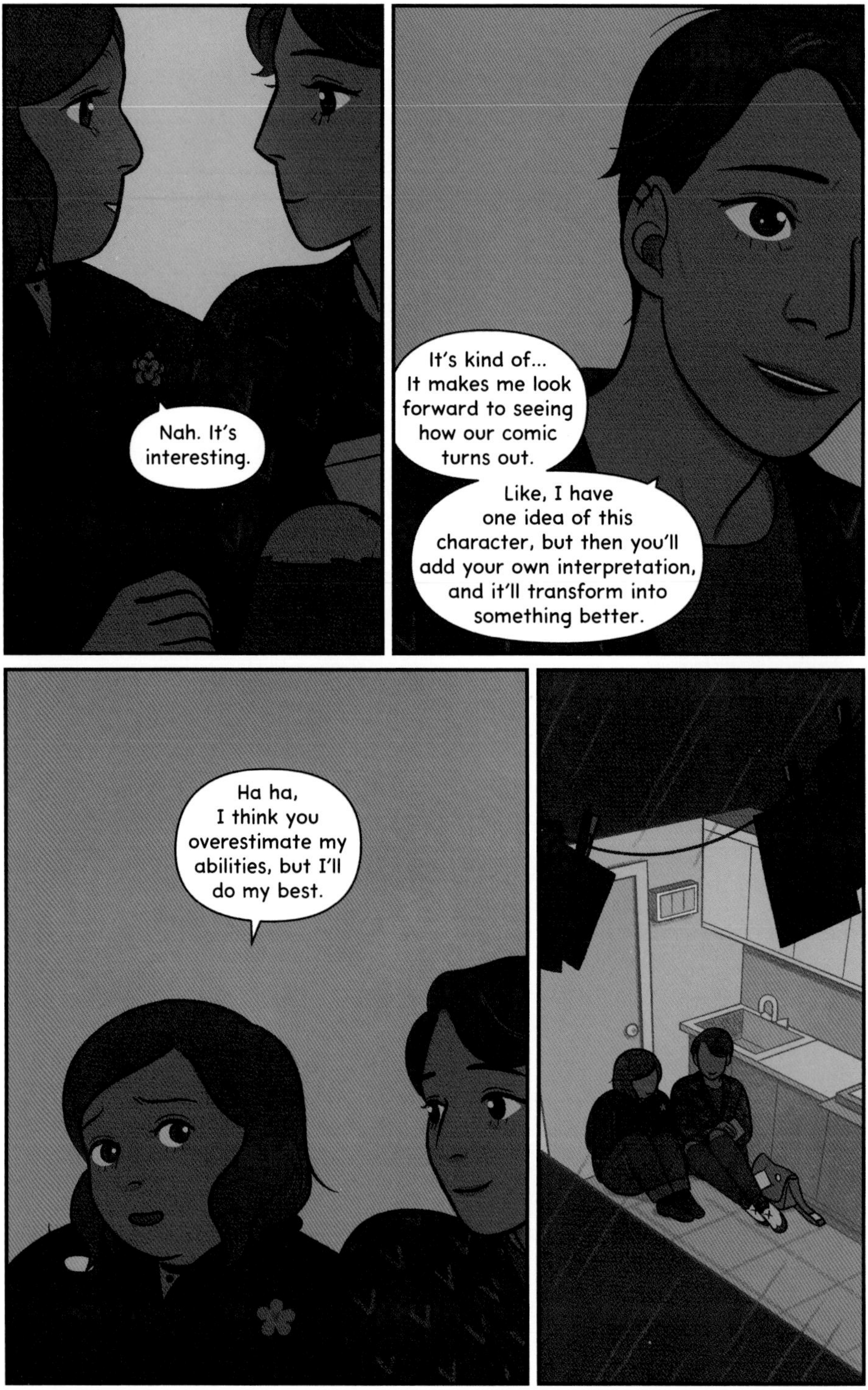

Nah. It's interesting.
It's kind of... It makes me look forward to seeing how our comic turns out.
Like, I have one idea of this character, but then you'll add your own interpretation, and it'll transform into something better.
Ha ha, I think you overestimate my abilities, but I'll do my best.

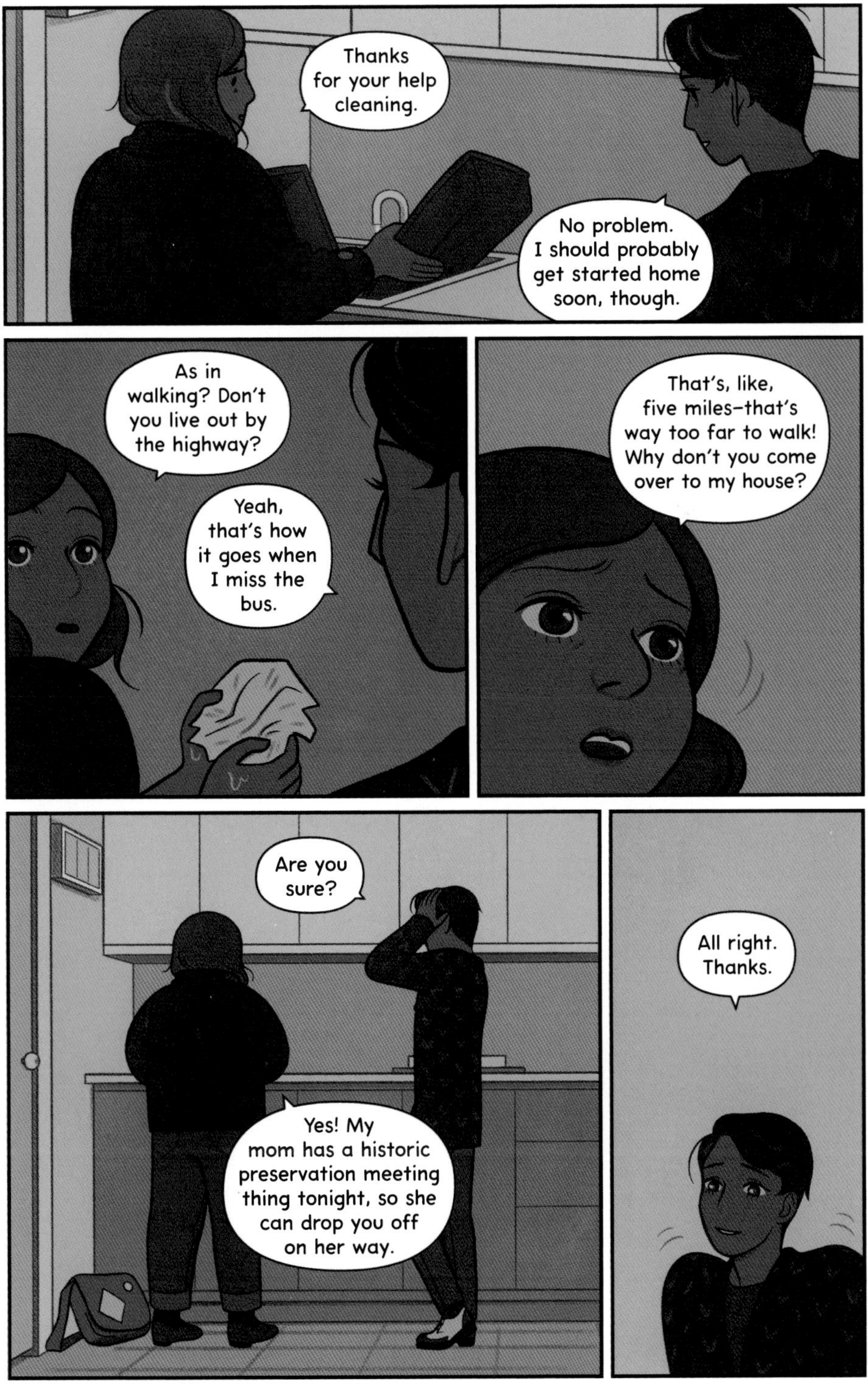
Thanks for your help cleaning.
No problem. I should probably get started home soon, though.
As in walking? Don't you live out by the highway?
Yeah, that's how it goes when I miss the bus.
That's, like, five miles–that's way too far to walk! Why don't you come over to my house?
Are you sure?
Yes! My mom has a historic preservation meeting thing tonight, so she can drop you off on her way.
All right. Thanks.

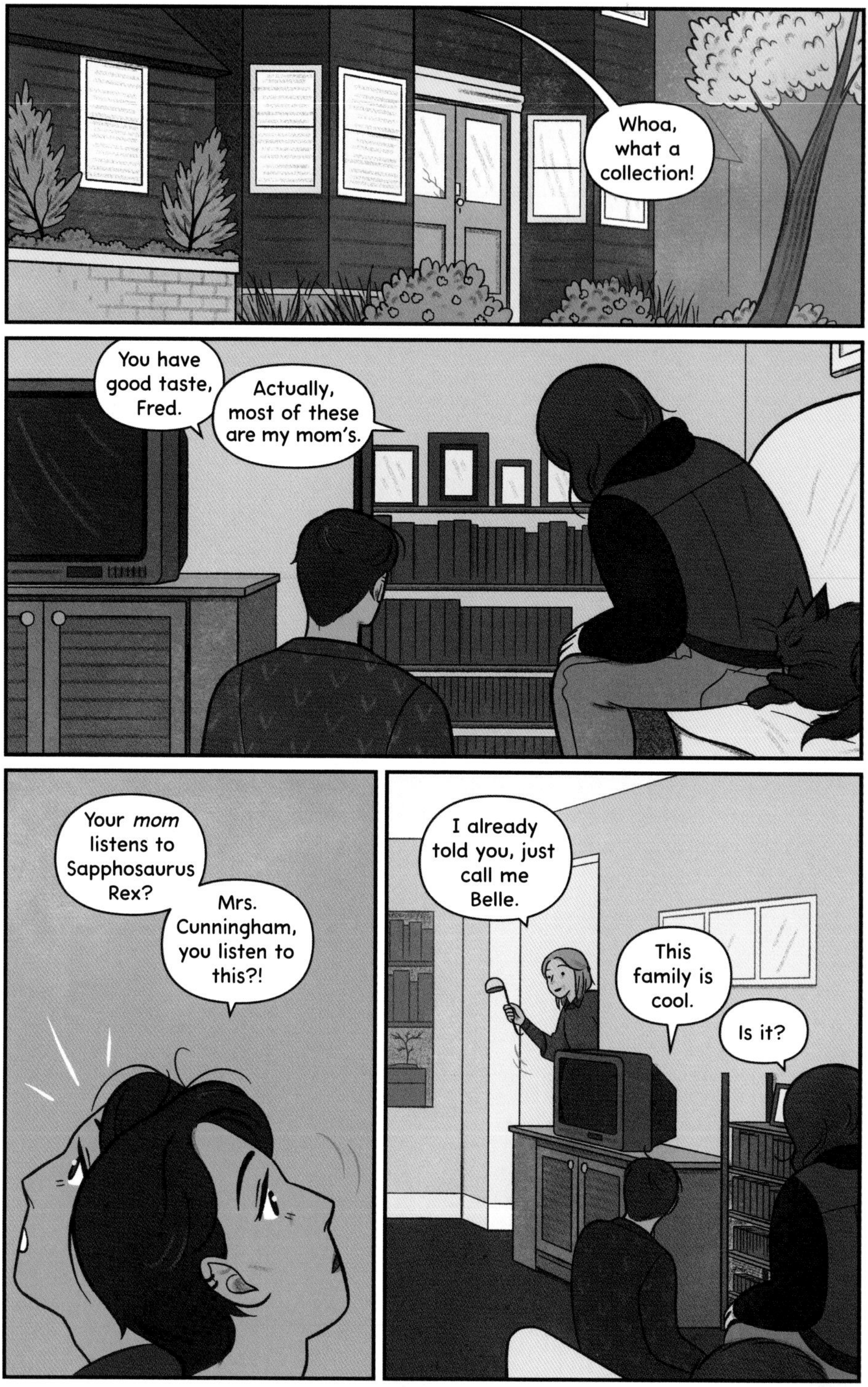
Whoa, what a collection!
You have good taste, Fred.
Actually, most of these are my mom's.
Your *mom* listens to Sapphosaurus Rex?
Mrs. Cunningham, you listen to this?!
I already told you, just call me Belle.
This family is cool.
Is it?

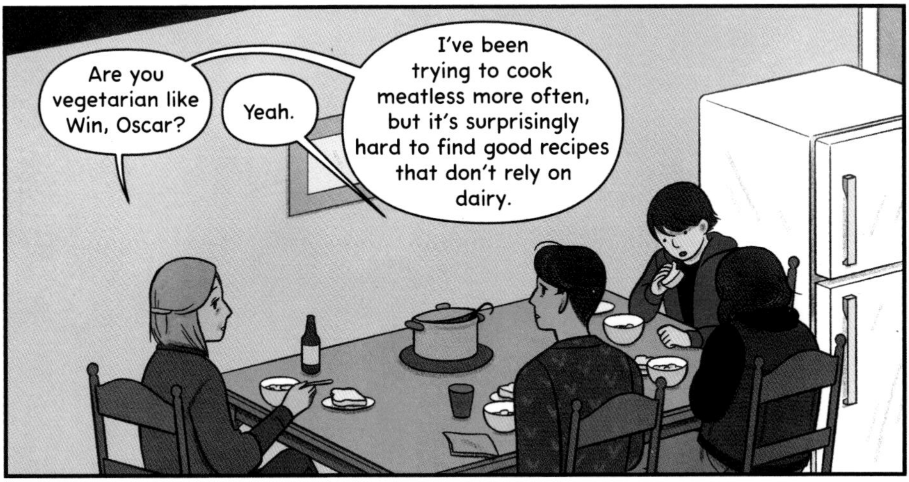
Are you vegetarian like Win, Oscar?
Yeah.
I've been trying to cook meatless more often, but it's surprisingly hard to find good recipes that don't rely on dairy.
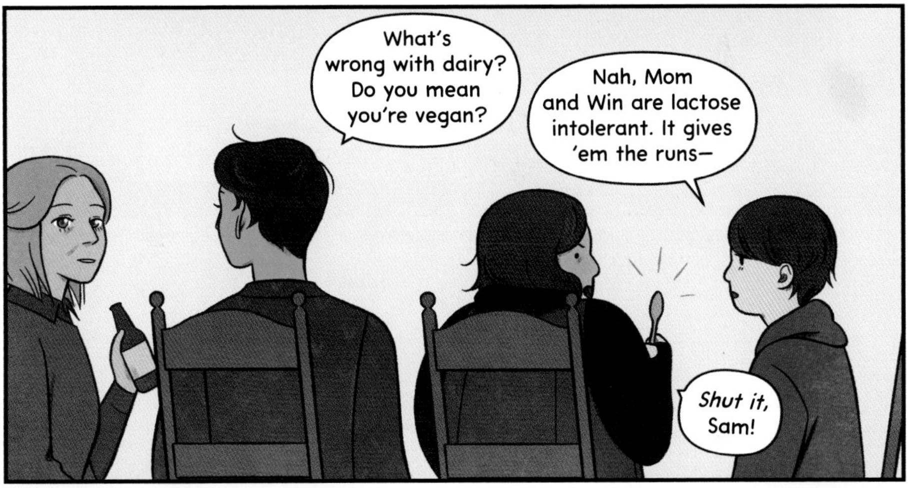
What's wrong with dairy? Do you mean you're vegan?
Nah, Mom and Win are lactose intolerant. It gives 'em the runs—
Shut it, Sam!
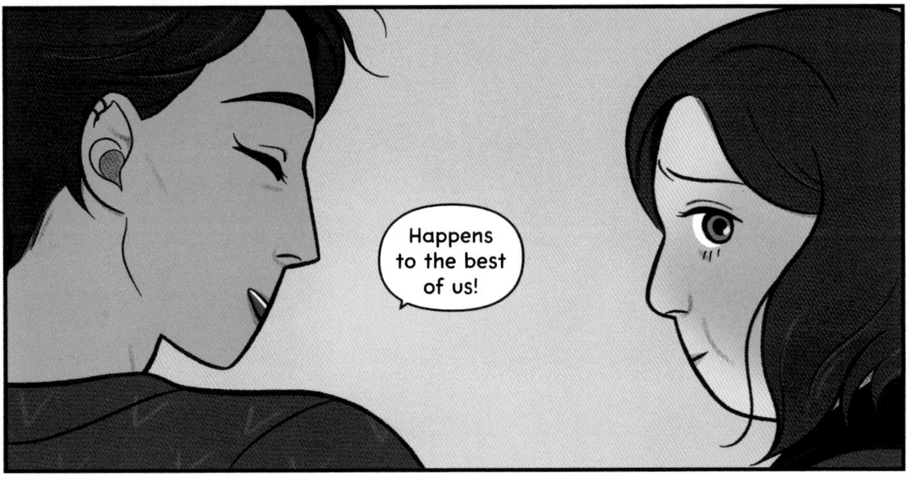
Happens to the best of us!

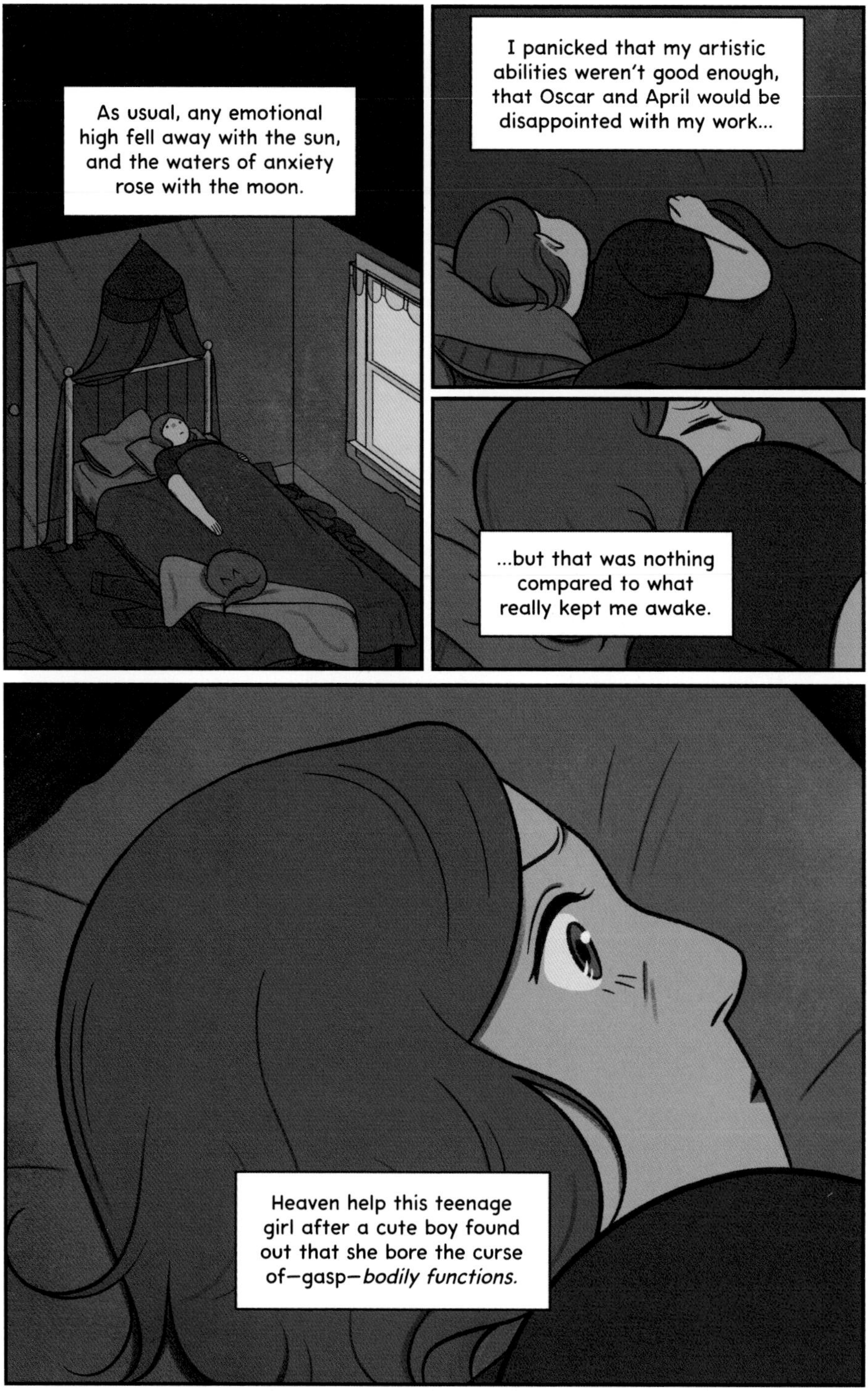
As usual, any emotional high fell away with the sun, and the waters of anxiety rose with the moon.
I panicked that my artistic abilities weren't good enough, that Oscar and April would be disappointed with my work...
...but that was nothing compared to what really kept me awake.
Heaven help this teenage girl after a cute boy found out that she bore the curse of—gasp—*bodily functions.*

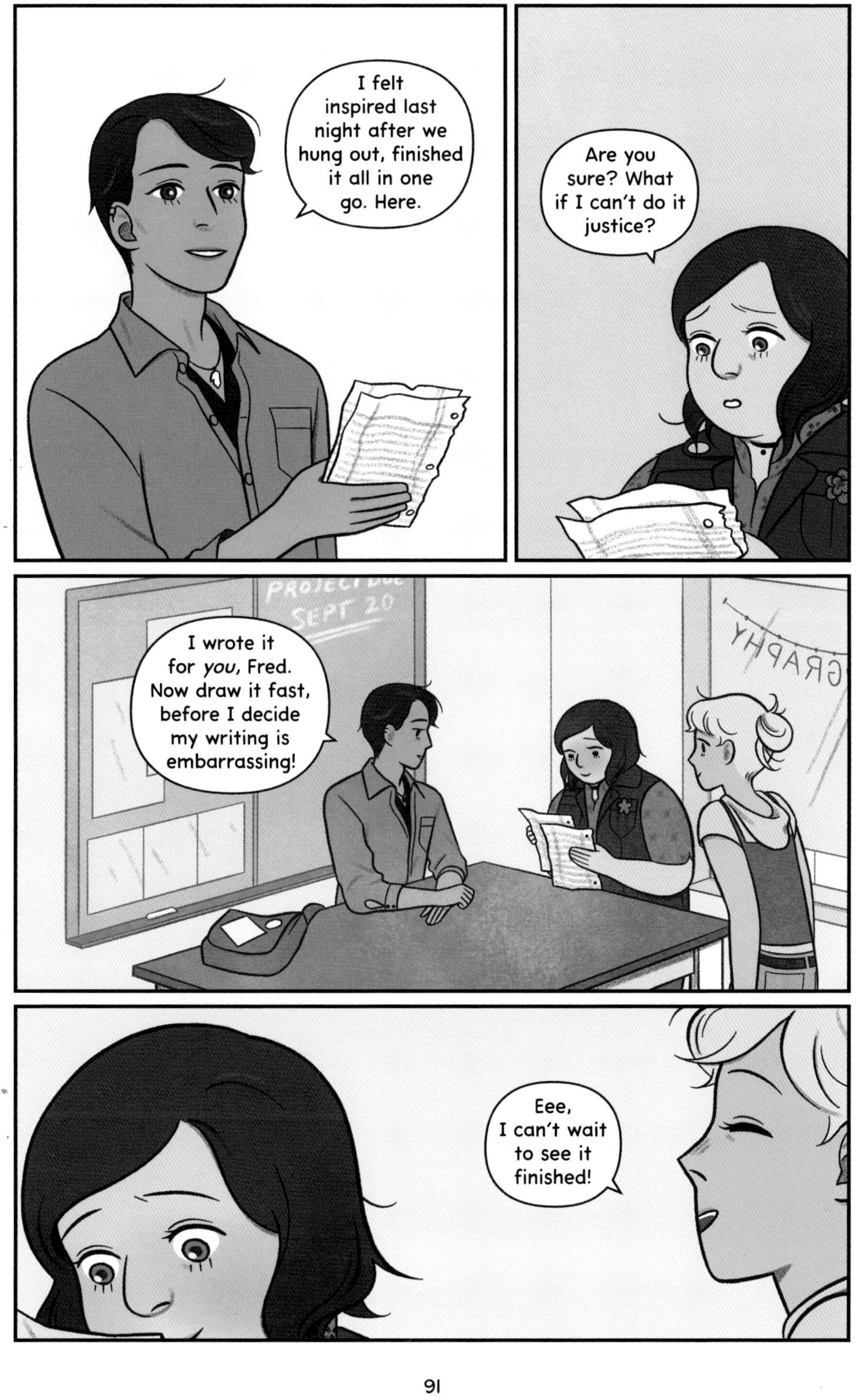
I felt inspired last night after we hung out, finished it all in one go. Here.
Are you sure? What if I can't do it justice?
I wrote it for *you*, Fred. Now draw it fast, before I decide my writing is embarrassing!
Eee, I can't wait to see it finished!

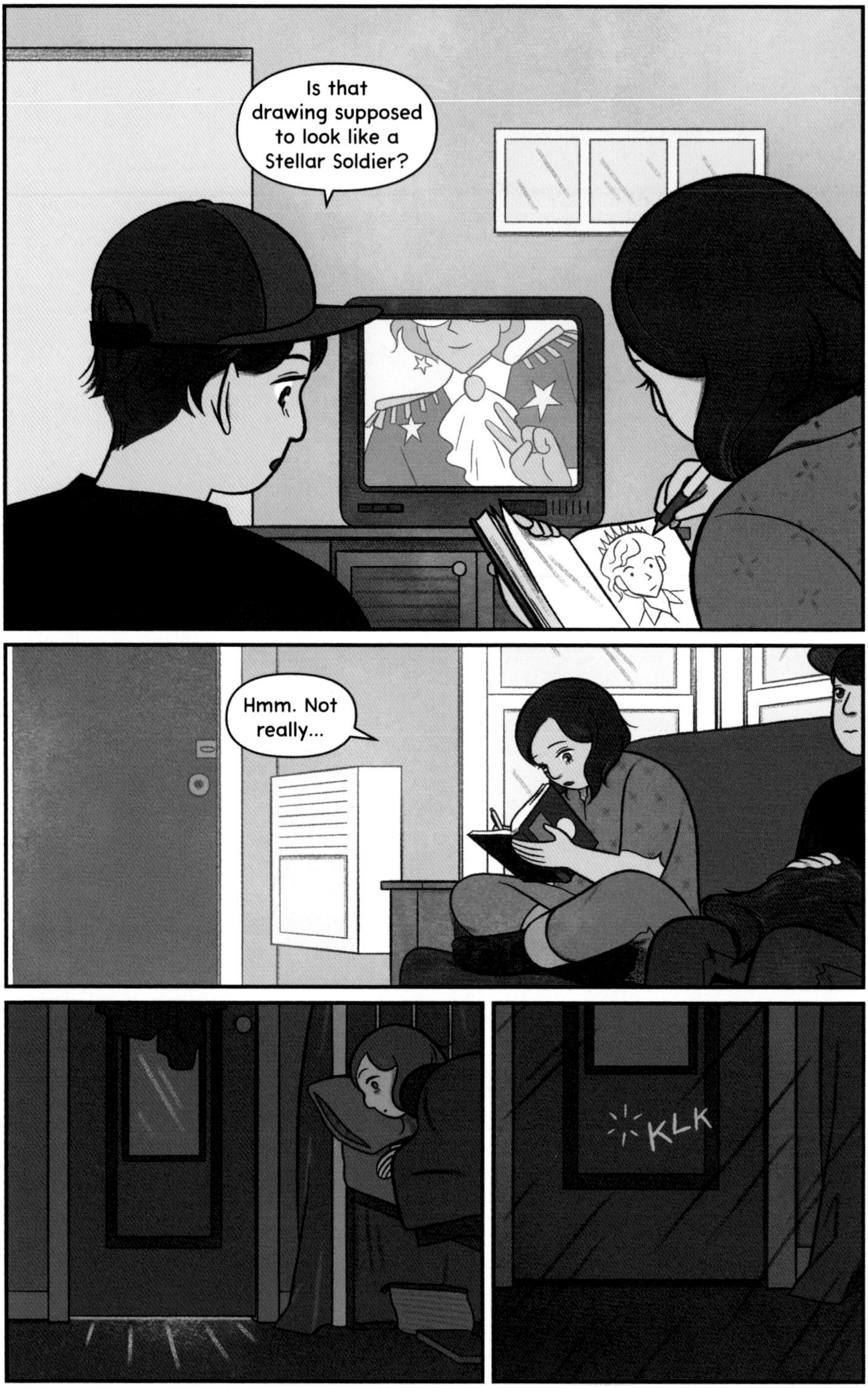
Is that drawing supposed to look like a Stellar Soldier?
Hmm. Not really...
KLK

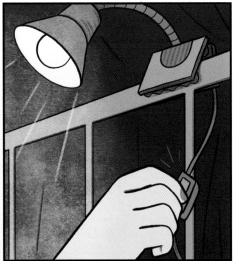

It's amazing what finding the right outlet did for my worries.

My brain was too busy designing characters and problem-solving panel compositions to dwell on much else...

Though even that wasn't without cost.

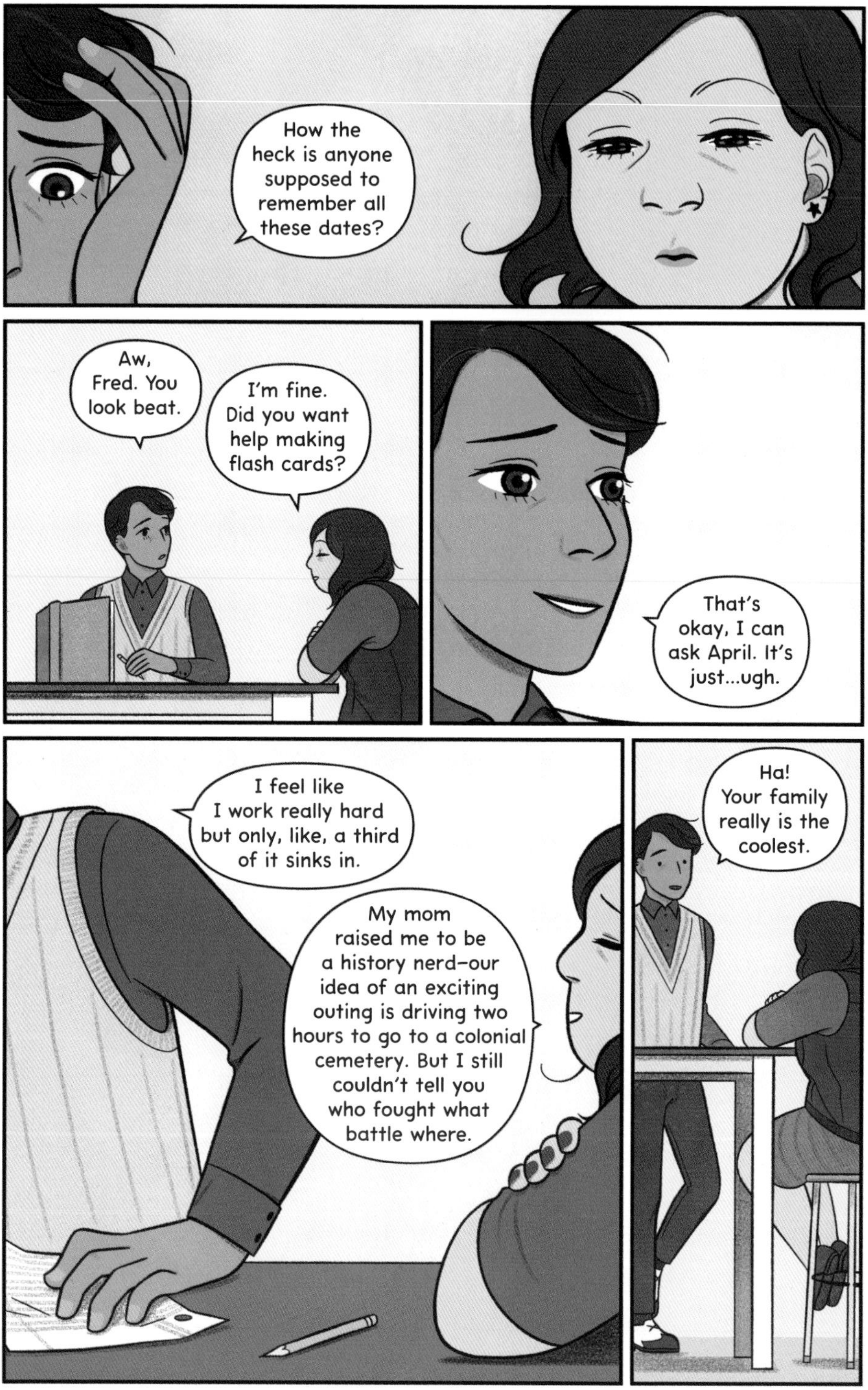
How the heck is anyone supposed to remember all these dates?
Aw, Fred. You look beat.
I'm fine. Did you want help making flash cards?
That's okay, I can ask April. It's just...ugh.
I feel like I work really hard but only, like, a third of it sinks in.
My mom raised me to be a history nerd—our idea of an exciting outing is driving two hours to go to a colonial cemetery. But I still couldn't tell you who fought what battle where.
Ha! Your family really is the coolest.

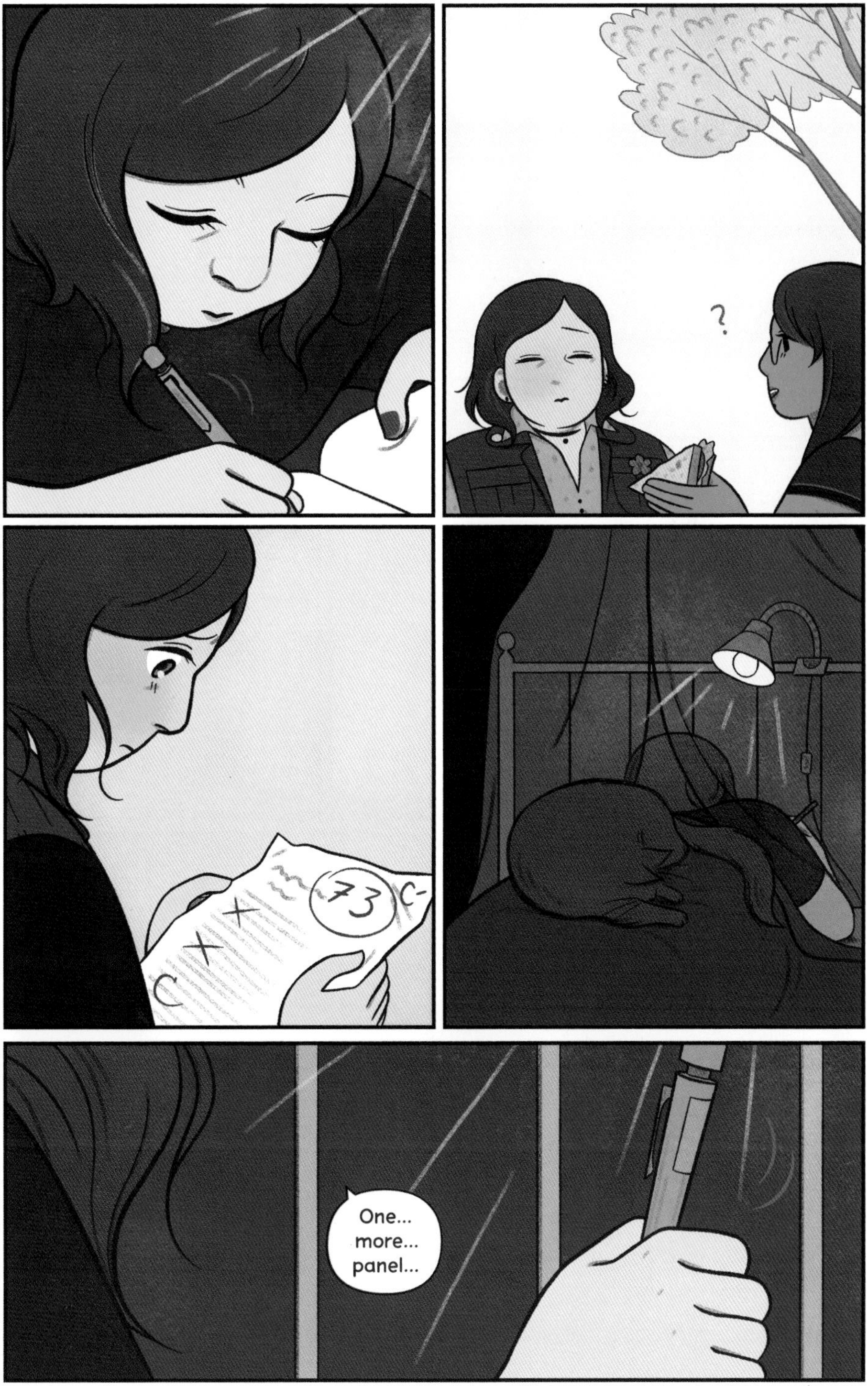
?
73
C-
One... more... panel...

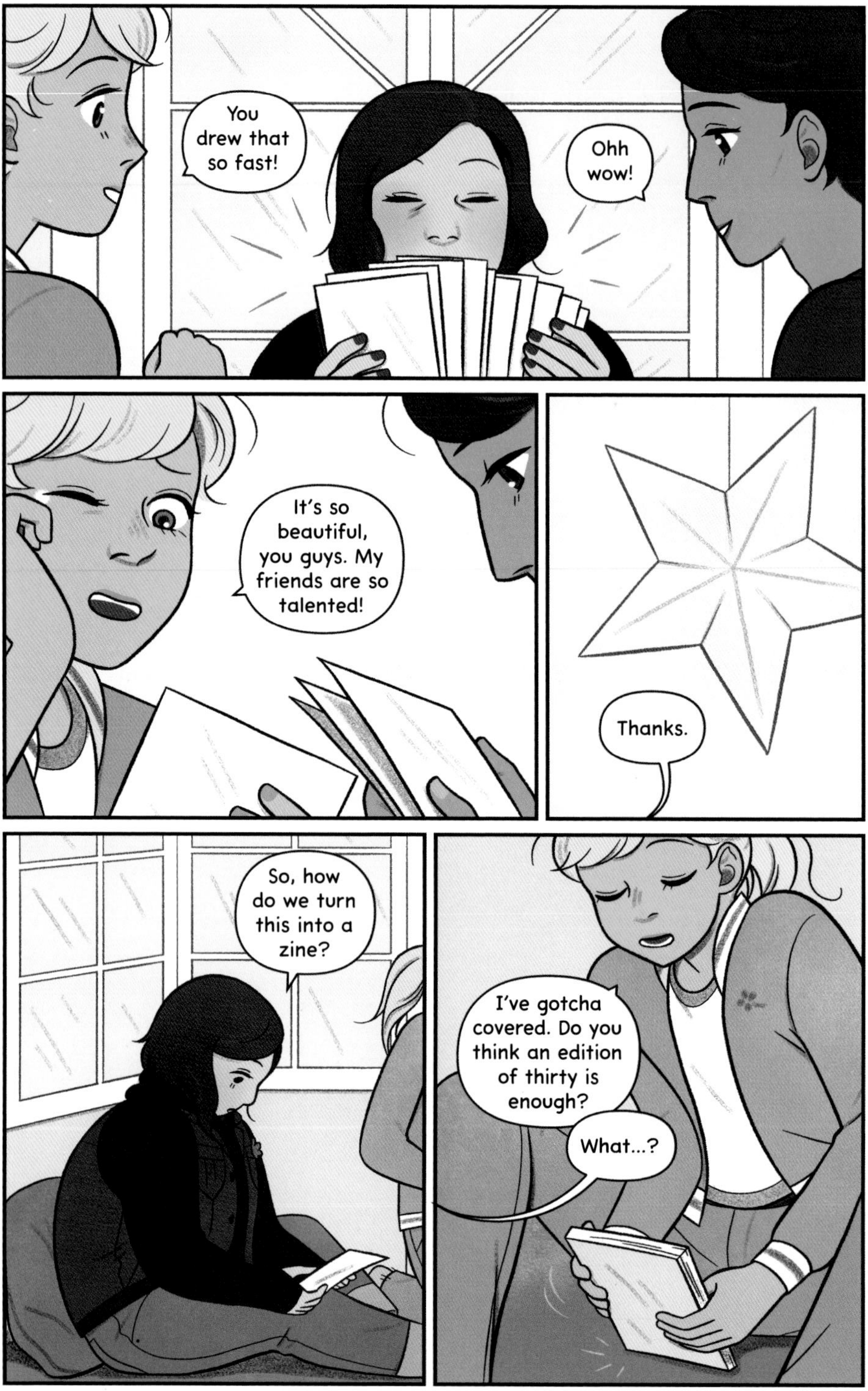
You drew that so fast!
Ohh wow!
It's so beautiful, you guys. My friends are so talented!
Thanks.
So, how do we turn this into a zine?
I've gotcha covered. Do you think an edition of thirty is enough?
What...?

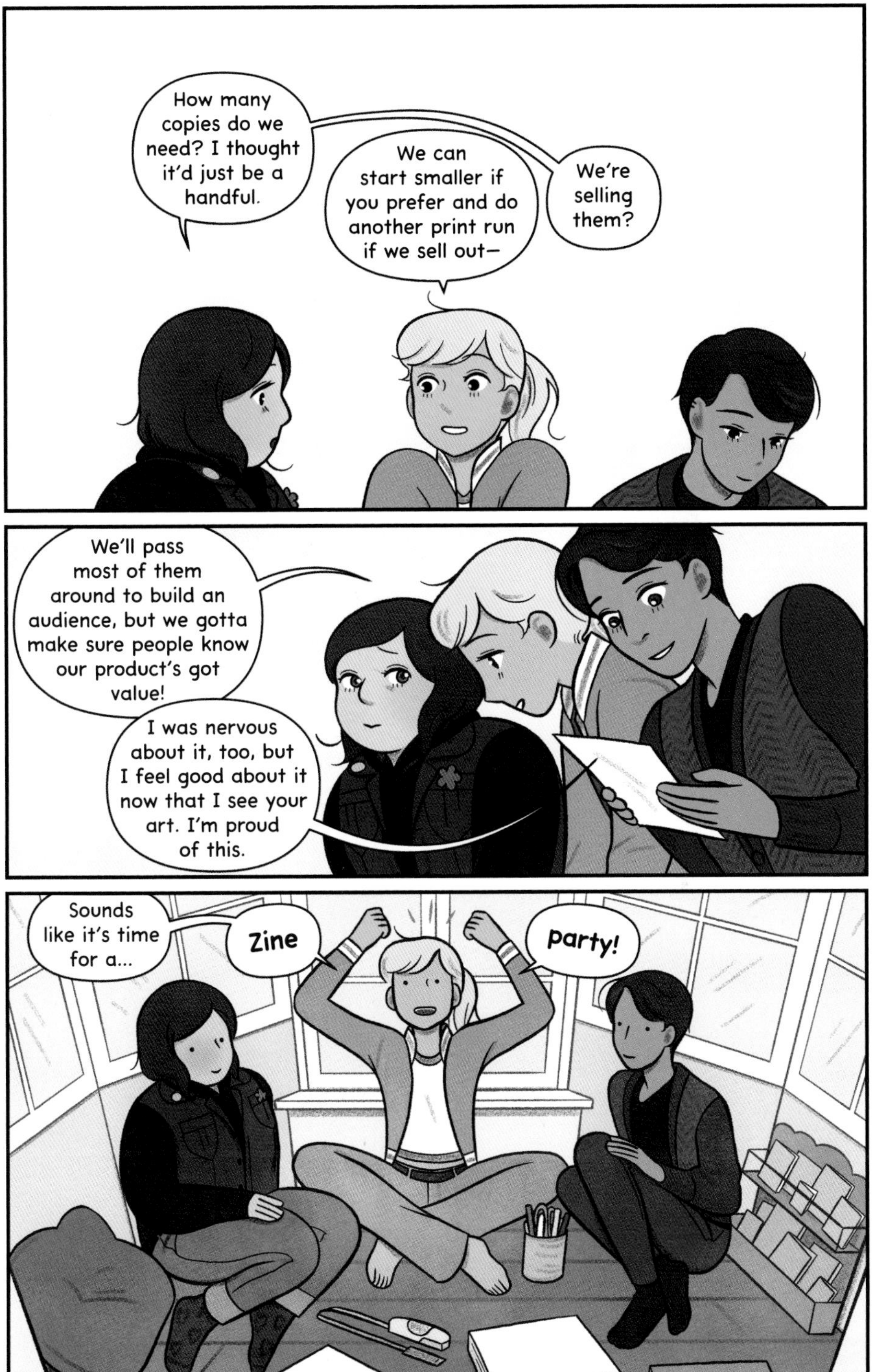
How many copies do we need? I thought it'd just be a handful.
We can start smaller if you prefer and do another print run if we sell out—
We're selling them?
We'll pass most of them around to build an audience, but we gotta make sure people know our product's got value!
I was nervous about it, too, but I feel good about it now that I see your art. I'm proud of this.
Sounds like it's time for a...
Zine
party!

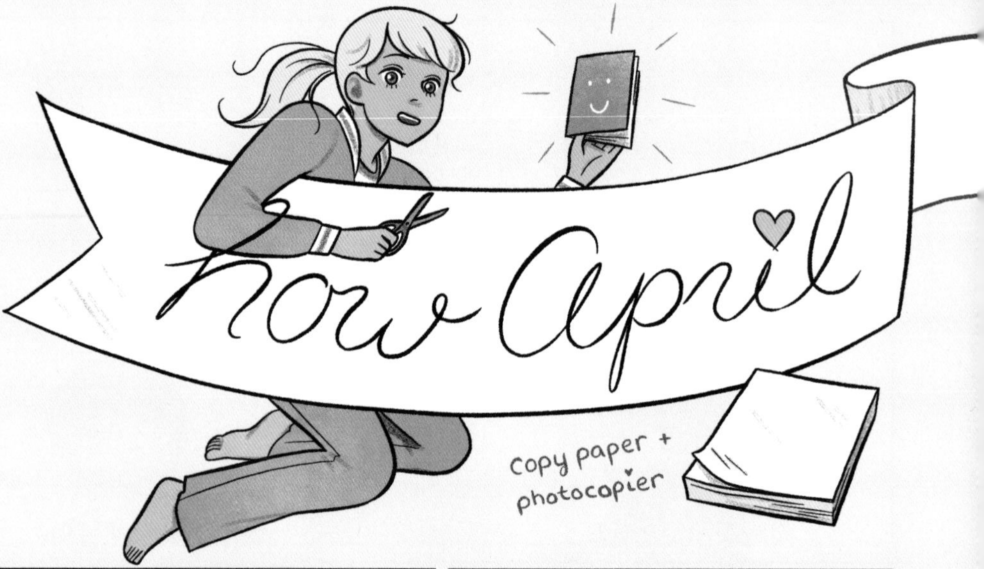
how April
copy paper +
photocopier

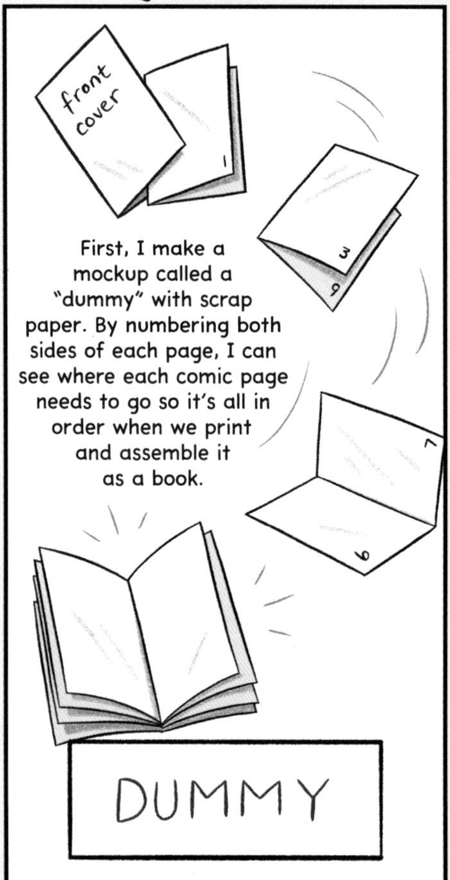
front cover
1
3
6
7
9
First, I make a mockup called a "dummy" with scrap paper. By numbering both sides of each page, I can see where each comic page needs to go so it's all in order when we print and assemble it as a book.
DUMMY

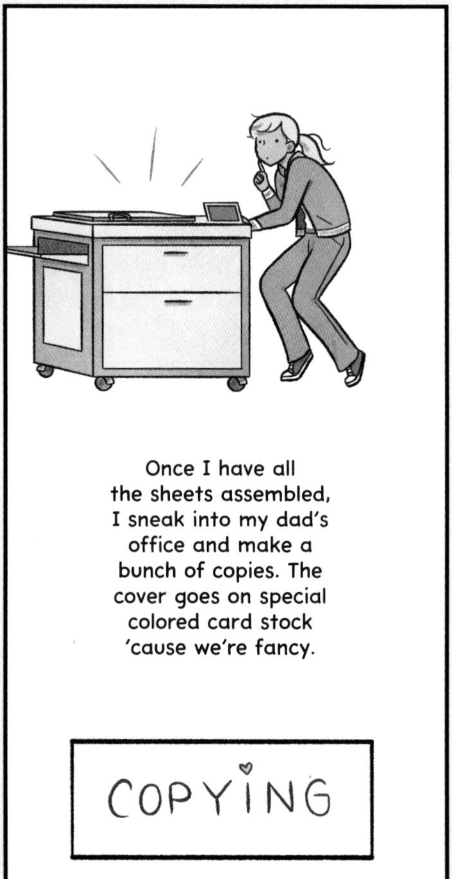
Once I have all the sheets assembled, I sneak into my dad's office and make a bunch of copies. The cover goes on special colored card stock 'cause we're fancy.
COPYING

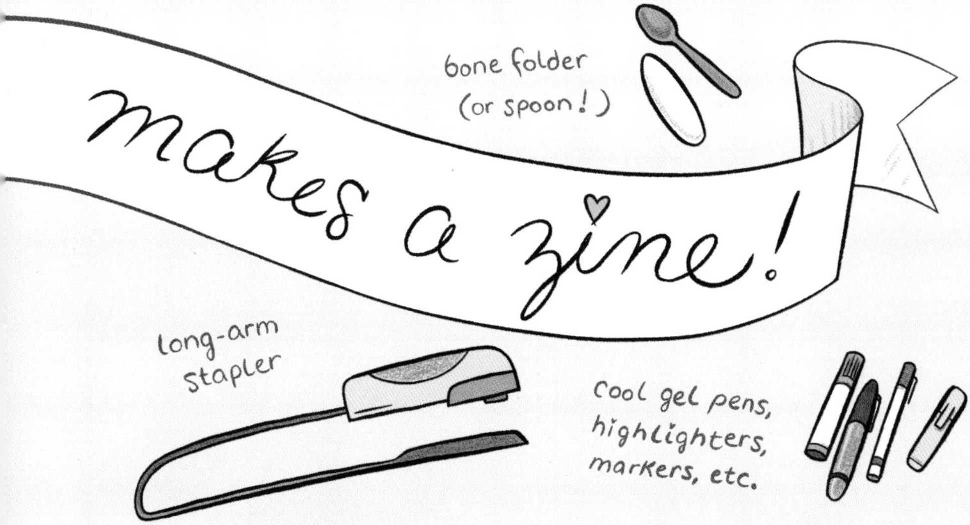
makes a zine!
bone folder (or spoon!)
long-arm stapler
cool gel pens, highlighters, markers, etc.

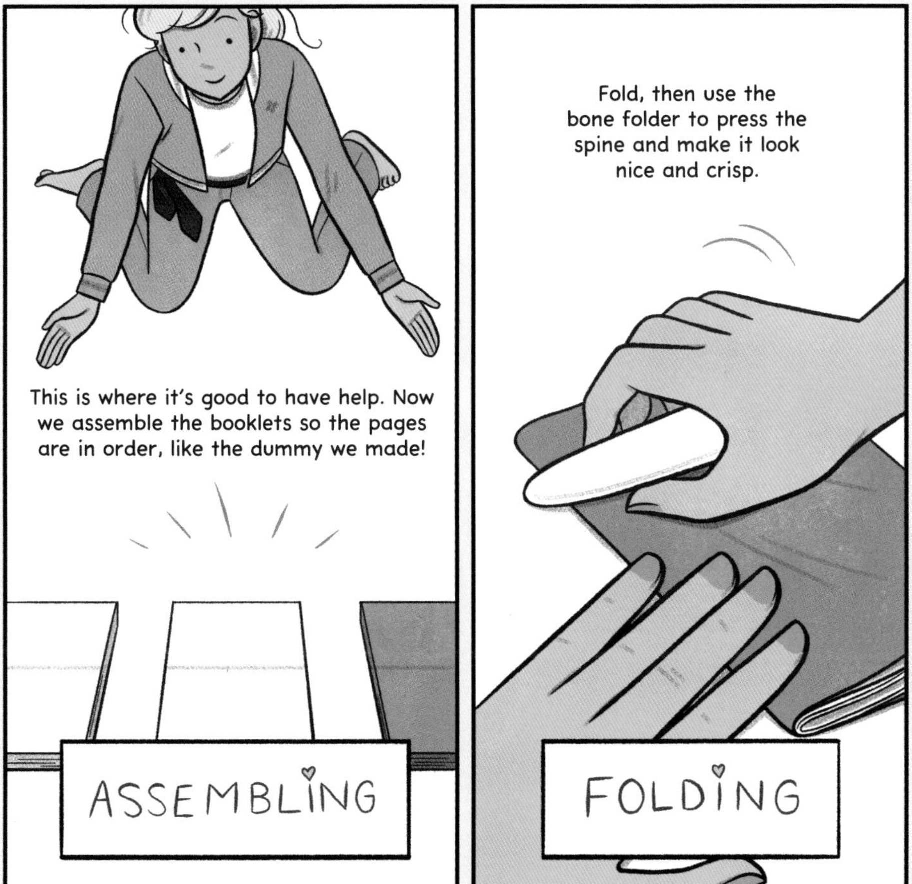
This is where it's good to have help. Now we assemble the booklets so the pages are in order, like the dummy we made!
ASSEMBLING
Fold, then use the bone folder to press the spine and make it look nice and crisp.
FOLDING

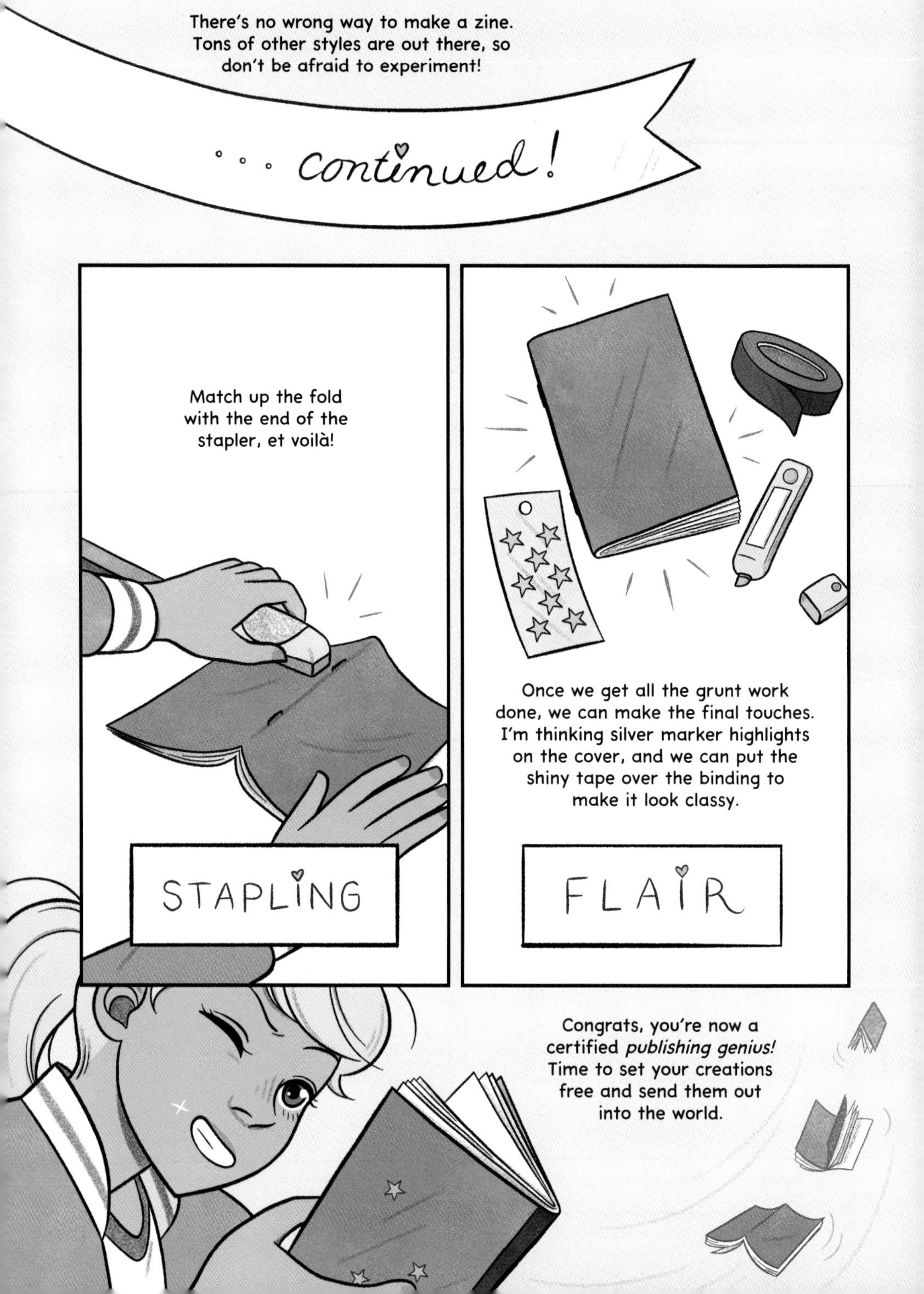
There's no wrong way to make a zine. Tons of other styles are out there, so don't be afraid to experiment!
. . . continued!
Match up the fold with the end of the stapler, et voilà!
STAPLING
Once we get all the grunt work done, we can make the final touches. I'm thinking silver marker highlights on the cover, and we can put the shiny tape over the binding to make it look classy.
FLAIR
Congrats, you're now a certified *publishing genius!* Time to set your creations free and send them out into the world.

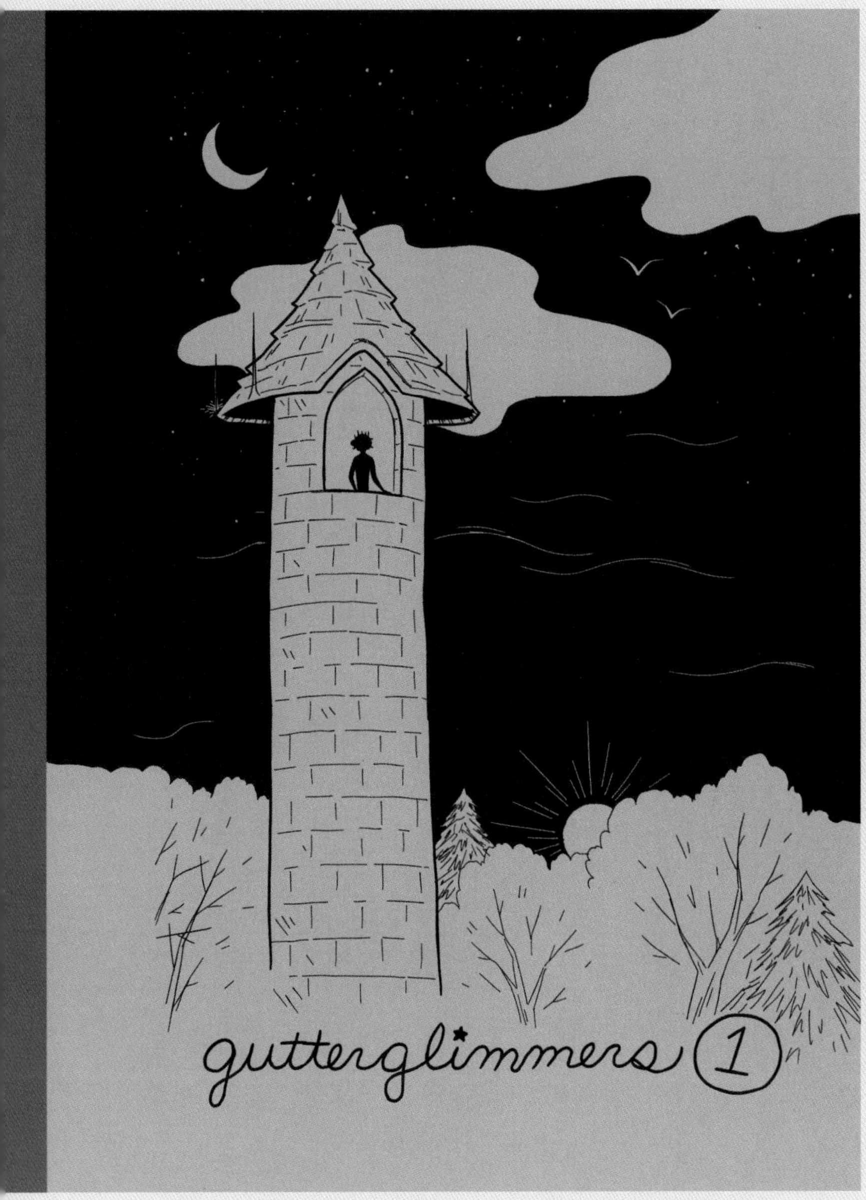
gutterglimmers 1

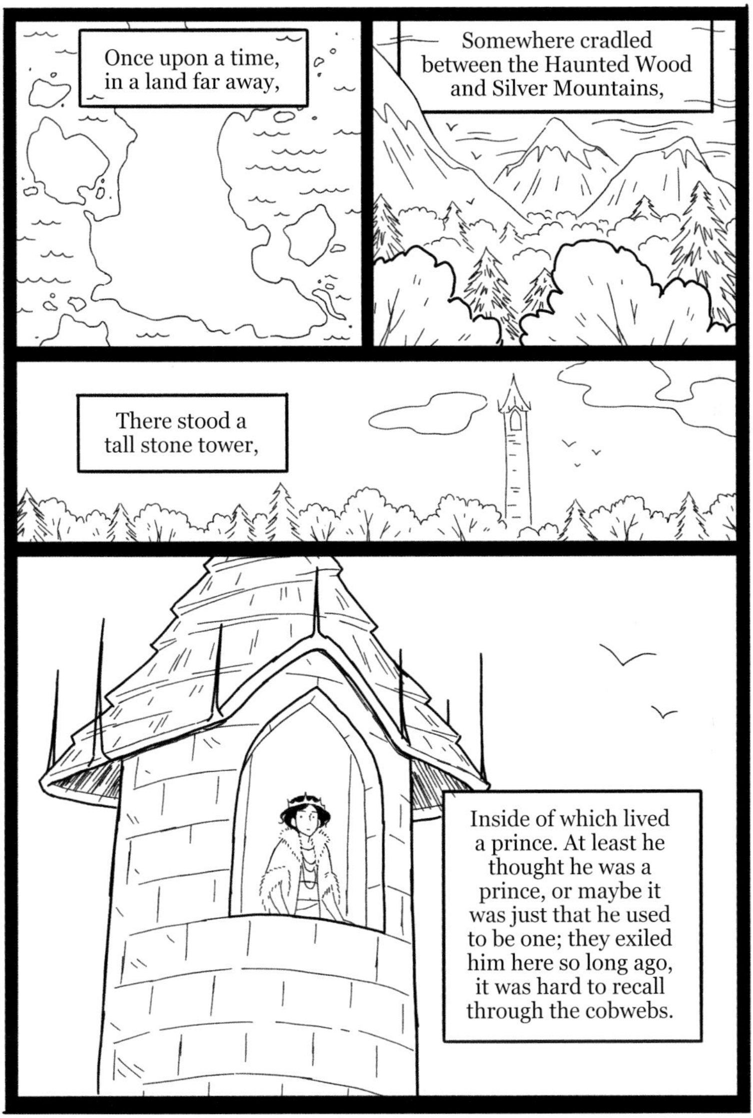
Once upon a time, in a land far away,
Somewhere cradled between the Haunted Wood and Silver Mountains,
There stood a tall stone tower,
Inside of which lived a prince. At least he thought he was a prince, or maybe it was just that he used to be one; they exiled him here so long ago, it was hard to recall through the cobwebs.

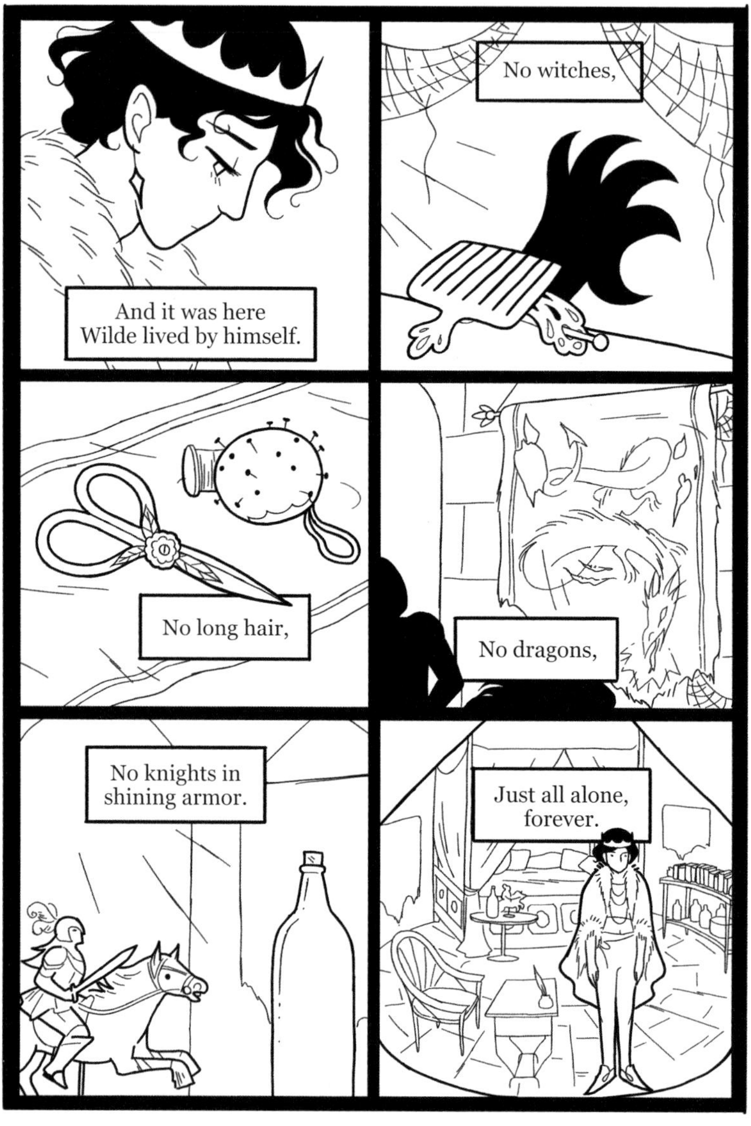
And it was here Wilde lived by himself.
No witches,
No long hair,
No dragons,
No knights in shining armor.
Just all alone, forever.

But each night,
as he slept,

He dreamt,

And in his dreams,
his soul was free...

To explore the
world outside.

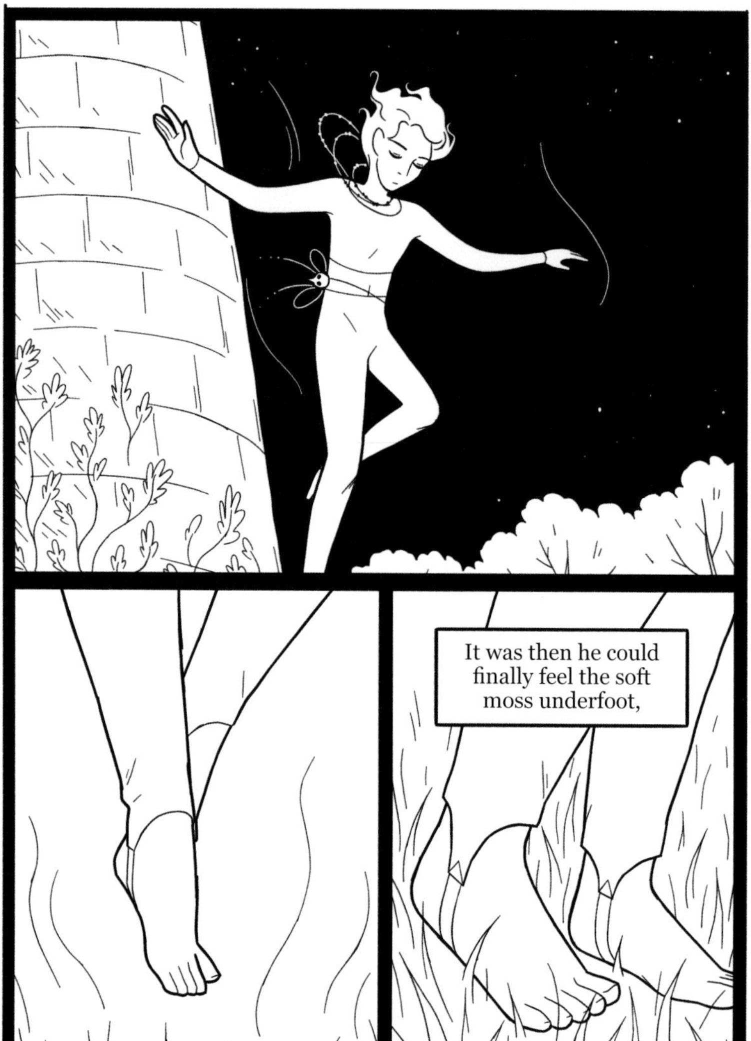
It was then he could
finally feel the soft
moss underfoot,

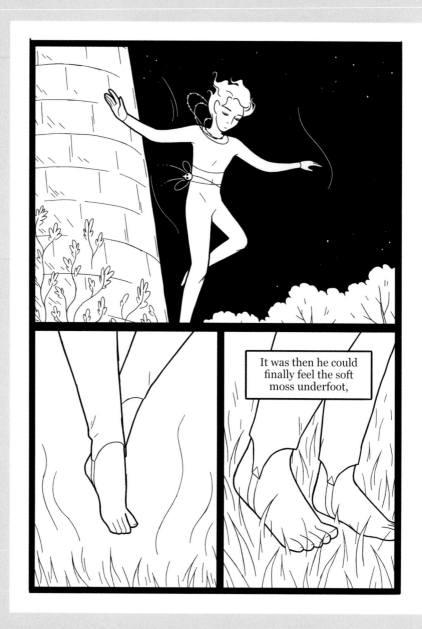

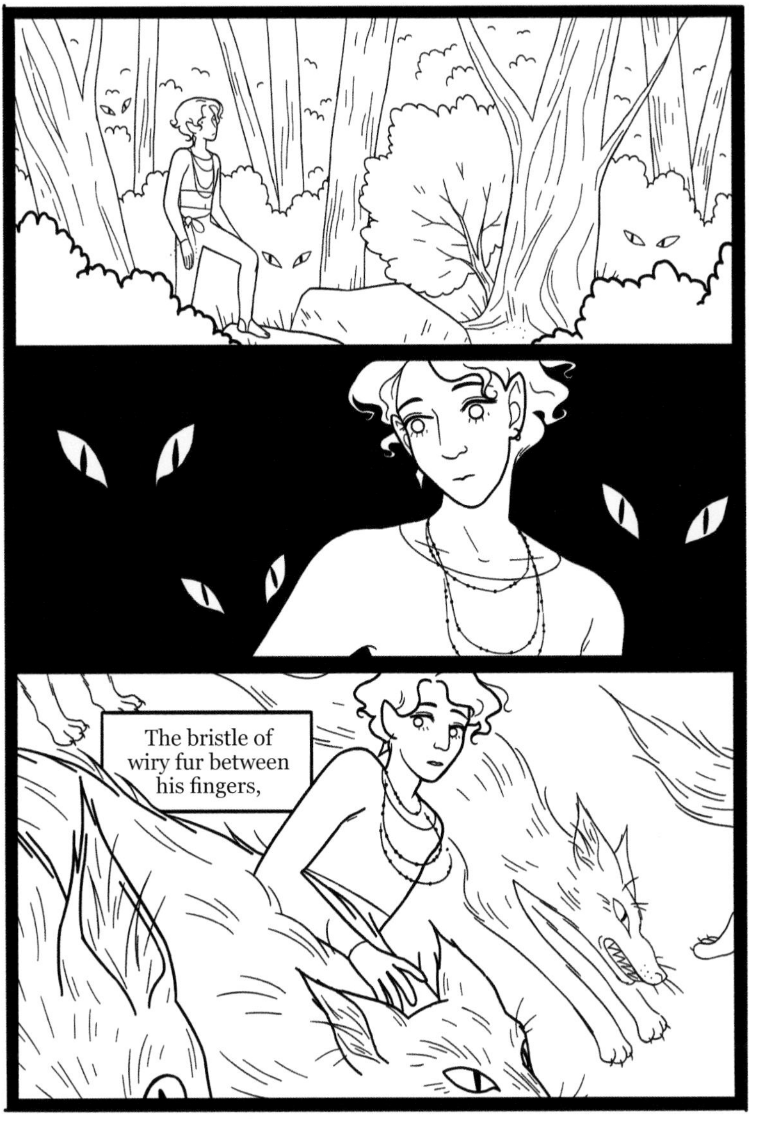
The bristle of wiry fur between his fingers,

And he could run until the salt of the sea filled his lungs and his legs gave out from underneath him.

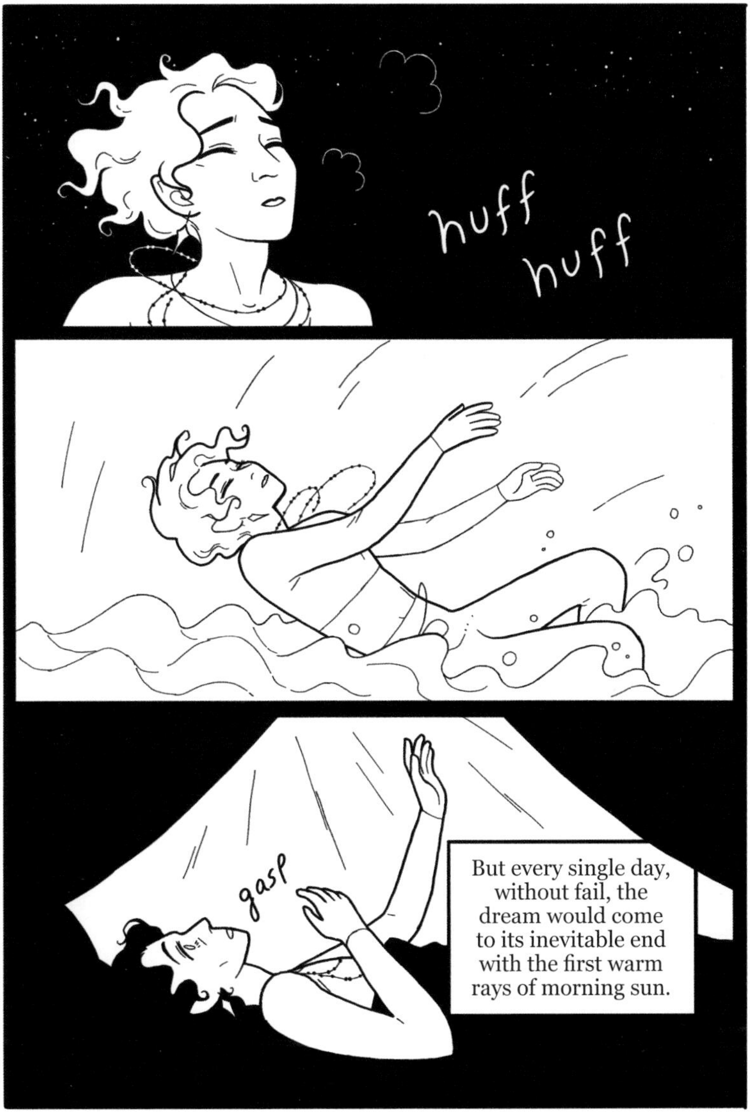
huff
huff
gasp
But every single day, without fail, the dream would come to its inevitable end with the first warm rays of morning sun.

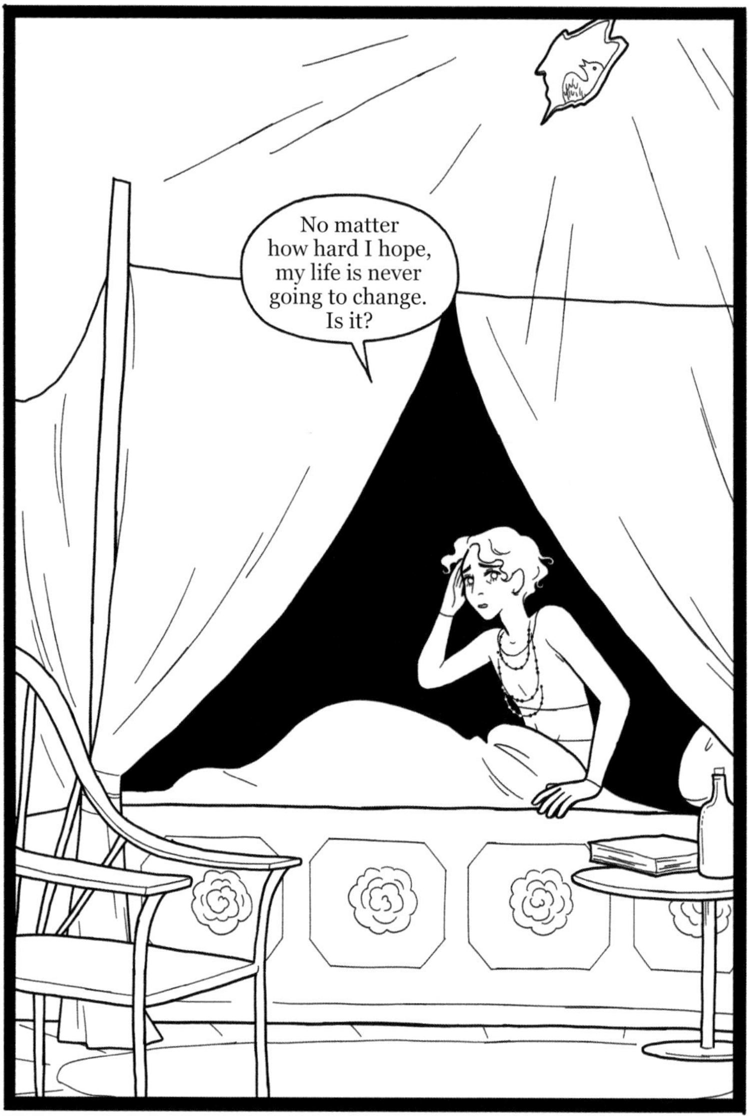
No matter how hard I hope, my life is never going to change. Is it?

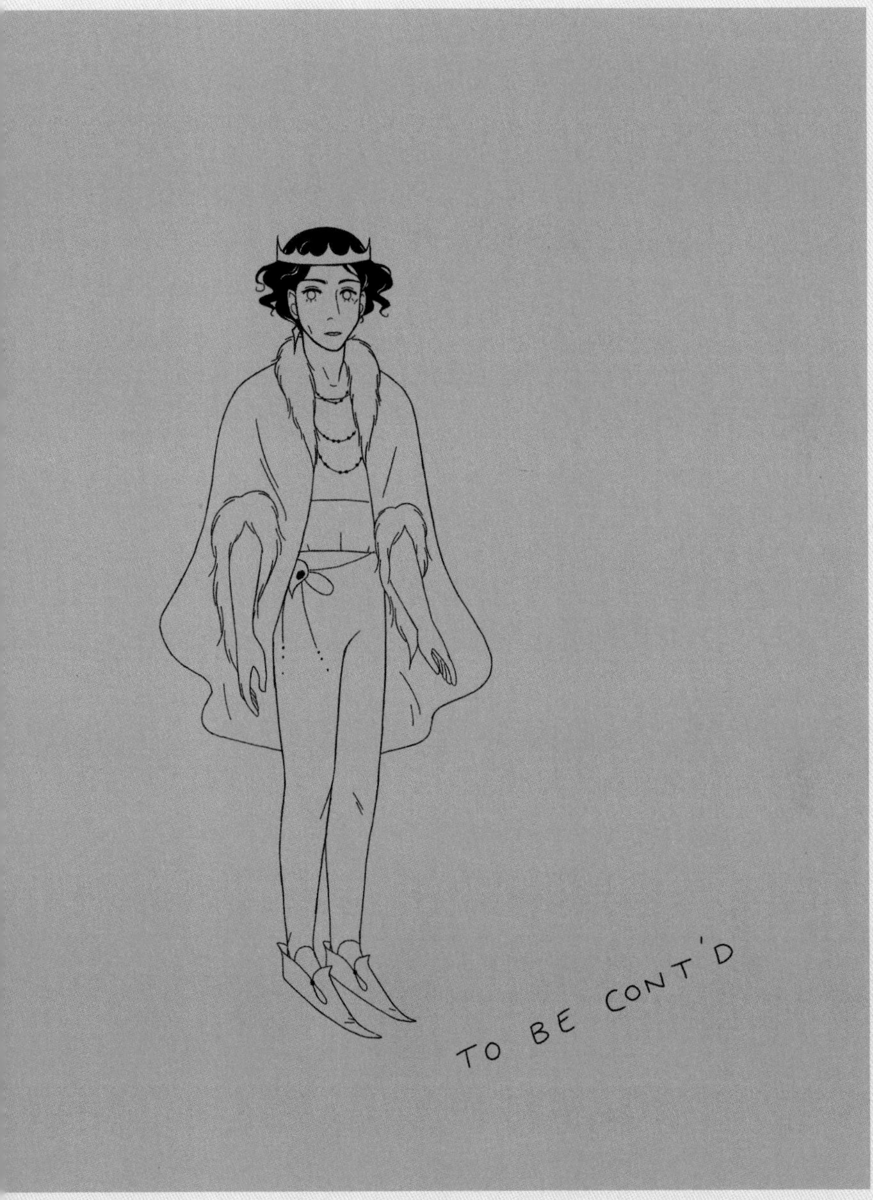
TO BE CONT'D

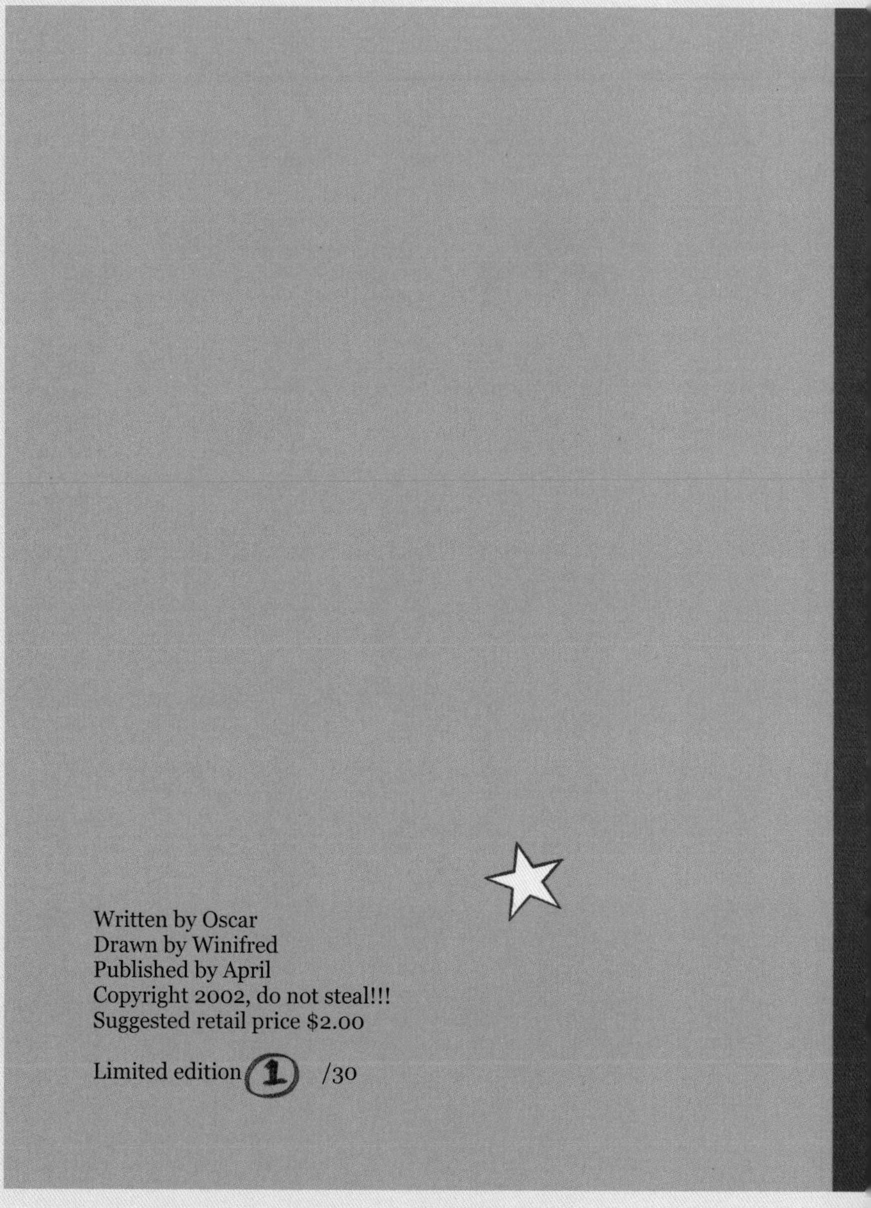
Written by Oscar
Drawn by Winifred
Published by April
Copyright 2002, do not steal!!!
Suggested retail price $2.00
Limited edition 1 /30

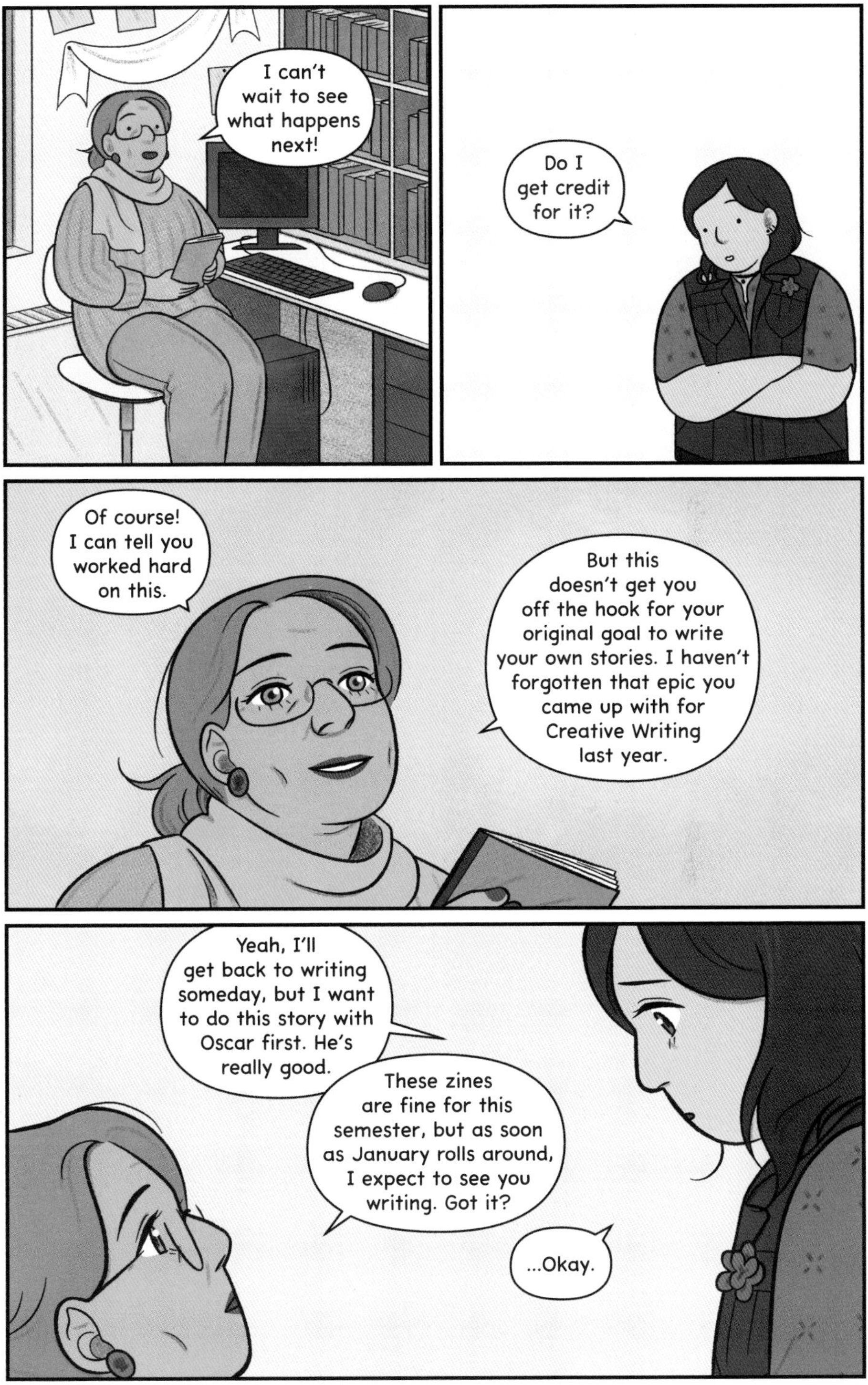
I can't wait to see what happens next!
Do I get credit for it?
Of course! I can tell you worked hard on this.
But this doesn't get you off the hook for your original goal to write your own stories. I haven't forgotten that epic you came up with for Creative Writing last year.
Yeah, I'll get back to writing someday, but I want to do this story with Oscar first. He's really good.
These zines are fine for this semester, but as soon as January rolls around, I expect to see you writing. Got it?
...Okay.

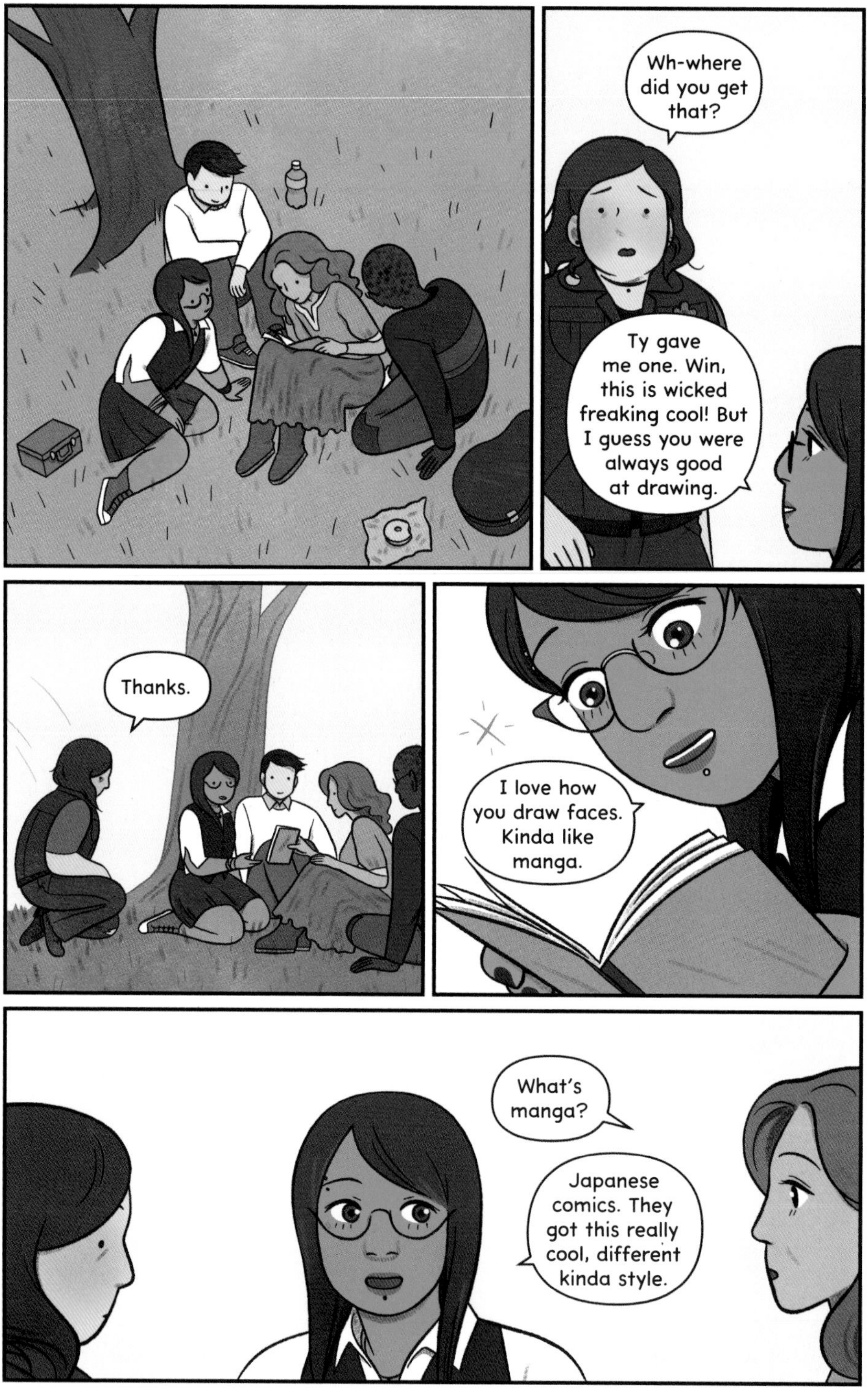
Wh-where did you get that?
Ty gave me one. Win, this is wicked freaking cool! But I guess you were always good at drawing.
Thanks.
I love how you draw faces. Kinda like manga.
What's manga?
Japanese comics. They got this really cool, different kinda style.

You read manga?

Yeah, discovered it over the summer!

Me too! Been trying to collect *Stellar Soldiers*, but I've only found a few scattered issues. The art's gorgeous, though.

I feel ya there. I'm in love with this series about dog demons, but I guess there's like a million volumes and it's taking them forever to translate it all.

Top secret, though, my sister's trying to convince our parents to let us use their credit card to order bootleg copies of the anime off this sketchy Chinese website.

Nice!

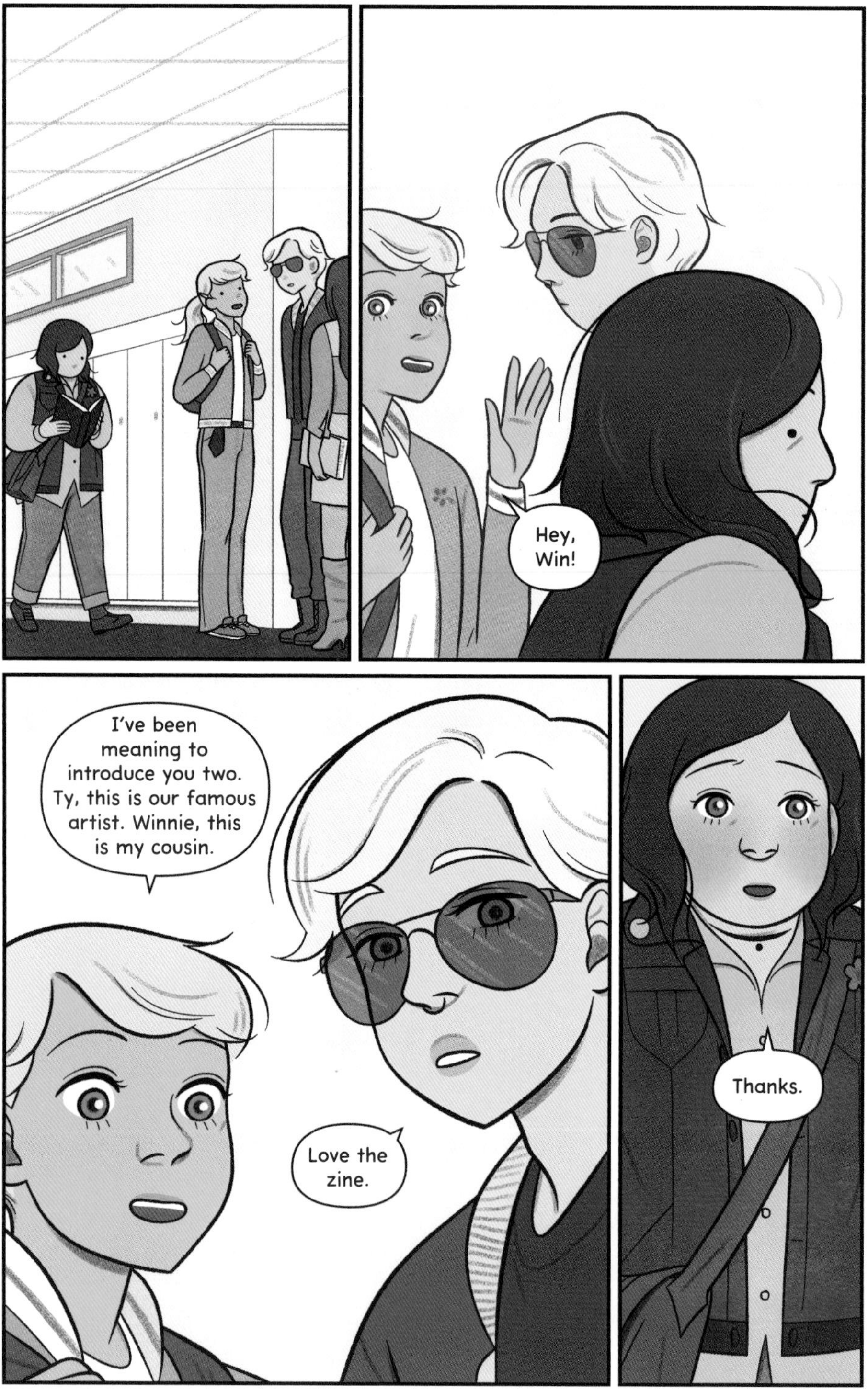
Hey, Win!
I've been meaning to introduce you two. Ty, this is our famous artist. Winnie, this is my cousin.
Love the zine.
Thanks.

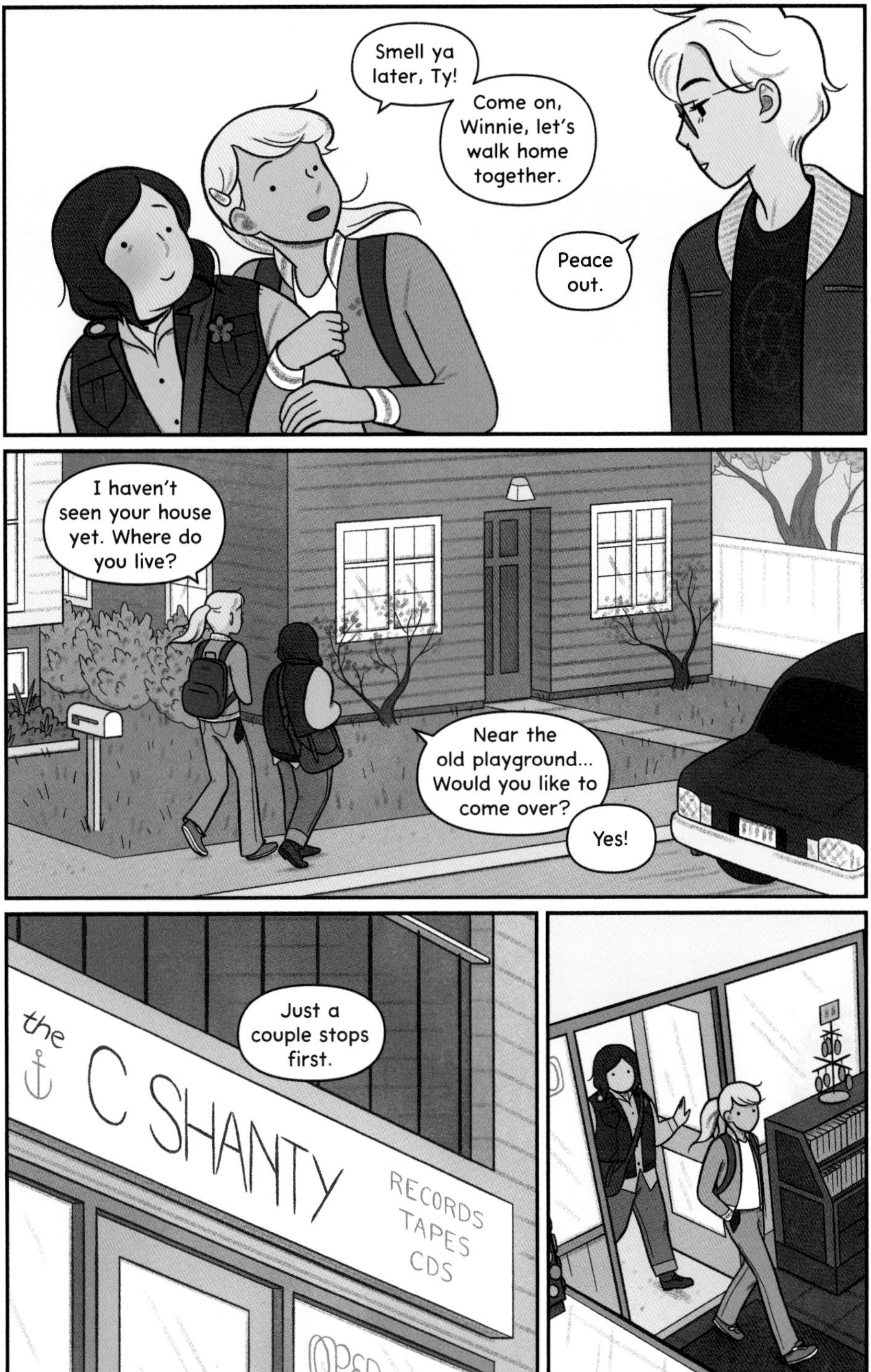
Smell ya later, Ty!
Come on, Winnie, let's walk home together.
Peace out.
I haven't seen your house yet. Where do you live?
Near the old playground... Would you like to come over?
Yes!
Just a couple stops first.
the C SHANTY
RECORDS TAPES CDS

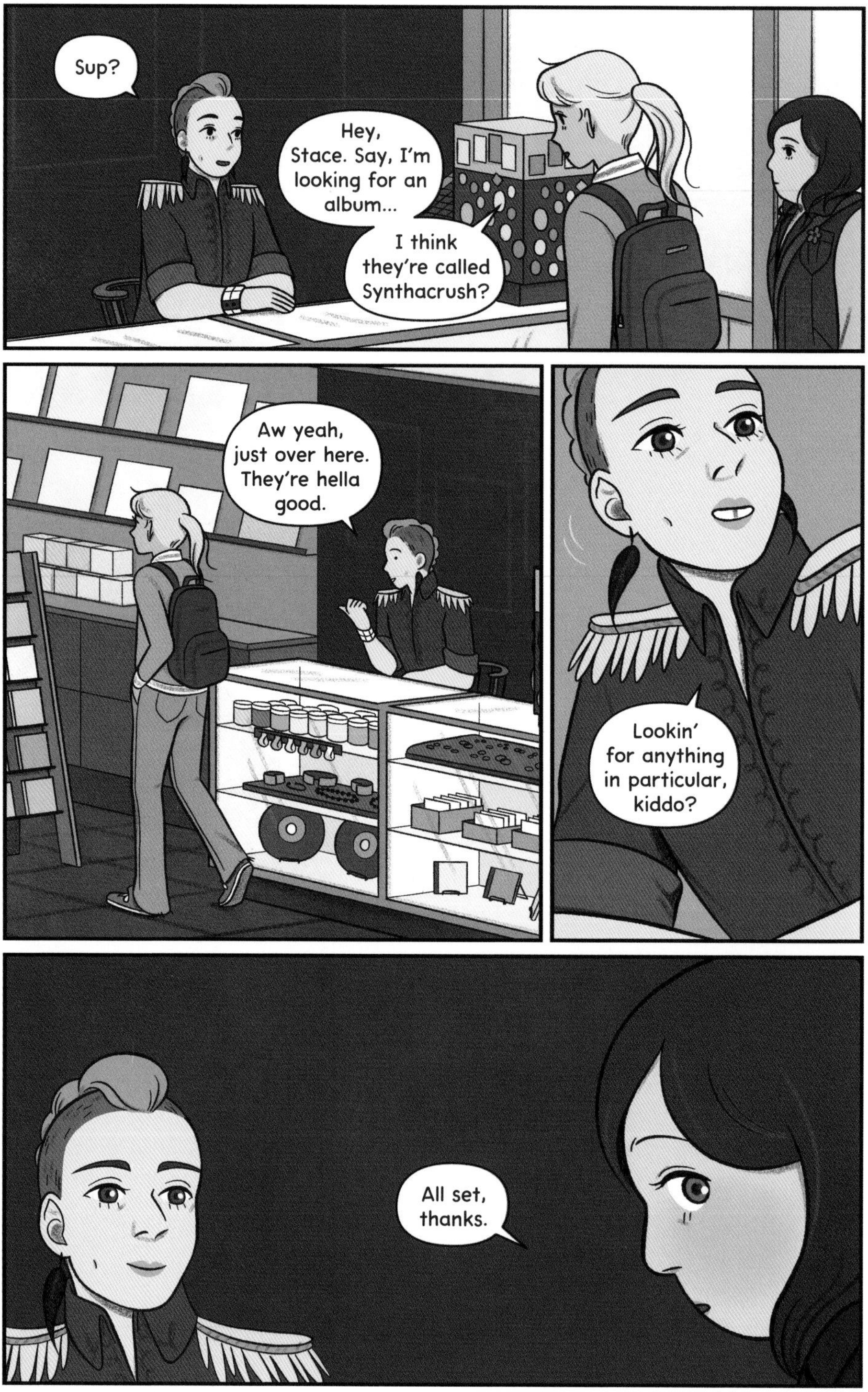
Sup?
Hey, Stace. Say, I'm looking for an album...
I think they're called Synthacrush?
Aw yeah, just over here. They're hella good.
Lookin' for anything in particular, kiddo?
All set, thanks.

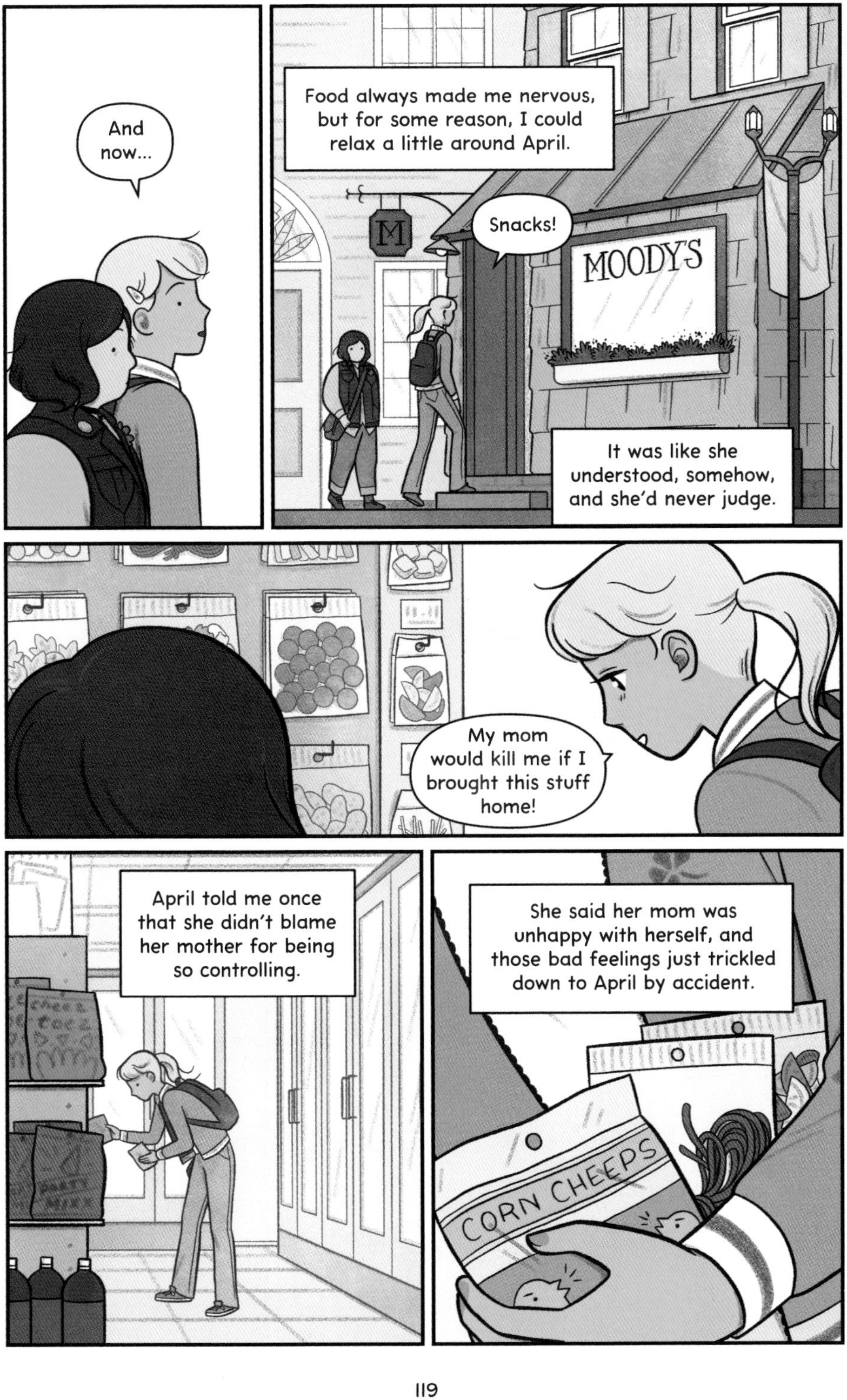
And now...
Food always made me nervous, but for some reason, I could relax a little around April.
M
Snacks!
MOODY'S
It was like she understood, somehow, and she'd never judge.
My mom would kill me if I brought this stuff home!
April told me once that she didn't blame her mother for being so controlling.
She said her mom was unhappy with herself, and those bad feelings just trickled down to April by accident.
CORN CHEEPS

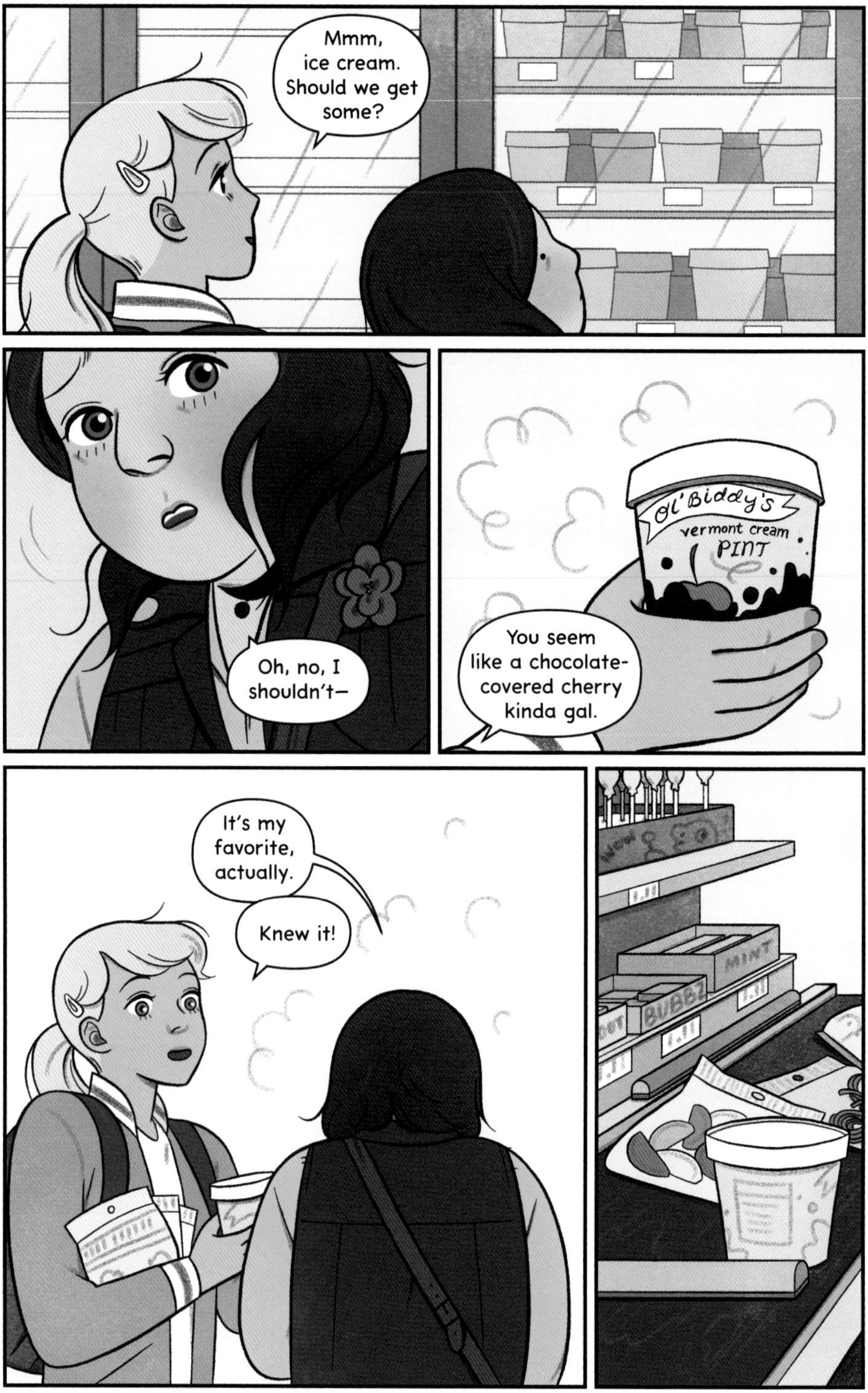
Mmm, ice cream. Should we get some?
Oh, no, I shouldn't—
Ol' Biddy's
vermont cream
PINT
You seem like a chocolate-covered cherry kinda gal.
It's my favorite, actually.
Knew it!
MINT
BUBBZ

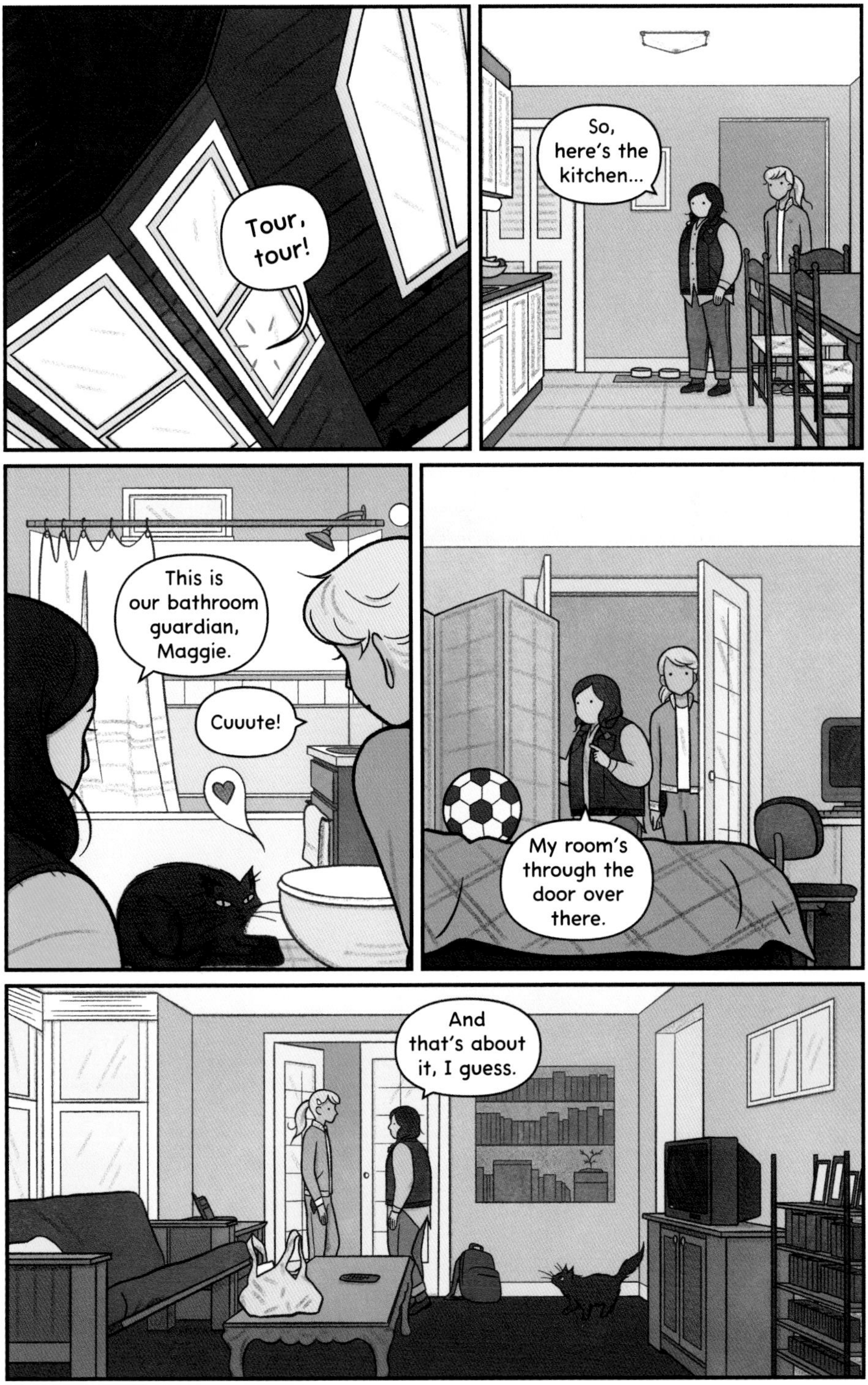
Tour, tour!
So, here's the kitchen...
This is our bathroom guardian, Maggie.
Cuuute!
My room's through the door over there.
And that's about it, I guess.

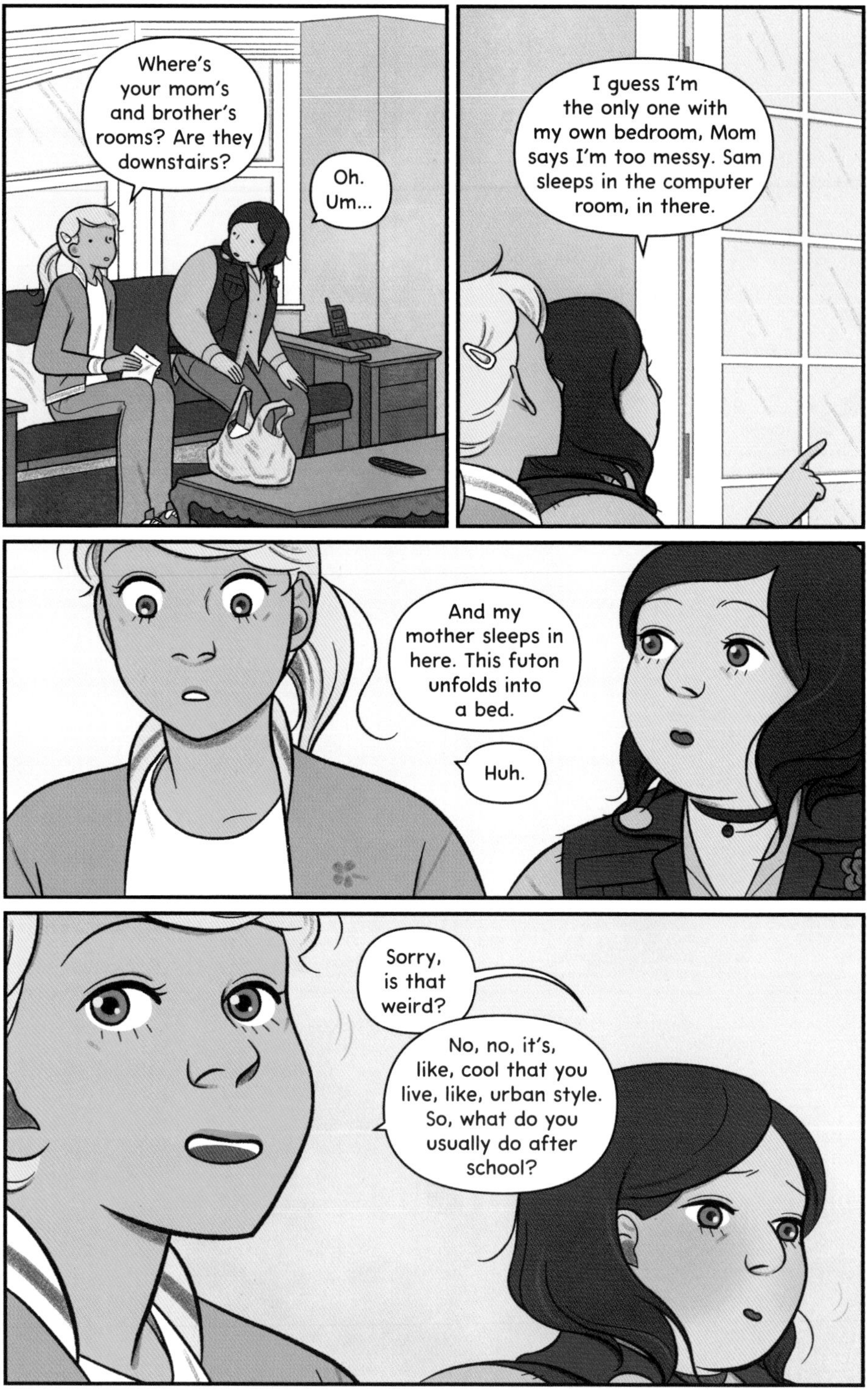
Where's your mom's and brother's rooms? Are they downstairs?
Oh. Um...
I guess I'm the only one with my own bedroom, Mom says I'm too messy. Sam sleeps in the computer room, in there.
And my mother sleeps in here. This futon unfolds into a bed.
Huh.
Sorry, is that weird?
No, no, it's, like, cool that you live, like, urban style. So, what do you usually do after school?

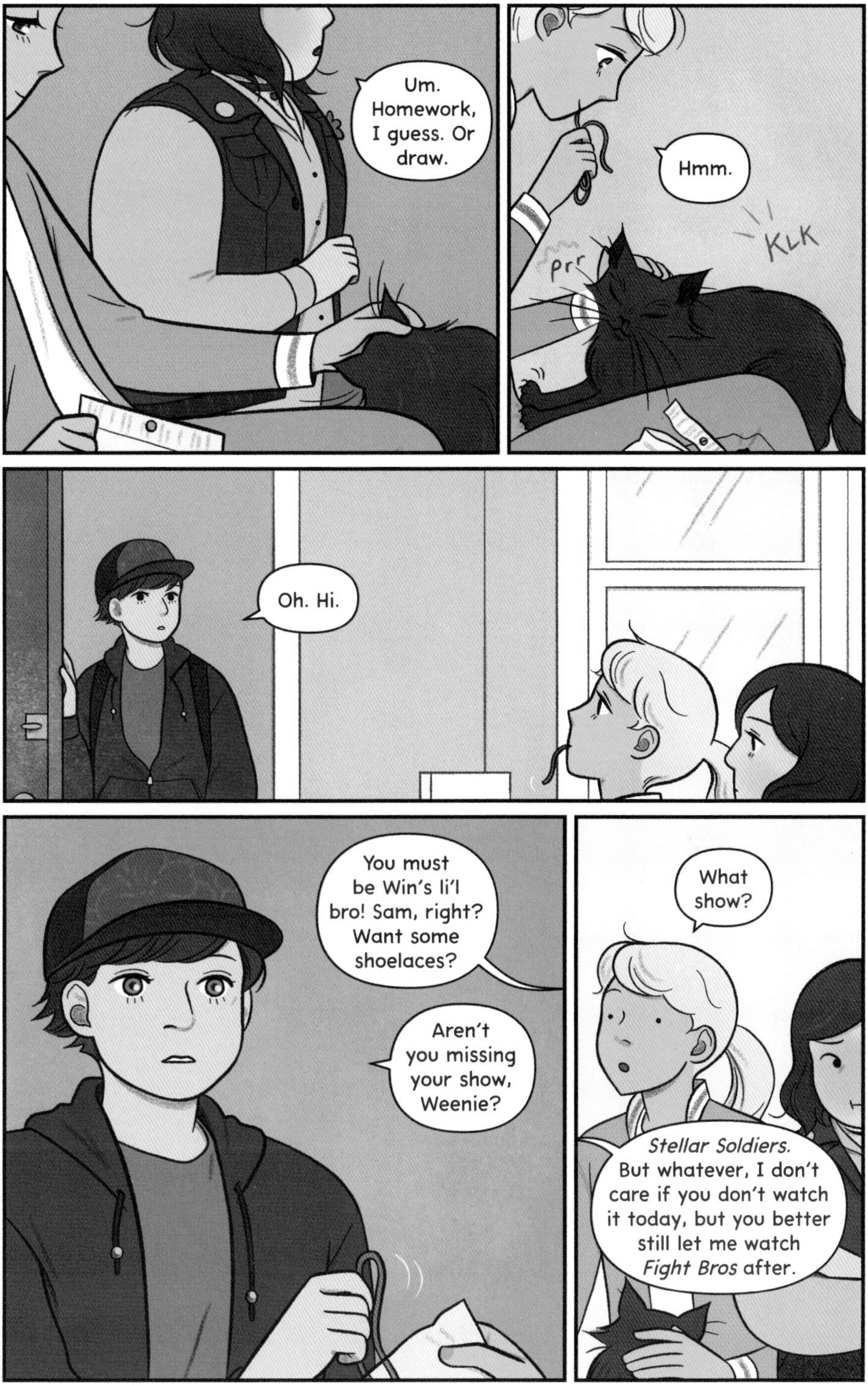
Um. Homework, I guess. Or draw.
Hmm.
prr
KLK
Oh. Hi.
You must be Win's li'l bro! Sam, right? Want some shoelaces?
Aren't you missing your show, Weenie?
What show?
Stellar Soldiers. But whatever, I don't care if you don't watch it today, but you better still let me watch *Fight Bros* after.

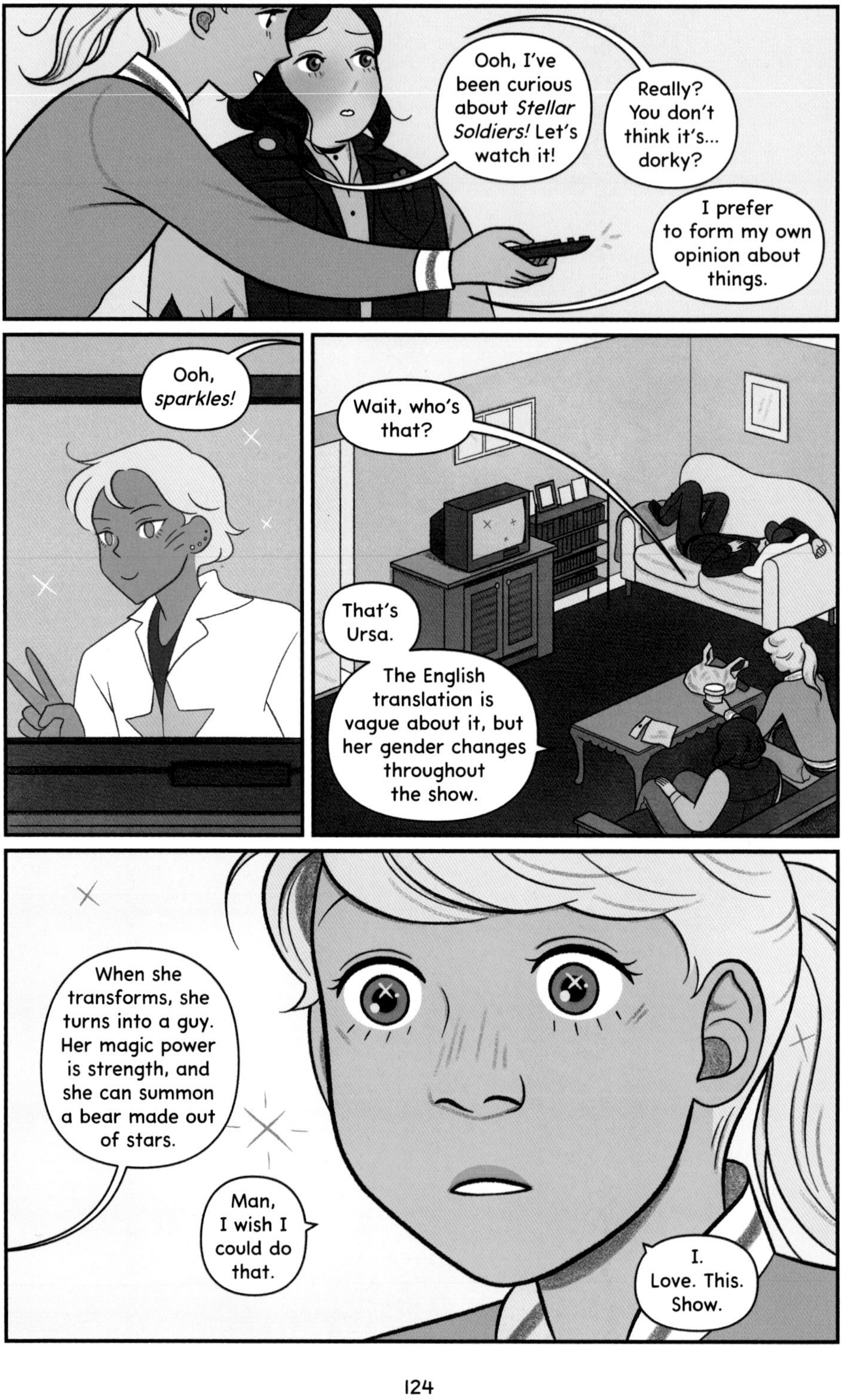
Ooh, I've been curious about *Stellar Soldiers!* Let's watch it!
Really? You don't think it's... dorky?
I prefer to form my own opinion about things.
Ooh, *sparkles!*
Wait, who's that?
That's Ursa.
The English translation is vague about it, but her gender changes throughout the show.
When she transforms, she turns into a guy. Her magic power is strength, and she can summon a bear made out of stars.
Man, I wish I could do that.
I. Love. This. Show.

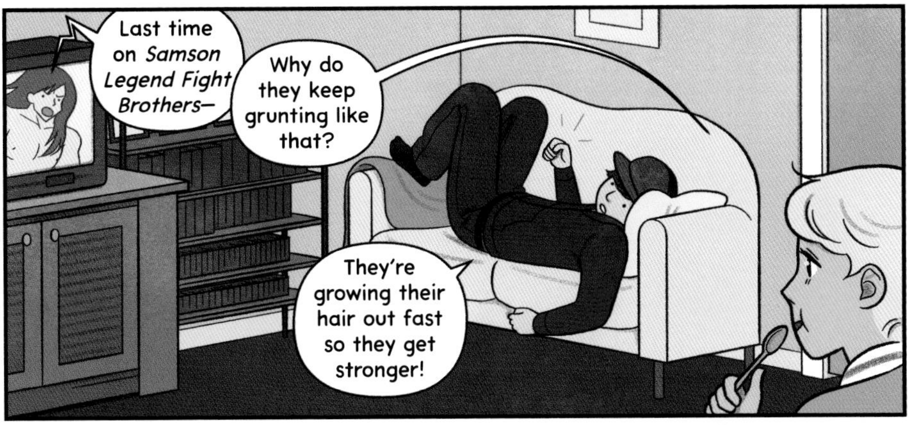
Last time on *Samson Legend Fight Brothers*—
Why do they keep grunting like that?
They're growing their hair out fast so they get stronger!

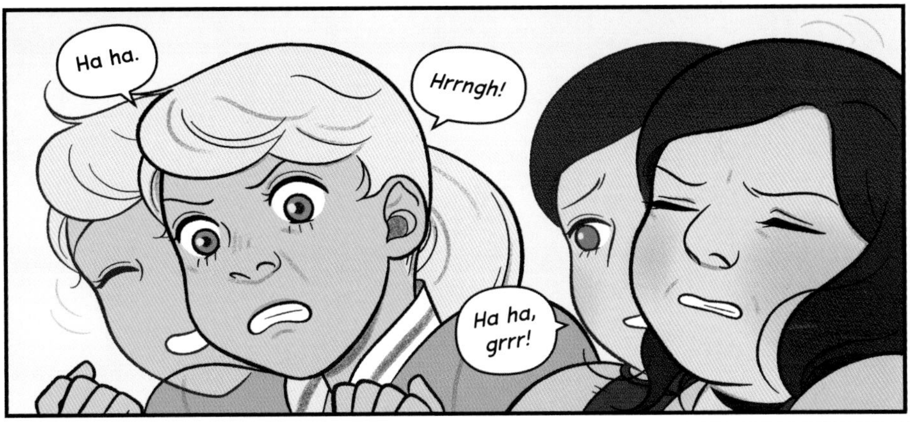
Ha ha.
Hrrngh!
Ha ha, grrr!

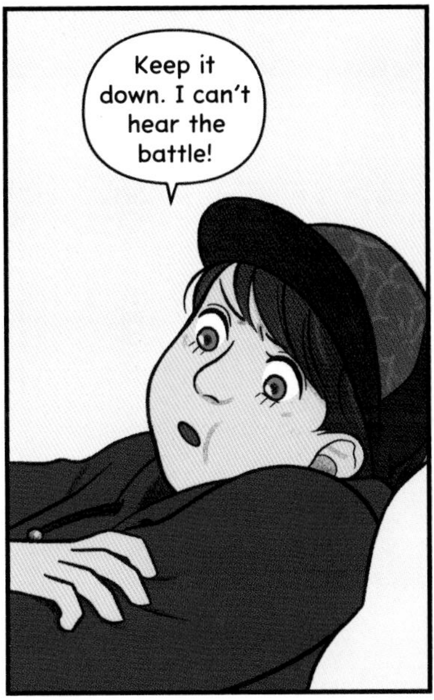
Keep it down. I can't hear the battle!

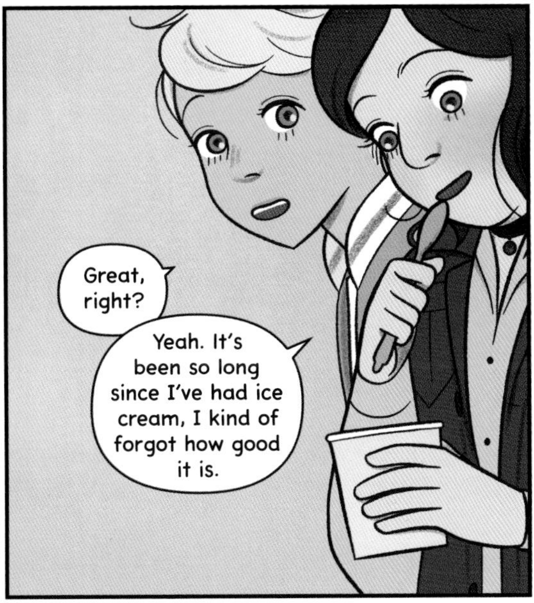
Great, right?
Yeah. It's been so long since I've had ice cream, I kind of forgot how good it is.

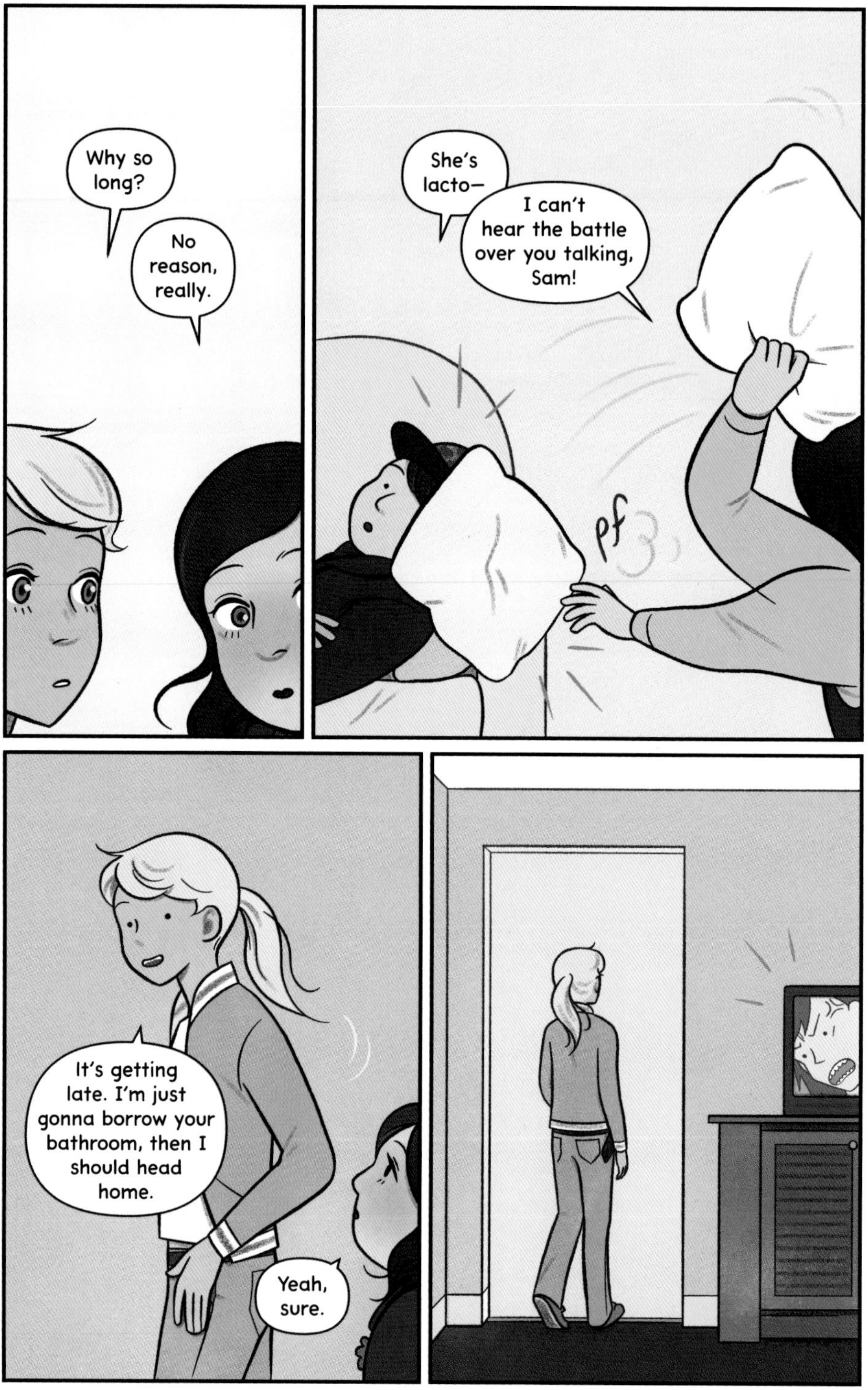
Why so long?
No reason, really.
She's lacto—
I can't hear the battle over you talking, Sam!
pf
It's getting late. I'm just gonna borrow your bathroom, then I should head home.
Yeah, sure.

Chili night! I think I'm getting better at this veggie thing.

Sorry, I'm not sure I want dinner tonight.

Hope you feel better soon, kitten.

Sam's embarrassing description of what dairy did to me was gentle compared to the reality.

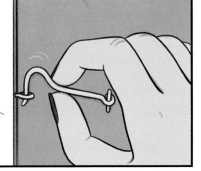

tK

It hit me like food poisoning, more than anything. First, cold sweats...

...then an ache in my abdomen that bloomed into dizzying nausea.

I figured this was what I deserved for indulging myself like that.

A dark feeling inside me told me that if I was going to act gross and fat, might as well eat something that would punish me later.

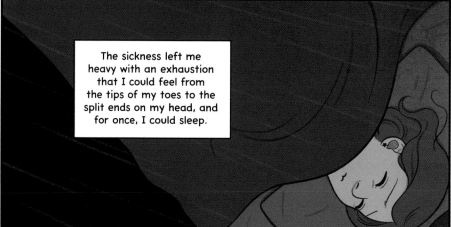

The sickness left me heavy with an exhaustion that I could feel from the tips of my toes to the split ends on my head, and for once, I could sleep.

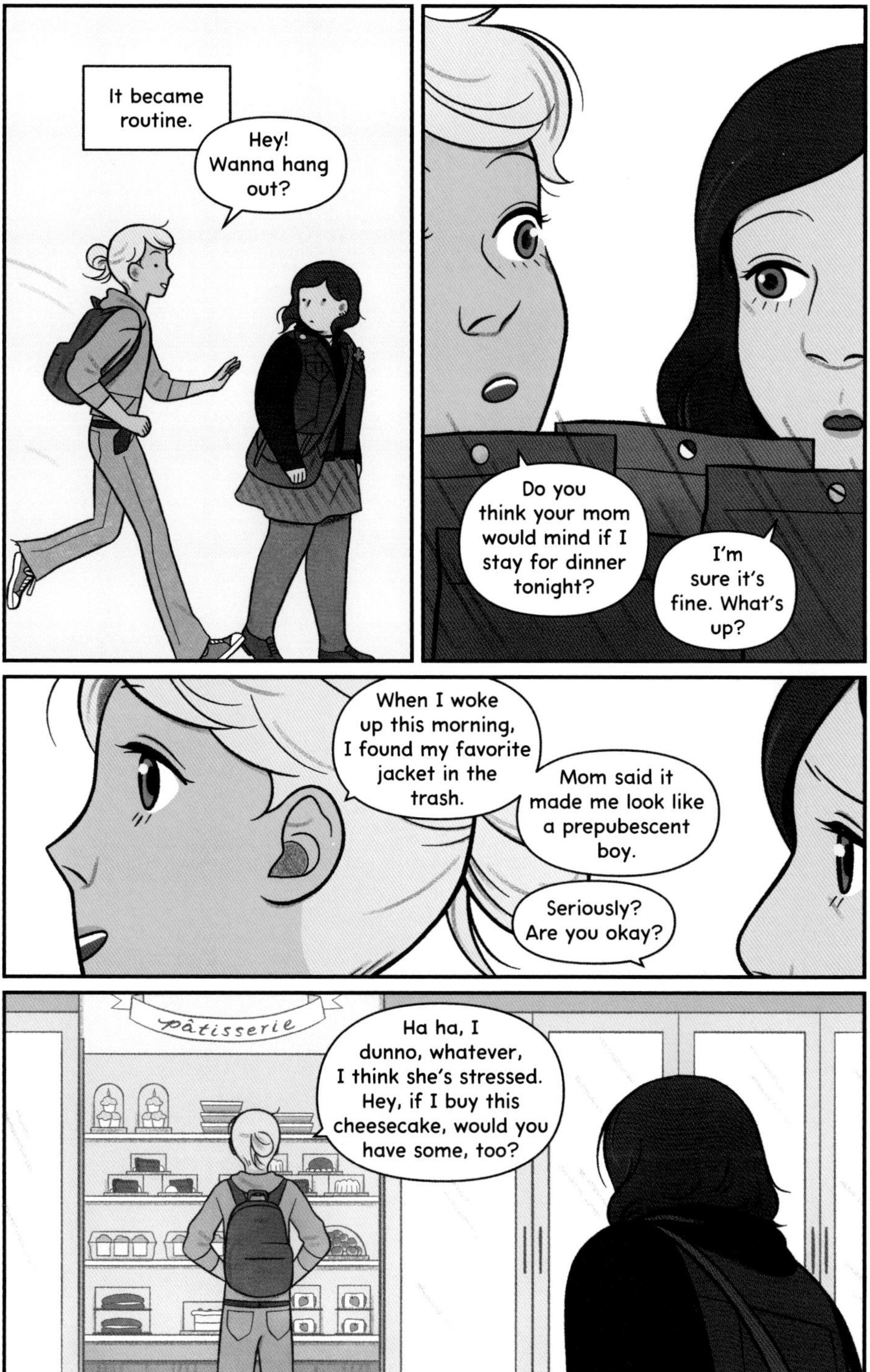
It became routine.
Hey! Wanna hang out?
Do you think your mom would mind if I stay for dinner tonight?
I'm sure it's fine. What's up?
When I woke up this morning, I found my favorite jacket in the trash.
Mom said it made me look like a prepubescent boy.
Seriously? Are you okay?
pâtisserie
Ha ha, I dunno, whatever, I think she's stressed. Hey, if I buy this cheesecake, would you have some, too?

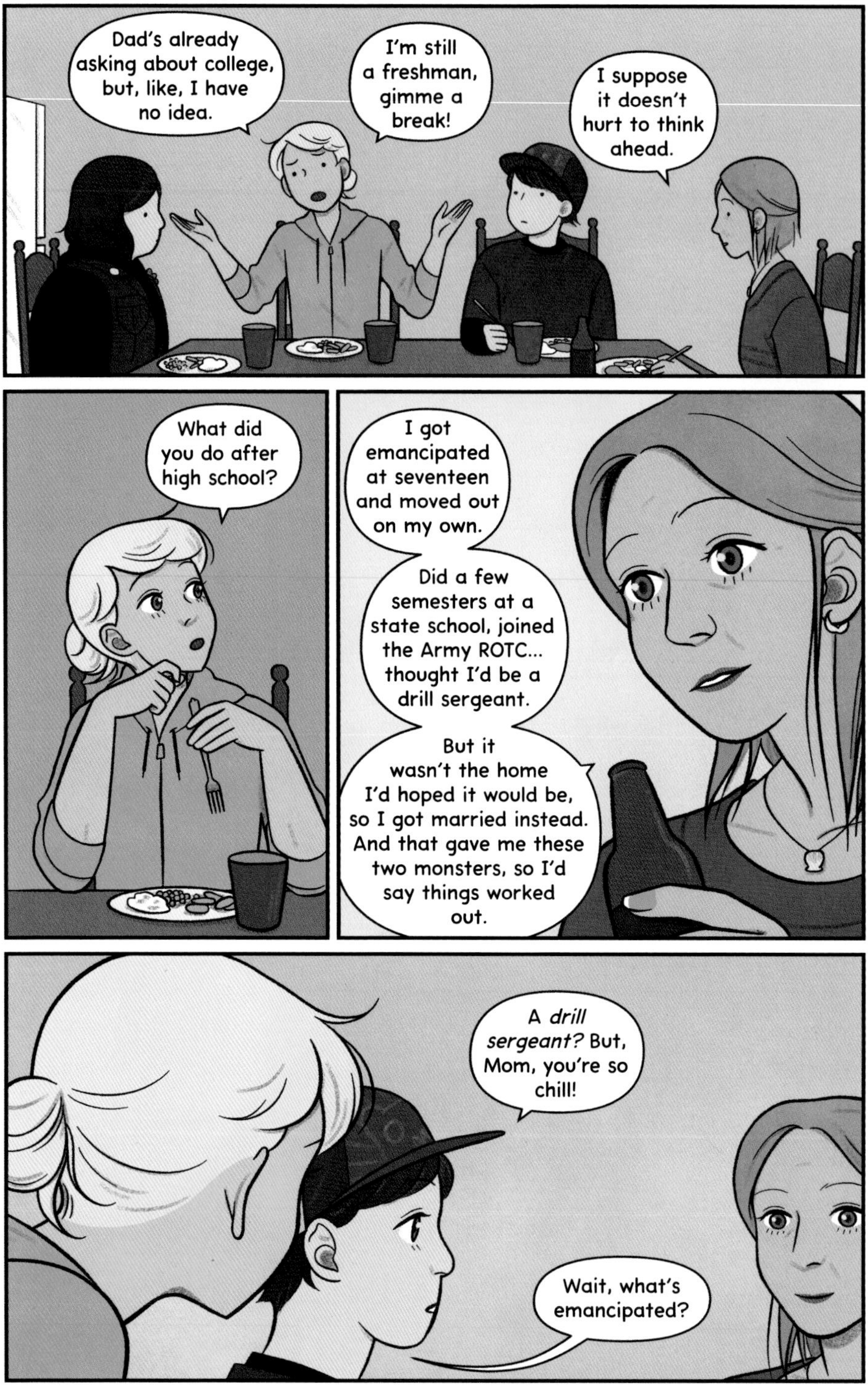
Dad's already asking about college, but, like, I have no idea.
I'm still a freshman, gimme a break!
I suppose it doesn't hurt to think ahead.
What did you do after high school?
I got emancipated at seventeen and moved out on my own.
Did a few semesters at a state school, joined the Army ROTC... thought I'd be a drill sergeant.
But it wasn't the home I'd hoped it would be, so I got married instead. And that gave me these two monsters, so I'd say things worked out.
A *drill sergeant?* But, Mom, you're so chill!
Wait, what's emancipated?

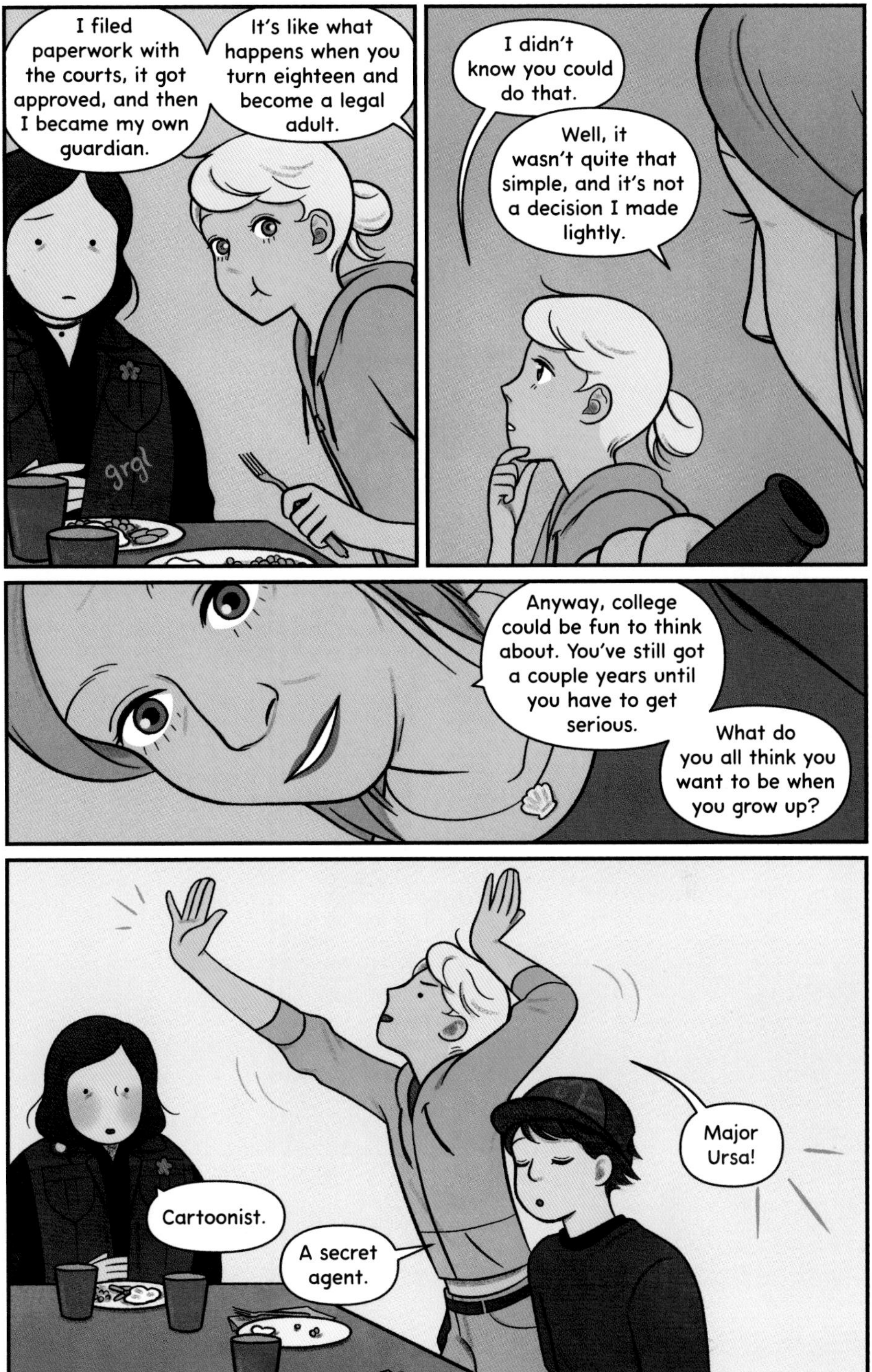
I filed paperwork with the courts, it got approved, and then I became my own guardian.
It's like what happens when you turn eighteen and become a legal adult.
grrl
I didn't know you could do that.
Well, it wasn't quite that simple, and it's not a decision I made lightly.
Anyway, college could be fun to think about. You've still got a couple years until you have to get serious.
What do you all think you want to be when you grow up?
Cartoonist.
A secret agent.
Major Ursa!

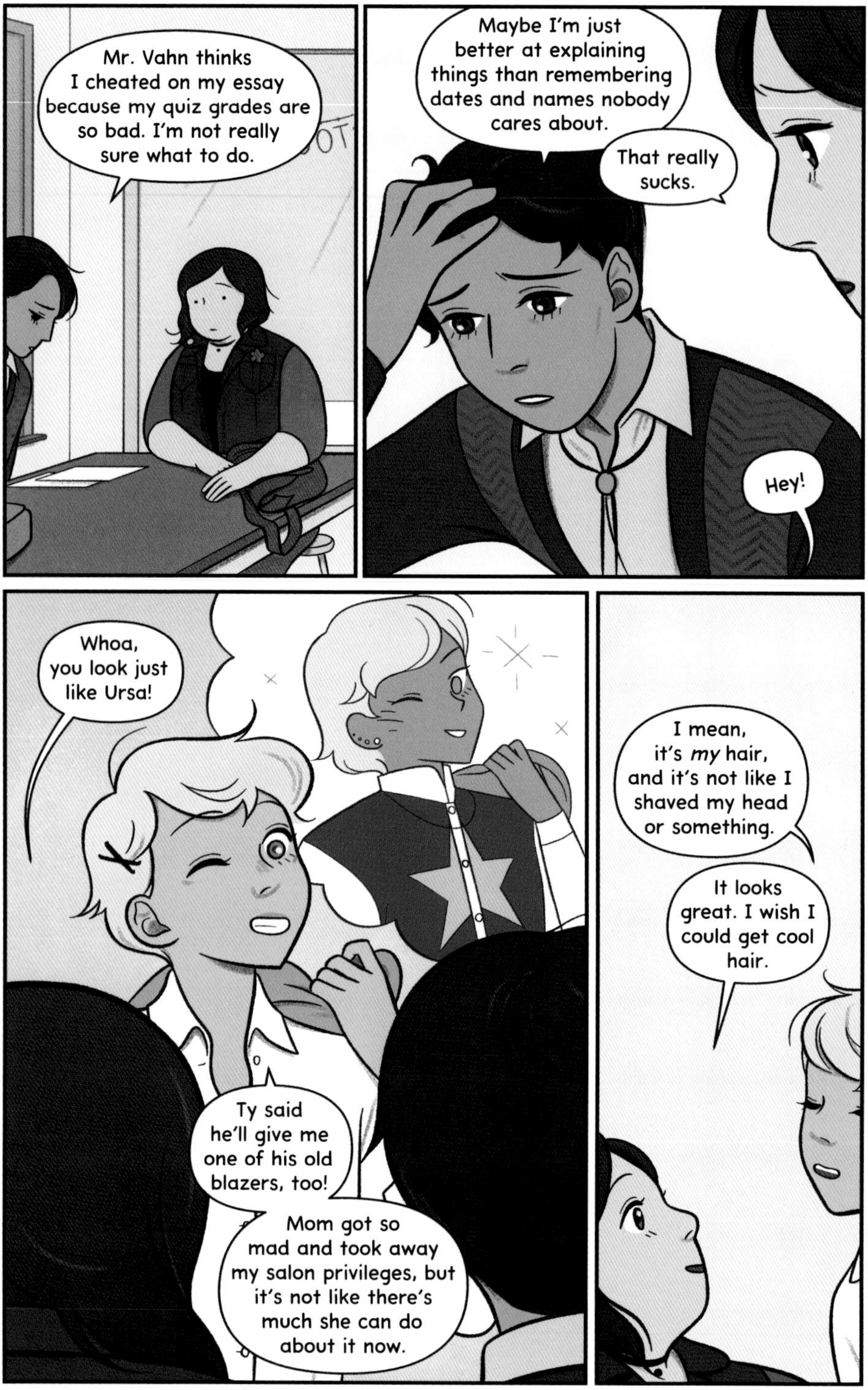
Mr. Vahn thinks I cheated on my essay because my quiz grades are so bad. I'm not really sure what to do.
Maybe I'm just better at explaining things than remembering dates and names nobody cares about.
That really sucks.
Hey!
Whoa, you look just like Ursa!
Ty said he'll give me one of his old blazers, too!
Mom got so mad and took away my salon privileges, but it's not like there's much she can do about it now.
I mean, it's *my* hair, and it's not like I shaved my head or something.
It looks great. I wish I could get cool hair.

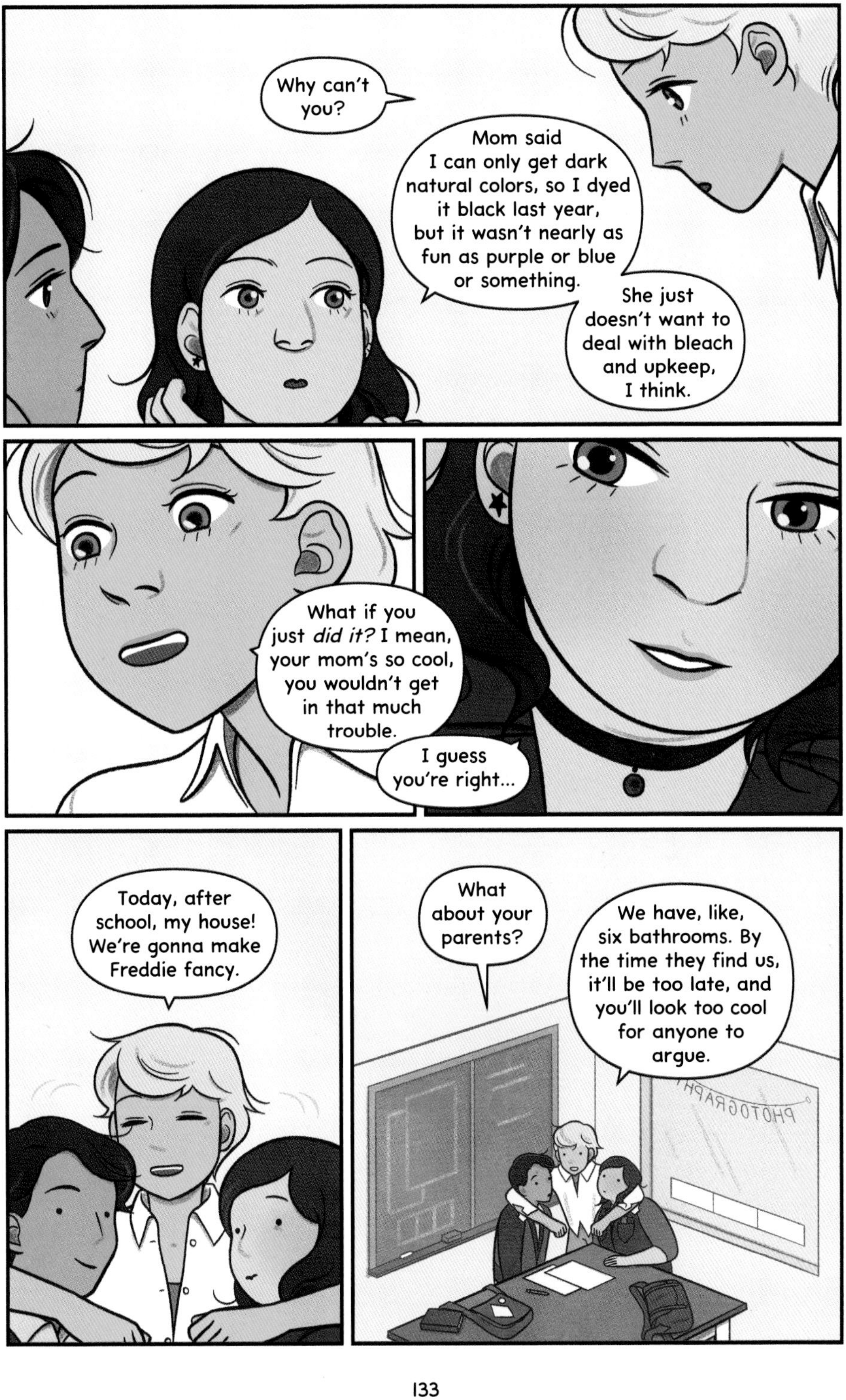
Why can't you?
Mom said I can only get dark natural colors, so I dyed it black last year, but it wasn't nearly as fun as purple or blue or something.
She just doesn't want to deal with bleach and upkeep, I think.
What if you just *did it?* I mean, your mom's so cool, you wouldn't get in that much trouble.
I guess you're right...
Today, after school, my house! We're gonna make Freddie fancy.
What about your parents?
We have, like, six bathrooms. By the time they find us, it'll be too late, and you'll look too cool for anyone to argue.

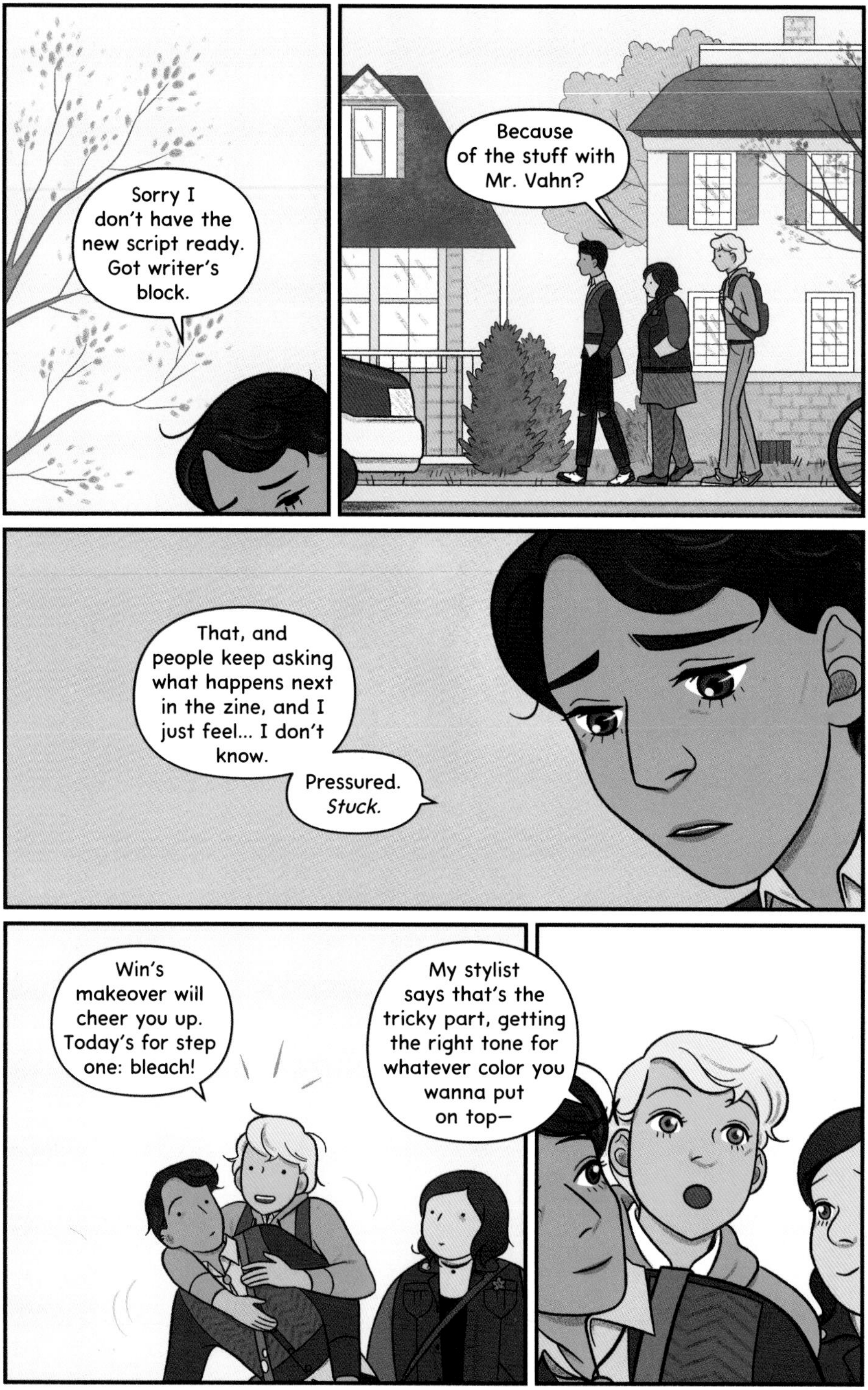
Sorry I don't have the new script ready. Got writer's block.
Because of the stuff with Mr. Vahn?
That, and people keep asking what happens next in the zine, and I just feel... I don't know.
Pressured. *Stuck.*
Win's makeover will cheer you up. Today's for step one: bleach!
My stylist says that's the tricky part, getting the right tone for whatever color you wanna put on top—

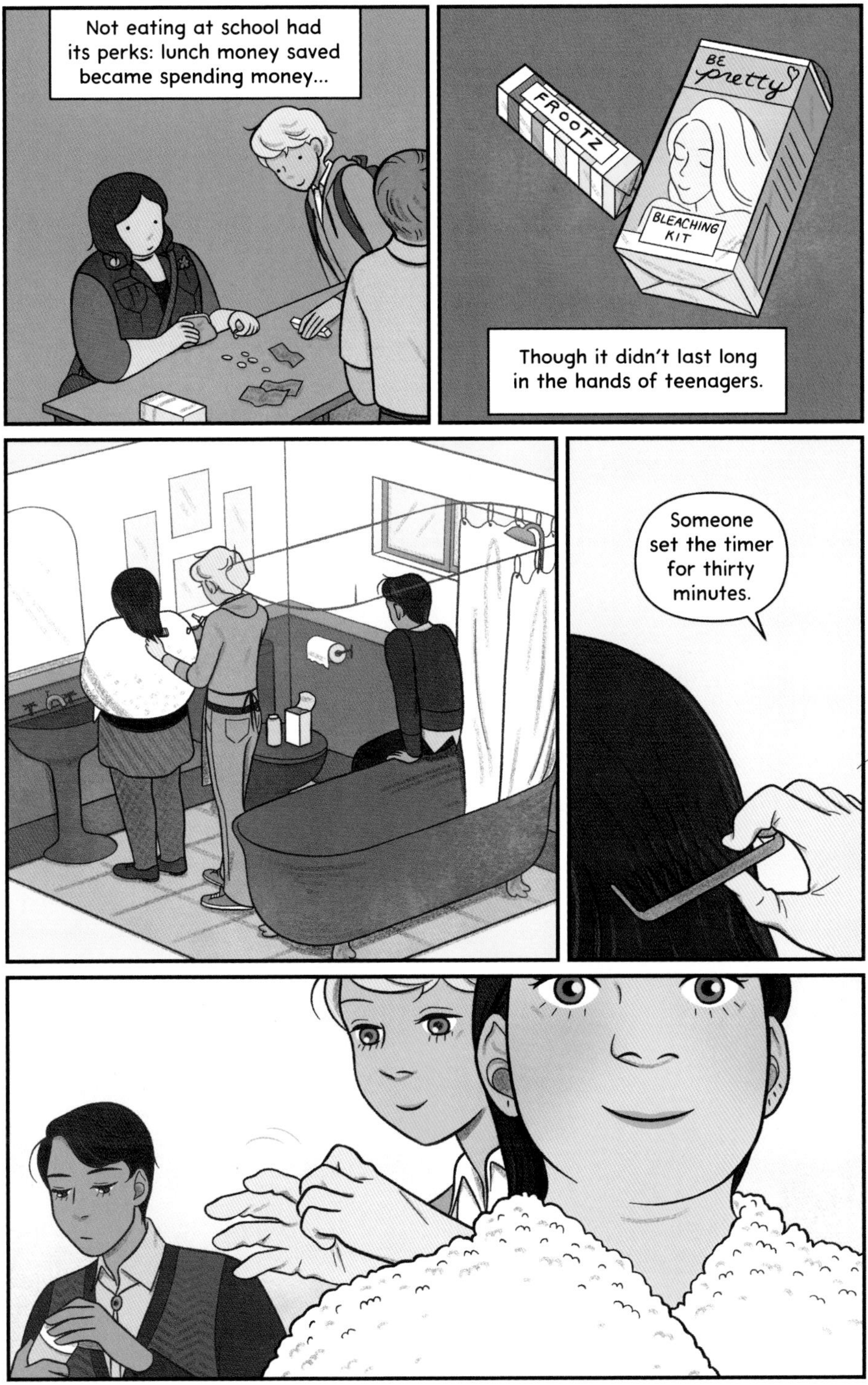
Not eating at school had its perks: lunch money saved became spending money...
FROOTZ
BE pretty
BLEACHING KIT
Though it didn't last long in the hands of teenagers.
Someone set the timer for thirty minutes.

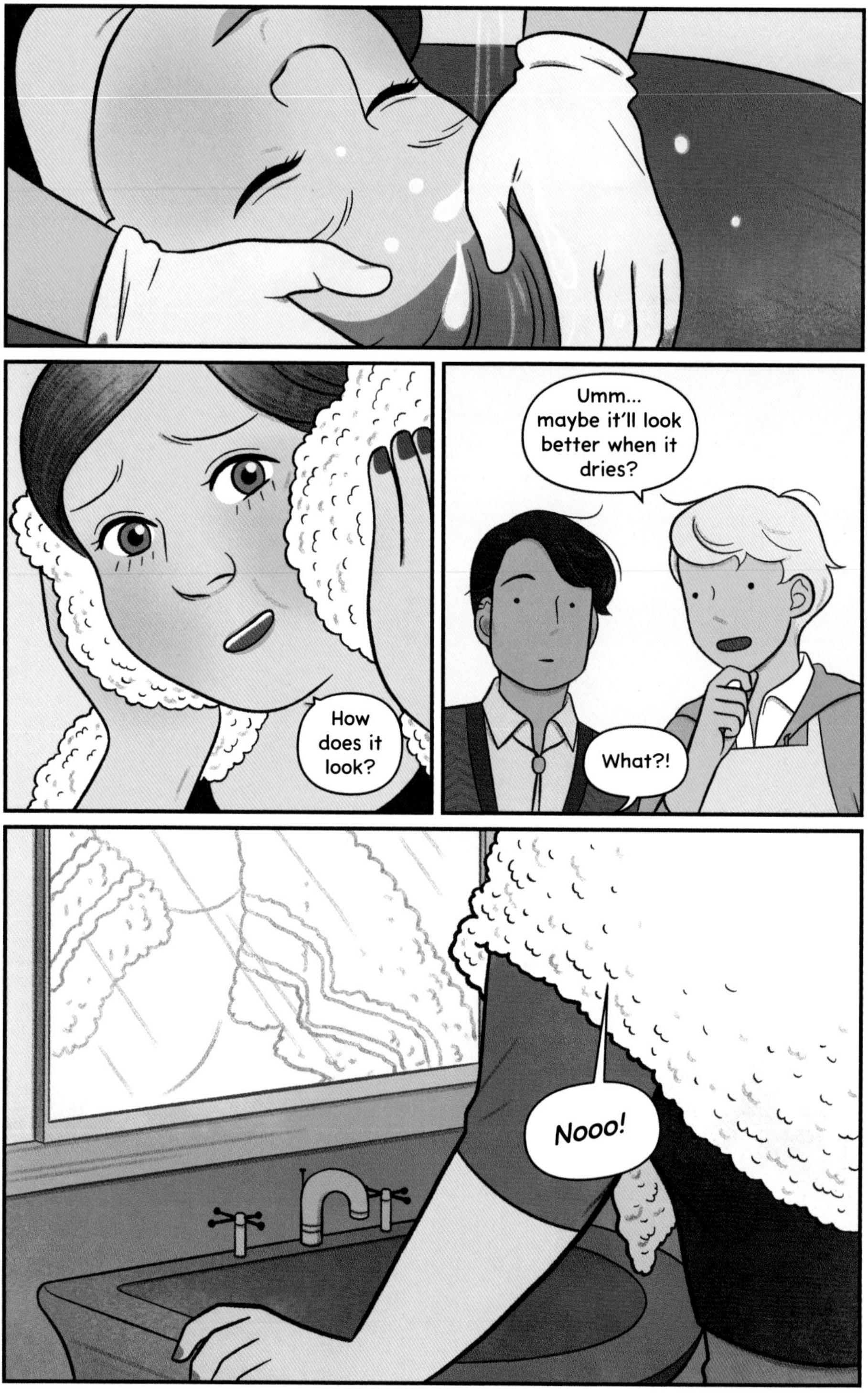

How does it look?
Umm... maybe it'll look better when it dries?
What?!
Nooo!

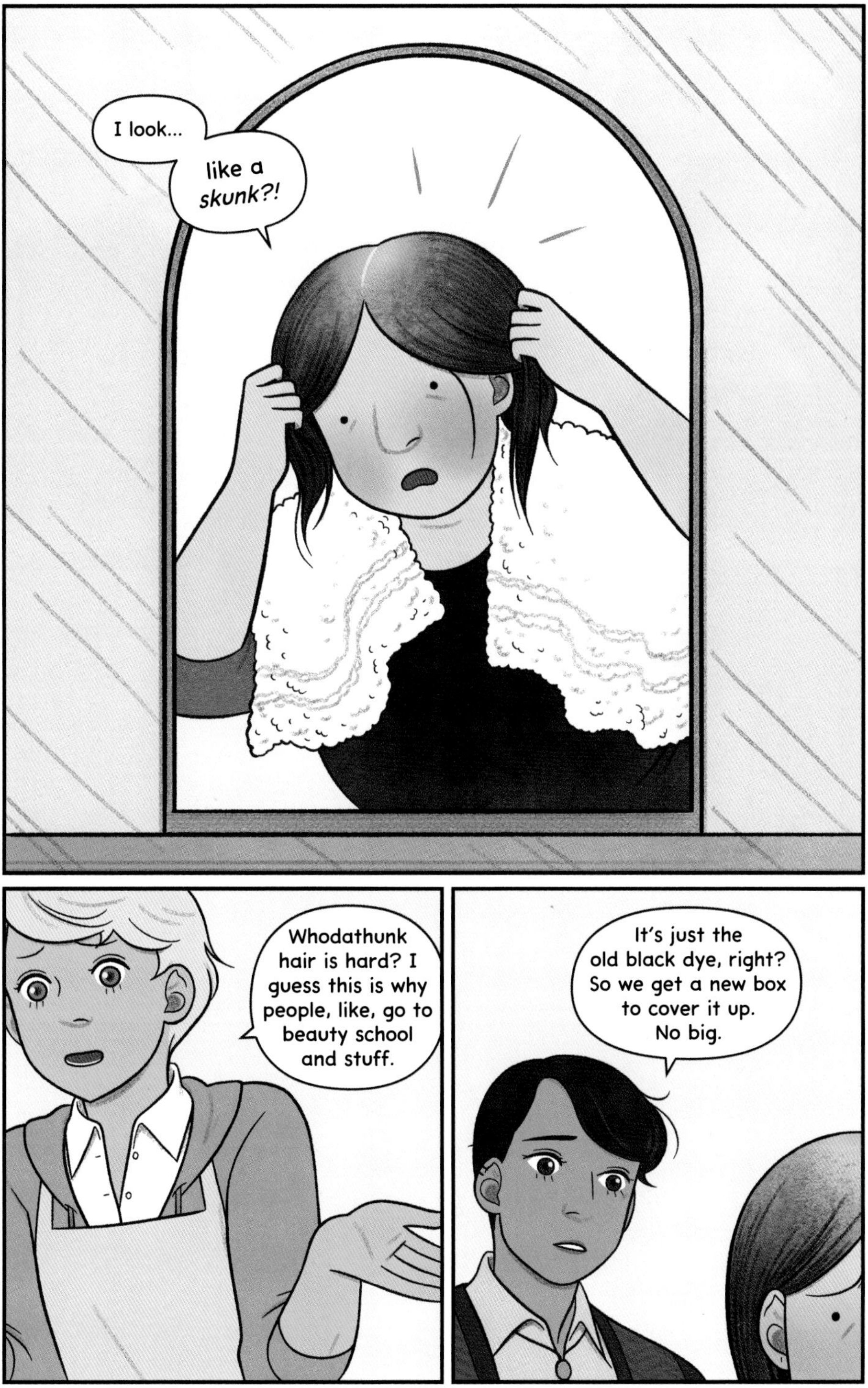
I look...
like a *skunk*?!
Whodathunk hair is hard? I guess this is why people, like, go to beauty school and stuff.
It's just the old black dye, right? So we get a new box to cover it up. No big.

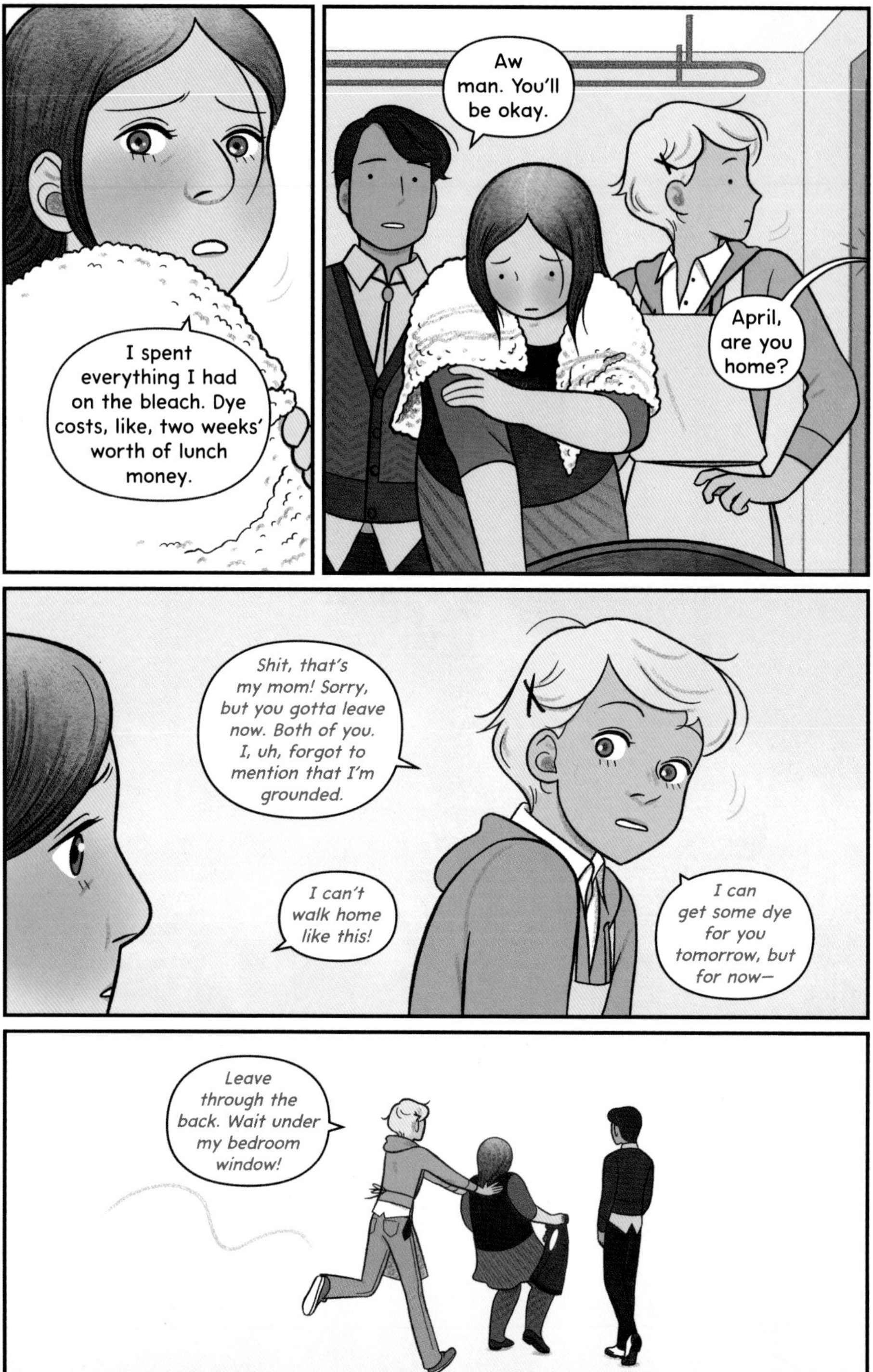
I spent everything I had on the bleach. Dye costs, like, two weeks' worth of lunch money.
Aw man. You'll be okay.
April, are you home?
Shit, that's my mom! Sorry, but you gotta leave now. Both of you. I, uh, forgot to mention that I'm grounded.
I can't walk home like this!
I can get some dye for you tomorrow, but for now—
Leave through the back. Wait under my bedroom window!

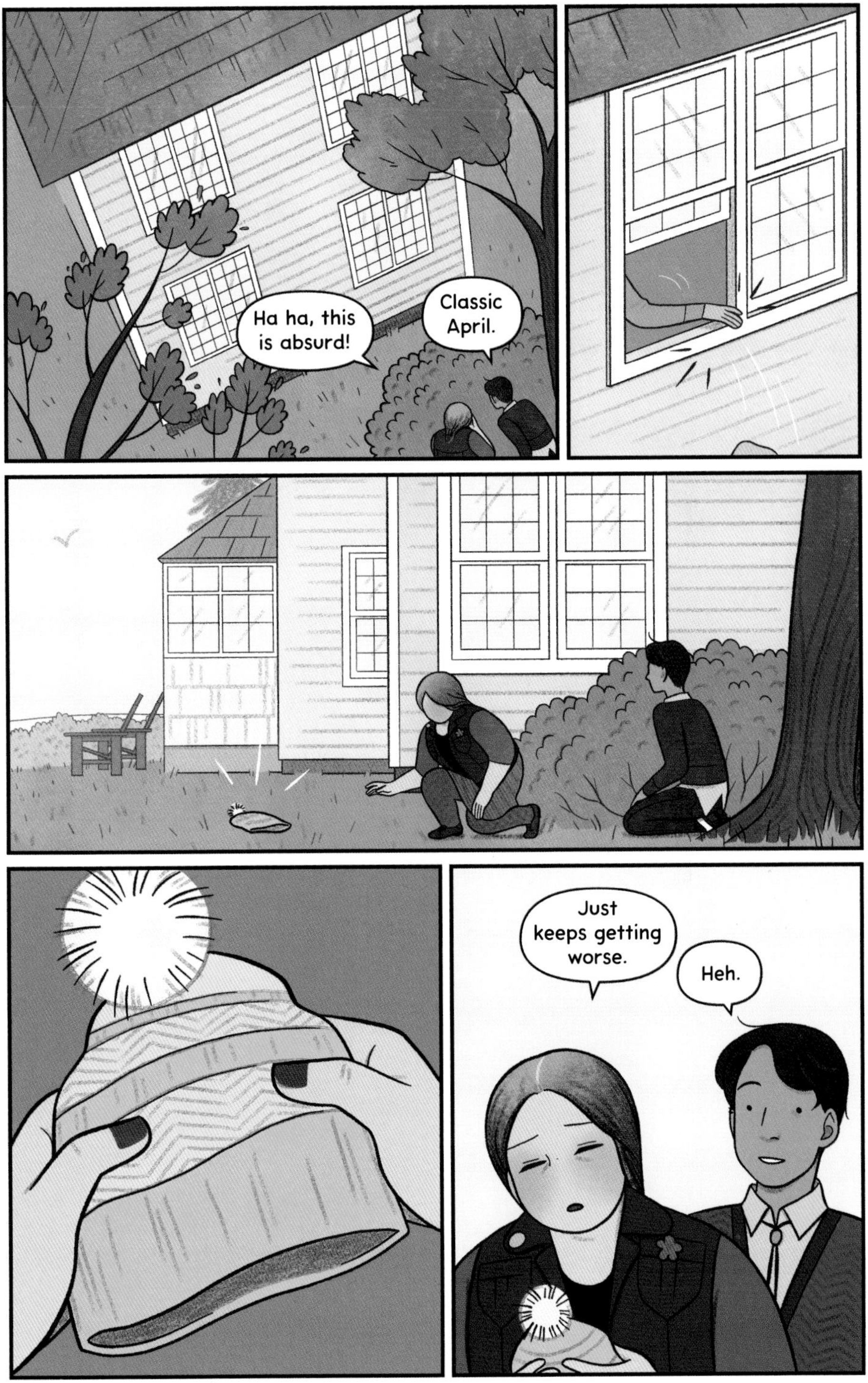
Ha ha, this is absurd!
Classic April.
Just keeps getting worse.
Heh.

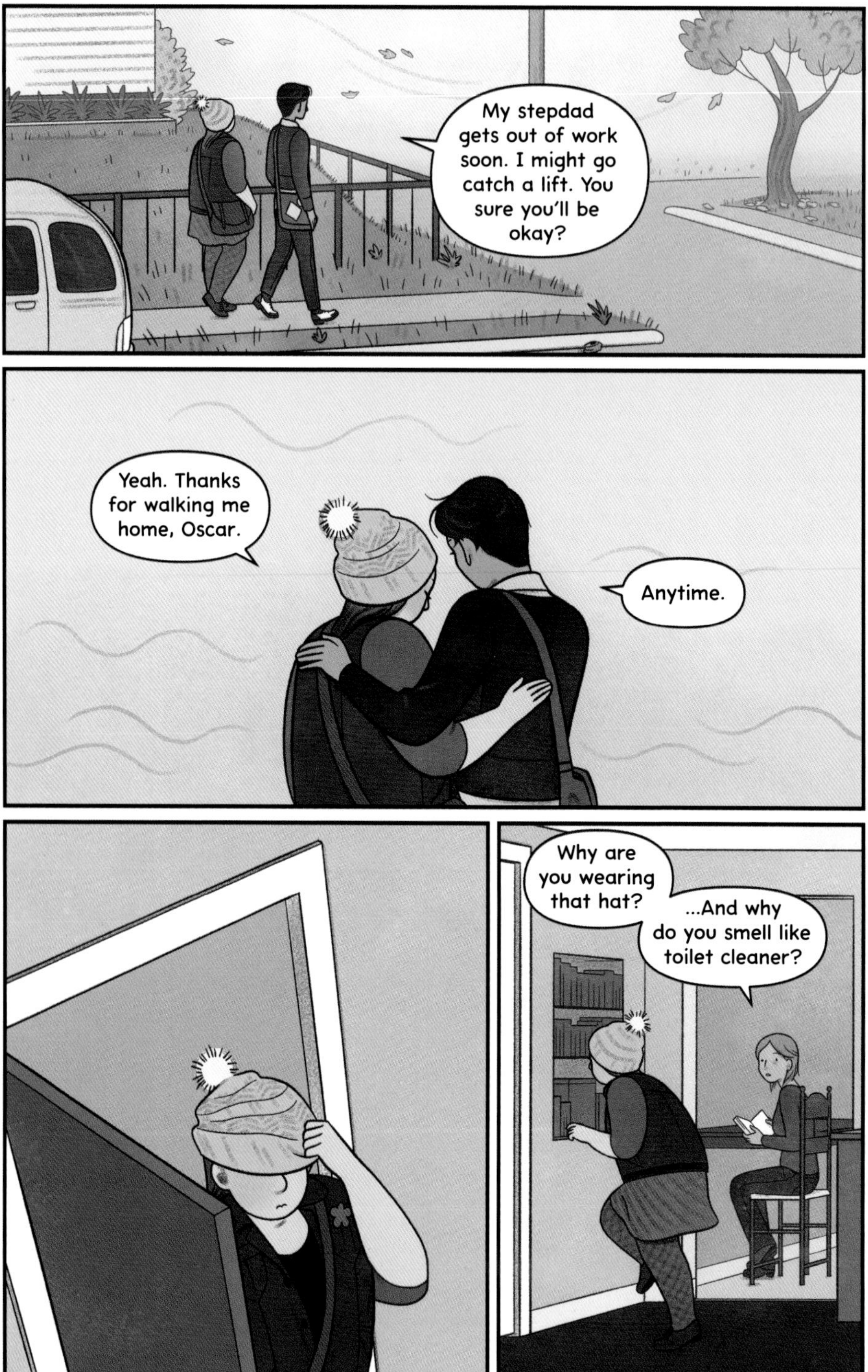
My stepdad gets out of work soon. I might go catch a lift. You sure you'll be okay?
Yeah. Thanks for walking me home, Oscar.
Anytime.
Why are you wearing that hat?
...And why do you smell like toilet cleaner?

Promise you won't laugh.

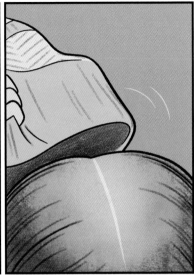

I'm sorry, I just...

snrk

Ha ha.

Mama, don't laugh! I know I should've listened to you.

Oh honey. If this is your terrible attempt at teen rebellion, I'll take it.

Now, how about we make a deal.

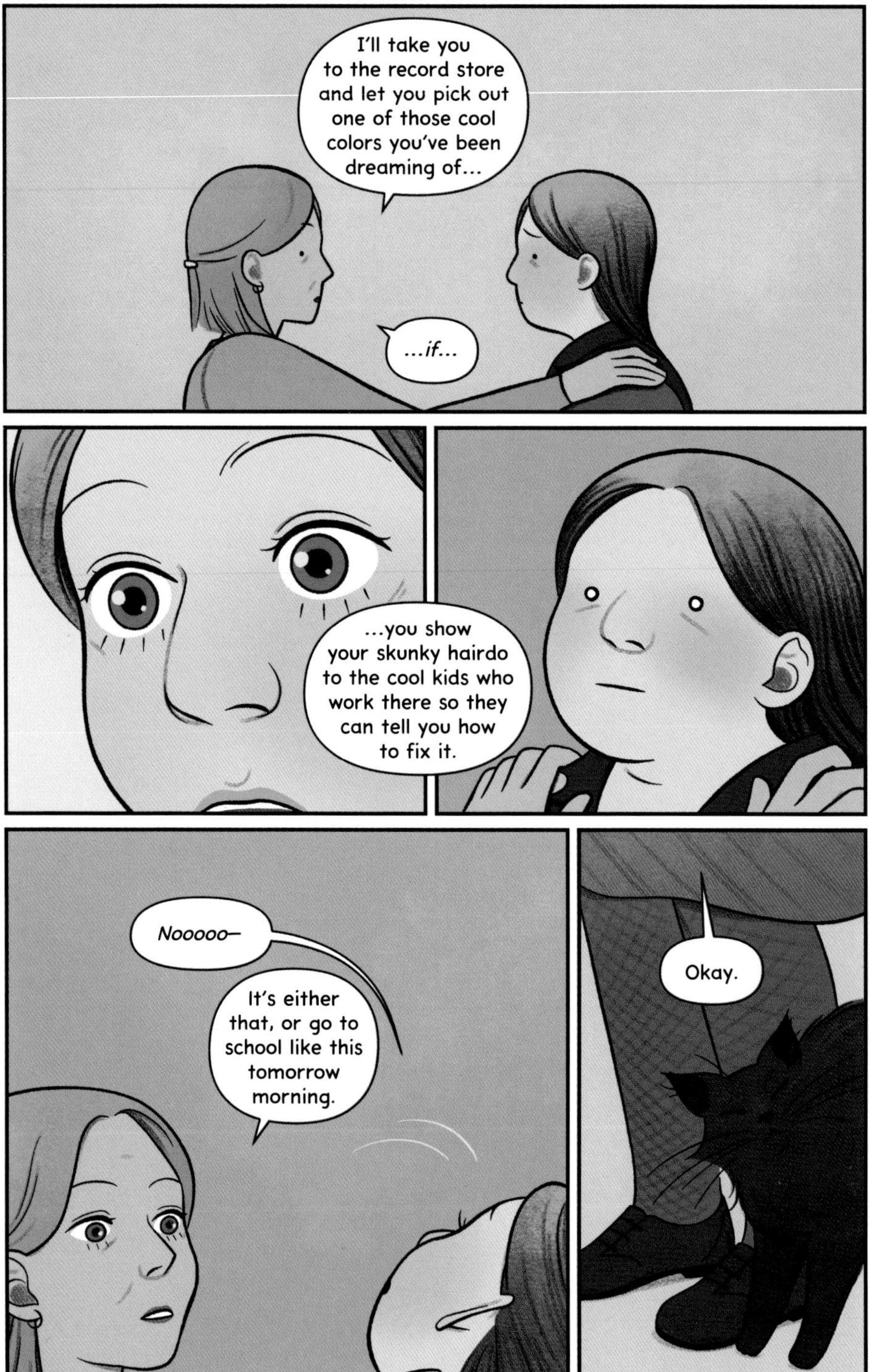
I'll take you to the record store and let you pick out one of those cool colors you've been dreaming of...
...*if*...
...you show your skunky hairdo to the cool kids who work there so they can tell you how to fix it.
Nooooo—
It's either that, or go to school like this tomorrow morning.
Okay.

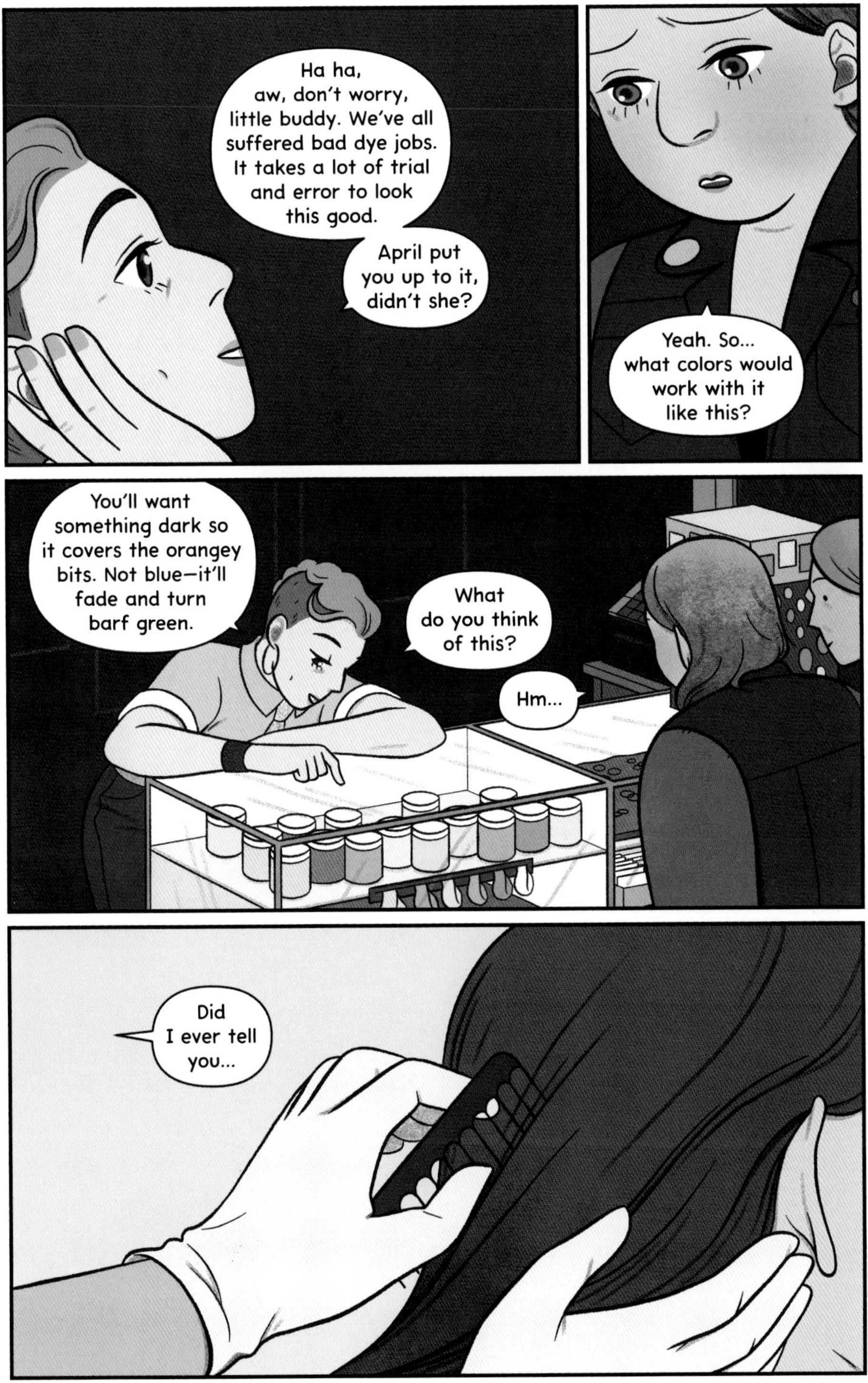
Ha ha, aw, don't worry, little buddy. We've all suffered bad dye jobs. It takes a lot of trial and error to look this good.
April put you up to it, didn't she?
Yeah. So... what colors would work with it like this?
You'll want something dark so it covers the orangey bits. Not blue—it'll fade and turn barf green.
What do you think of this?
Hm...
Did I ever tell you...

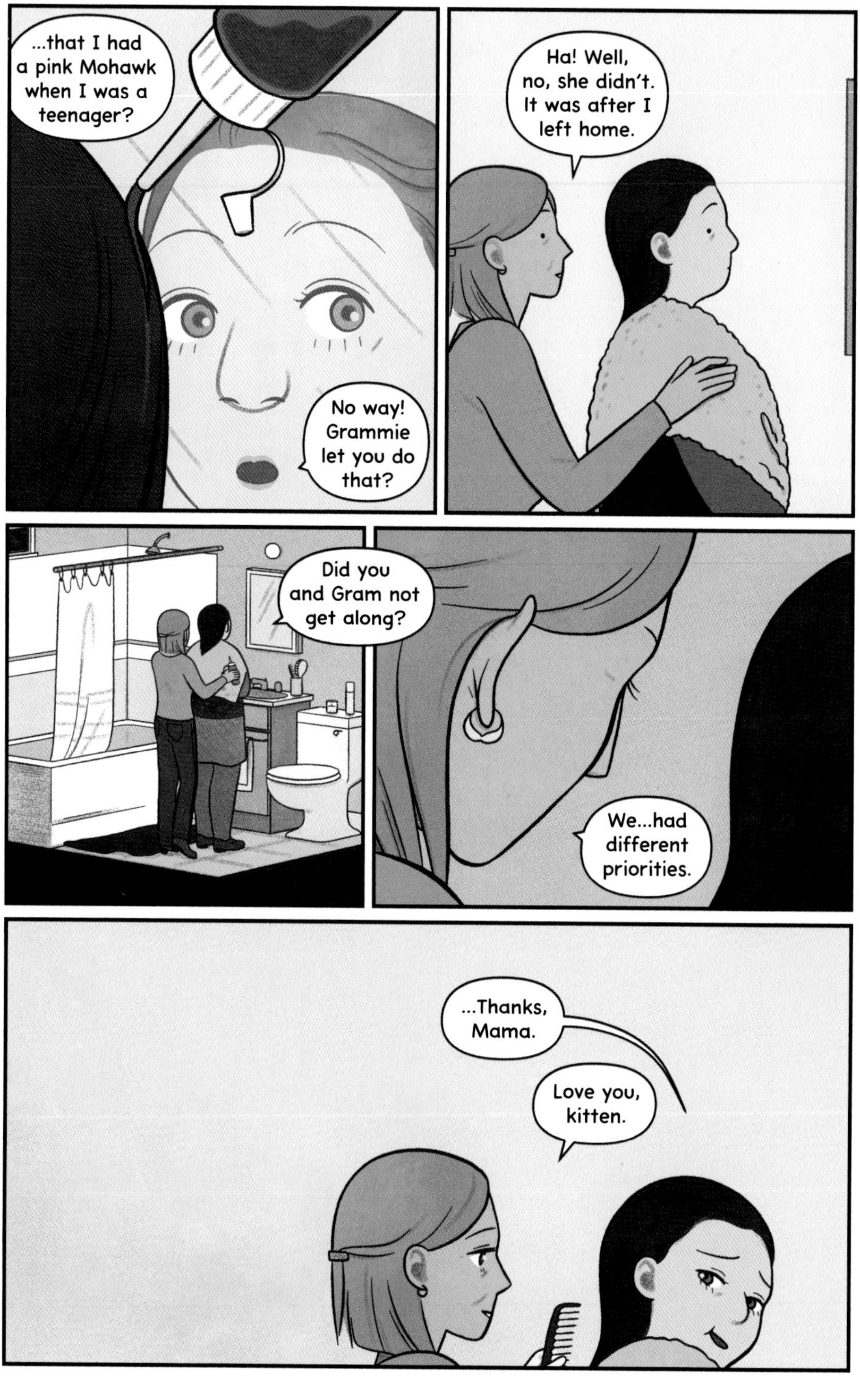
...that I had a pink Mohawk when I was a teenager?
No way! Grammie let you do that?
Ha! Well, no, she didn't. It was after I left home.
Did you and Gram not get along?
We...had different priorities.
...Thanks, Mama.
Love you, kitten.

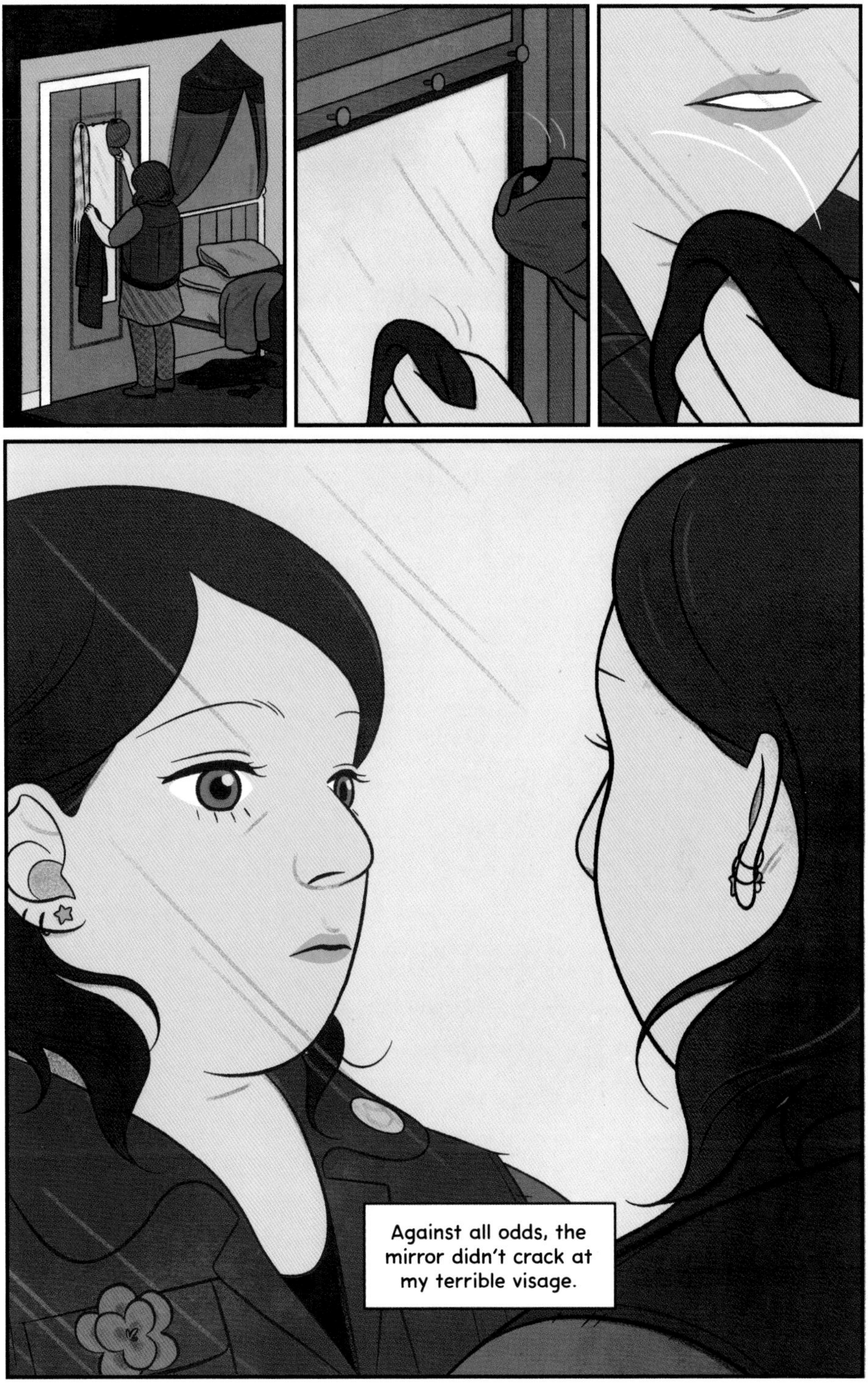
Against all odds, the
mirror didn't crack at
my terrible visage.

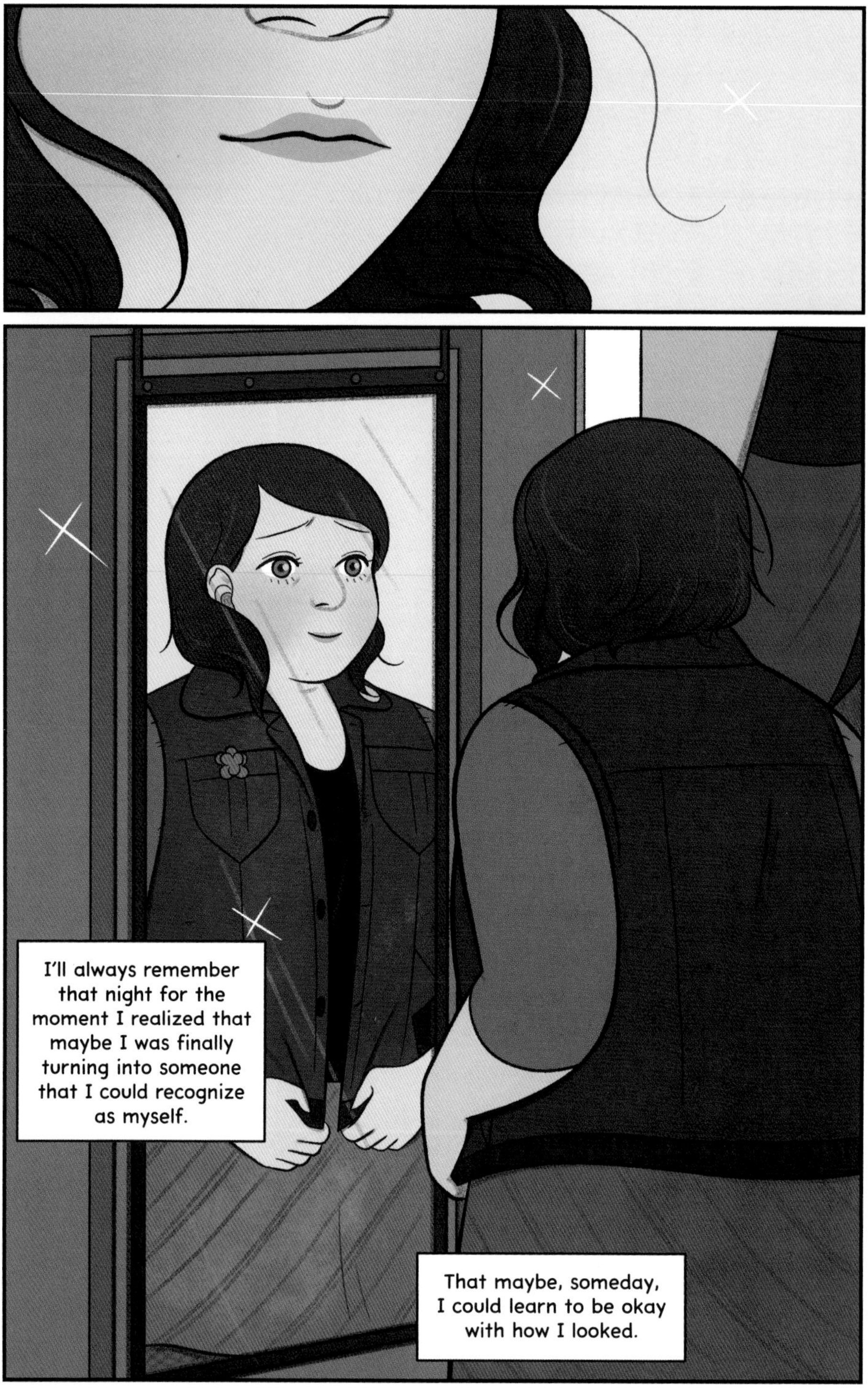
I'll always remember that night for the moment I realized that maybe I was finally turning into someone that I could recognize as myself.
That maybe, someday, I could learn to be okay with how I looked.

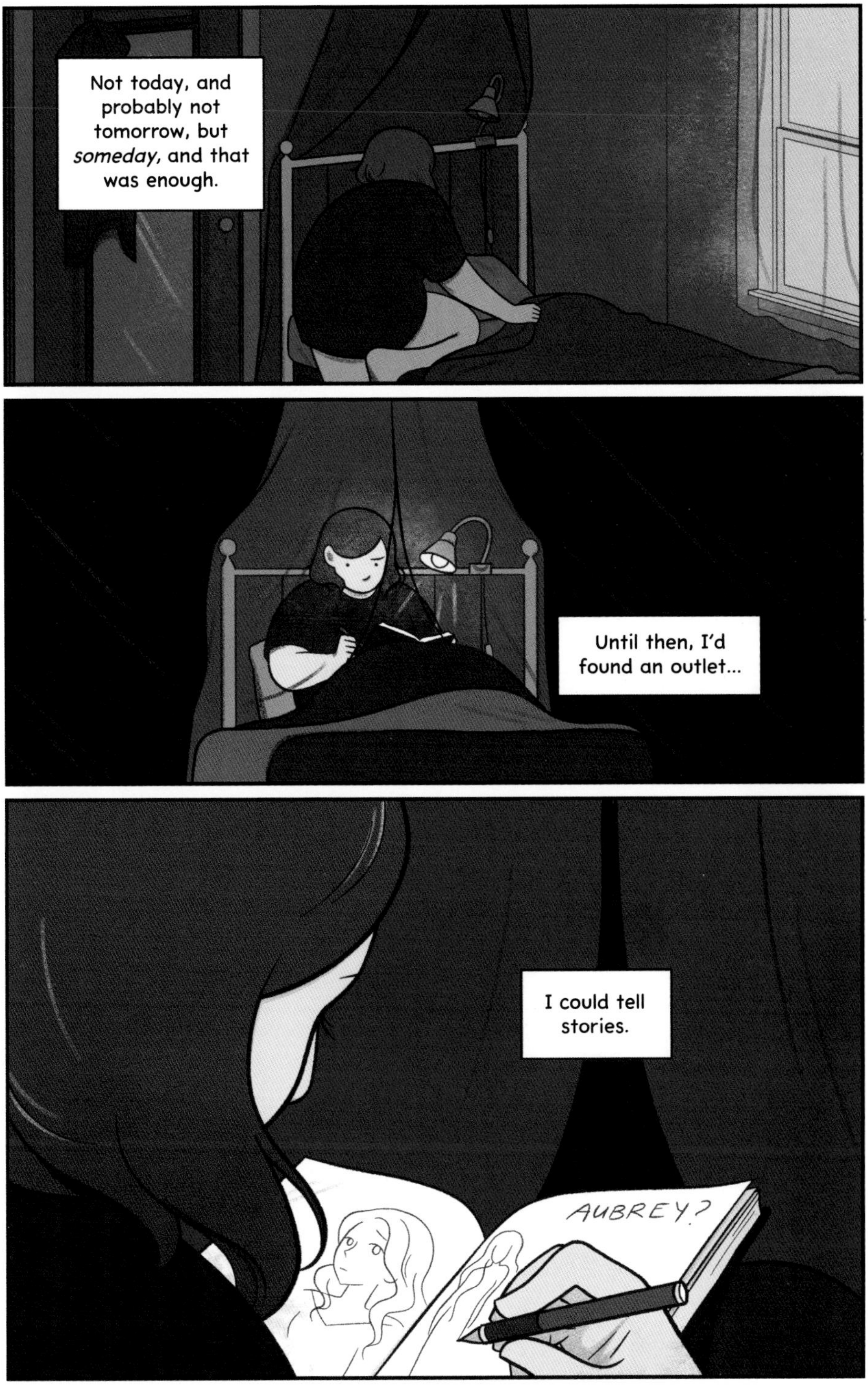
Not today, and probably not tomorrow, but *someday,* and that was enough.
Until then, I'd found an outlet...
I could tell stories.
AUBREY?

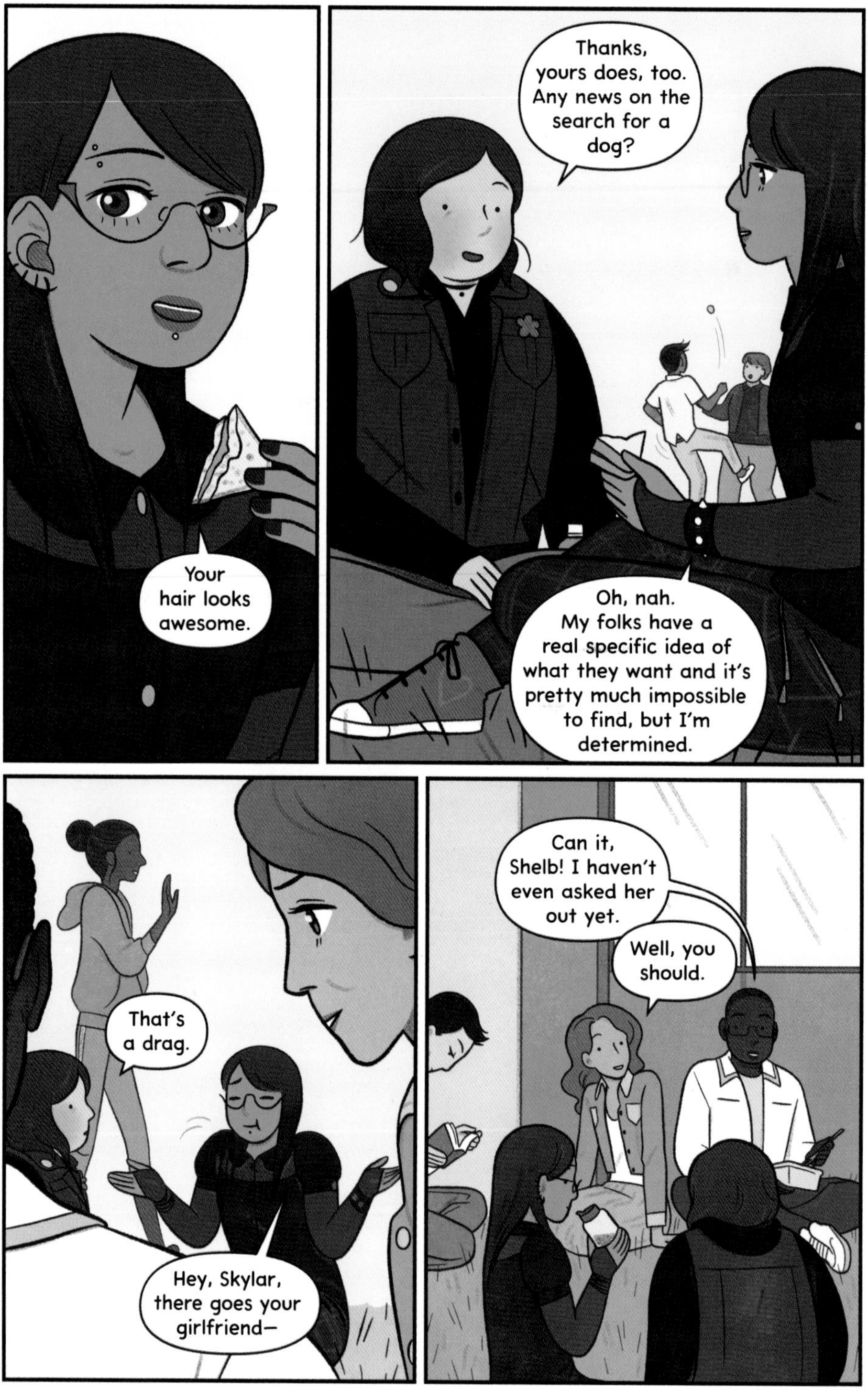
Your hair looks awesome.
Thanks, yours does, too. Any news on the search for a dog?
Oh, nah. My folks have a real specific idea of what they want and it's pretty much impossible to find, but I'm determined.
That's a drag.
Hey, Skylar, there goes your girlfriend—
Can it, Shelb! I haven't even asked her out yet.
Well, you should.

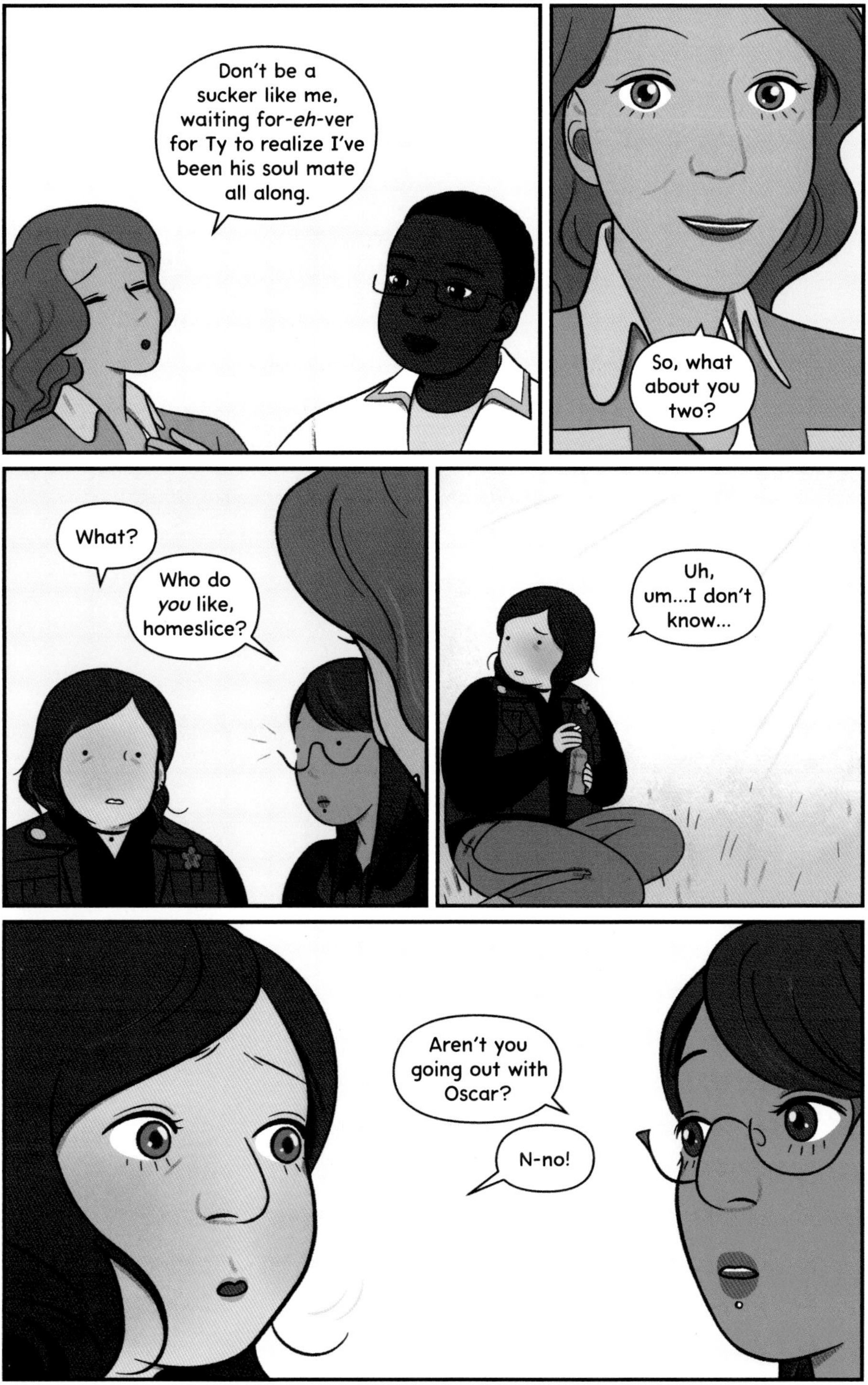
Don't be a sucker like me, waiting for-*eh*-ver for Ty to realize I've been his soul mate all along.
So, what about you two?
What?
Who do *you* like, homeslice?
Uh, um...I don't know...
Aren't you going out with Oscar?
N-no!

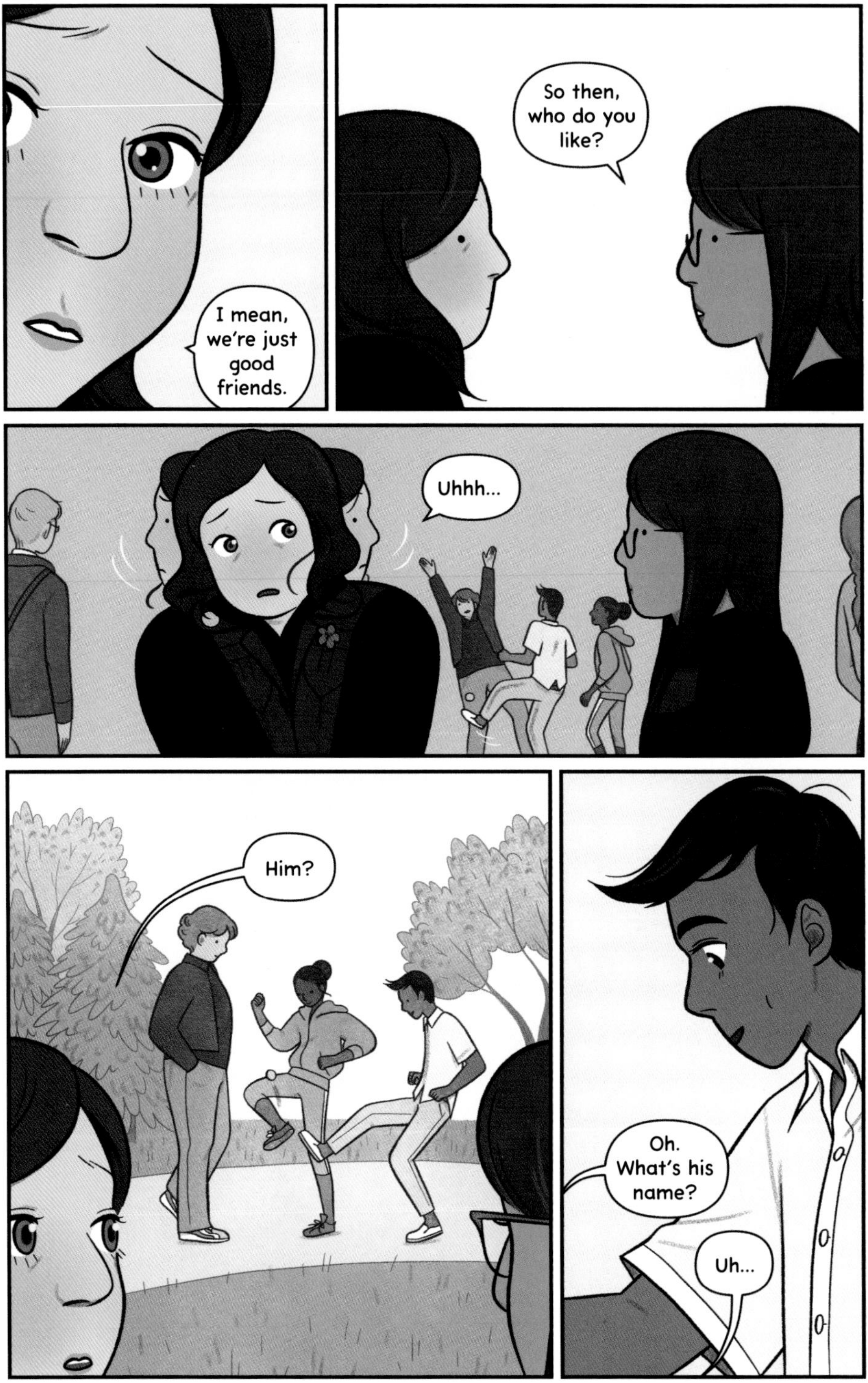
I mean, we're just good friends.
So then, who do you like?
Uhhh...
Him?
Oh. What's his name?
Uh...

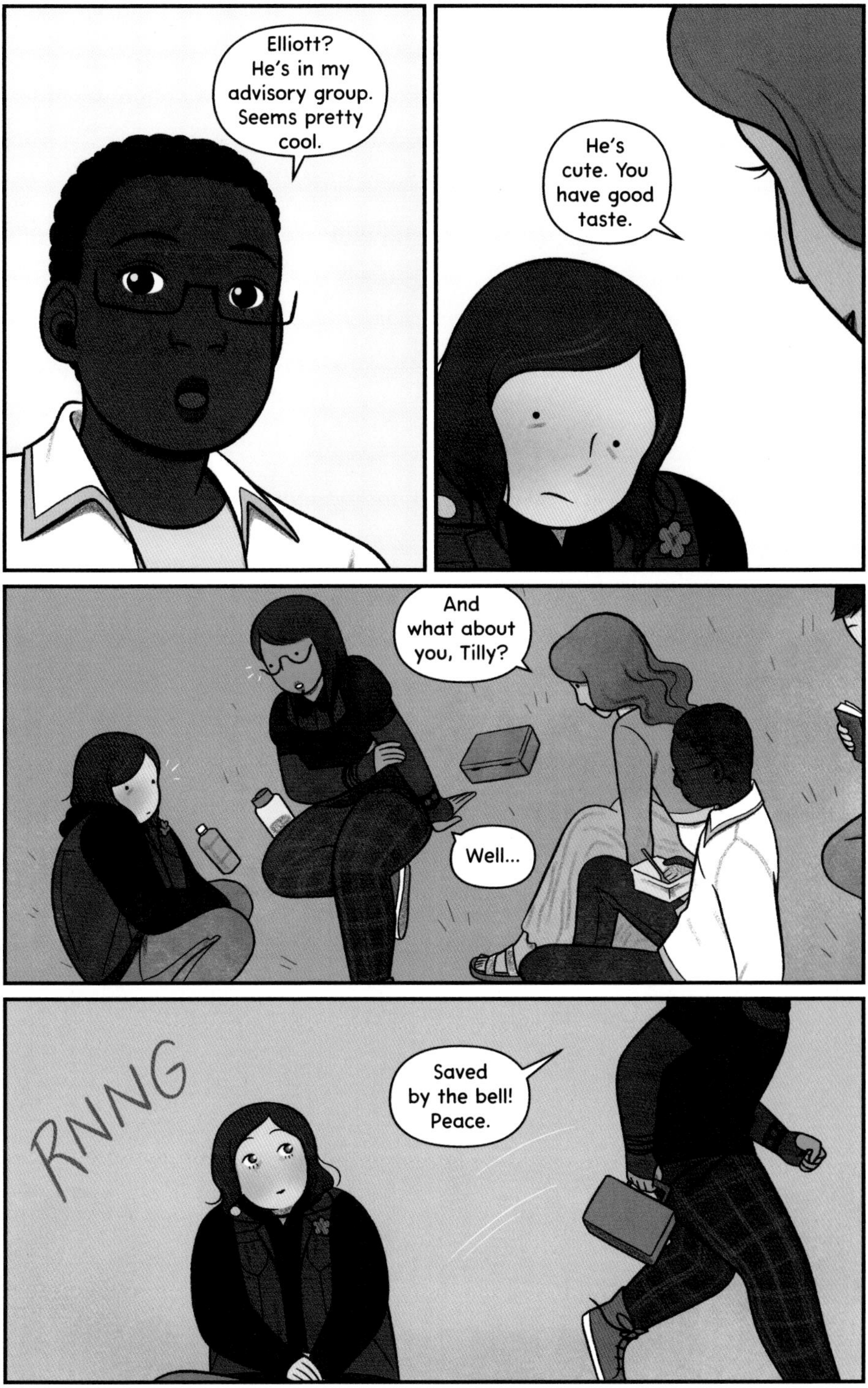
Elliott? He's in my advisory group. Seems pretty cool.
He's cute. You have good taste.
And what about you, Tilly?
Well...
RNNG
Saved by the bell! Peace.

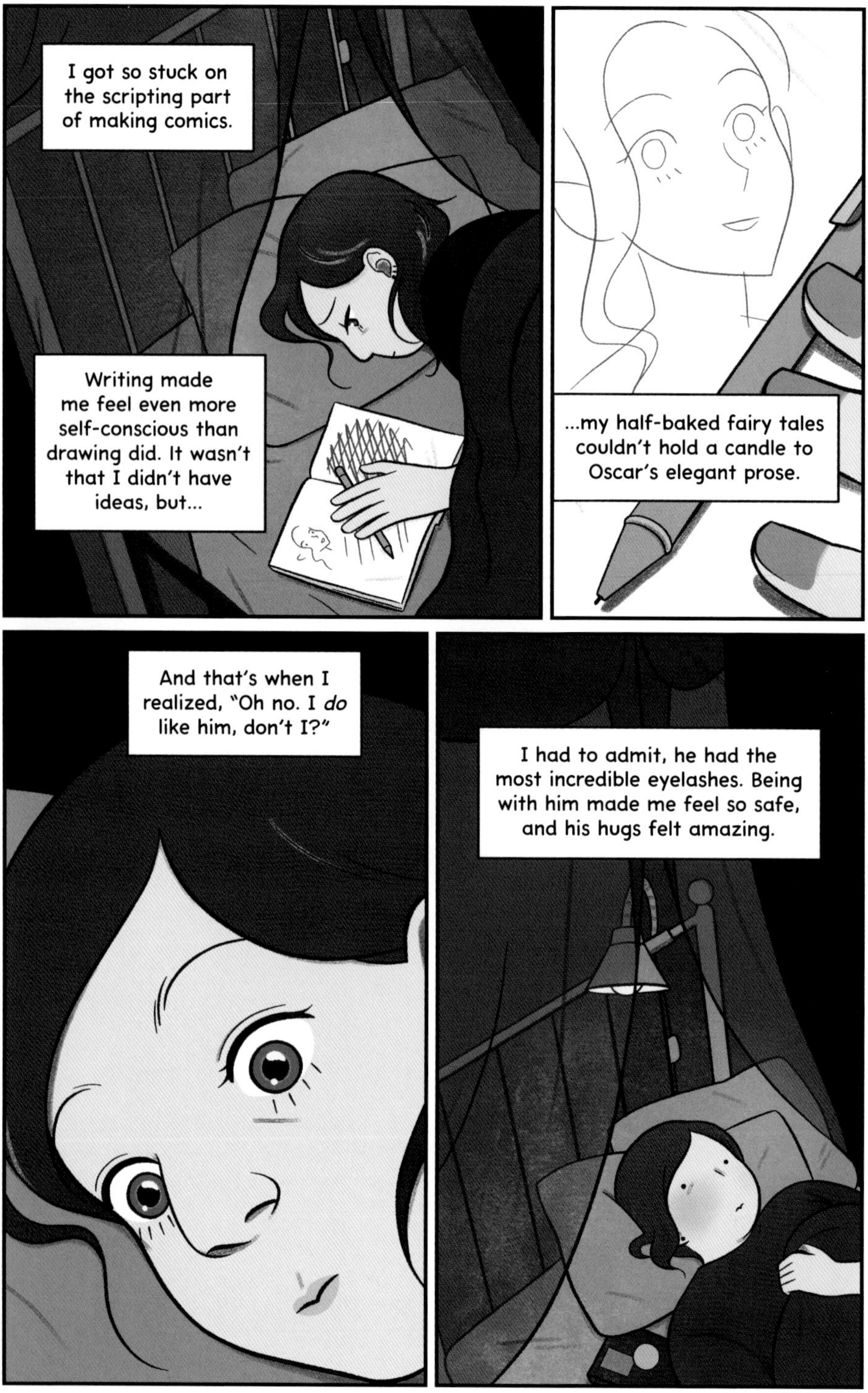
I got so stuck on the scripting part of making comics.
Writing made me feel even more self-conscious than drawing did. It wasn't that I didn't have ideas, but...
...my half-baked fairy tales couldn't hold a candle to Oscar's elegant prose.
And that's when I realized, "Oh no. I *do* like him, don't I?"
I had to admit, he had the most incredible eyelashes. Being with him made me feel so safe, and his hugs felt amazing.

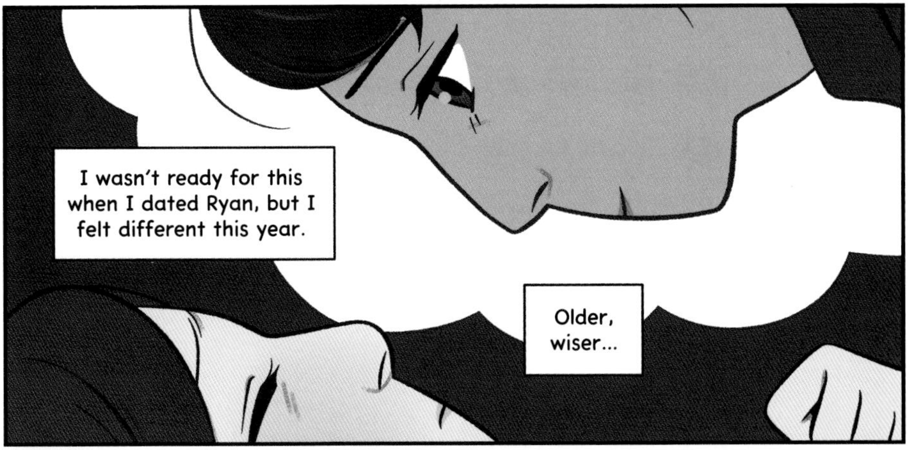
I wasn't ready for this when I dated Ryan, but I felt different this year.
Older, wiser...

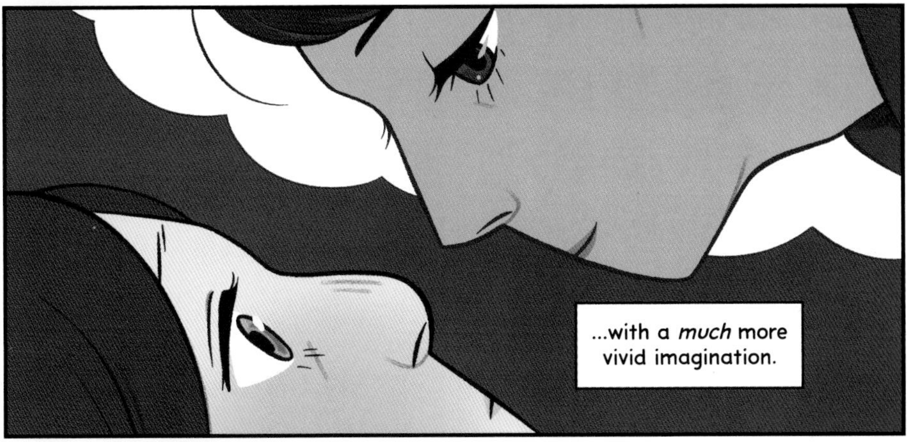
...with a *much* more vivid imagination.

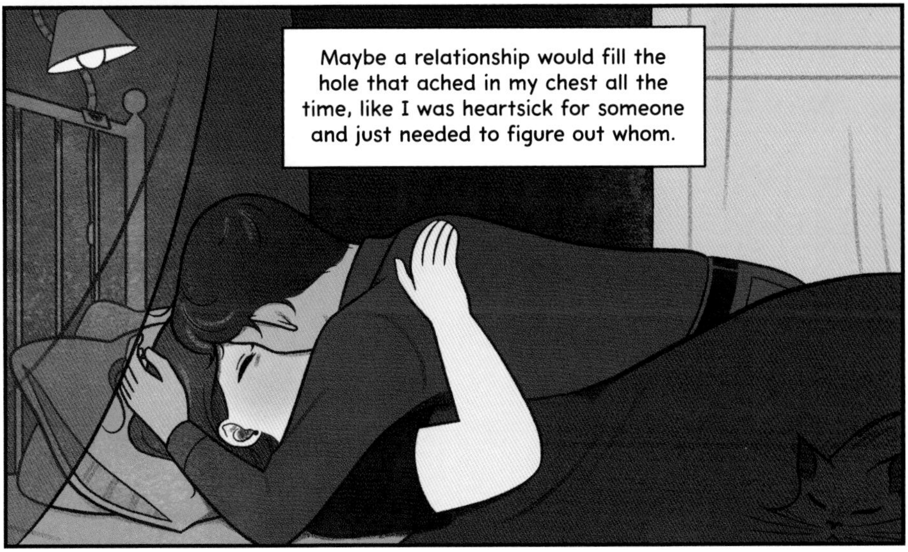
Maybe a relationship would fill the hole that ached in my chest all the time, like I was heartsick for someone and just needed to figure out whom.

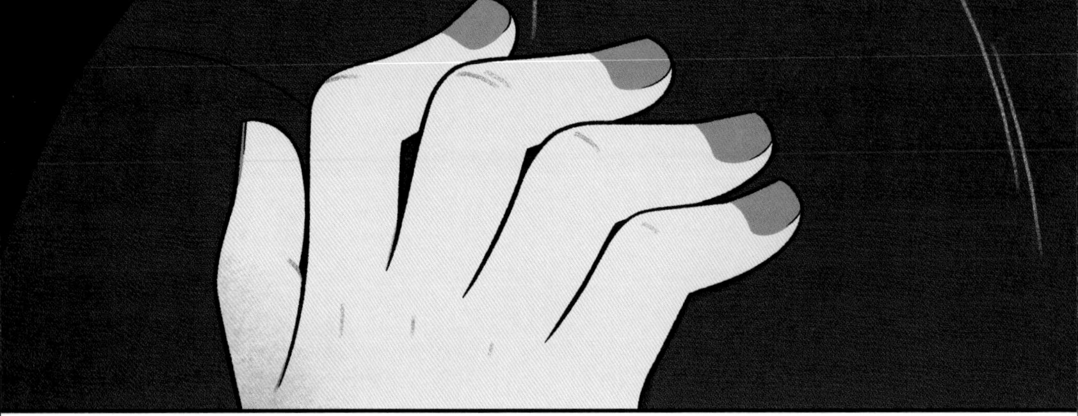
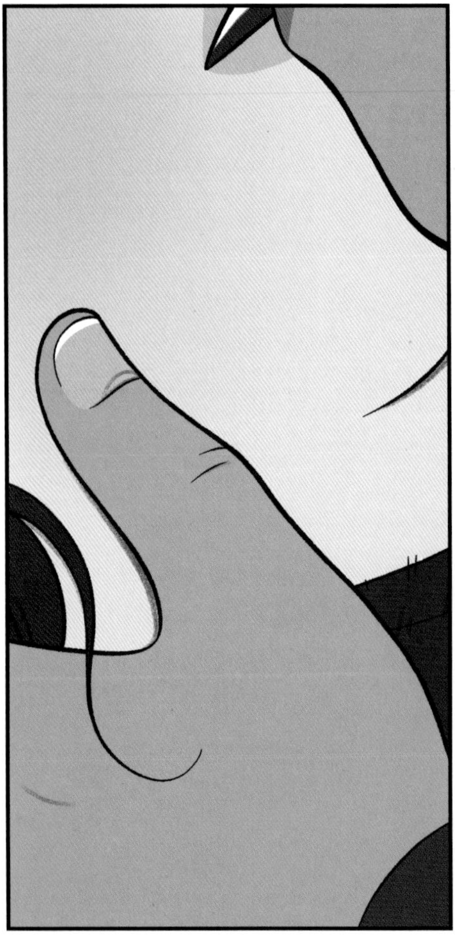
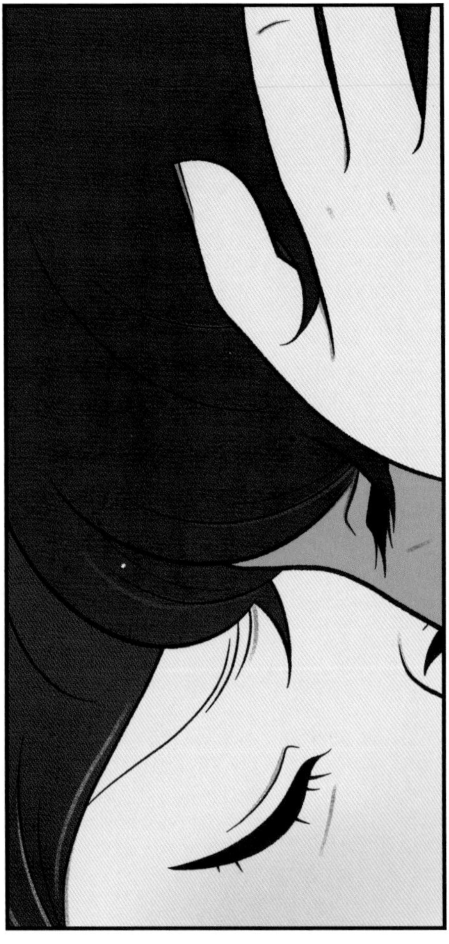

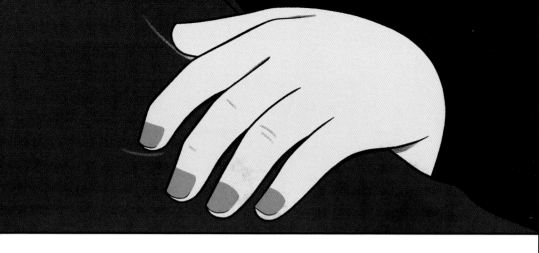

Tilly?

Hoo boy.

155

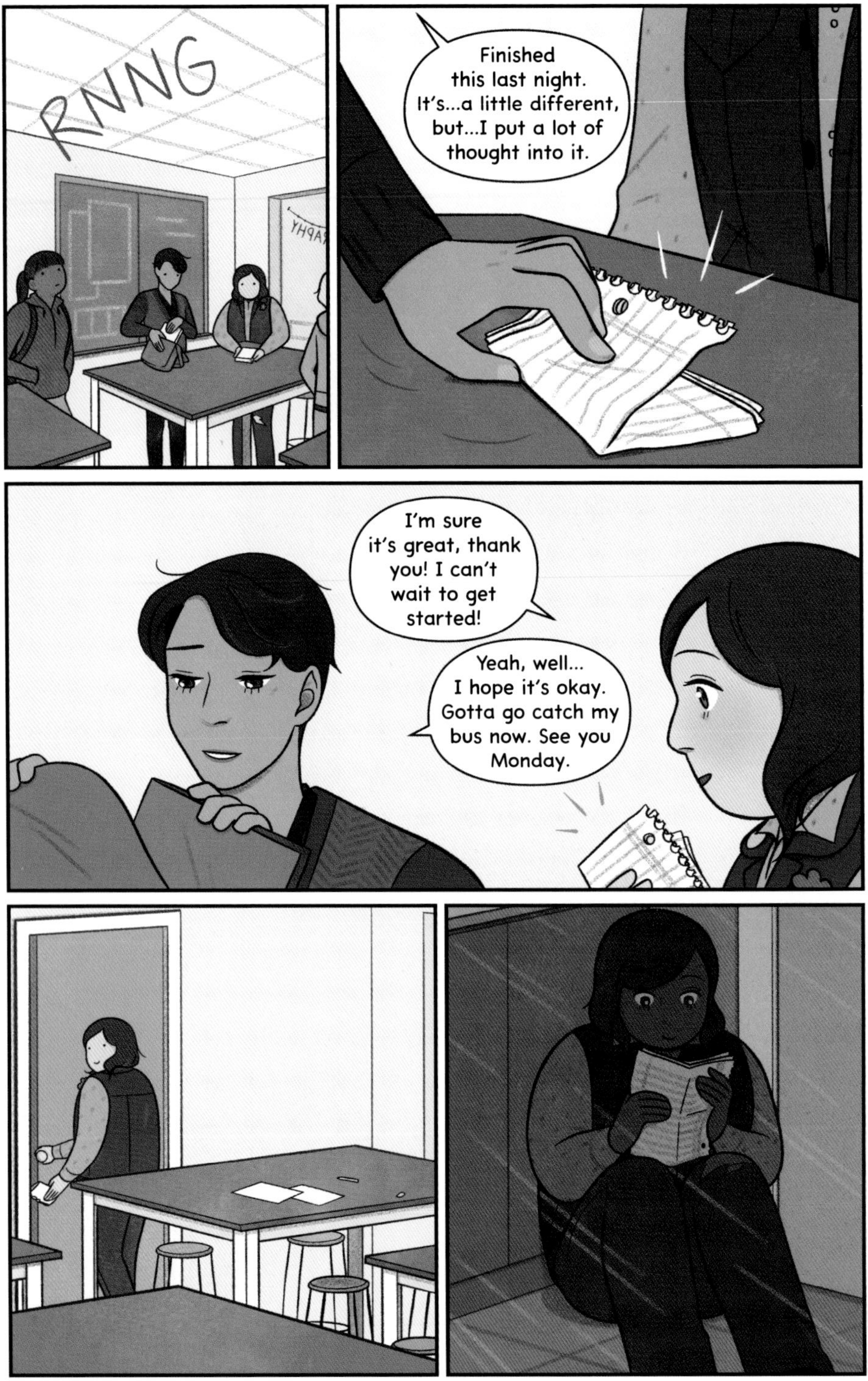
RNNG
Finished this last night. It's...a little different, but...I put a lot of thought into it.
I'm sure it's great, thank you! I can't wait to get started!
Yeah, well... I hope it's okay. Gotta go catch my bus now. See you Monday.

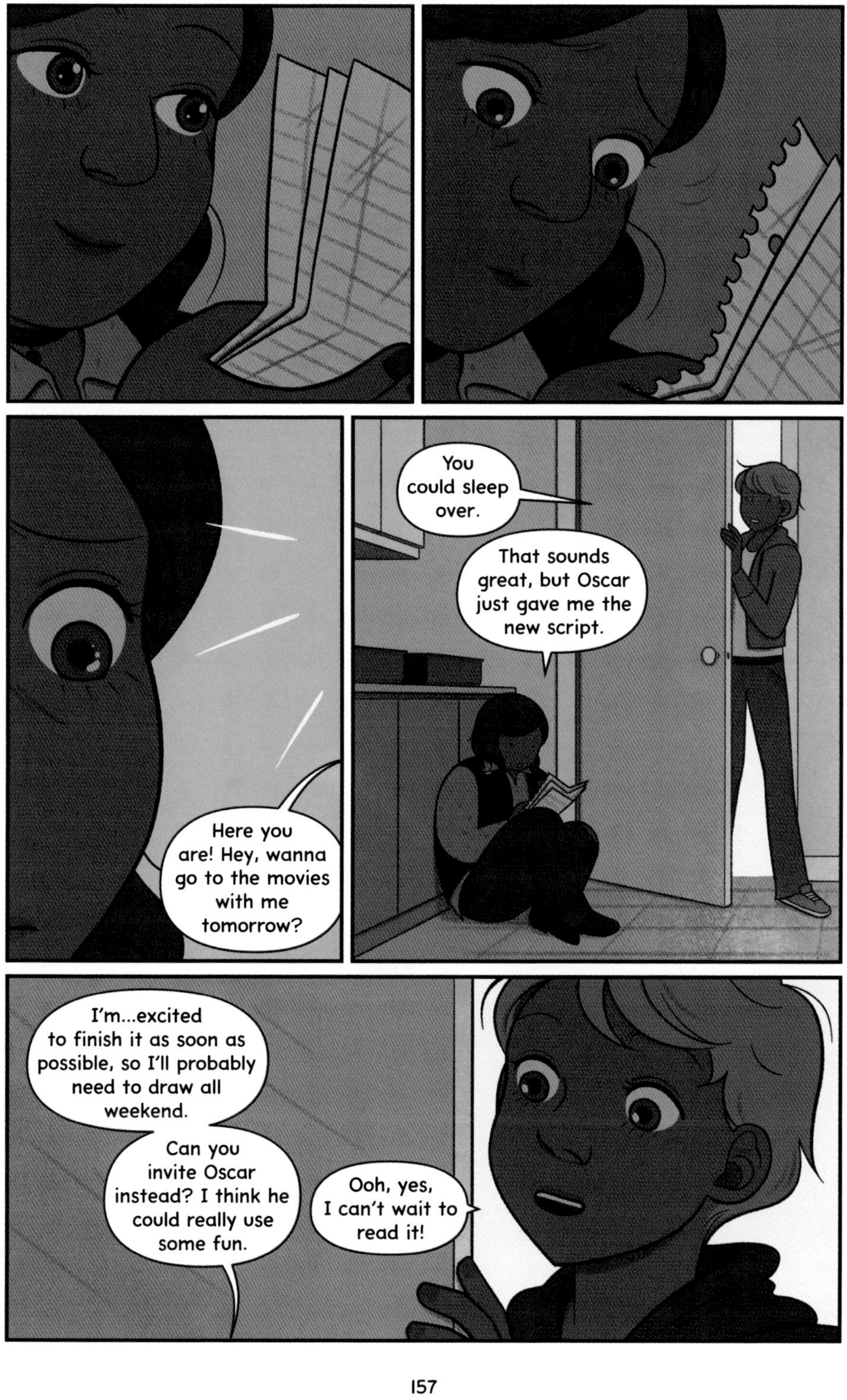
Here you are! Hey, wanna go to the movies with me tomorrow?
You could sleep over.
That sounds great, but Oscar just gave me the new script.
I'm...excited to finish it as soon as possible, so I'll probably need to draw all weekend.
Can you invite Oscar instead? I think he could really use some fun.
Ooh, yes, I can't wait to read it!

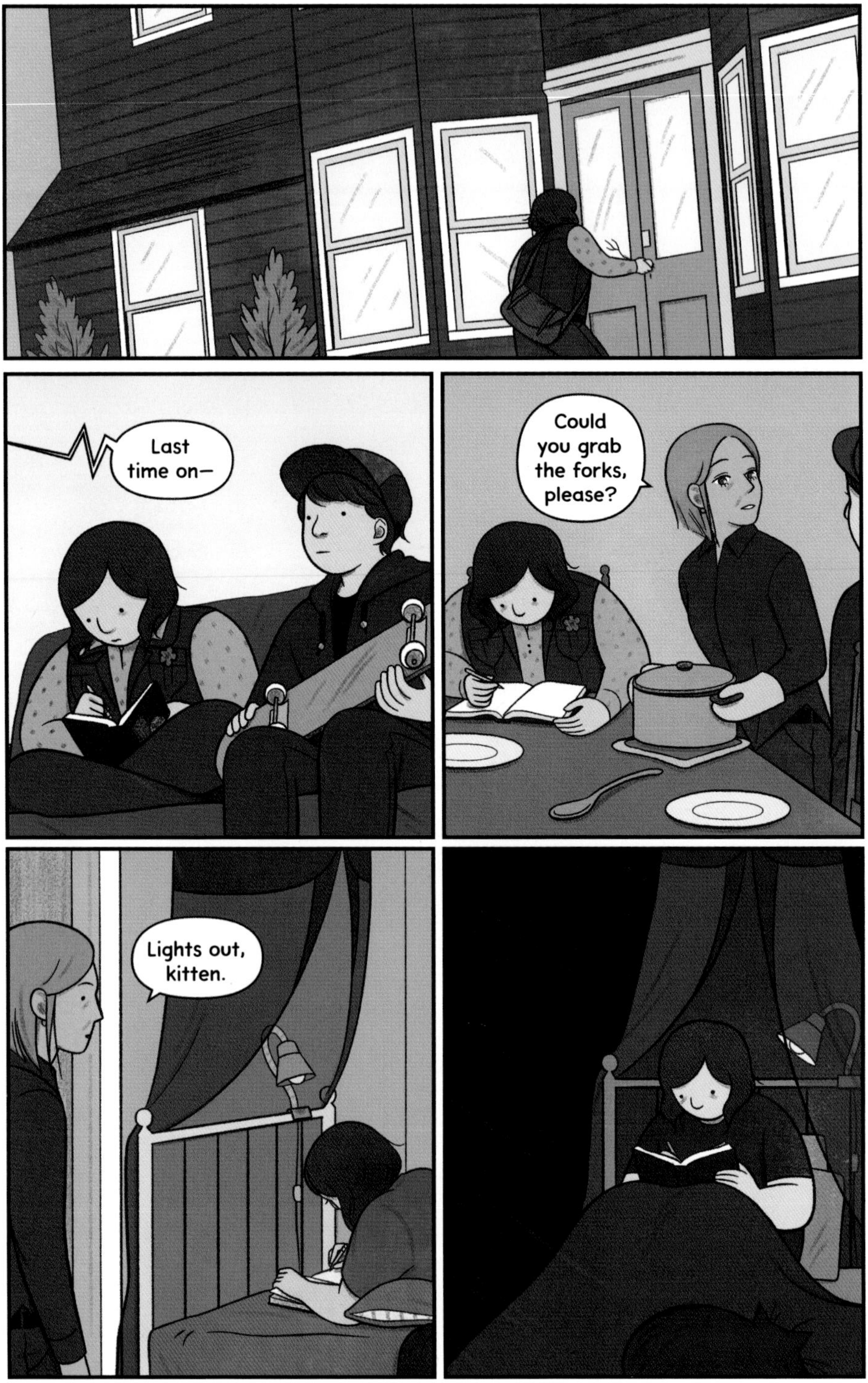
Last time on—
Could you grab the forks, please?
Lights out, kitten.

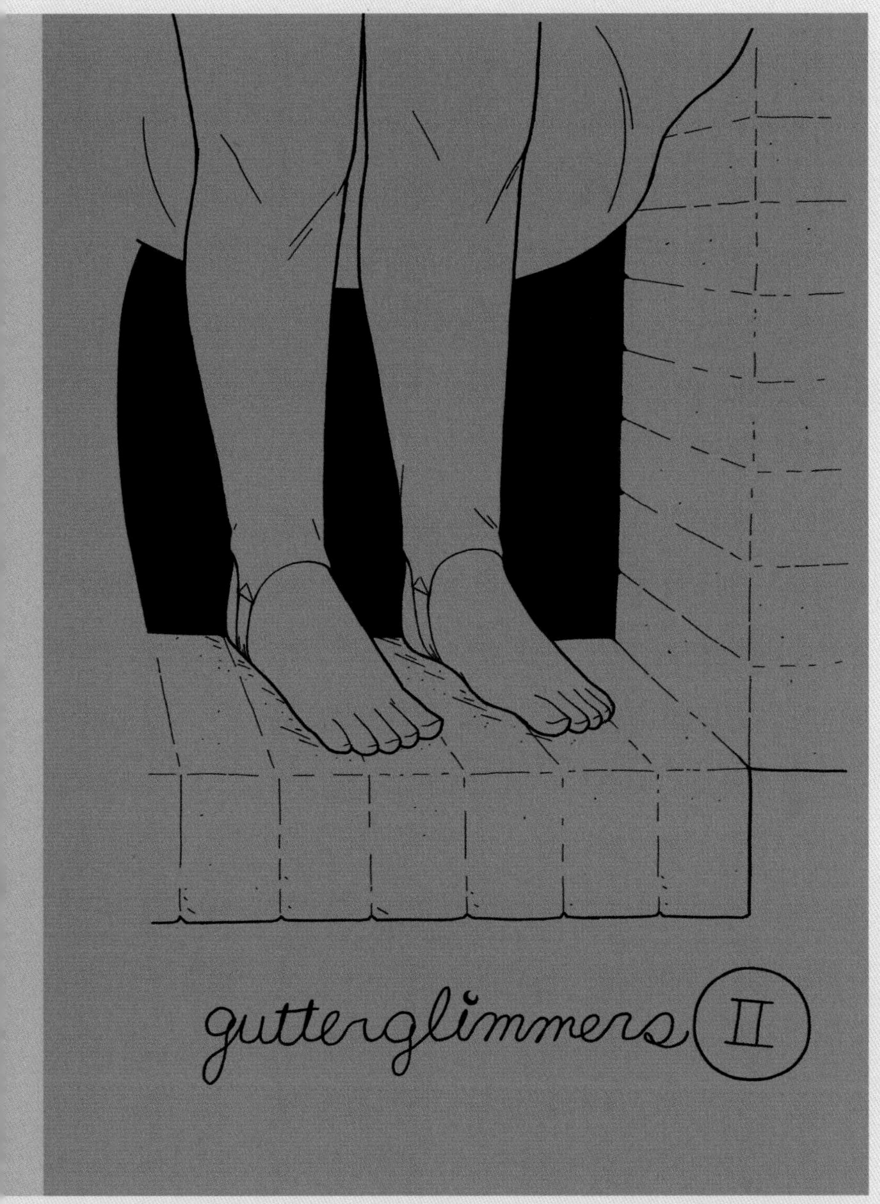
gutterglimmers II

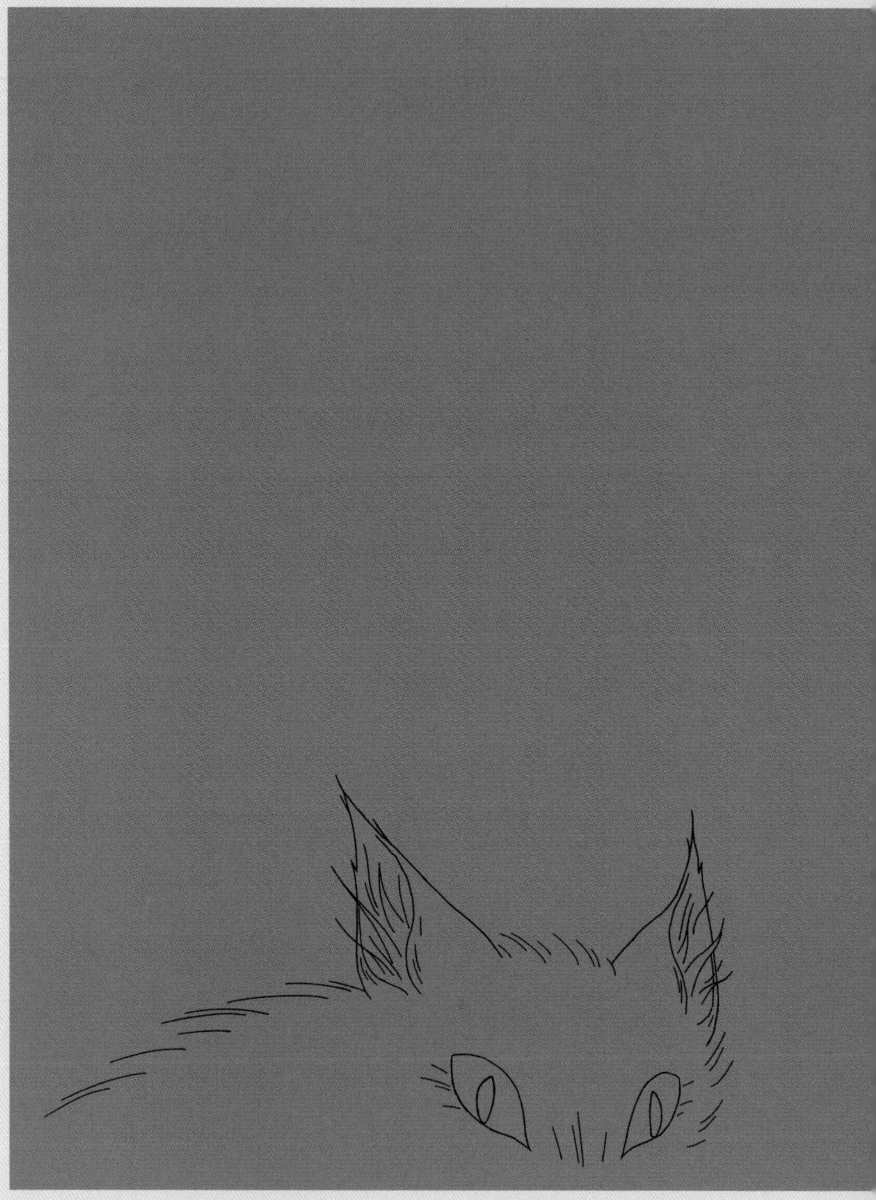

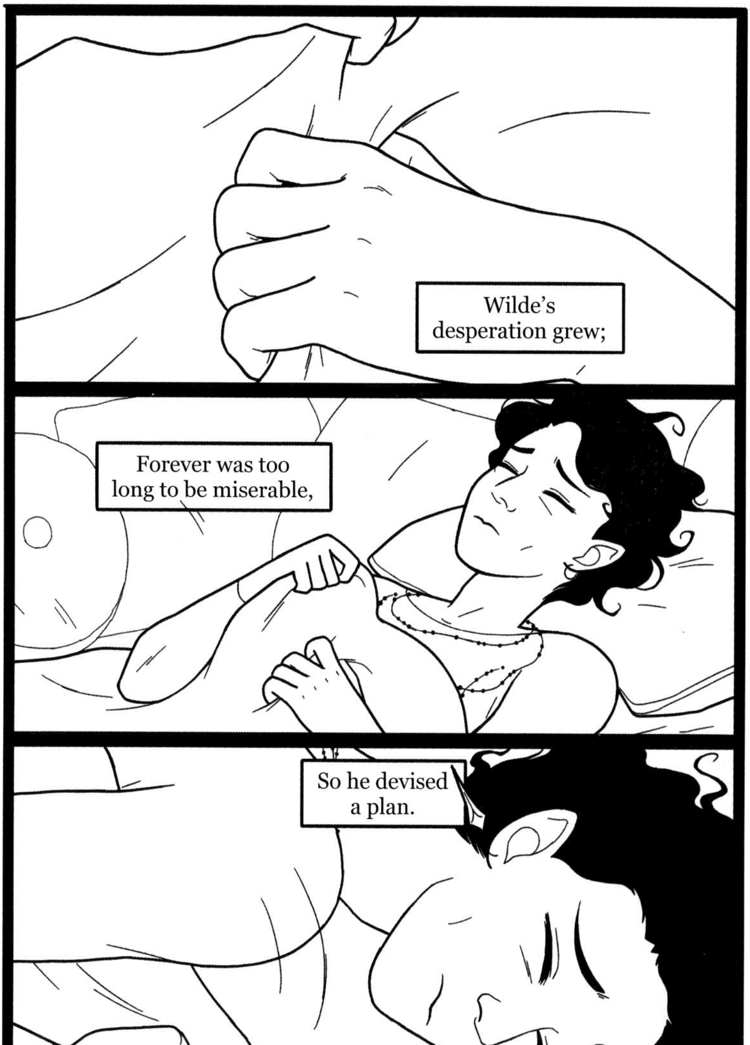
Wilde's desperation grew;
Forever was too long to be miserable,
So he devised a plan.

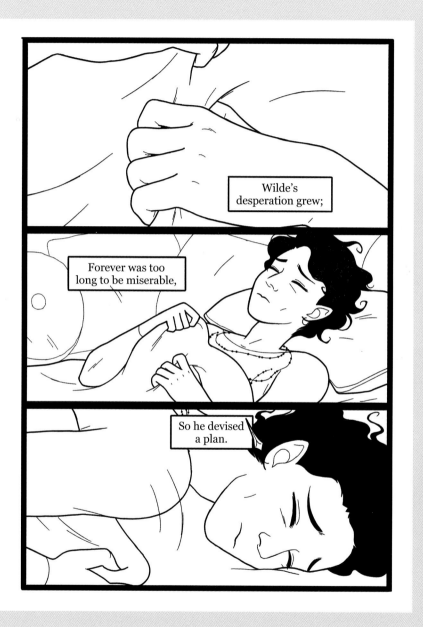

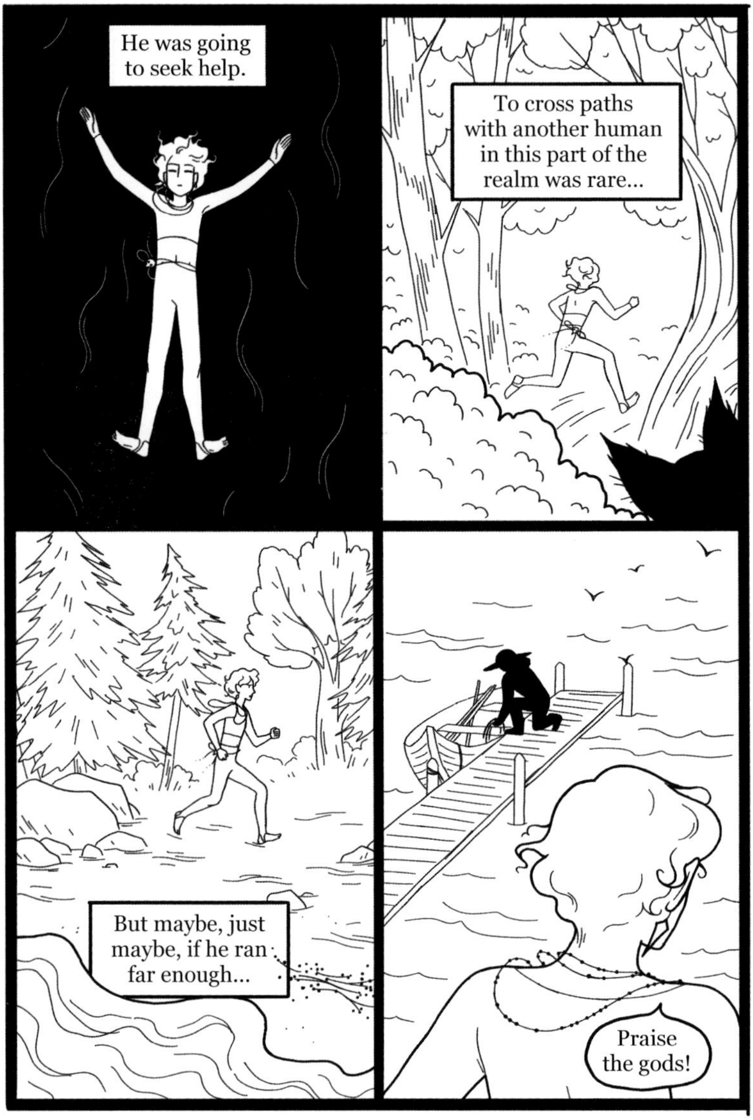
He was going to seek help.
To cross paths with another human in this part of the realm was rare...
But maybe, just maybe, if he ran far enough...
Praise the gods!

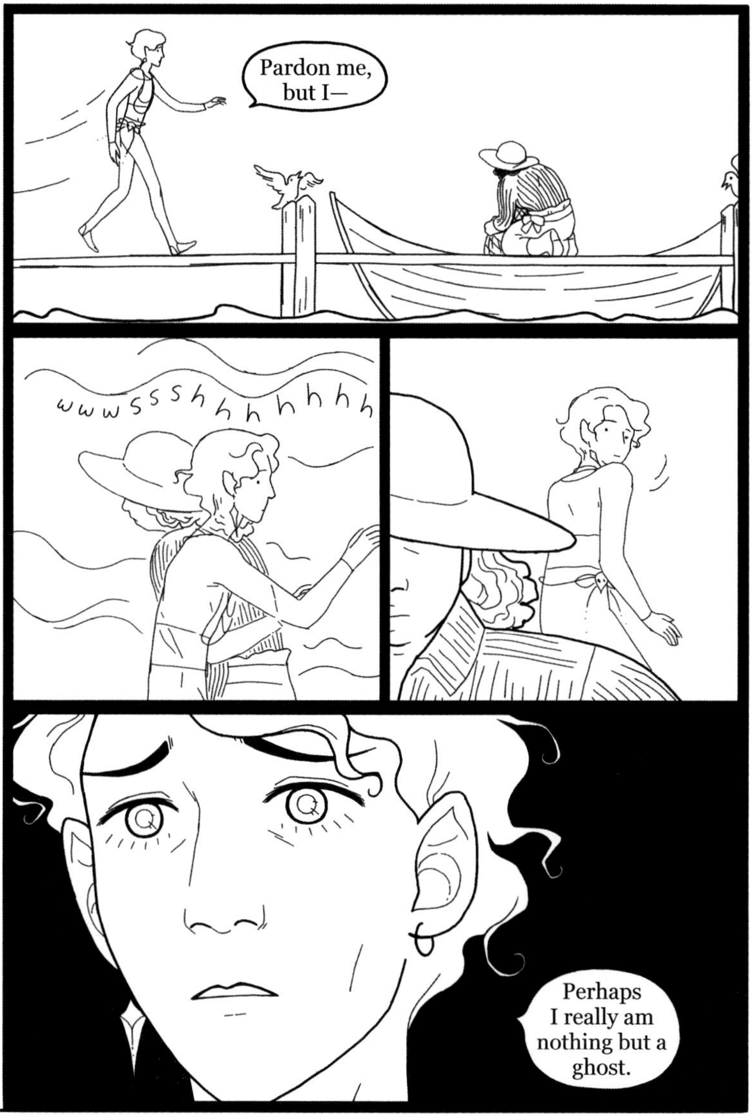
Pardon me, but I—
wwwssshhhhhhh
Perhaps I really am nothing but a ghost.

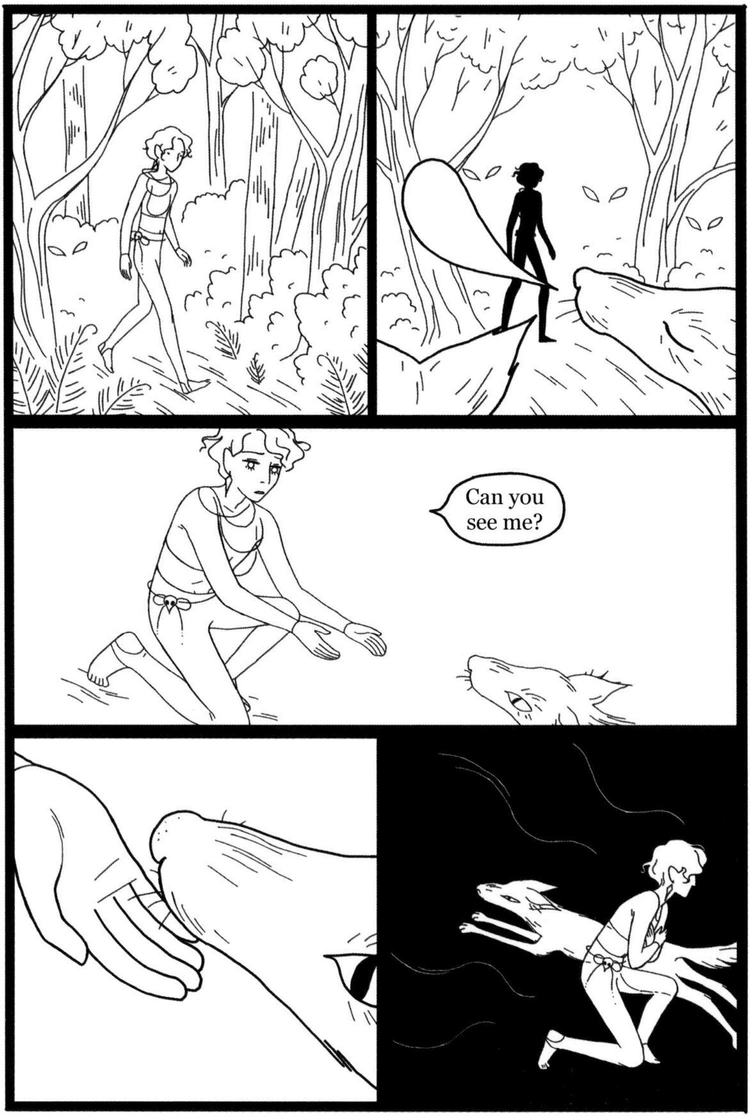
Can you see me?

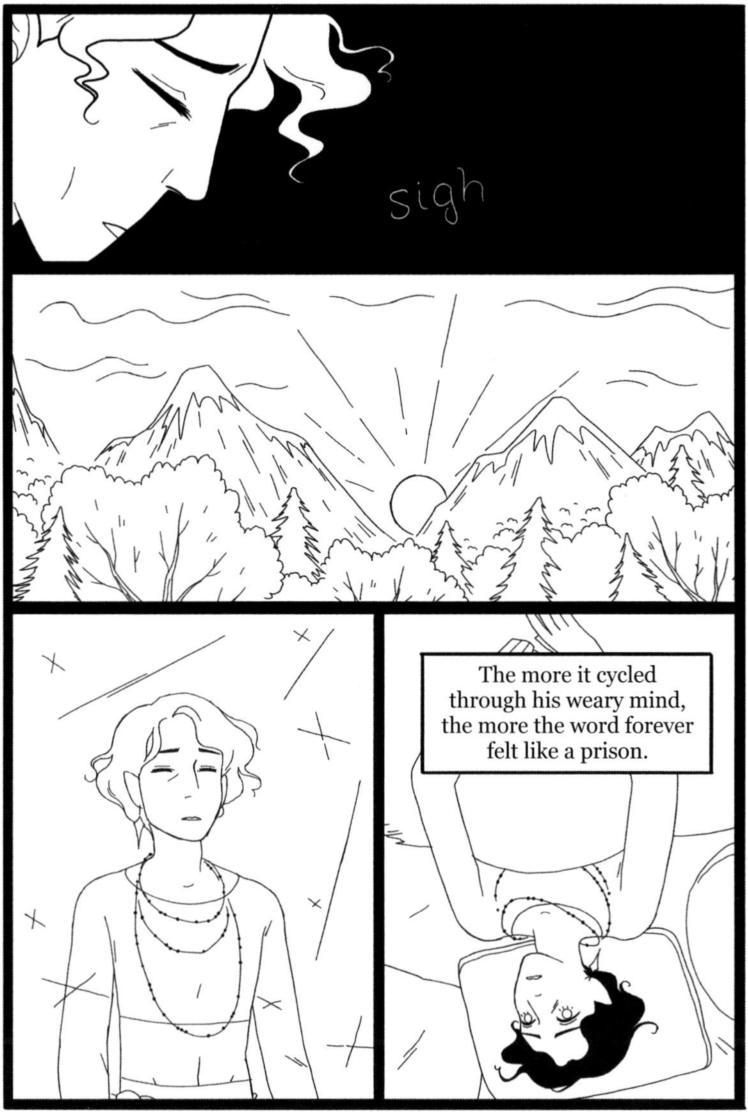
sigh
The more it cycled through his weary mind, the more the word forever felt like a prison.

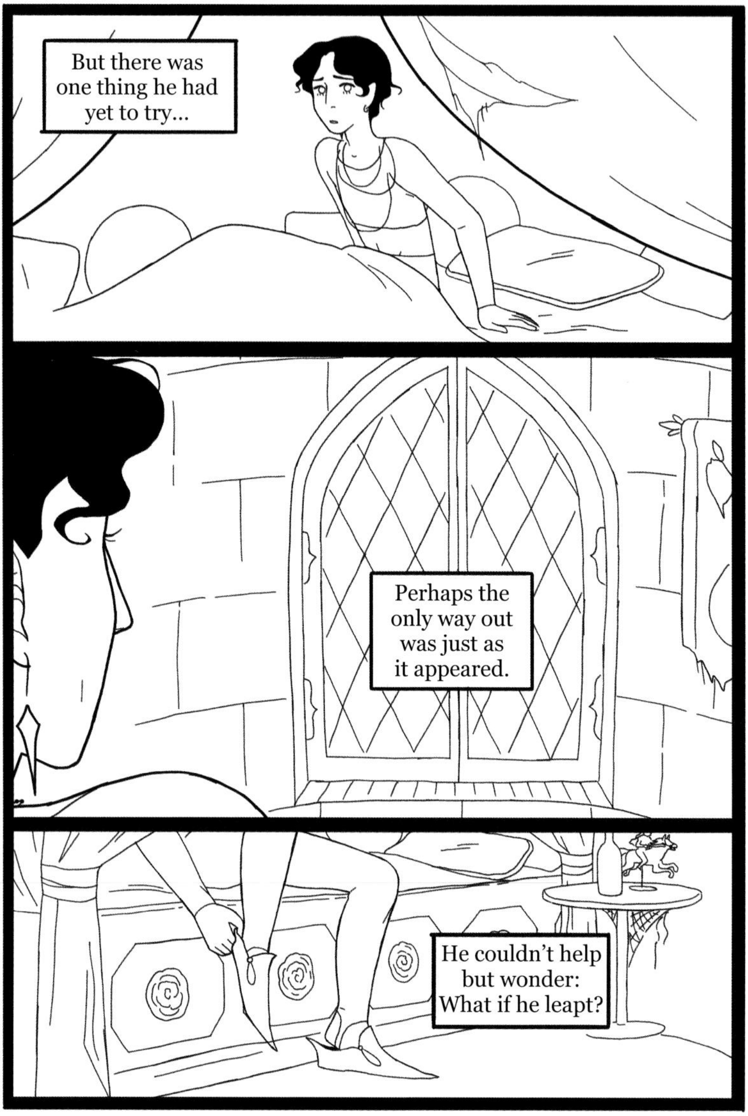
But there was one thing he had yet to try...
Perhaps the only way out was just as it appeared.
He couldn't help but wonder: What if he leapt?

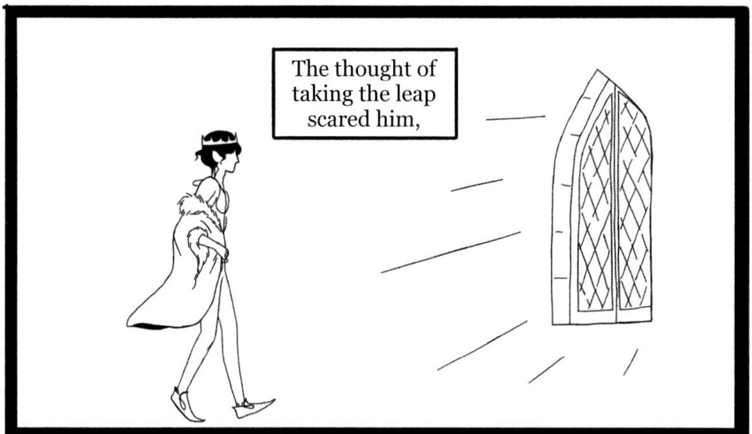
The thought of taking the leap scared him,

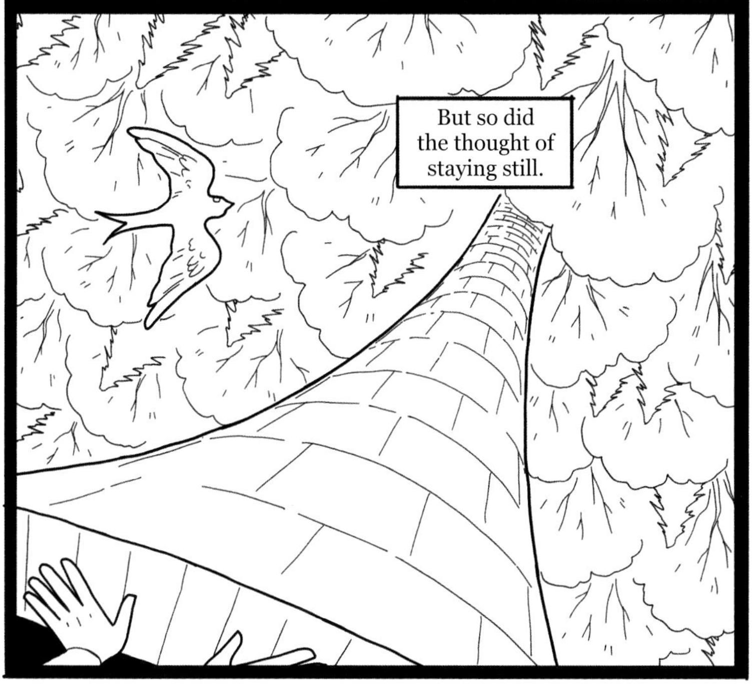
But so did the thought of staying still.

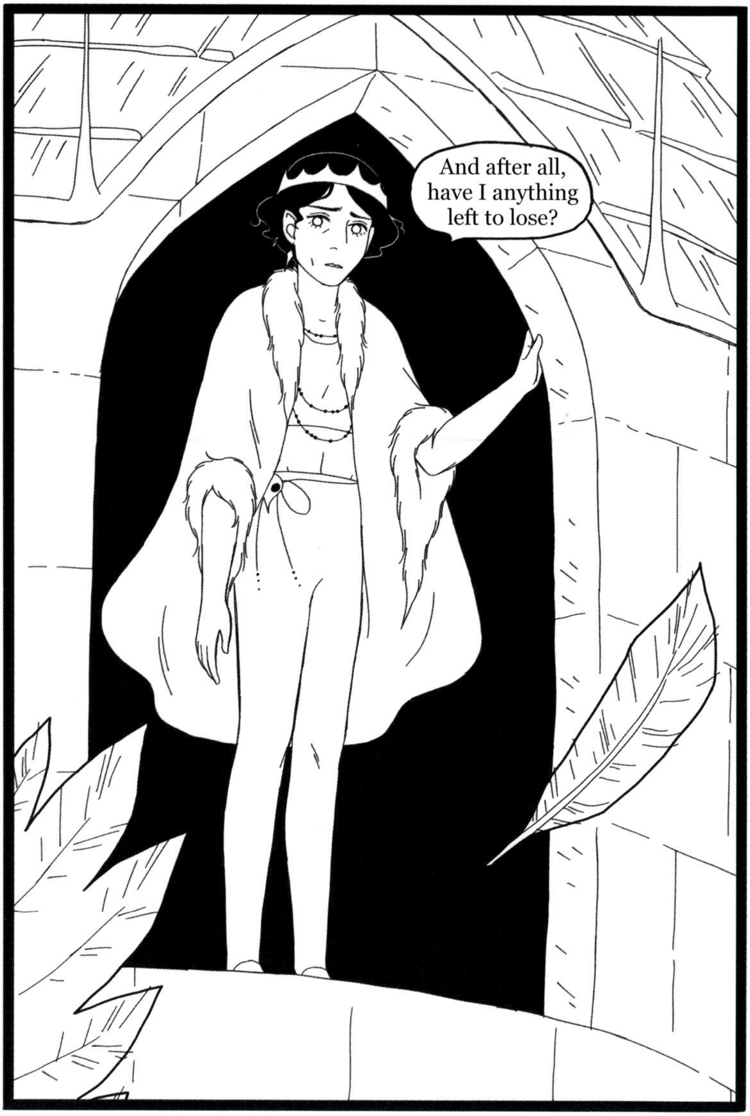
And after all, have I anything left to lose?

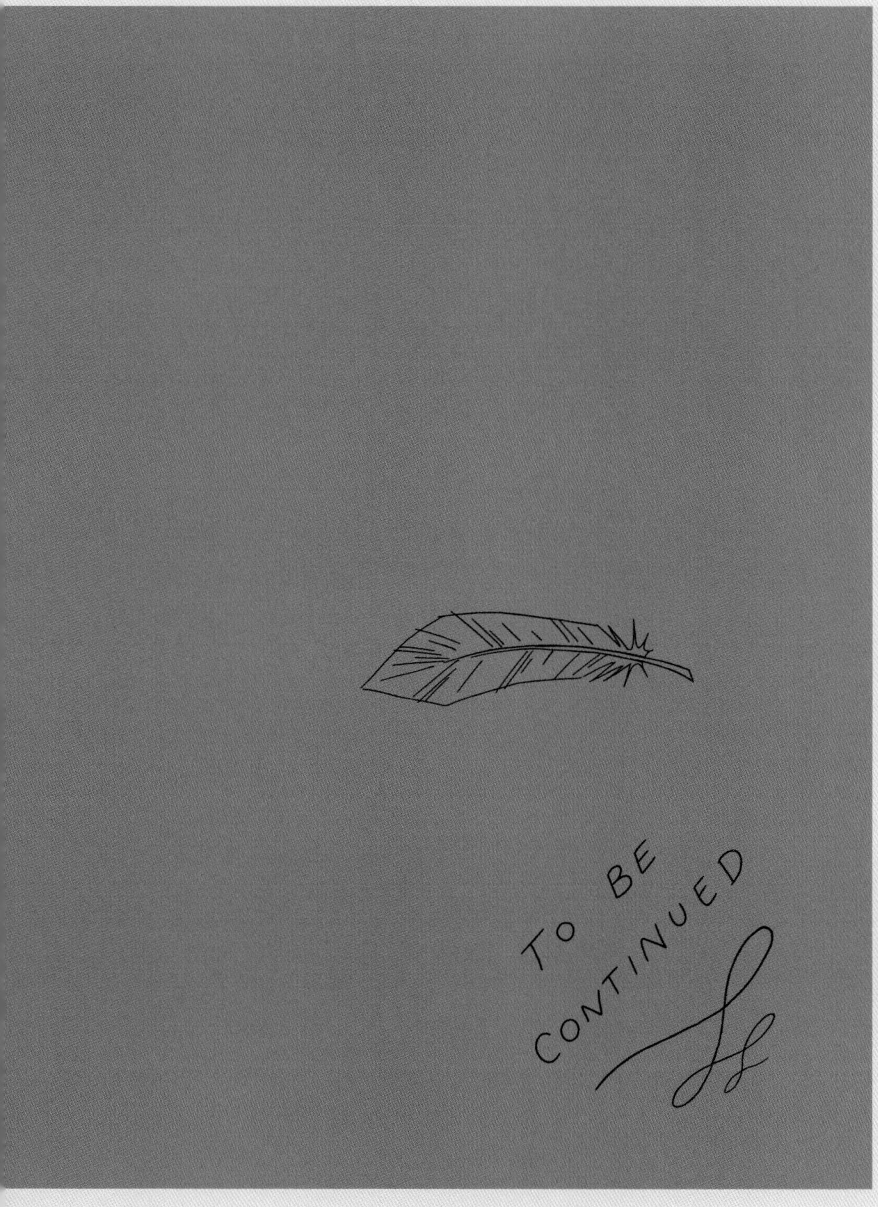
TO BE CONTINUED

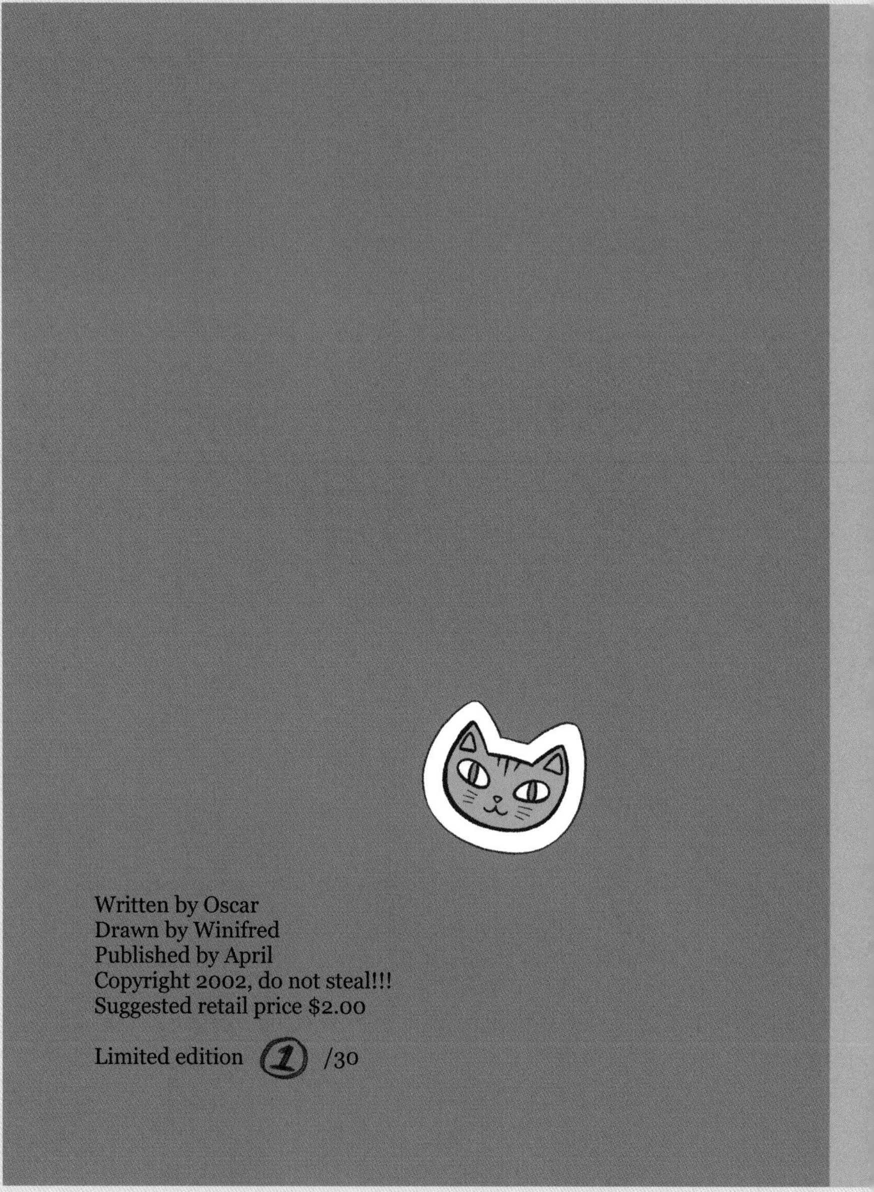
Written by Oscar
Drawn by Winifred
Published by April
Copyright 2002, do not steal!!!
Suggested retail price $2.00
Limited edition 1 /30

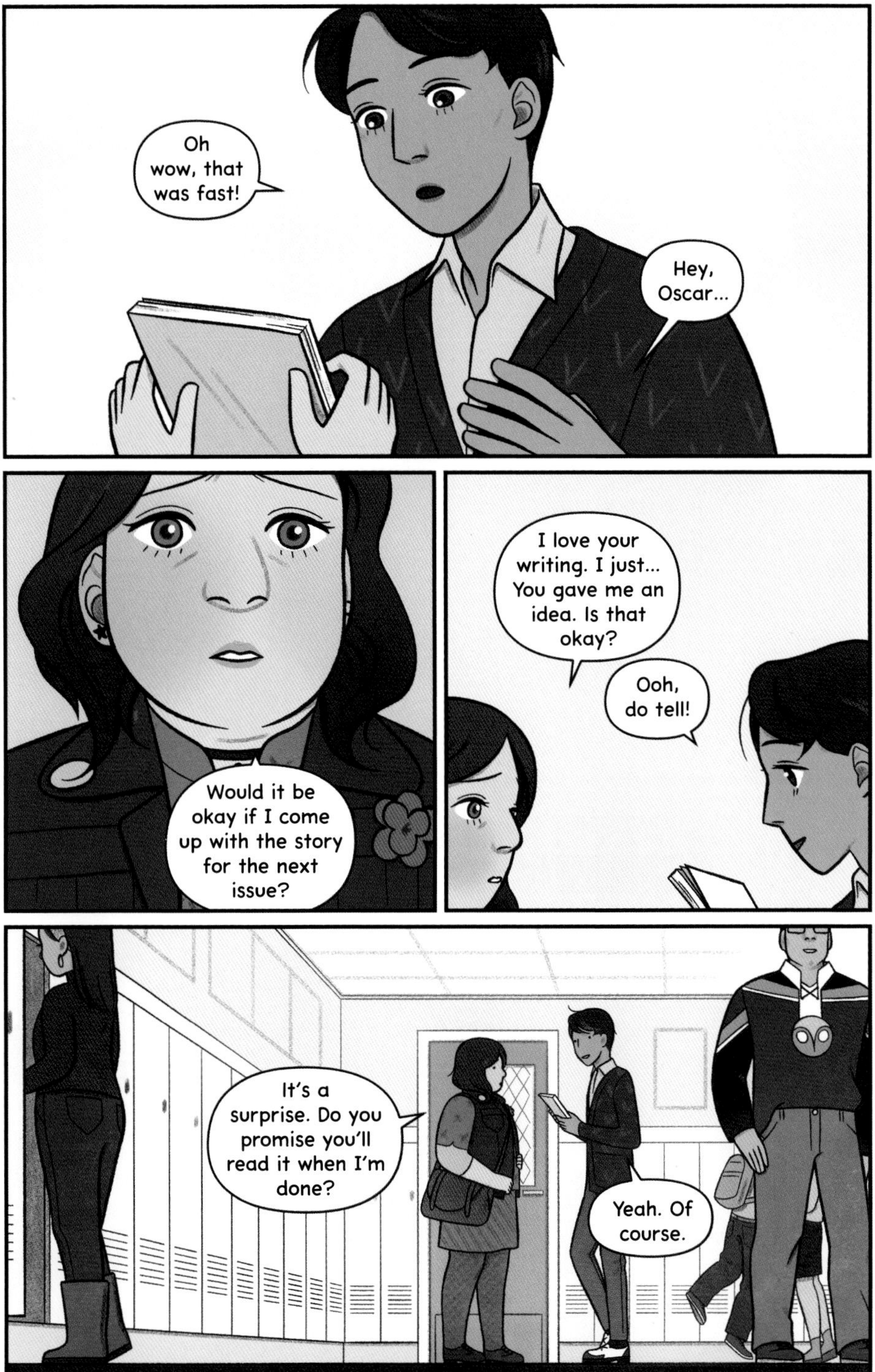
Oh wow, that was fast!
Hey, Oscar...
Would it be okay if I come up with the story for the next issue?
I love your writing. I just... You gave me an idea. Is that okay?
Ooh, do tell!
It's a surprise. Do you promise you'll read it when I'm done?
Yeah. Of course.

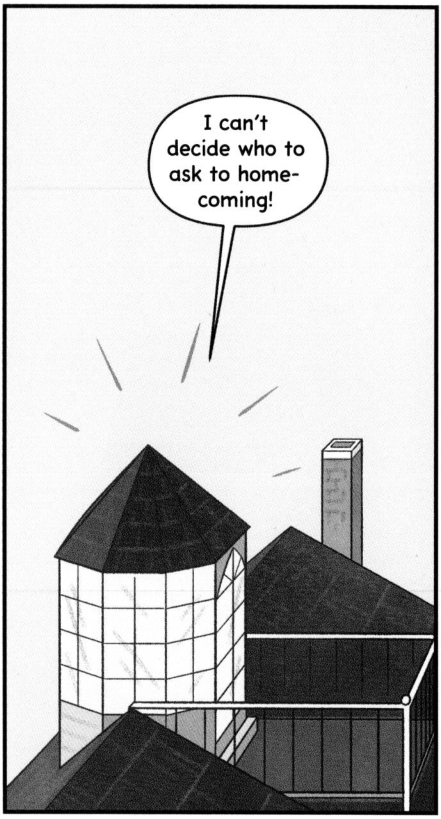
I can't decide who to ask to home-coming!

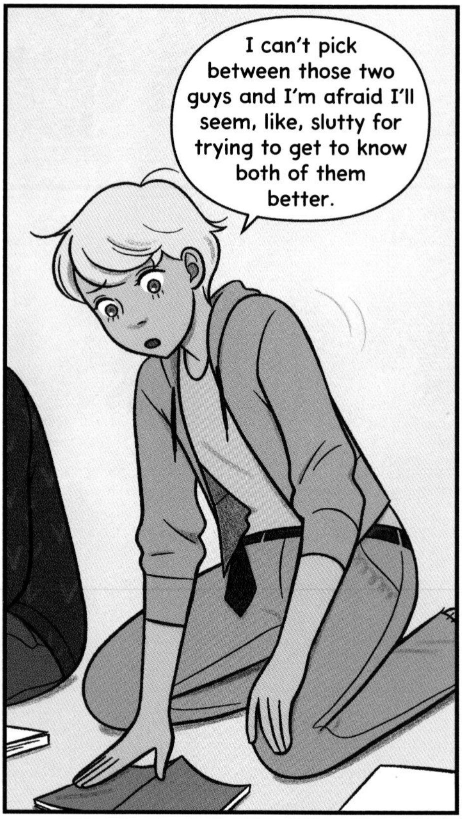
I can't pick between those two guys and I'm afraid I'll seem, like, slutty for trying to get to know both of them better.

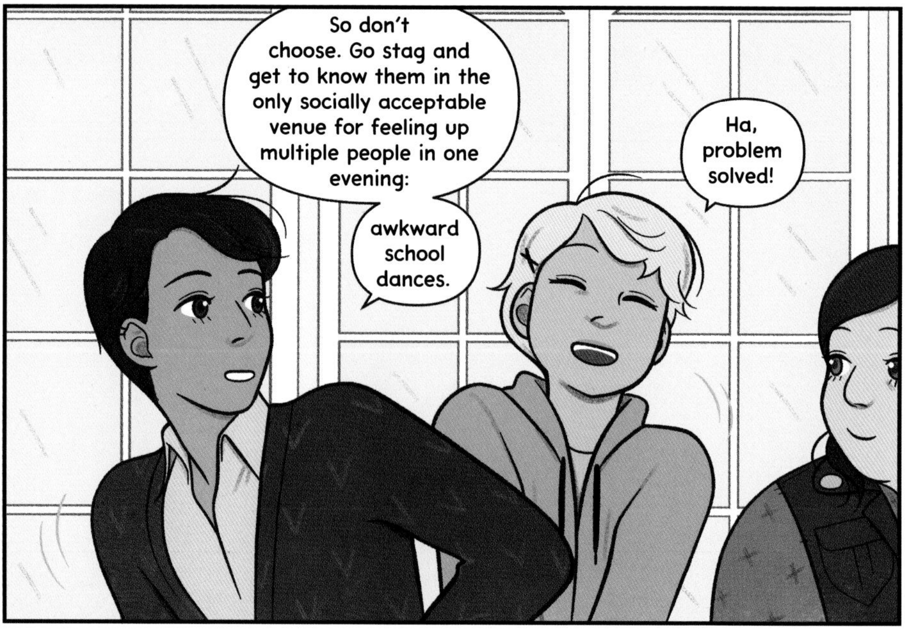
So don't choose. Go stag and get to know them in the only socially acceptable venue for feeling up multiple people in one evening:
awkward school dances.
Ha, problem solved!

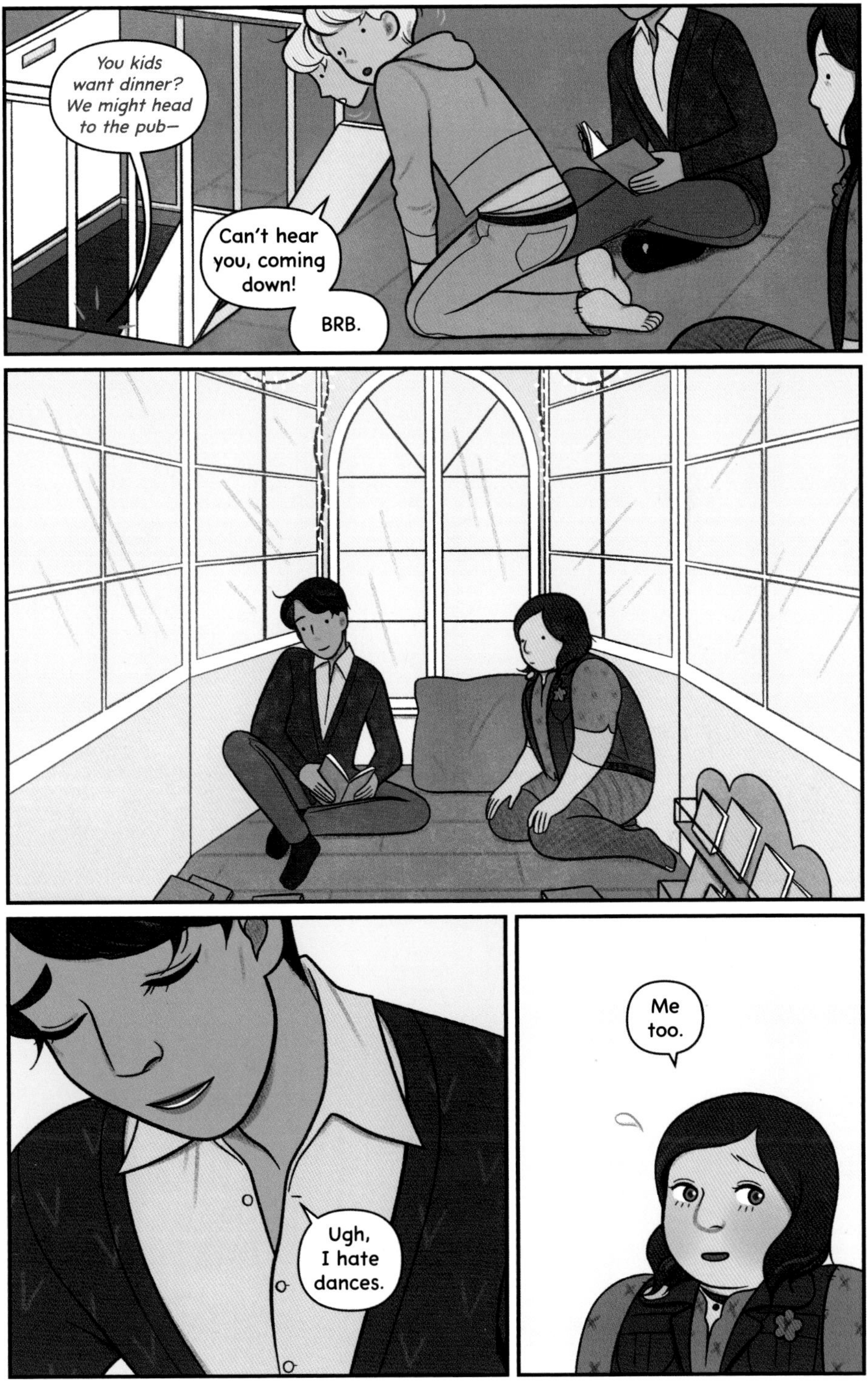
You kids want dinner? We might head to the pub—
Can't hear you, coming down!
BRB.
Ugh, I hate dances.
Me too.

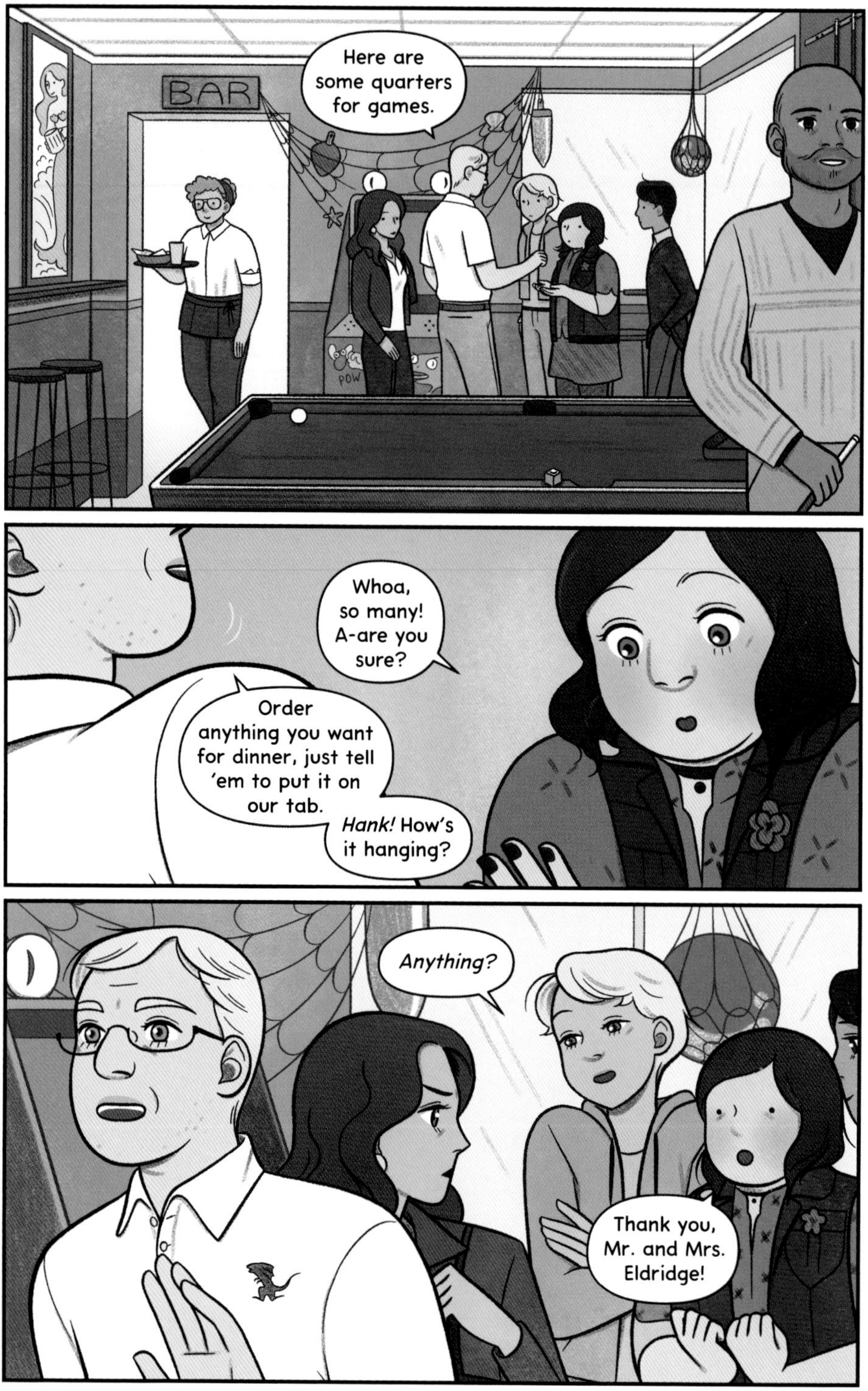
BAR
Here are some quarters for games.
POW
Whoa, so many! A-are you sure?
Order anything you want for dinner, just tell 'em to put it on our tab.
Hank! How's it hanging?
Anything?
Thank you, Mr. and Mrs. Eldridge!

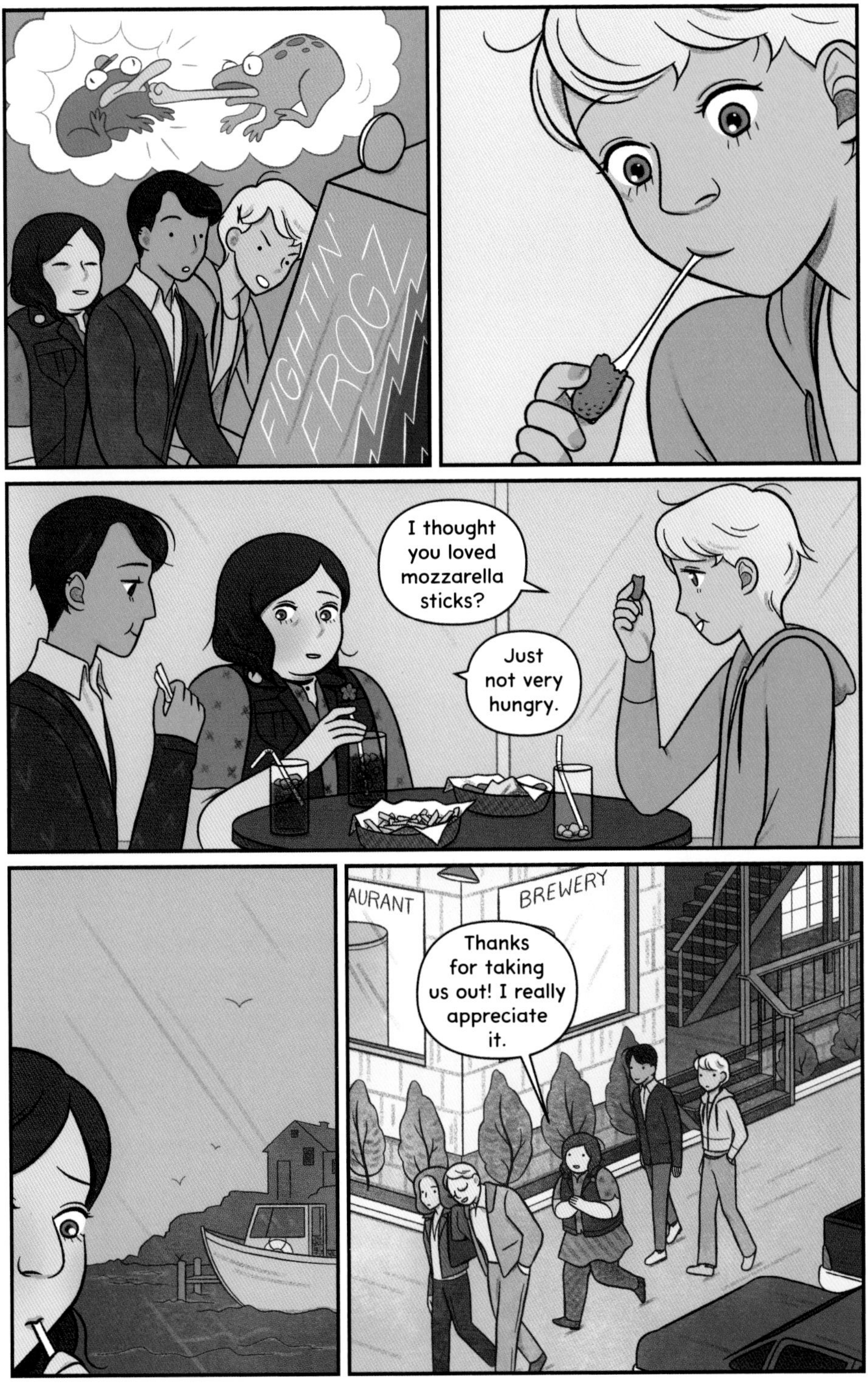
FIGHTIN' FROG
I thought you loved mozzarella sticks?
Just not very hungry.
AURANT
BREWERY
Thanks for taking us out! I really appreciate it.

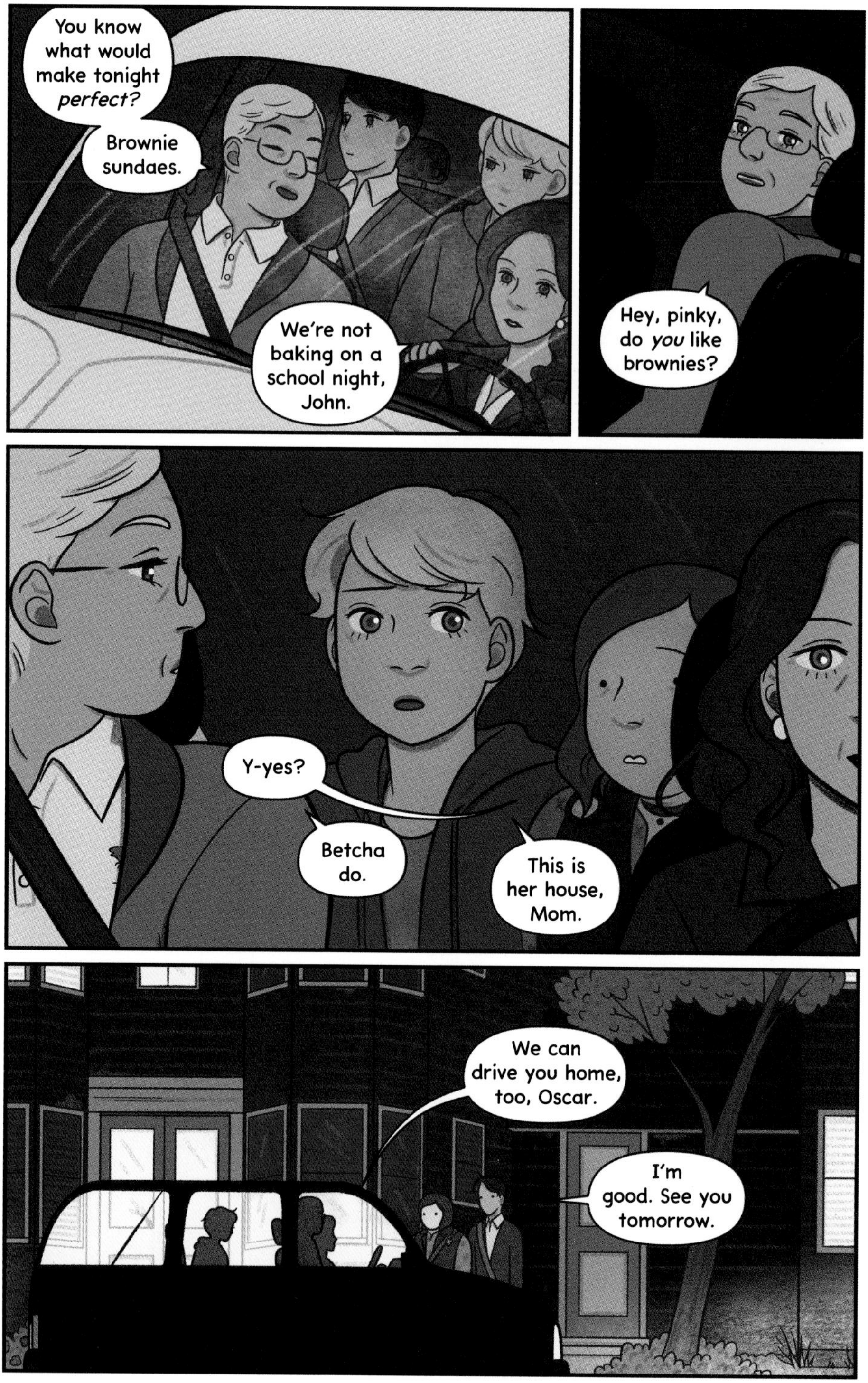
You know what would make tonight *perfect?*
Brownie sundaes.
We're not baking on a school night, John.
Hey, pinky, do *you* like brownies?
Y-yes?
Betcha do.
This is her house, Mom.
We can drive you home, too, Oscar.
I'm good. See you tomorrow.

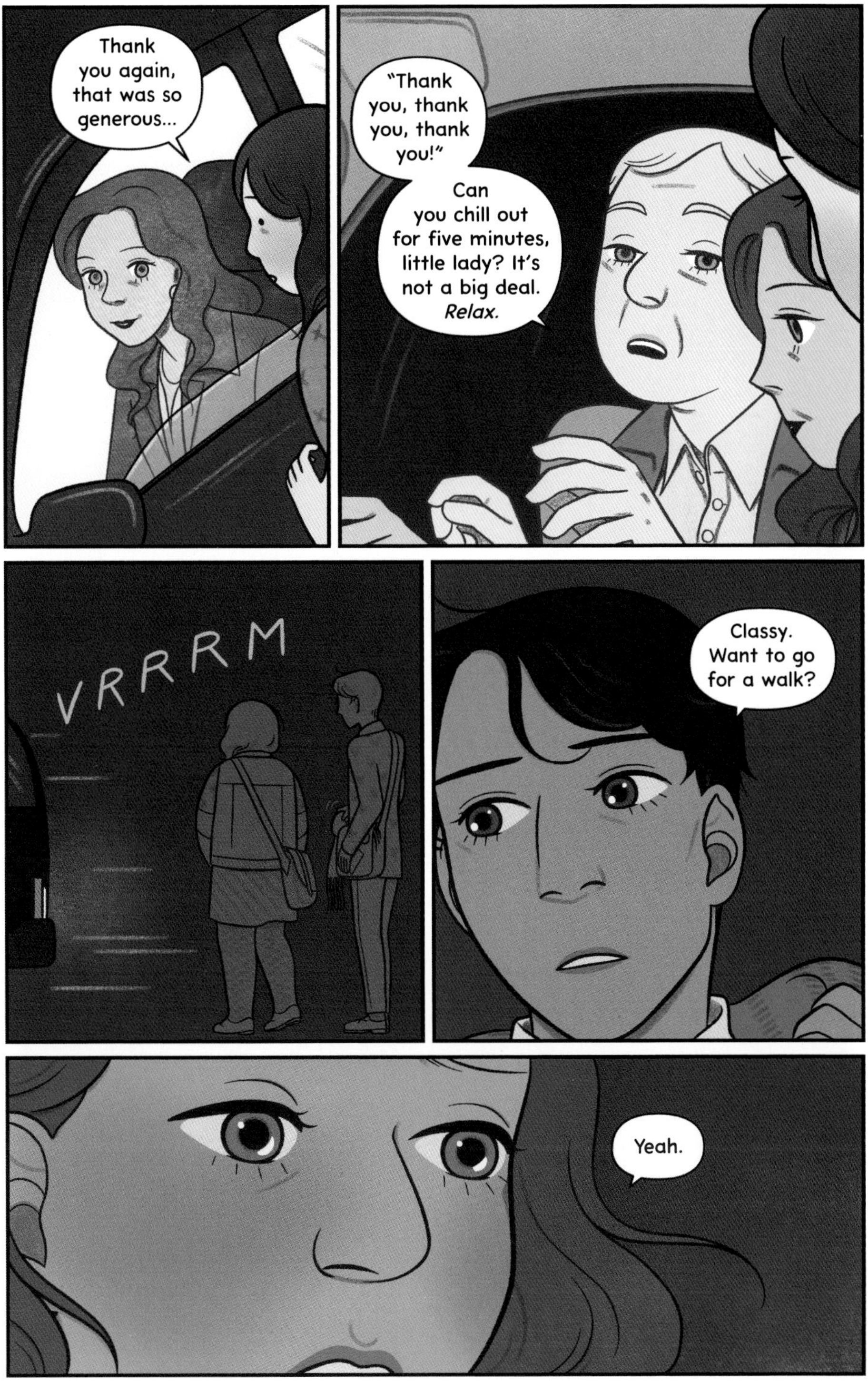
Thank you again, that was so generous...
"Thank you, thank you, thank you!"
Can you chill out for five minutes, little lady? It's not a big deal. *Relax.*
VRRRM
Classy. Want to go for a walk?
Yeah.

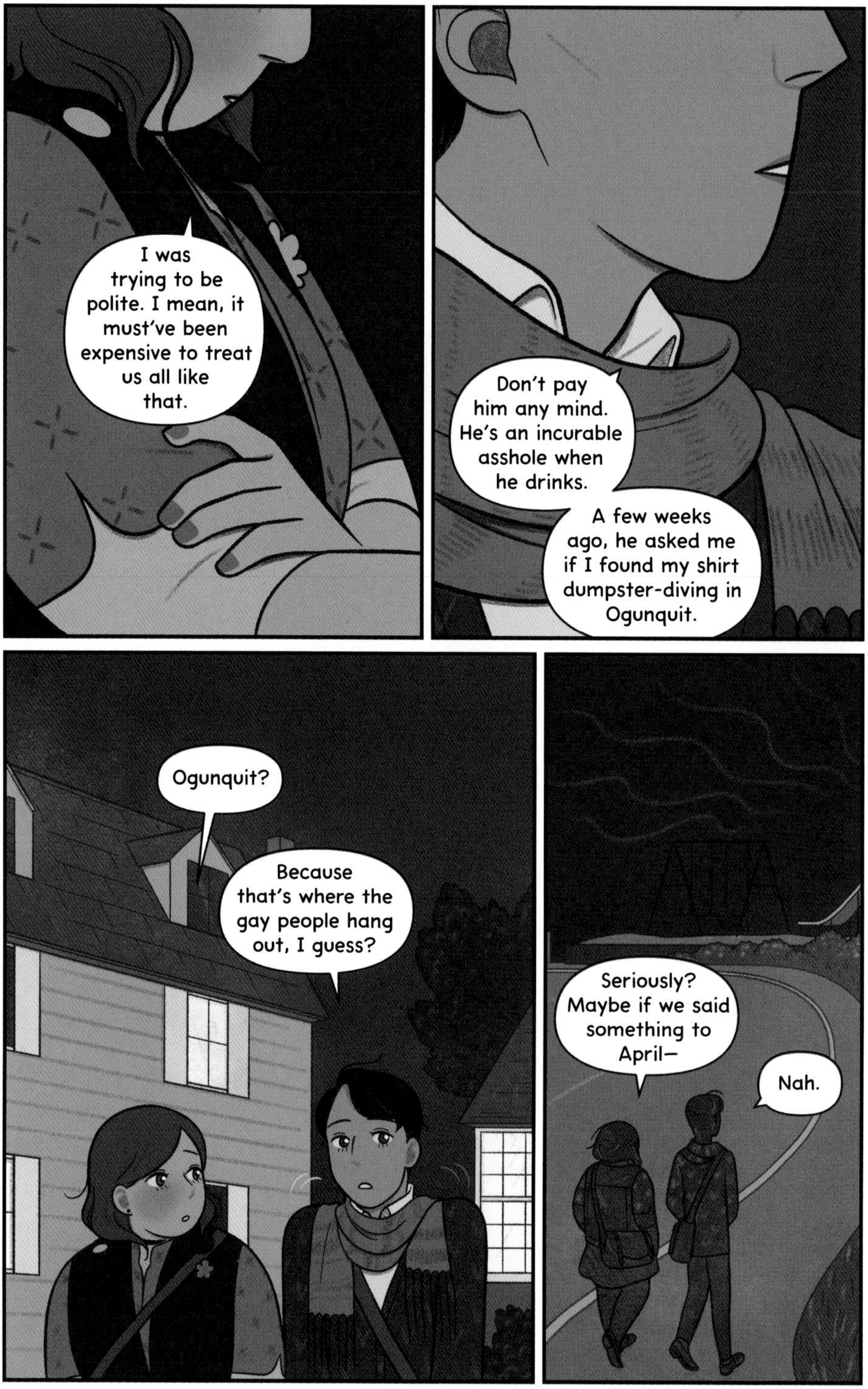
I was trying to be polite. I mean, it must've been expensive to treat us all like that.
Don't pay him any mind. He's an incurable asshole when he drinks.
A few weeks ago, he asked me if I found my shirt dumpster-diving in Ogunquit.
Ogunquit?
Because that's where the gay people hang out, I guess?
Seriously? Maybe if we said something to April—
Nah.

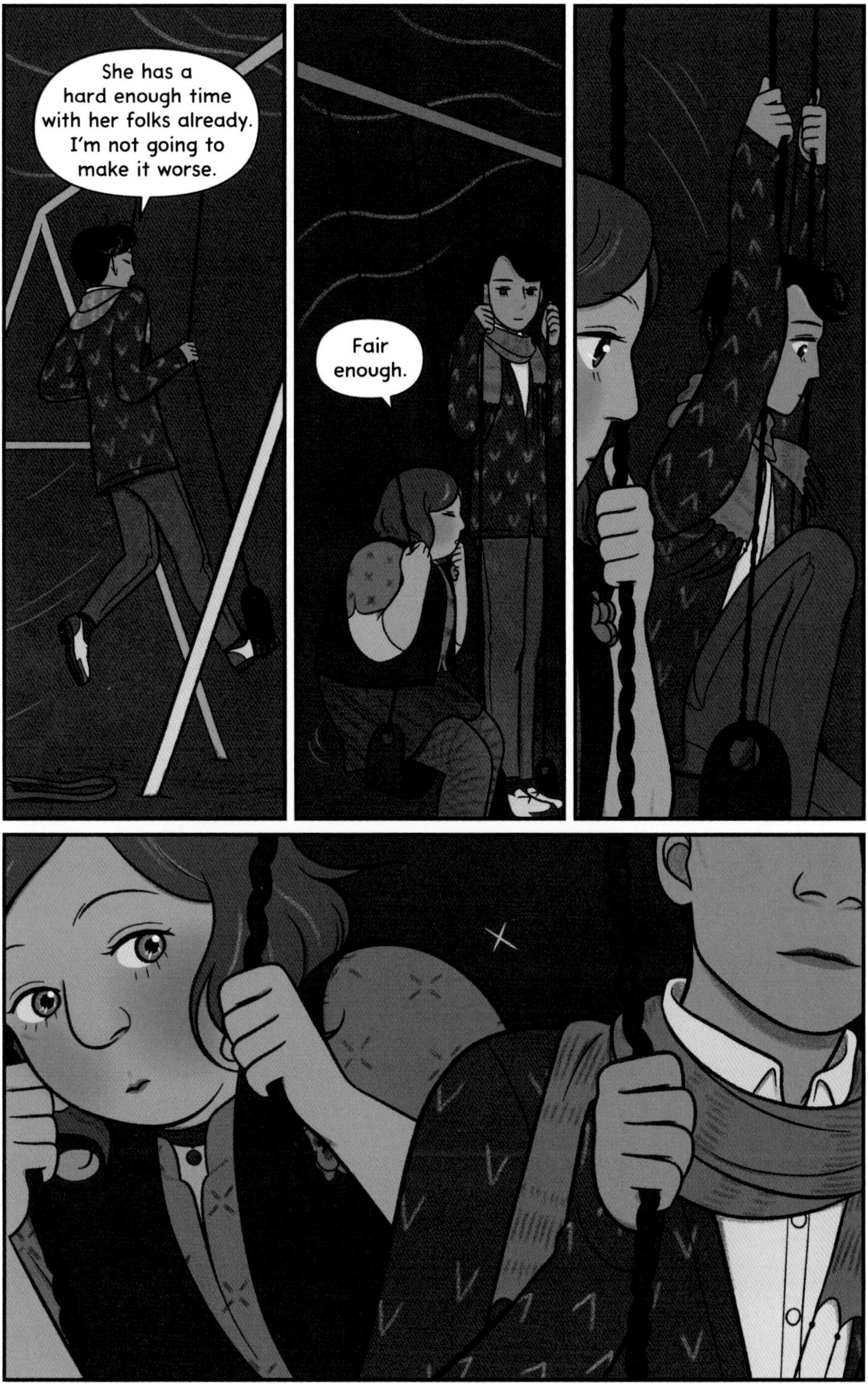
She has a hard enough time with her folks already. I'm not going to make it worse.
Fair enough.

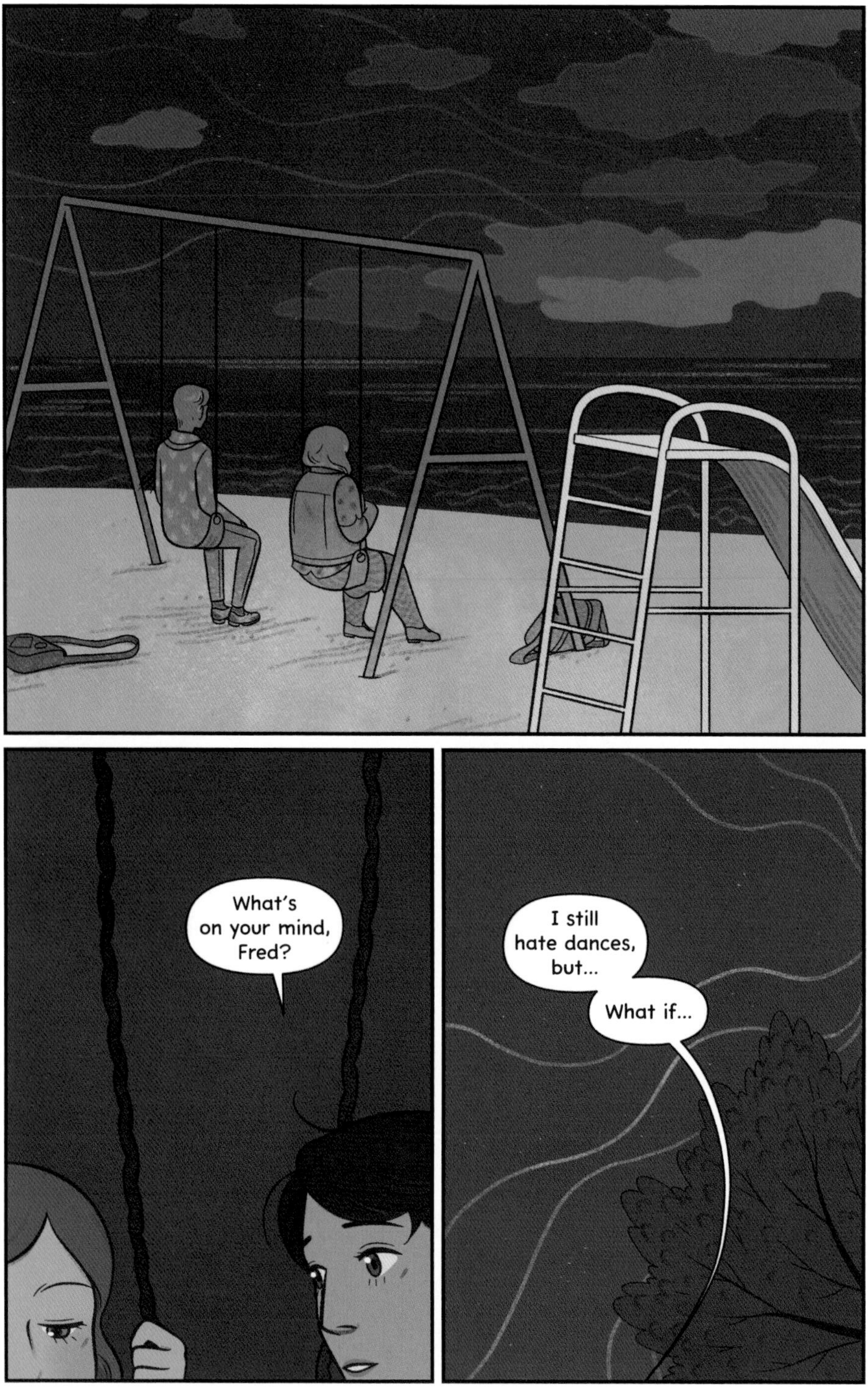
What's on your mind, Fred?
I still hate dances, but...
What if...

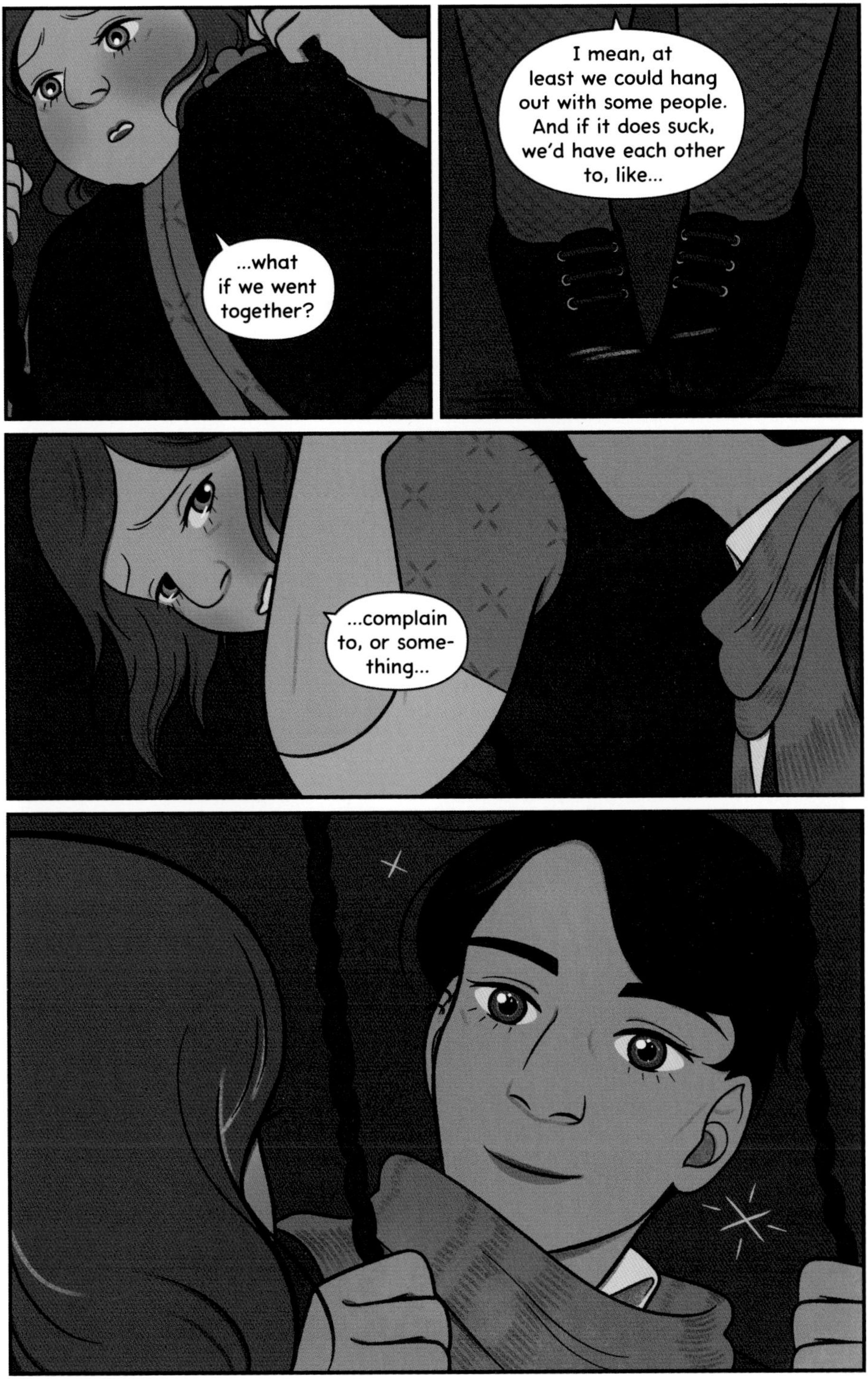
...what if we went together?
I mean, at least we could hang out with some people. And if it does suck, we'd have each other to, like...
...complain to, or some-thing...

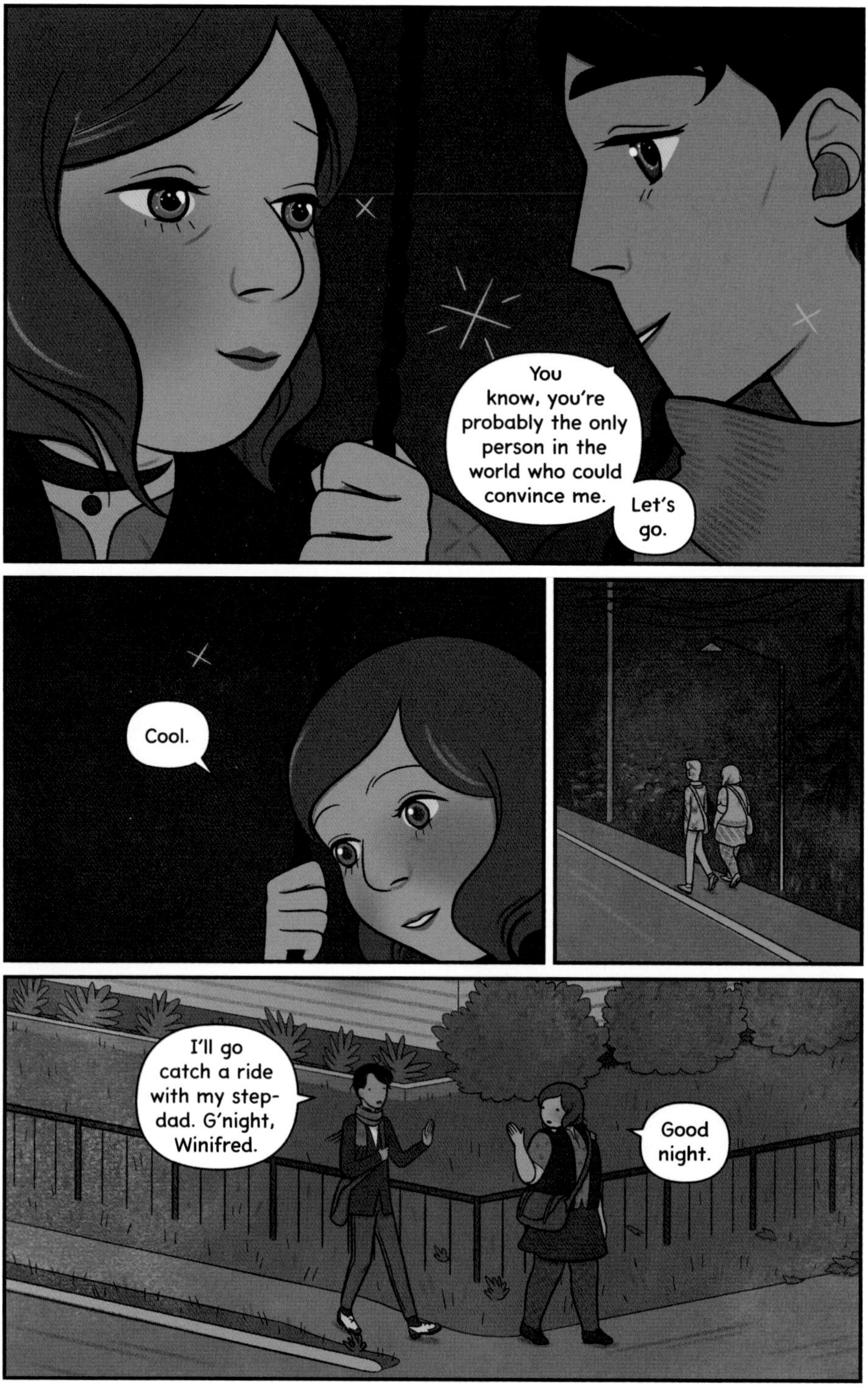
You know, you're probably the only person in the world who could convince me.
Let's go.
Cool.
I'll go catch a ride with my step-dad. G'night, Winifred.
Good night.

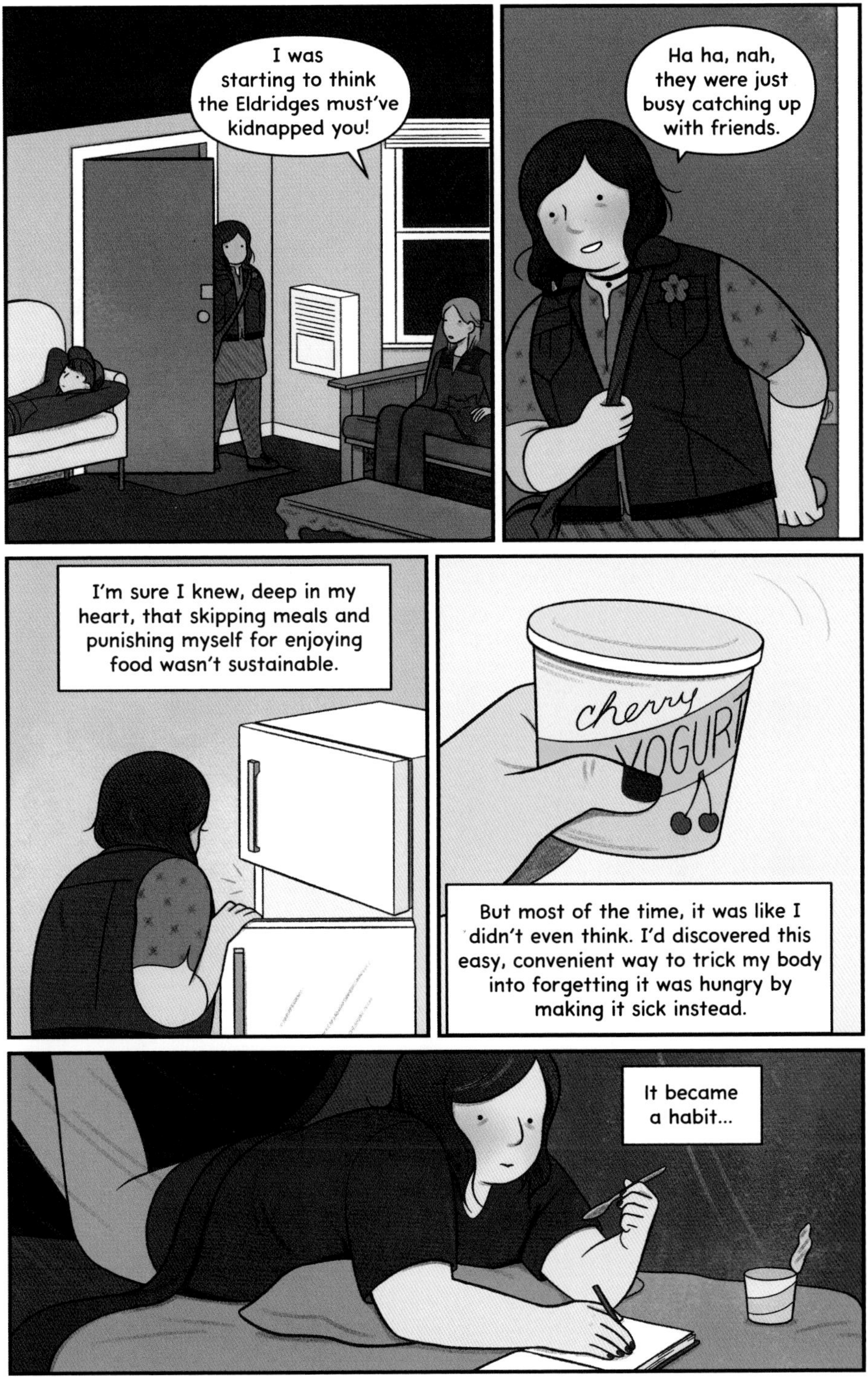
I was starting to think the Eldridges must've kidnapped you!
Ha ha, nah, they were just busy catching up with friends.
I'm sure I knew, deep in my heart, that skipping meals and punishing myself for enjoying food wasn't sustainable.
cherry
YOGURT
But most of the time, it was like I didn't even think. I'd discovered this easy, convenient way to trick my body into forgetting it was hungry by making it sick instead.
It became a habit...

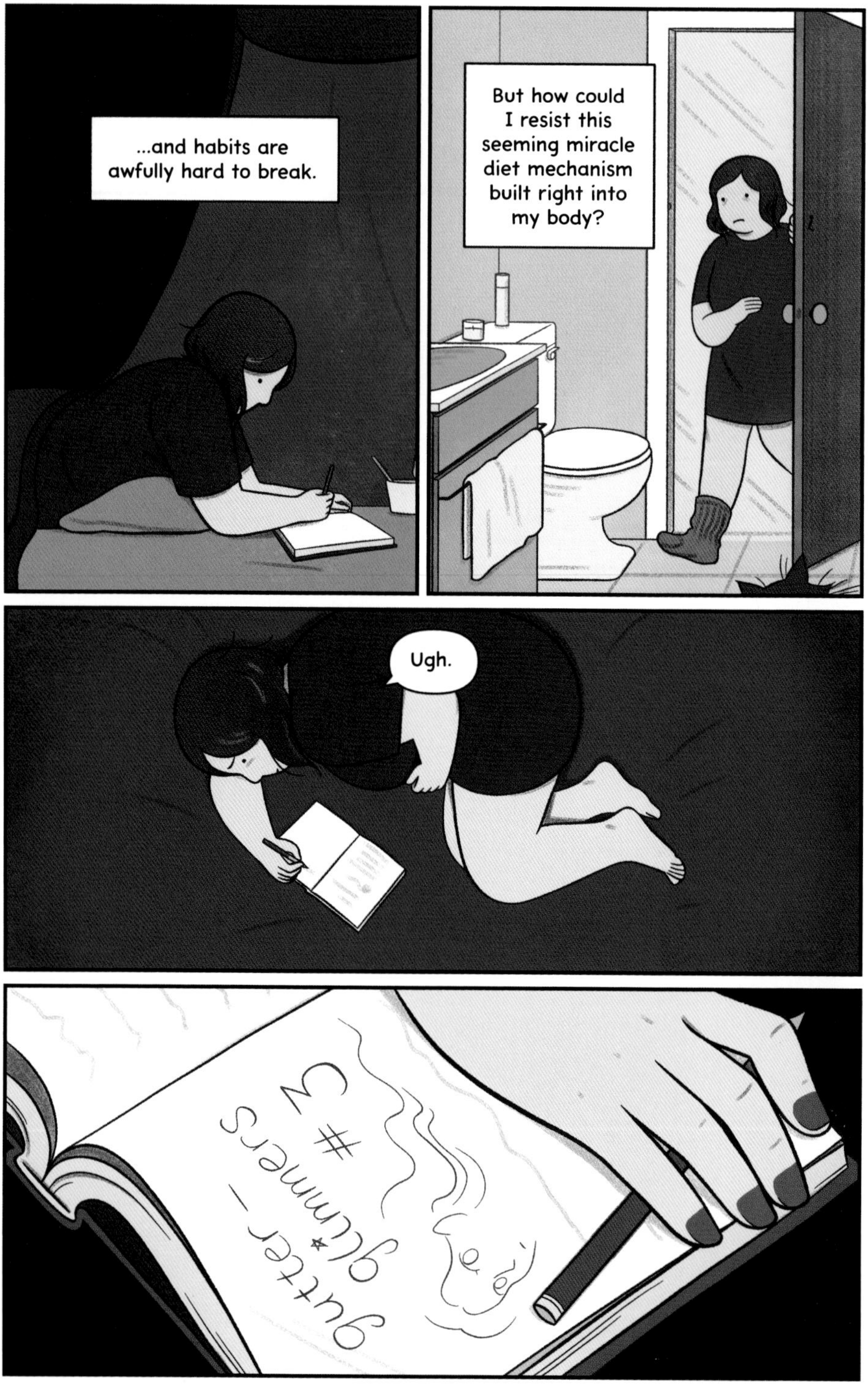
...and habits are awfully hard to break.
But how could I resist this seeming miracle diet mechanism built right into my body?
Ugh.
gutter_ glimmers #3

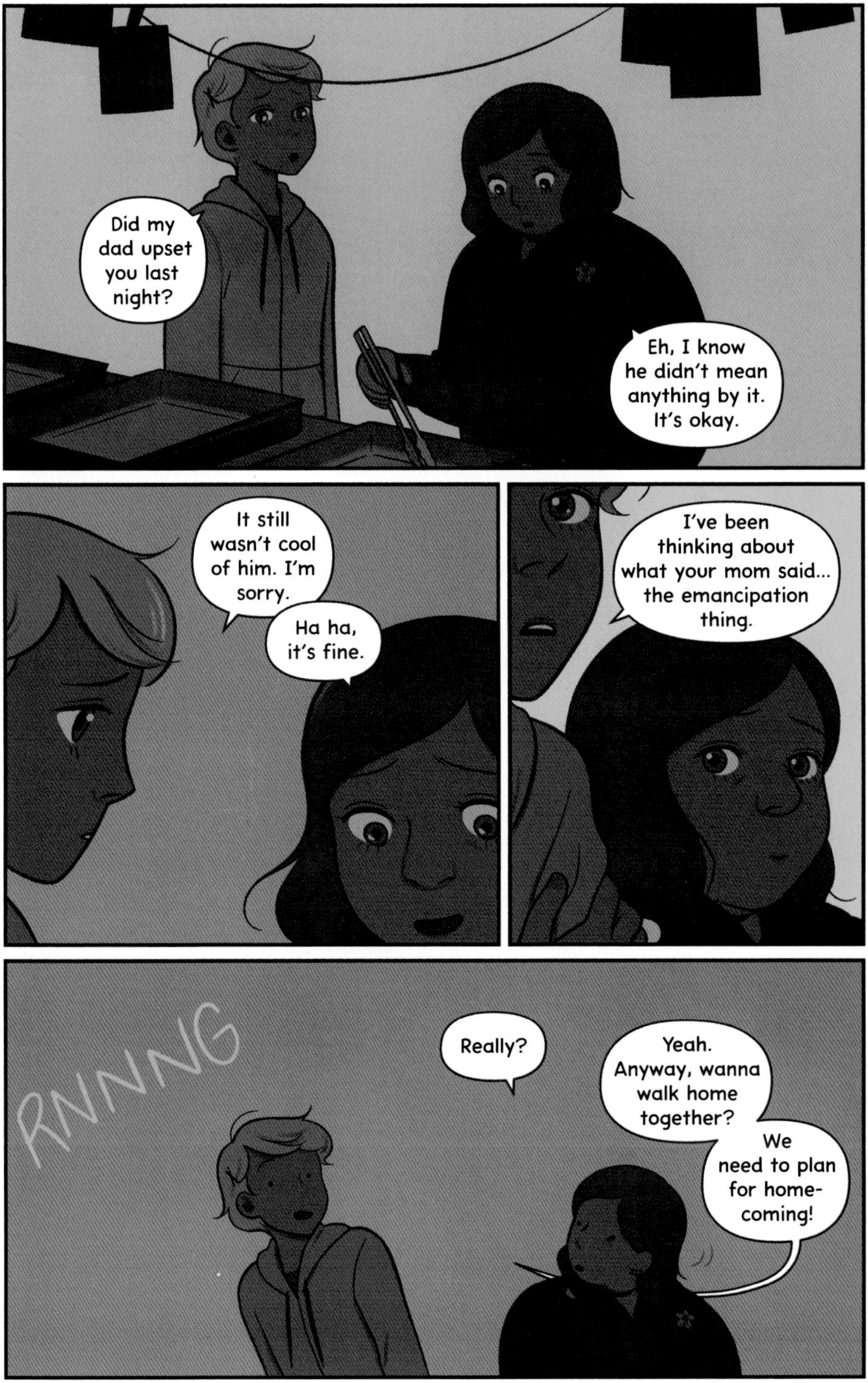

Did my dad upset you last night?
Eh, I know he didn't mean anything by it. It's okay.
It still wasn't cool of him. I'm sorry.
Ha ha, it's fine.
I've been thinking about what your mom said... the emancipation thing.
RNNNG
Really?
Yeah. Anyway, wanna walk home together?
We need to plan for home-coming!

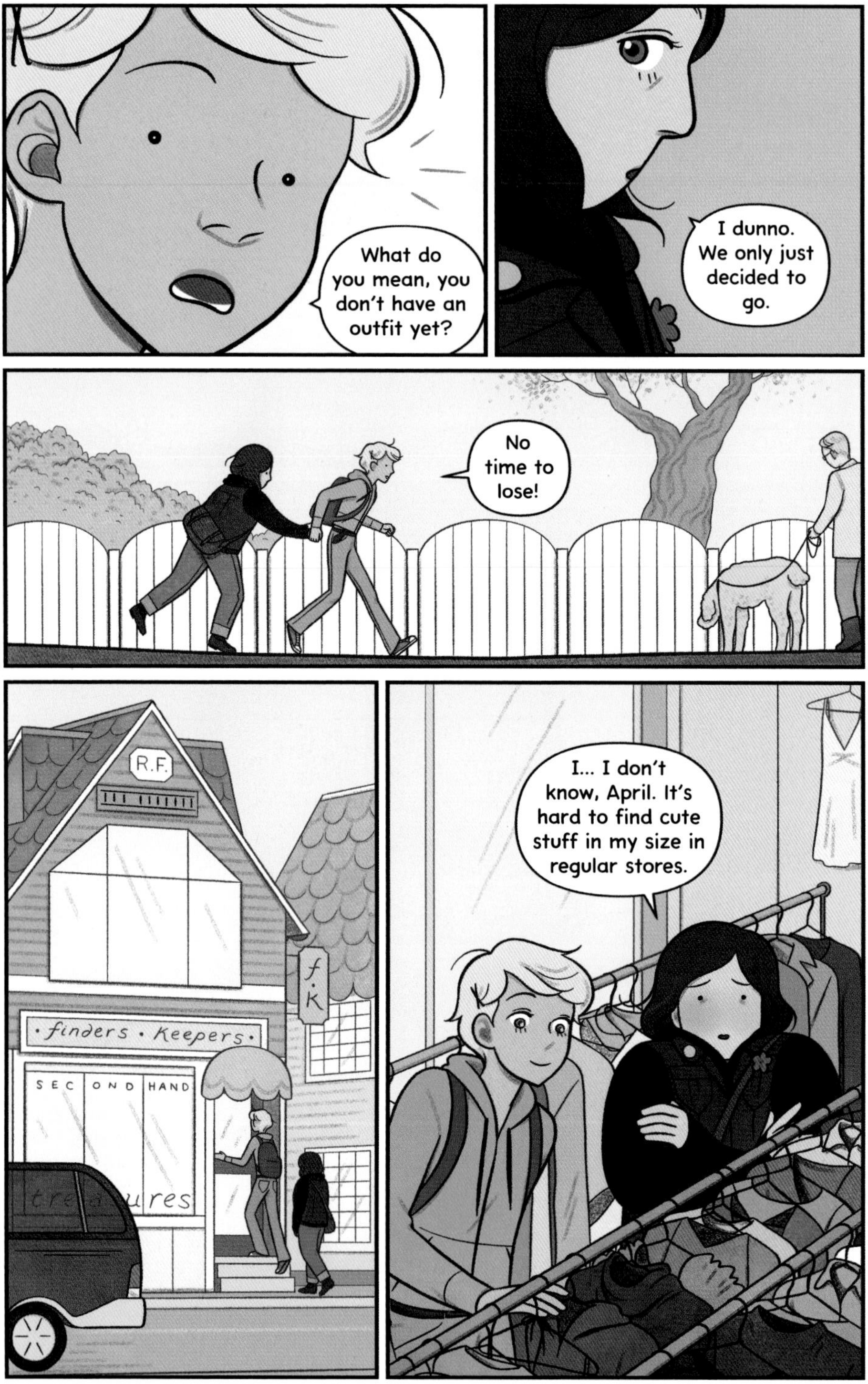
What do you mean, you don't have an outfit yet?
I dunno. We only just decided to go.
No time to lose!
R.F.
finders • keepers
SECOND HAND
I... I don't know, April. It's hard to find cute stuff in my size in regular stores.

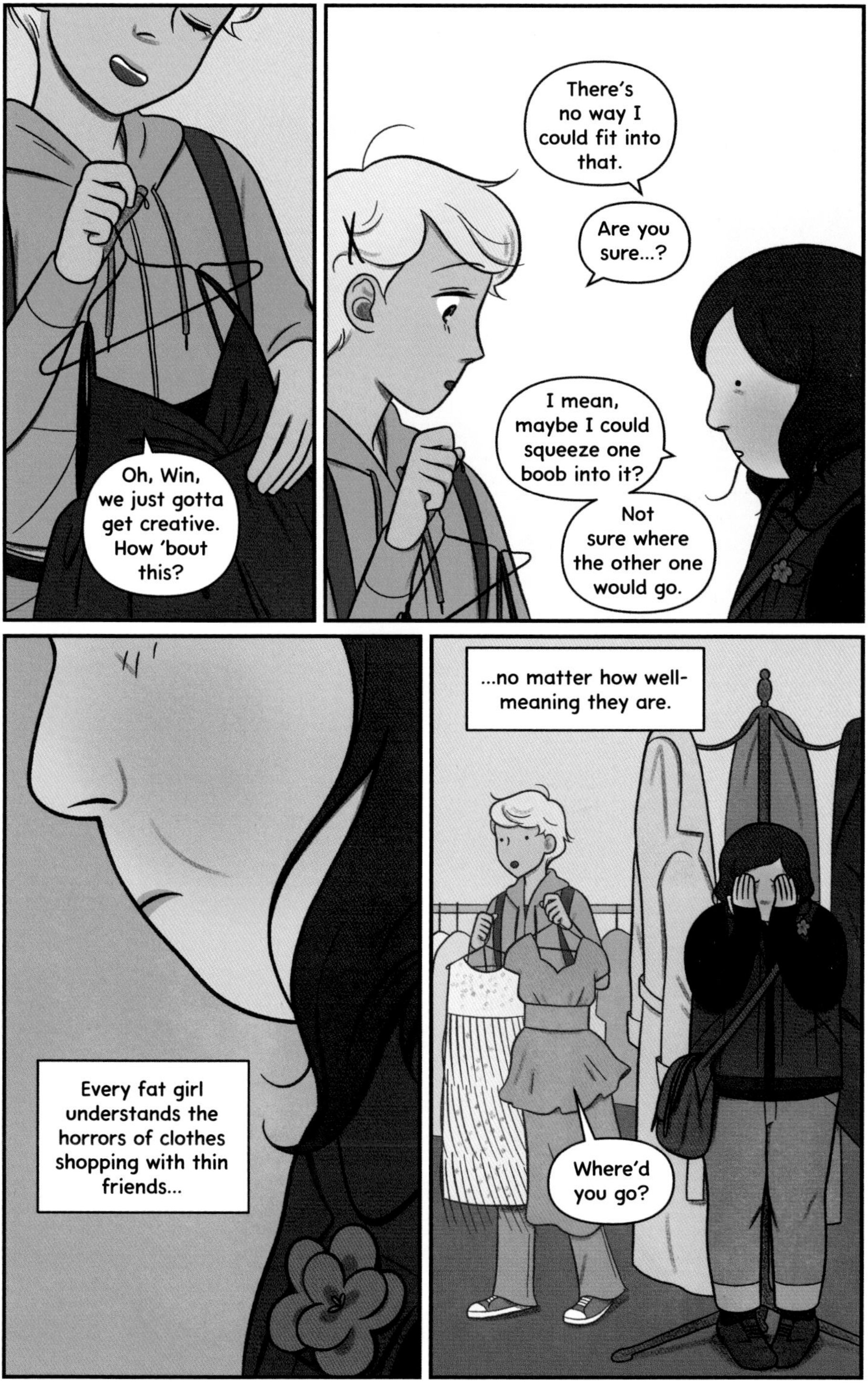
Oh, Win, we just gotta get creative. How 'bout this?
There's no way I could fit into that.
Are you sure...?
I mean, maybe I could squeeze one boob into it?
Not sure where the other one would go.
Every fat girl understands the horrors of clothes shopping with thin friends...
...no matter how well-meaning they are.
Where'd you go?

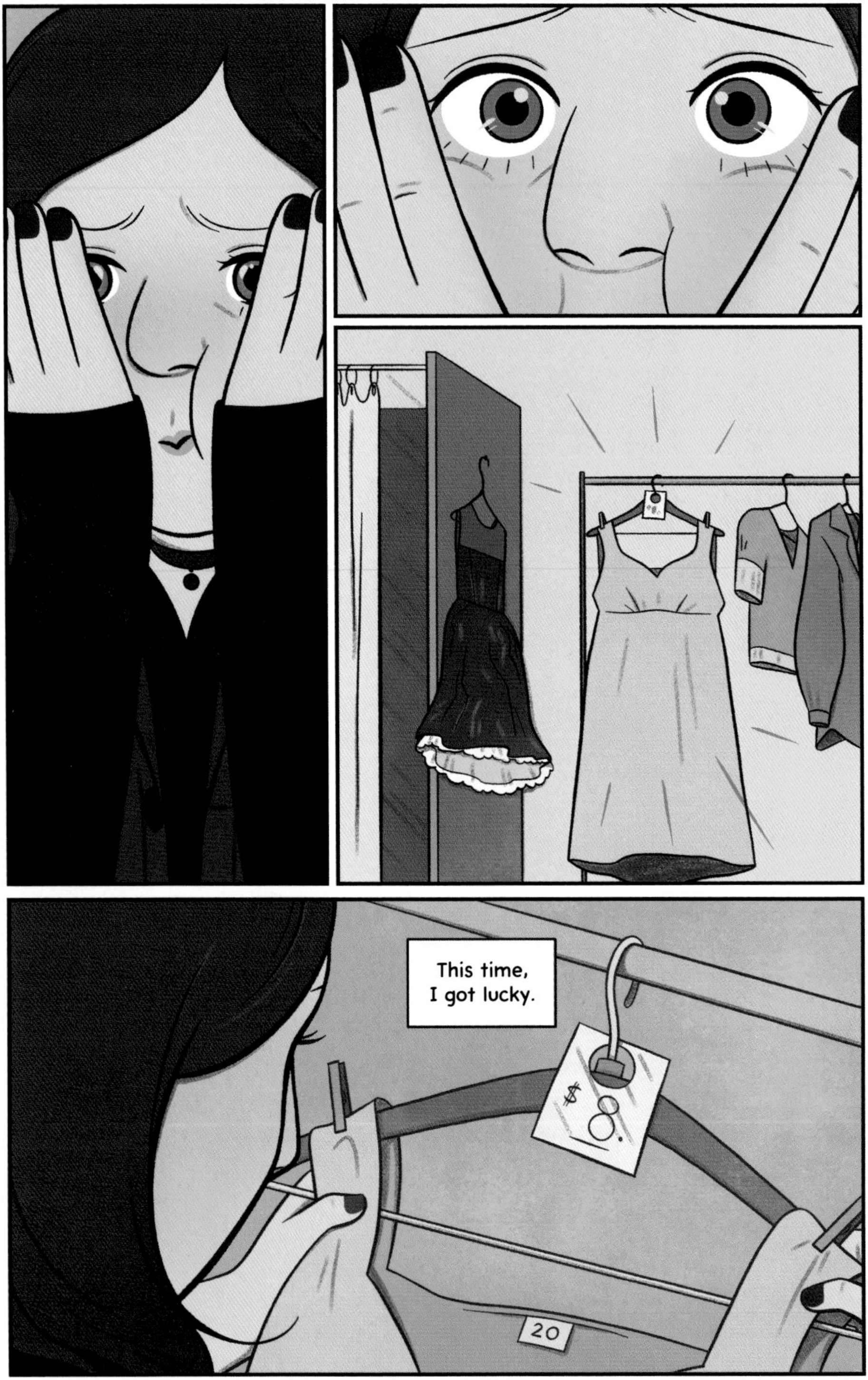
This time,
I got lucky.
$8.
20

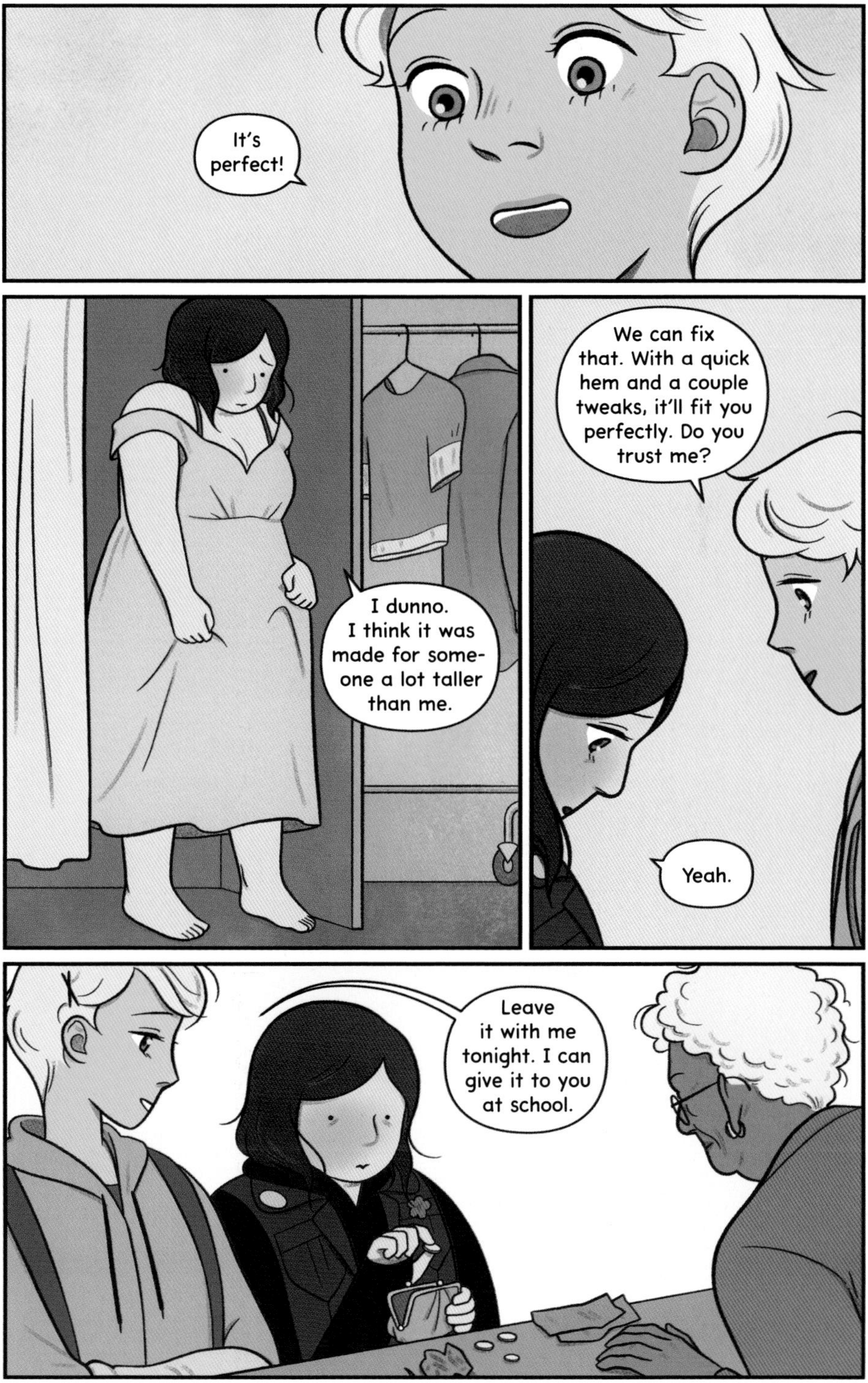
It's perfect!
I dunno. I think it was made for some-one a lot taller than me.
We can fix that. With a quick hem and a couple tweaks, it'll fit you perfectly. Do you trust me?
Yeah.
Leave it with me tonight. I can give it to you at school.

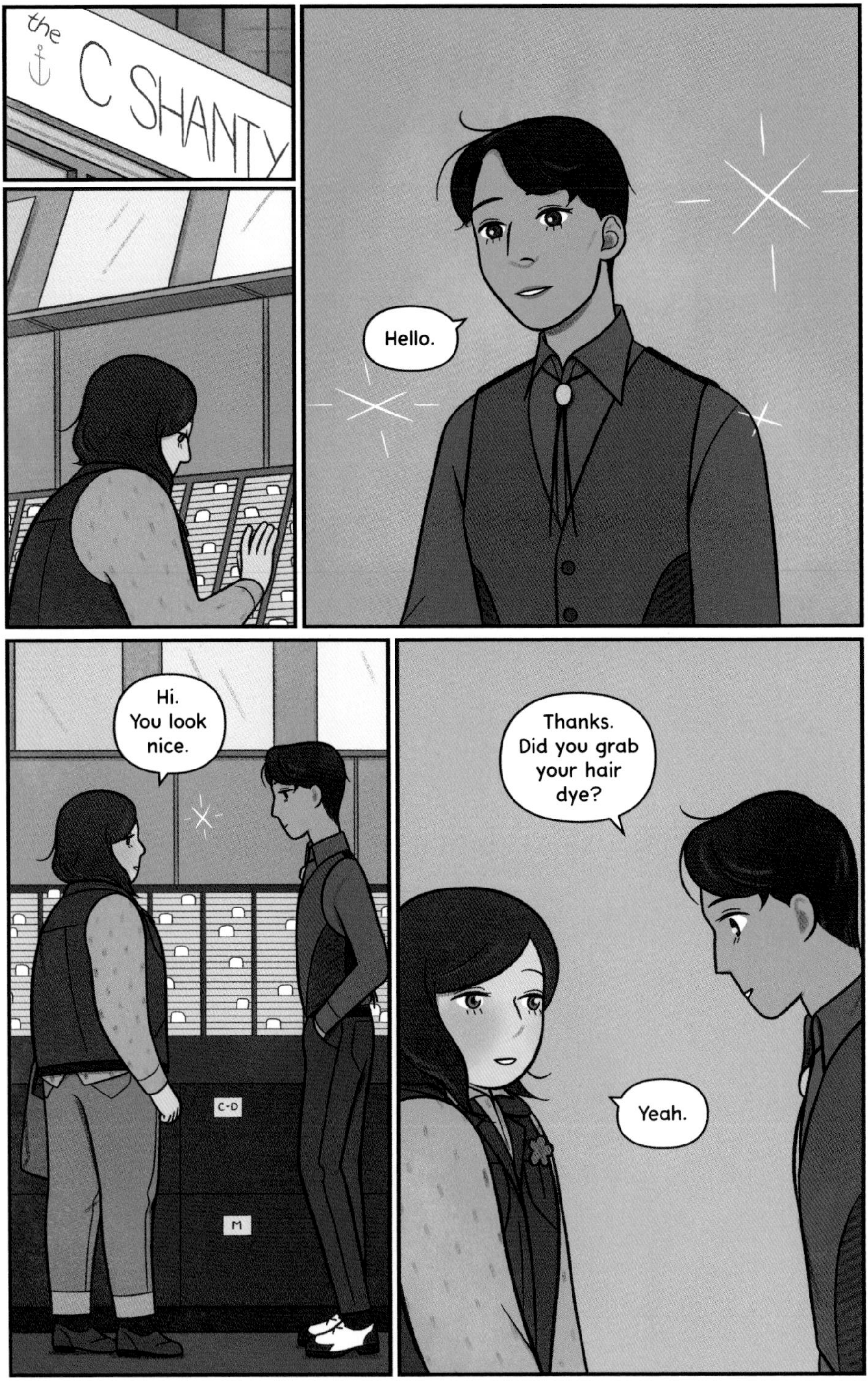
the C SHANTY
Hello.
Hi. You look nice.
C-D
M
Thanks. Did you grab your hair dye?
Yeah.

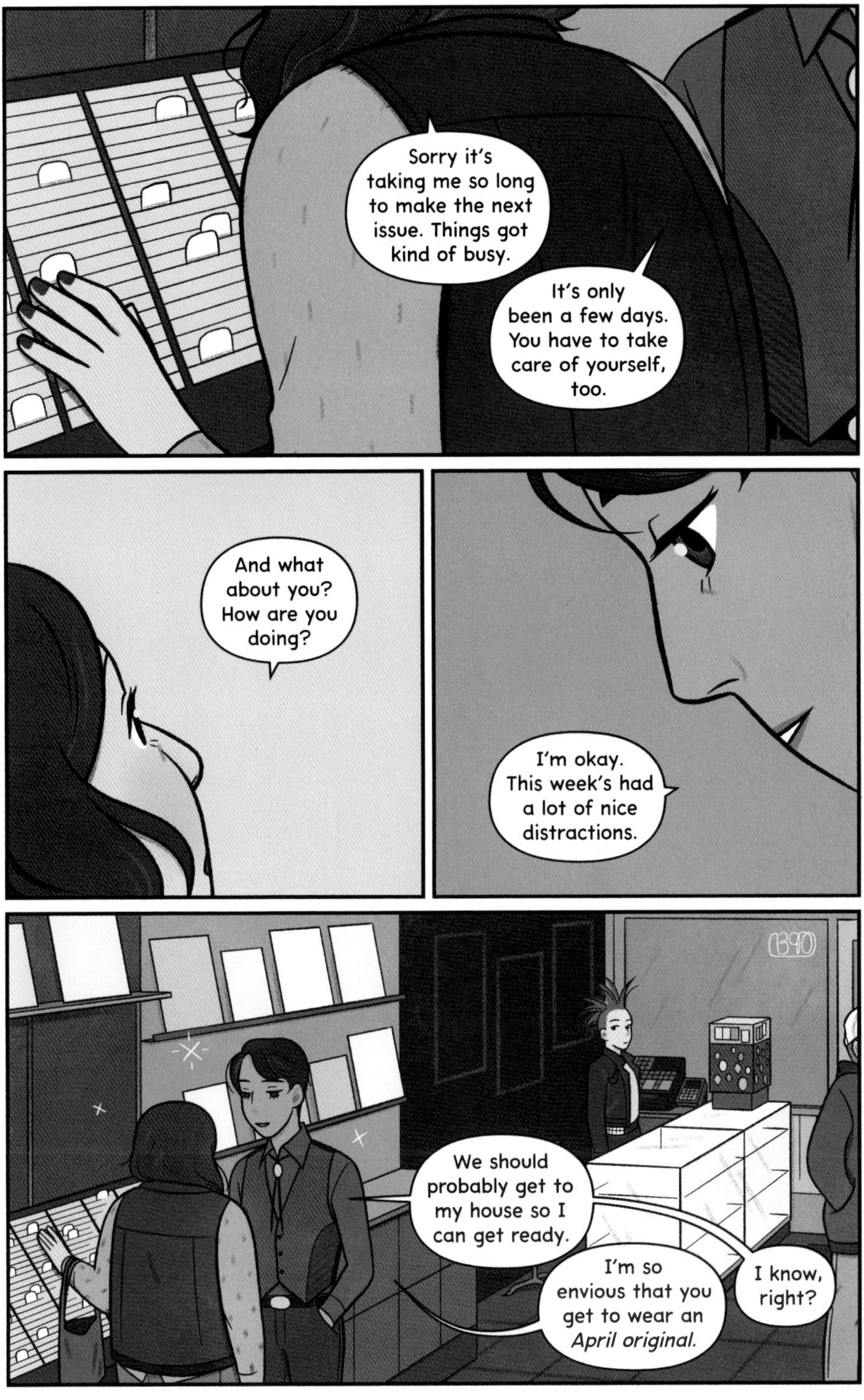
Sorry it's taking me so long to make the next issue. Things got kind of busy.
It's only been a few days. You have to take care of yourself, too.
And what about you? How are you doing?
I'm okay. This week's had a lot of nice distractions.
We should probably get to my house so I can get ready.
I'm so envious that you get to wear an *April original.*
I know, right?

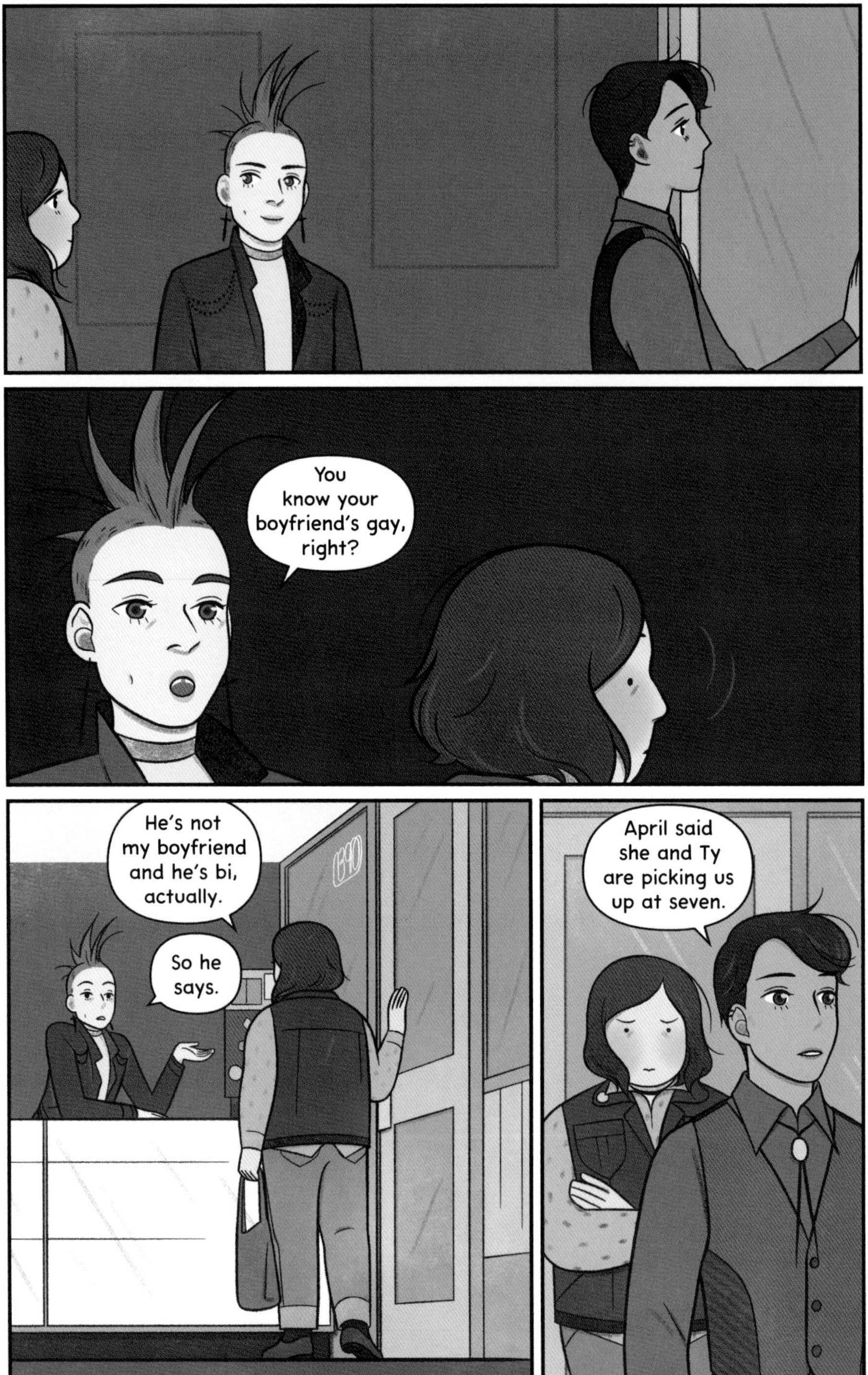
You know your boyfriend's gay, right?
He's not my boyfriend and he's bi, actually.
So he says.
April said she and Ty are picking us up at seven.

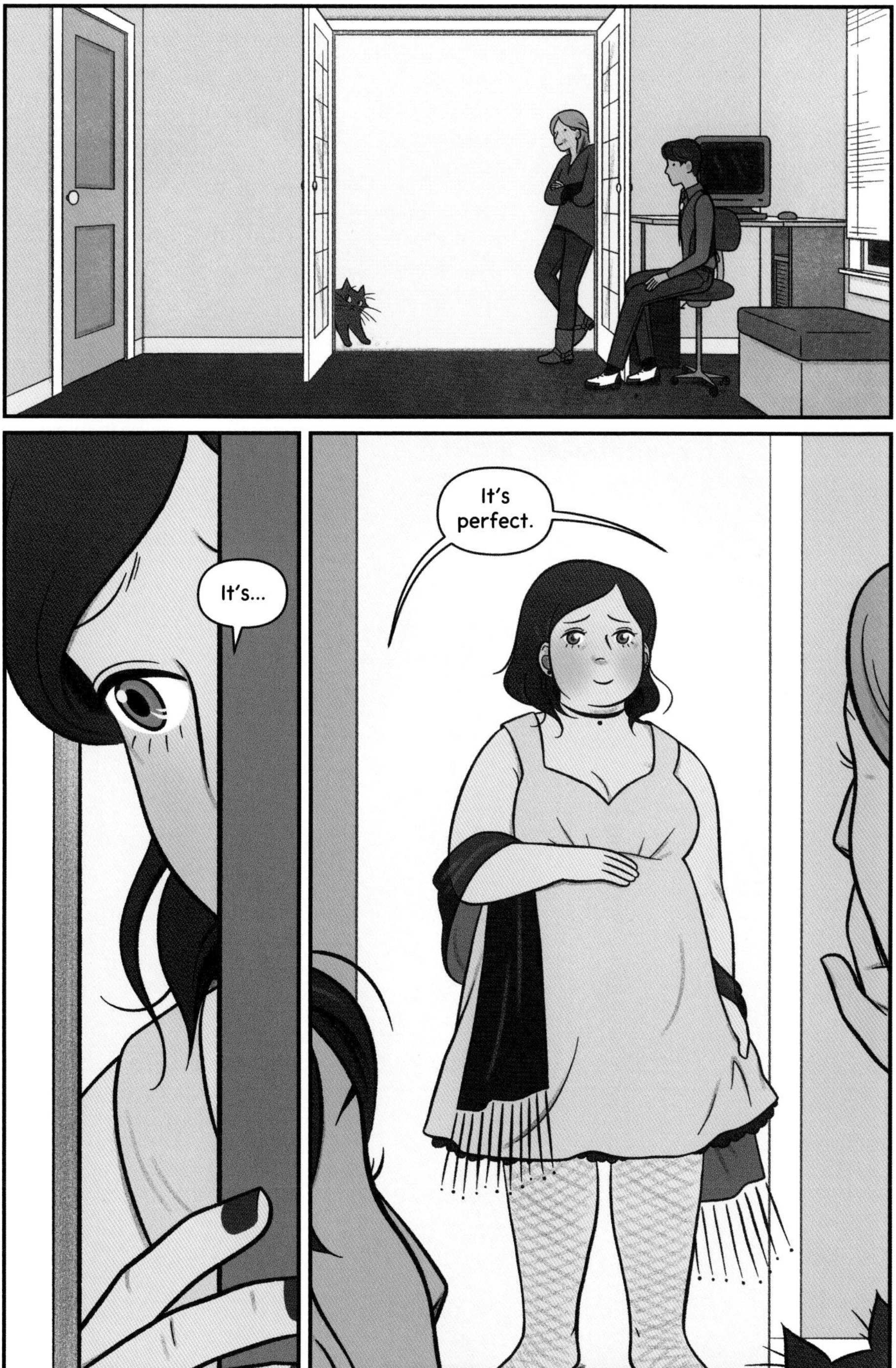
It's...
It's perfect.

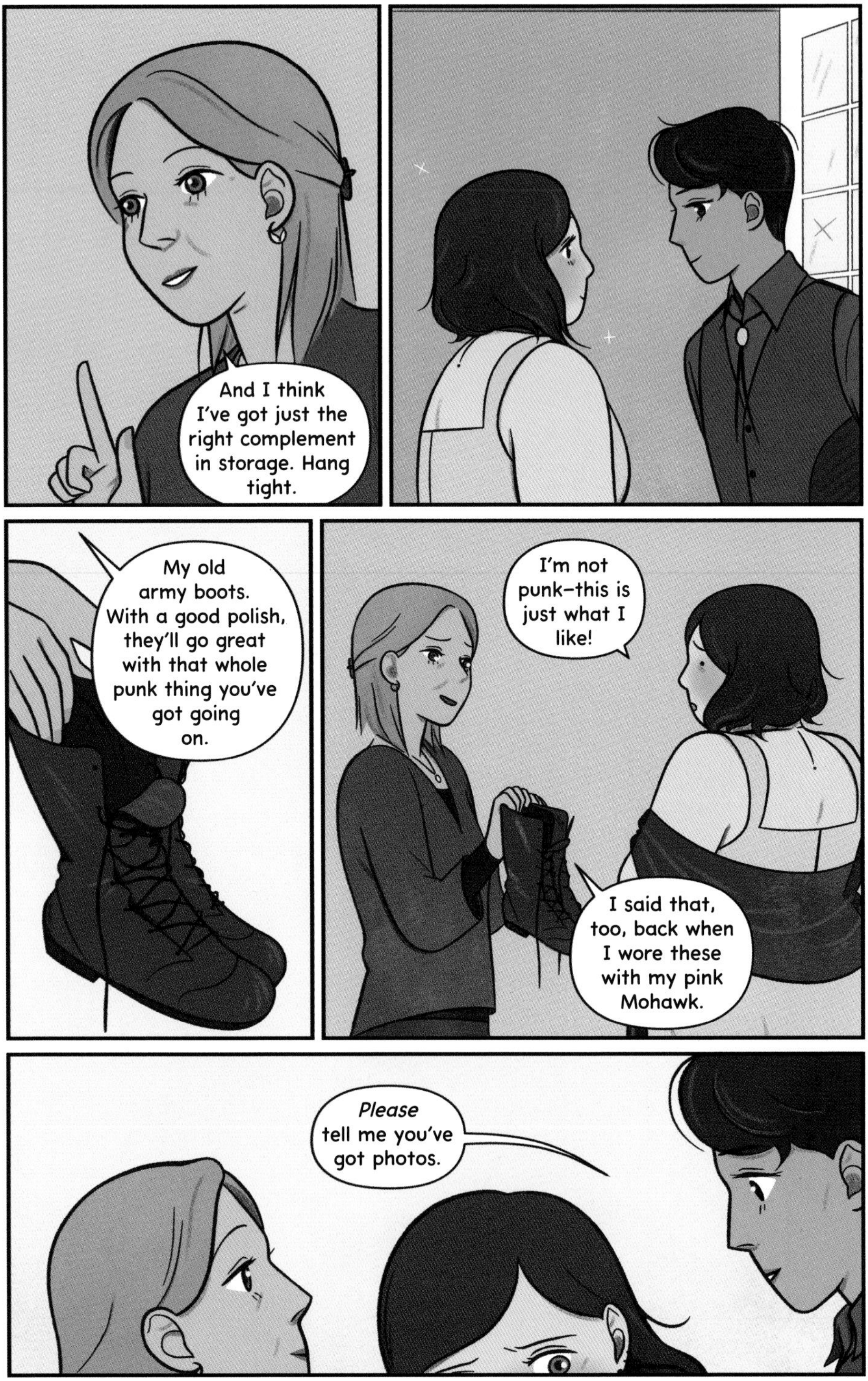
And I think I've got just the right complement in storage. Hang tight.
My old army boots. With a good polish, they'll go great with that whole punk thing you've got going on.
I'm not punk—this is just what I like!
I said that, too, back when I wore these with my pink Mohawk.
Please tell me you've got photos.

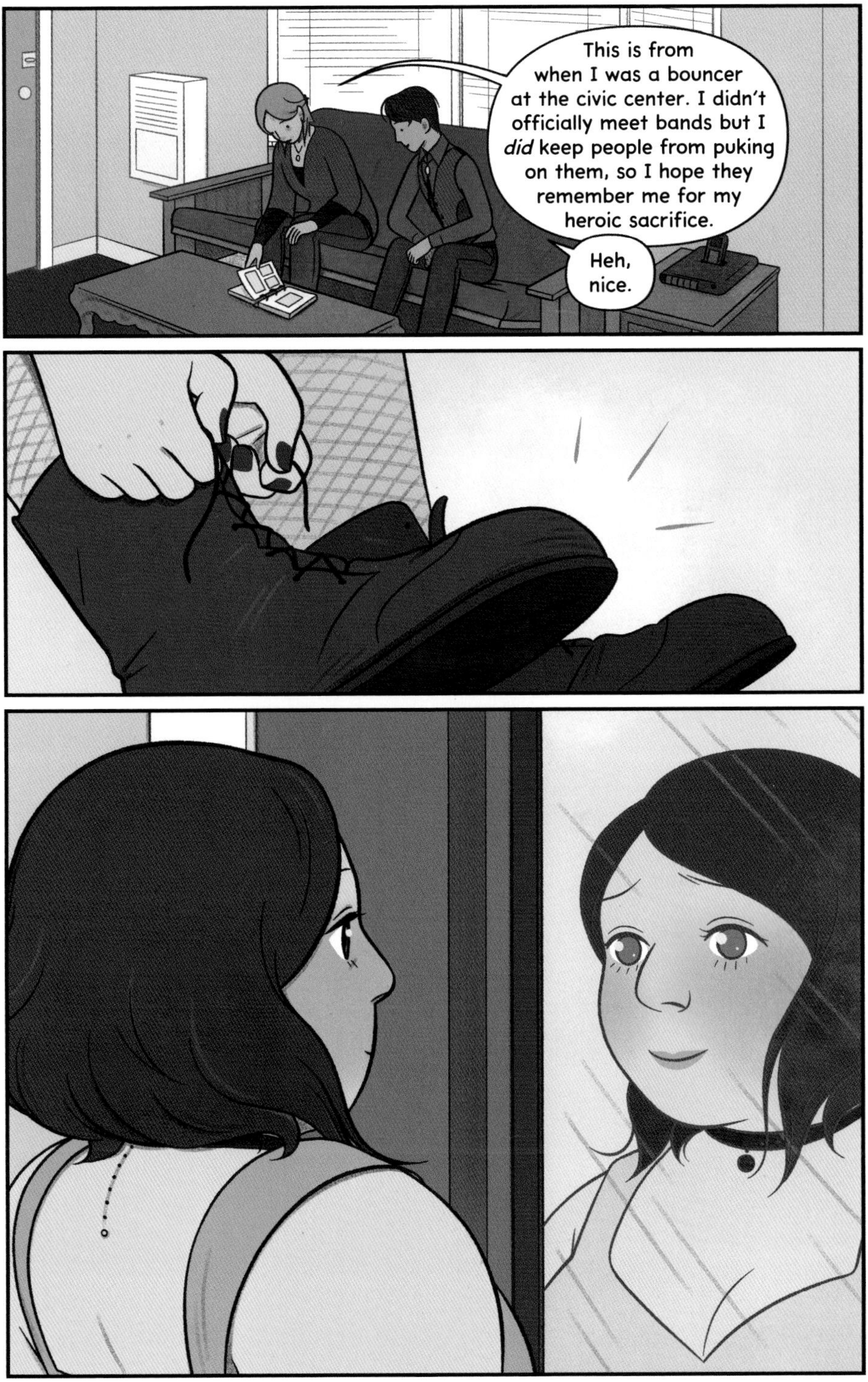
This is from when I was a bouncer at the civic center. I didn't officially meet bands but I *did* keep people from puking on them, so I hope they remember me for my heroic sacrifice.
Heh, nice.

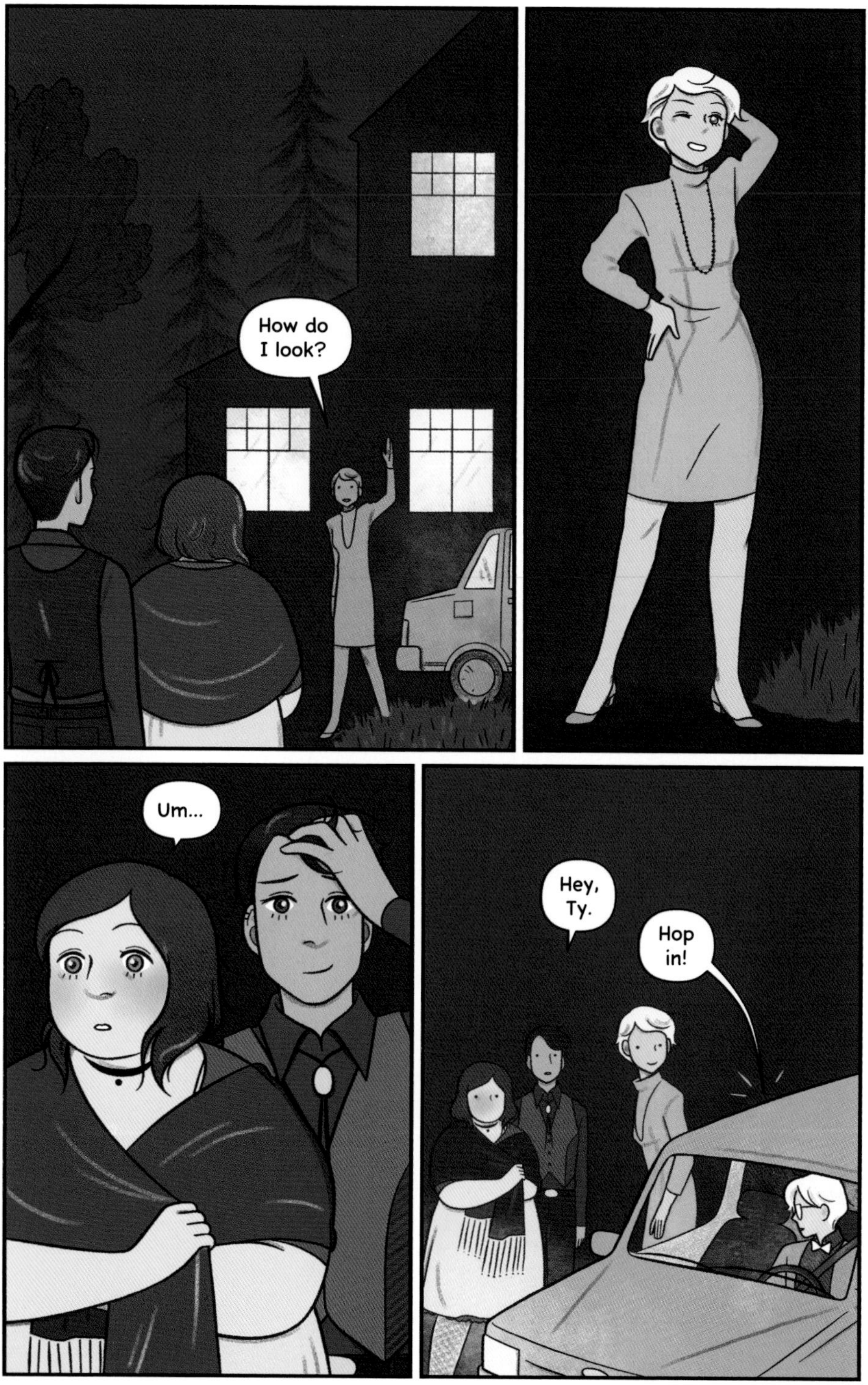
How do I look?
Um...
Hey, Ty.
Hop in!

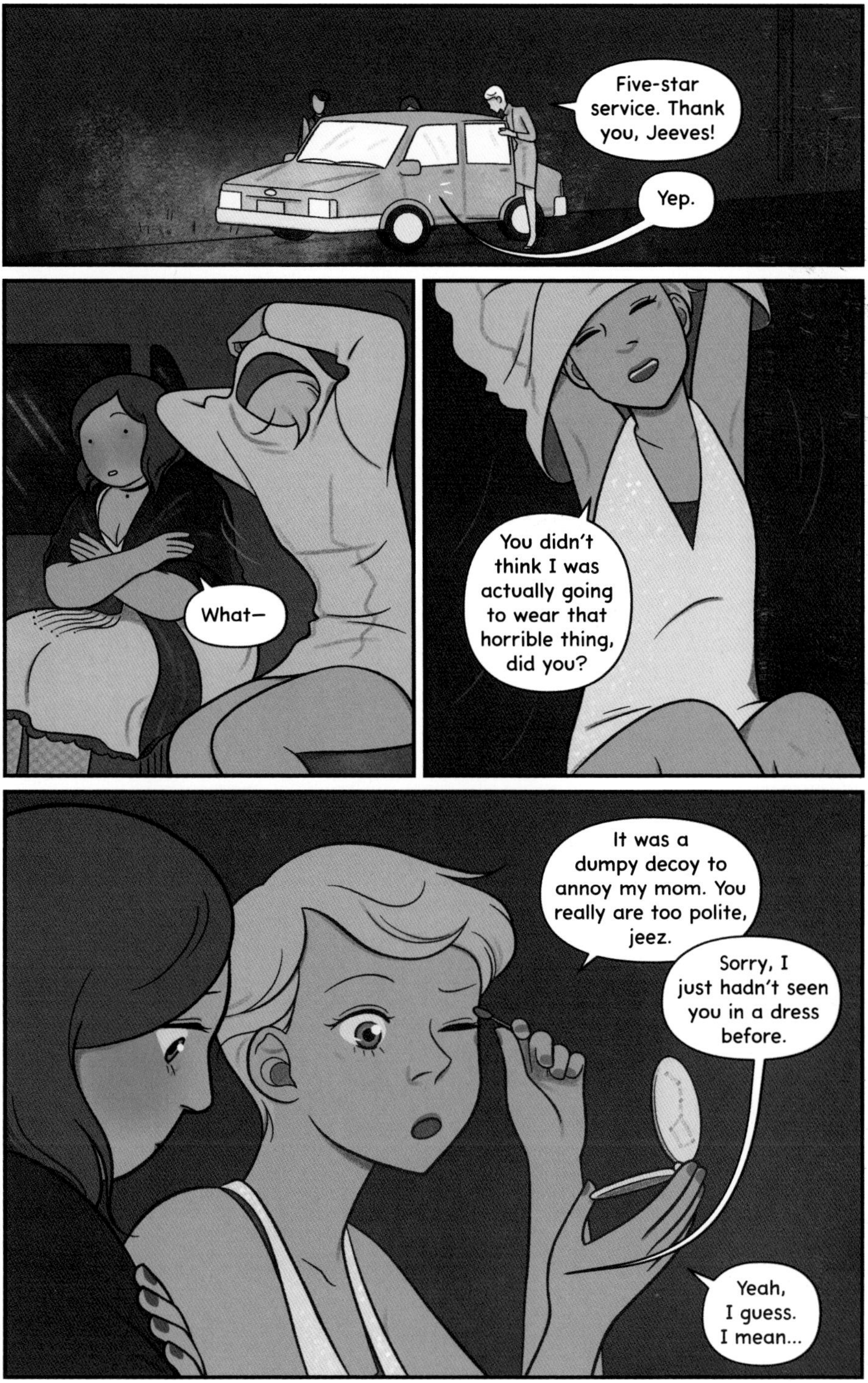
Five-star service. Thank you, Jeeves!
Yep.
What—
You didn't think I was actually going to wear that horrible thing, did you?
It was a dumpy decoy to annoy my mom. You really are too polite, jeez.
Sorry, I just hadn't seen you in a dress before.
Yeah, I guess. I mean...

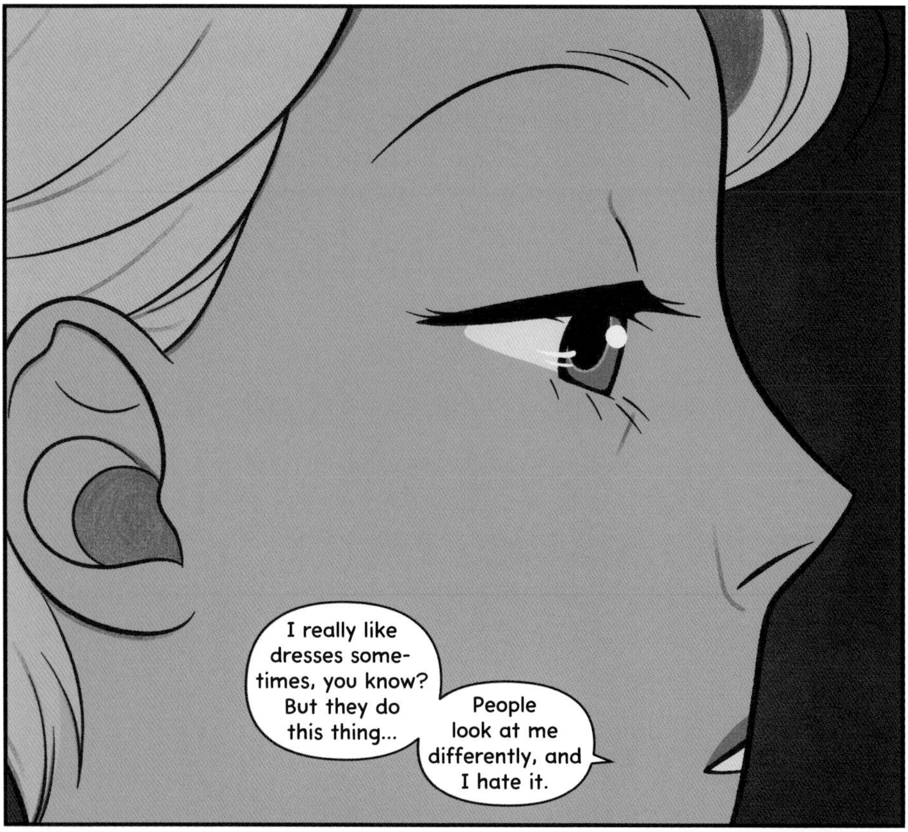
I really like dresses some-times, you know? But they do this thing...
People look at me differently, and I hate it.

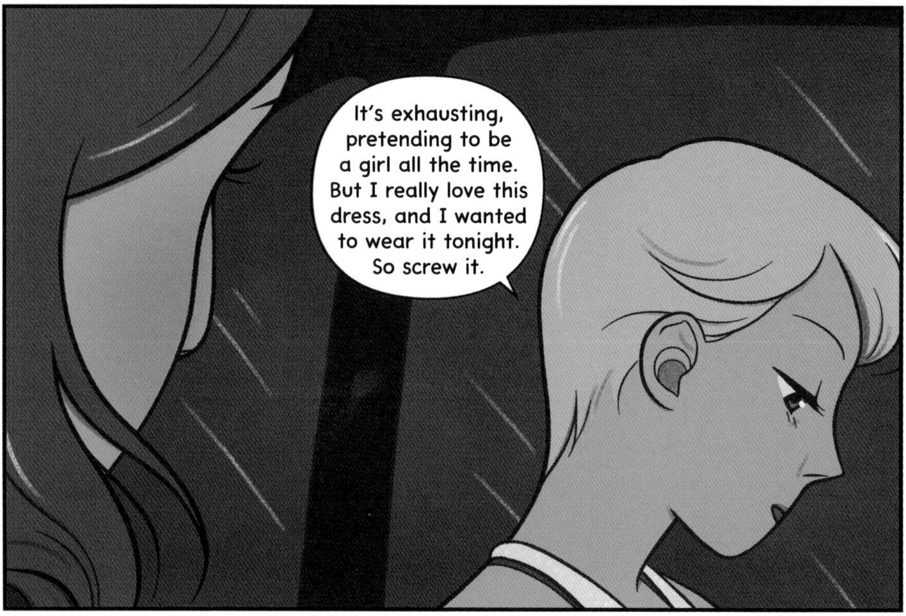
It's exhausting, pretending to be a girl all the time. But I really love this dress, and I wanted to wear it tonight. So screw it.

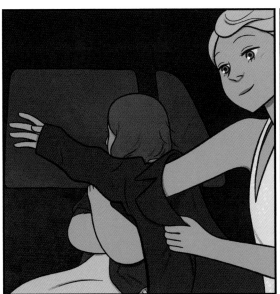

I couldn't believe what you did with this dress, April.

It's awesome. Thanks.

Really? You like it that much?

I'm so glad.

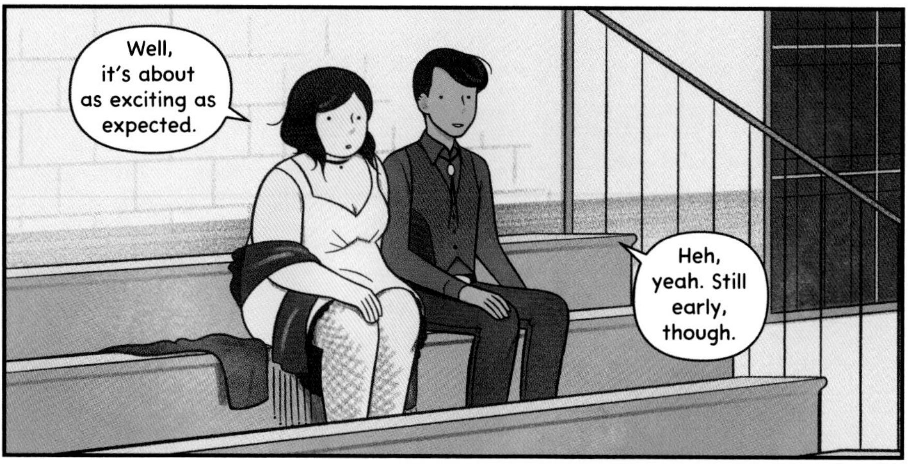
Well, it's about as exciting as expected.
Heh, yeah. Still early, though.

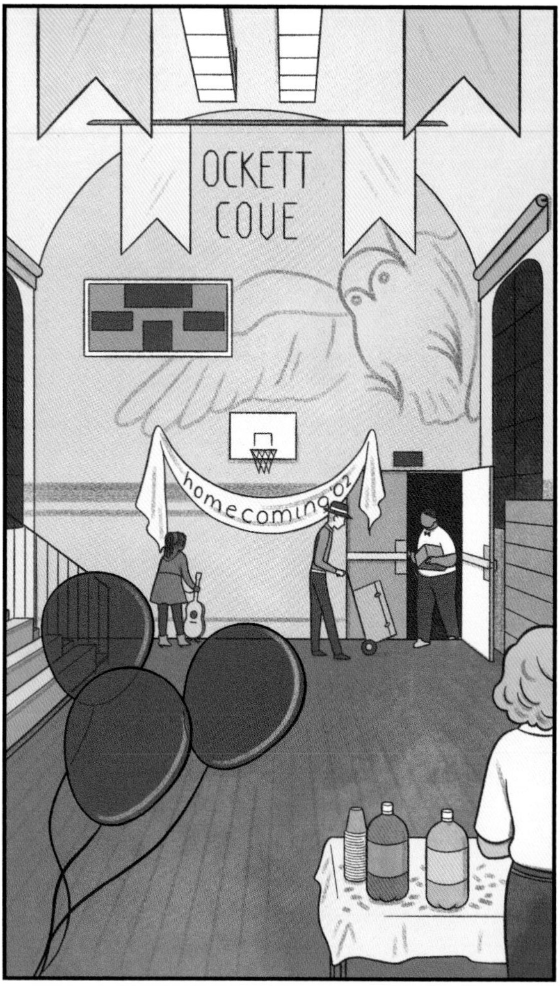
OCKETT COVE
homecoming '02

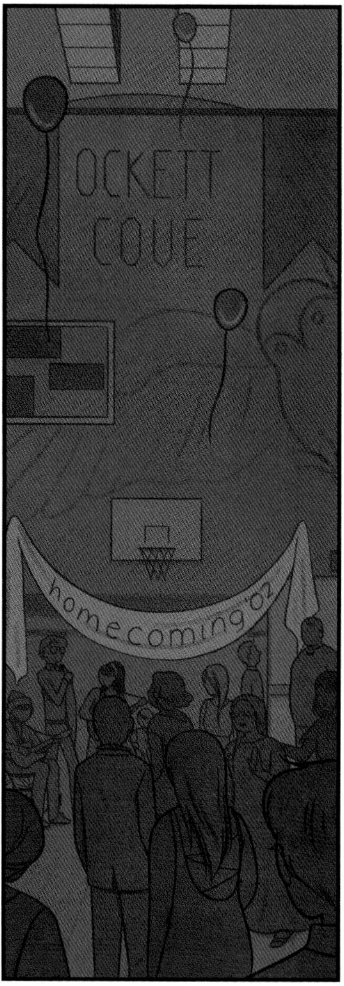
OCKETT COVE
homecoming '02

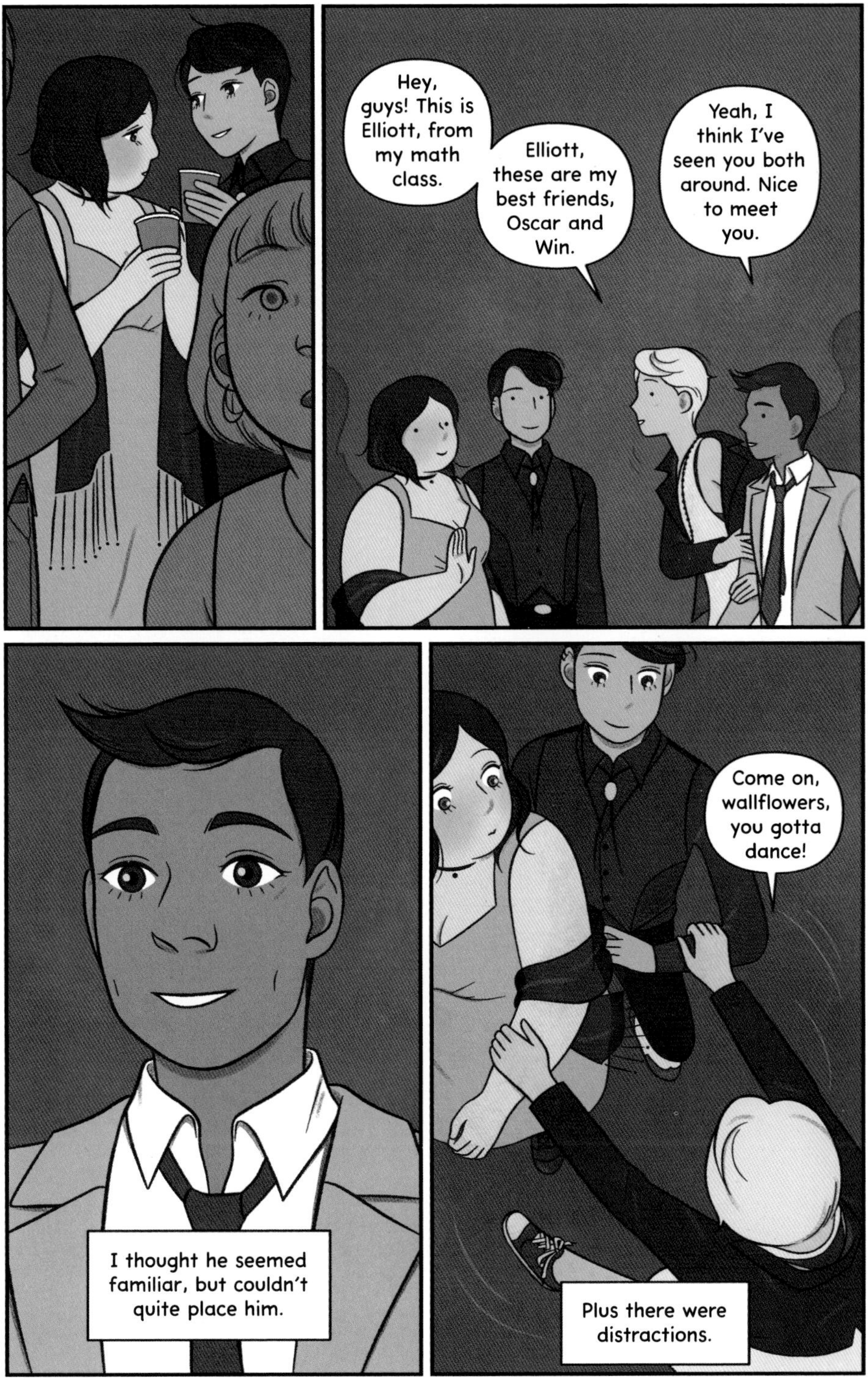
Hey, guys! This is Elliott, from my math class.
Elliott, these are my best friends, Oscar and Win.
Yeah, I think I've seen you both around. Nice to meet you.
I thought he seemed familiar, but couldn't quite place him.
Come on, wallflowers, you gotta dance!
Plus there were distractions.

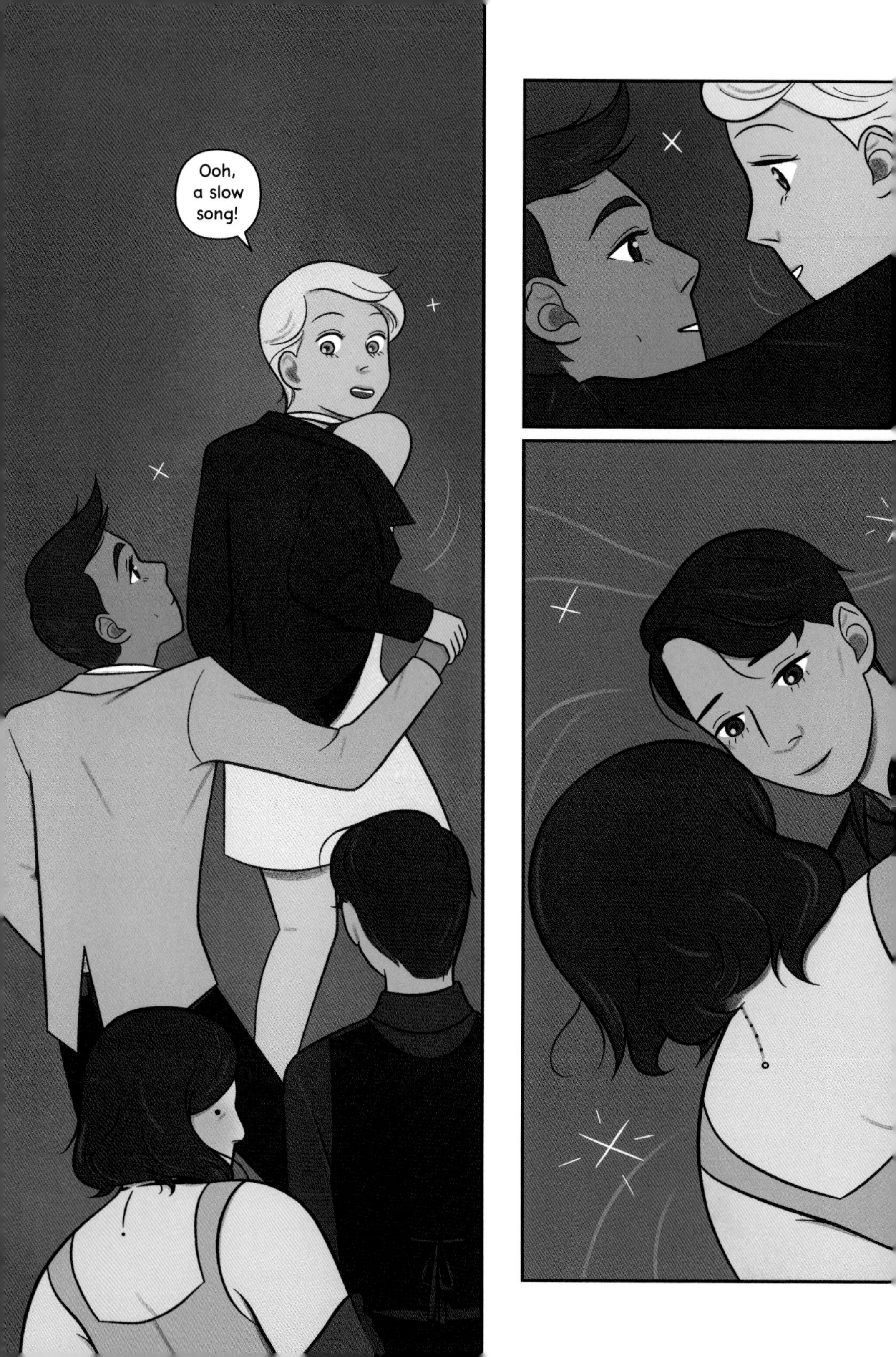
Ooh, a slow song!

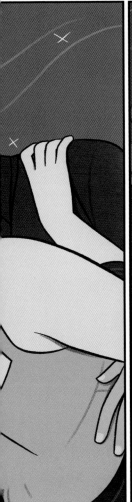

We came together without thinking, like it was the most natural thing we could do.

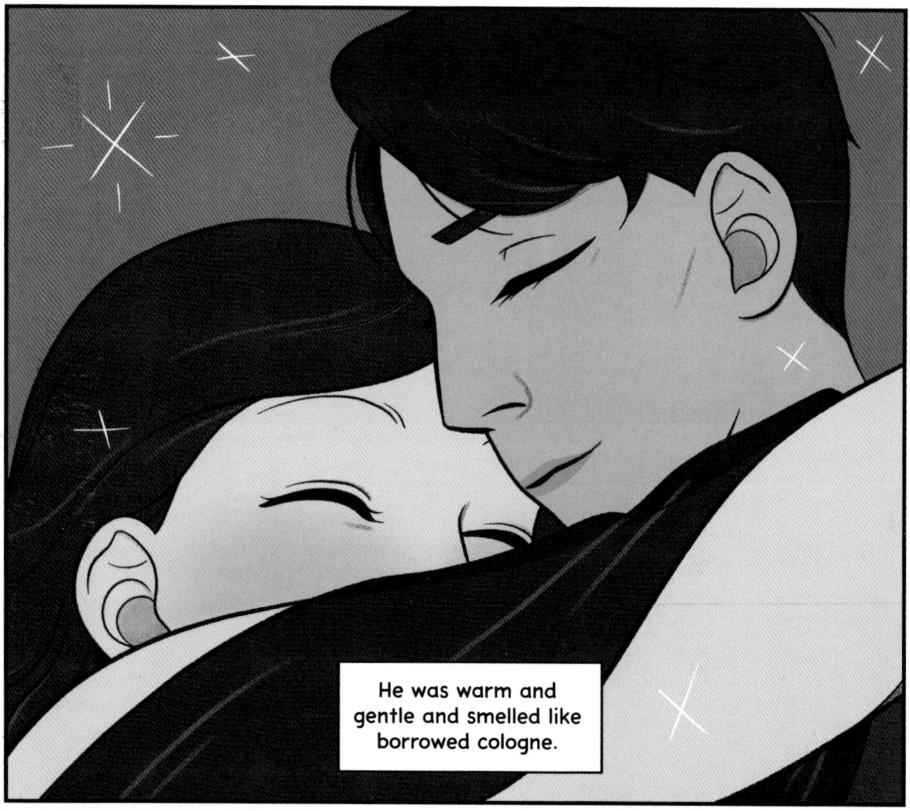
He was warm and gentle and smelled like borrowed cologne.
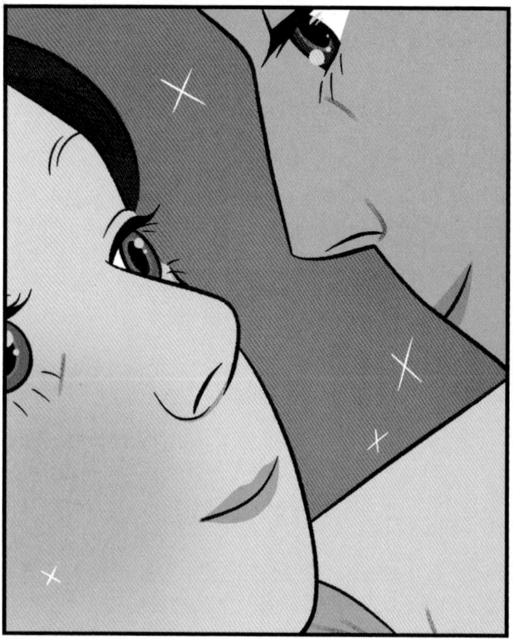
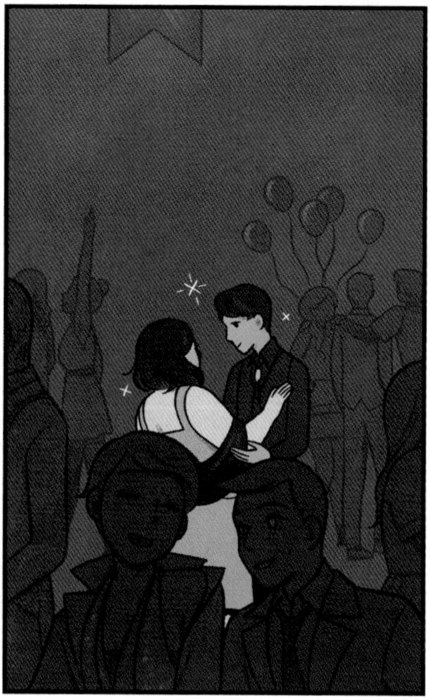

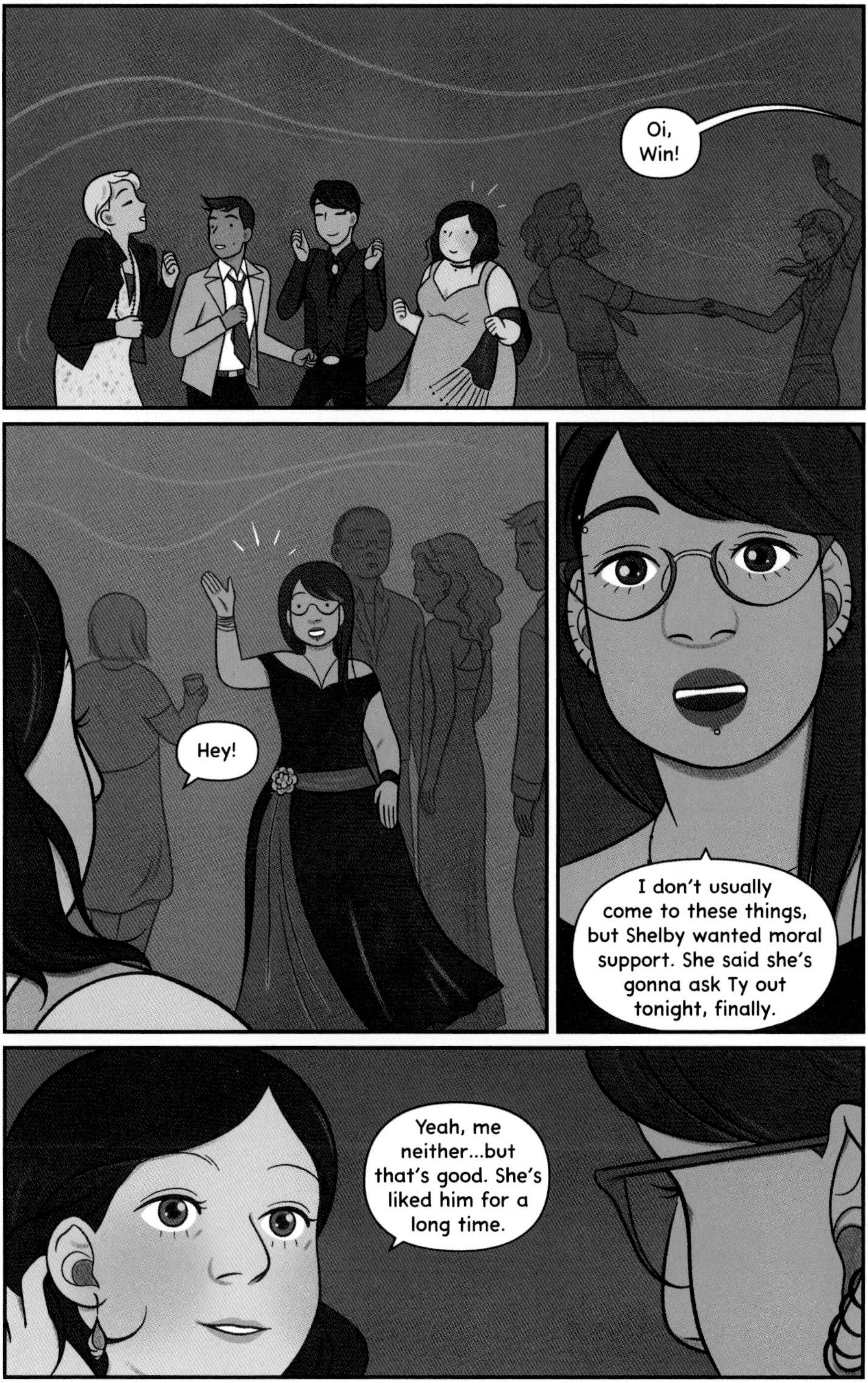
Oi, Win!
Hey!
I don't usually come to these things, but Shelby wanted moral support. She said she's gonna ask Ty out tonight, finally.
Yeah, me neither...but that's good. She's liked him for a long time.

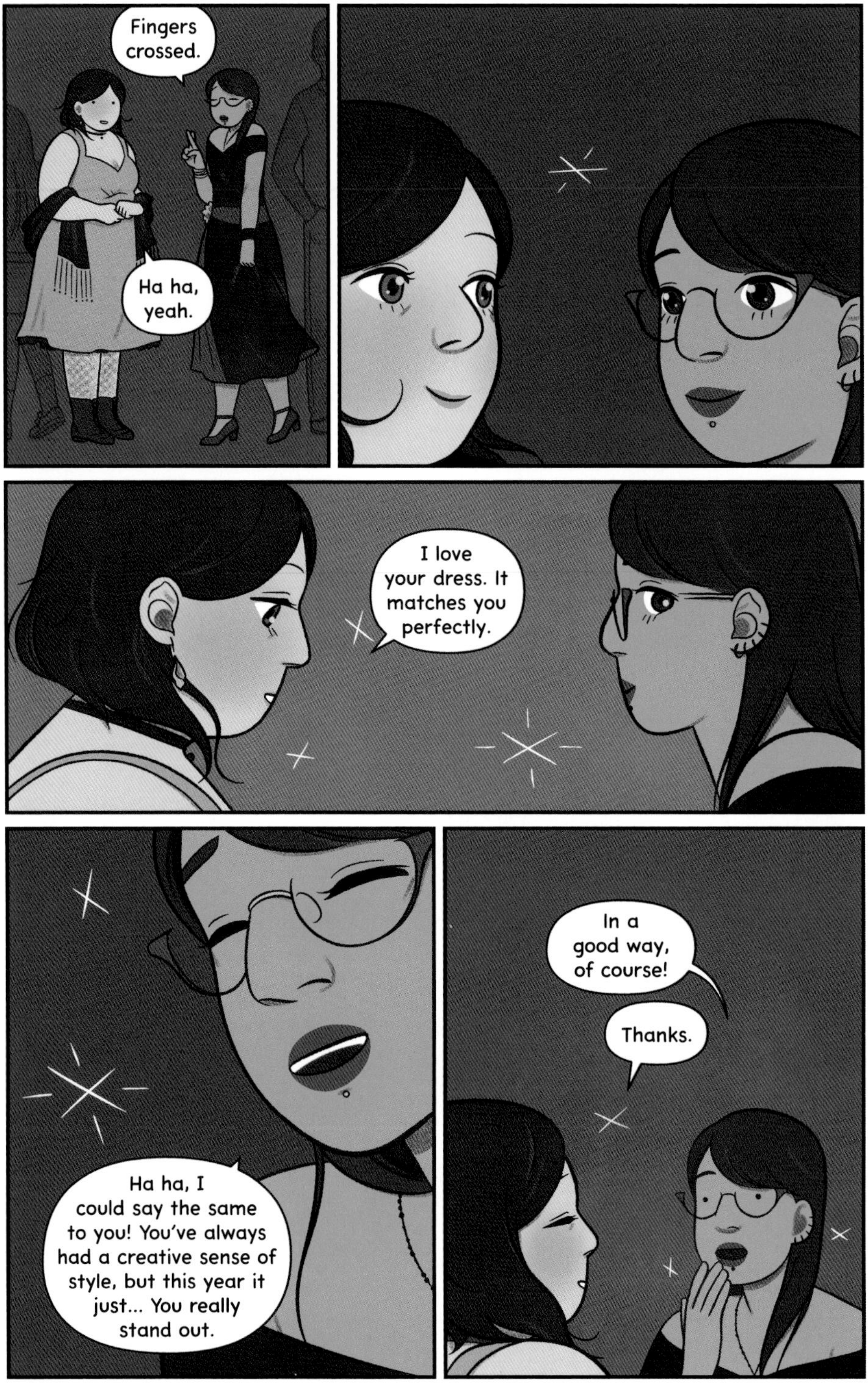
Fingers crossed.
Ha ha, yeah.
I love your dress. It matches you perfectly.
Ha ha, I could say the same to you! You've always had a creative sense of style, but this year it just... You really stand out.
In a good way, of course!
Thanks.

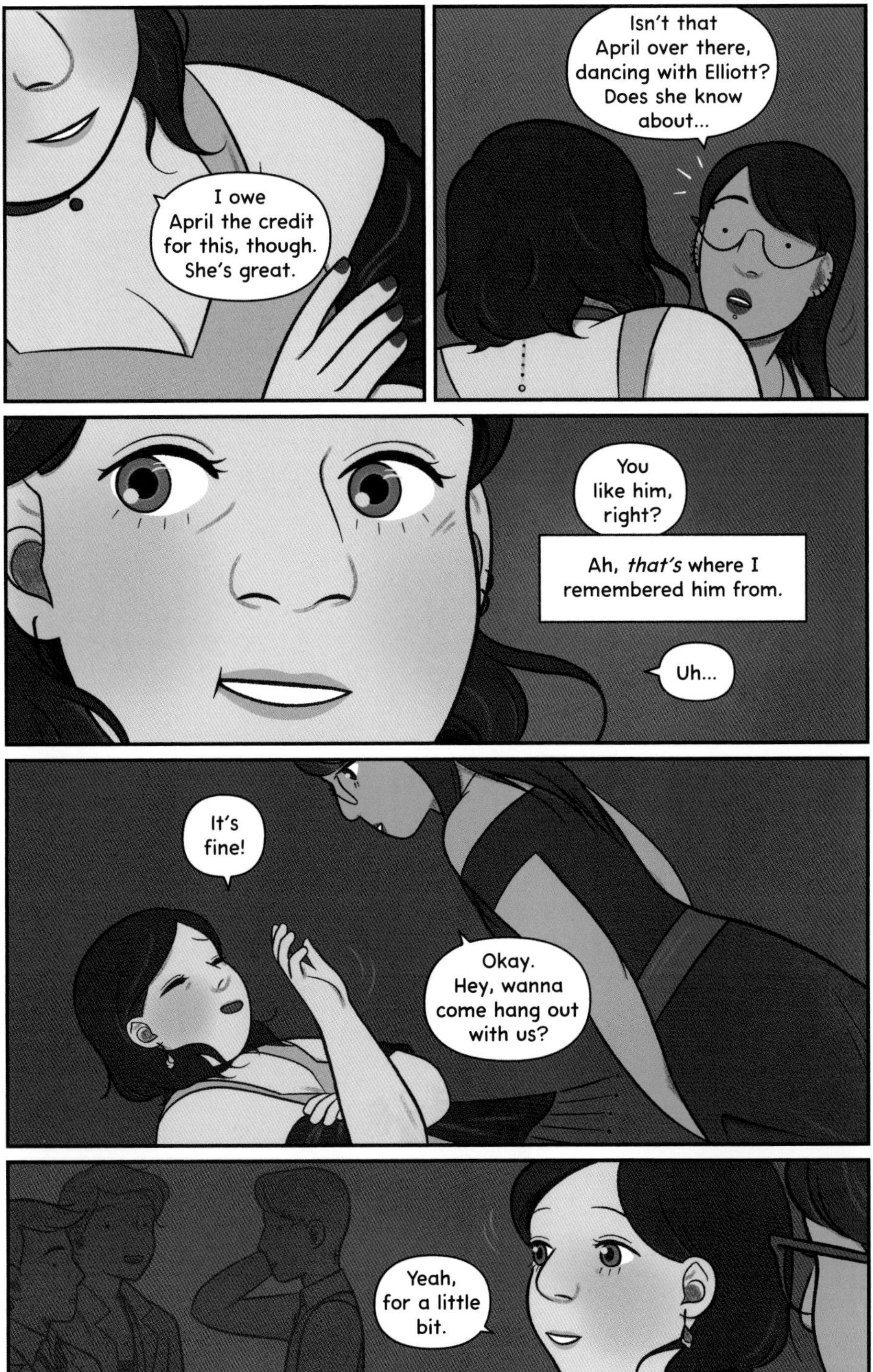
I owe April the credit for this, though. She's great.
Isn't that April over there, dancing with Elliott? Does she know about...
You like him, right?
Ah, *that's* where I remembered him from.
Uh...
It's fine!
Okay. Hey, wanna come hang out with us?
Yeah, for a little bit.

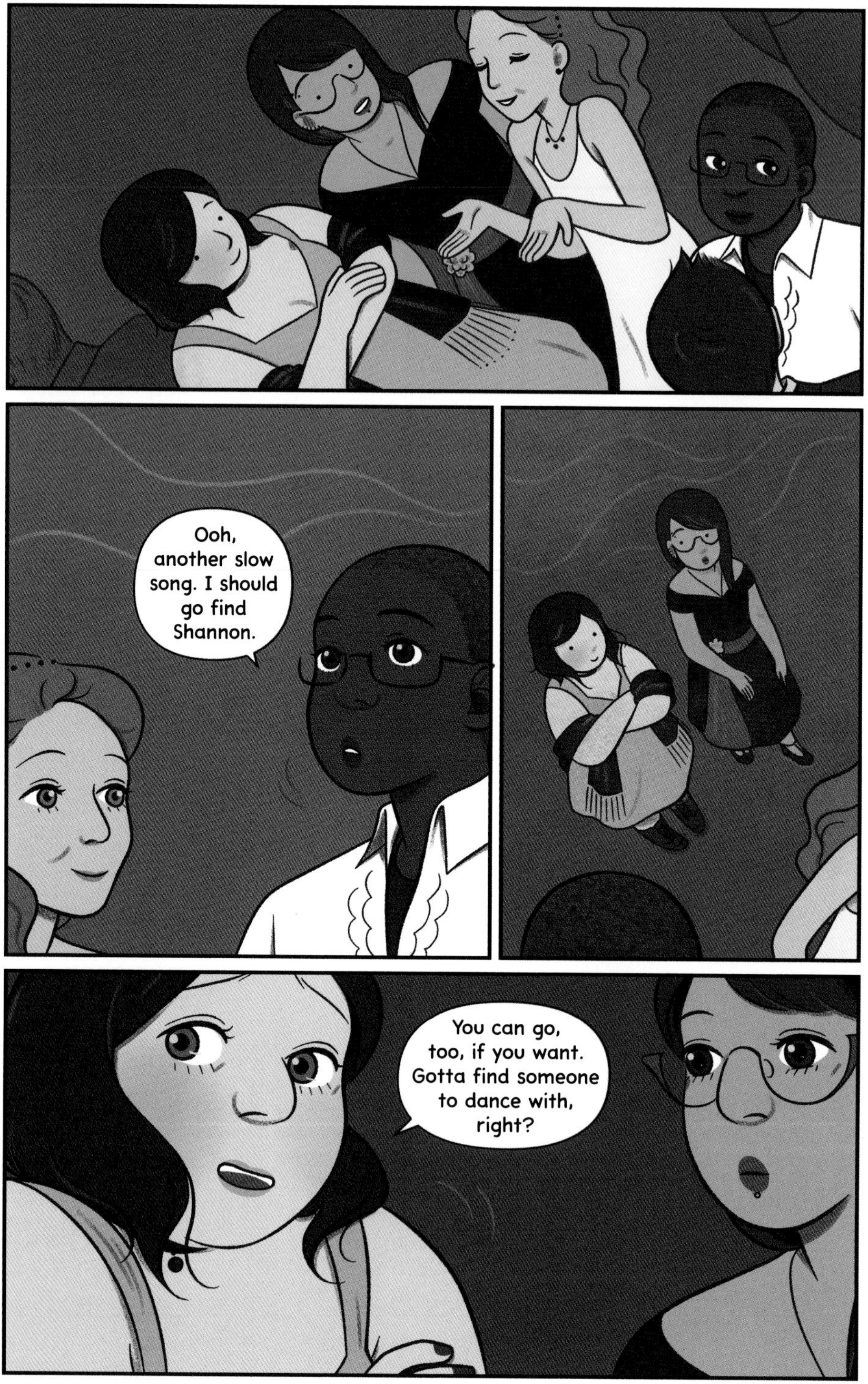
Ooh, another slow song. I should go find Shannon.
You can go, too, if you want. Gotta find someone to dance with, right?

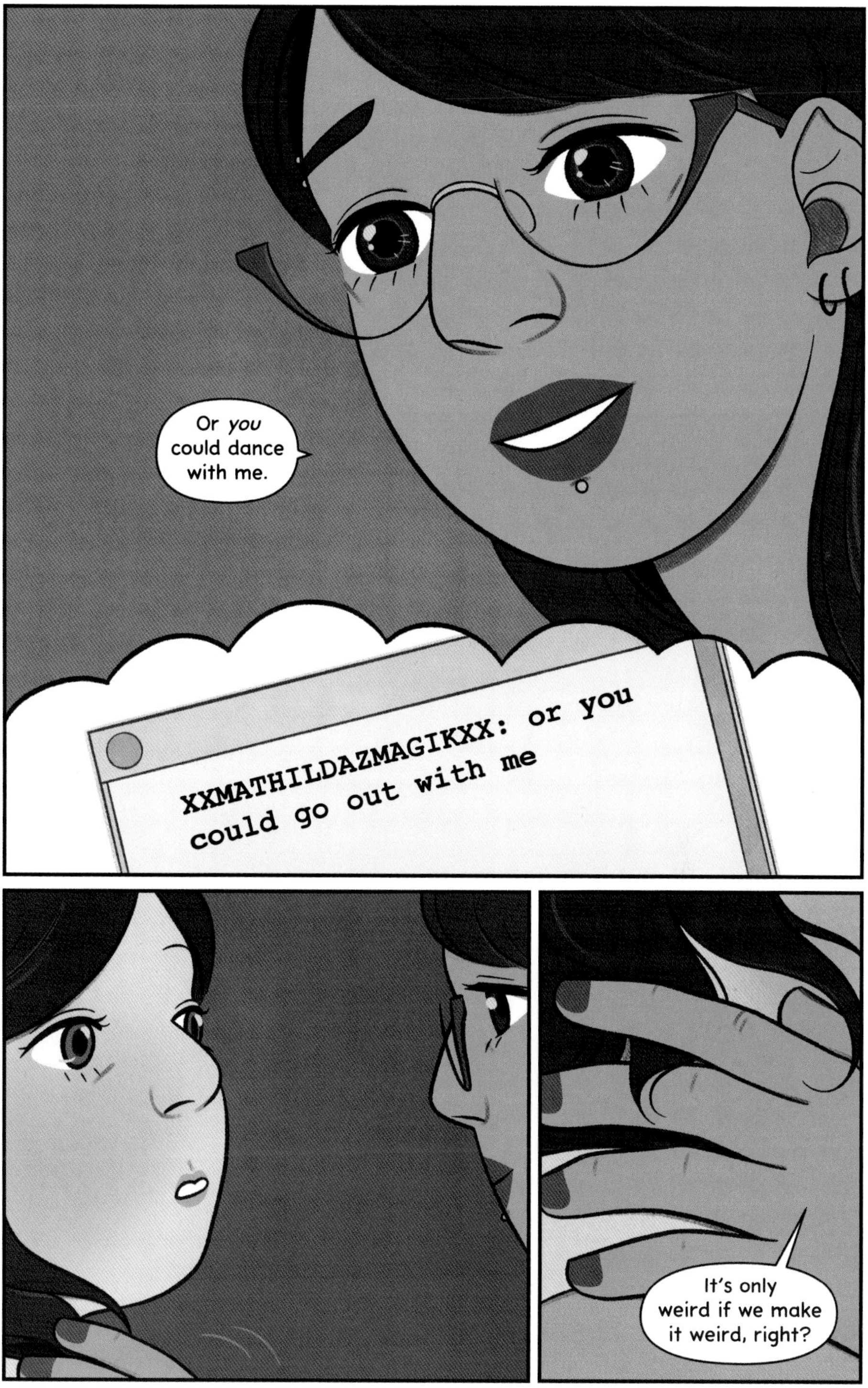
Or *you* could dance with me.
XXMATHILDAZMAGIKXX: or you could go out with me
It's only weird if we make it weird, right?

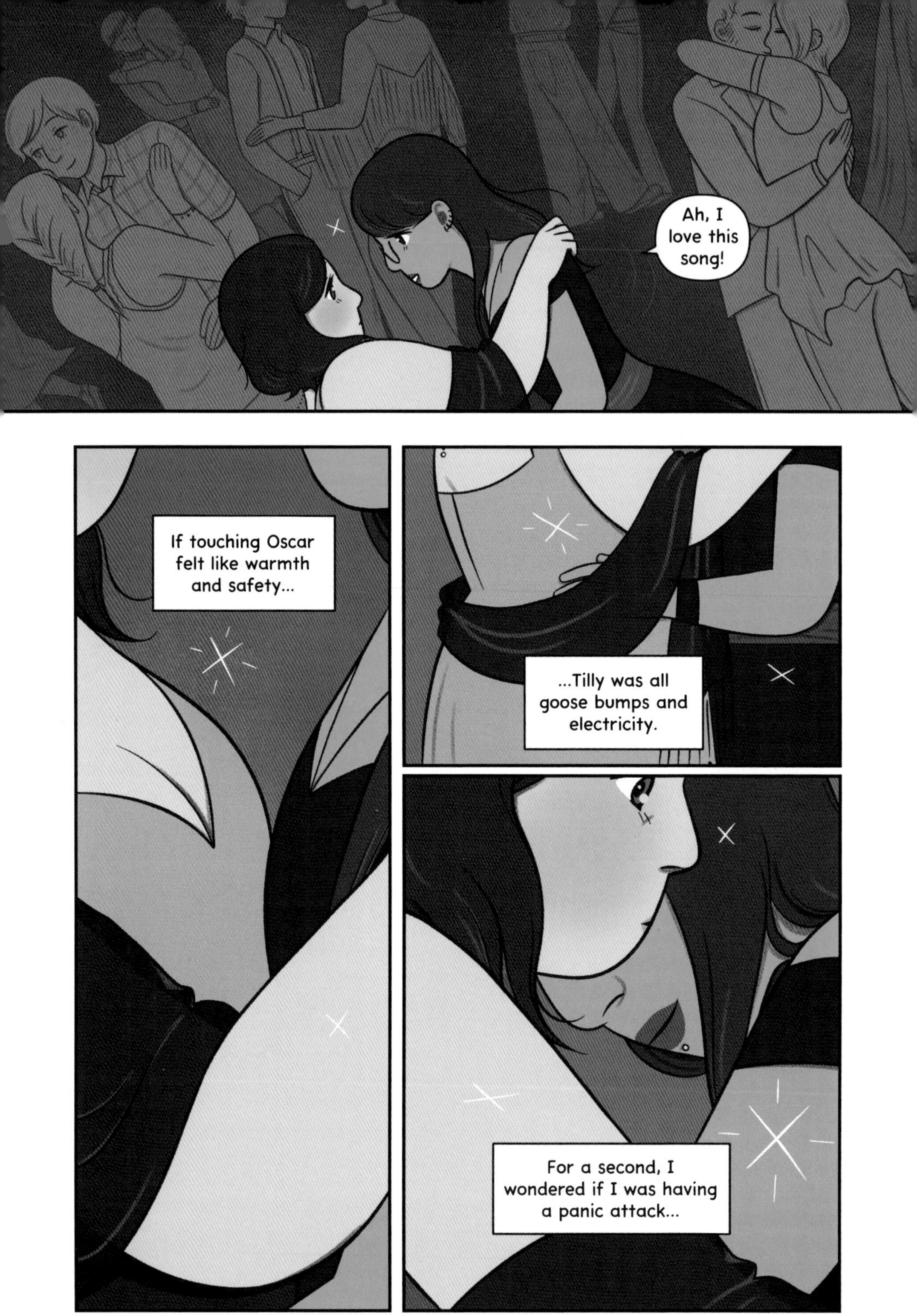
Ah, I love this song!
If touching Oscar felt like warmth and safety...
...Tilly was all goose bumps and electricity.
For a second, I wondered if I was having a panic attack...

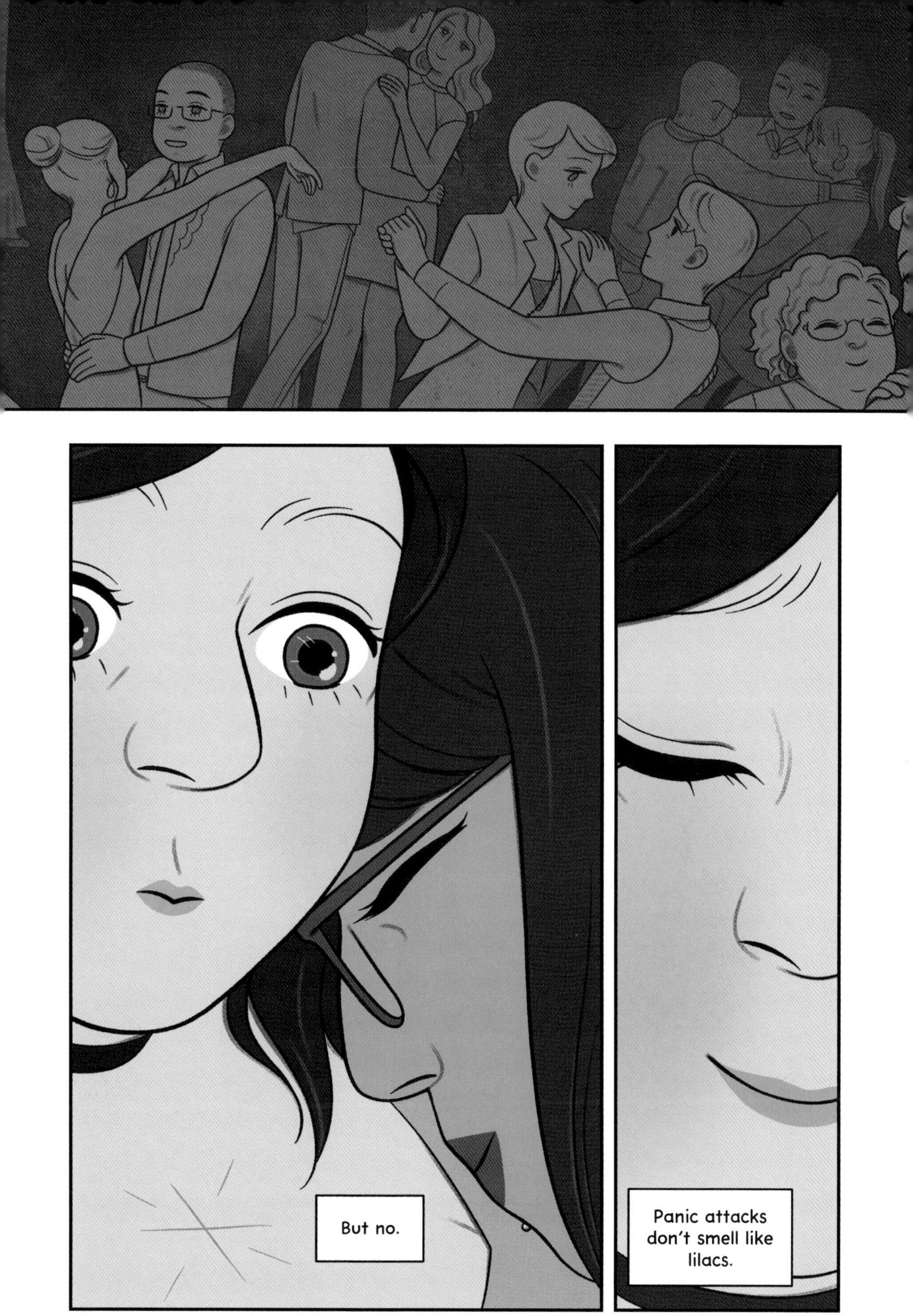
But no.
Panic attacks don't smell like lilacs.

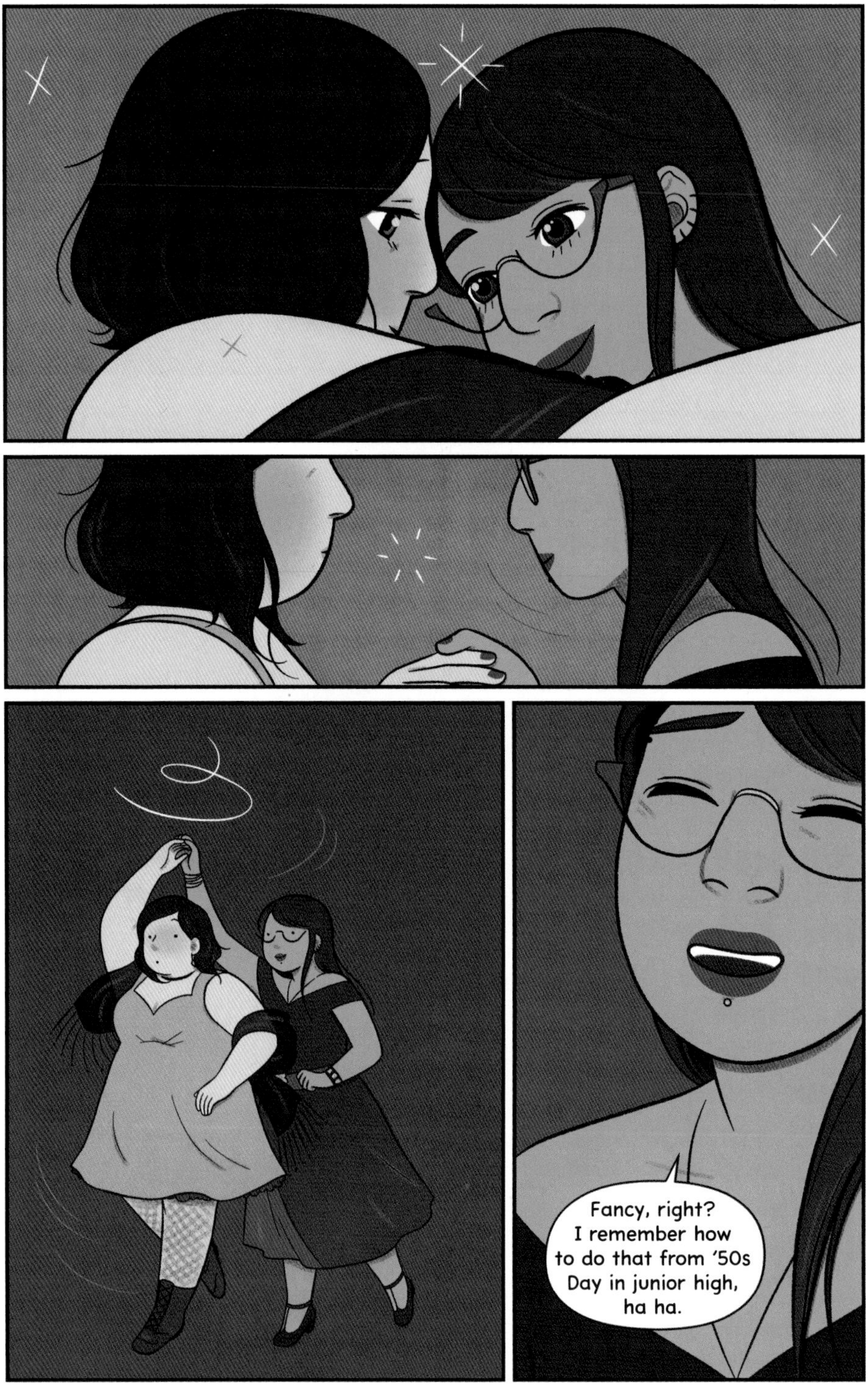
Fancy, right? I remember how to do that from '50s Day in junior high, ha ha.

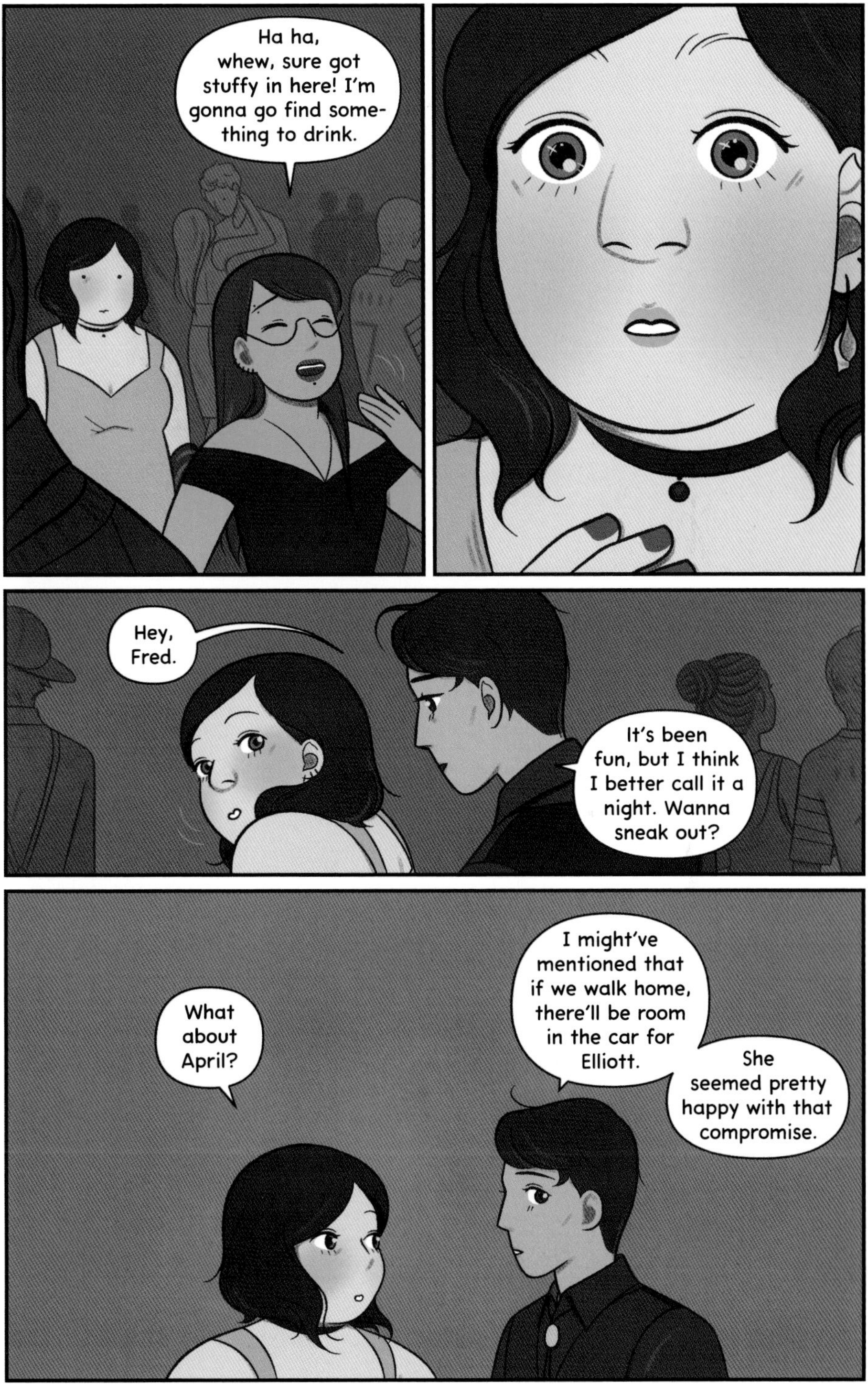
Ha ha, whew, sure got stuffy in here! I'm gonna go find some-thing to drink.
Hey, Fred.
It's been fun, but I think I better call it a night. Wanna sneak out?
What about April?
I might've mentioned that if we walk home, there'll be room in the car for Elliott.
She seemed pretty happy with that compromise.

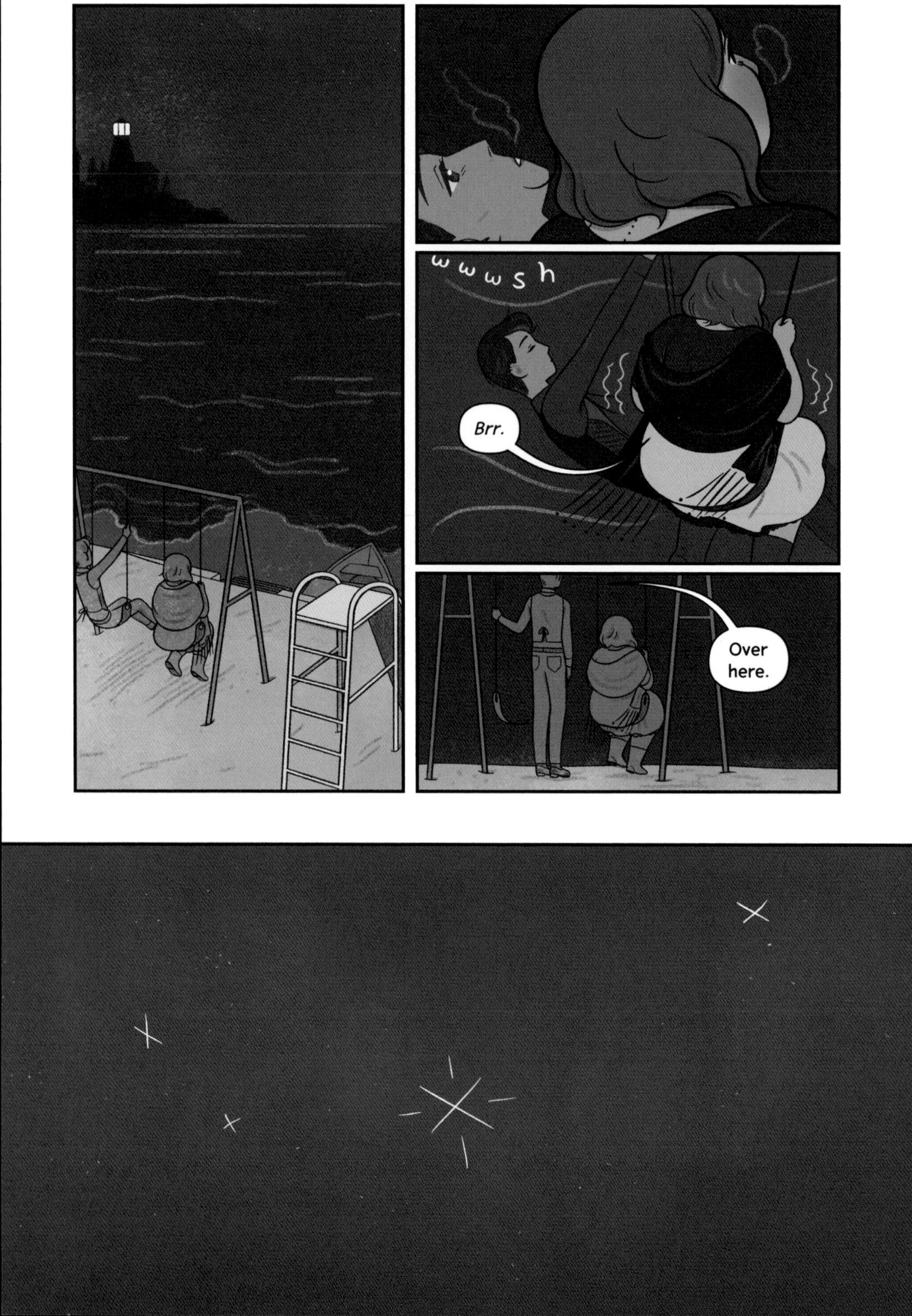
wwwsh
Brr.
Over here.

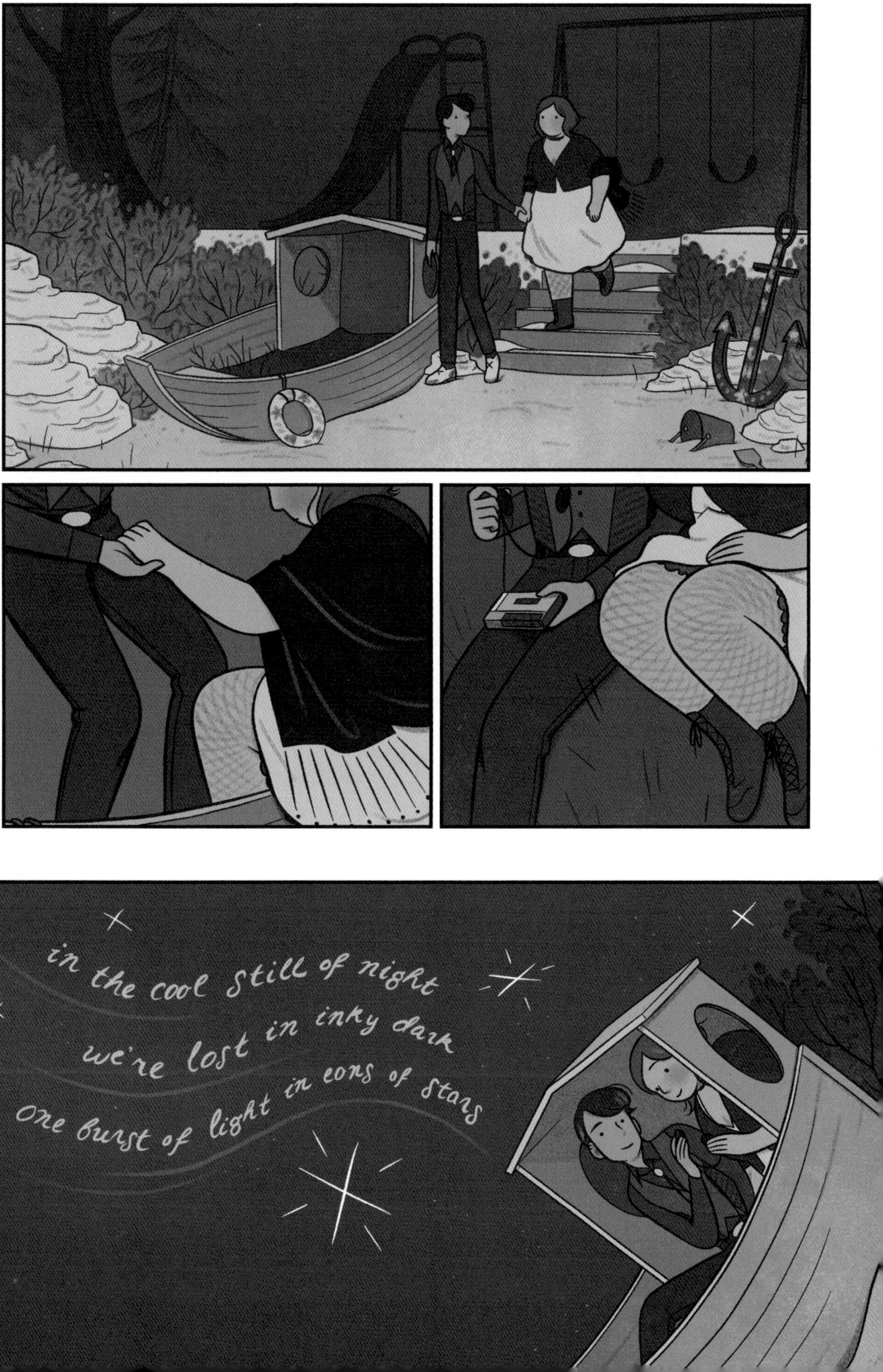
in the cool still of night
we're lost in inky dark
one burst of light in eons of stars

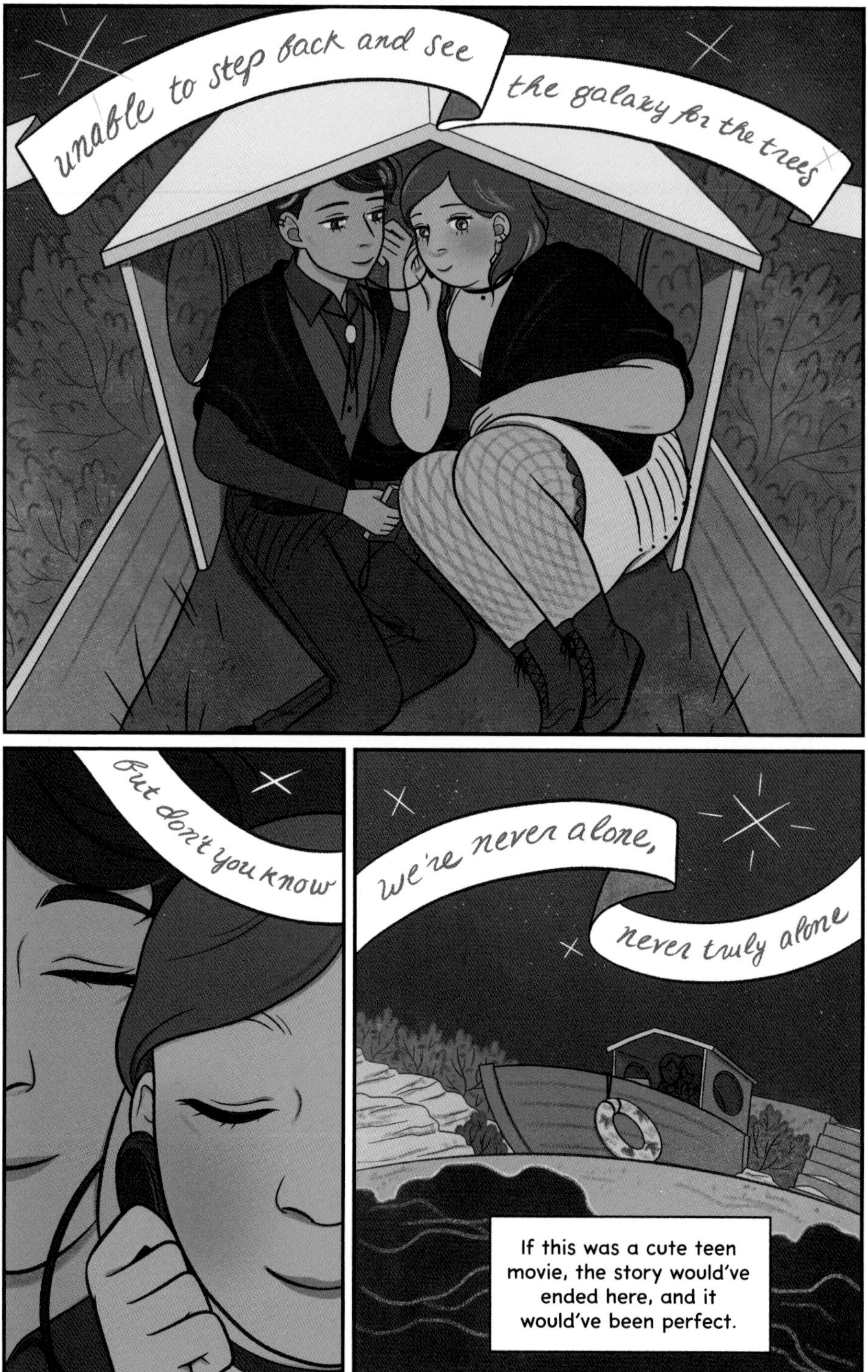
unable to step back and see
the galaxy for the trees
But don't you know
we're never alone,
never truly alone
If this was a cute teen movie, the story would've ended here, and it would've been perfect.

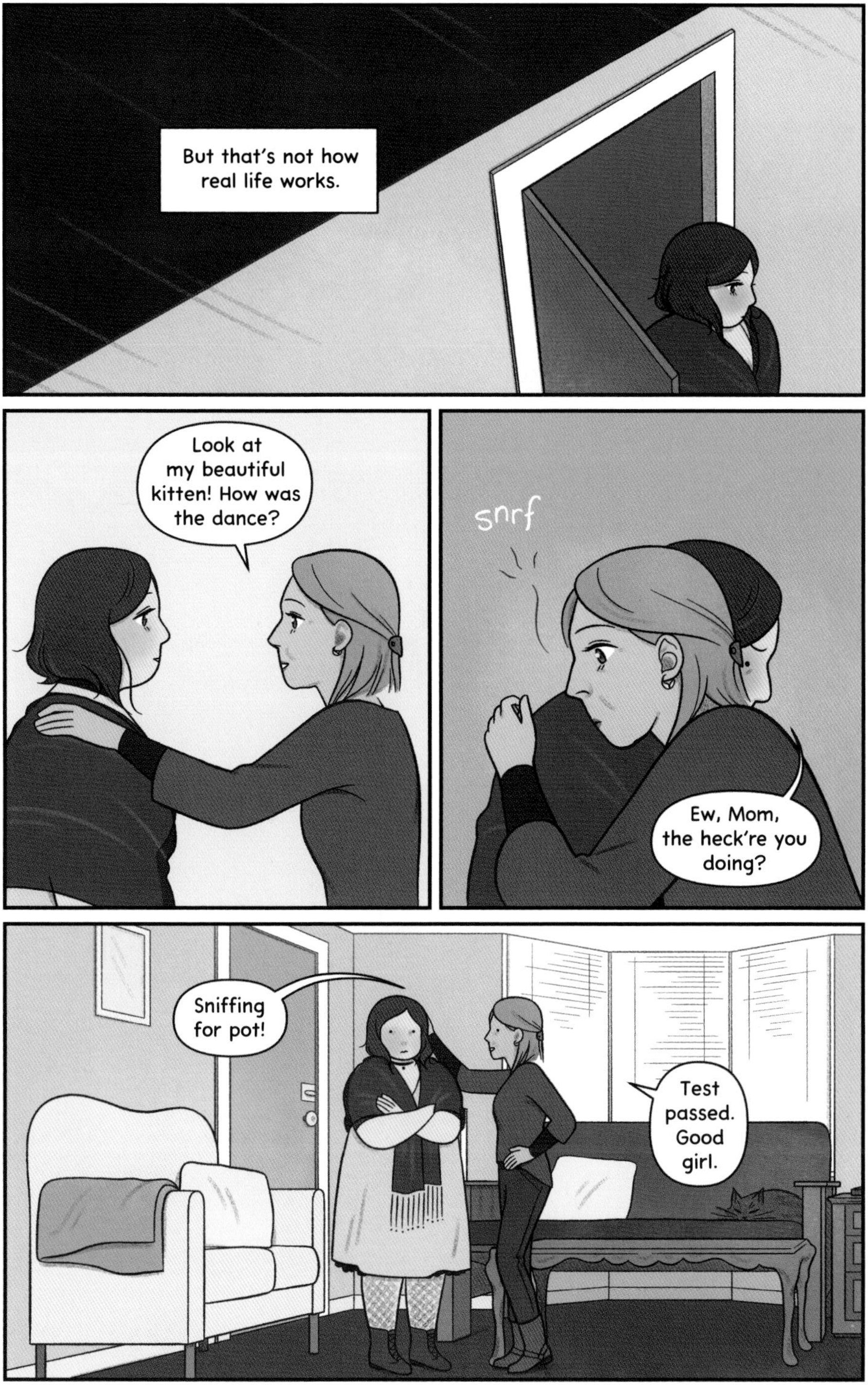
But that's not how real life works.
Look at my beautiful kitten! How was the dance?
snrf
Ew, Mom, the heck're you doing?
Sniffing for pot!
Test passed. Good girl.

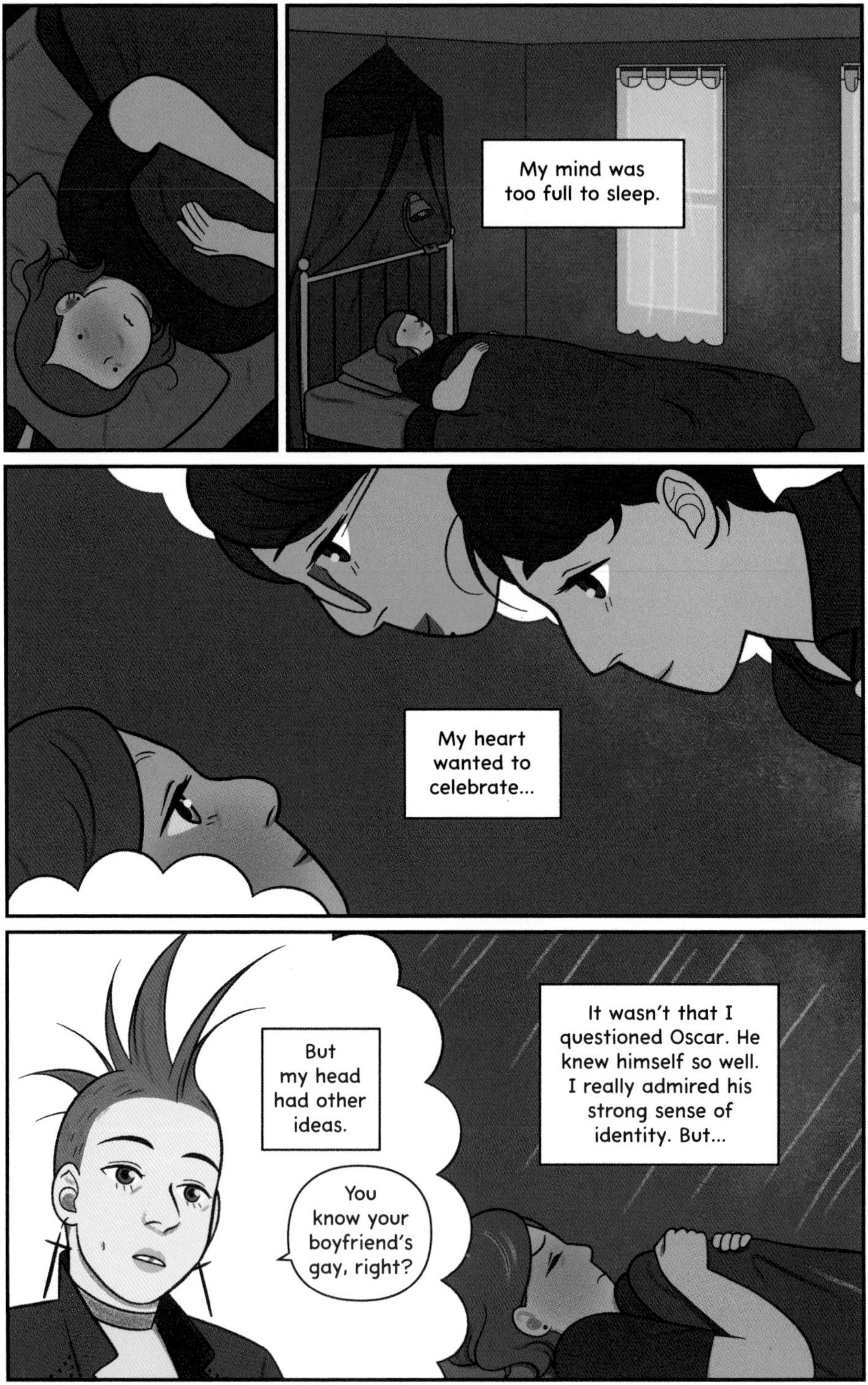
My mind was too full to sleep.
My heart wanted to celebrate...
But my head had other ideas.
You know your boyfriend's gay, right?
It wasn't that I questioned Oscar. He knew himself so well. I really admired his strong sense of identity. But...

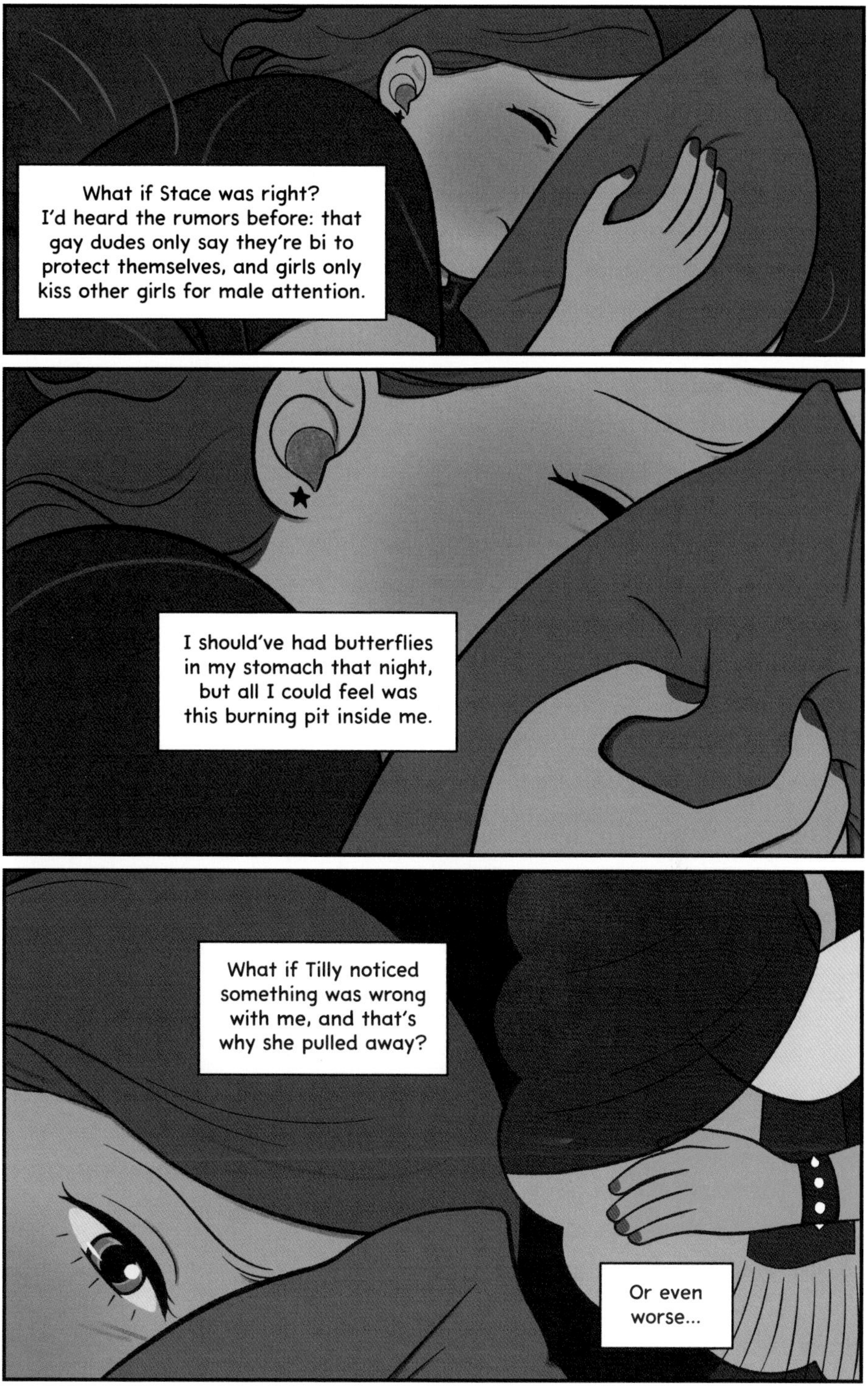
What if Stace was right?
I'd heard the rumors before: that gay dudes only say they're bi to protect themselves, and girls only kiss other girls for male attention.
I should've had butterflies in my stomach that night, but all I could feel was this burning pit inside me.
What if Tilly noticed something was wrong with me, and that's why she pulled away?
Or even worse...

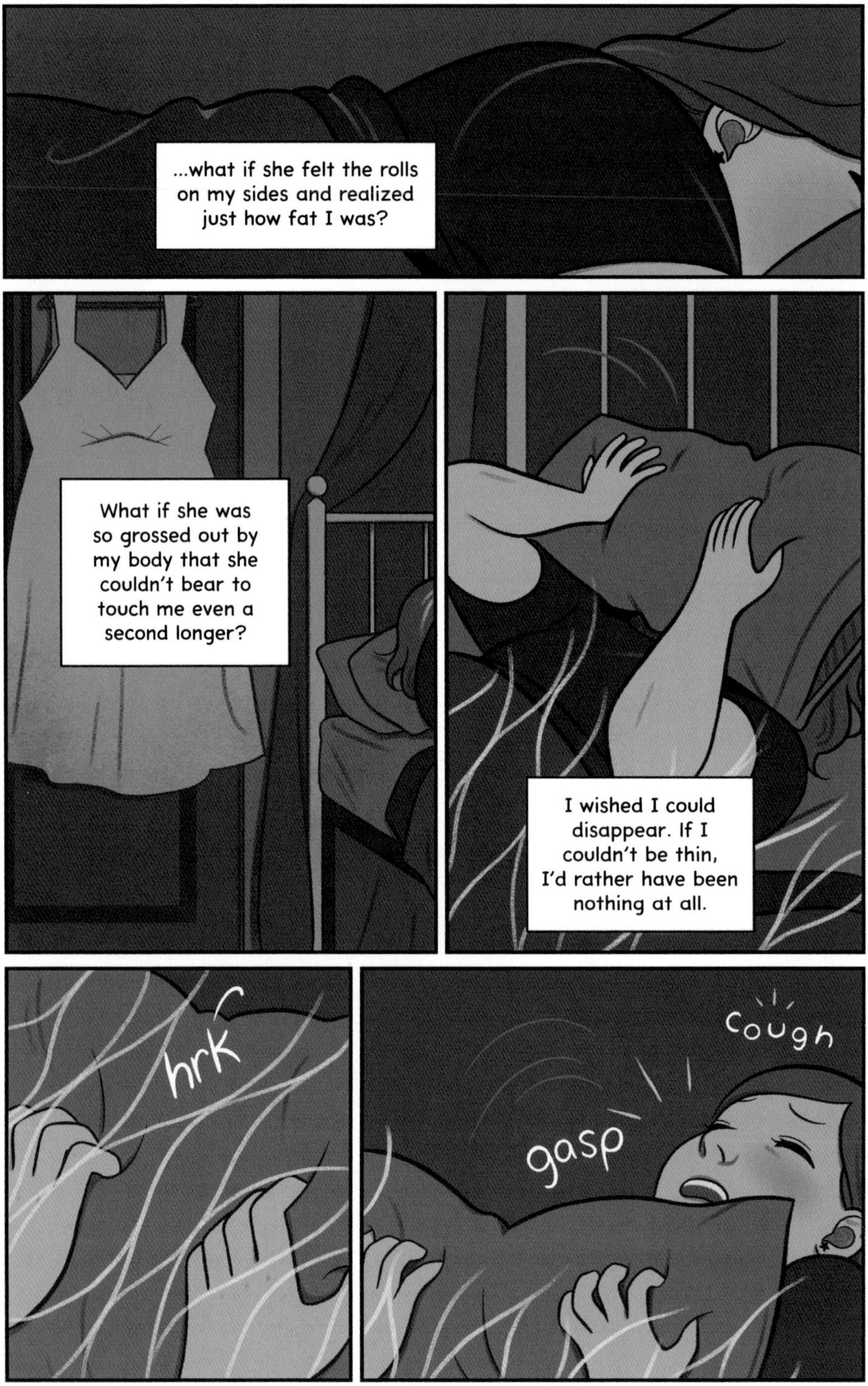
...what if she felt the rolls on my sides and realized just how fat I was?
What if she was so grossed out by my body that she couldn't bear to touch me even a second longer?
I wished I could disappear. If I couldn't be thin, I'd rather have been nothing at all.
hrk
cough
gasp

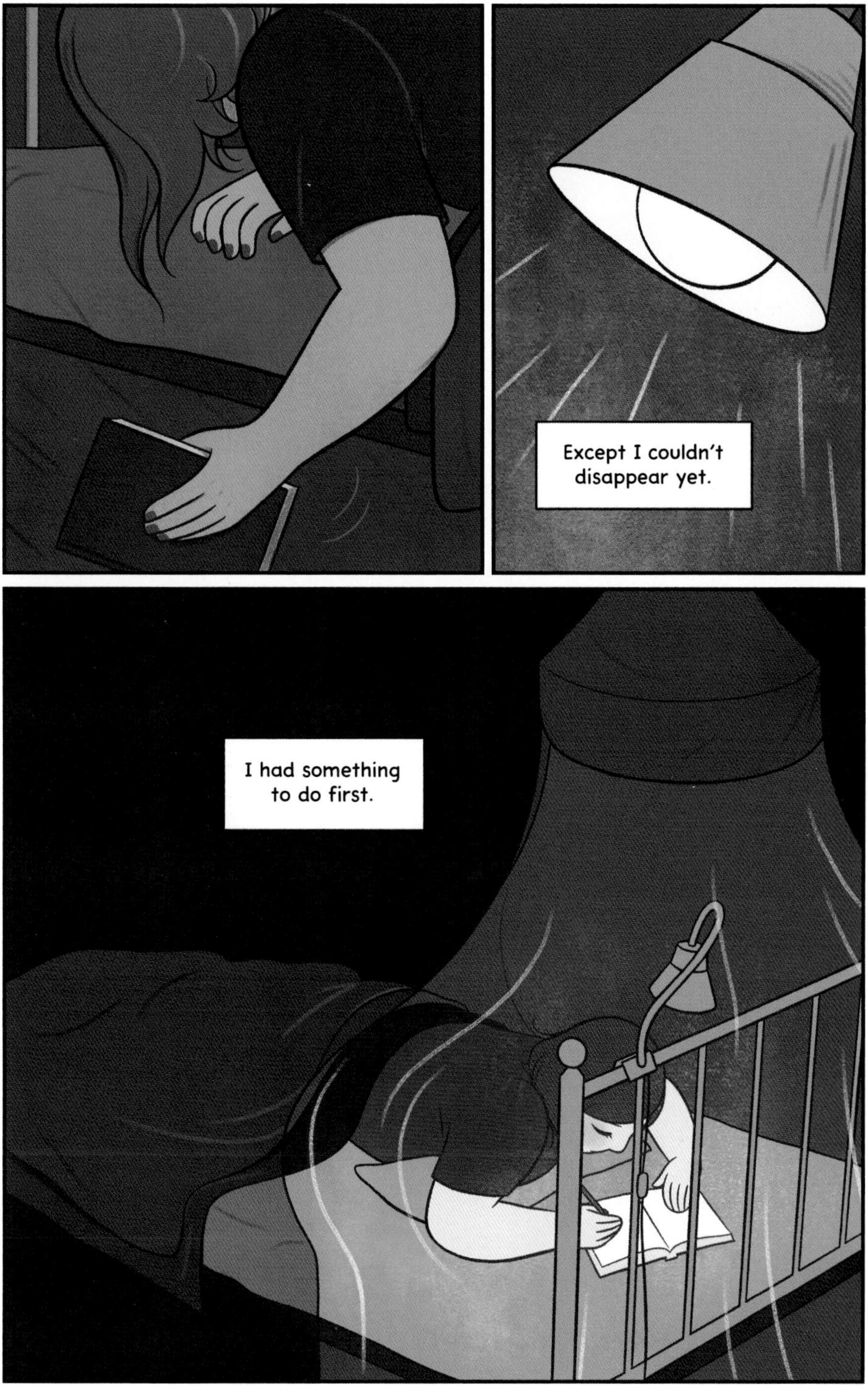
Except I couldn't
disappear yet.
I had something
to do first.

Oh, hey.

How long have you been in here? Did you skip class?

I'm always here to listen, you know.

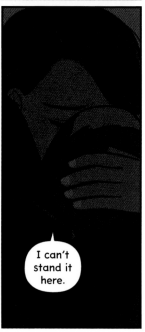

I can't stand it here.

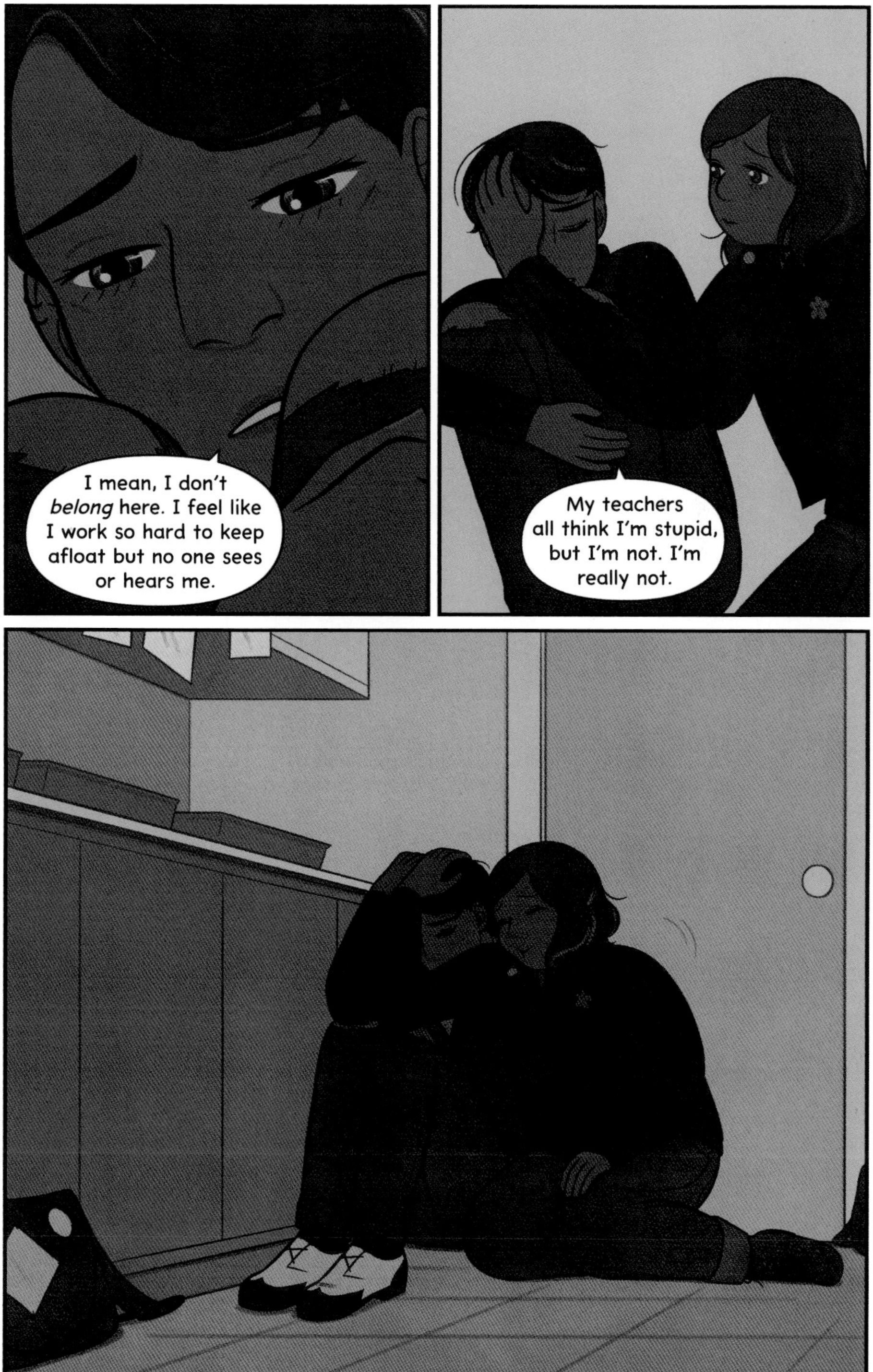
I mean, I don't *belong* here. I feel like I work so hard to keep afloat but no one sees or hears me.
My teachers all think I'm stupid, but I'm not. I'm really not.

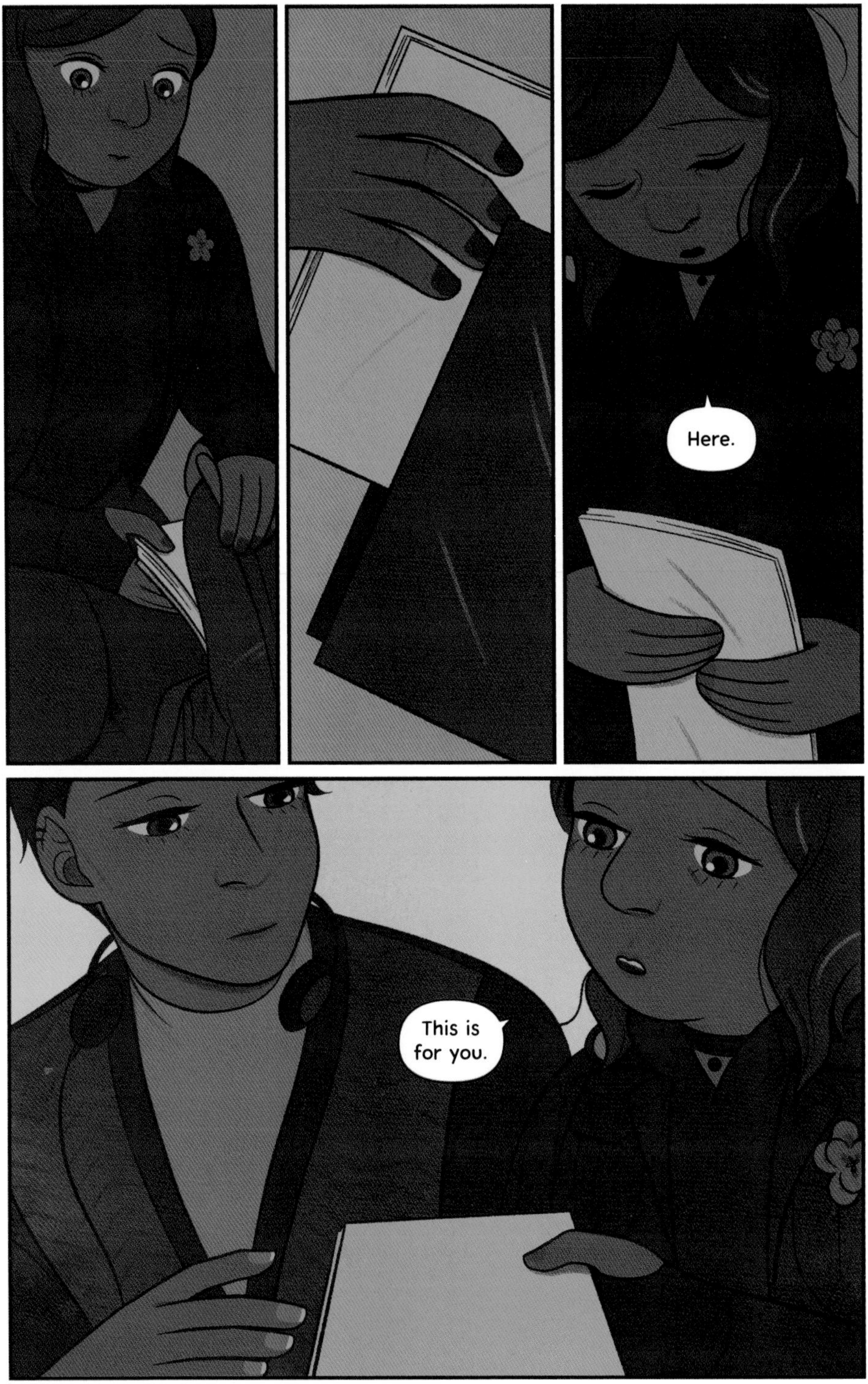
Here.
This is for you.

gutterglimmers III

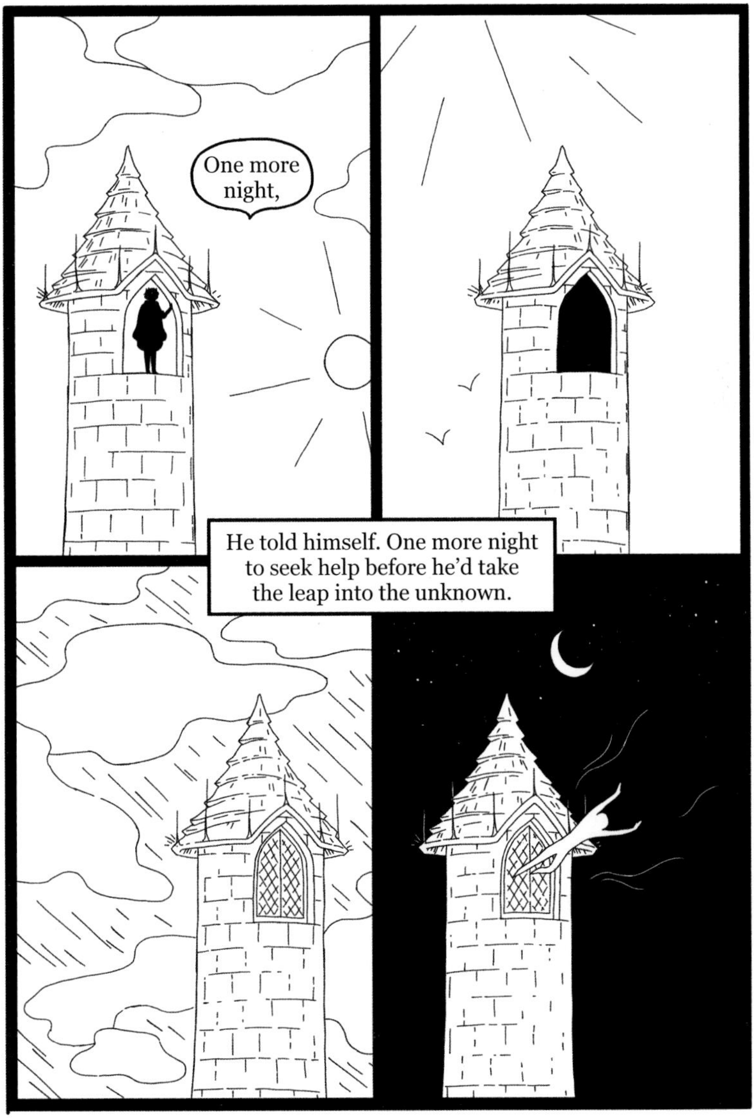
One more night,
He told himself. One more night to seek help before he'd take the leap into the unknown.

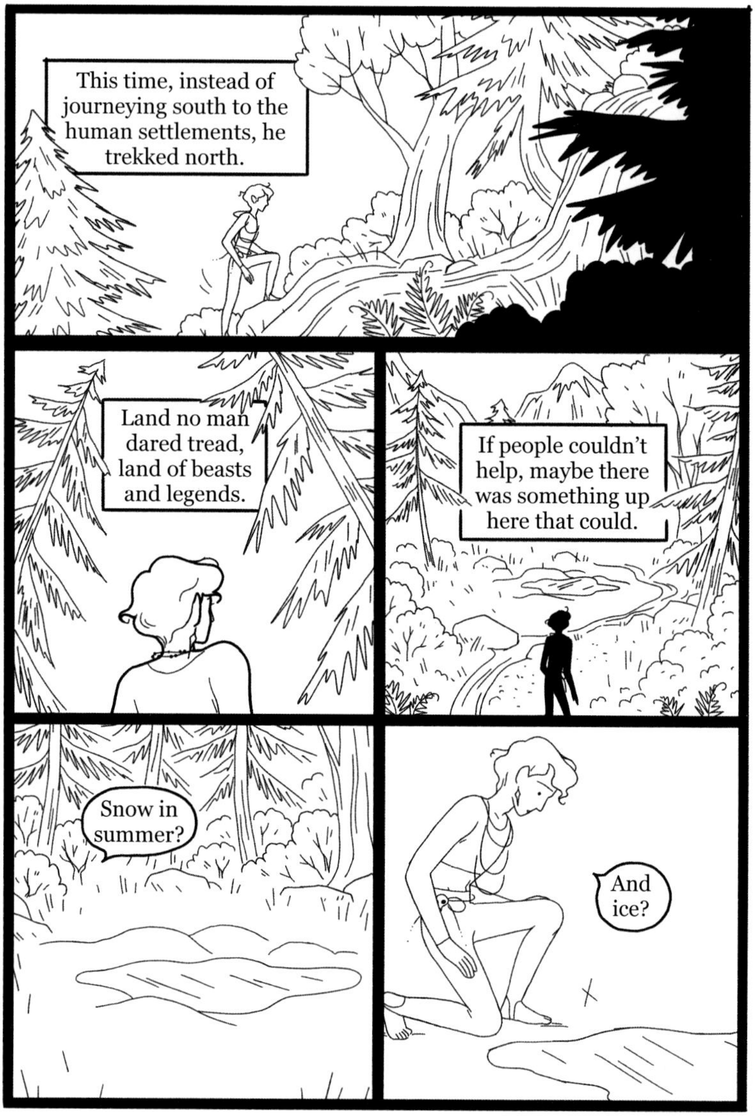
This time, instead of journeying south to the human settlements, he trekked north.
Land no man dared tread, land of beasts and legends.
If people couldn't help, maybe there was something up here that could.
Snow in summer?
And ice?

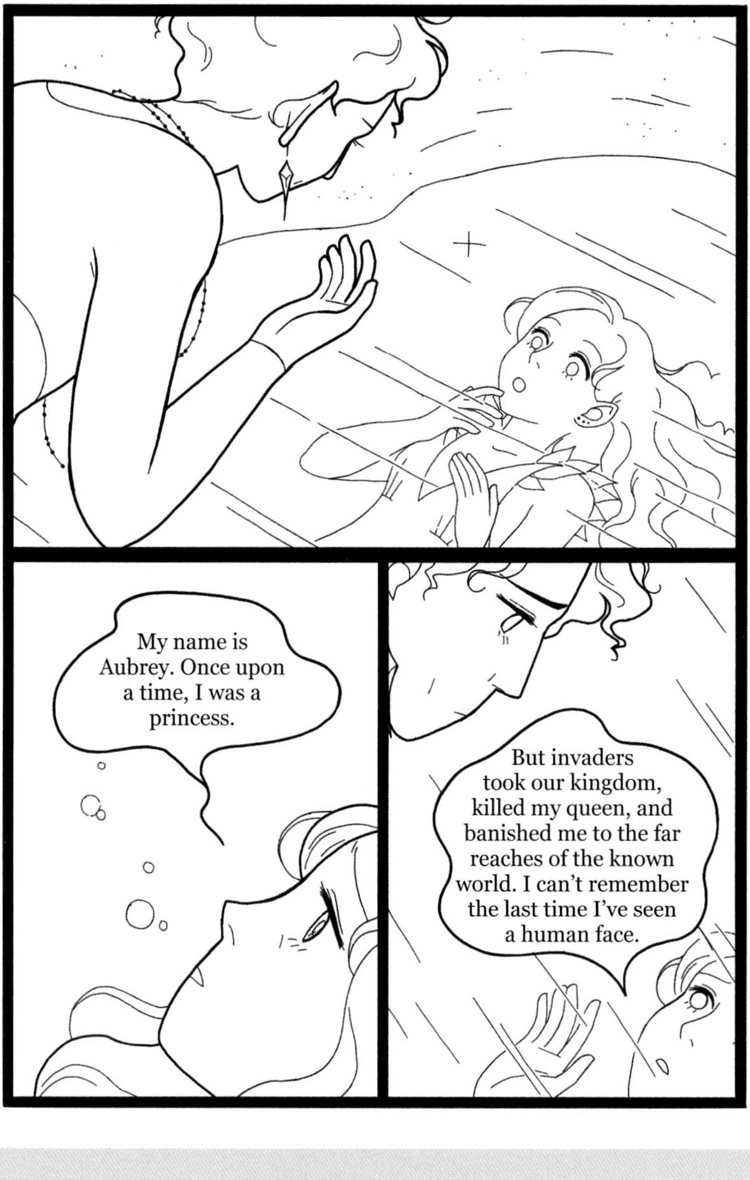
My name is Aubrey. Once upon a time, I was a princess.
But invaders took our kingdom, killed my queen, and banished me to the far reaches of the known world. I can't remember the last time I've seen a human face.

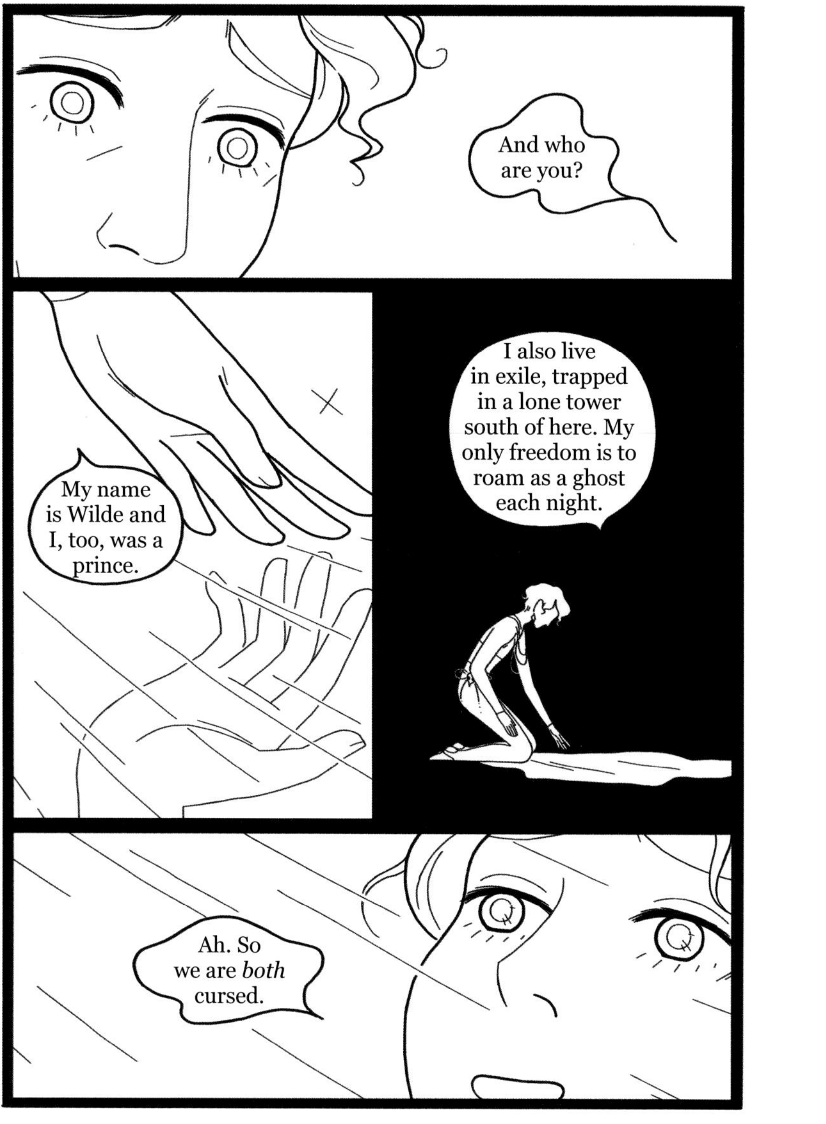
And who are you?
My name is Wilde and I, too, was a prince.
I also live in exile, trapped in a lone tower south of here. My only freedom is to roam as a ghost each night.
Ah. So we are *both* cursed.

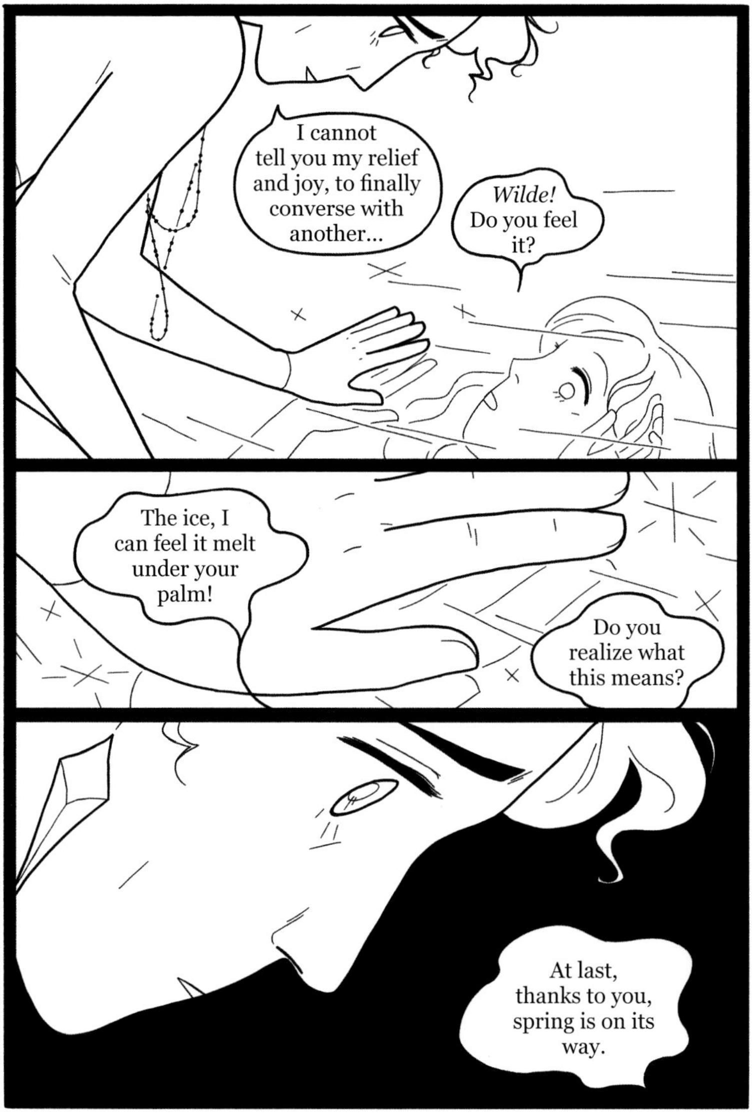
I cannot tell you my relief and joy, to finally converse with another...
Wilde! Do you feel it?
The ice, I can feel it melt under your palm!
Do you realize what this means?
At last, thanks to you, spring is on its way.

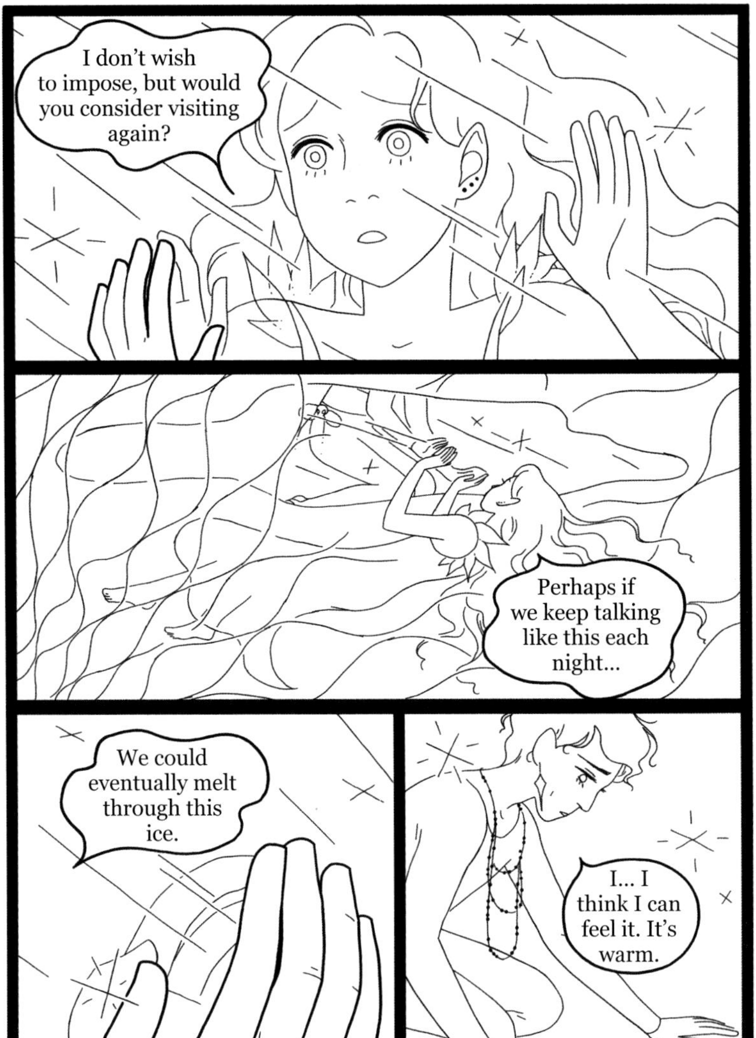
I don't wish to impose, but would you consider visiting again?
Perhaps if we keep talking like this each night...
We could eventually melt through this ice.
I... I think I can feel it. It's warm.

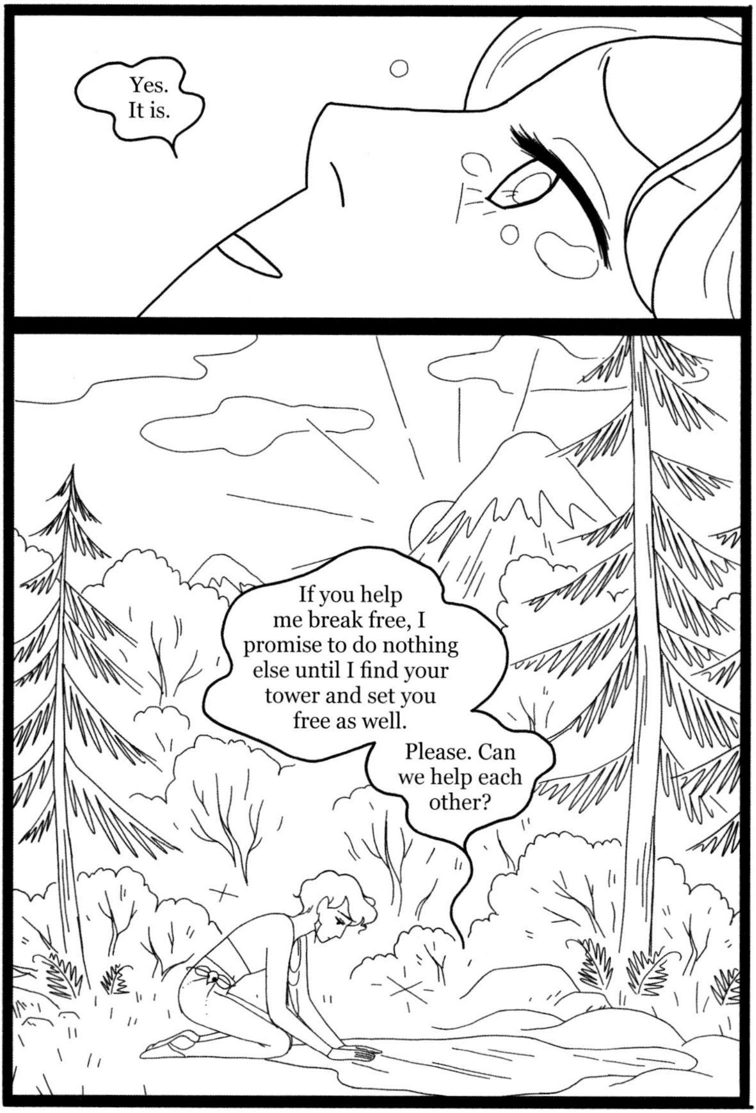
Yes. It is.
If you help me break free, I promise to do nothing else until I find your tower and set you free as well.
Please. Can we help each other?

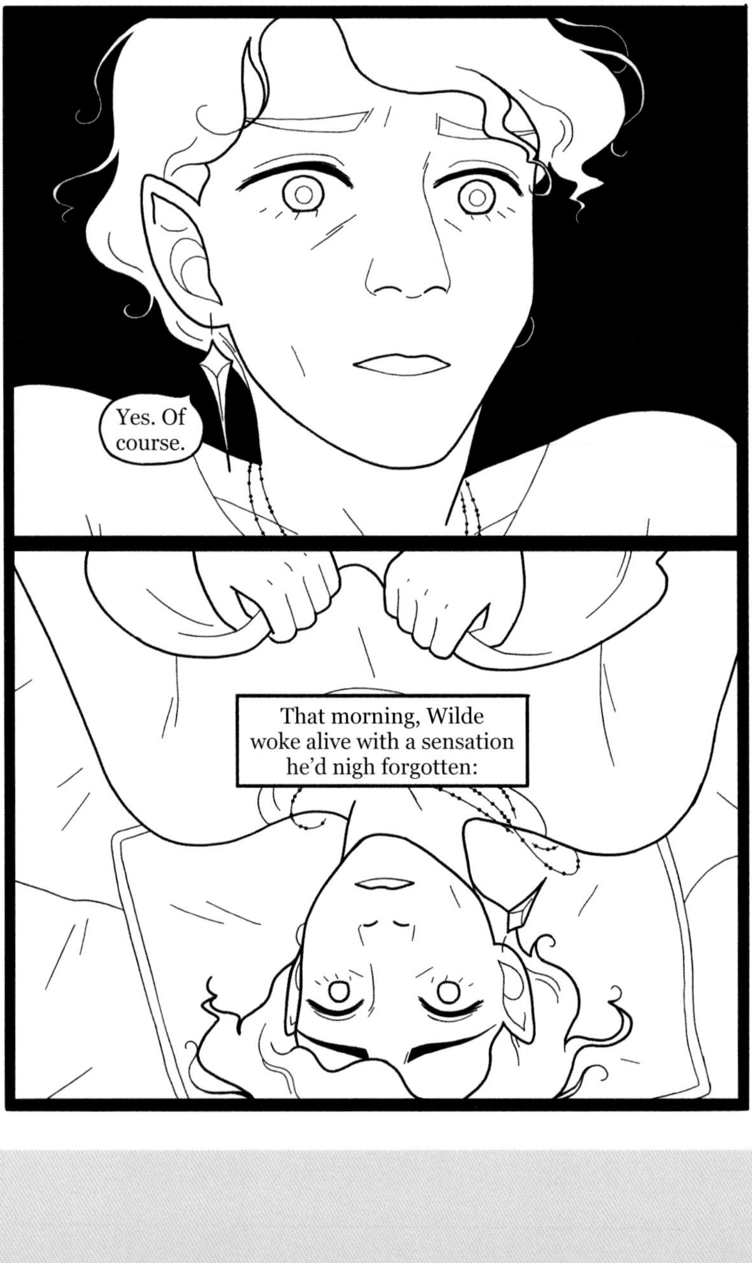
Yes. Of course.
That morning, Wilde woke alive with a sensation he'd nigh forgotten:

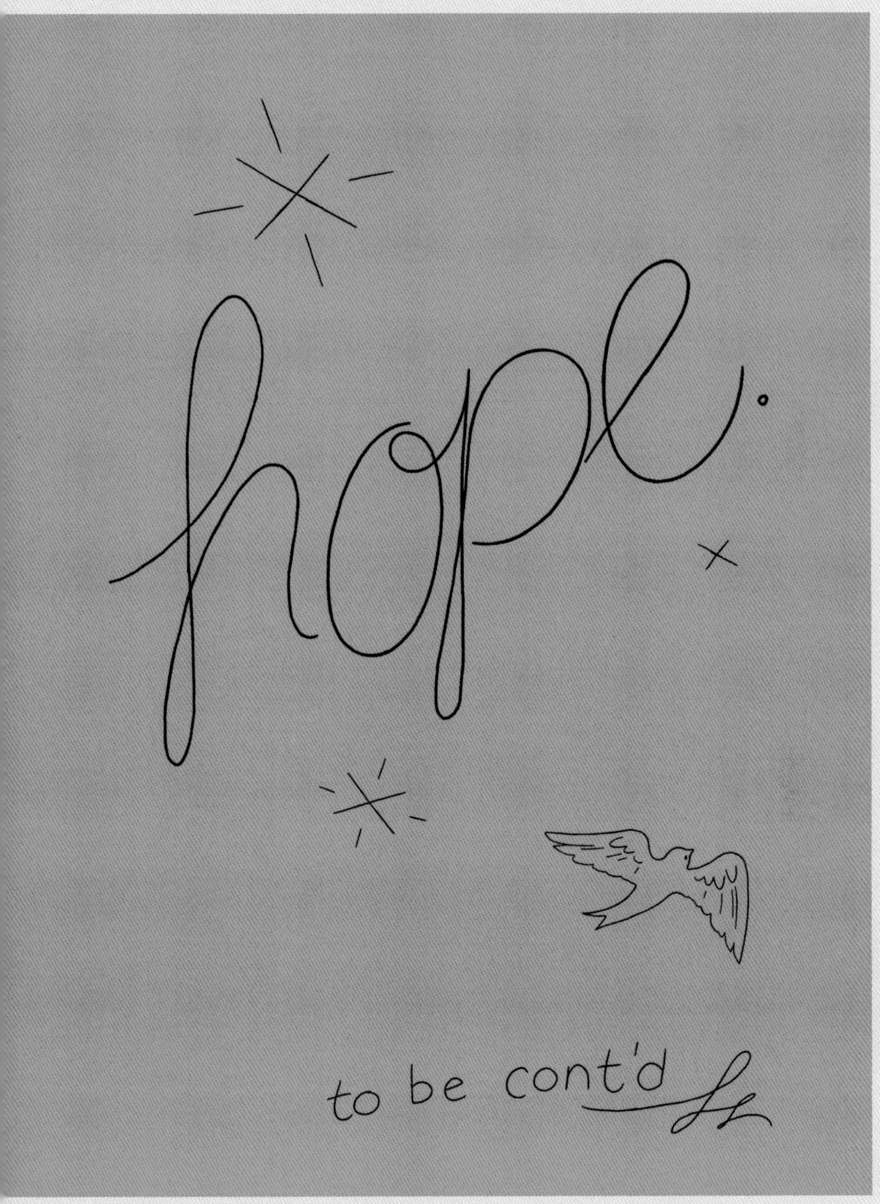
hope.
to be cont'd

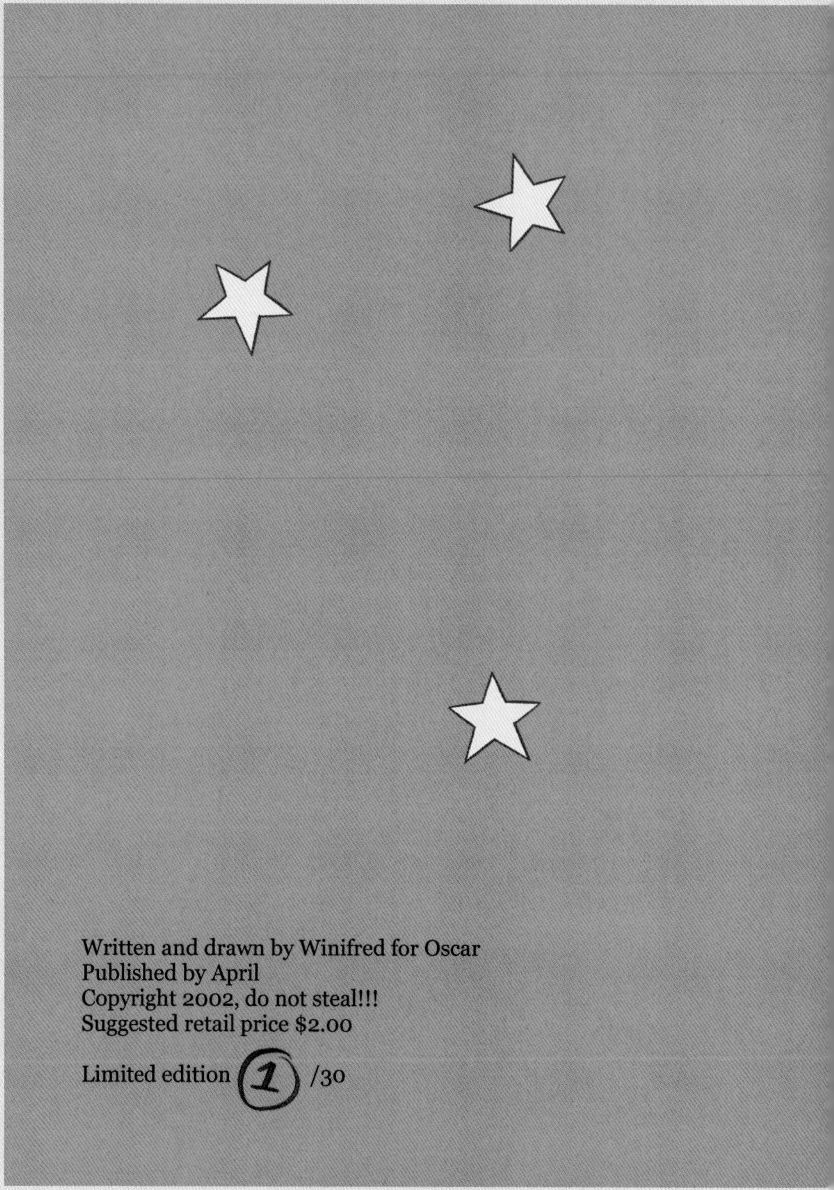
Written and drawn by Winifred for Oscar
Published by April
Copyright 2002, do not steal!!!
Suggested retail price $2.00
Limited edition 1 /30

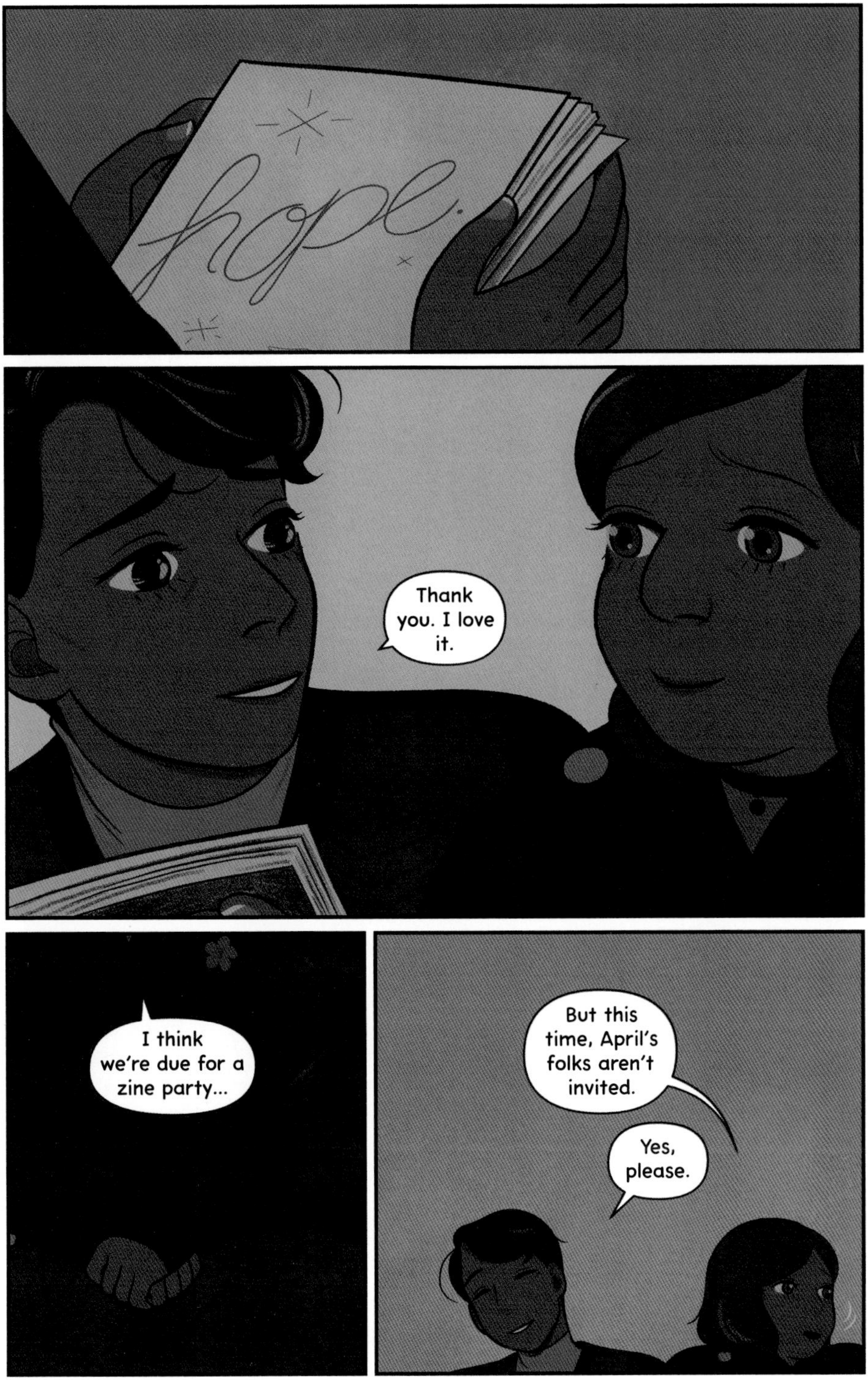
hope.
Thank you. I love it.
I think we're due for a zine party...
But this time, April's folks aren't invited.
Yes, please.

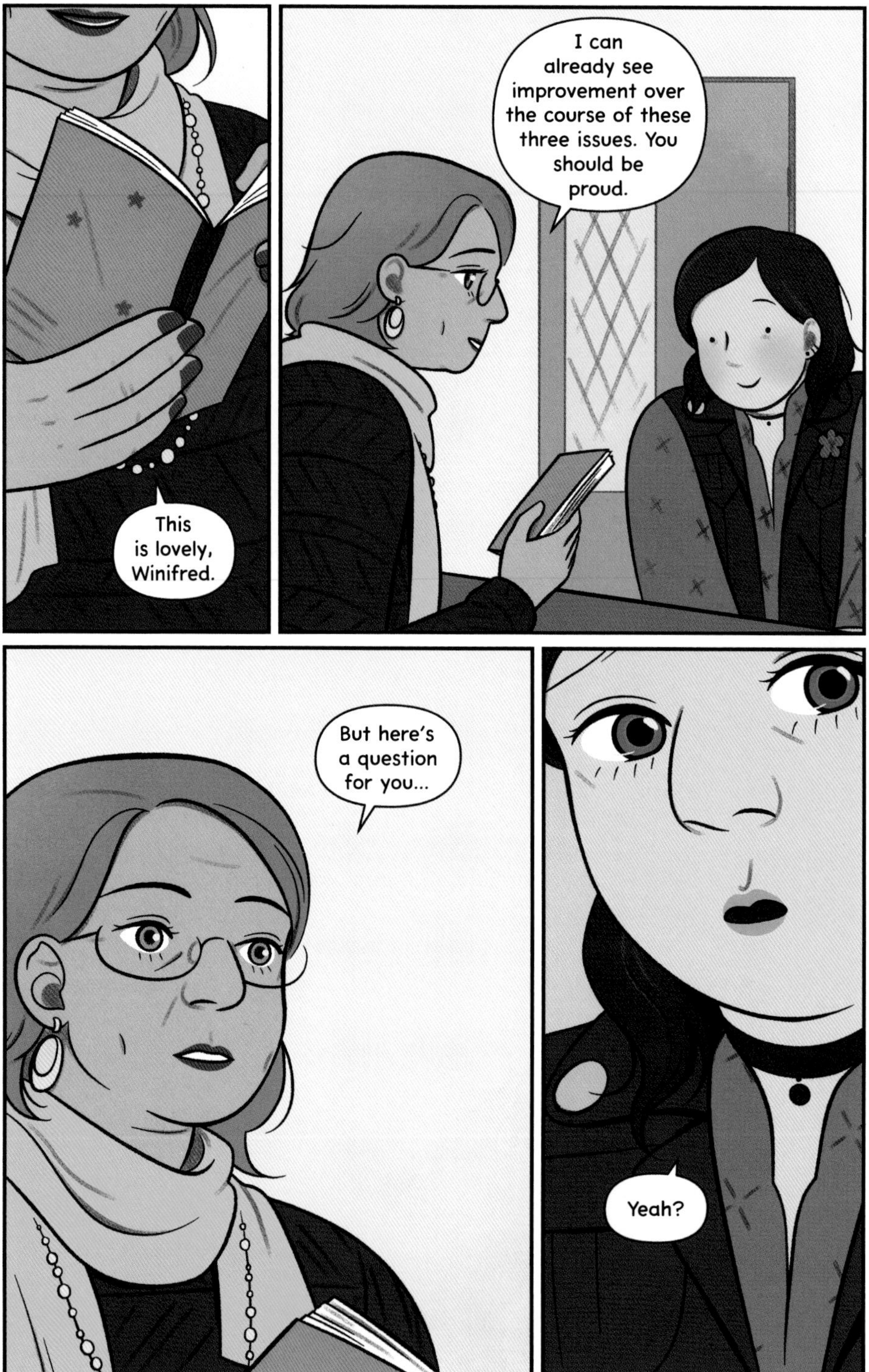
This is lovely, Winifred.
I can already see improvement over the course of these three issues. You should be proud.
But here's a question for you...
Yeah?

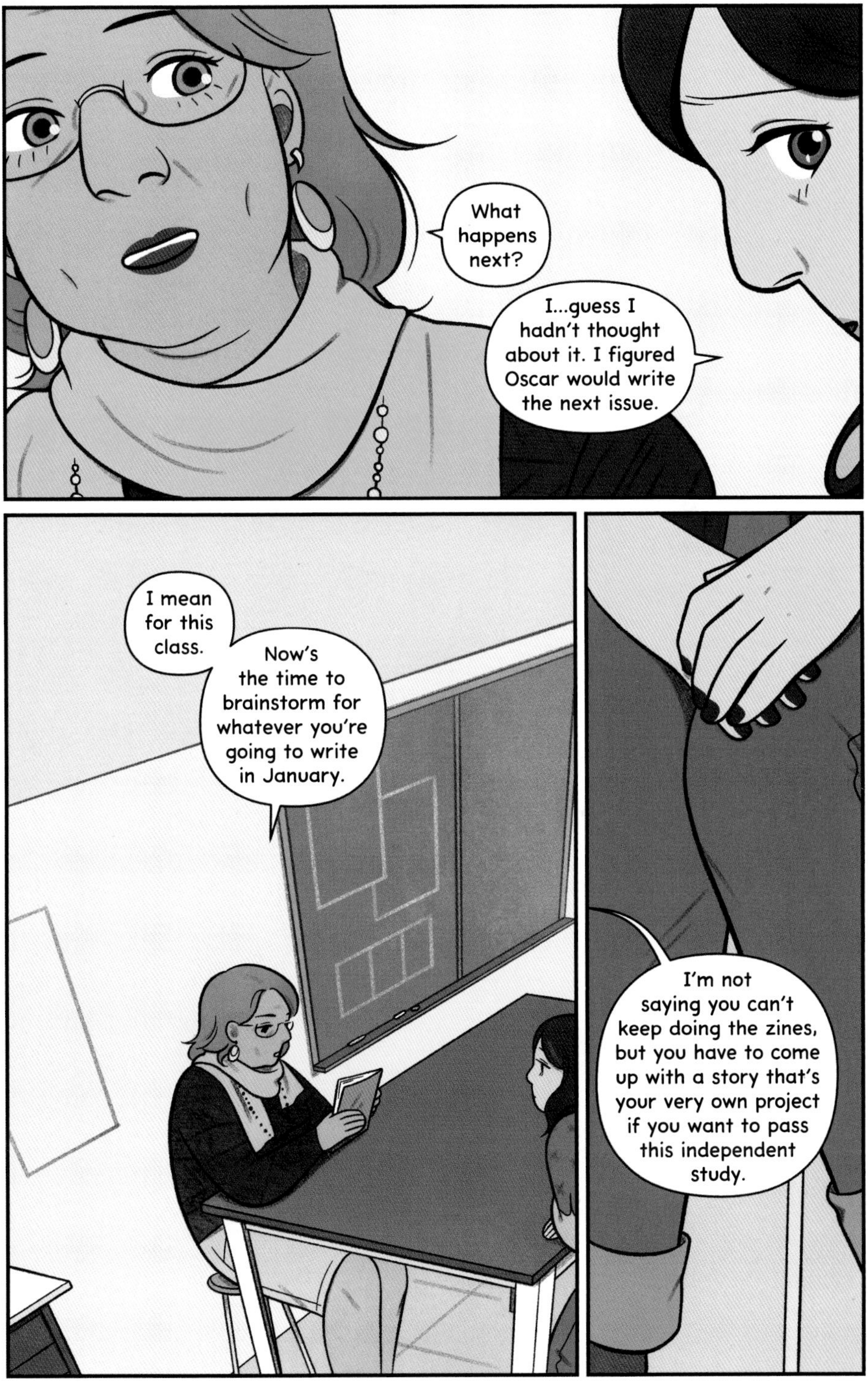
What happens next?
I...guess I hadn't thought about it. I figured Oscar would write the next issue.
I mean for this class.
Now's the time to brainstorm for whatever you're going to write in January.
I'm not saying you can't keep doing the zines, but you have to come up with a story that's your very own project if you want to pass this independent study.

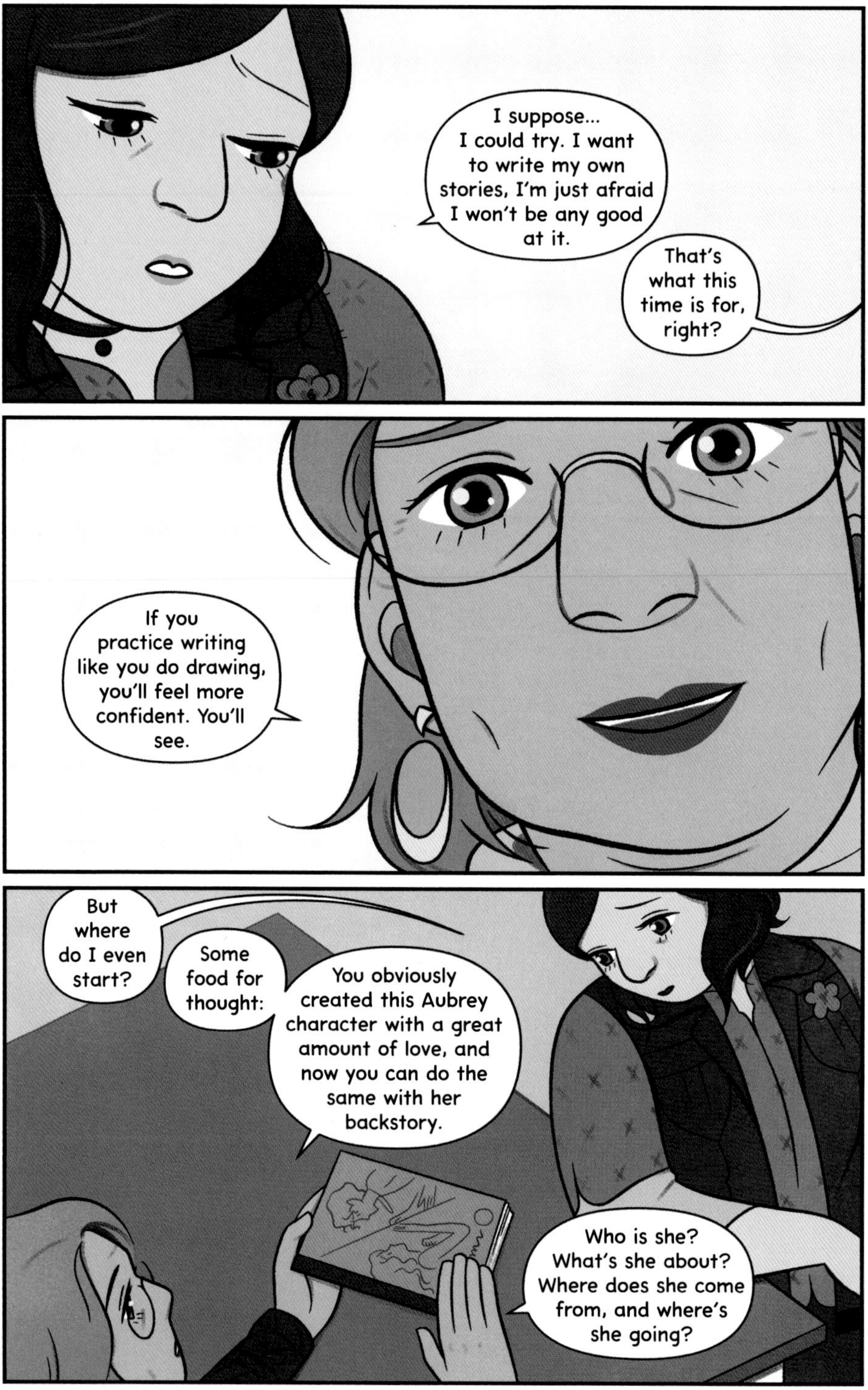
I suppose... I could try. I want to write my own stories, I'm just afraid I won't be any good at it.
That's what this time is for, right?
If you practice writing like you do drawing, you'll feel more confident. You'll see.
But where do I even start?
Some food for thought:
You obviously created this Aubrey character with a great amount of love, and now you can do the same with her backstory.
Who is she? What's she about? Where does she come from, and where's she going?

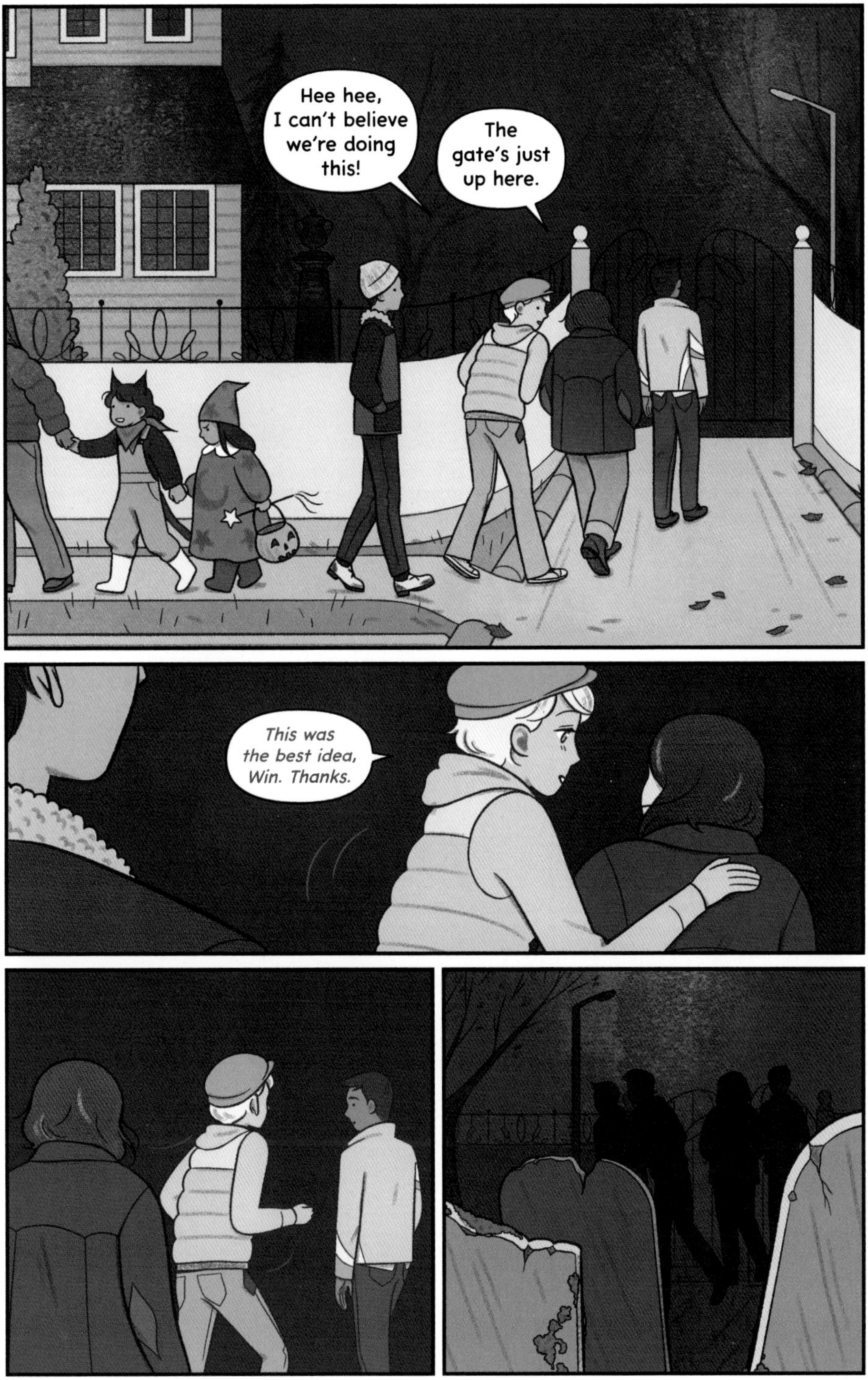
Hee hee, I can't believe we're doing this!
The gate's just up here.
This was the best idea, Win. Thanks.

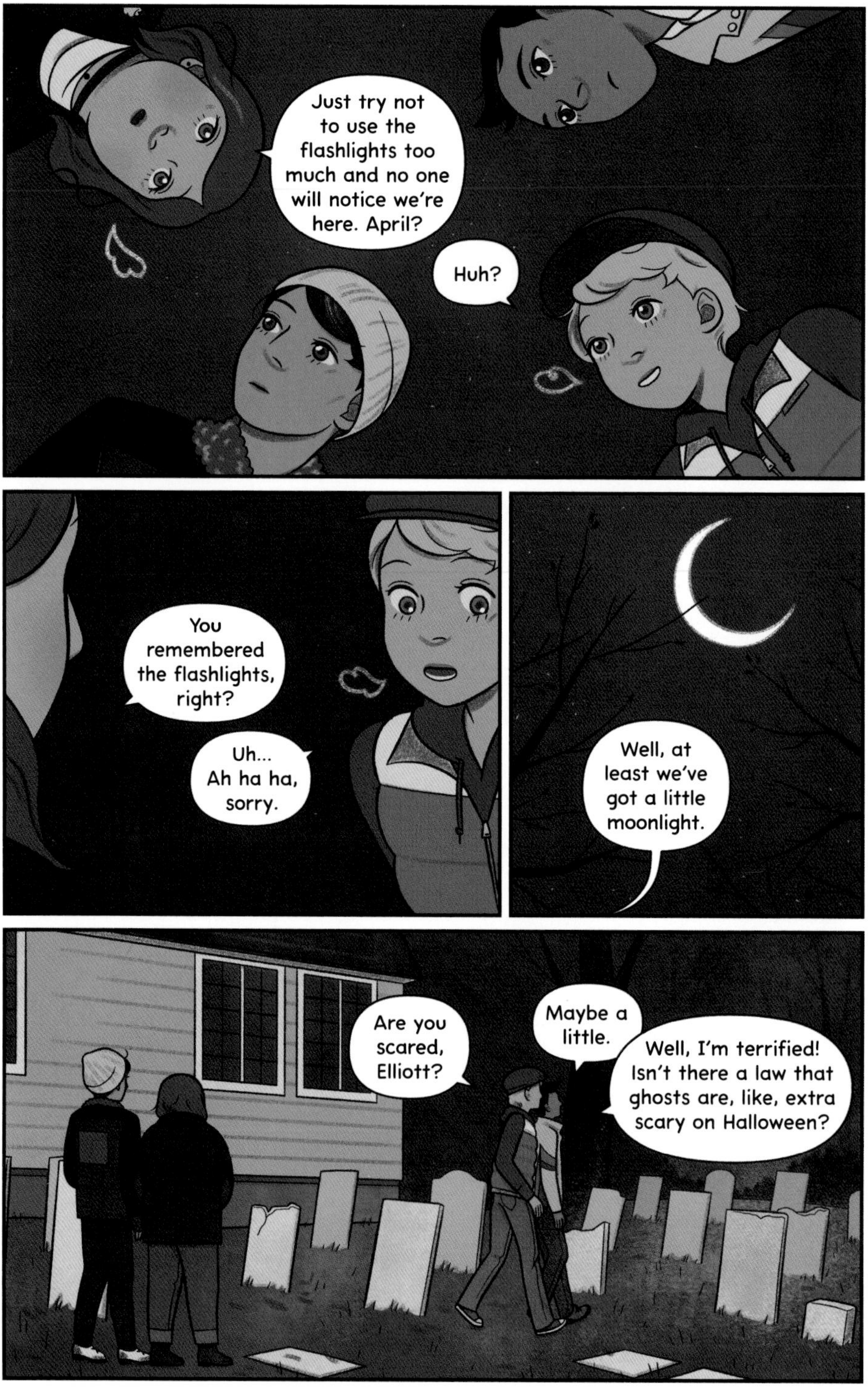
Just try not to use the flashlights too much and no one will notice we're here. April?
Huh?
You remembered the flashlights, right?
Uh... Ah ha ha, sorry.
Well, at least we've got a little moonlight.
Are you scared, Elliott?
Maybe a little.
Well, I'm terrified! Isn't there a law that ghosts are, like, extra scary on Halloween?

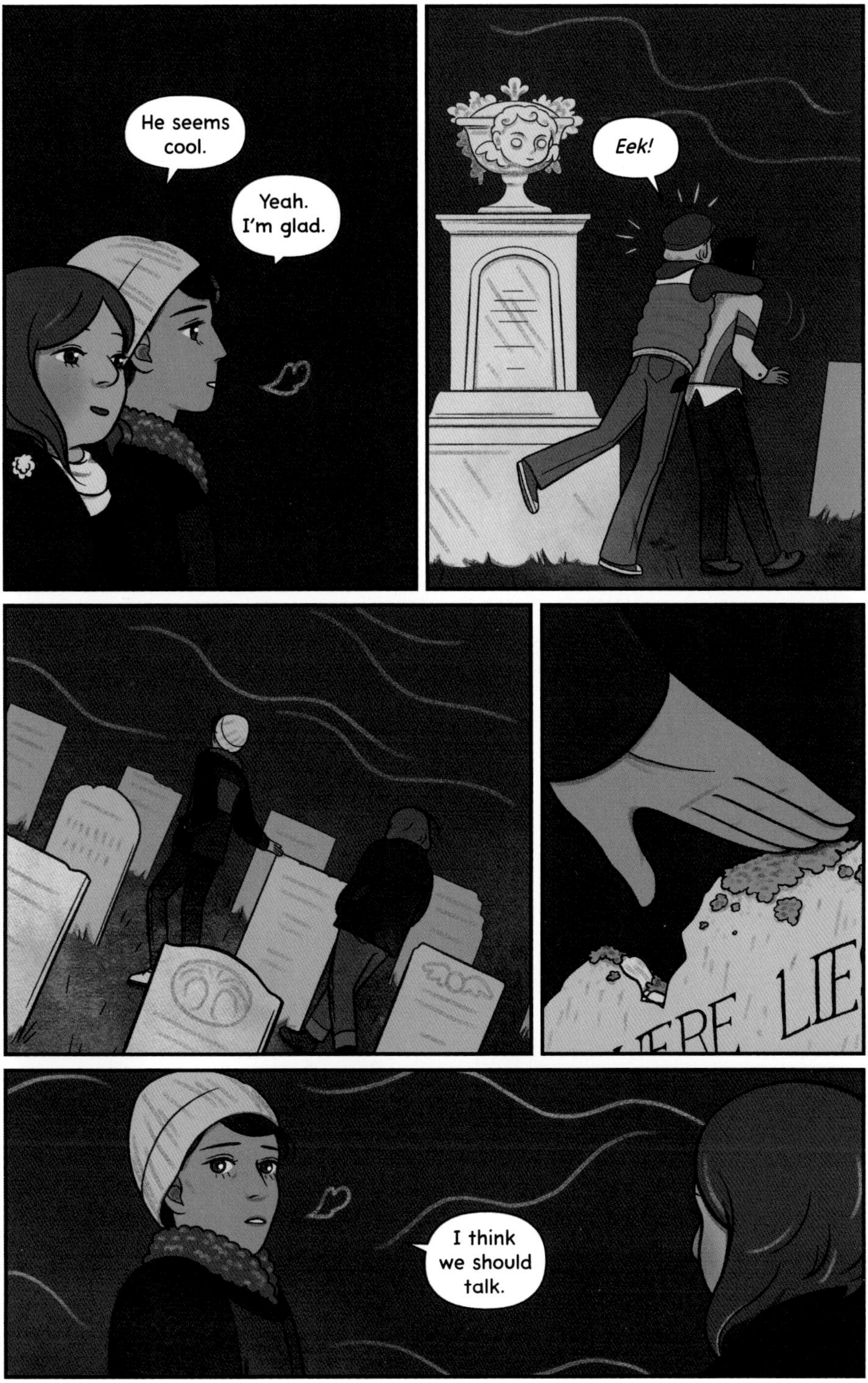
He seems cool.
Yeah. I'm glad.
Eek!
I think we should talk.

What's on your mind?

I... I get the feeling that you like me. And I'd be lying if I said I didn't have feelings for you, too.

But I'm afraid I'm leading you on. I'm not sure I'm ready for a new relationship. Not when I'm so messed up over all this other stuff.

That's not fair to you.

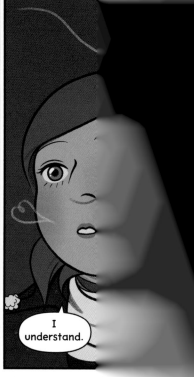

I understand.

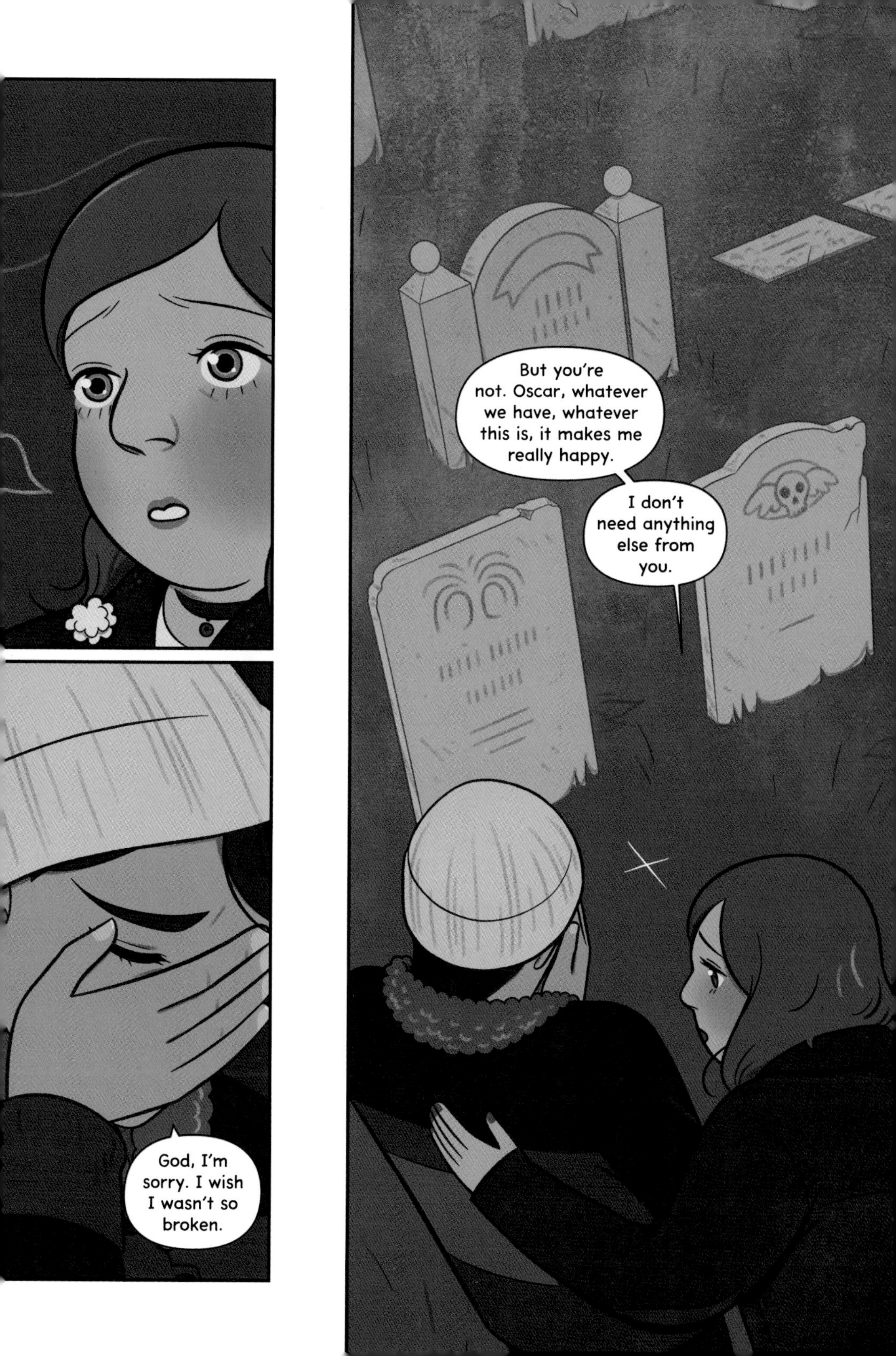
God, I'm sorry. I wish I wasn't so broken.
But you're not. Oscar, whatever we have, whatever this is, it makes me really happy.
I don't need anything else from you.

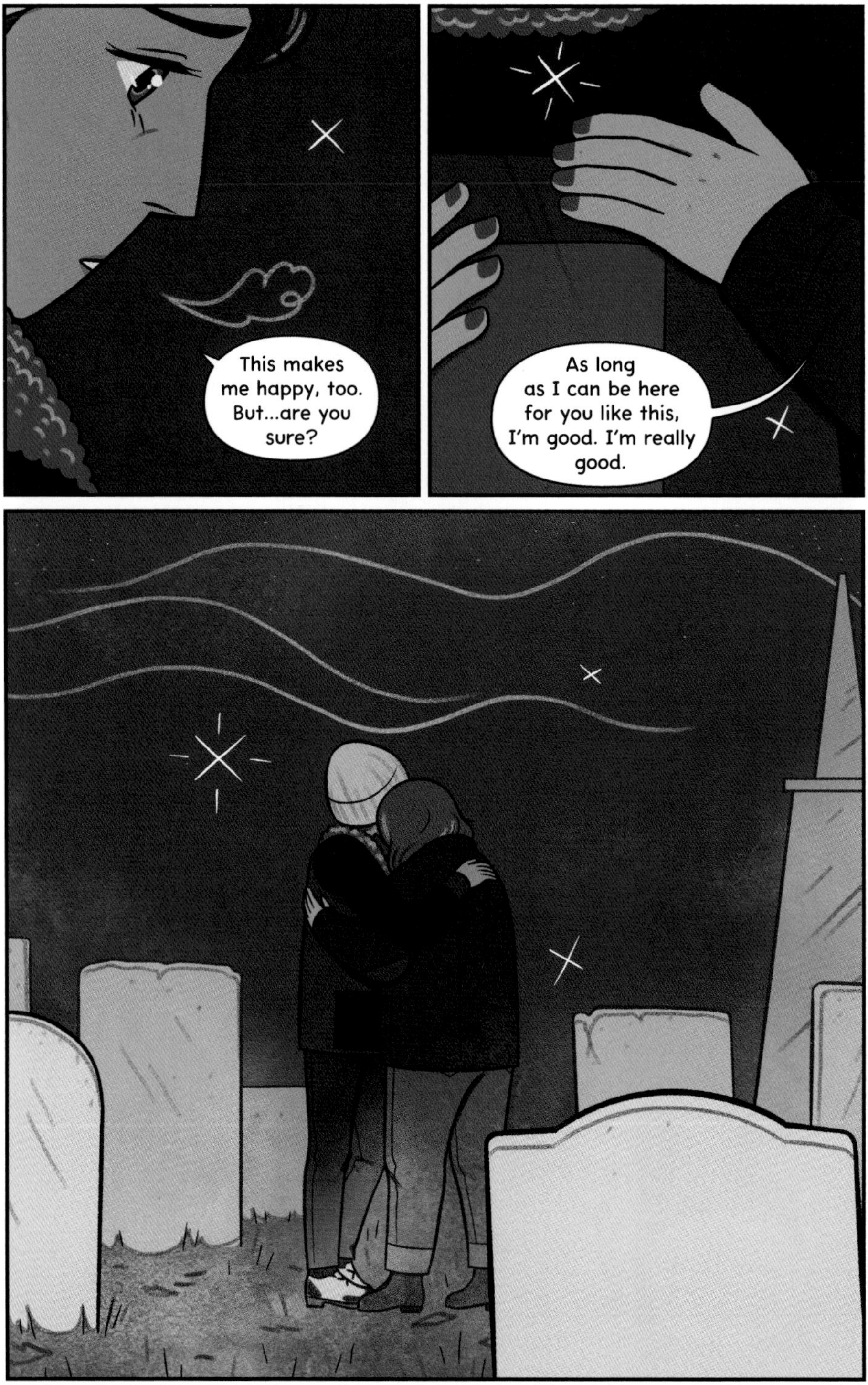
This makes me happy, too. But...are you sure?
As long as I can be here for you like this, I'm good. I'm really good.

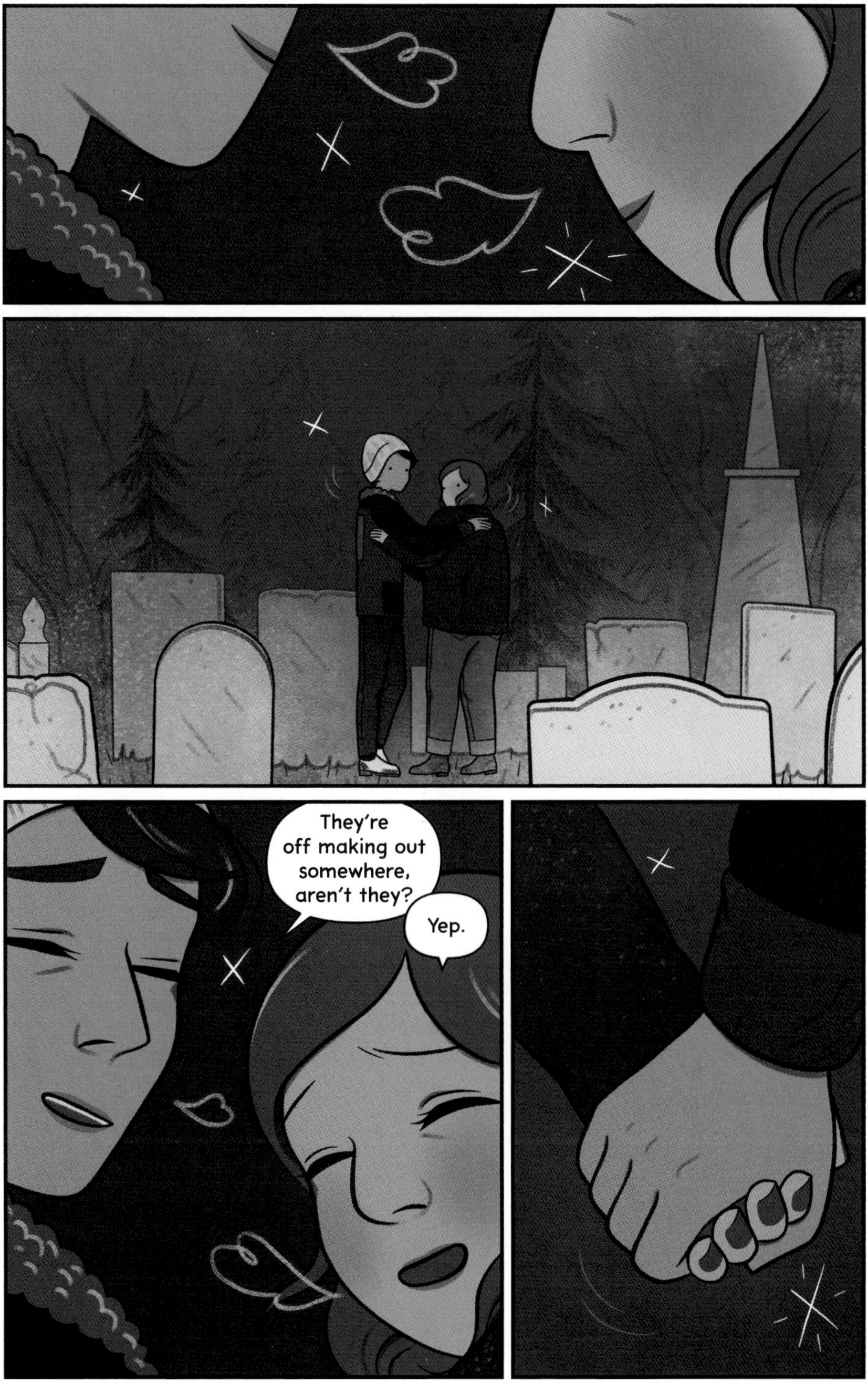
They're off making out somewhere, aren't they?
Yep.

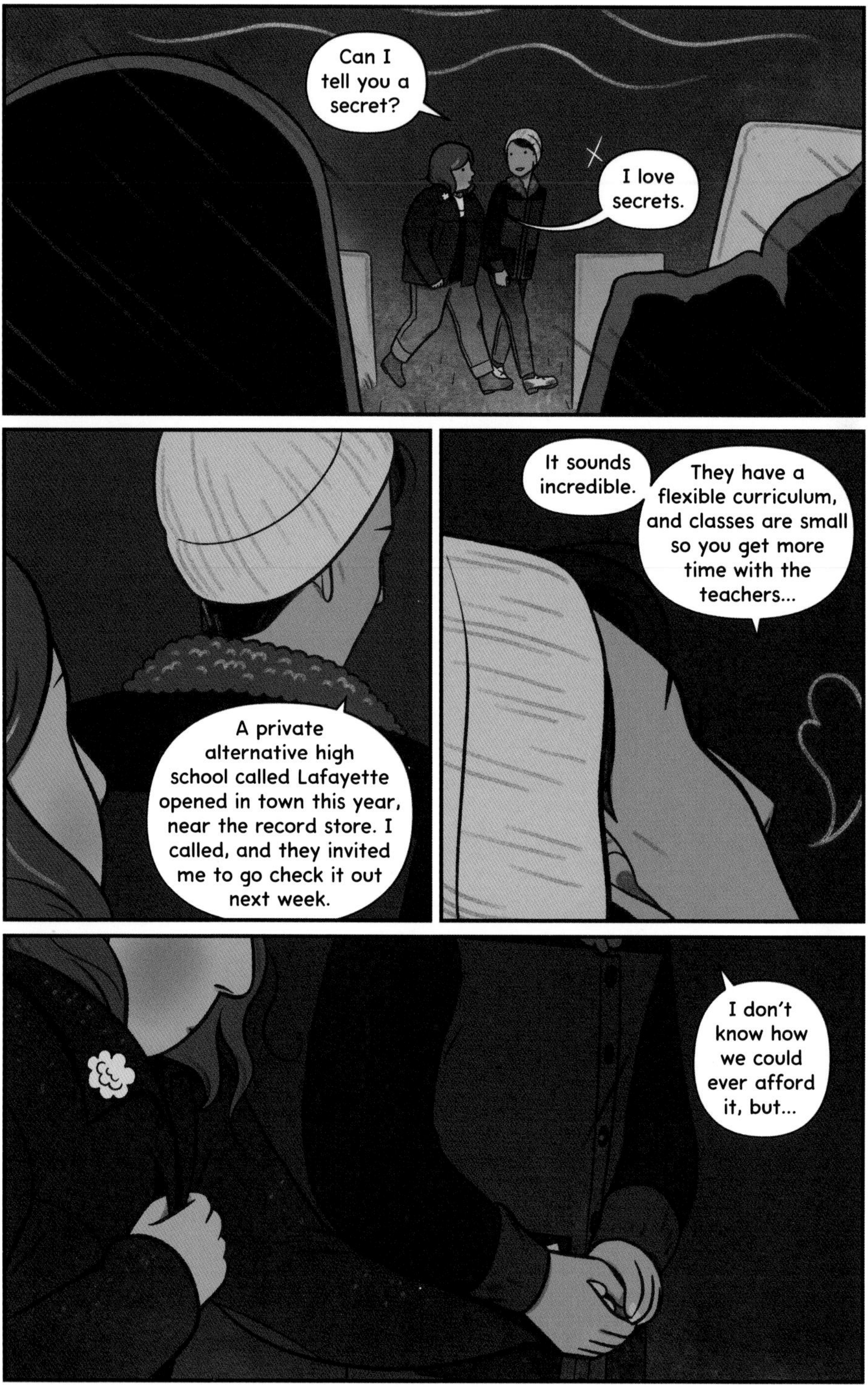
Can I tell you a secret?
I love secrets.
A private alternative high school called Lafayette opened in town this year, near the record store. I called, and they invited me to go check it out next week.
It sounds incredible.
They have a flexible curriculum, and classes are small so you get more time with the teachers...
I don't know how we could ever afford it, but...

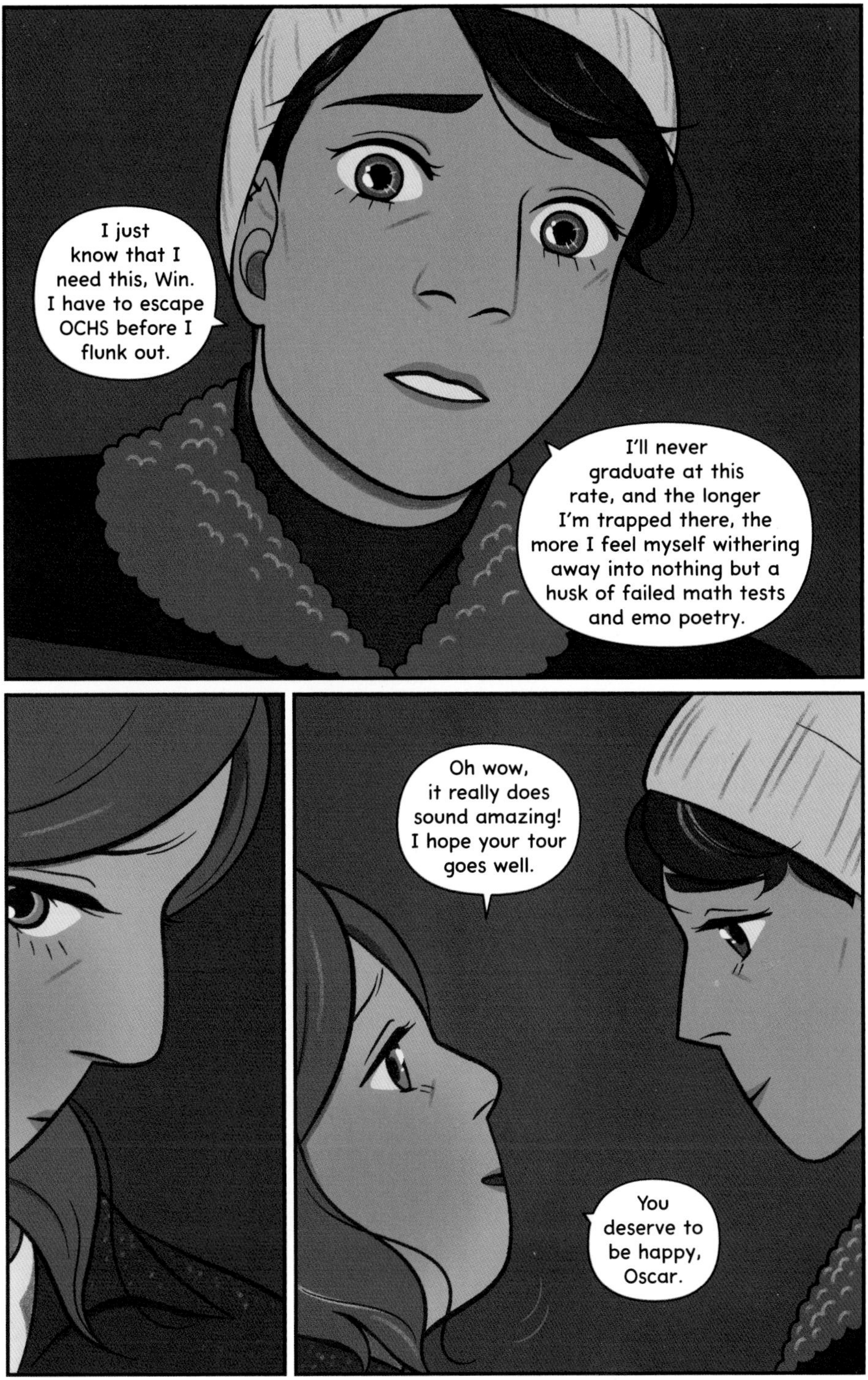
I just know that I need this, Win. I have to escape OCHS before I flunk out.
I'll never graduate at this rate, and the longer I'm trapped there, the more I feel myself withering away into nothing but a husk of failed math tests and emo poetry.
Oh wow, it really does sound amazing! I hope your tour goes well.
You deserve to be happy, Oscar.

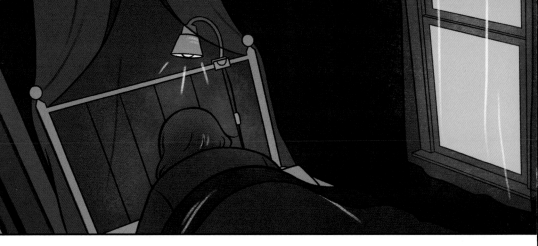

SNP

Ugh!

sigh

No wonder I couldn't come up with interesting stories. I was too much of a boring failure of a person to write anything different.

No wonder Oscar didn't want to be with me. No wonder he wanted to leave.

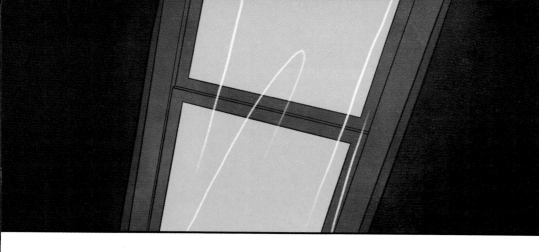

No. I wasn't so self-centered that I thought this was about me. He had a chance at happiness at a new school, and there was no way I'd begrudge him that.

But I knew how it went. There was no way our friendship could possibly stay the same if he left.

Just like what happened with Jayme and Jess. We hadn't talked in months.

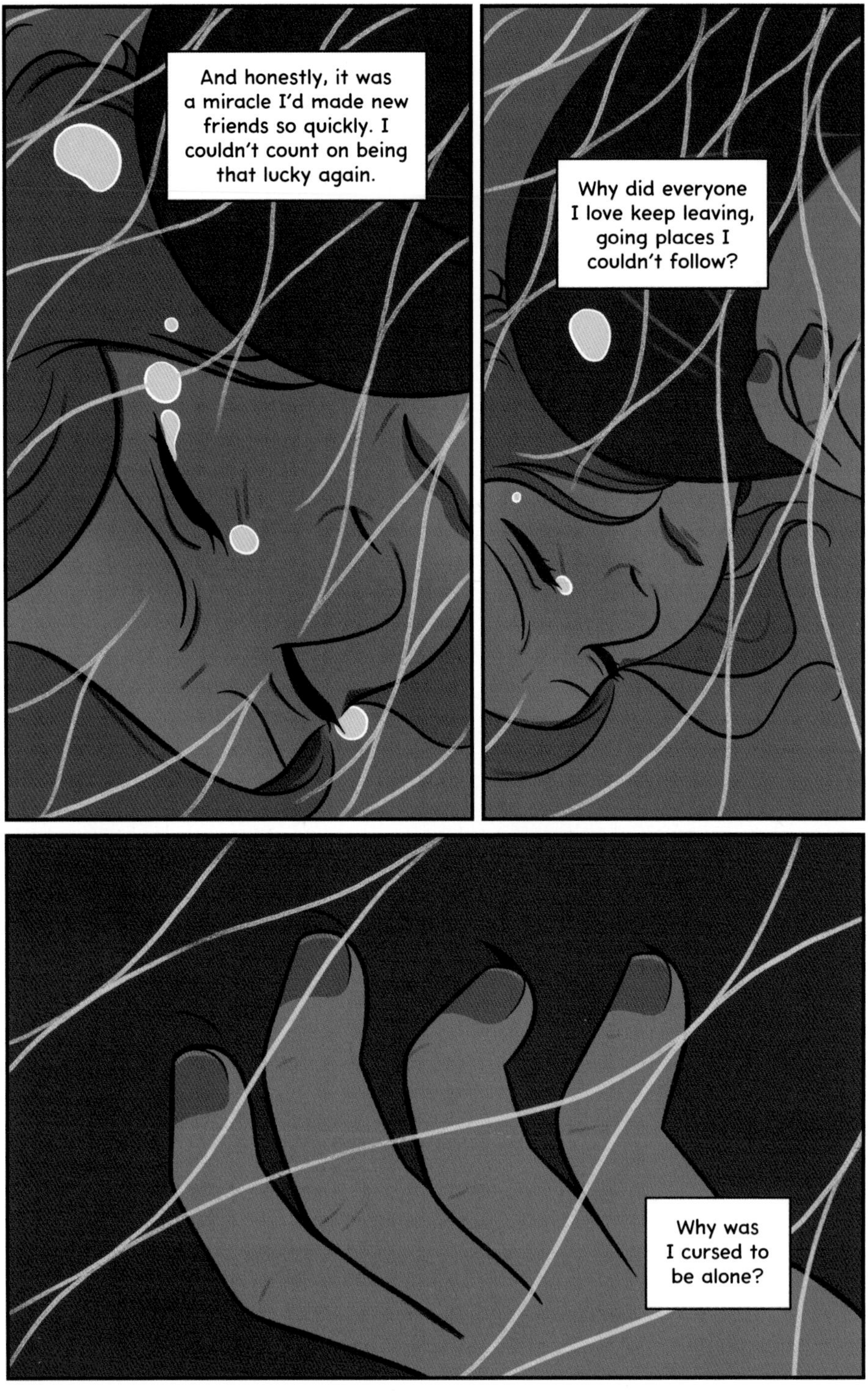
And honestly, it was a miracle I'd made new friends so quickly. I couldn't count on being that lucky again.
Why did everyone I love keep leaving, going places I couldn't follow?
Why was I cursed to be alone?

BEEP
BEEP
BEE-
clk
Oops.

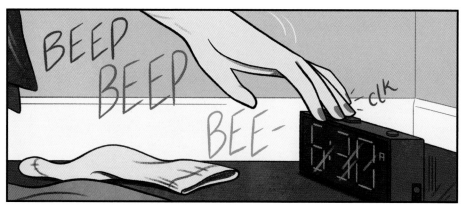

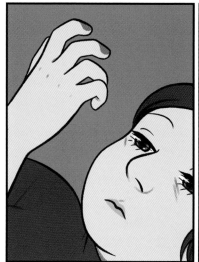

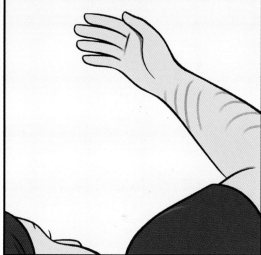

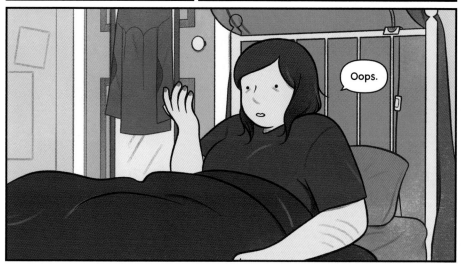

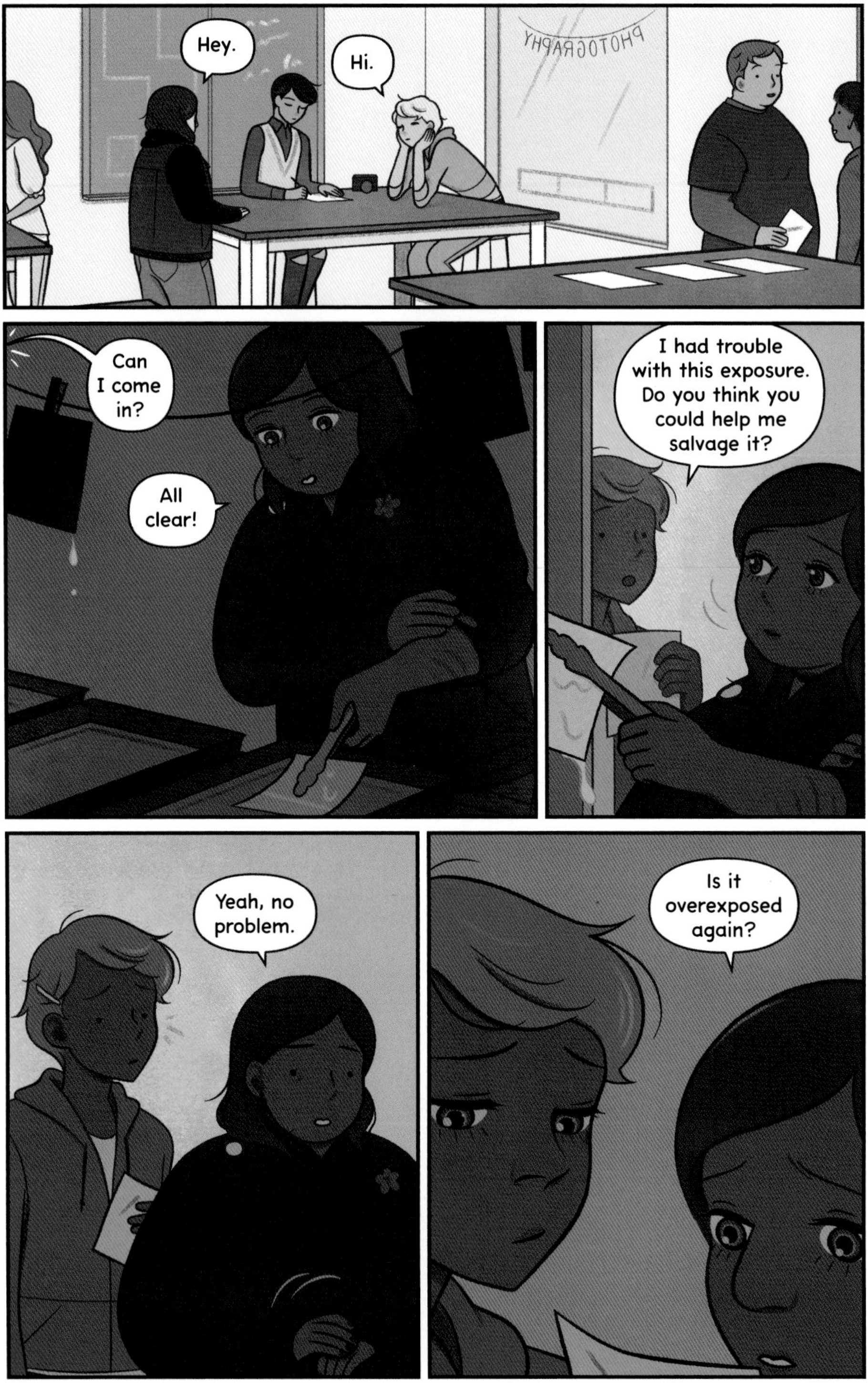
Hey.
Hi.
PHOTOGRAPHY
Can I come in?
All clear!
I had trouble with this exposure. Do you think you could help me salvage it?
Yeah, no problem.
Is it overexposed again?

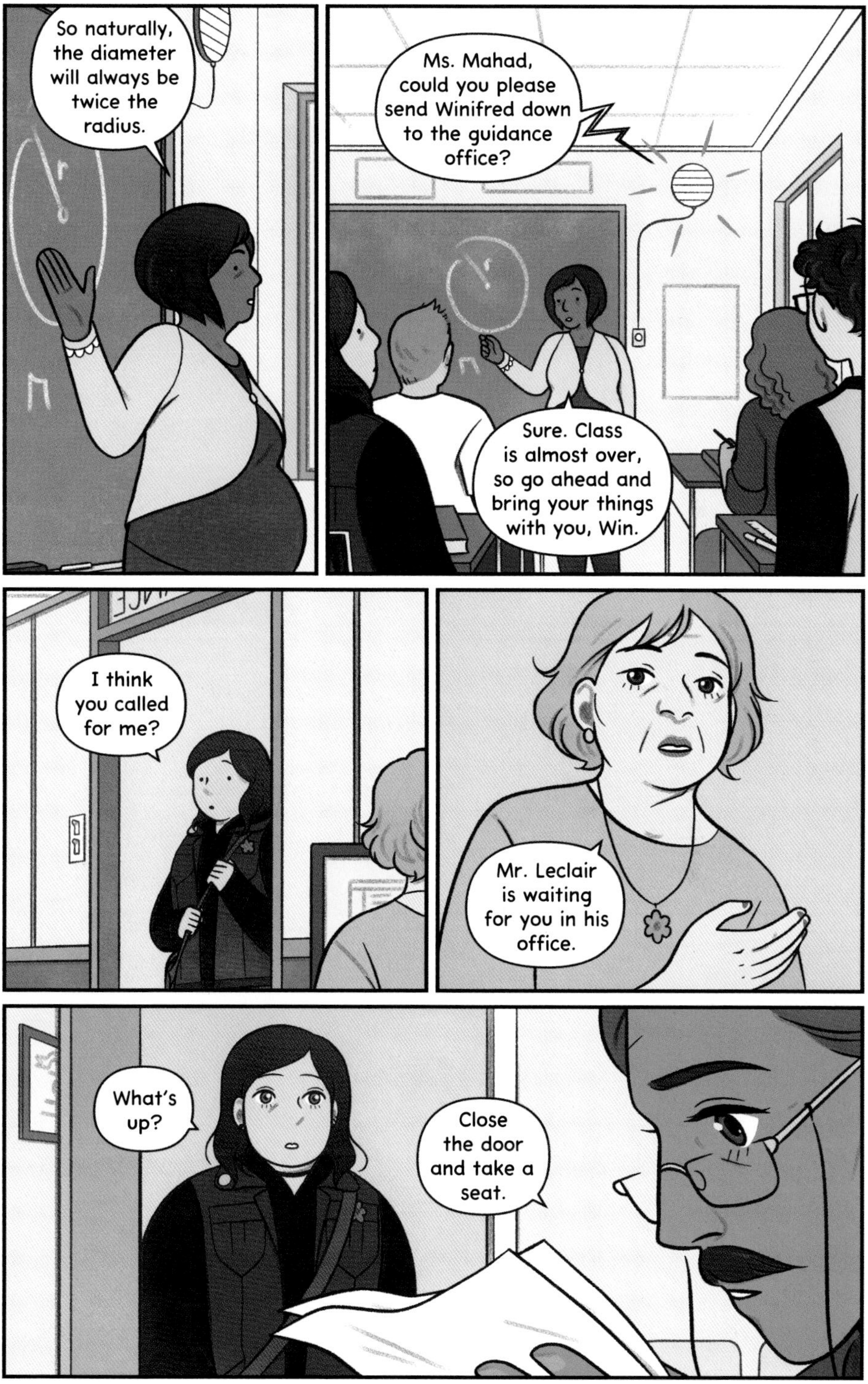

So naturally, the diameter will always be twice the radius.
Ms. Mahad, could you please send Winifred down to the guidance office?
Sure. Class is almost over, so go ahead and bring your things with you, Win.
I think you called for me?
Mr. Leclair is waiting for you in his office.
What's up?
Close the door and take a seat.

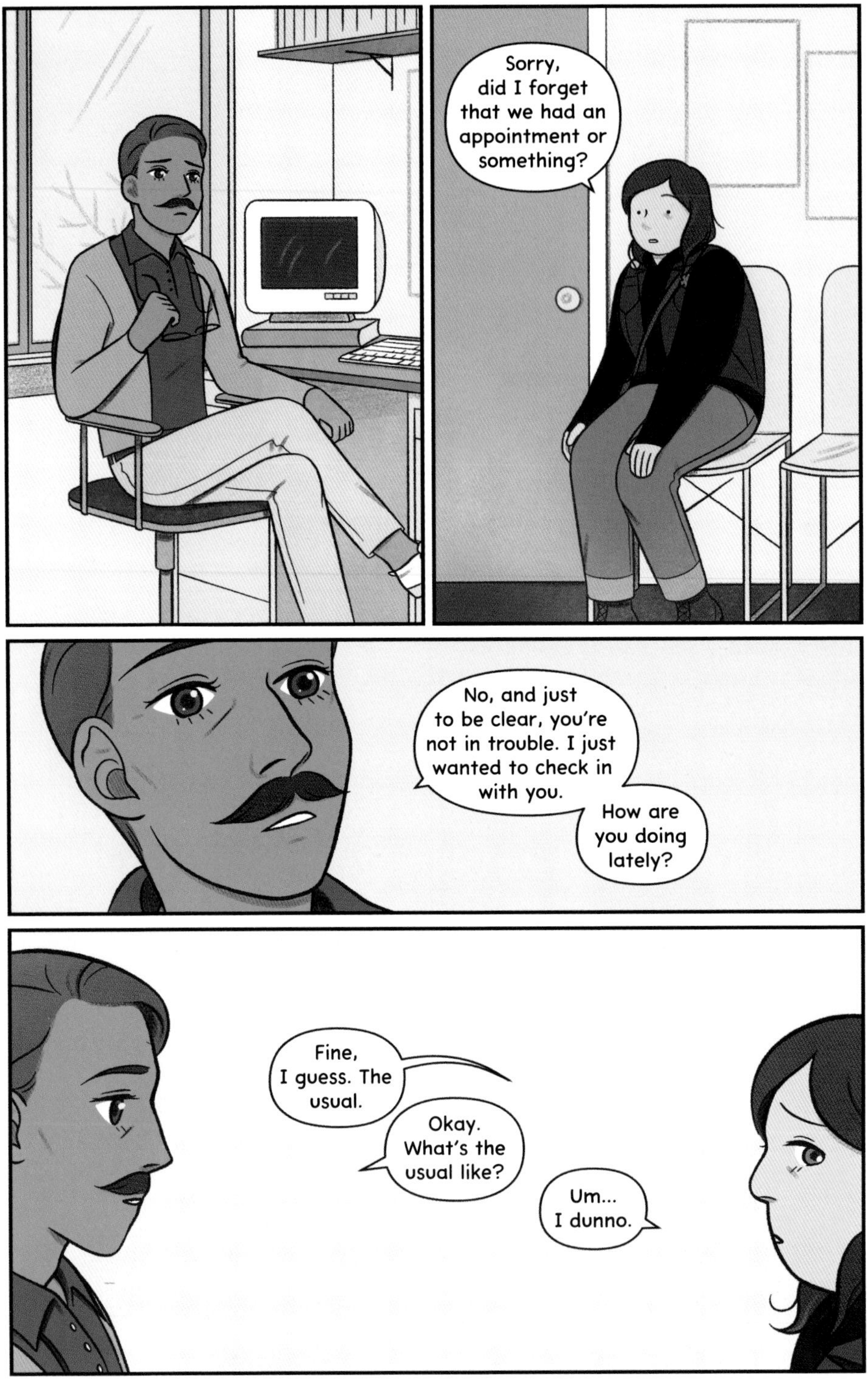
Sorry, did I forget that we had an appointment or something?
No, and just to be clear, you're not in trouble. I just wanted to check in with you.
How are you doing lately?
Fine, I guess. The usual.
Okay. What's the usual like?
Um... I dunno.

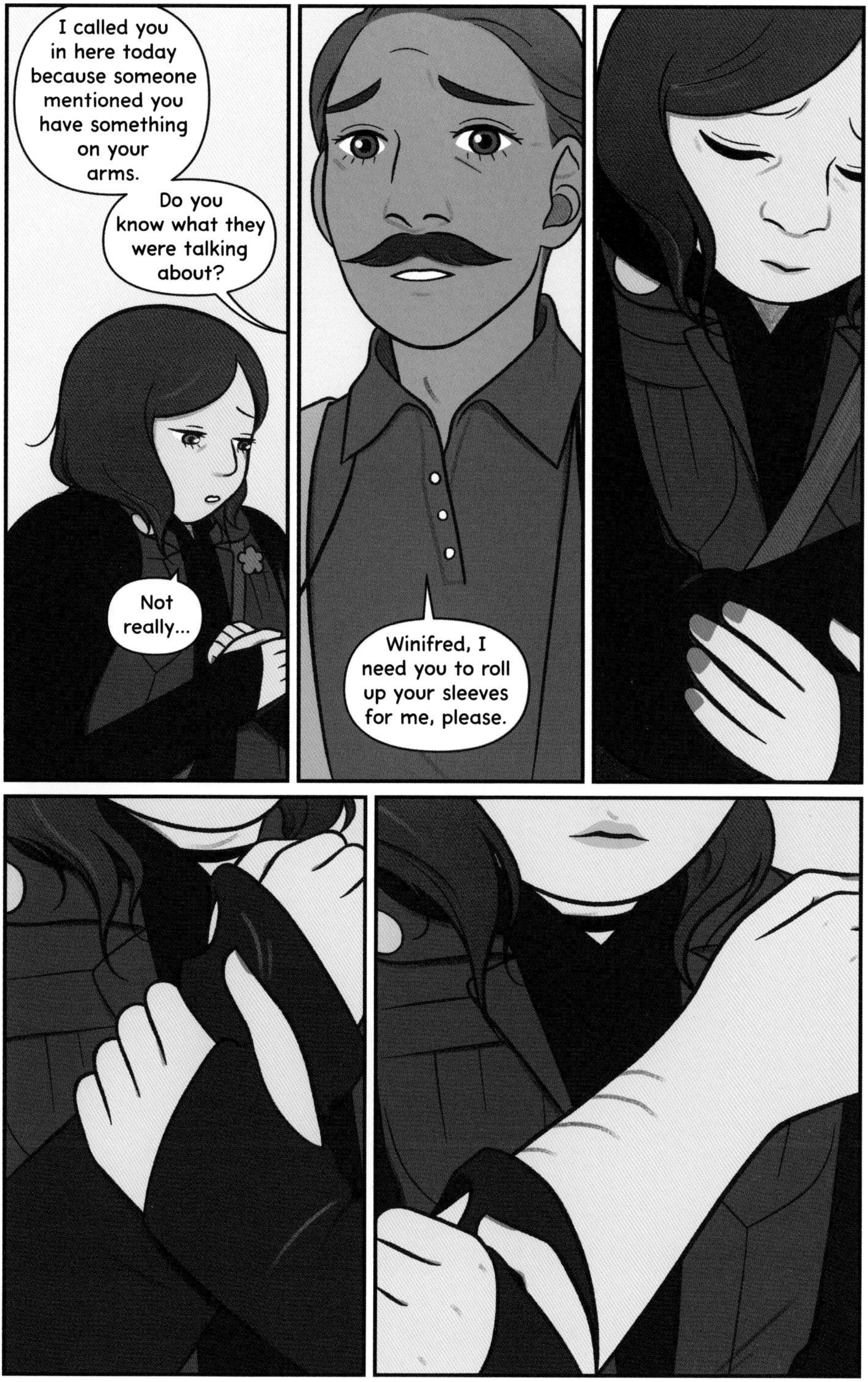
I called you in here today because someone mentioned you have something on your arms.
Do you know what they were talking about?
Not really...
Winifred, I need you to roll up your sleeves for me, please.

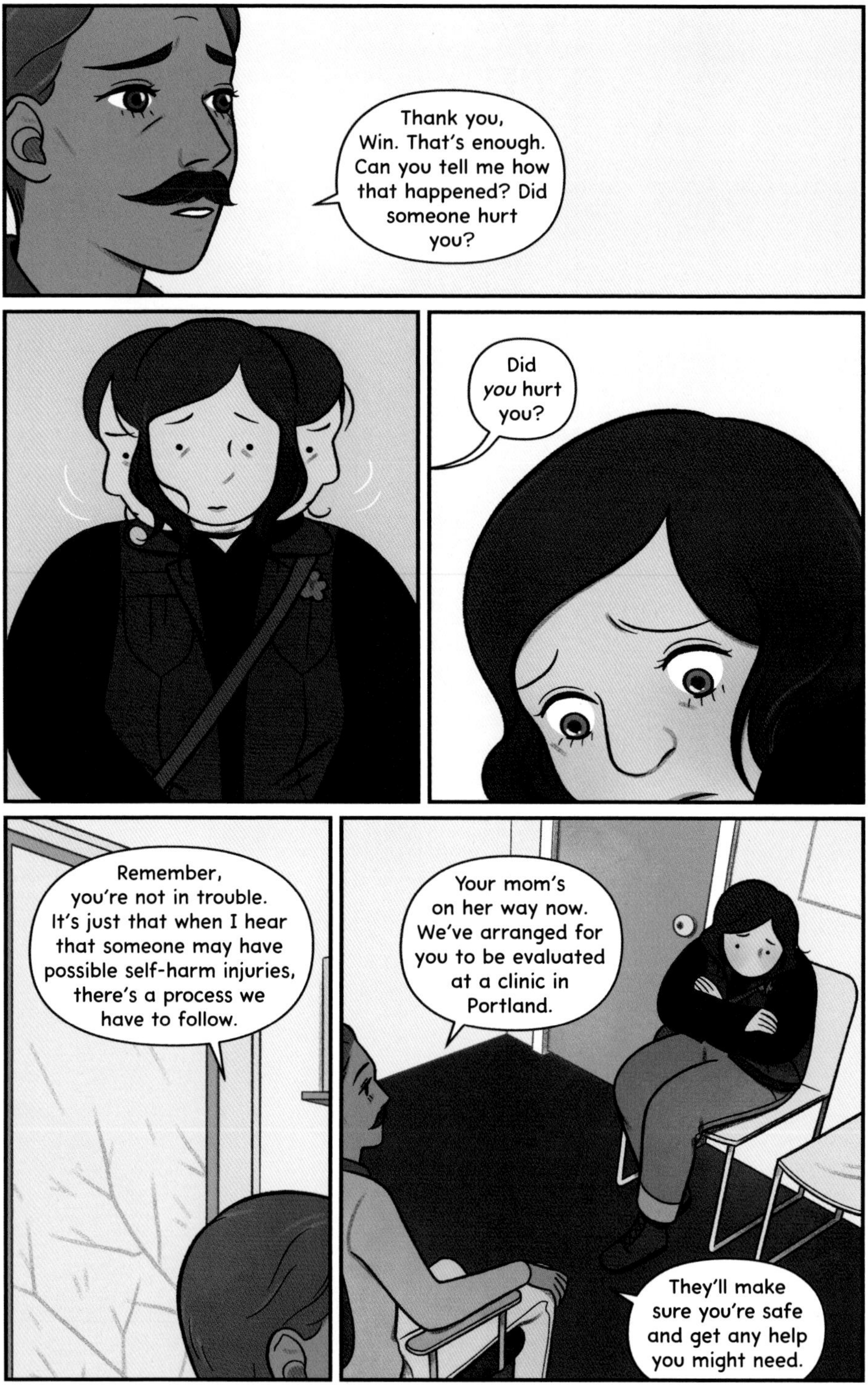
Thank you, Win. That's enough. Can you tell me how that happened? Did someone hurt you?
Did *you* hurt you?
Remember, you're not in trouble. It's just that when I hear that someone may have possible self-harm injuries, there's a process we have to follow.
Your mom's on her way now. We've arranged for you to be evaluated at a clinic in Portland.
They'll make sure you're safe and get any help you might need.

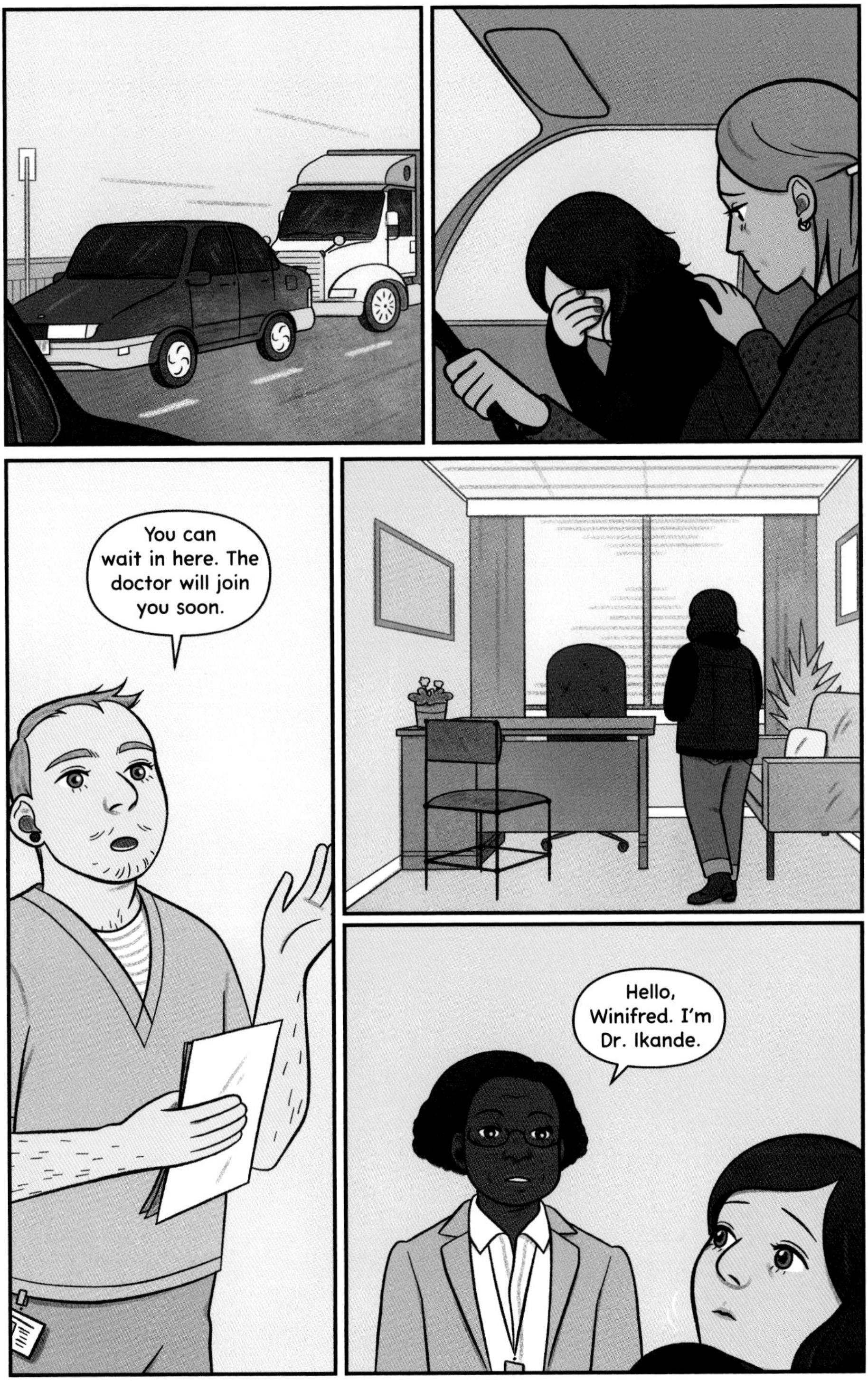
You can wait in here. The doctor will join you soon.
Hello, Winifred. I'm Dr. Ikande.

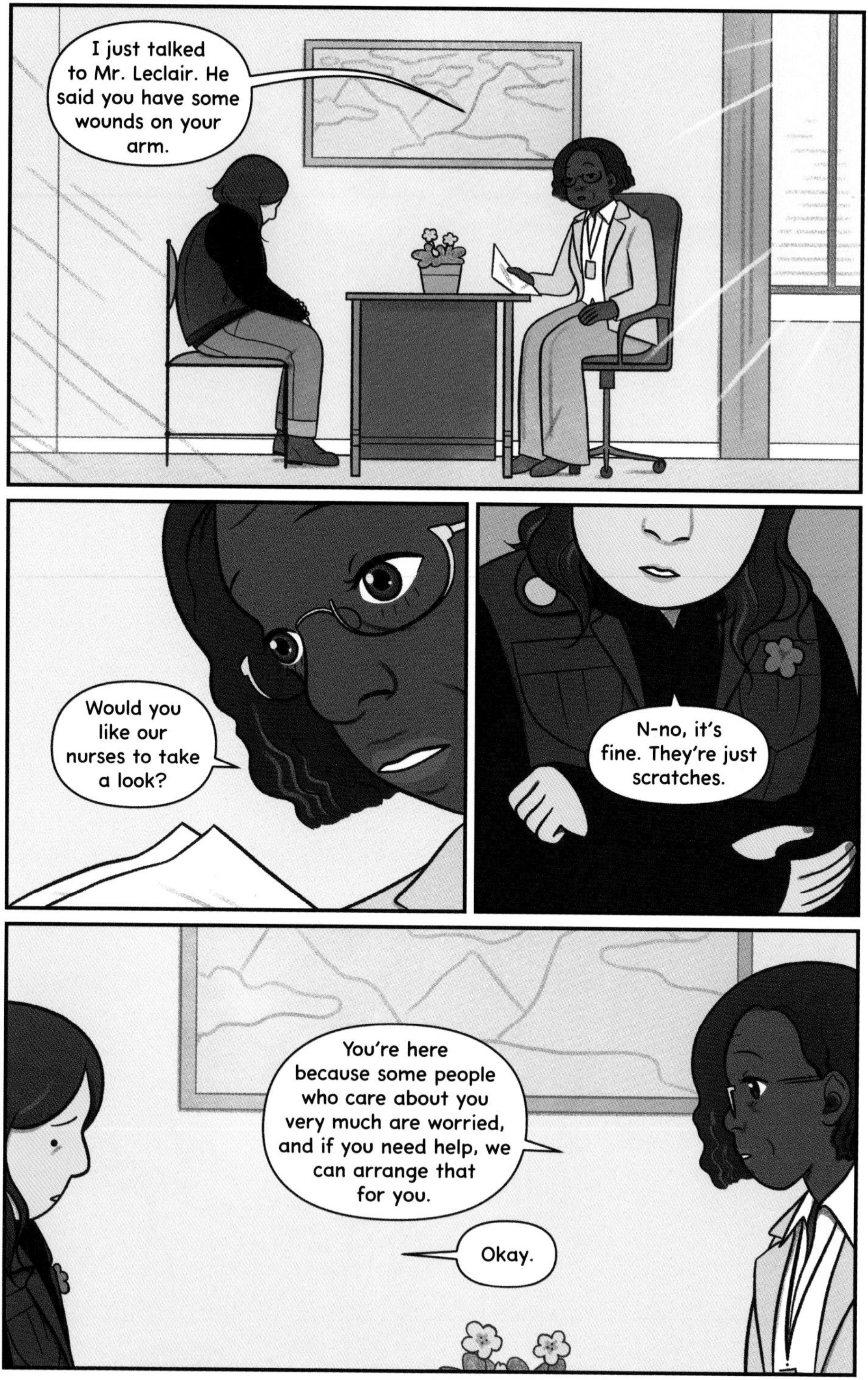
I just talked to Mr. Leclair. He said you have some wounds on your arm.
Would you like our nurses to take a look?
N-no, it's fine. They're just scratches.
You're here because some people who care about you very much are worried, and if you need help, we can arrange that for you.
Okay.

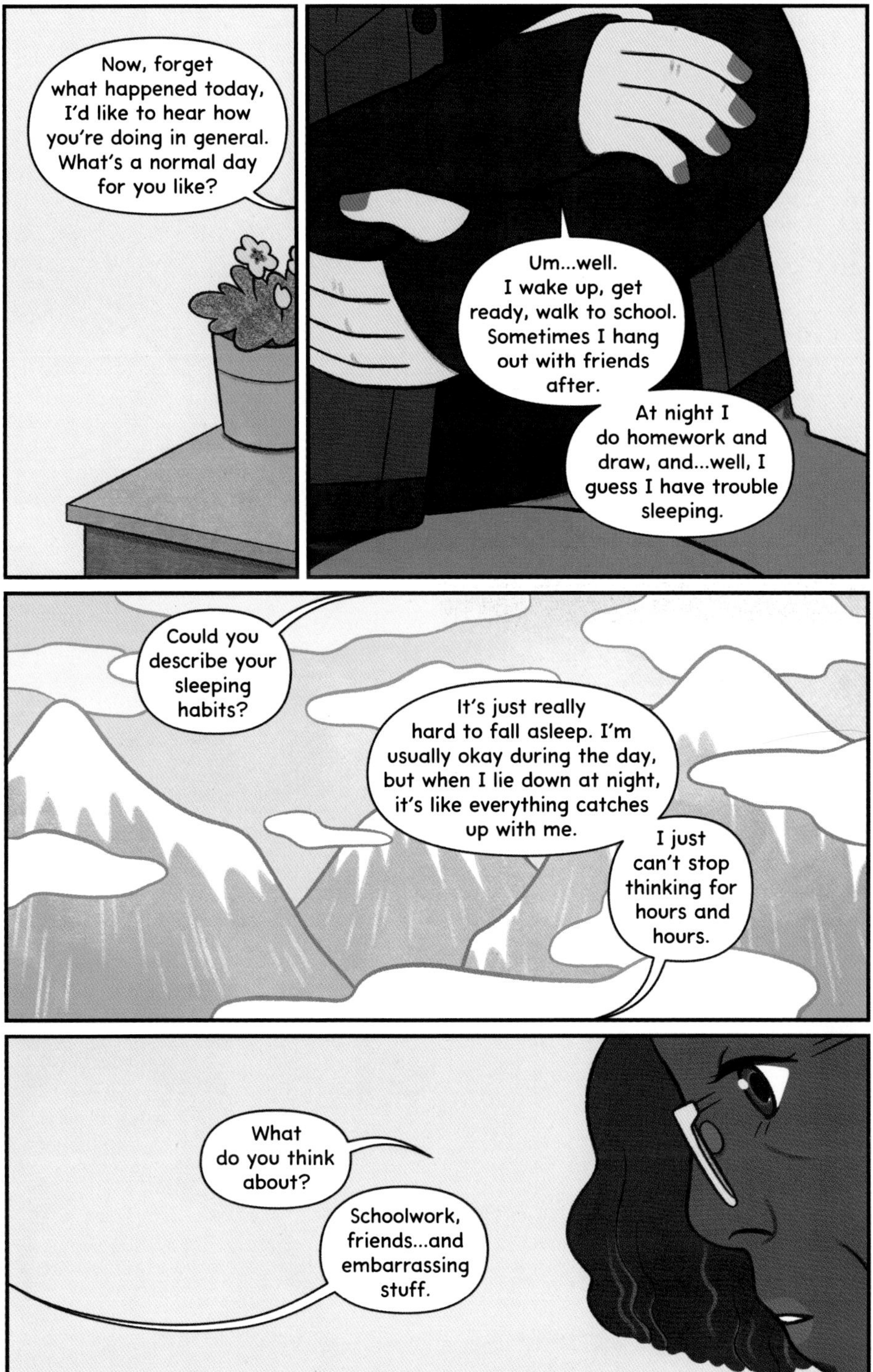
Now, forget what happened today, I'd like to hear how you're doing in general. What's a normal day for you like?
Um...well. I wake up, get ready, walk to school. Sometimes I hang out with friends after.
At night I do homework and draw, and...well, I guess I have trouble sleeping.
Could you describe your sleeping habits?
It's just really hard to fall asleep. I'm usually okay during the day, but when I lie down at night, it's like everything catches up with me.
I just can't stop thinking for hours and hours.
What do you think about?
Schoolwork, friends...and embarrassing stuff.

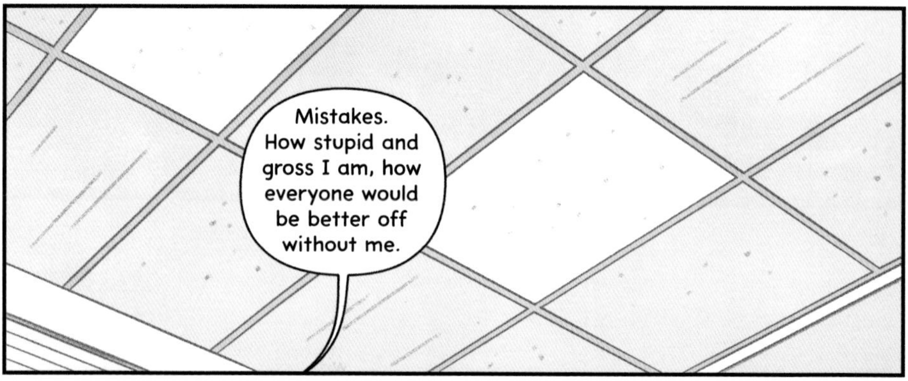
Mistakes. How stupid and gross I am, how everyone would be better off without me.

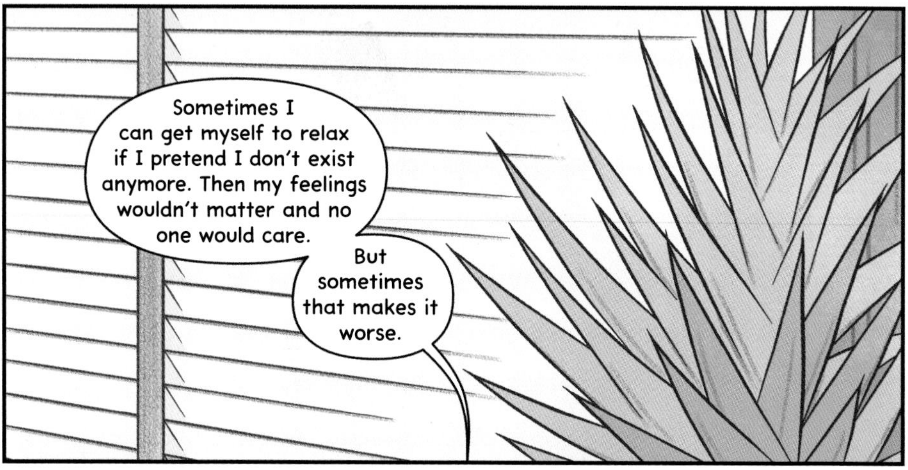
Sometimes I can get myself to relax if I pretend I don't exist anymore. Then my feelings wouldn't matter and no one would care.
But sometimes that makes it worse.

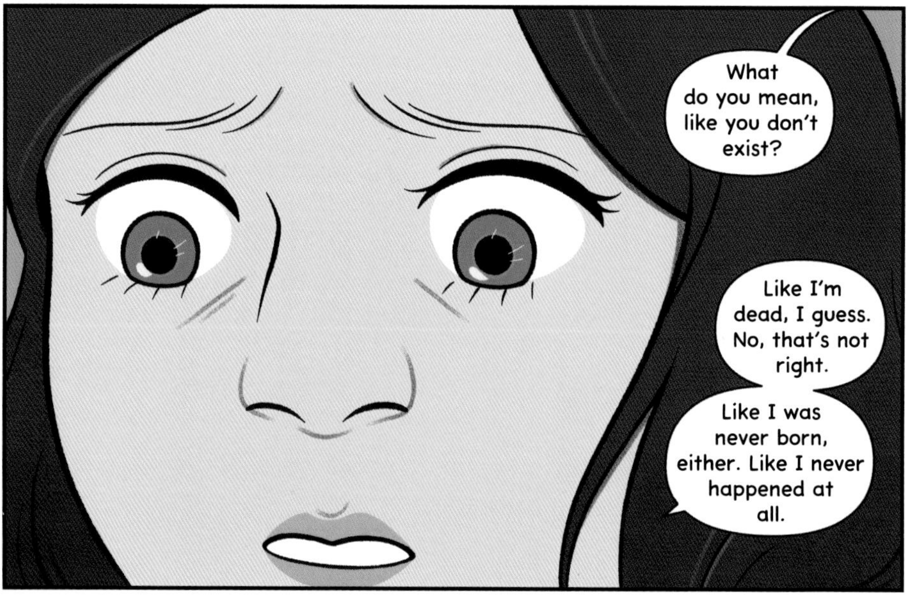
What do you mean, like you don't exist?
Like I'm dead, I guess. No, that's not right.
Like I was never born, either. Like I never happened at all.

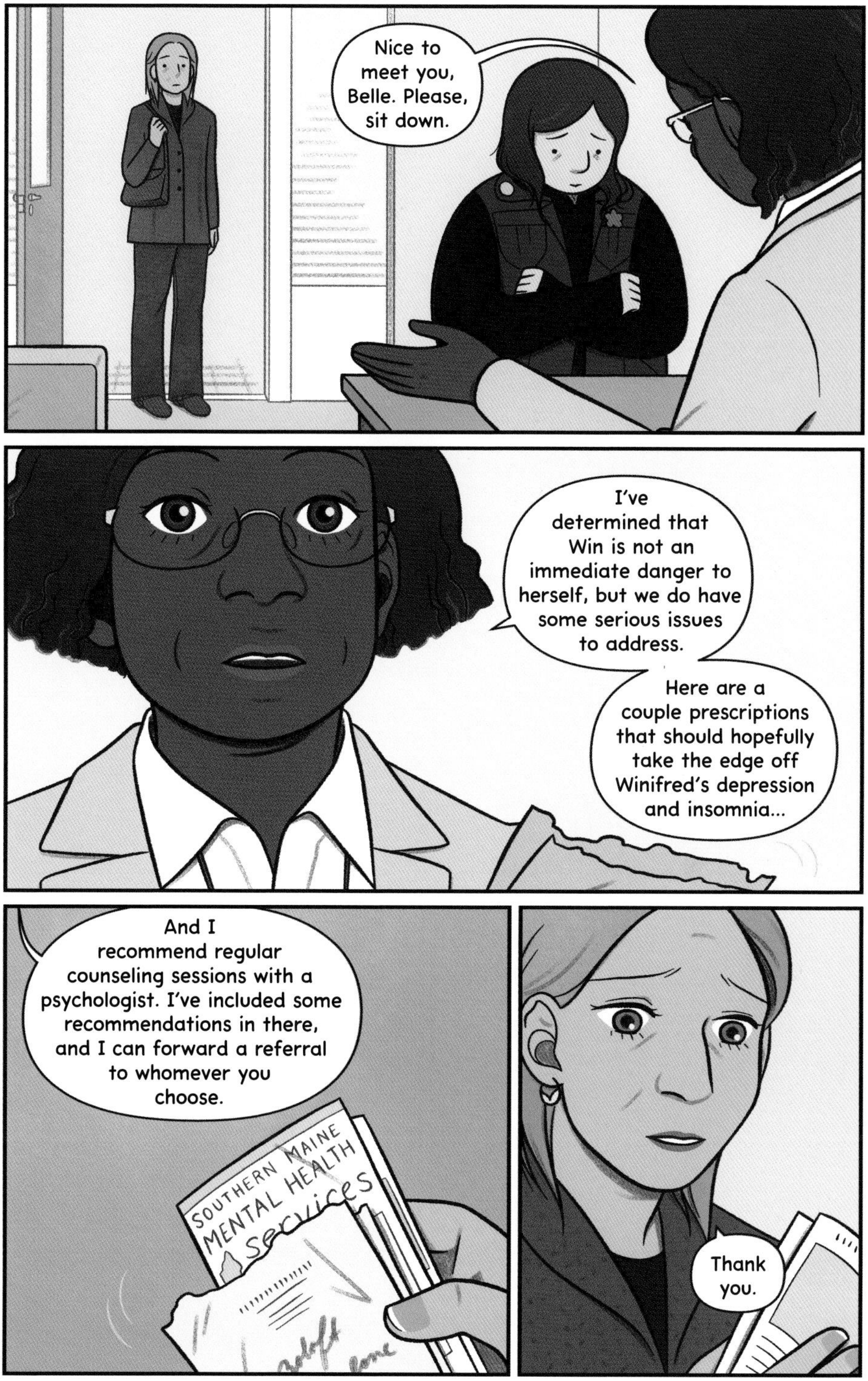
Nice to meet you, Belle. Please, sit down.
I've determined that Win is not an immediate danger to herself, but we do have some serious issues to address.
Here are a couple prescriptions that should hopefully take the edge off Winifred's depression and insomnia...
And I recommend regular counseling sessions with a psychologist. I've included some recommendations in there, and I can forward a referral to whomever you choose.
SOUTHERN MAINE MENTAL HEALTH Services
Thank you.

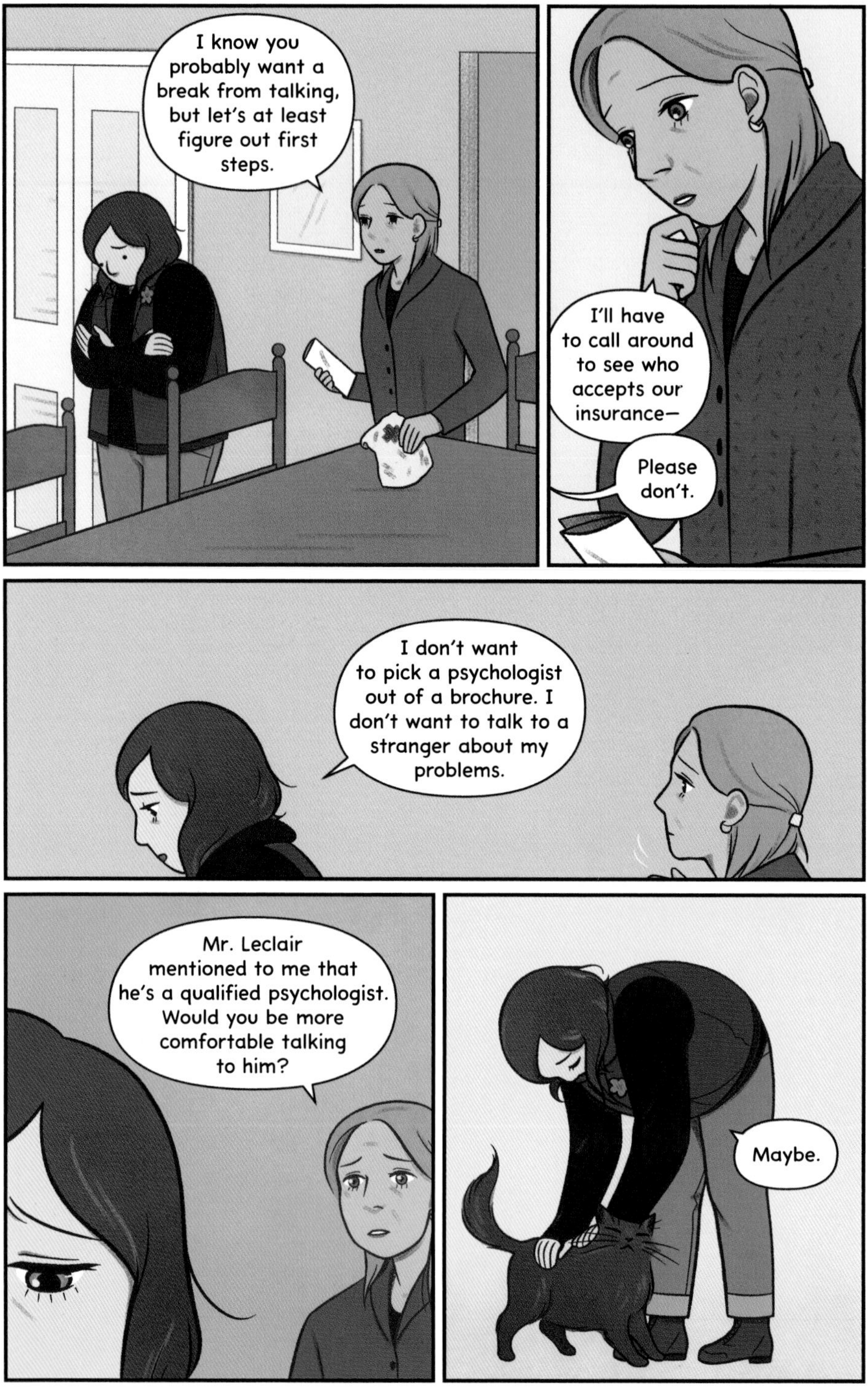
I know you probably want a break from talking, but let's at least figure out first steps.
I'll have to call around to see who accepts our insurance—
Please don't.
I don't want to pick a psychologist out of a brochure. I don't want to talk to a stranger about my problems.
Mr. Leclair mentioned to me that he's a qualified psychologist. Would you be more comfortable talking to him?
Maybe.

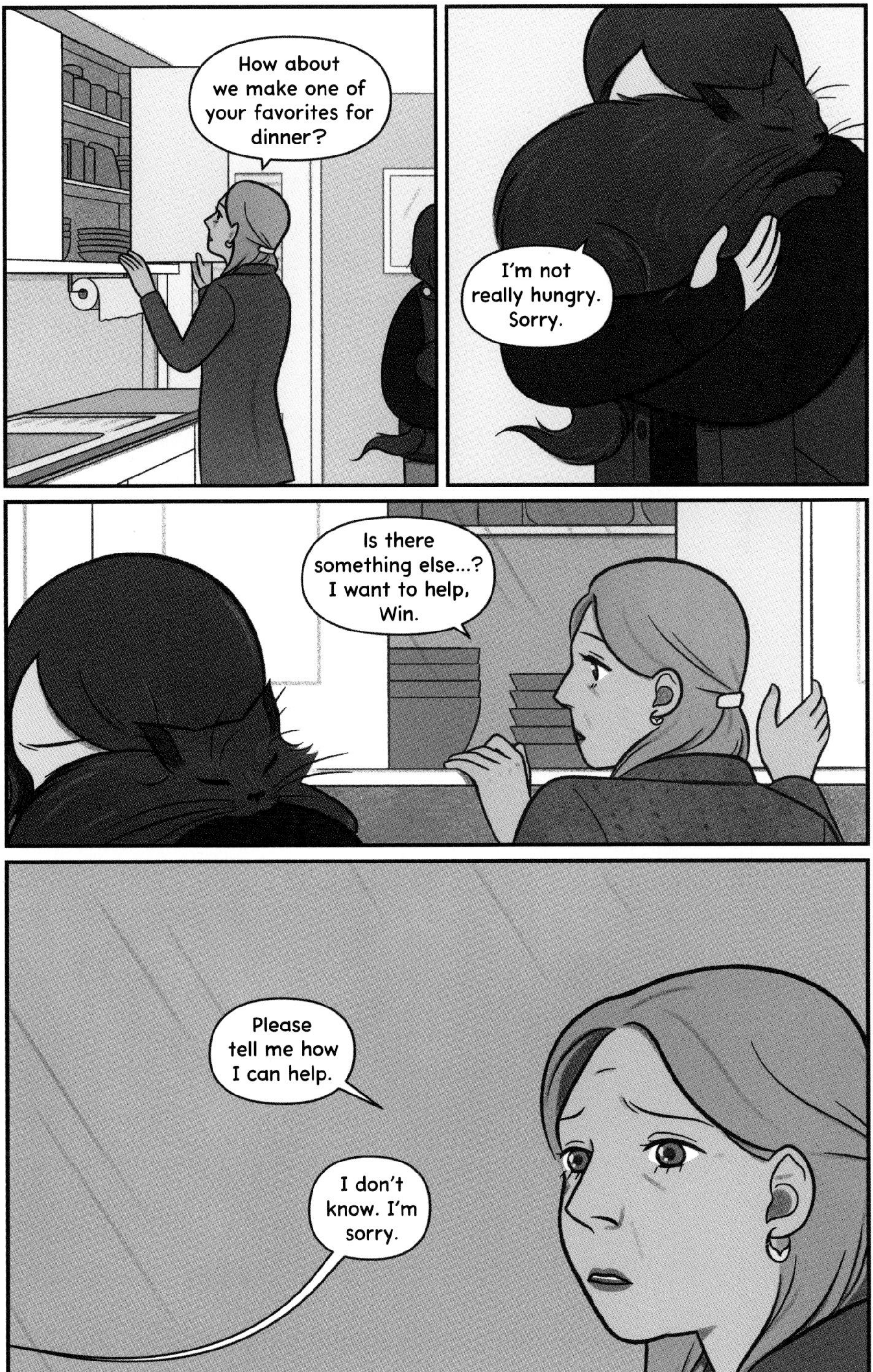
How about we make one of your favorites for dinner?
I'm not really hungry. Sorry.
Is there something else...? I want to help, Win.
Please tell me how I can help.
I don't know. I'm sorry.

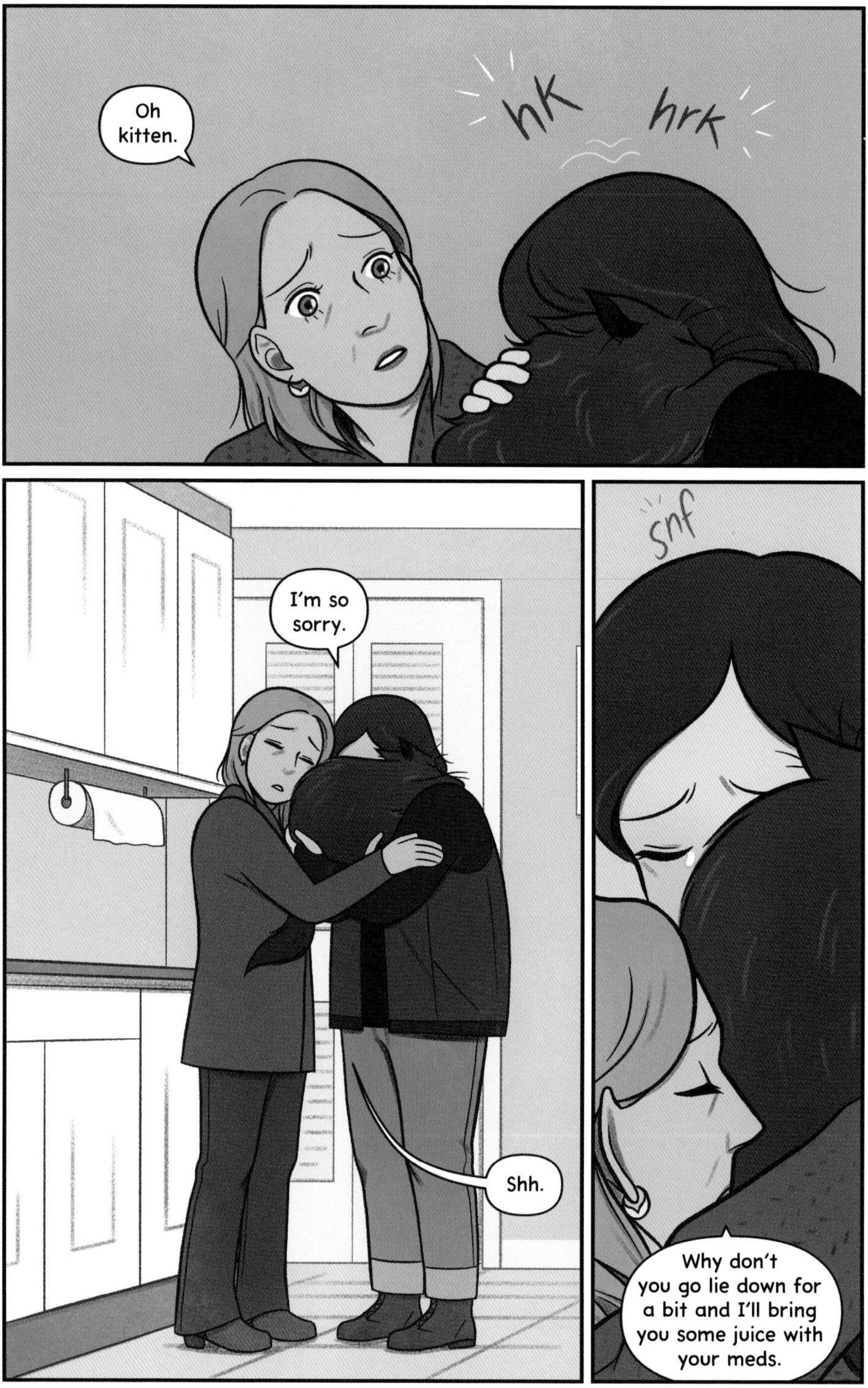
Oh kitten.
hk
hrk
I'm so sorry.
Shh.
snf
Why don't you go lie down for a bit and I'll bring you some juice with your meds.

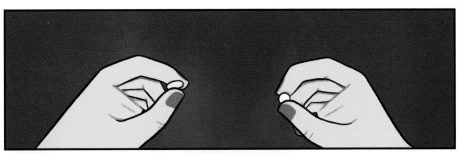

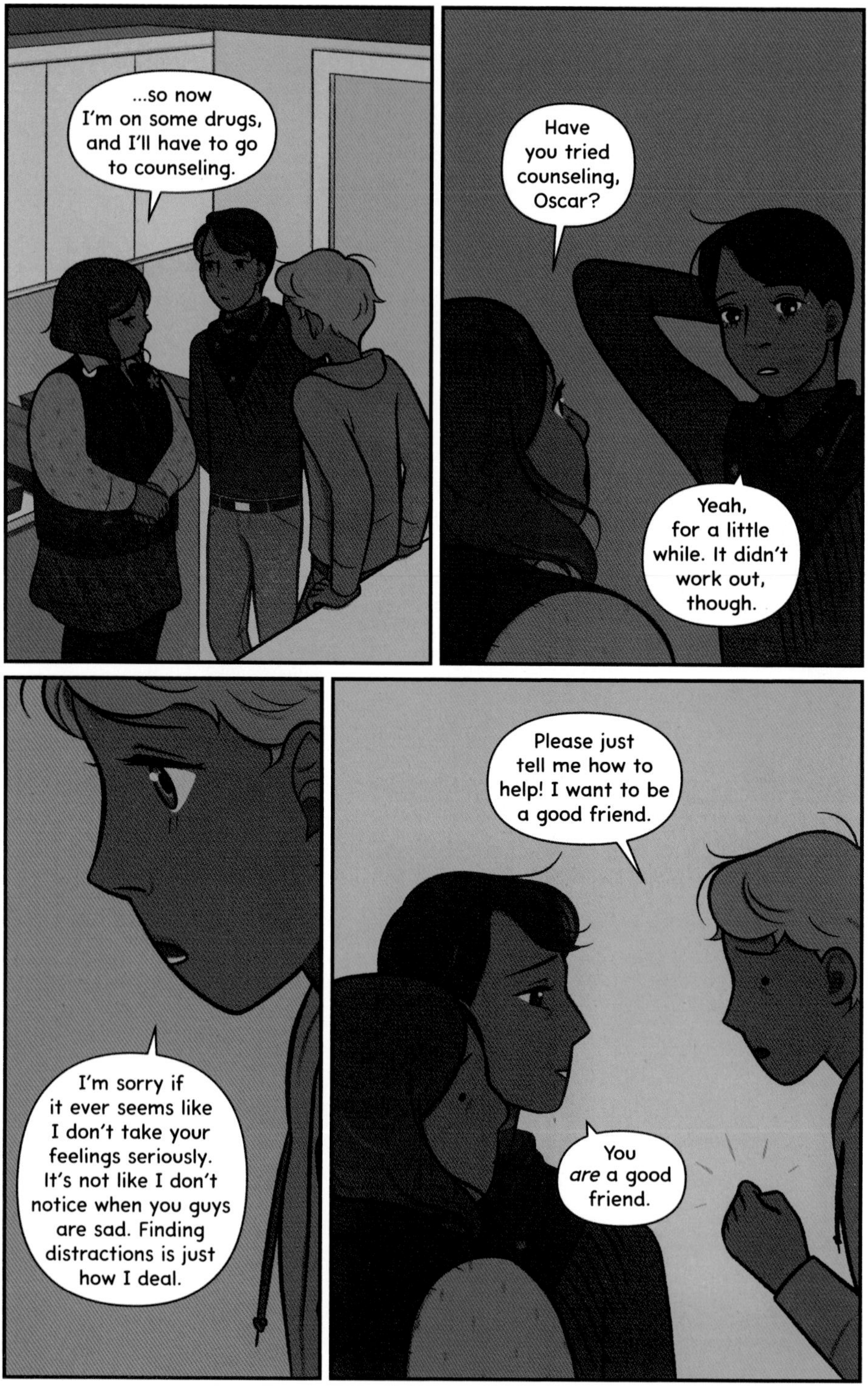
...so now I'm on some drugs, and I'll have to go to counseling.
Have you tried counseling, Oscar?
Yeah, for a little while. It didn't work out, though.
I'm sorry if it ever seems like I don't take your feelings seriously. It's not like I don't notice when you guys are sad. Finding distractions is just how I deal.
Please just tell me how to help! I want to be a good friend.
You *are* a good friend.

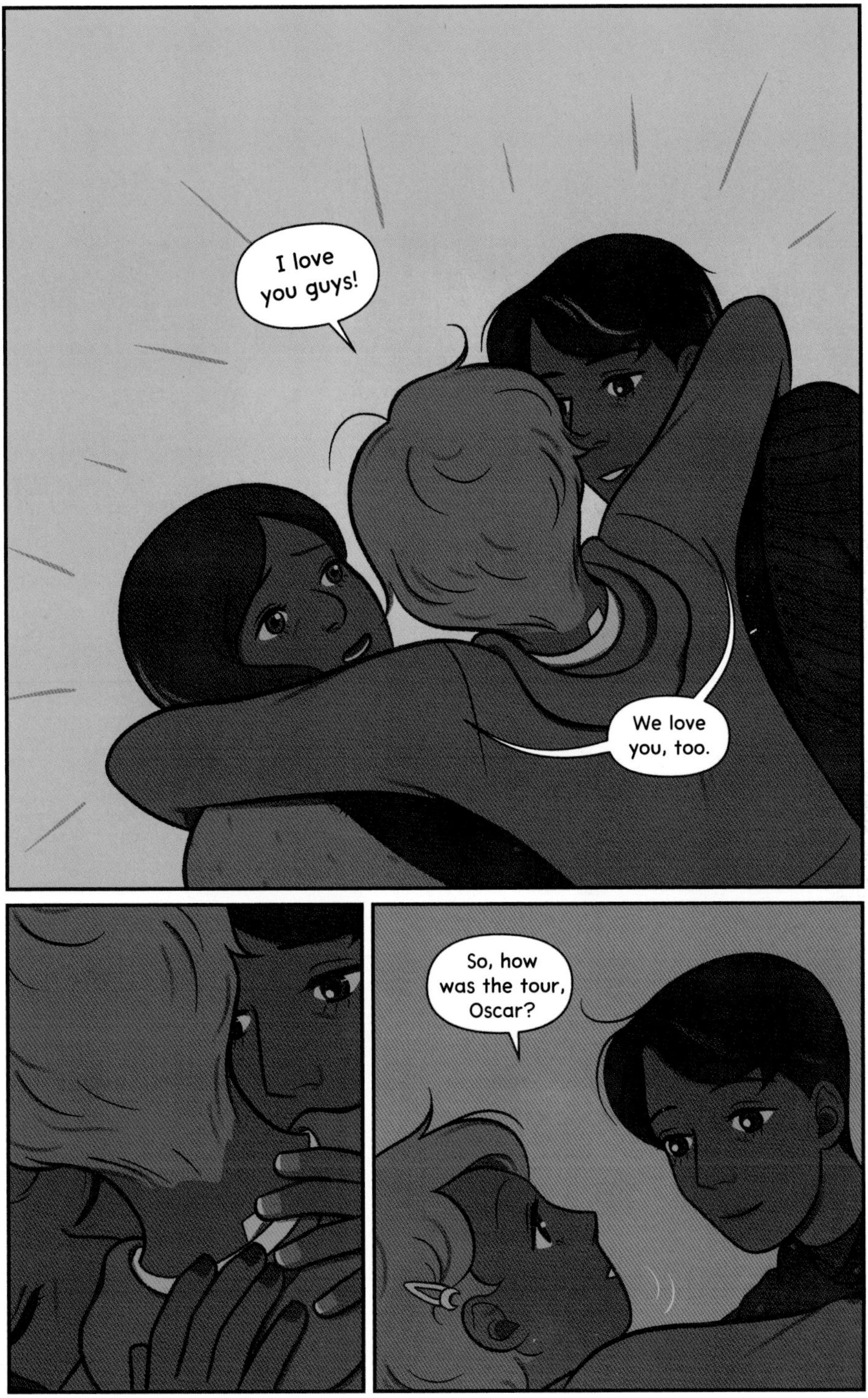
I love you guys!
We love you, too.
So, how was the tour, Oscar?

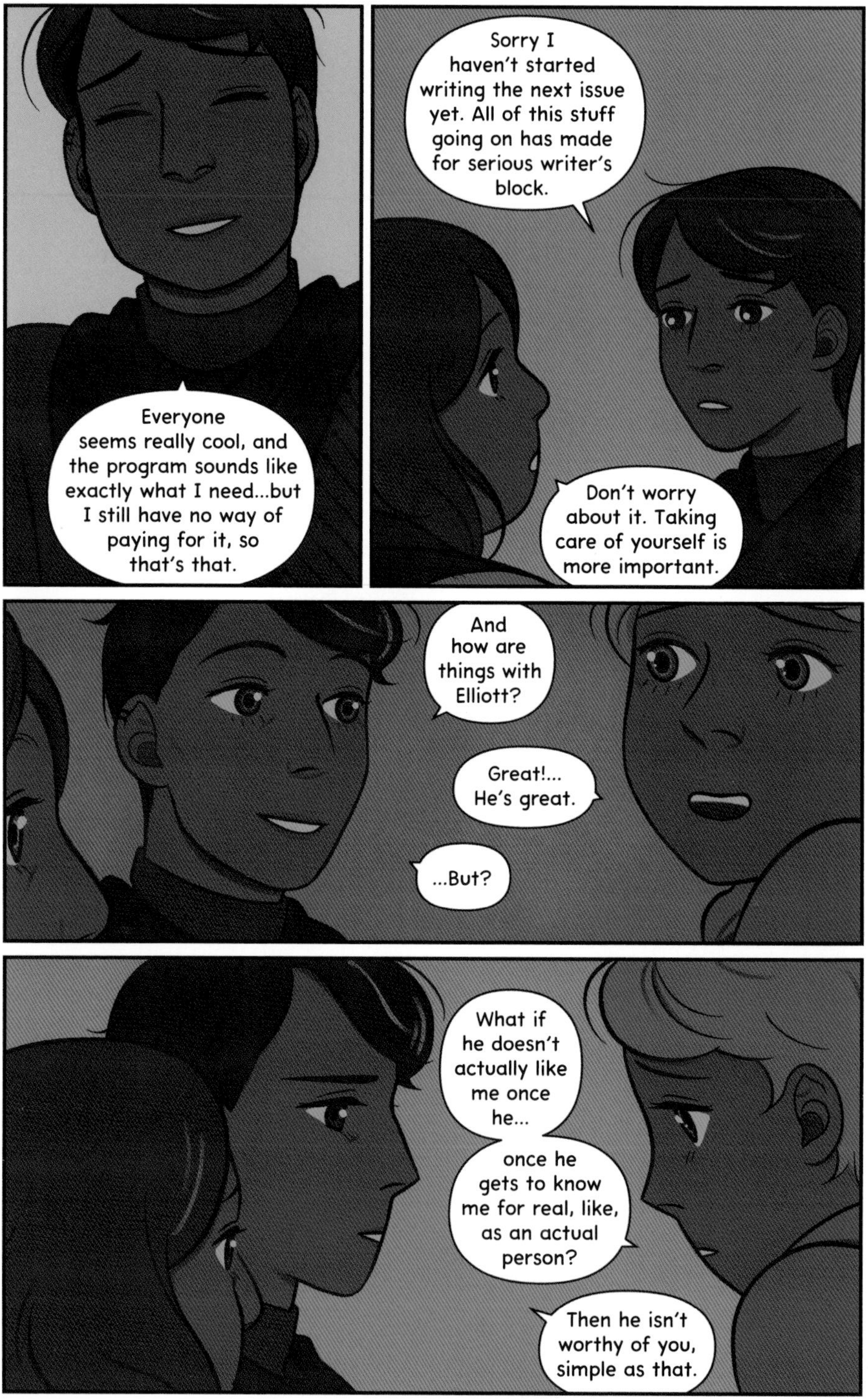
Everyone seems really cool, and the program sounds like exactly what I need...but I still have no way of paying for it, so that's that.
Sorry I haven't started writing the next issue yet. All of this stuff going on has made for serious writer's block.
Don't worry about it. Taking care of yourself is more important.
And how are things with Elliott?
Great!... He's great.
...But?
What if he doesn't actually like me once he...
once he gets to know me for real, like, as an actual person?
Then he isn't worthy of you, simple as that.

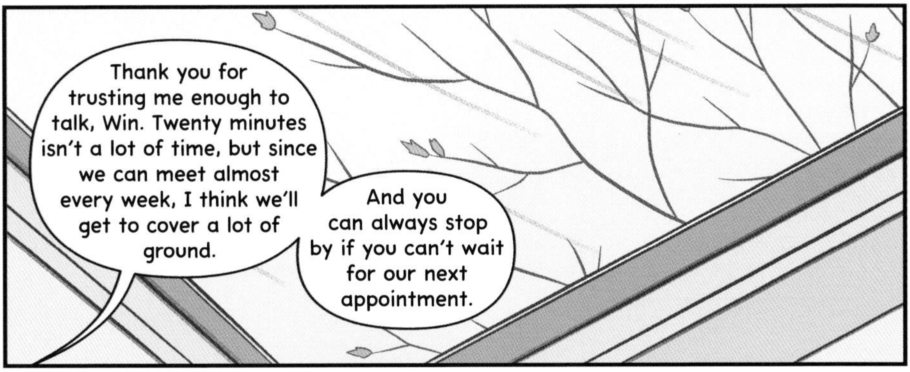
Thank you for trusting me enough to talk, Win. Twenty minutes isn't a lot of time, but since we can meet almost every week, I think we'll get to cover a lot of ground.
And you can always stop by if you can't wait for our next appointment.

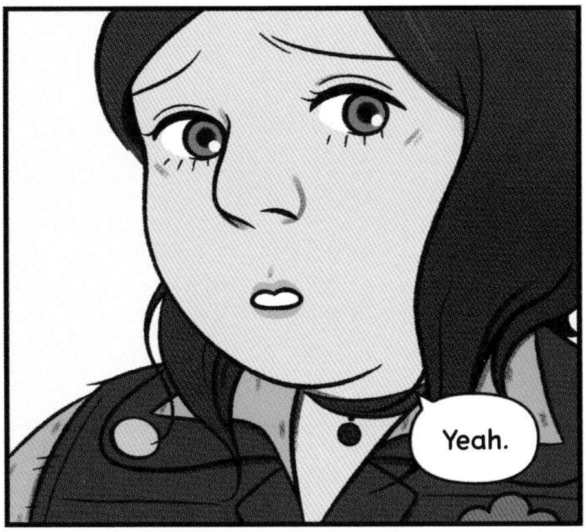
Yeah.

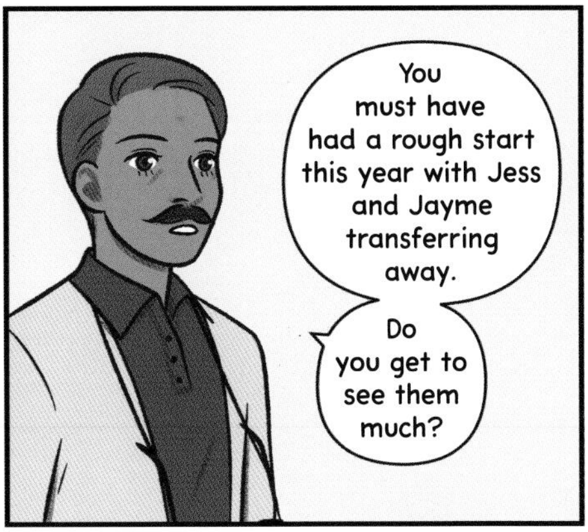
You must have had a rough start this year with Jess and Jayme transferring away.
Do you get to see them much?

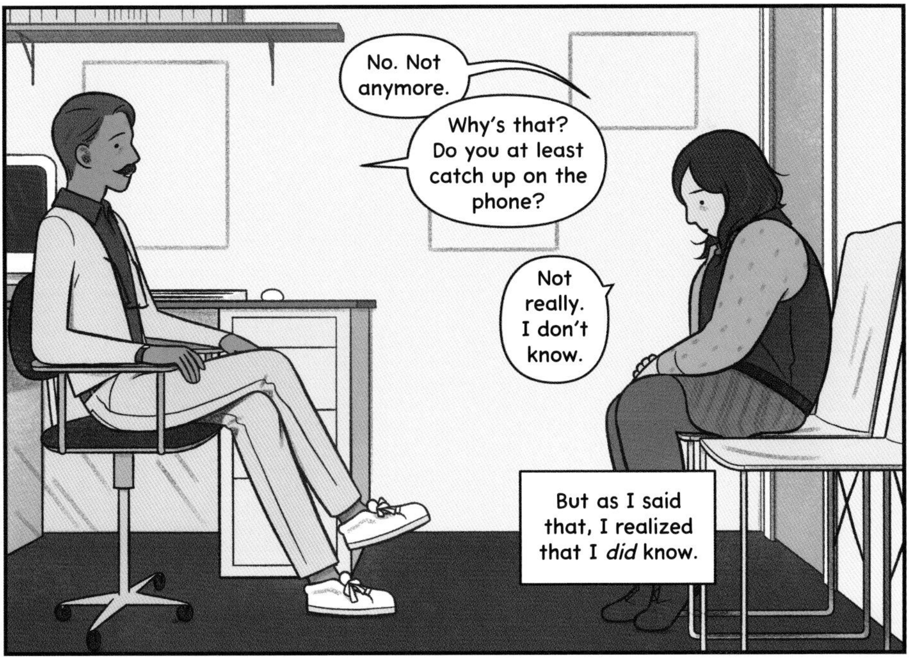
No. Not anymore.
Why's that? Do you at least catch up on the phone?
Not really. I don't know.
But as I said that, I realized that I *did* know.

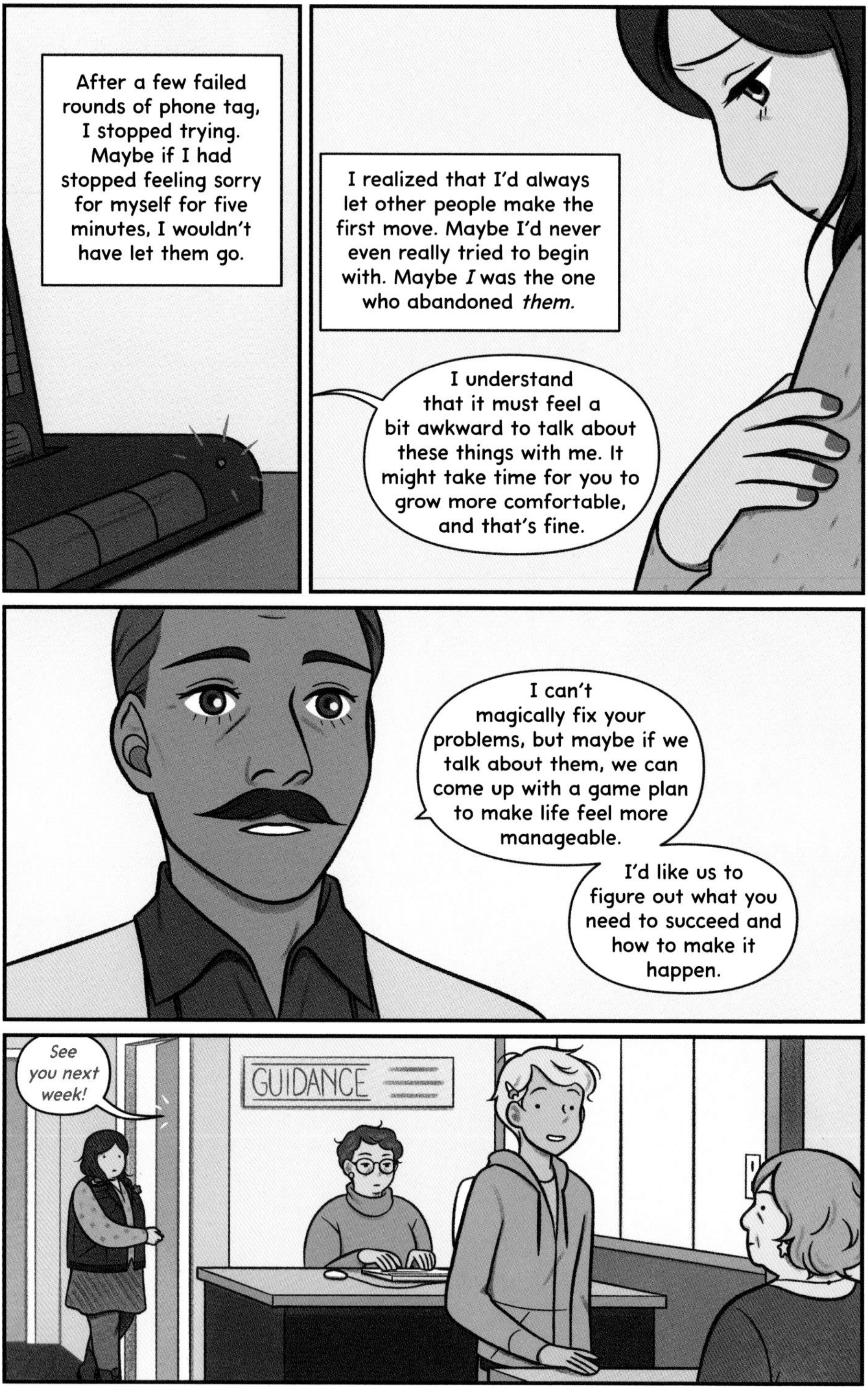
After a few failed rounds of phone tag, I stopped trying. Maybe if I had stopped feeling sorry for myself for five minutes, I wouldn't have let them go.
I realized that I'd always let other people make the first move. Maybe I'd never even really tried to begin with. Maybe *I* was the one who abandoned *them.*
I understand that it must feel a bit awkward to talk about these things with me. It might take time for you to grow more comfortable, and that's fine.
I can't magically fix your problems, but maybe if we talk about them, we can come up with a game plan to make life feel more manageable.
I'd like us to figure out what you need to succeed and how to make it happen.
See you next week!
GUIDANCE

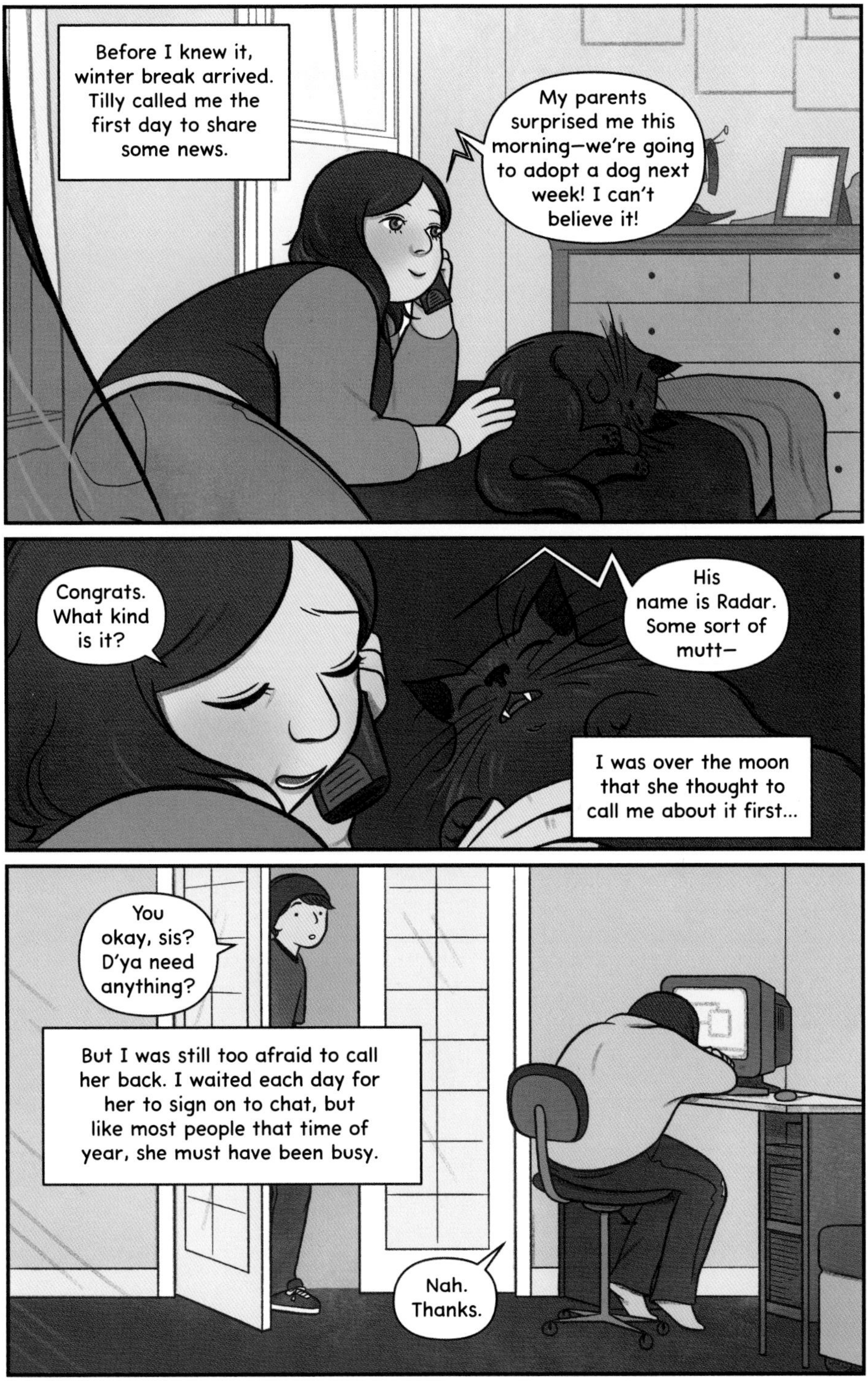
Before I knew it, winter break arrived. Tilly called me the first day to share some news.
My parents surprised me this morning—we're going to adopt a dog next week! I can't believe it!
Congrats. What kind is it?
His name is Radar. Some sort of mutt—
I was over the moon that she thought to call me about it first...
You okay, sis? D'ya need anything?
But I was still too afraid to call her back. I waited each day for her to sign on to chat, but like most people that time of year, she must have been busy.
Nah. Thanks.

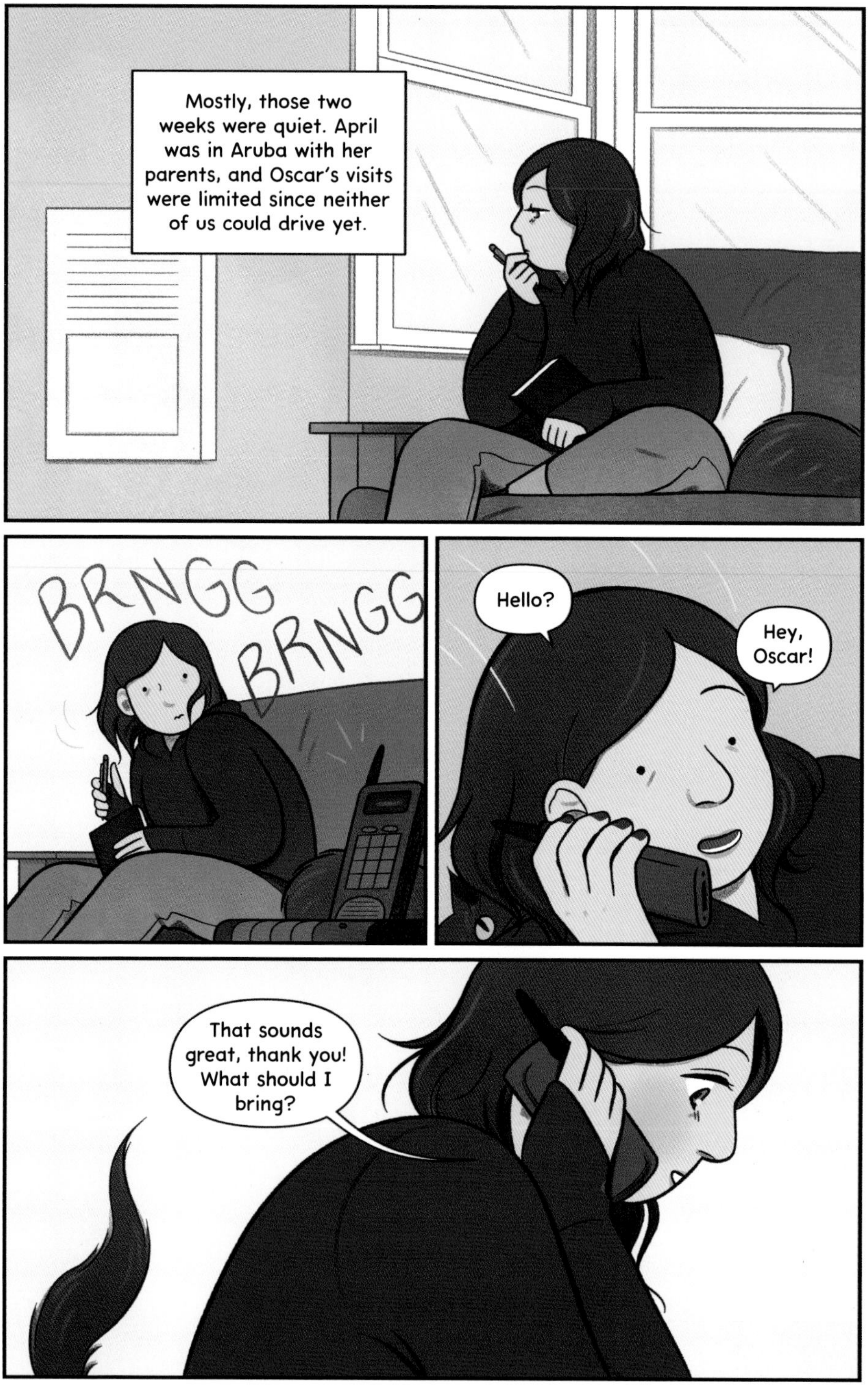
Mostly, those two weeks were quiet. April was in Aruba with her parents, and Oscar's visits were limited since neither of us could drive yet.
BRNGG BRNGG
Hello?
Hey, Oscar!
That sounds great, thank you! What should I bring?

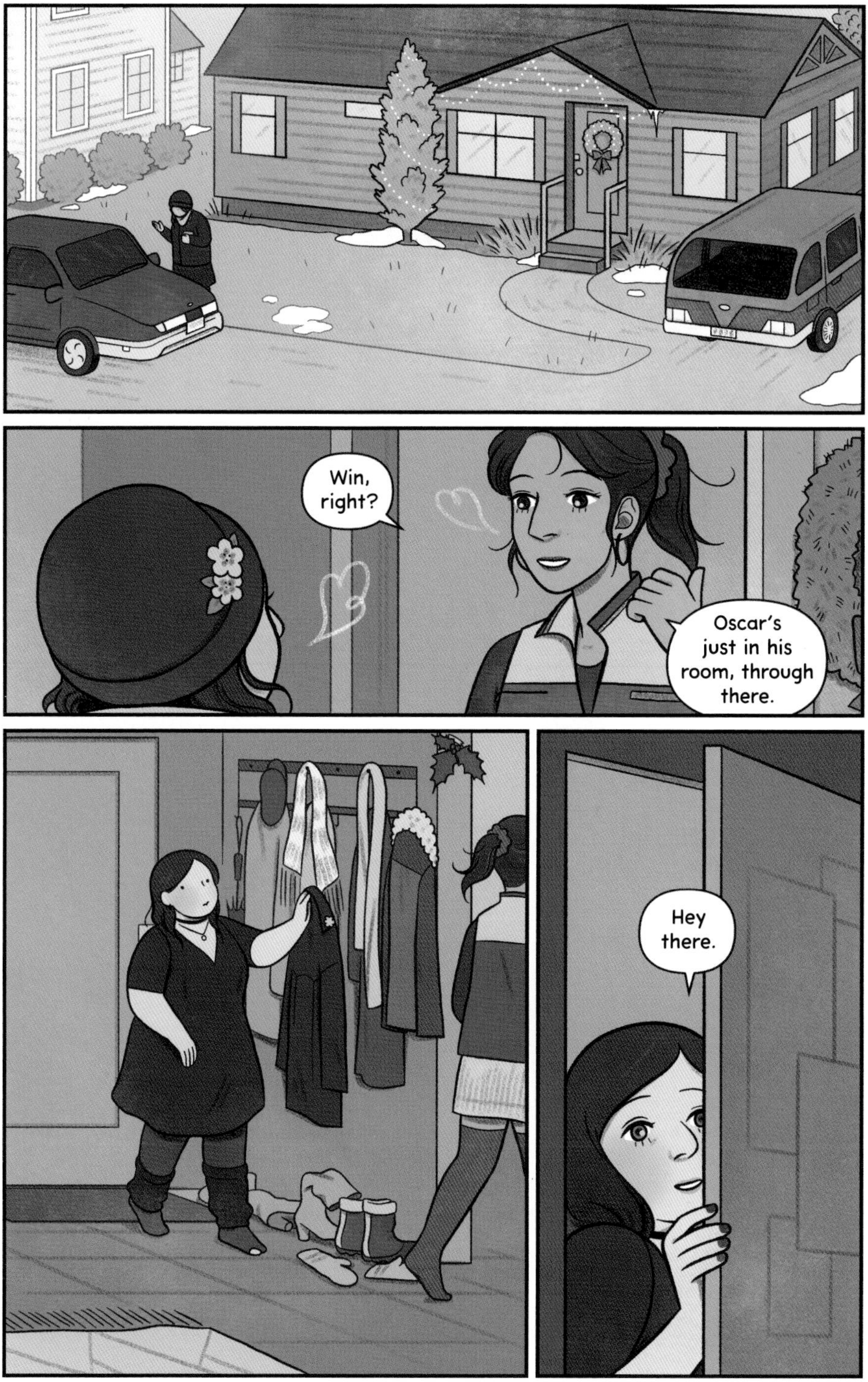
Win, right?
Oscar's just in his room, through there.
Hey there.

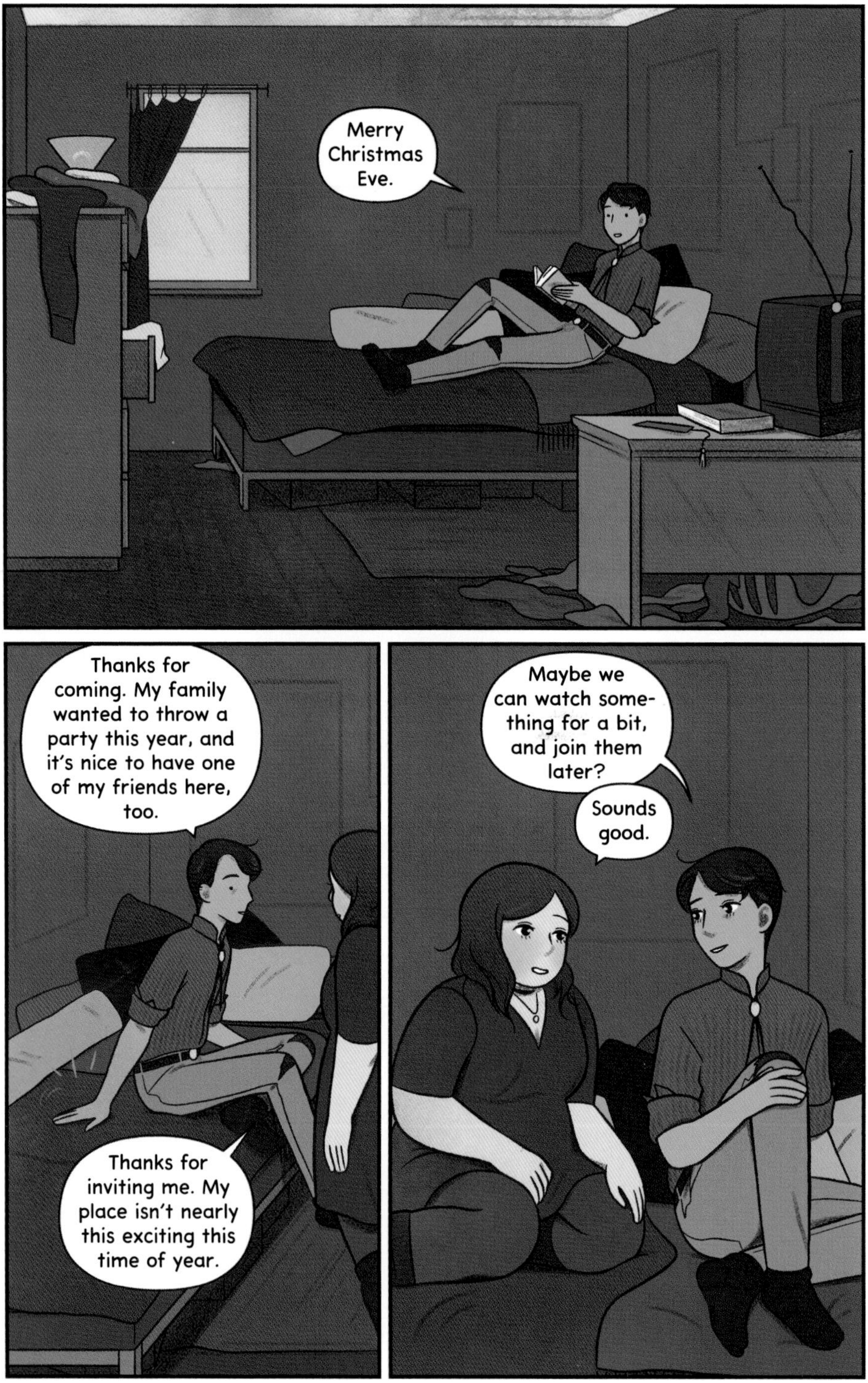
Merry Christmas Eve.
Thanks for coming. My family wanted to throw a party this year, and it's nice to have one of my friends here, too.
Thanks for inviting me. My place isn't nearly this exciting this time of year.
Maybe we can watch something for a bit, and join them later?
Sounds good.

To see myself through your eyes, as I look to someone who loves me...

...it has simply been the greatest thing.

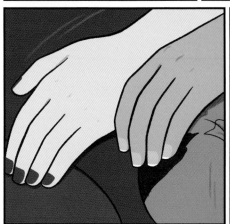

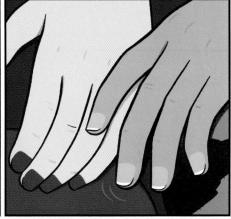

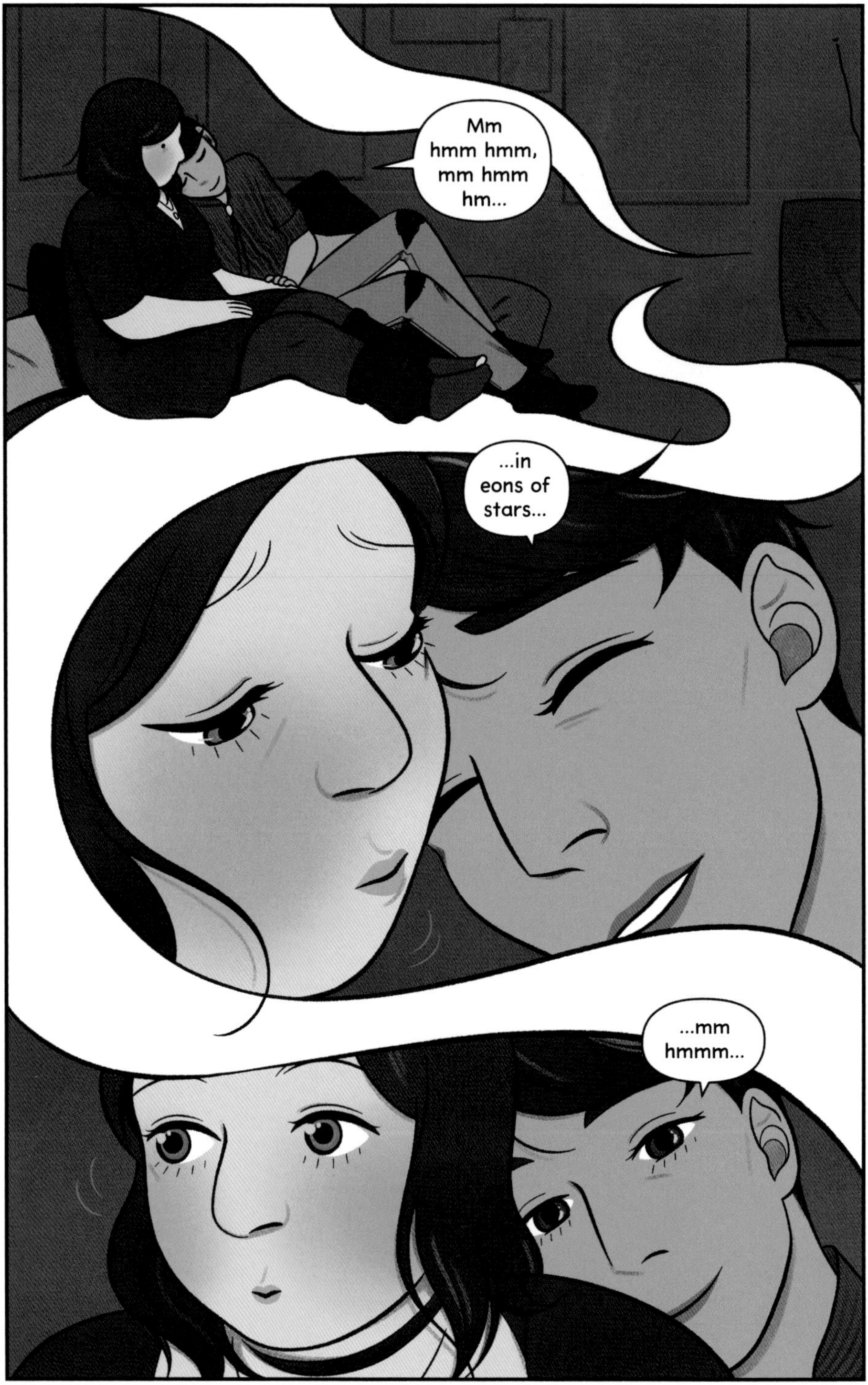
Mm hmm hmm, mm hmm hm...
...in eons of stars...
...mm hmmm...

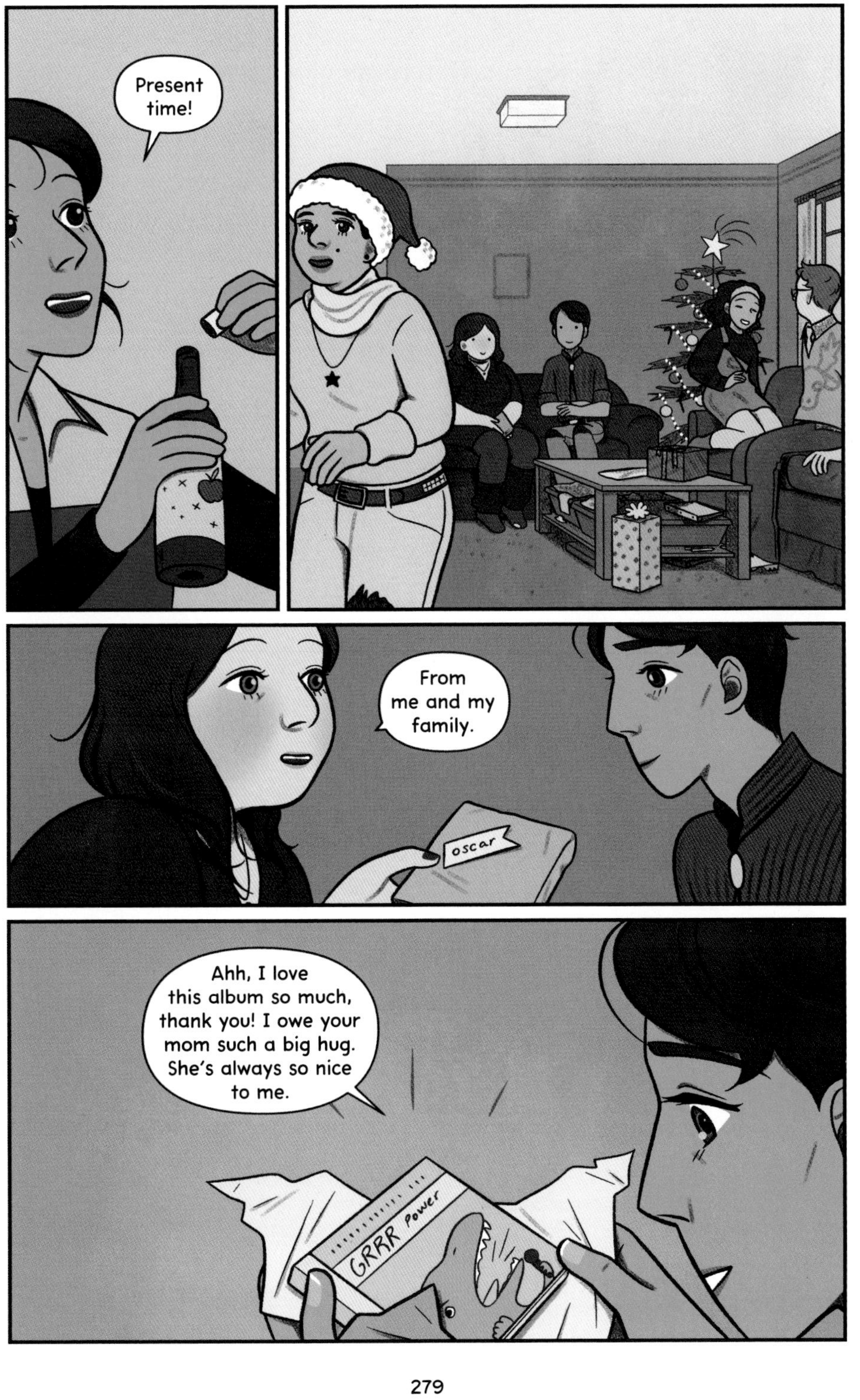
Present time!
From me and my family.
oscar
Ahh, I love this album so much, thank you! I owe your mom such a big hug. She's always so nice to me.
GRRR Power

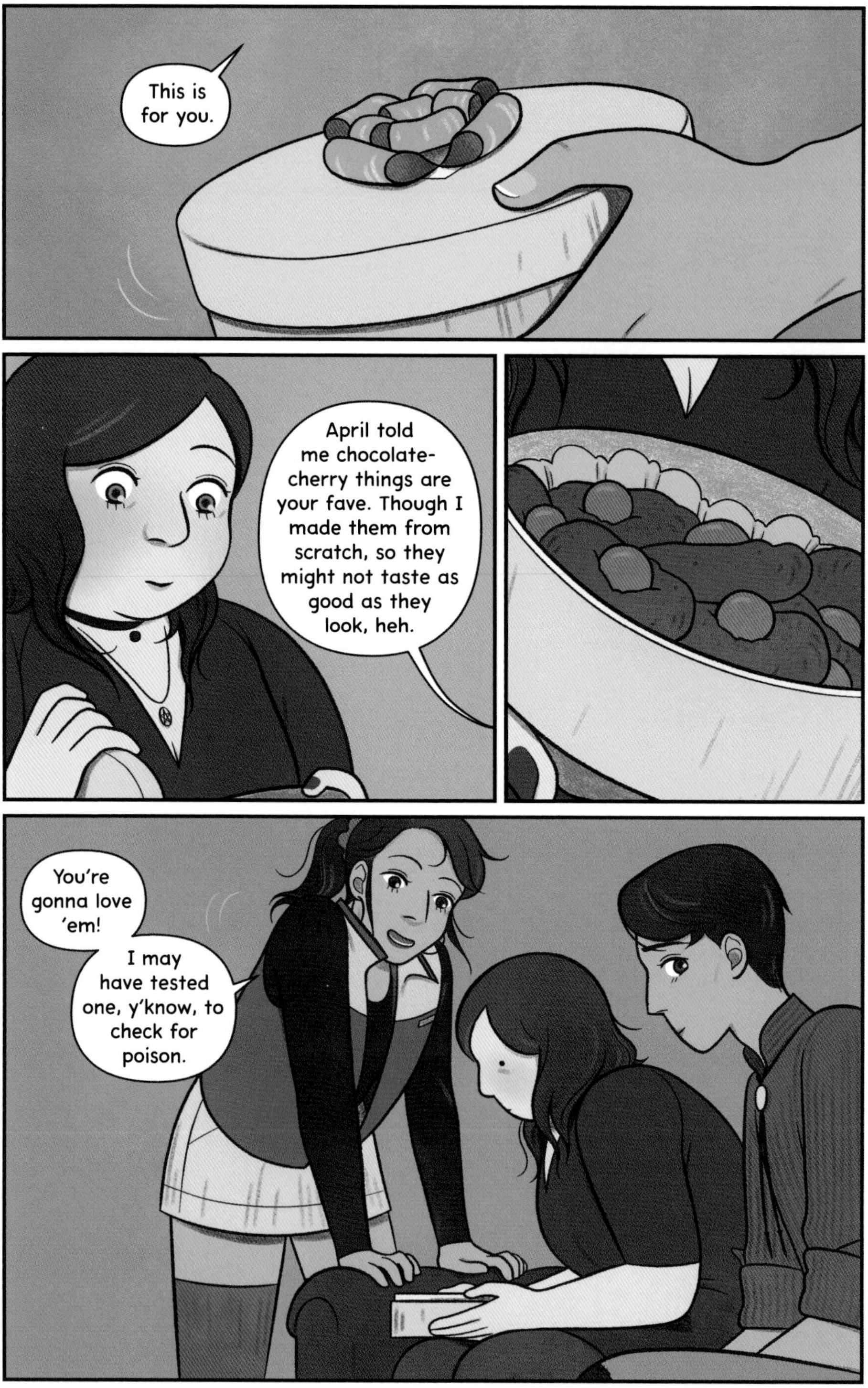

This is for you.
April told me chocolate-cherry things are your fave. Though I made them from scratch, so they might not taste as good as they look, heh.
You're gonna love 'em!
I may have tested one, y'know, to check for poison.

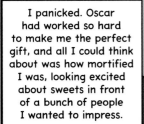

I panicked. Oscar had worked so hard to make me the perfect gift, and all I could think about was how mortified I was, looking excited about sweets in front of a bunch of people I wanted to impress.

The room spun and my stomach churned along with it, an acrid taste creeping up the back of my throat.

My heart seized in my chest and I was truly convinced, at least for a second, that I was dying.

The ultimate humiliation: a fat girl literally dying of glee over chocolate.

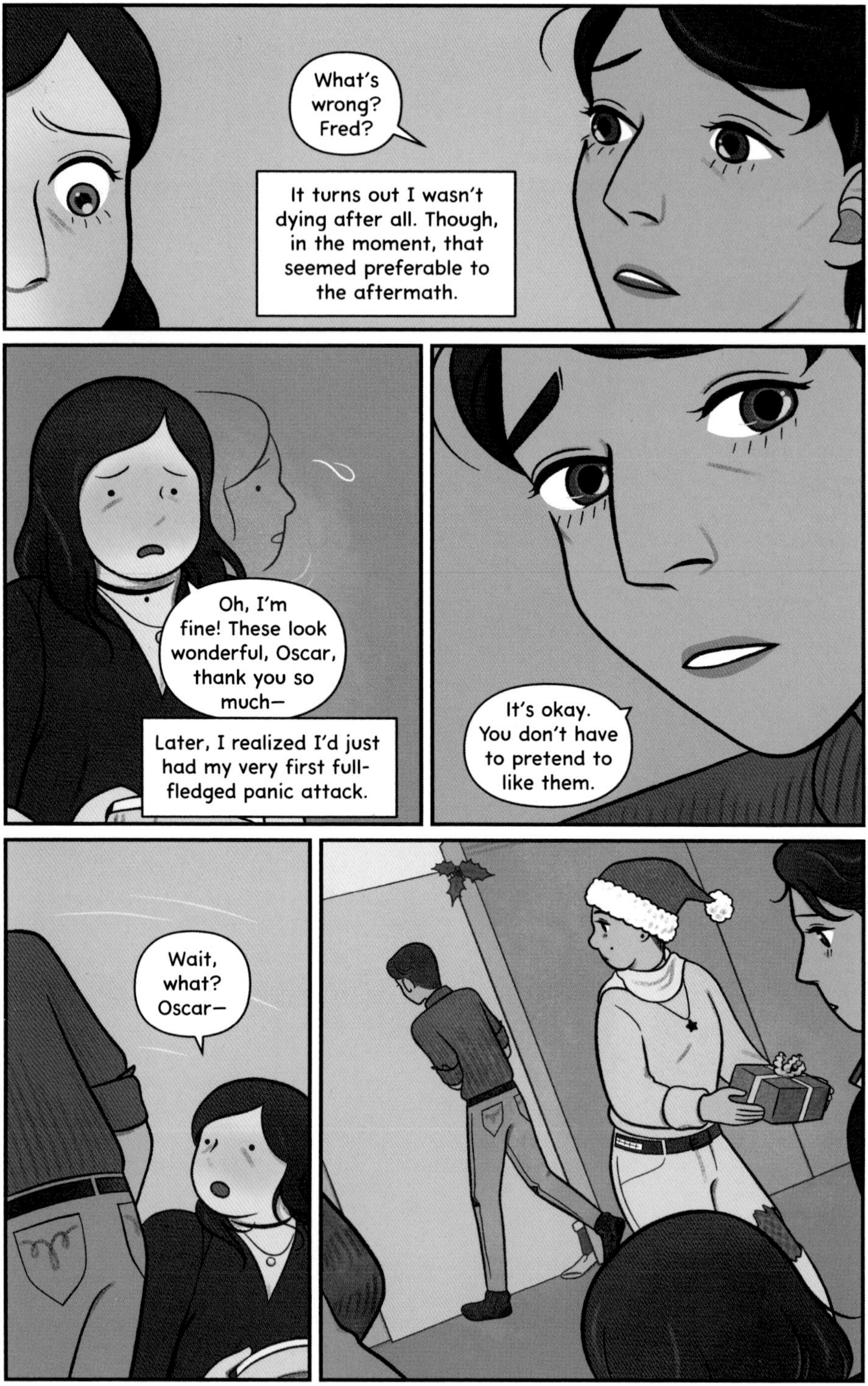
What's wrong? Fred?
It turns out I wasn't dying after all. Though, in the moment, that seemed preferable to the aftermath.
Oh, I'm fine! These look wonderful, Oscar, thank you so much—
Later, I realized I'd just had my very first full-fledged panic attack.
It's okay. You don't have to pretend to like them.
Wait, what? Oscar—

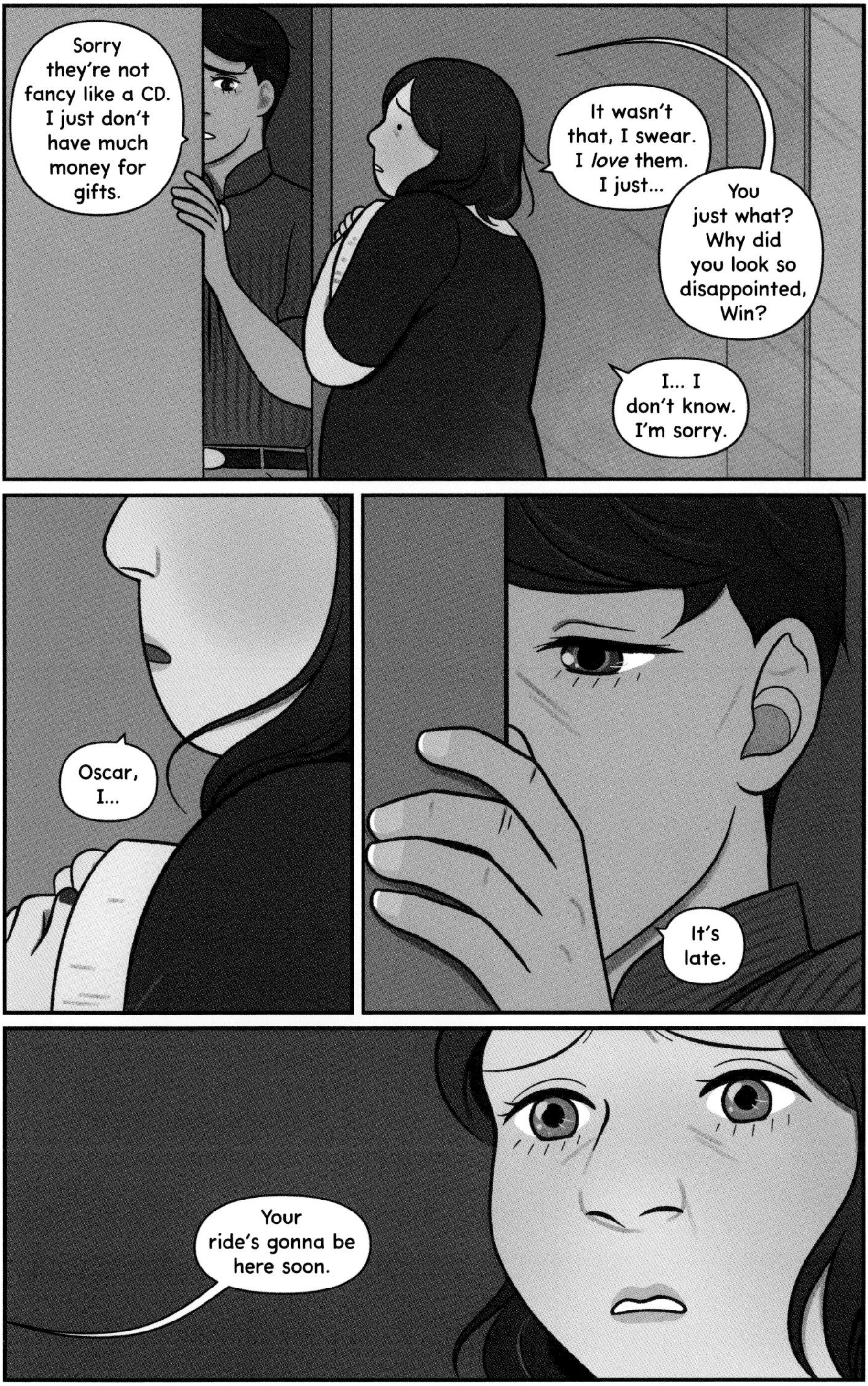
Sorry they're not fancy like a CD. I just don't have much money for gifts.
It wasn't that, I swear. I *love* them. I just...
You just what? Why did you look so disappointed, Win?
I... I don't know. I'm sorry.
Oscar, I...
It's late.
Your ride's gonna be here soon.

When I call your names for attendance, come up to my desk to grab your new schedules.

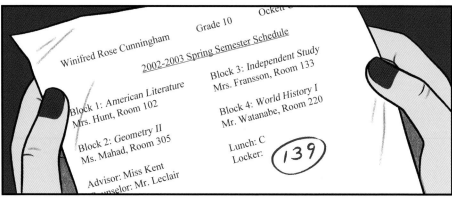

Winifred Rose Cunningham Grade 10 Ockett

2002-2003 Spring Semester Schedule

Block 1: American Literature
Mrs. Hunt, Room 102

Block 2: Geometry II
Ms. Mahad, Room 305

Block 3: Independent Study
Mrs. Fransson, Room 133

Block 4: World History I
Mr. Watanabe, Room 220

Lunch: C
Locker: 139

Advisor: Miss Kent
Counselor: Mr. Leclair

—nie! Winnie, can you hear me?

Hey! I already miss having last period with you. Photo class was the best. How was your break?

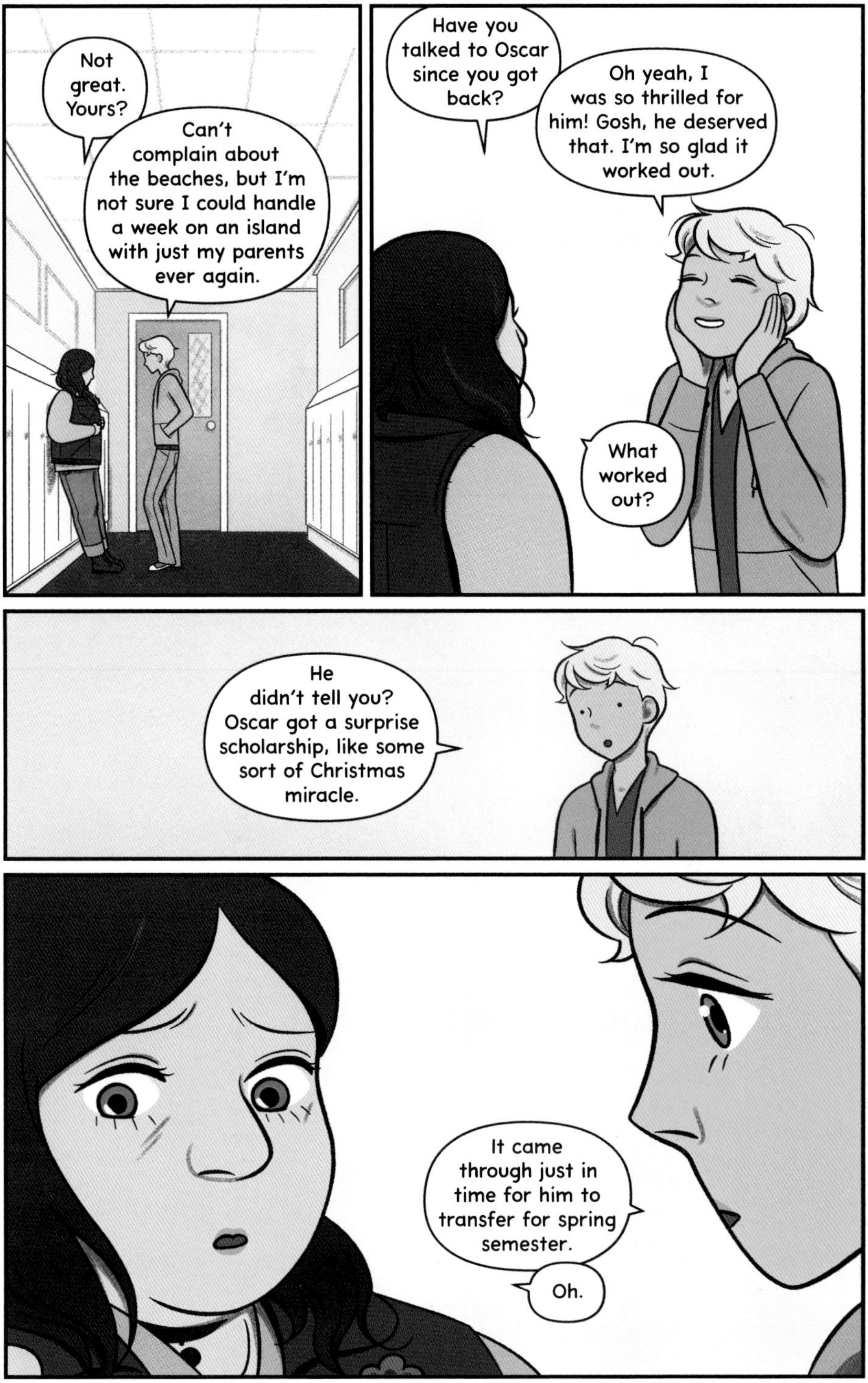
Not great. Yours?
Can't complain about the beaches, but I'm not sure I could handle a week on an island with just my parents ever again.
Have you talked to Oscar since you got back?
Oh yeah, I was so thrilled for him! Gosh, he deserved that. I'm so glad it worked out.
What worked out?
He didn't tell you? Oscar got a surprise scholarship, like some sort of Christmas miracle.
It came through just in time for him to transfer for spring semester.
Oh.

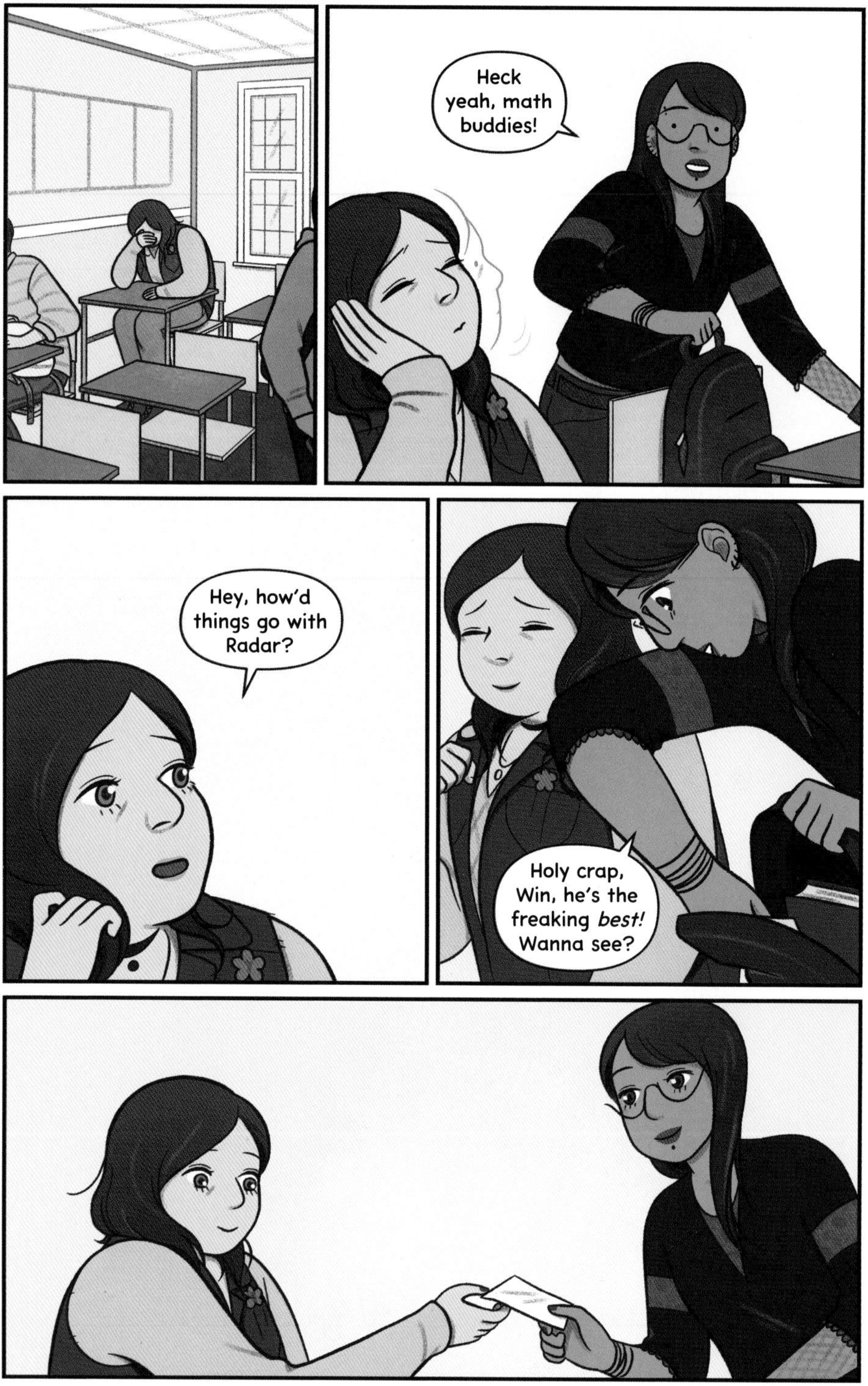
Heck yeah, math buddies!
Hey, how'd things go with Radar?
Holy crap, Win, he's the freaking *best!* Wanna see?

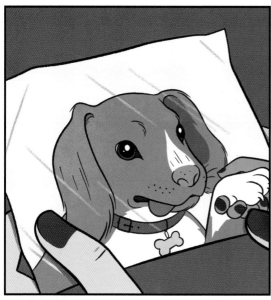

He's adorable.

He's such a good boy. Doesn't bark at anything—

And he likes chicken adobo almost as much as I do...

So I'm pretty sure we're soul mates.

Oh, and I discovered this cool manga about this girl who gets transported back through time to ancient Japan...

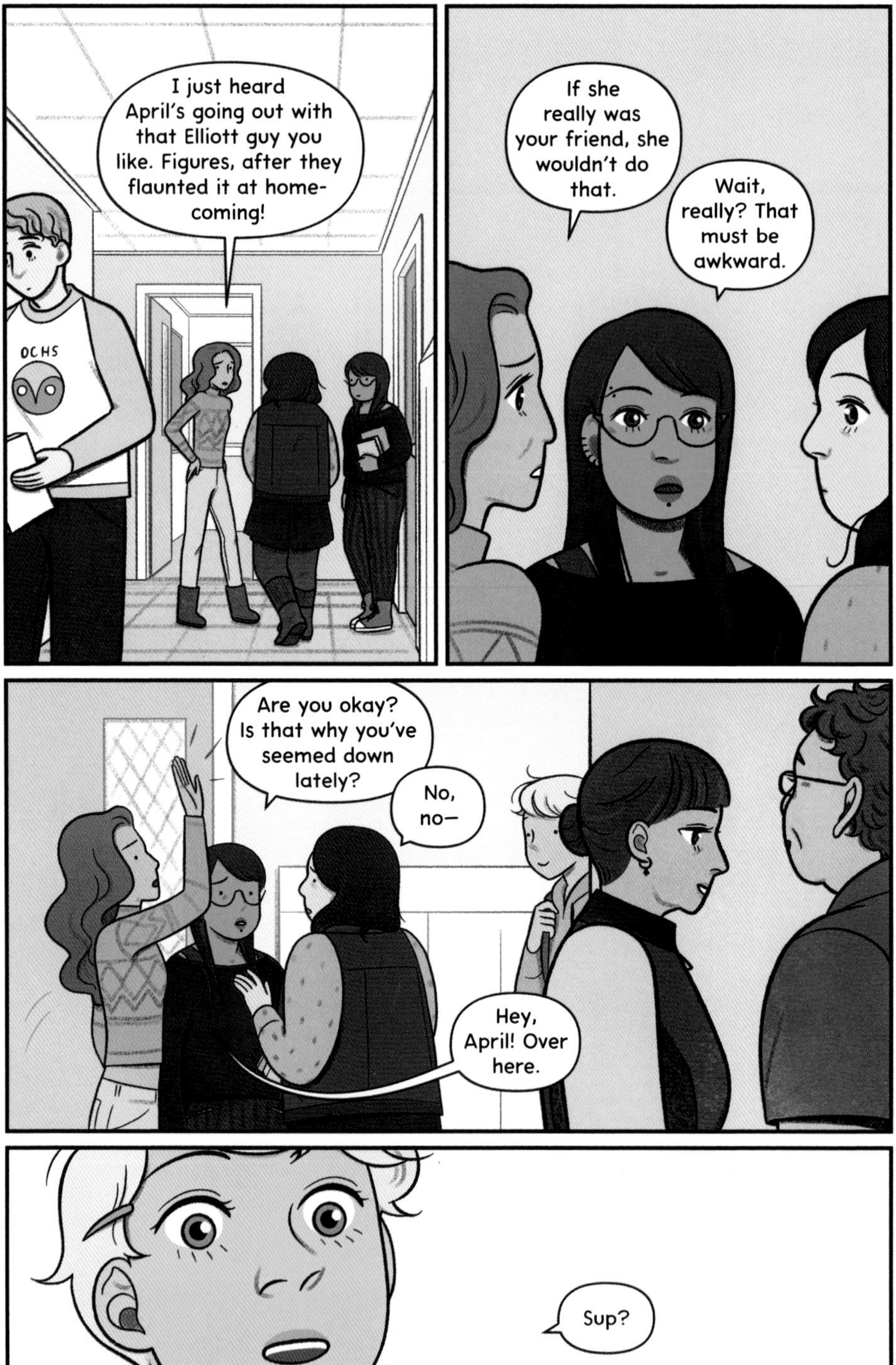
I just heard April's going out with that Elliott guy you like. Figures, after they flaunted it at home-coming!
OCHS
If she really was your friend, she wouldn't do that.
Wait, really? That must be awkward.
Are you okay? Is that why you've seemed down lately?
No, no—
Hey, April! Over here.
Sup?

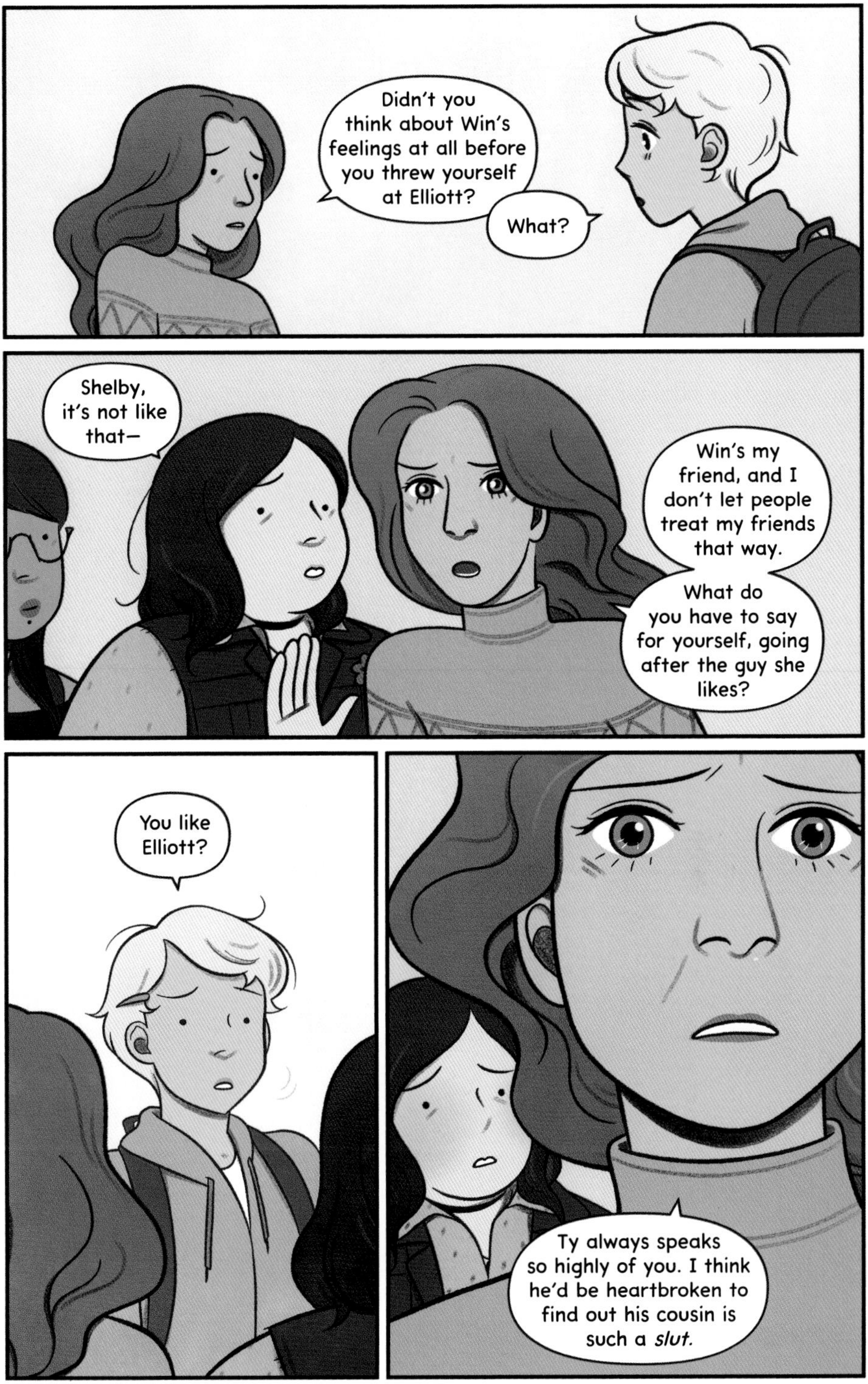
Didn't you think about Win's feelings at all before you threw yourself at Elliott?
What?
Shelby, it's not like that—
Win's my friend, and I don't let people treat my friends that way.
What do you have to say for yourself, going after the guy she likes?
You like Elliott?
Ty always speaks so highly of you. I think he'd be heartbroken to find out his cousin is such a *slut.*

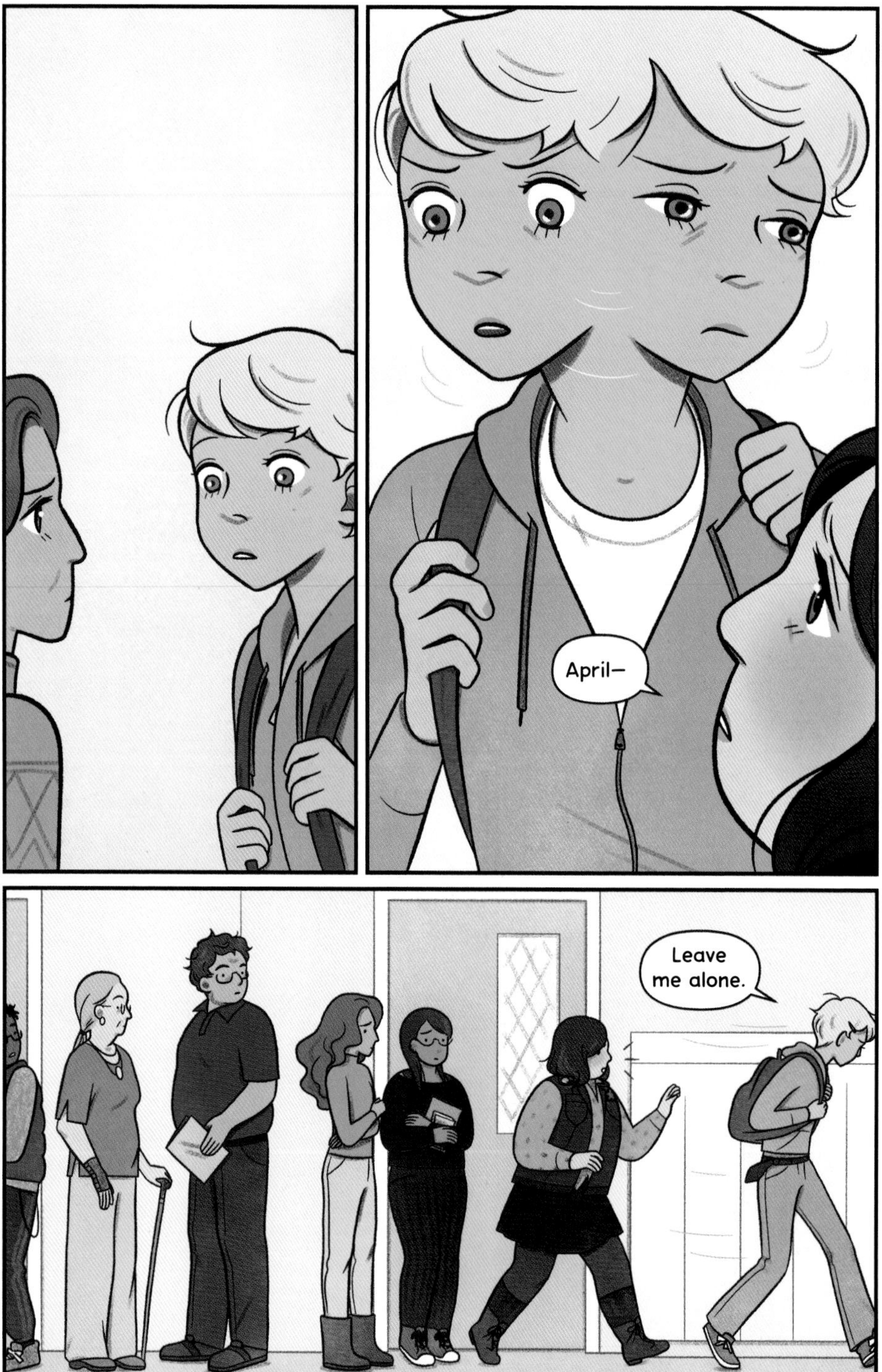
April—
Leave me alone.

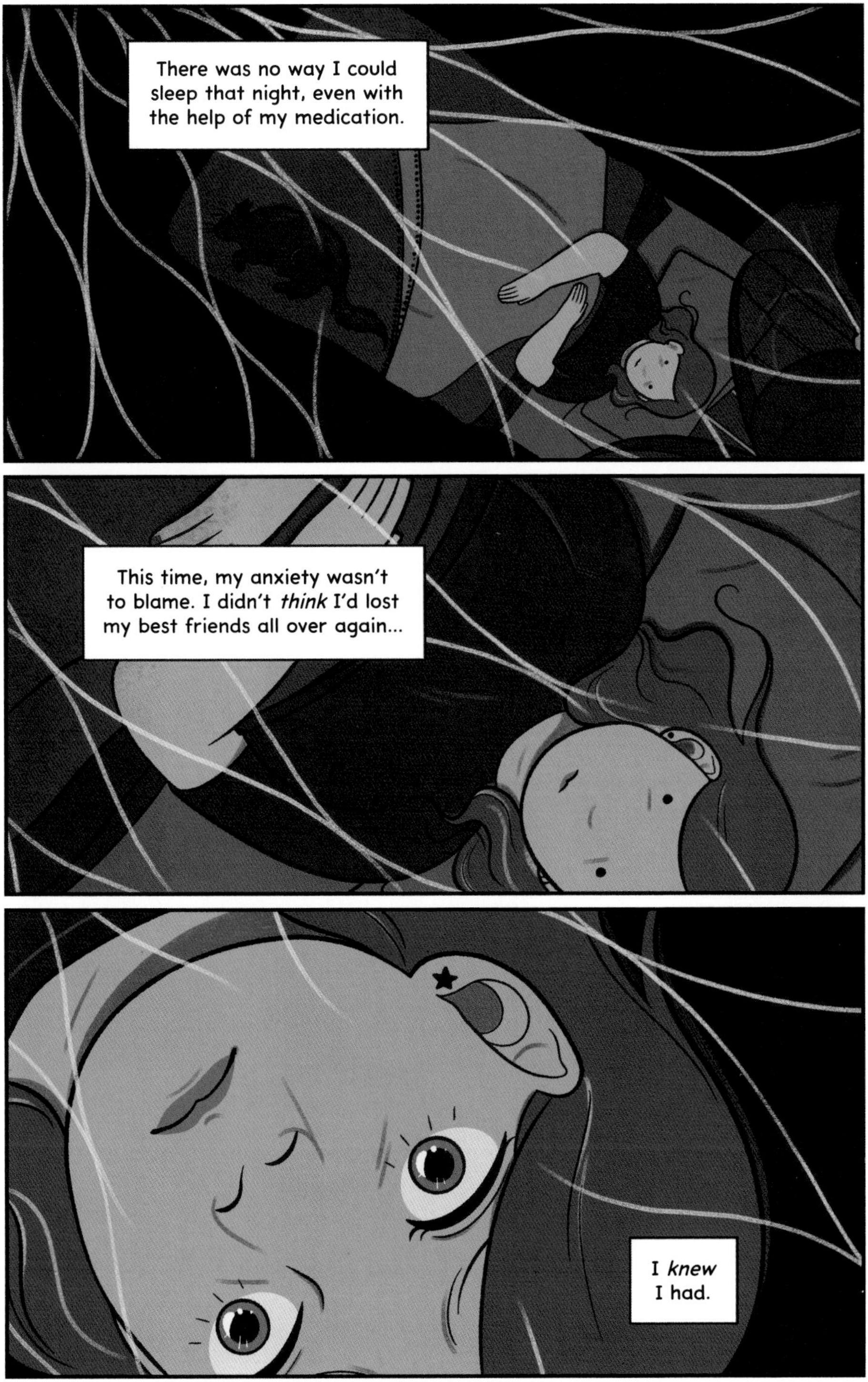
There was no way I could sleep that night, even with the help of my medication.
This time, my anxiety wasn't to blame. I didn't *think* I'd lost my best friends all over again...
I *knew* I had.

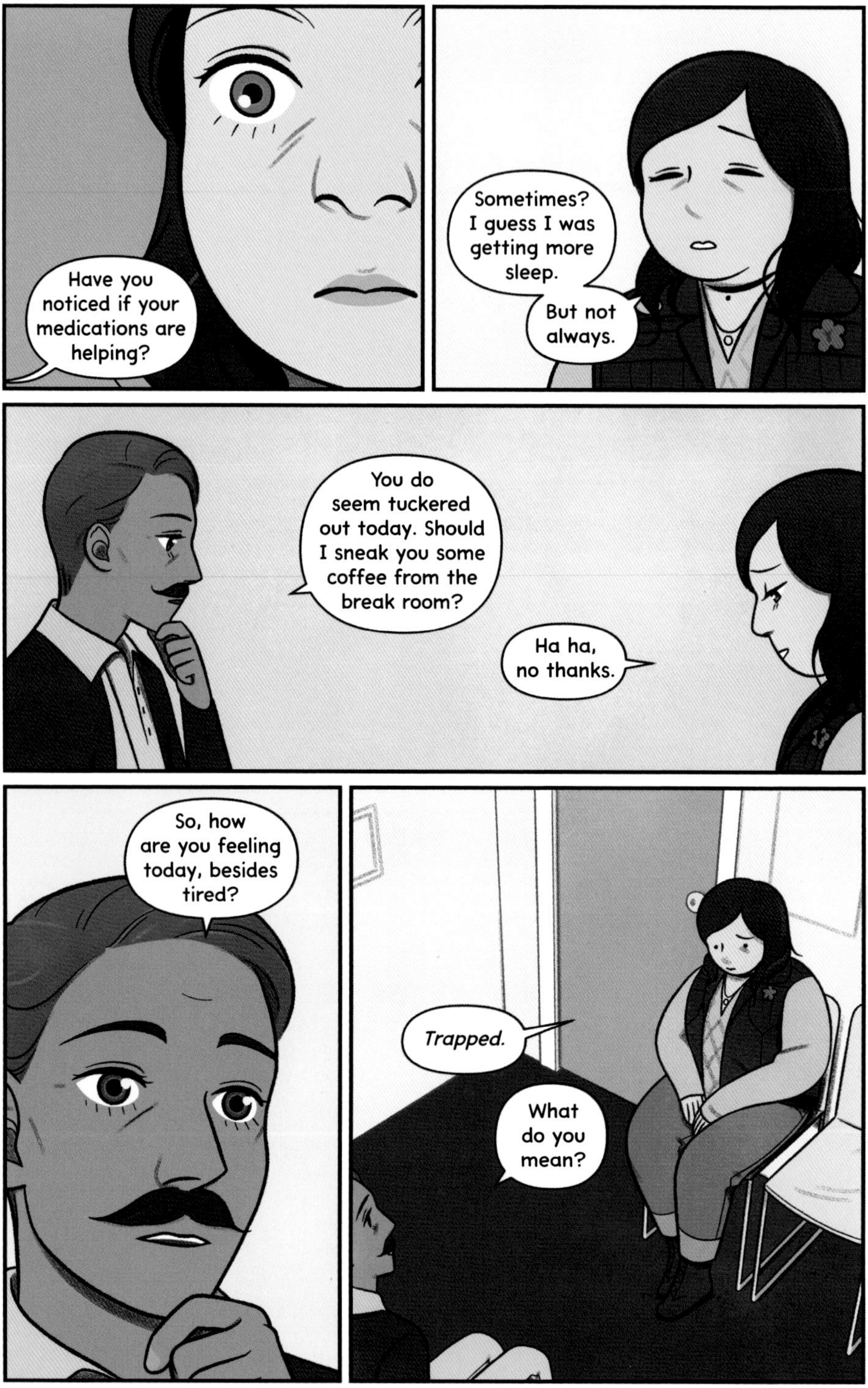

Have you noticed if your medications are helping?
Sometimes? I guess I was getting more sleep.
But not always.
You do seem tuckered out today. Should I sneak you some coffee from the break room?
Ha ha, no thanks.
So, how are you feeling today, besides tired?
Trapped.
What do you mean?

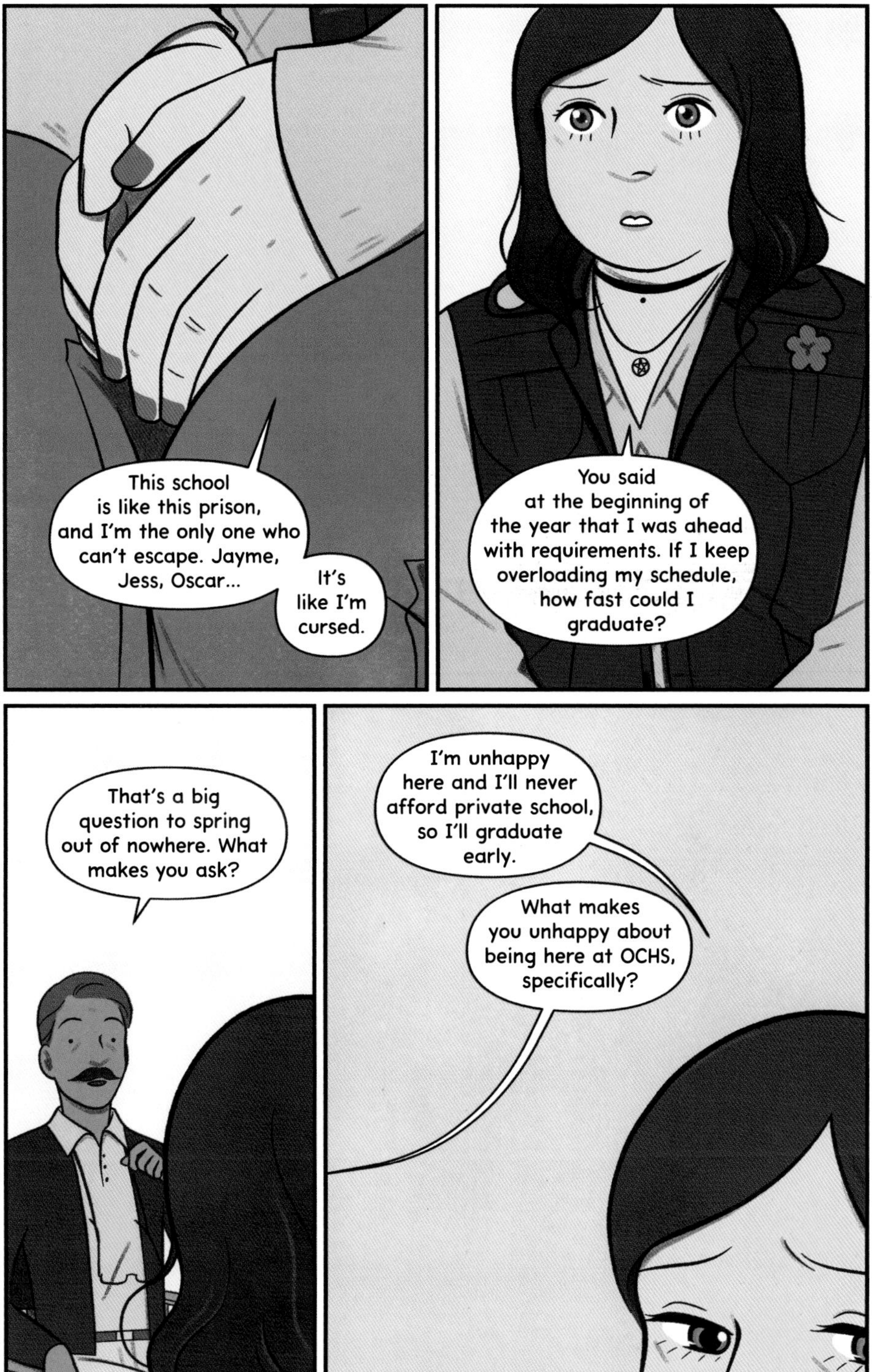
This school is like this prison, and I'm the only one who can't escape. Jayme, Jess, Oscar...
It's like I'm cursed.
You said at the beginning of the year that I was ahead with requirements. If I keep overloading my schedule, how fast could I graduate?
That's a big question to spring out of nowhere. What makes you ask?
I'm unhappy here and I'll never afford private school, so I'll graduate early.
What makes you unhappy about being here at OCHS, specifically?

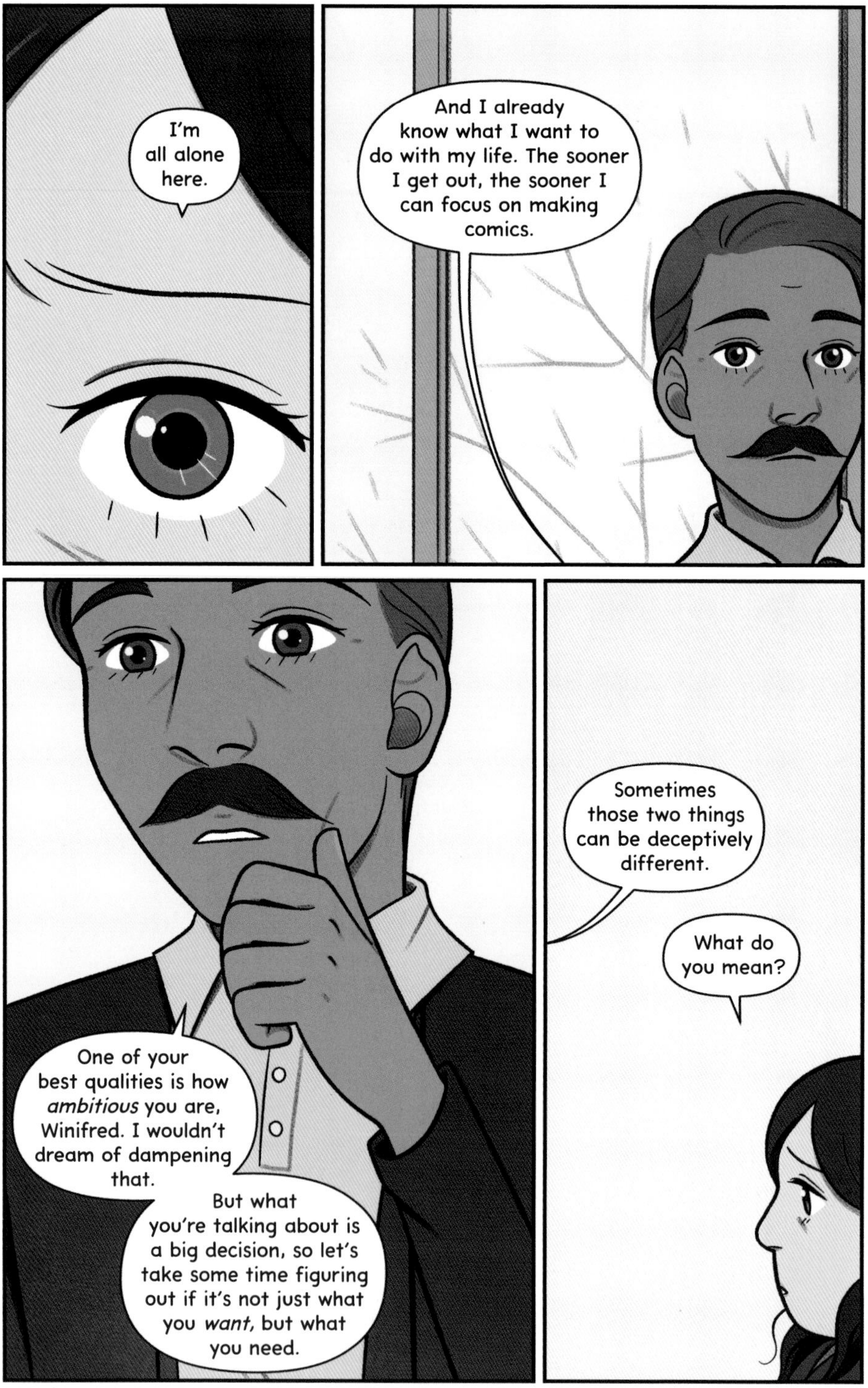
I'm all alone here.
And I already know what I want to do with my life. The sooner I get out, the sooner I can focus on making comics.
One of your best qualities is how *ambitious* you are, Winifred. I wouldn't dream of dampening that.
But what you're talking about is a big decision, so let's take some time figuring out if it's not just what you *want*, but what you need.
Sometimes those two things can be deceptively different.
What do you mean?

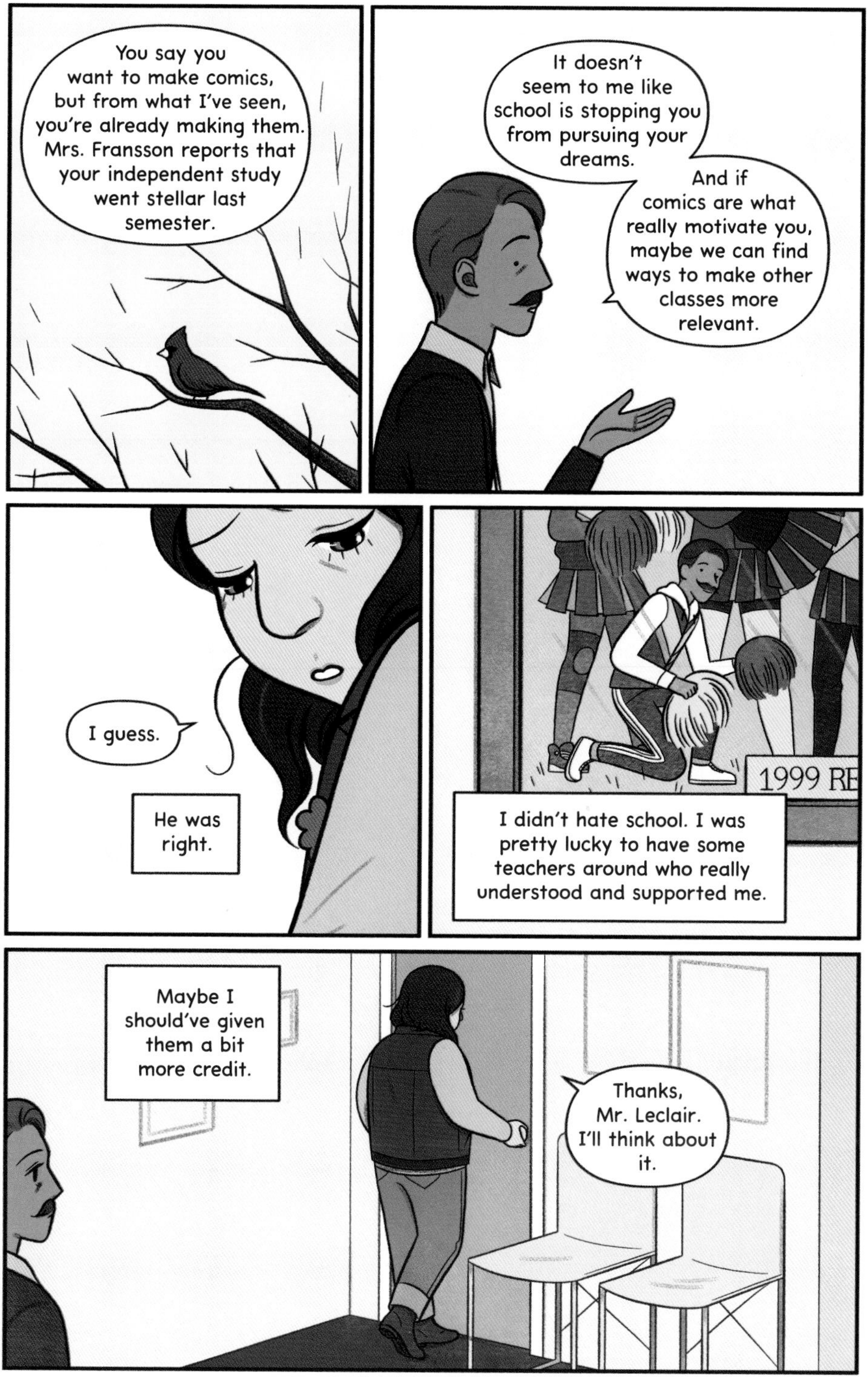
You say you want to make comics, but from what I've seen, you're already making them. Mrs. Fransson reports that your independent study went stellar last semester.
It doesn't seem to me like school is stopping you from pursuing your dreams.
And if comics are what really motivate you, maybe we can find ways to make other classes more relevant.
I guess.
He was right.
1999 RE
I didn't hate school. I was pretty lucky to have some teachers around who really understood and supported me.
Maybe I should've given them a bit more credit.
Thanks, Mr. Leclair. I'll think about it.

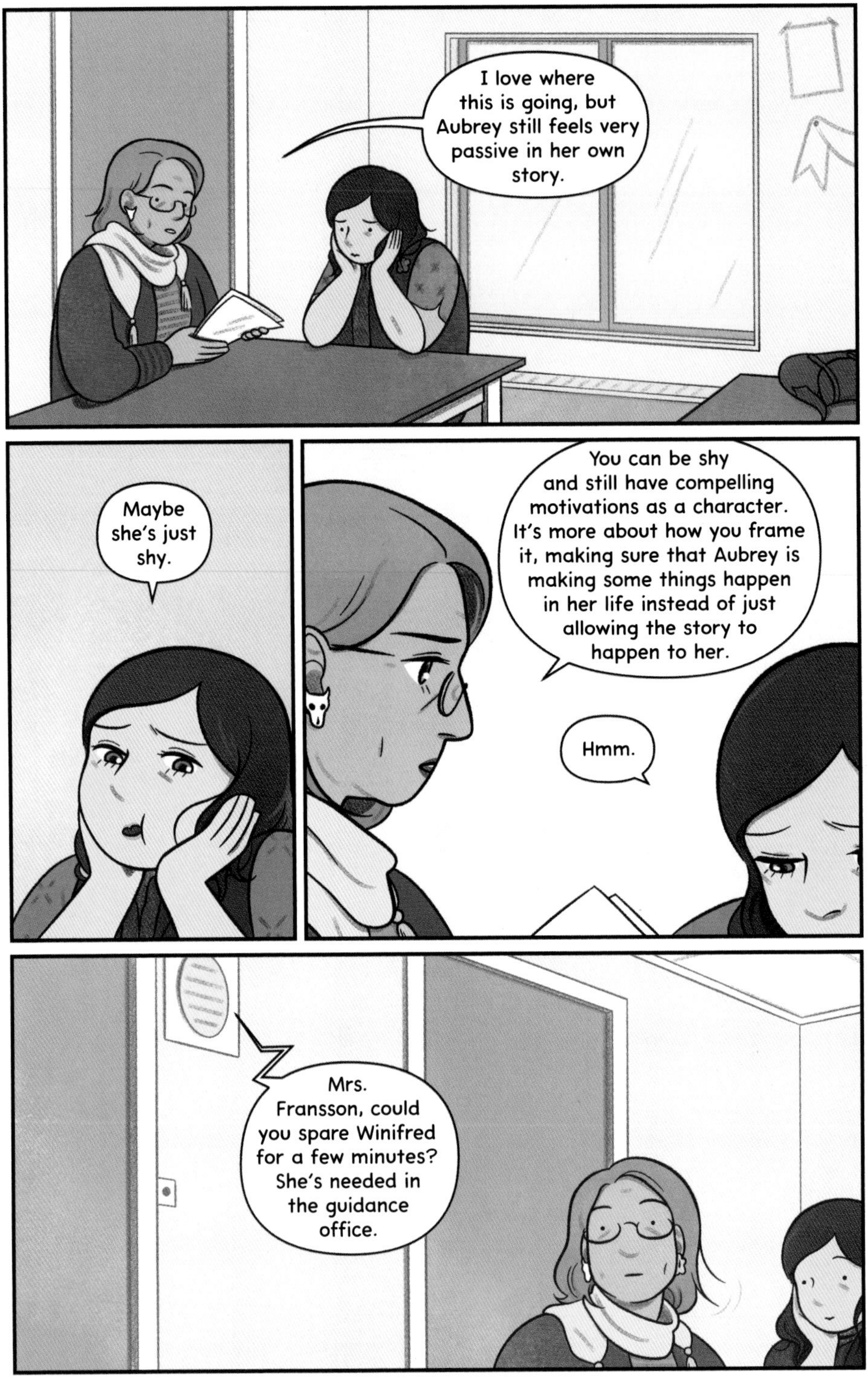
I love where this is going, but Aubrey still feels very passive in her own story.
Maybe she's just shy.
You can be shy and still have compelling motivations as a character. It's more about how you frame it, making sure that Aubrey is making some things happen in her life instead of just allowing the story to happen to her.
Hmm.
Mrs. Fransson, could you spare Winifred for a few minutes? She's needed in the guidance office.

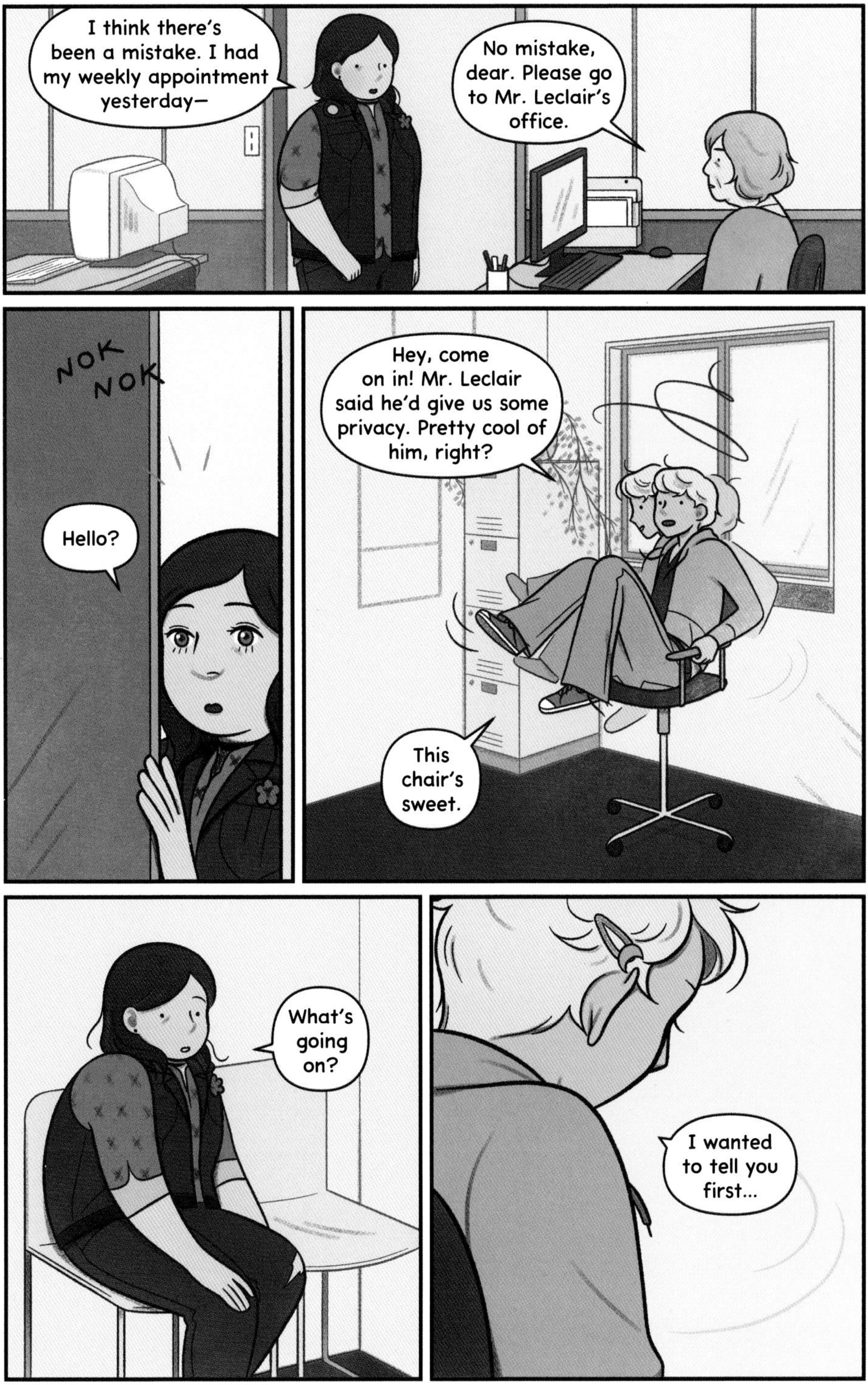
I think there's been a mistake. I had my weekly appointment yesterday—
No mistake, dear. Please go to Mr. Leclair's office.
NOK NOK
Hello?
Hey, come on in! Mr. Leclair said he'd give us some privacy. Pretty cool of him, right?
This chair's sweet.
What's going on?
I wanted to tell you first...

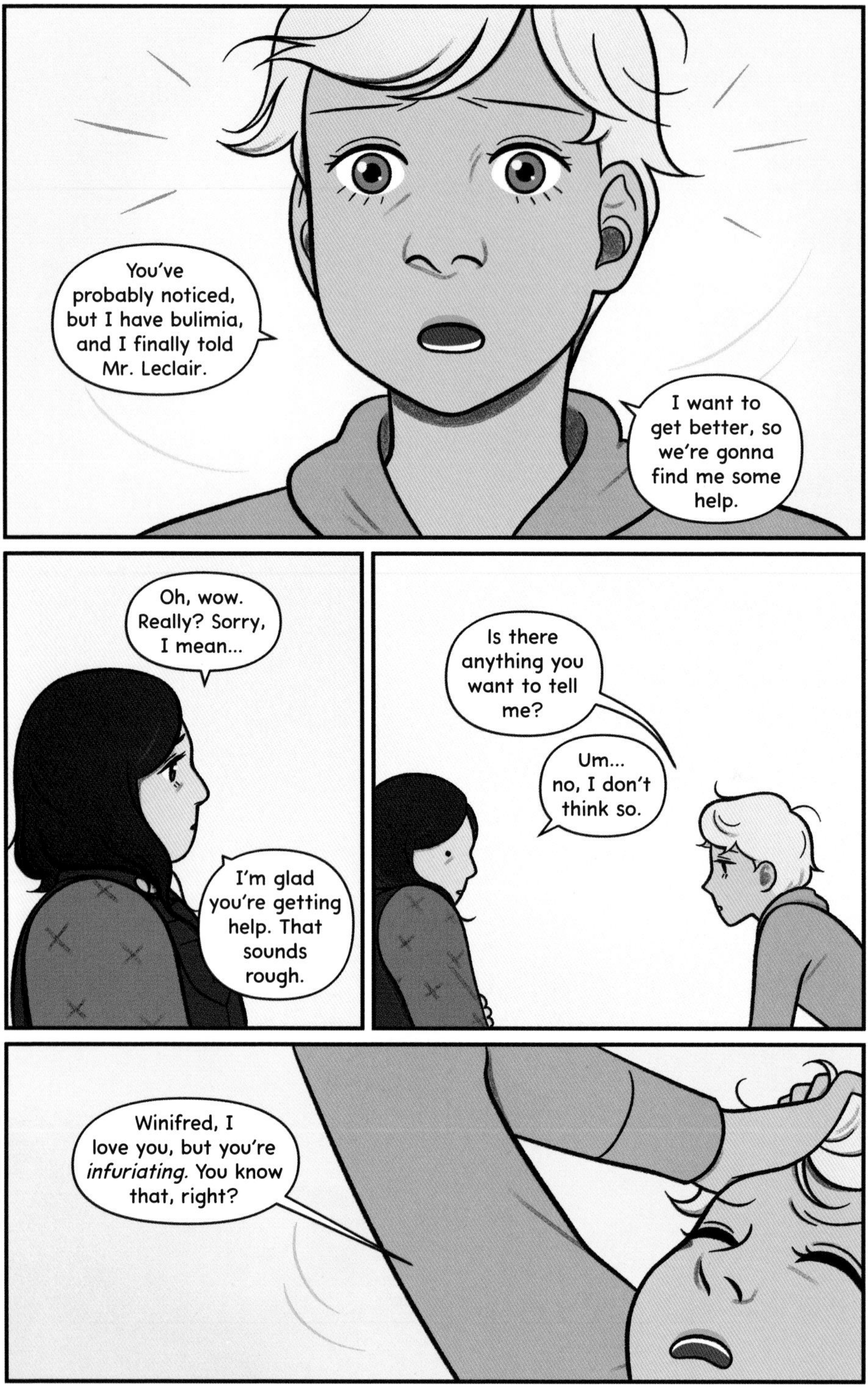
You've probably noticed, but I have bulimia, and I finally told Mr. Leclair.
I want to get better, so we're gonna find me some help.
Oh, wow. Really? Sorry, I mean...
I'm glad you're getting help. That sounds rough.
Is there anything you want to tell me?
Um... no, I don't think so.
Winifred, I love you, but you're *infuriating.* You know that, right?

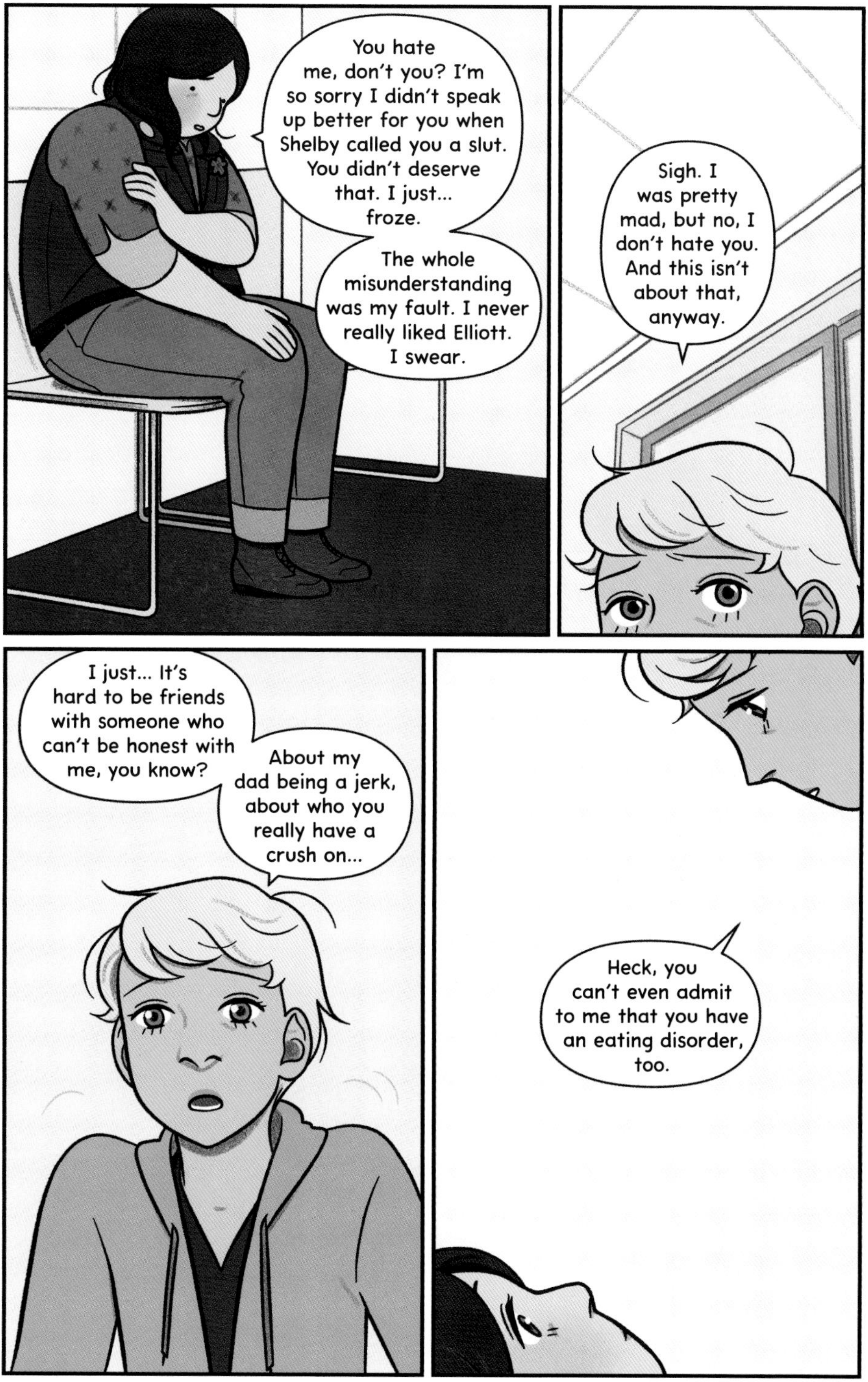

You hate me, don't you? I'm so sorry I didn't speak up better for you when Shelby called you a slut. You didn't deserve that. I just... froze.
The whole misunderstanding was my fault. I never really liked Elliott. I swear.
Sigh. I was pretty mad, but no, I don't hate you. And this isn't about that, anyway.
I just... It's hard to be friends with someone who can't be honest with me, you know?
About my dad being a jerk, about who you really have a crush on...
Heck, you can't even admit to me that you have an eating disorder, too.

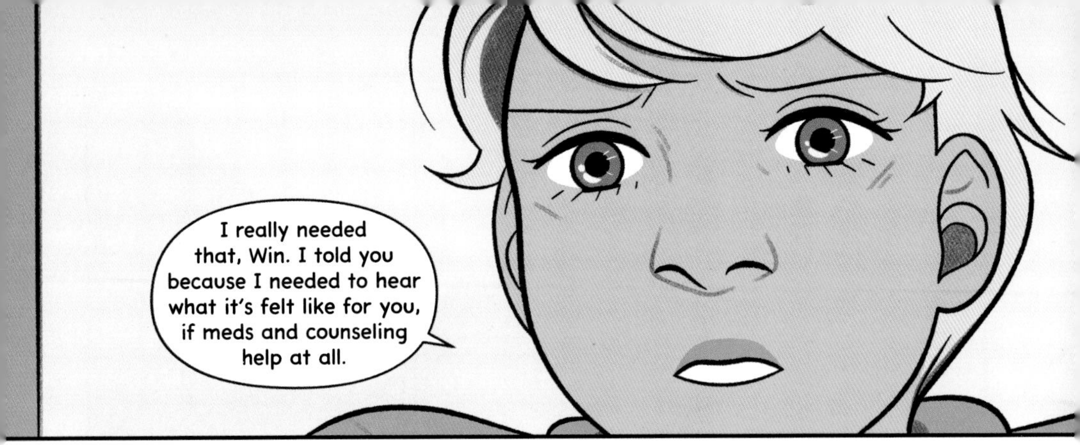
I really needed that, Win. I told you because I needed to hear what it's felt like for you, if meds and counseling help at all.

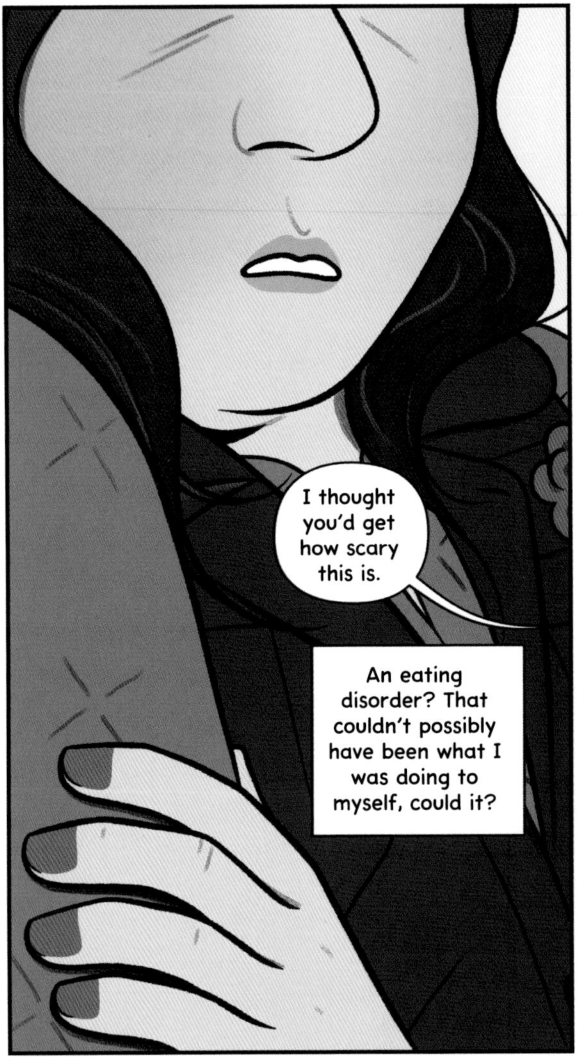
I thought you'd get how scary this is.
An eating disorder? That couldn't possibly have been what I was doing to myself, could it?

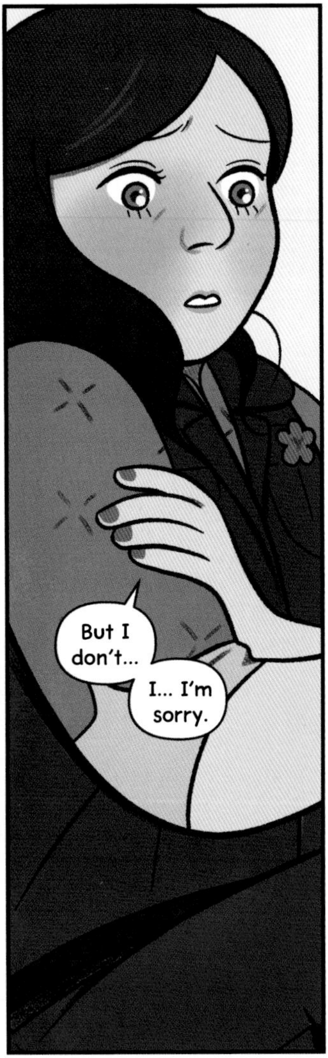
But I don't...
I... I'm sorry.

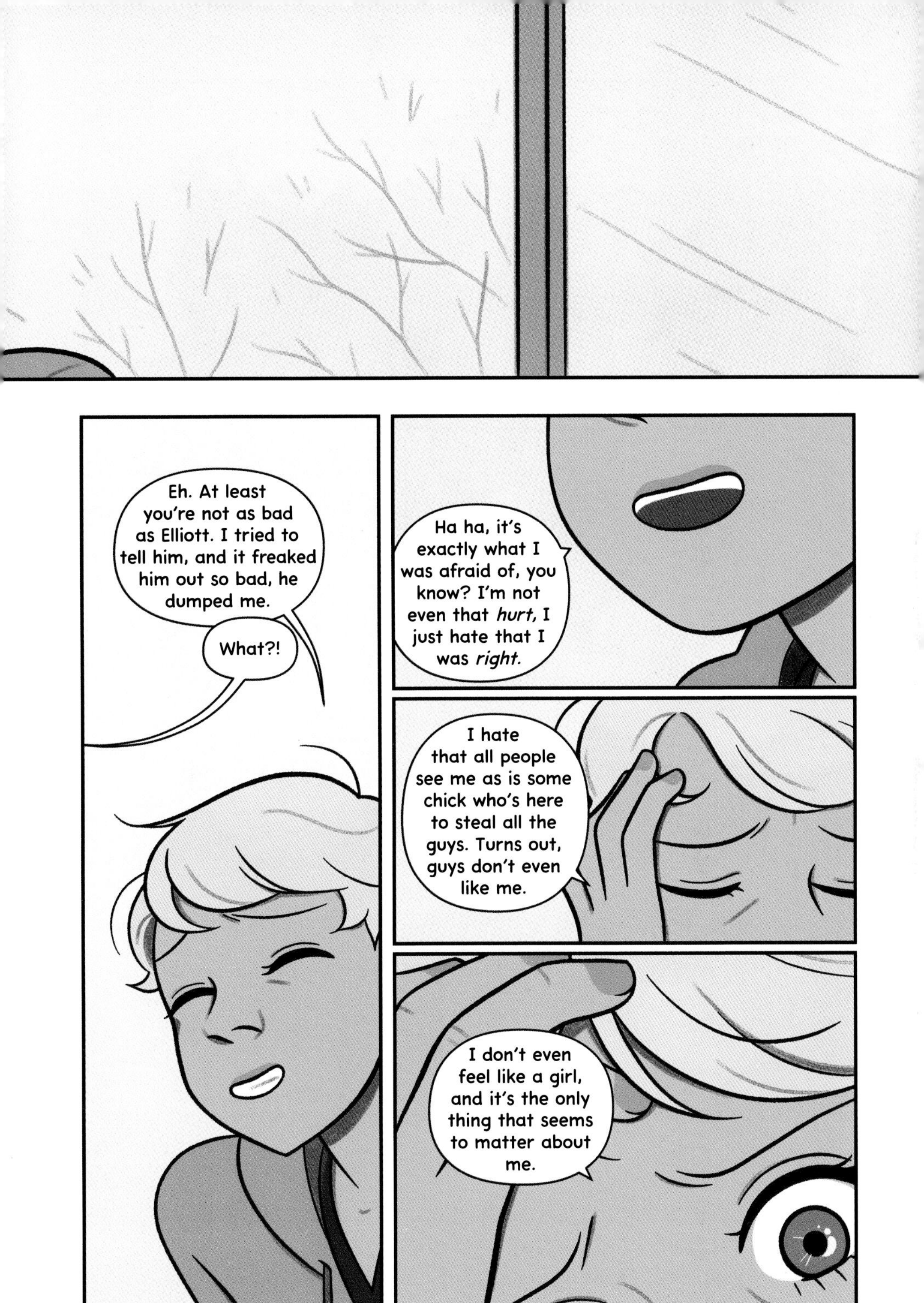
Eh. At least you're not as bad as Elliott. I tried to tell him, and it freaked him out so bad, he dumped me.
What?!
Ha ha, it's exactly what I was afraid of, you know? I'm not even that *hurt,* I just hate that I was *right.*
I hate that all people see me as is some chick who's here to steal all the guys. Turns out, guys don't even like me.
I don't even feel like a girl, and it's the only thing that seems to matter about me.

Do you mean... Are you like Mrs. Fransson? Except instead of realizing you're a girl, you're a boy instead?

No. Mrs. Fransson knows exactly who she is... but I don't think I'm a girl or a boy. I'm not sure I'm anything.

That sounds hard. I'm sorry.

Yeah. You said that already.

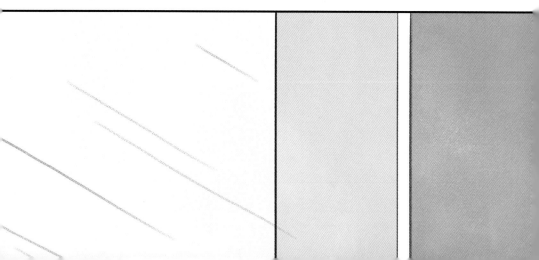

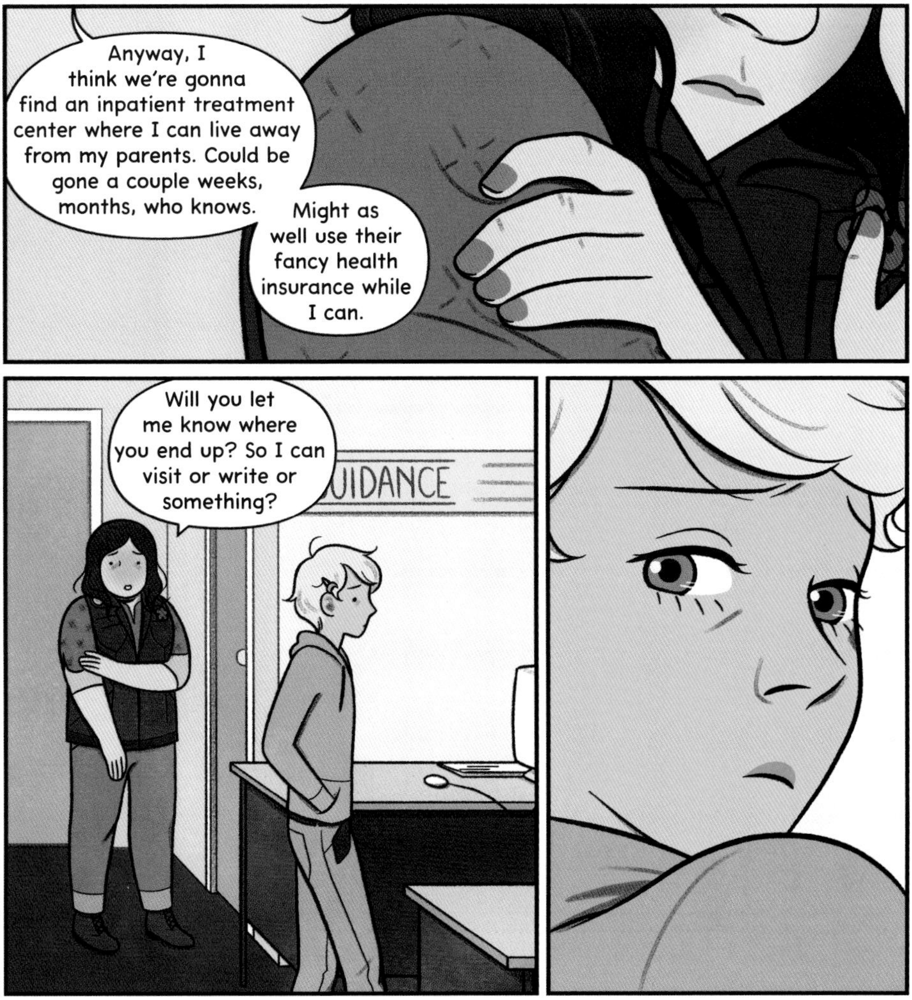
Anyway, I think we're gonna find an inpatient treatment center where I can live away from my parents. Could be gone a couple weeks, months, who knows.
Might as well use their fancy health insurance while I can.
Will you let me know where you end up? So I can visit or write or something?
UIDANCE

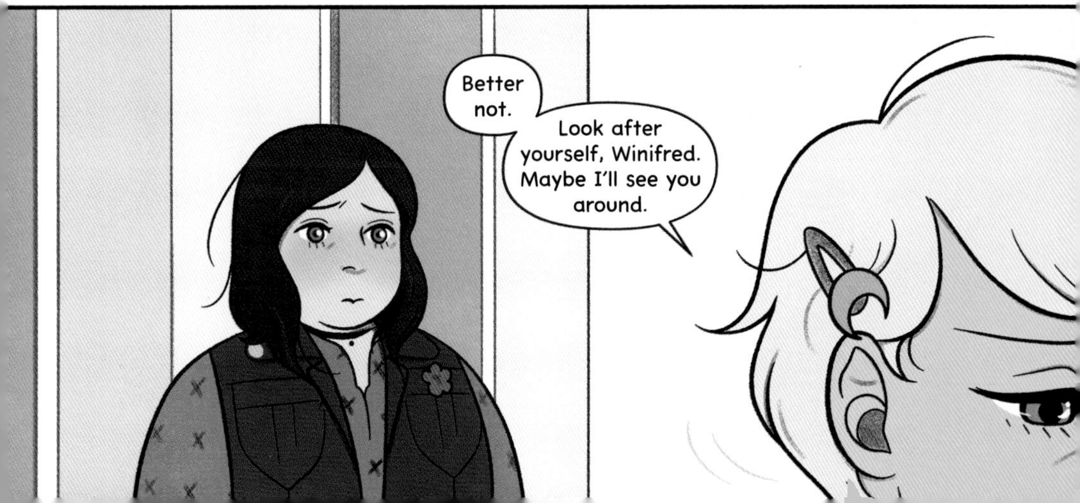
Better not.
Look after yourself, Winifred. Maybe I'll see you around.

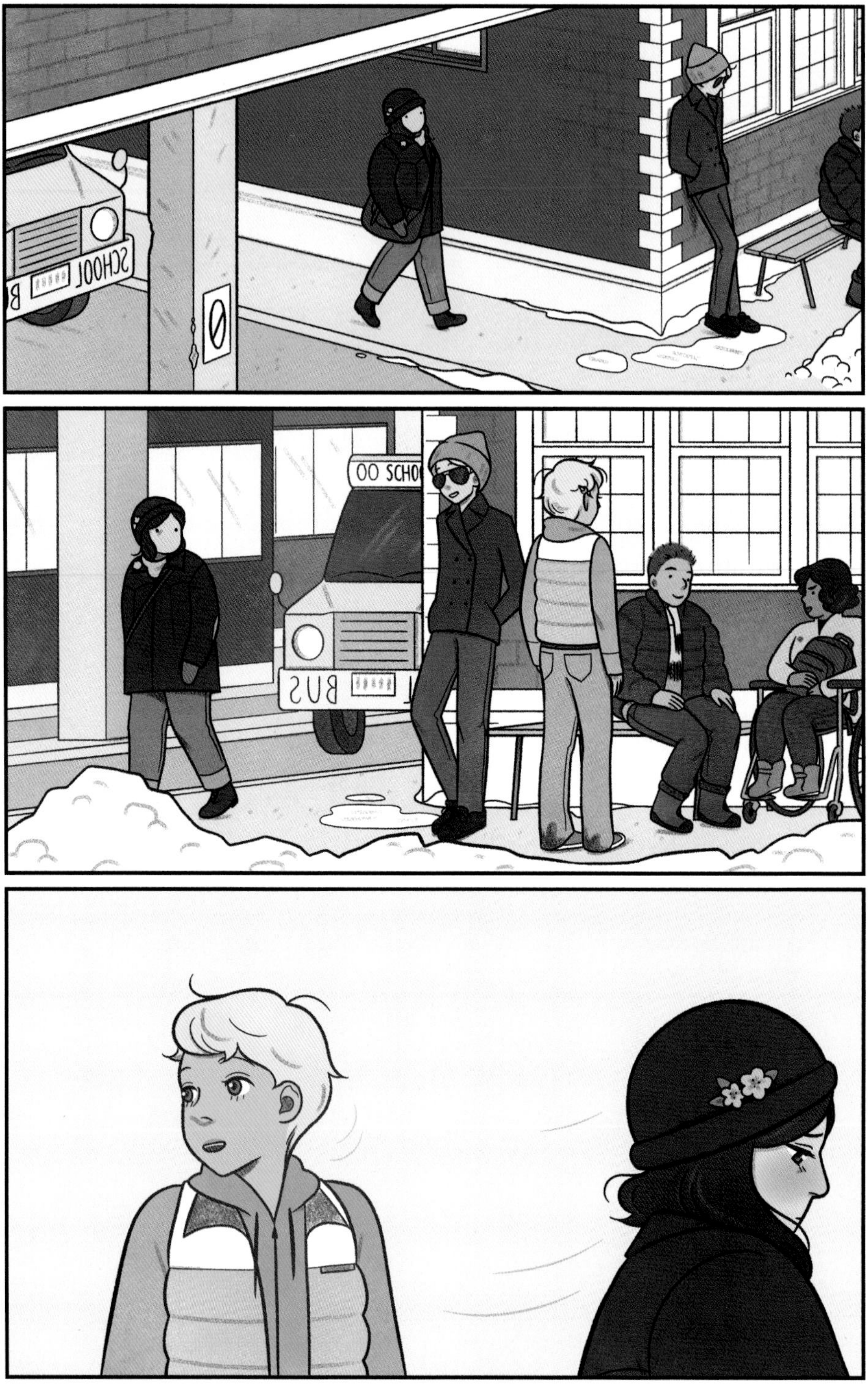
OO SCHO

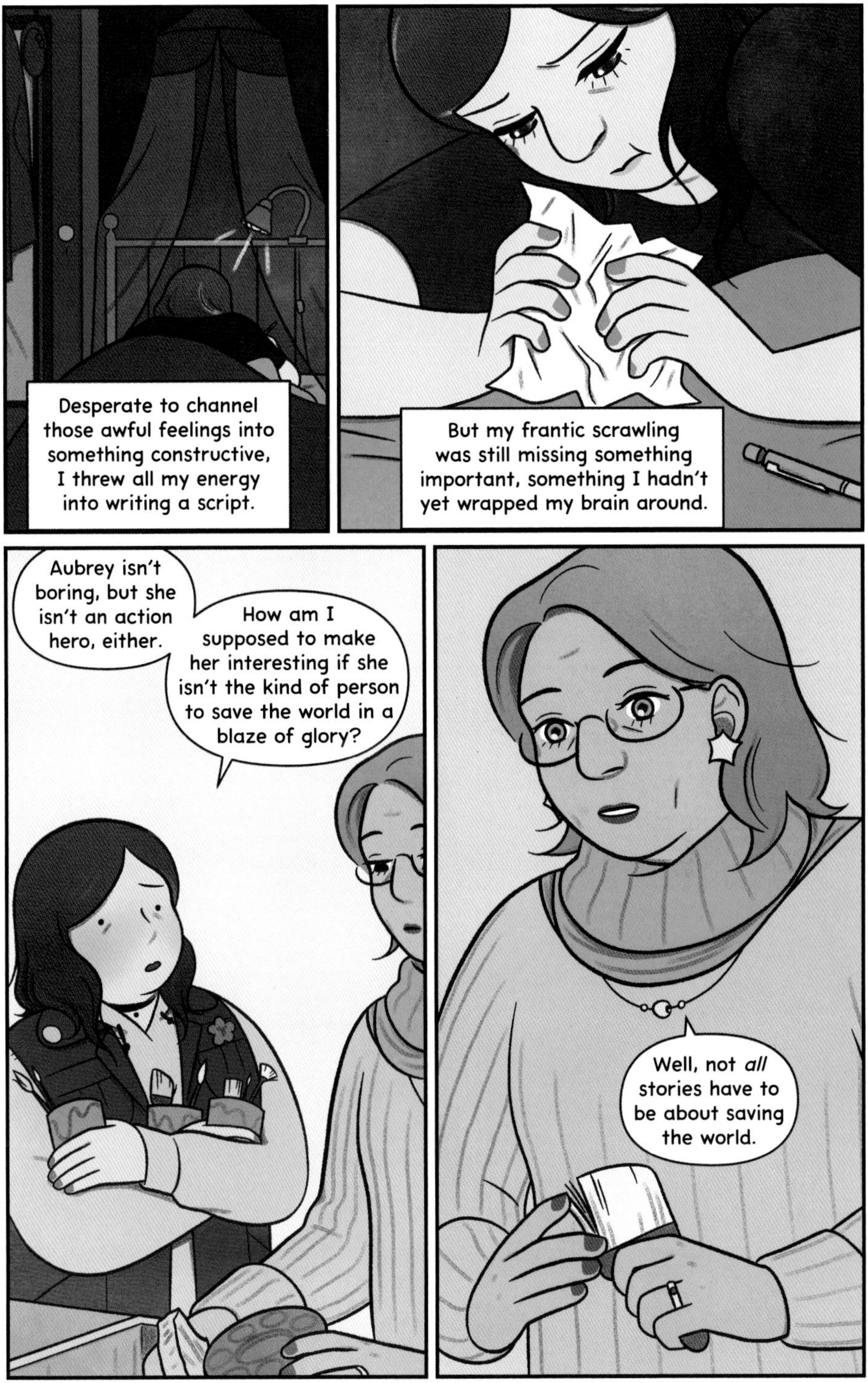
Desperate to channel those awful feelings into something constructive, I threw all my energy into writing a script.
But my frantic scrawling was still missing something important, something I hadn't yet wrapped my brain around.
Aubrey isn't boring, but she isn't an action hero, either.
How am I supposed to make her interesting if she isn't the kind of person to save the world in a blaze of glory?
Well, not *all* stories have to be about saving the world.

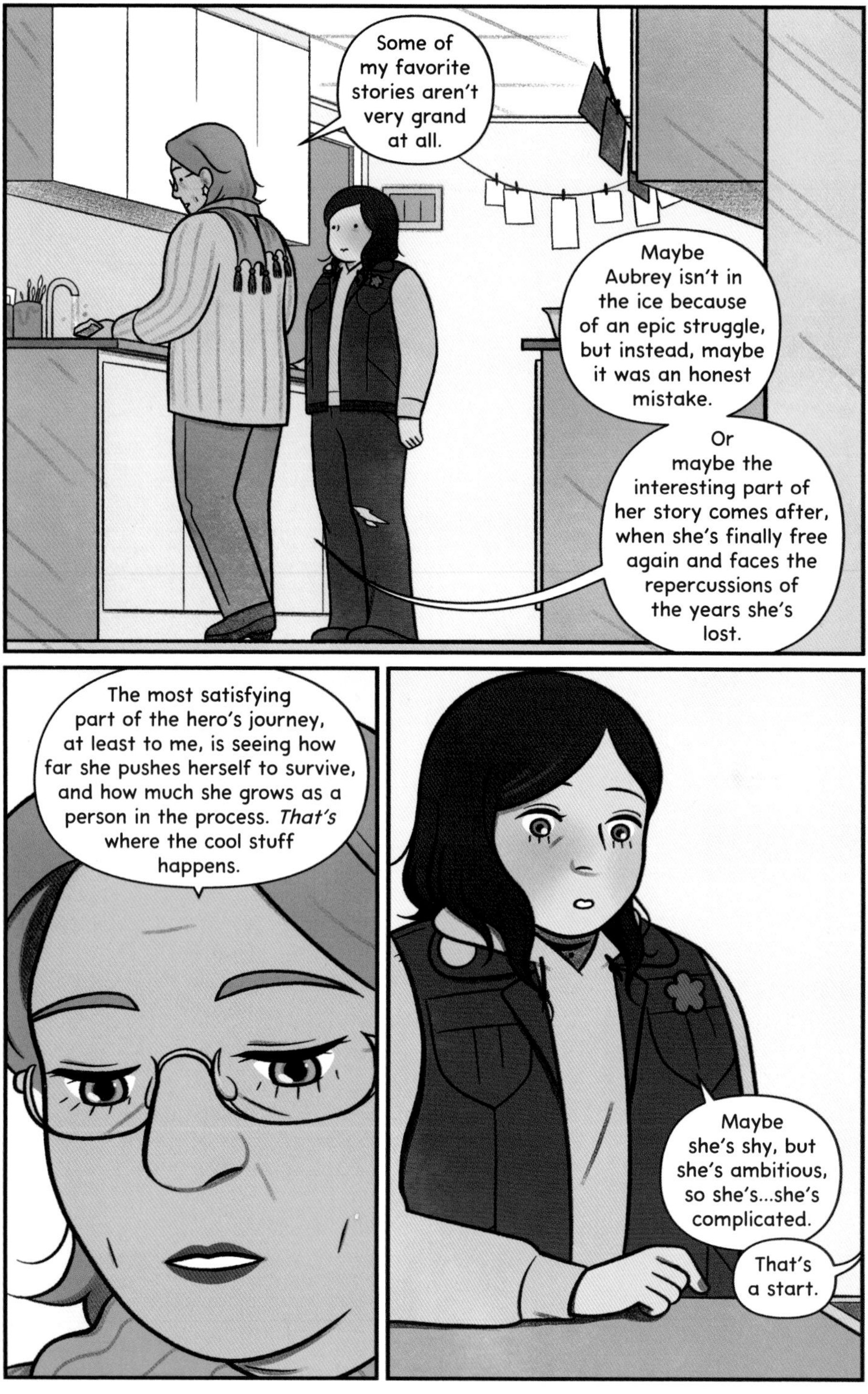
Some of my favorite stories aren't very grand at all.
Maybe Aubrey isn't in the ice because of an epic struggle, but instead, maybe it was an honest mistake.
Or maybe the interesting part of her story comes after, when she's finally free again and faces the repercussions of the years she's lost.
The most satisfying part of the hero's journey, at least to me, is seeing how far she pushes herself to survive, and how much she grows as a person in the process. *That's* where the cool stuff happens.
Maybe she's shy, but she's ambitious, so she's...she's complicated.
That's a start.

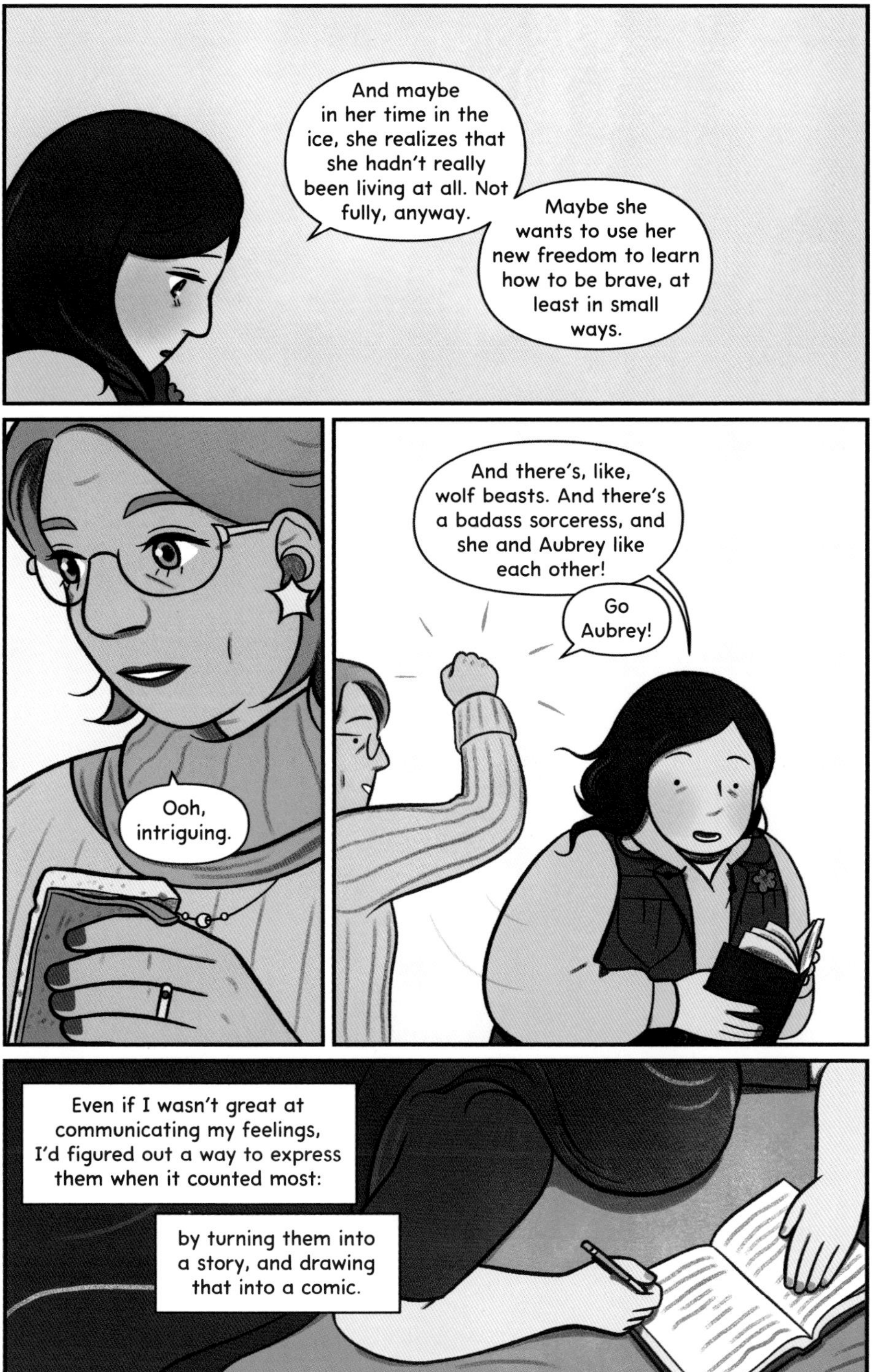
And maybe in her time in the ice, she realizes that she hadn't really been living at all. Not fully, anyway.
Maybe she wants to use her new freedom to learn how to be brave, at least in small ways.
Ooh, intriguing.
And there's, like, wolf beasts. And there's a badass sorceress, and she and Aubrey like each other!
Go Aubrey!
Even if I wasn't great at communicating my feelings, I'd figured out a way to express them when it counted most:
by turning them into a story, and drawing that into a comic.

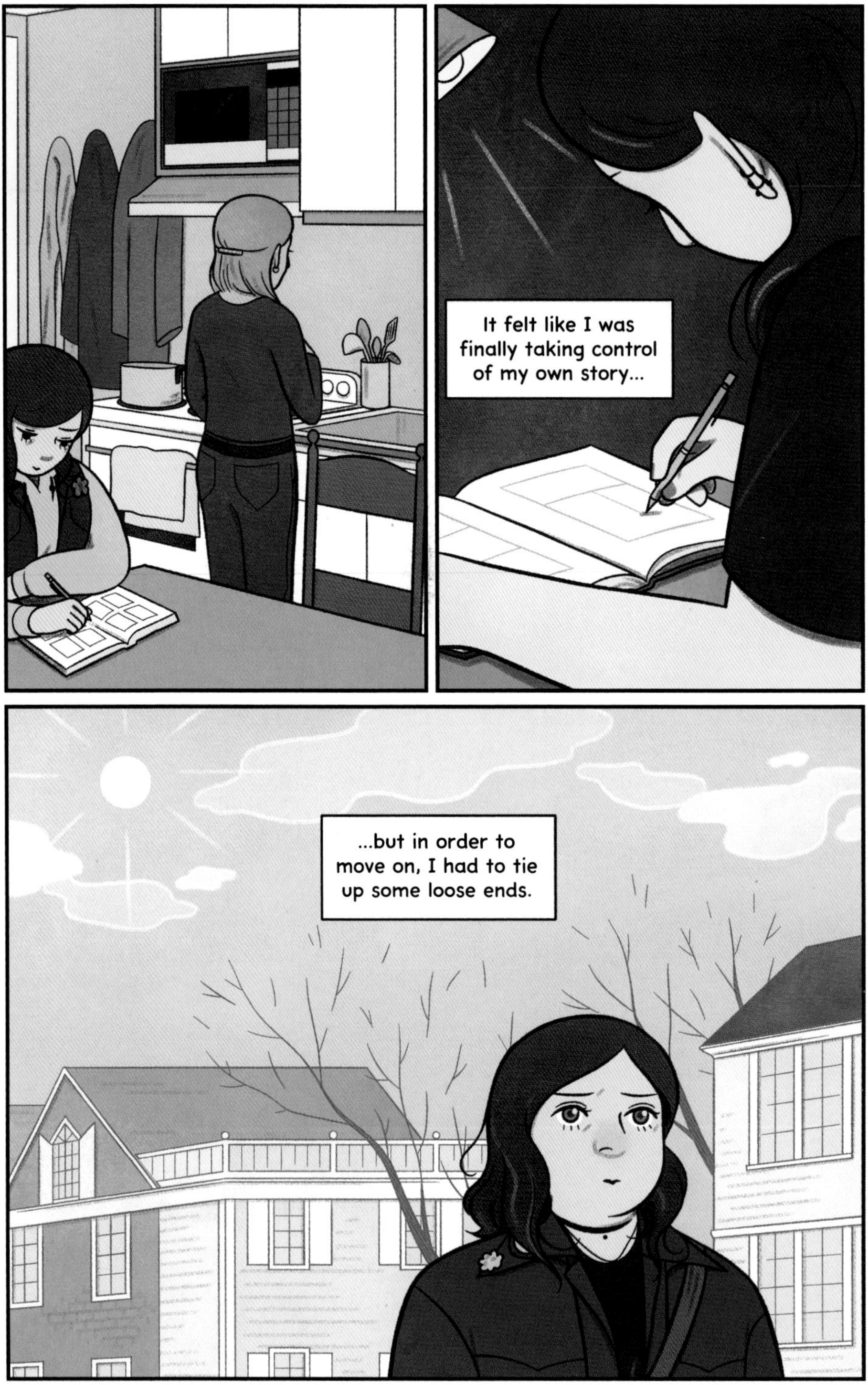
It felt like I was finally taking control of my own story...
...but in order to move on, I had to tie up some loose ends.

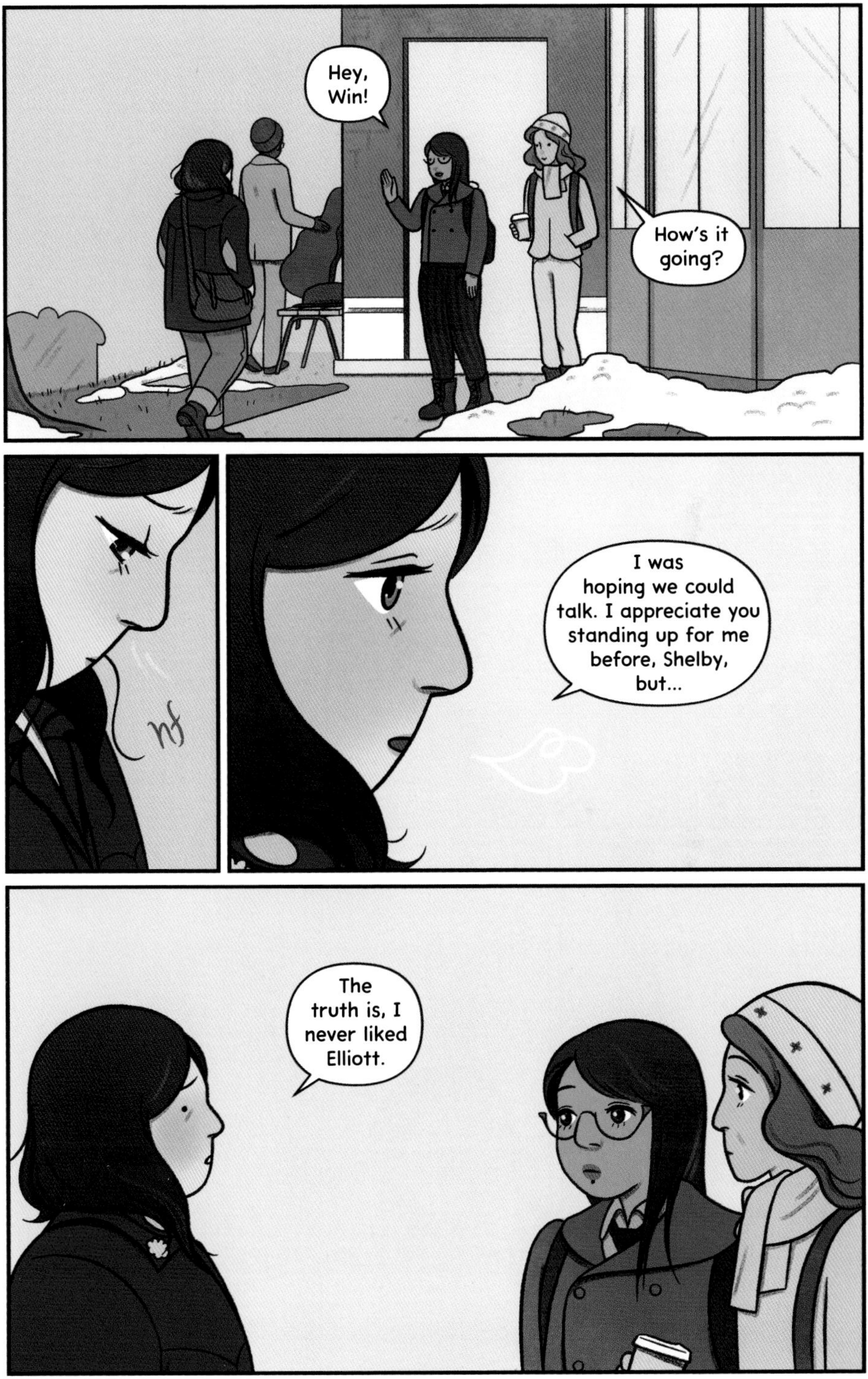
Hey, Win!
How's it going?
I was hoping we could talk. I appreciate you standing up for me before, Shelby, but...
The truth is, I never liked Elliott.

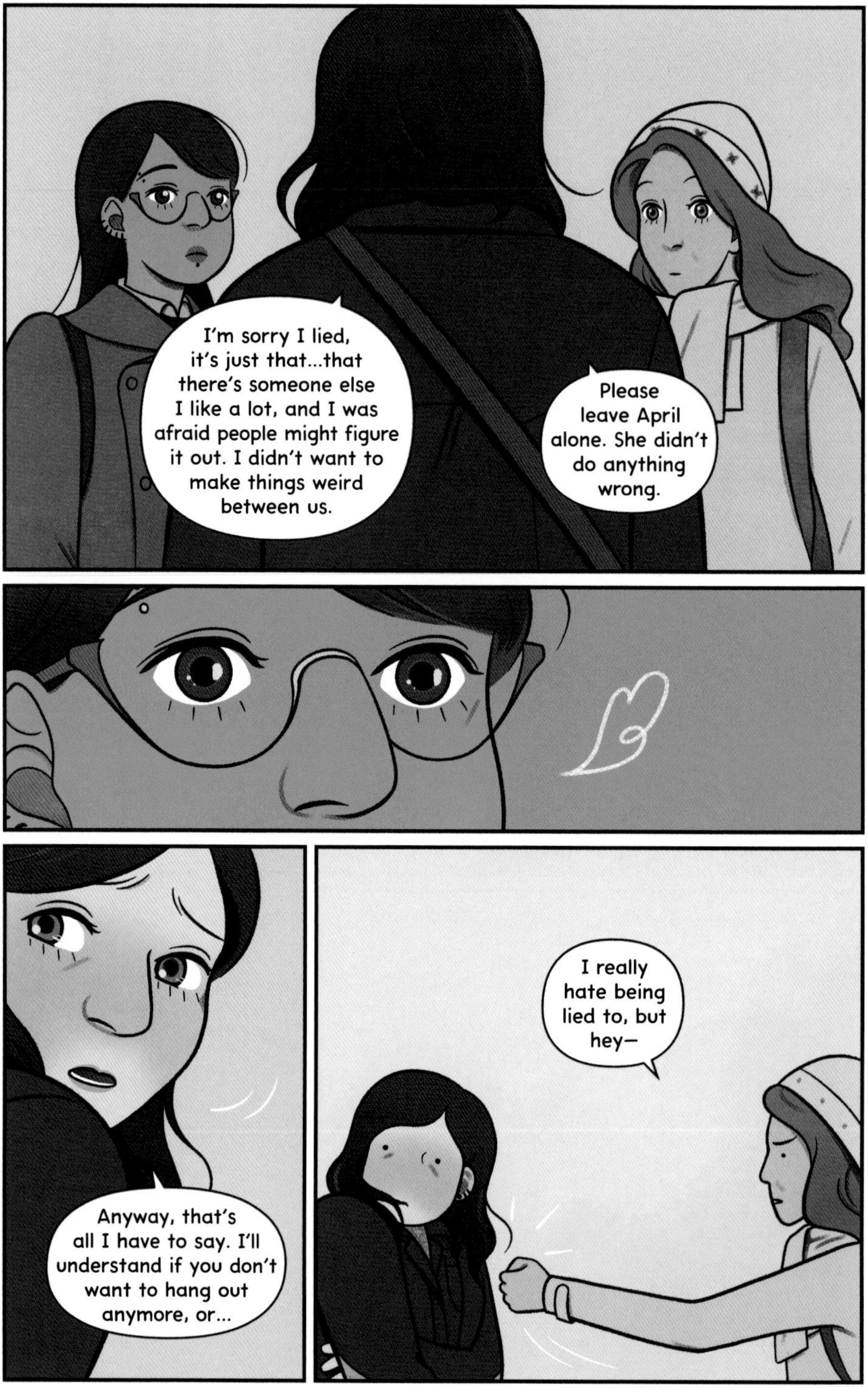
I'm sorry I lied, it's just that...that there's someone else I like a lot, and I was afraid people might figure it out. I didn't want to make things weird between us.
Please leave April alone. She didn't do anything wrong.
Anyway, that's all I have to say. I'll understand if you don't want to hang out anymore, or...
I really hate being lied to, but hey—

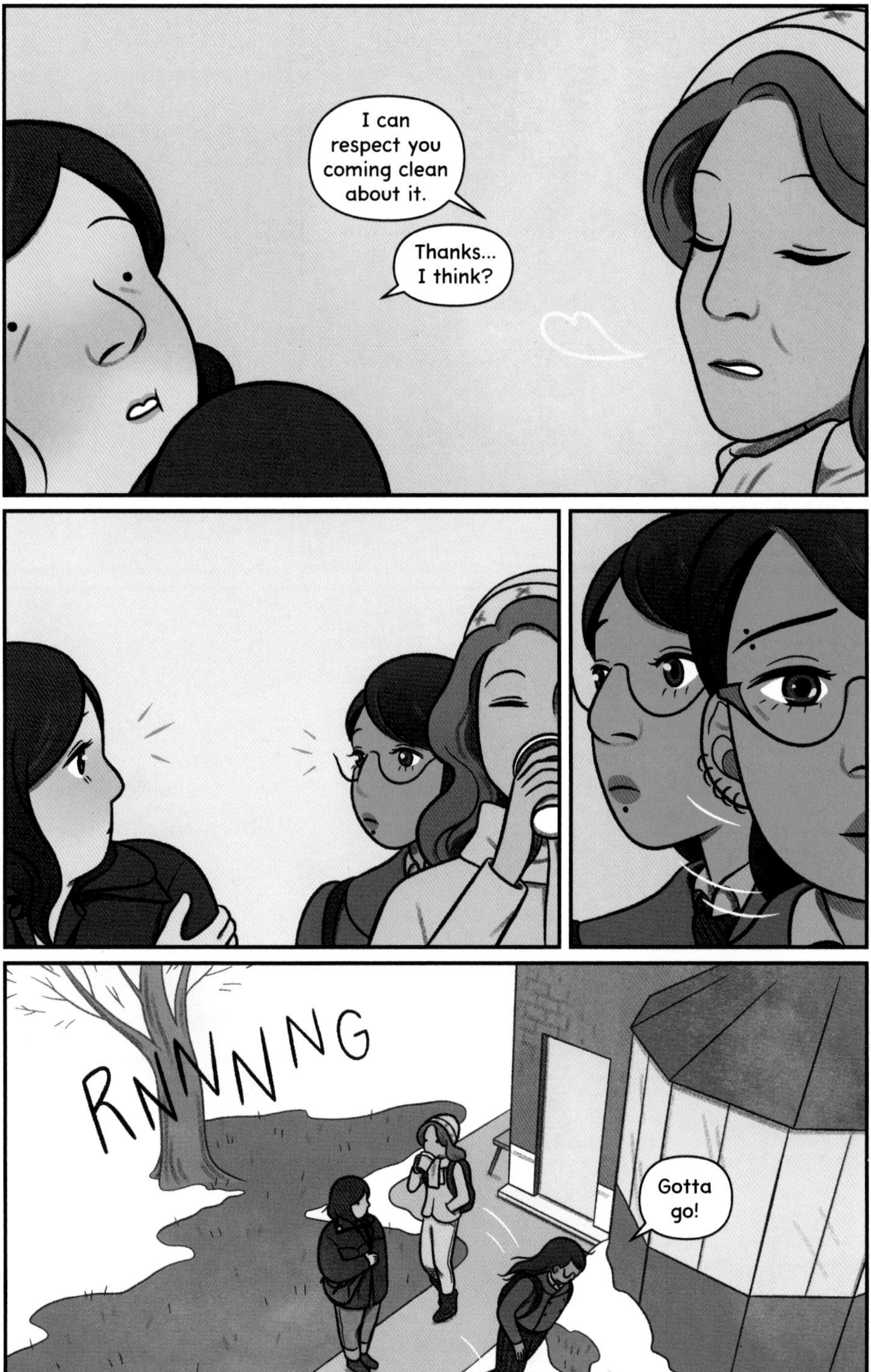
I can respect you coming clean about it.
Thanks... I think?
RNNNNG
Gotta go!

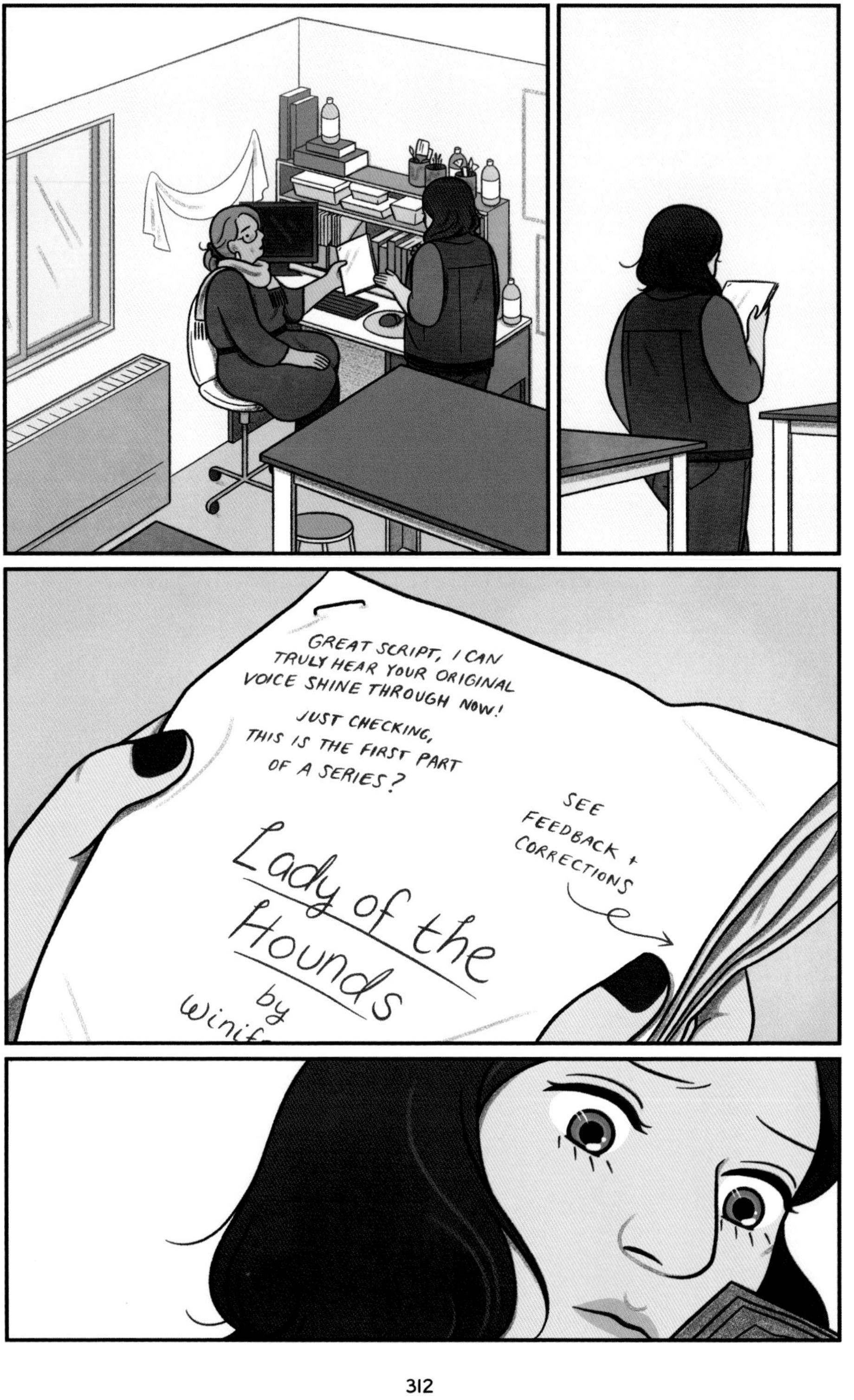
GREAT SCRIPT, I CAN TRULY HEAR YOUR ORIGINAL VOICE SHINE THROUGH NOW!
JUST CHECKING, THIS IS THE FIRST PART OF A SERIES?
SEE FEEDBACK + CORRECTIONS
Lady of the Hounds
by

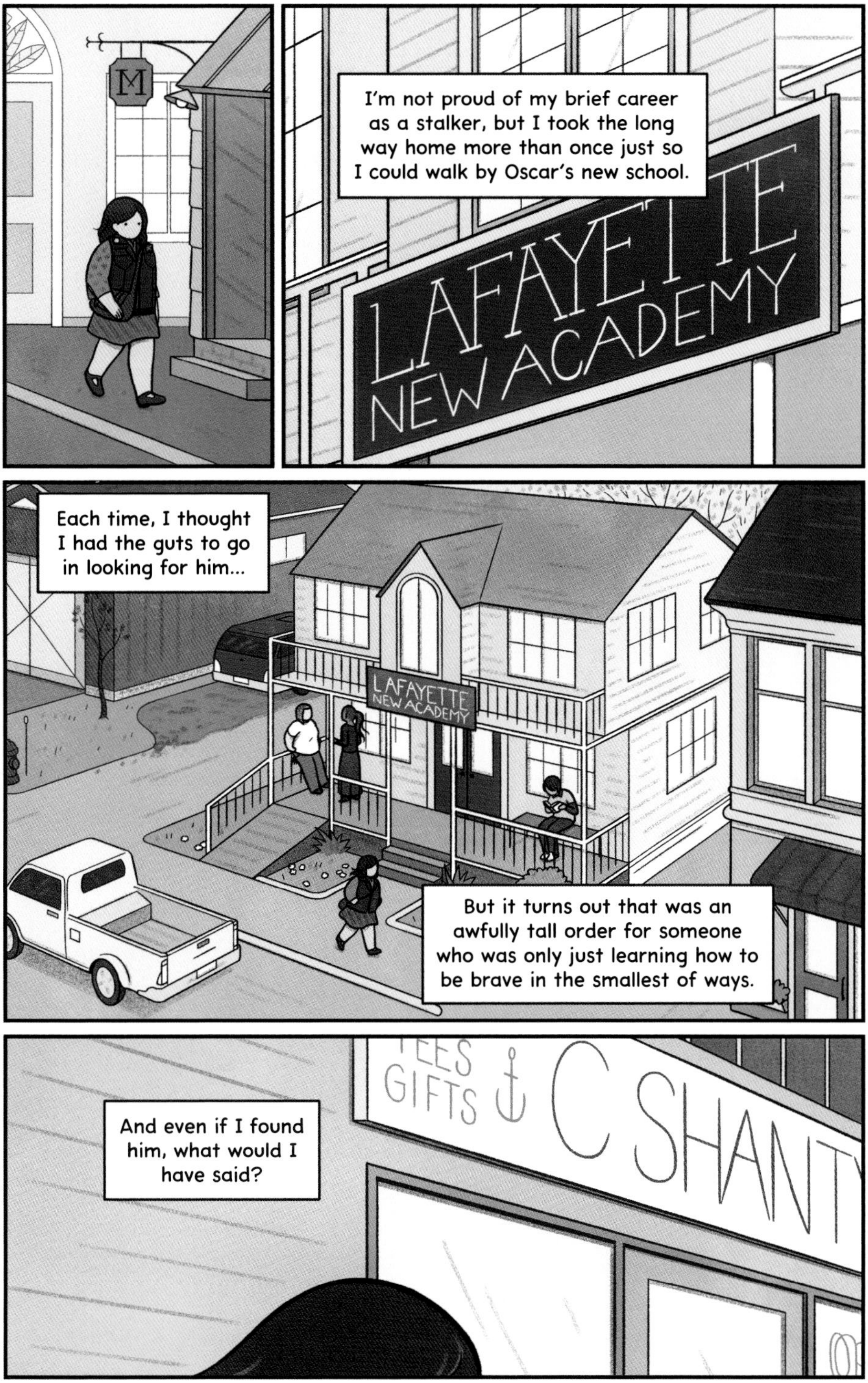
M
I'm not proud of my brief career as a stalker, but I took the long way home more than once just so I could walk by Oscar's new school.
LAFAYETTE NEW ACADEMY
Each time, I thought I had the guts to go in looking for him...
LAFAYETTE NEW ACADEMY
But it turns out that was an awfully tall order for someone who was only just learning how to be brave in the smallest of ways.
GIFTS
C SHANT
And even if I found him, what would I have said?

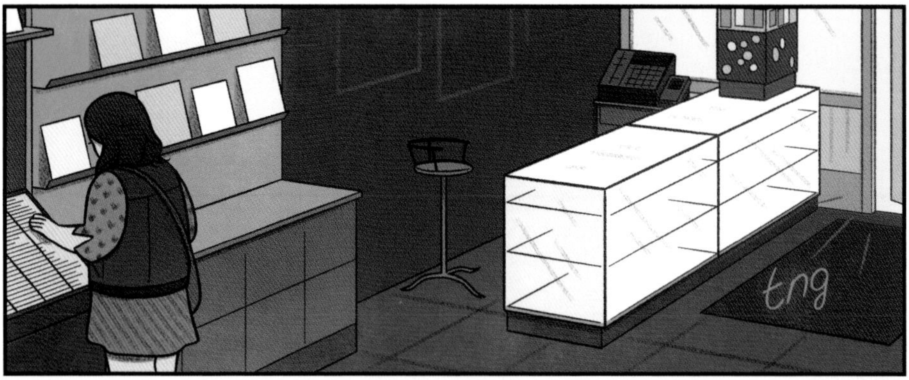
tng

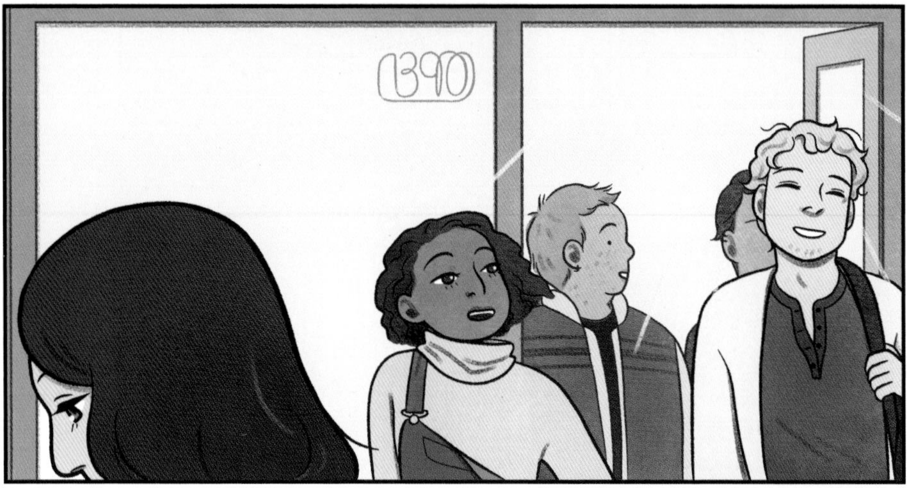
1390

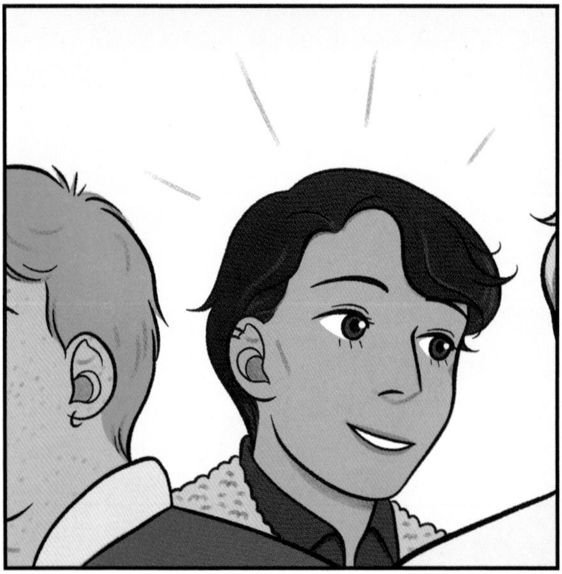

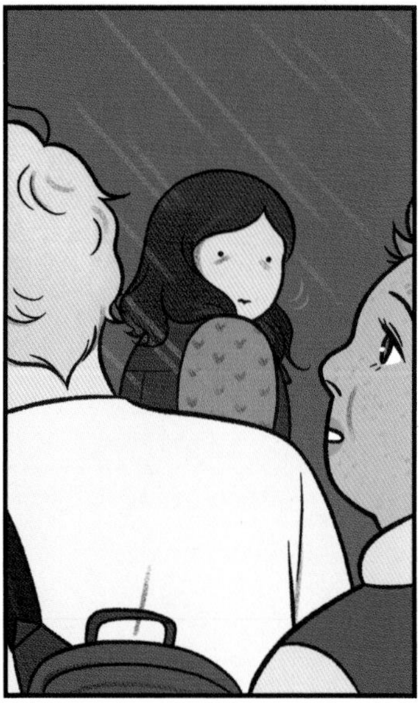

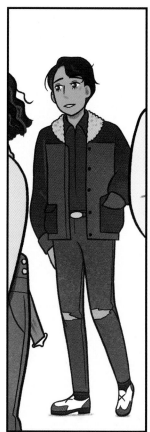

Oh my gosh, it's Fred!

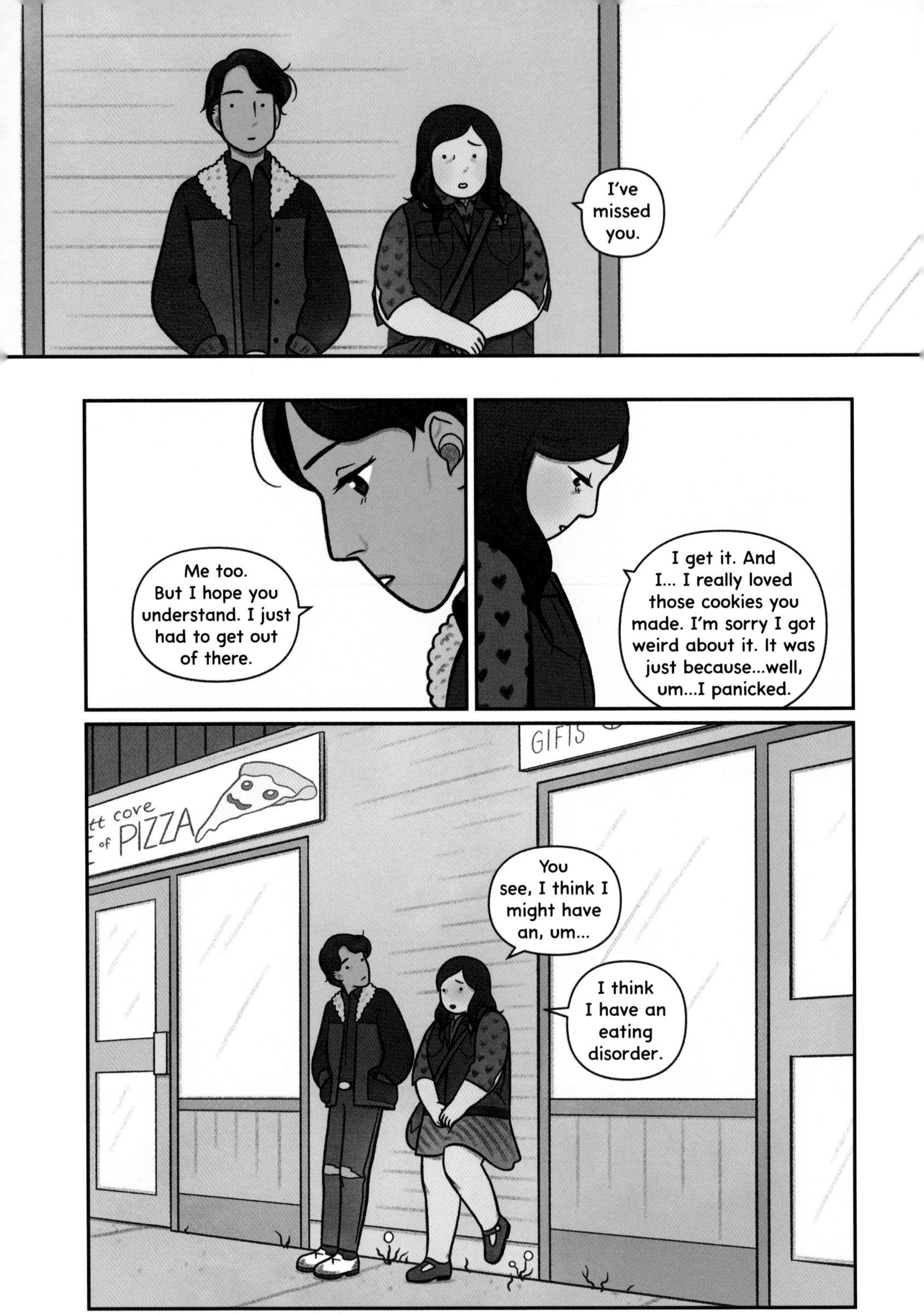
I've missed you.
Me too. But I hope you understand. I just had to get out of there.
I get it. And I... I really loved those cookies you made. I'm sorry I got weird about it. It was just because...well, um...I panicked.
PIZZA
You see, I think I might have an, um...
I think I have an eating disorder.

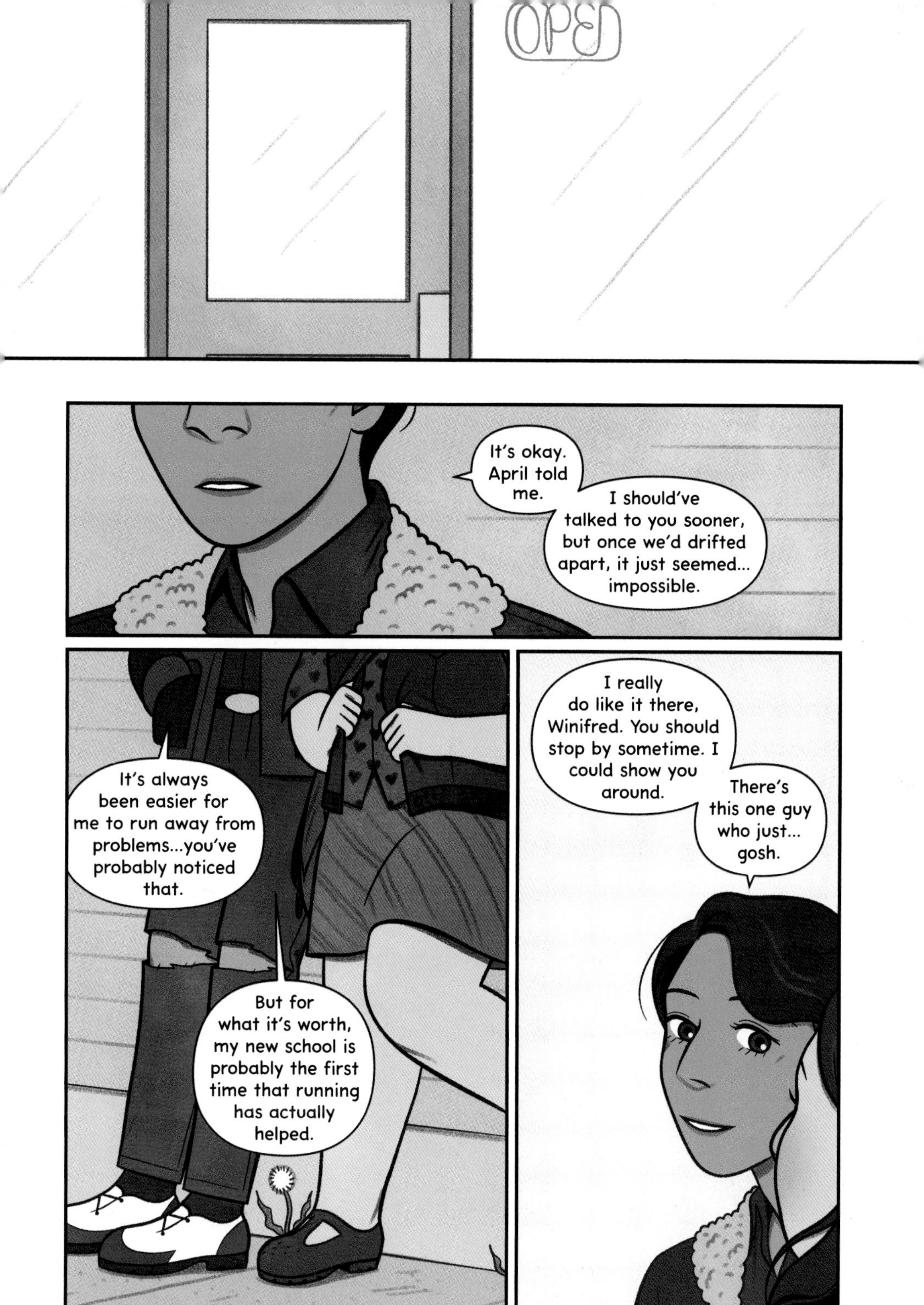
It's okay. April told me.
I should've talked to you sooner, but once we'd drifted apart, it just seemed... impossible.
It's always been easier for me to run away from problems...you've probably noticed that.
But for what it's worth, my new school is probably the first time that running has actually helped.
I really do like it there, Winifred. You should stop by sometime. I could show you around.
There's this one guy who just... gosh.

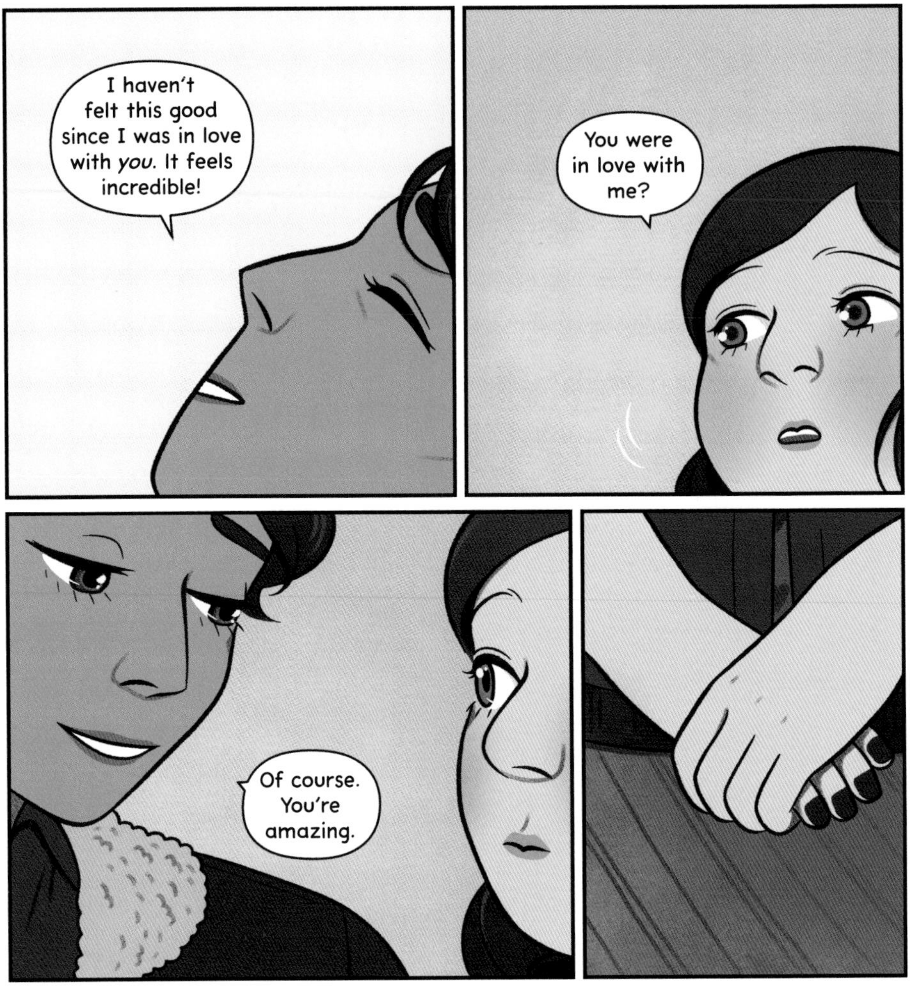
I haven't felt this good since I was in love with *you*. It feels incredible!
You were in love with me?
Of course. You're amazing.

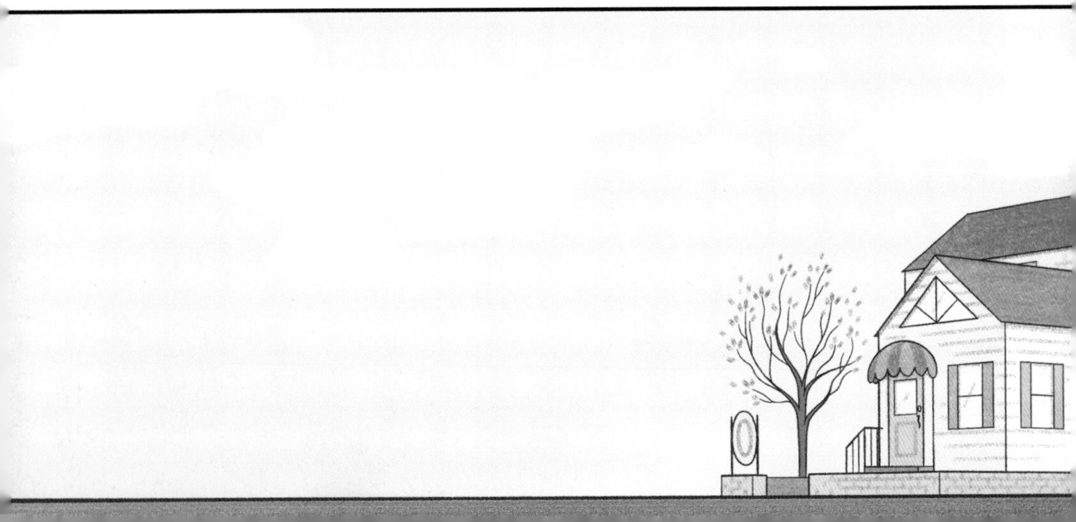

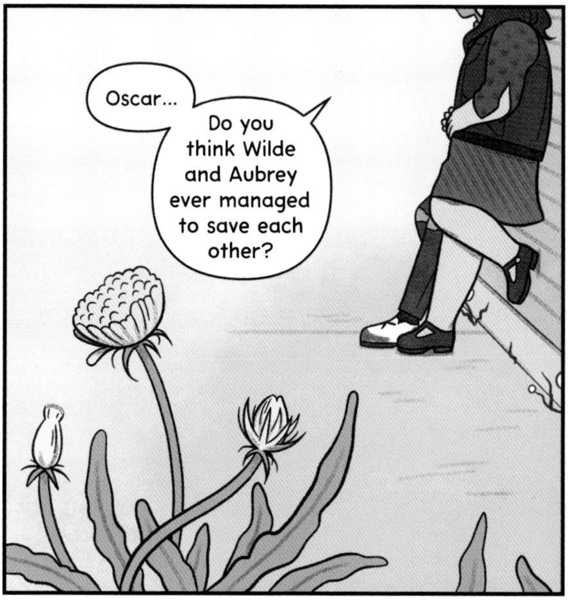
Oscar...
Do you think Wilde and Aubrey ever managed to save each other?

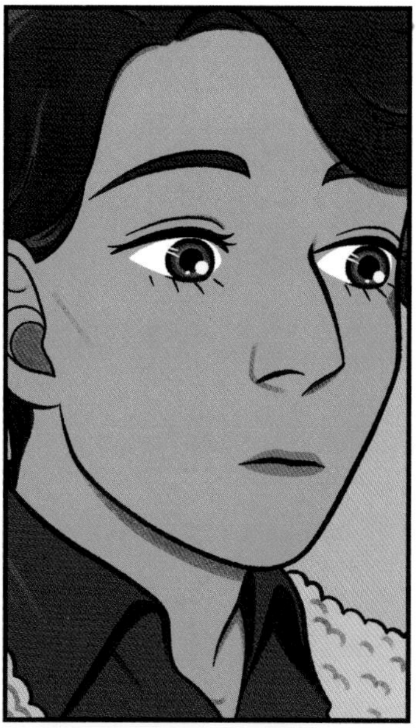

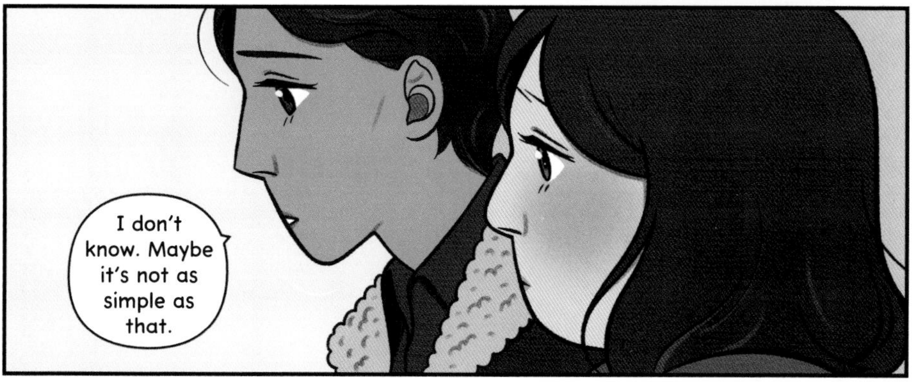
I don't know. Maybe it's not as simple as that.

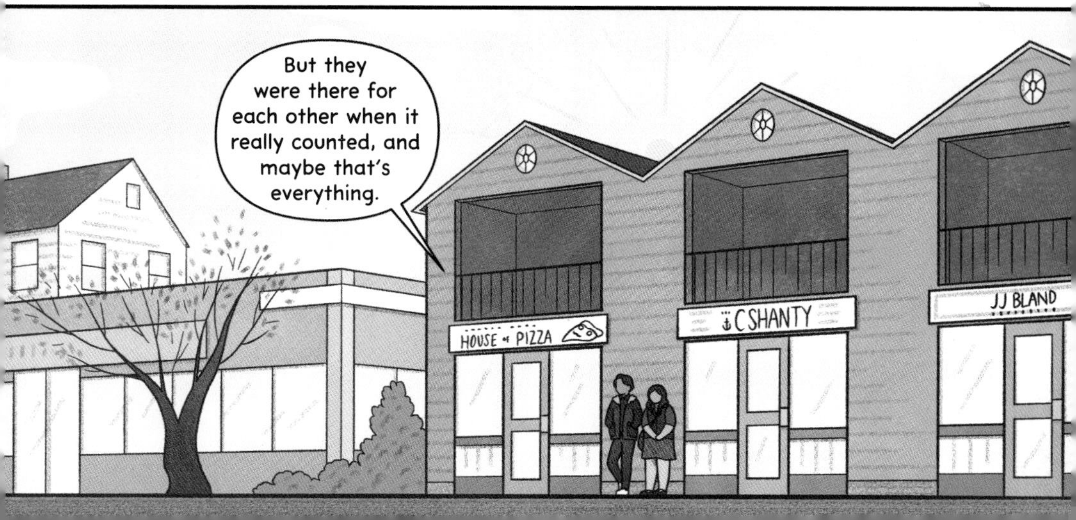
But they were there for each other when it really counted, and maybe that's everything.
HOUSE of PIZZA
C SHANTY
JJ BLAND

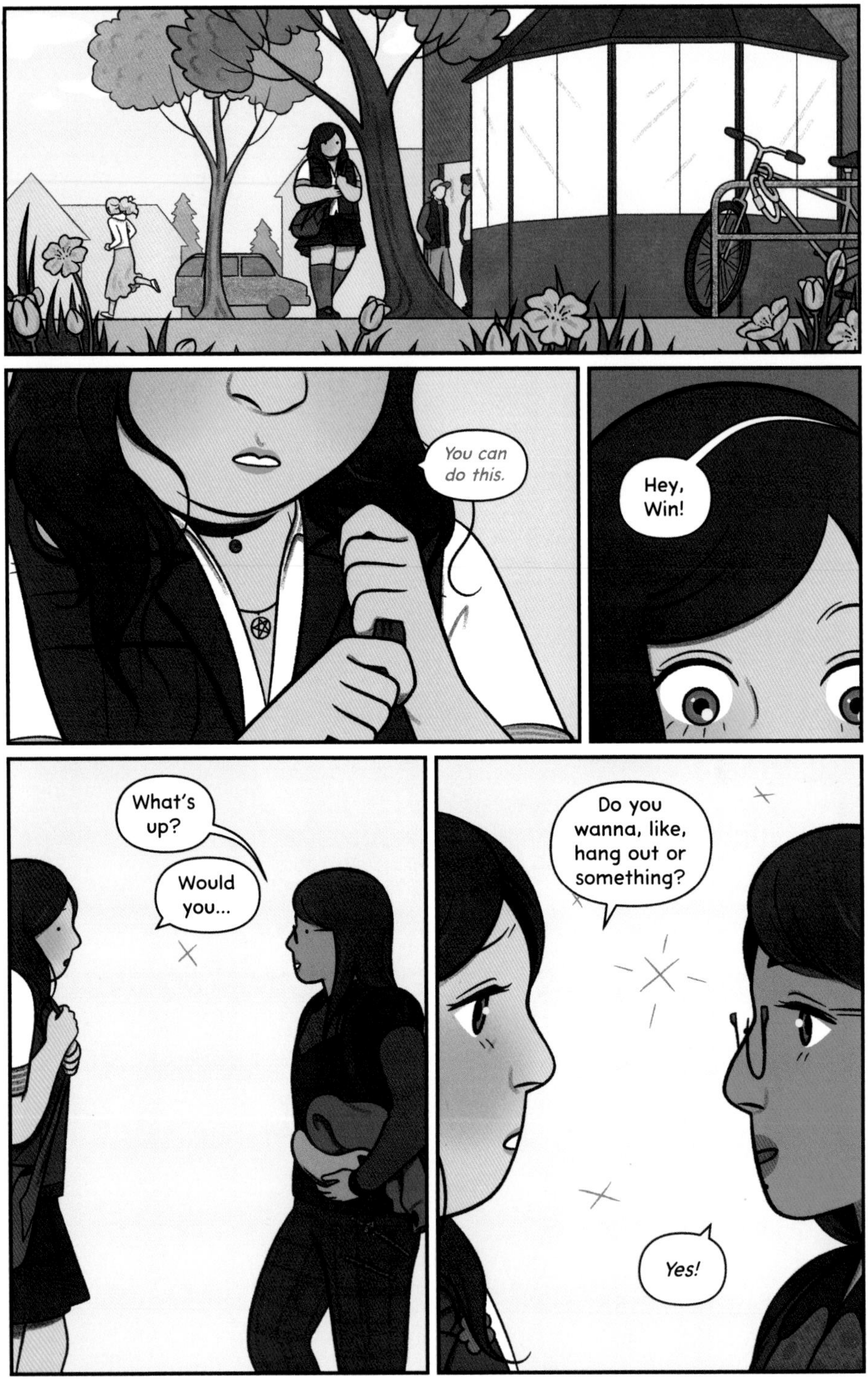
You can do this.
Hey, Win!
What's up?
Would you...
Do you wanna, like, hang out or something?
Yes!

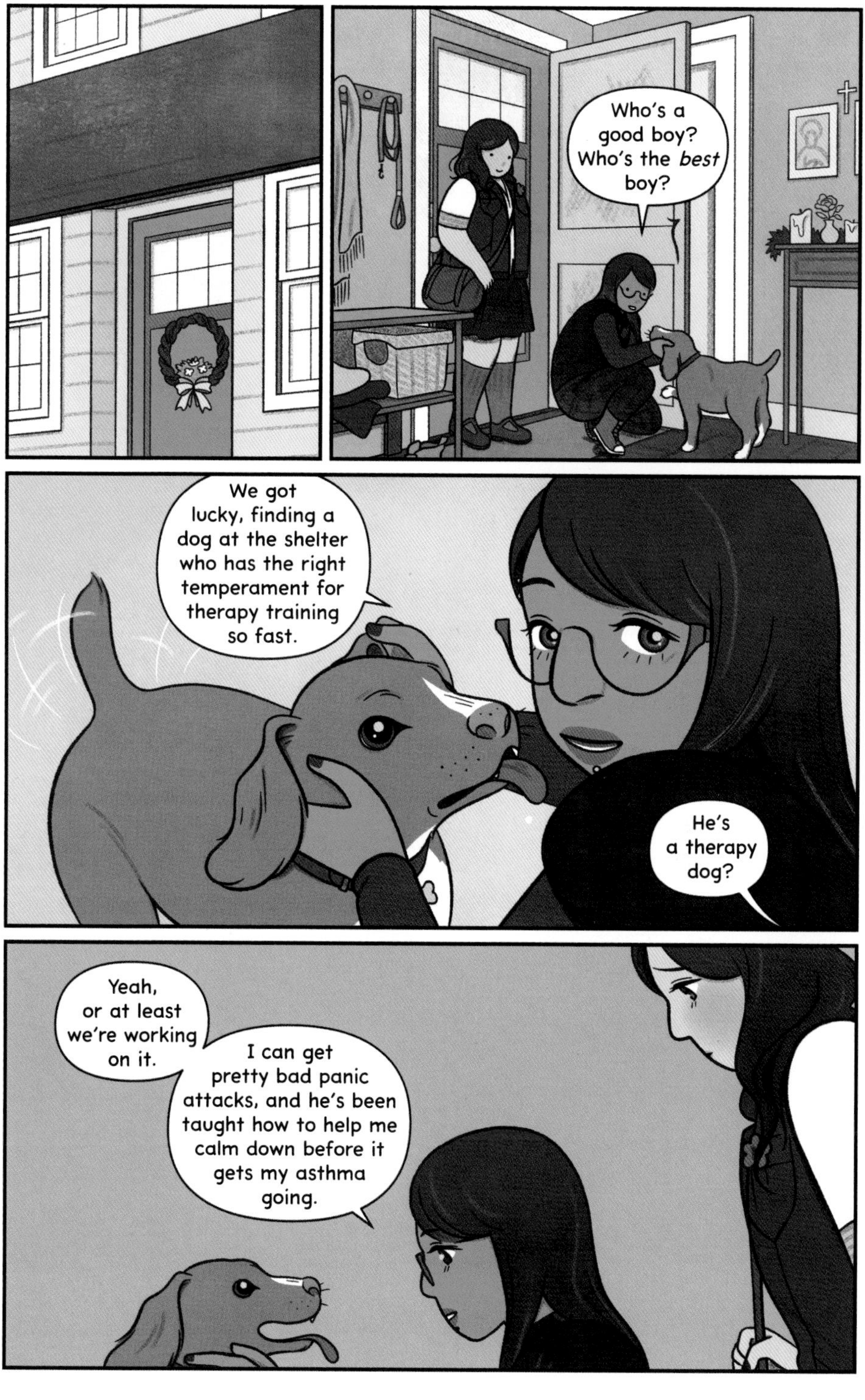
Who's a good boy? Who's the *best* boy?
We got lucky, finding a dog at the shelter who has the right temperament for therapy training so fast.
He's a therapy dog?
Yeah, or at least we're working on it.
I can get pretty bad panic attacks, and he's been taught how to help me calm down before it gets my asthma going.

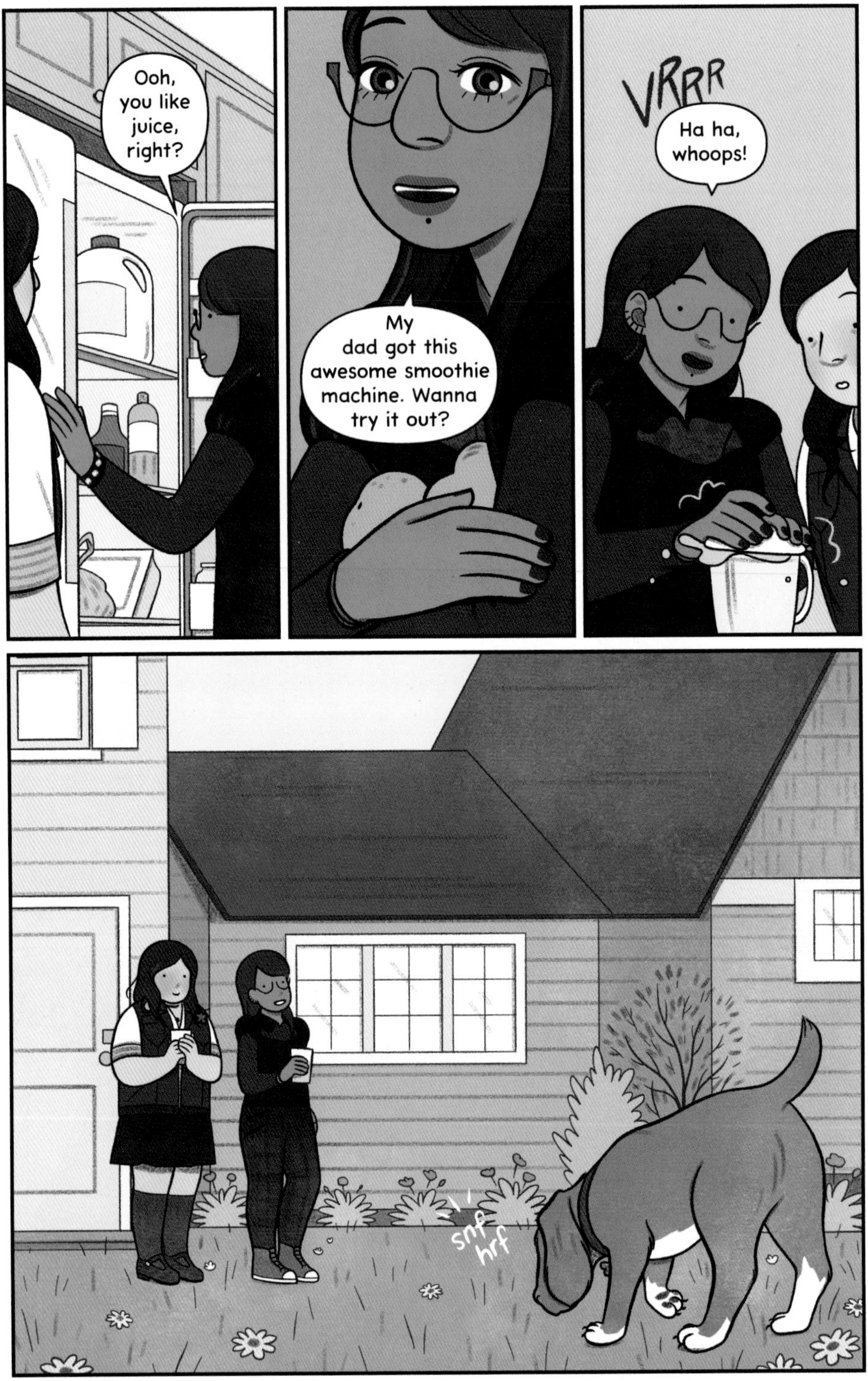
Ooh, you like juice, right?
My dad got this awesome smoothie machine. Wanna try it out?
VRRR
Ha ha, whoops!
snf hrf

In this one, I hear two of the female characters get to kiss!

But I'm afraid it's gonna take a million freaking volumes to get there.

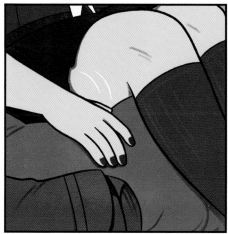

Hey, Tilly...

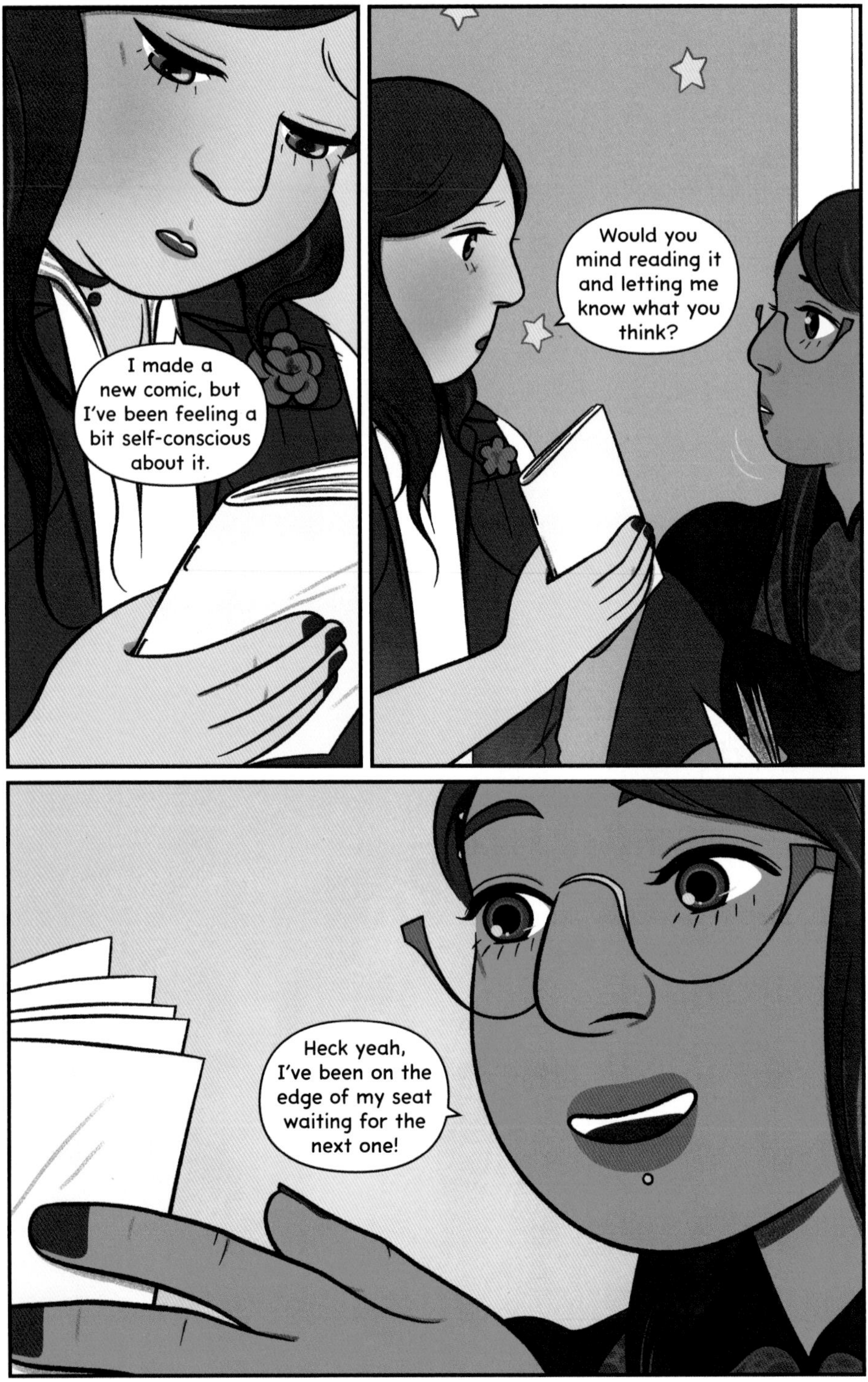
I made a new comic, but I've been feeling a bit self-conscious about it.
Would you mind reading it and letting me know what you think?
Heck yeah, I've been on the edge of my seat waiting for the next one!

gutterglimmers:
LADY OF THE
HOUNDS

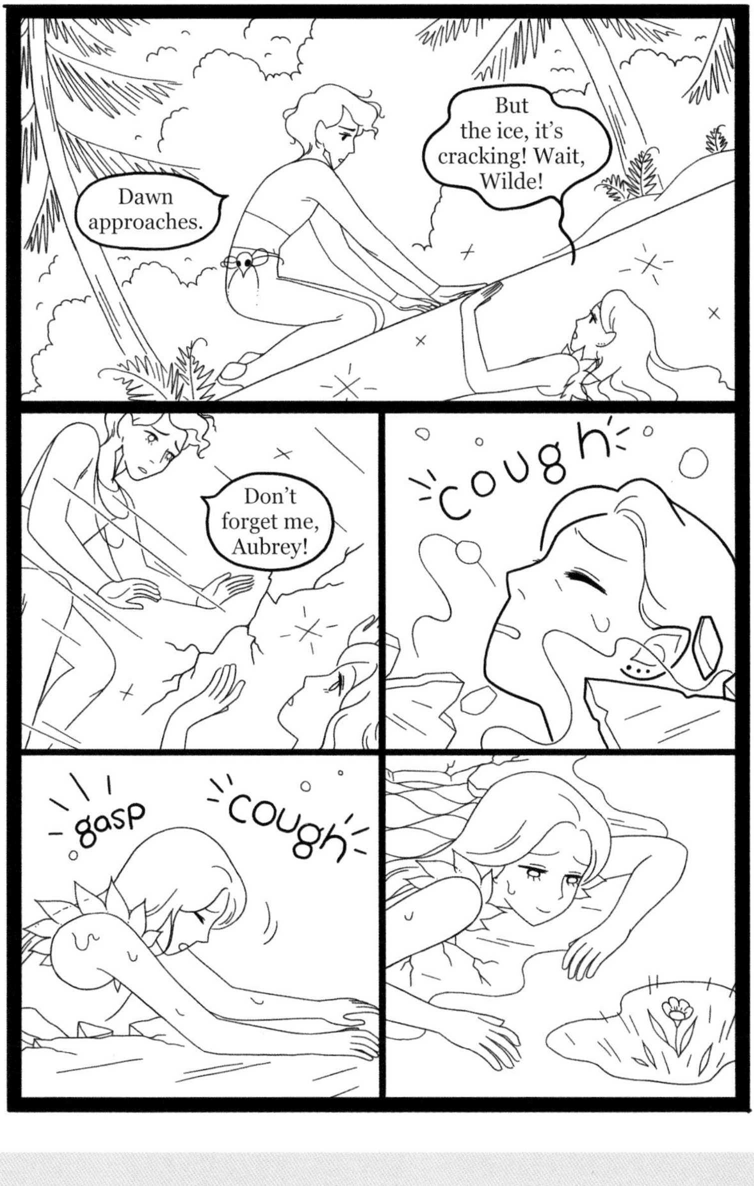
Dawn approaches.
But the ice, it's cracking! Wait, Wilde!
Don't forget me, Aubrey!
cough
gasp
cough

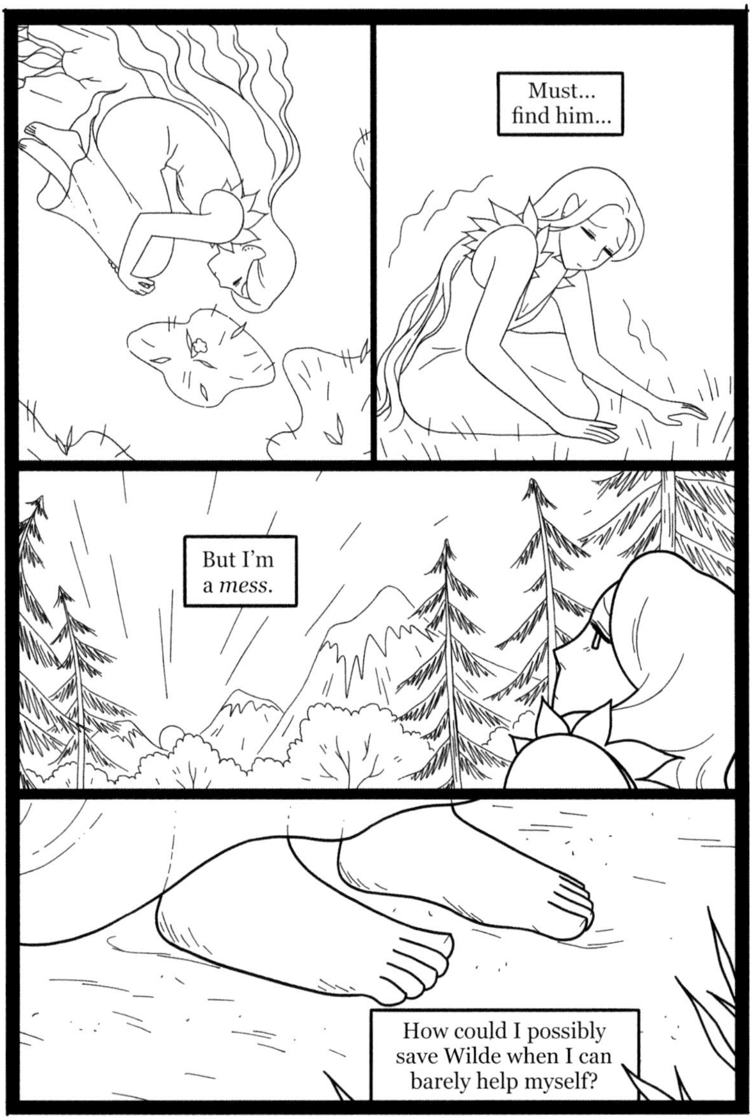
Must...
find him...
But I'm
a *mess*.
How could I possibly
save Wilde when I can
barely help myself?

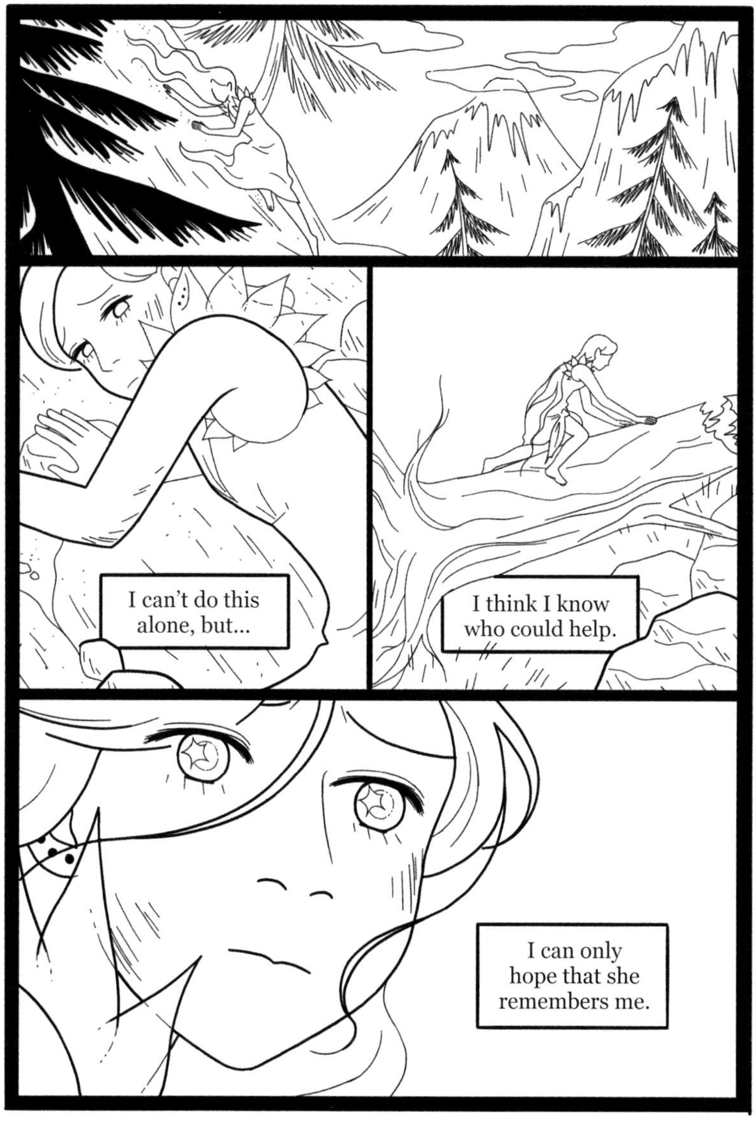
I can't do this alone, but...
I think I know who could help.
I can only hope that she remembers me.

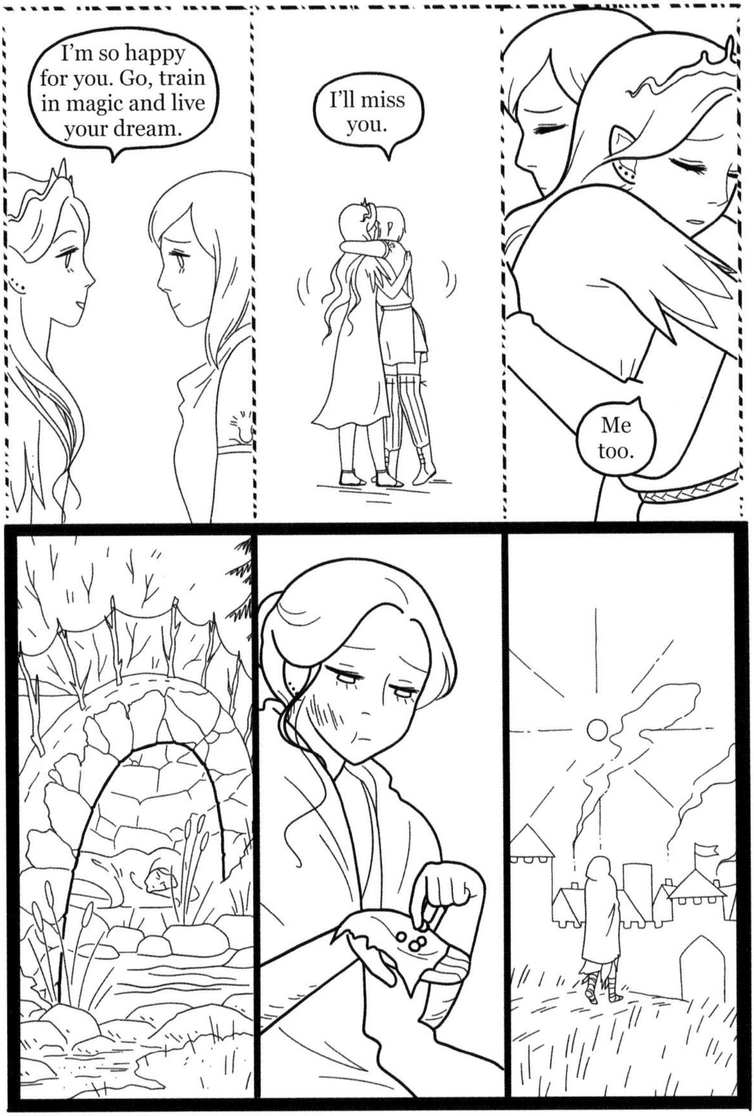
I'm so happy for you. Go, train in magic and live your dream.
I'll miss you.
Me too.

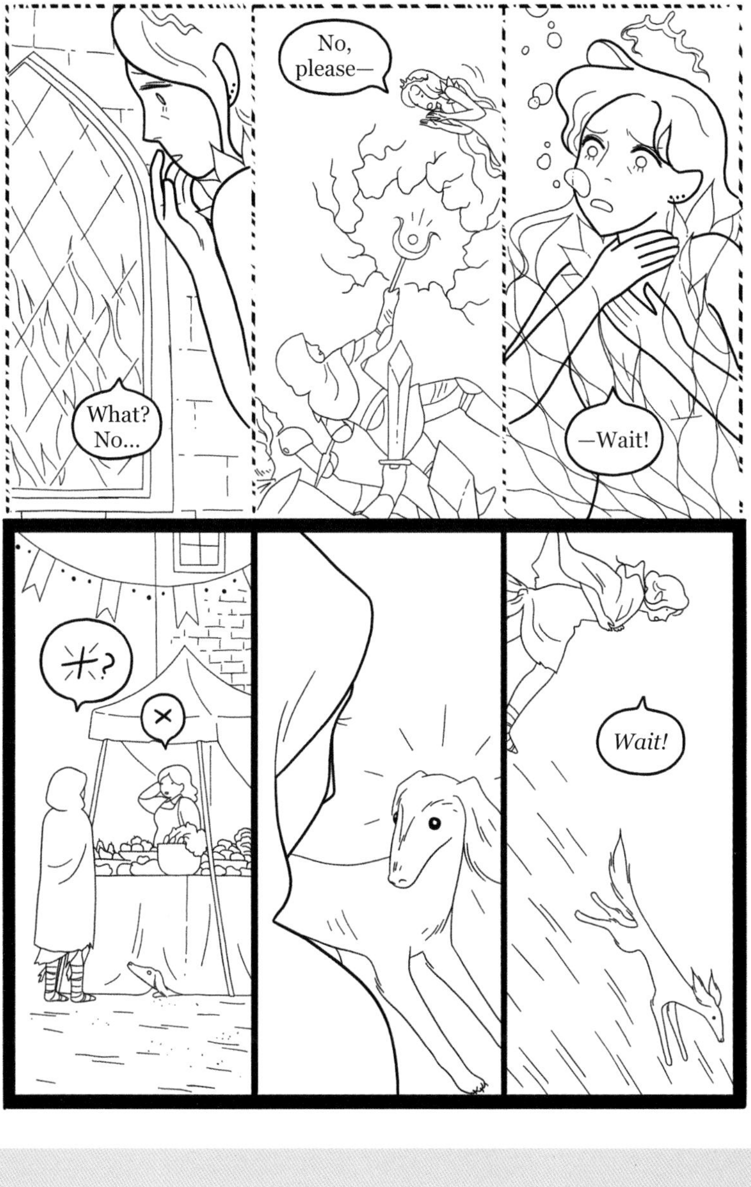
What? No...
No, please—
—Wait!
Wait!

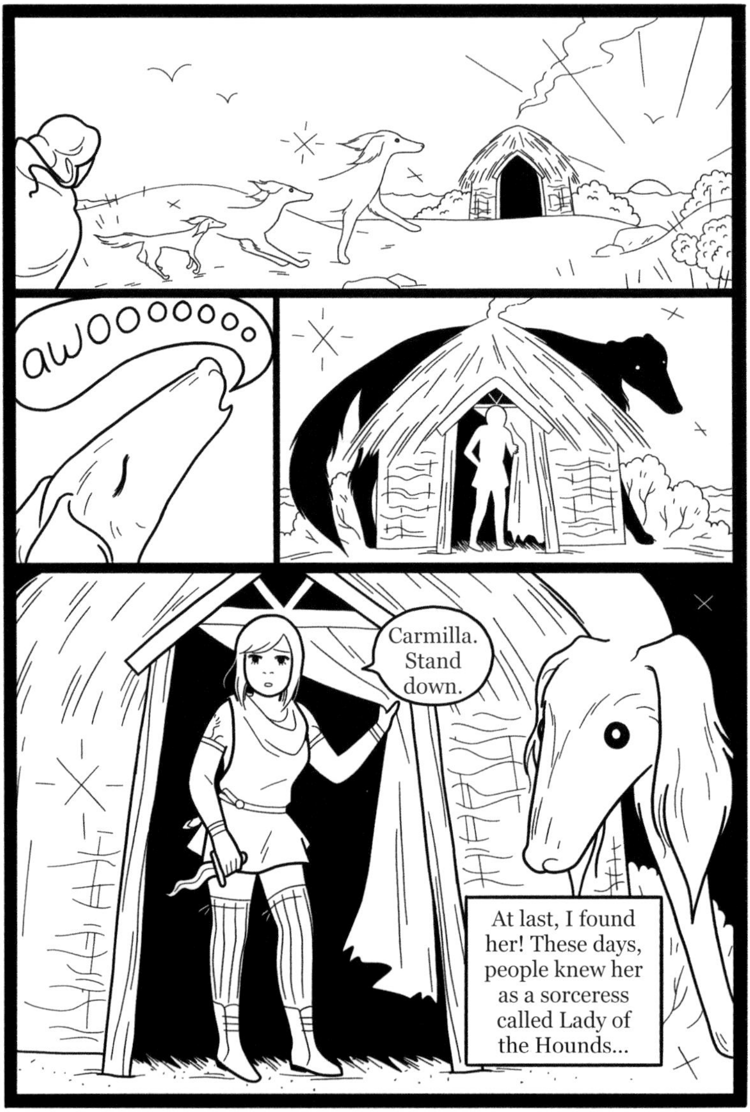
awooooooo
Carmilla. Stand down.
At last, I found her! These days, people knew her as a sorceress called Lady of the Hounds...

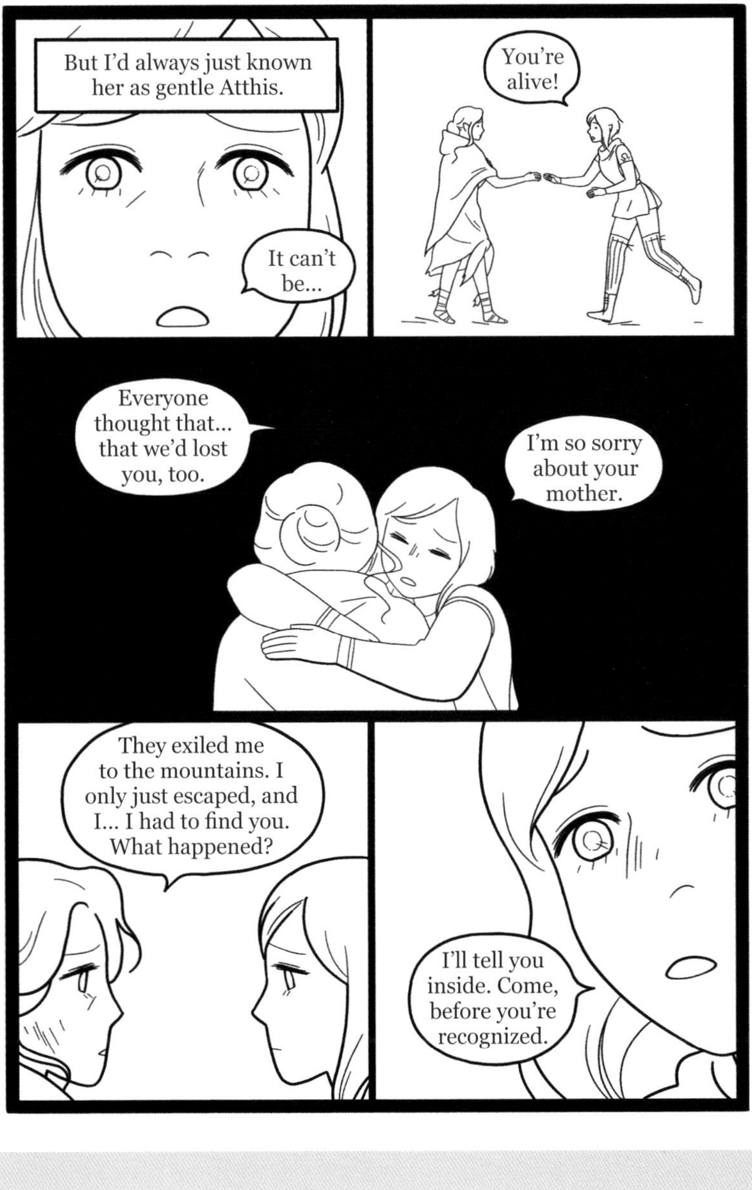
But I'd always just known her as gentle Atthis.
It can't be...
You're alive!
Everyone thought that... that we'd lost you, too.
I'm so sorry about your mother.
They exiled me to the mountains. I only just escaped, and I... I had to find you. What happened?
I'll tell you inside. Come, before you're recognized.

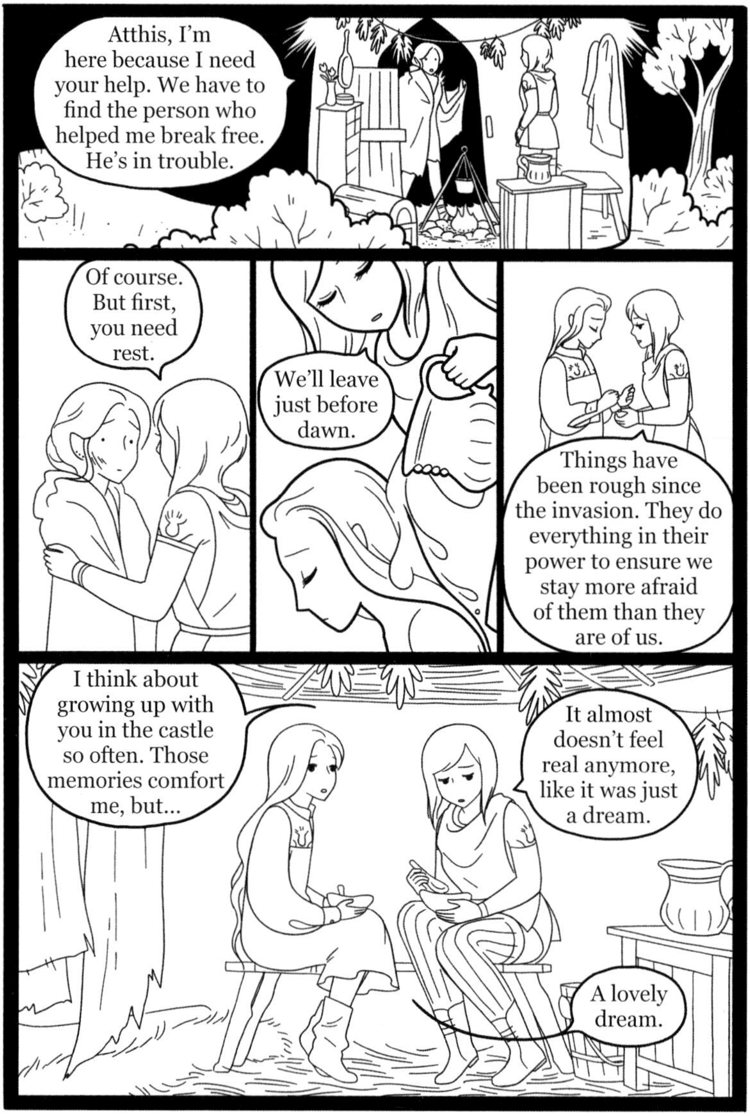
Atthis, I'm here because I need your help. We have to find the person who helped me break free. He's in trouble.
Of course. But first, you need rest.
We'll leave just before dawn.
Things have been rough since the invasion. They do everything in their power to ensure we stay more afraid of them than they are of us.
I think about growing up with you in the castle so often. Those memories comfort me, but...
It almost doesn't feel real anymore, like it was just a dream.
A lovely dream.

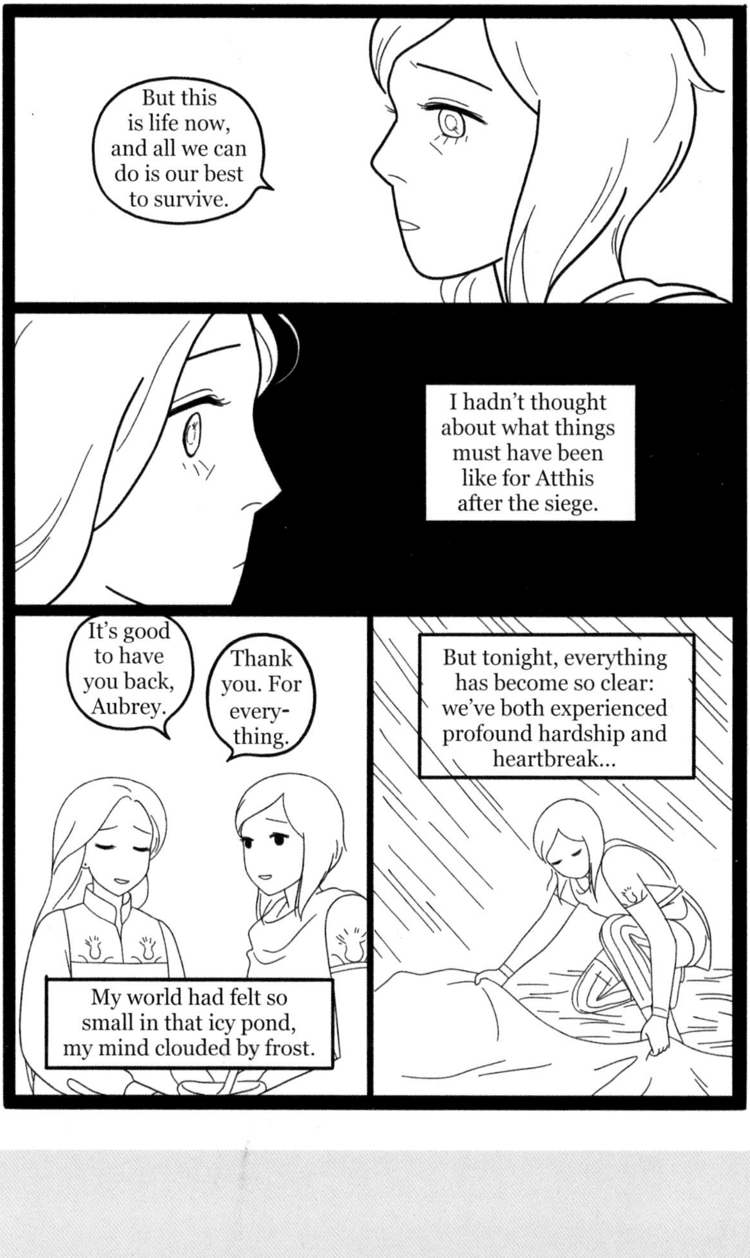

But this is life now, and all we can do is our best to survive.
I hadn't thought about what things must have been like for Atthis after the siege.
It's good to have you back, Aubrey.
Thank you. For every-thing.
My world had felt so small in that icy pond, my mind clouded by frost.
But tonight, everything has become so clear: we've both experienced profound hardship and heartbreak...

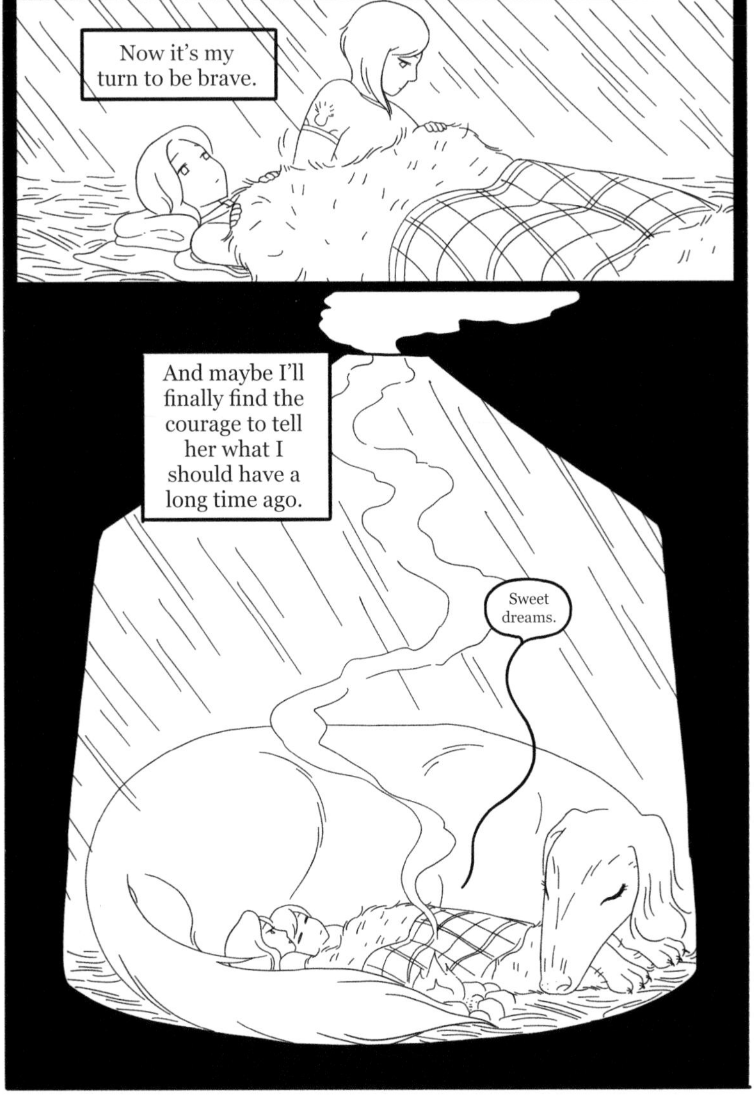
Now it's my turn to be brave.
And maybe I'll finally find the courage to tell her what I should have a long time ago.
Sweet dreams.

Written and Drawn by Win
Copyright 2003

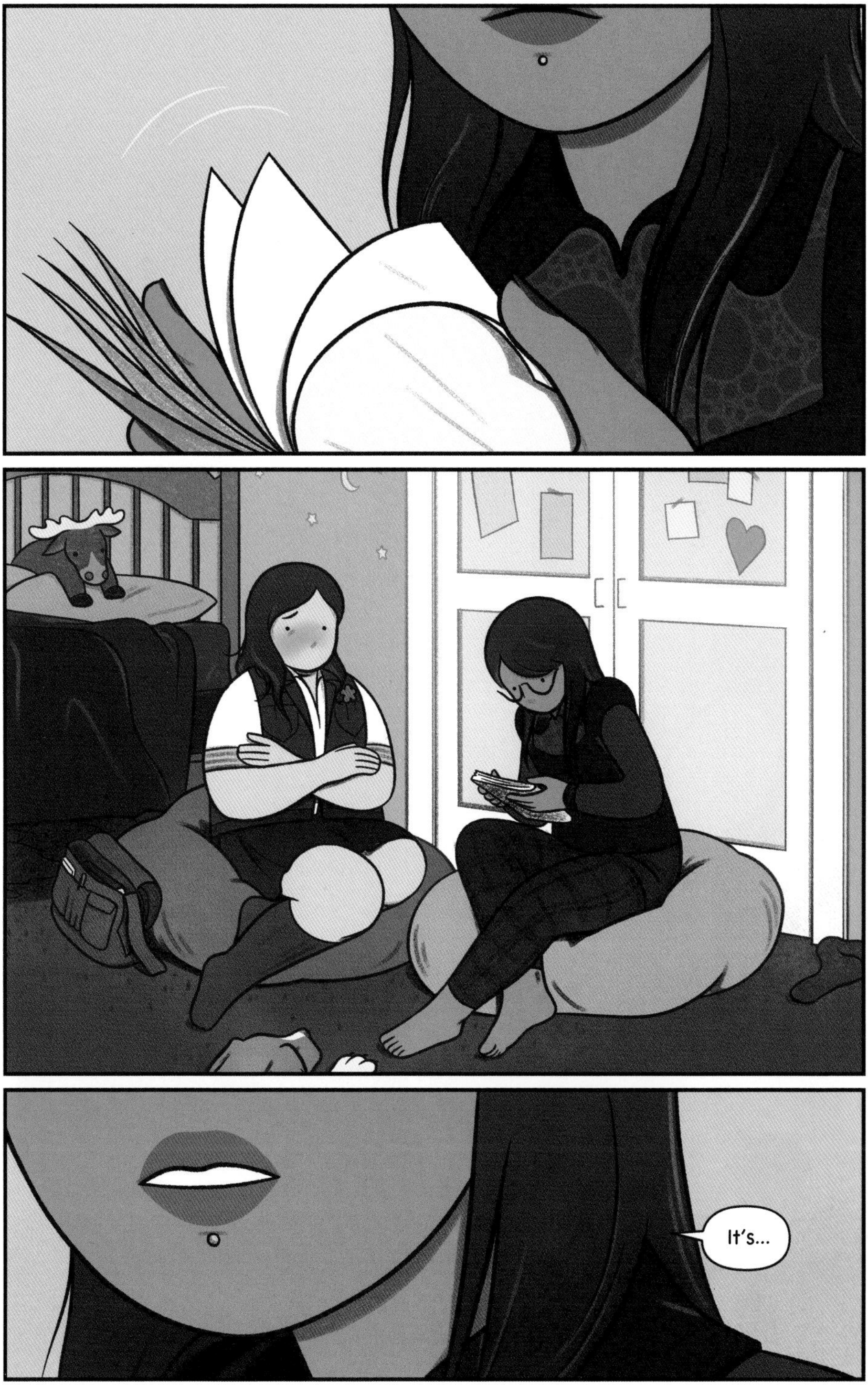
It's...

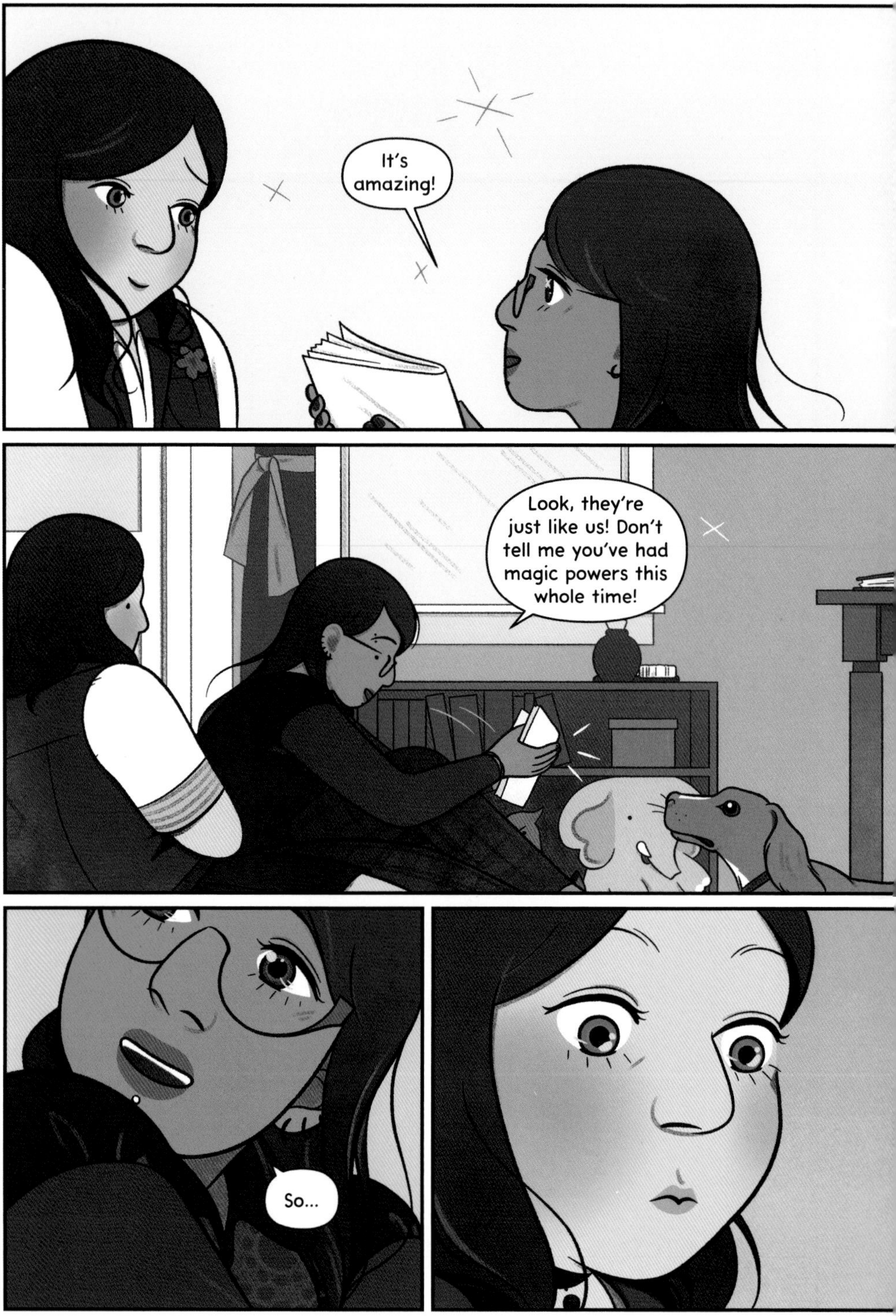
It's amazing!
Look, they're just like us! Don't tell me you've had magic powers this whole time!
So...

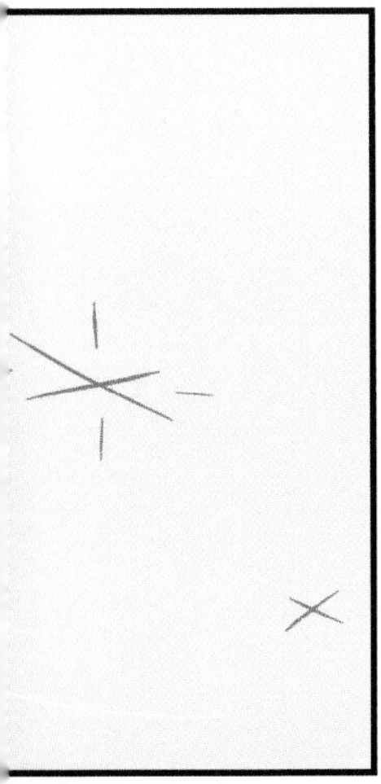
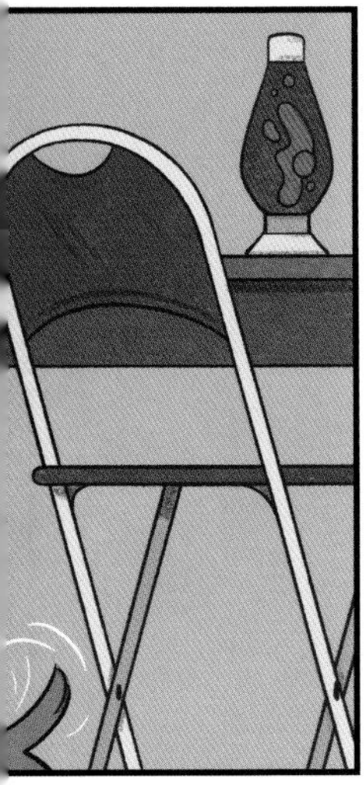
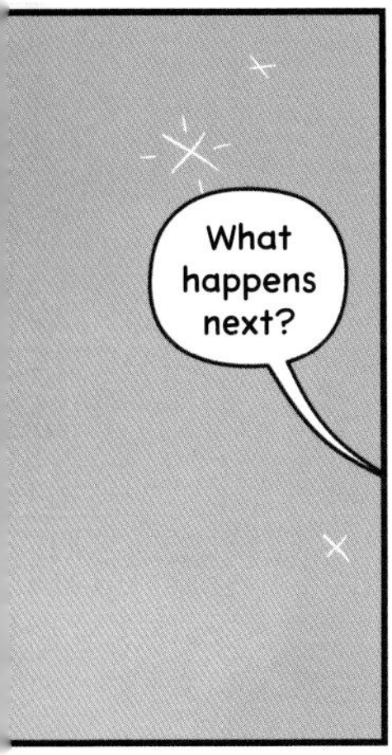
What happens next?
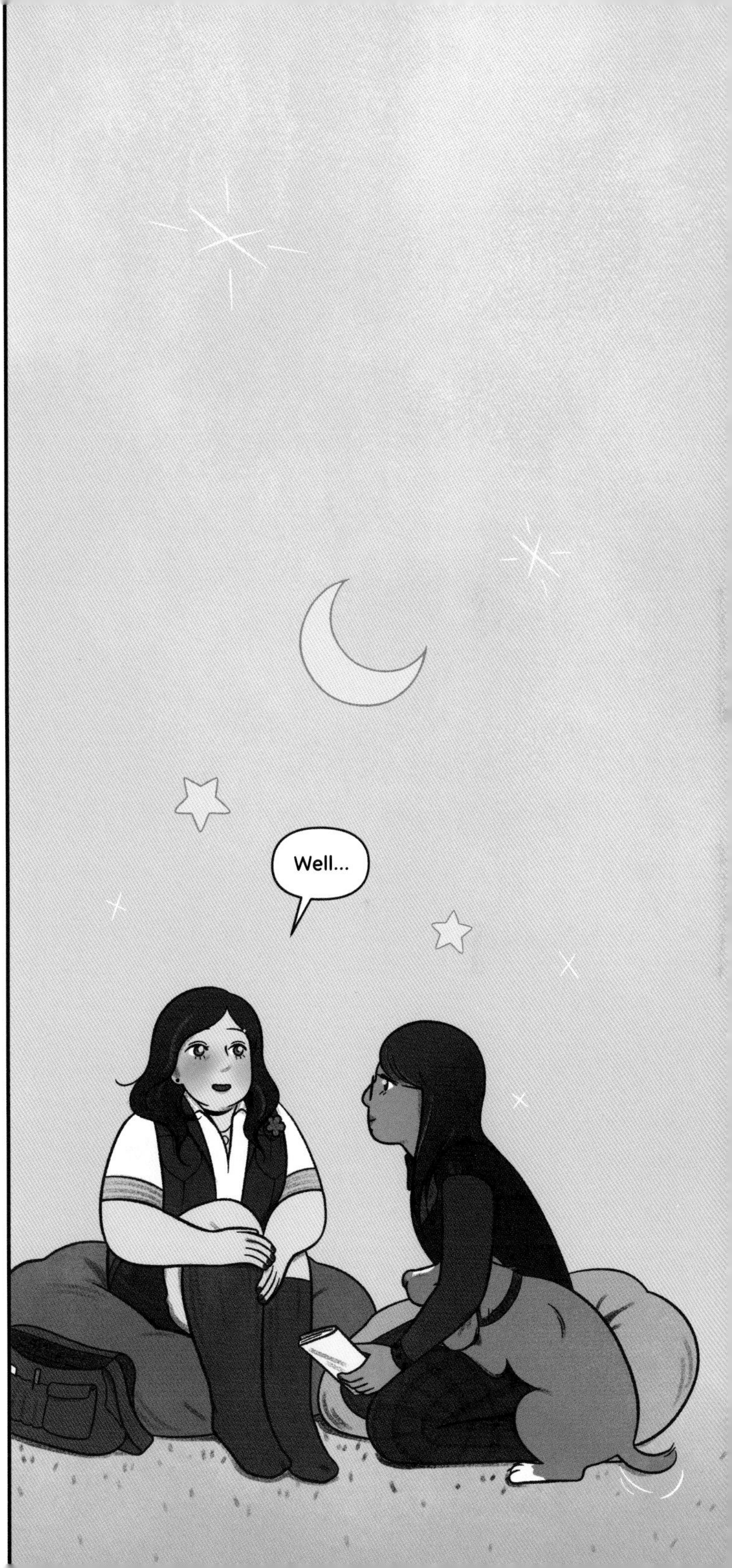
Well...

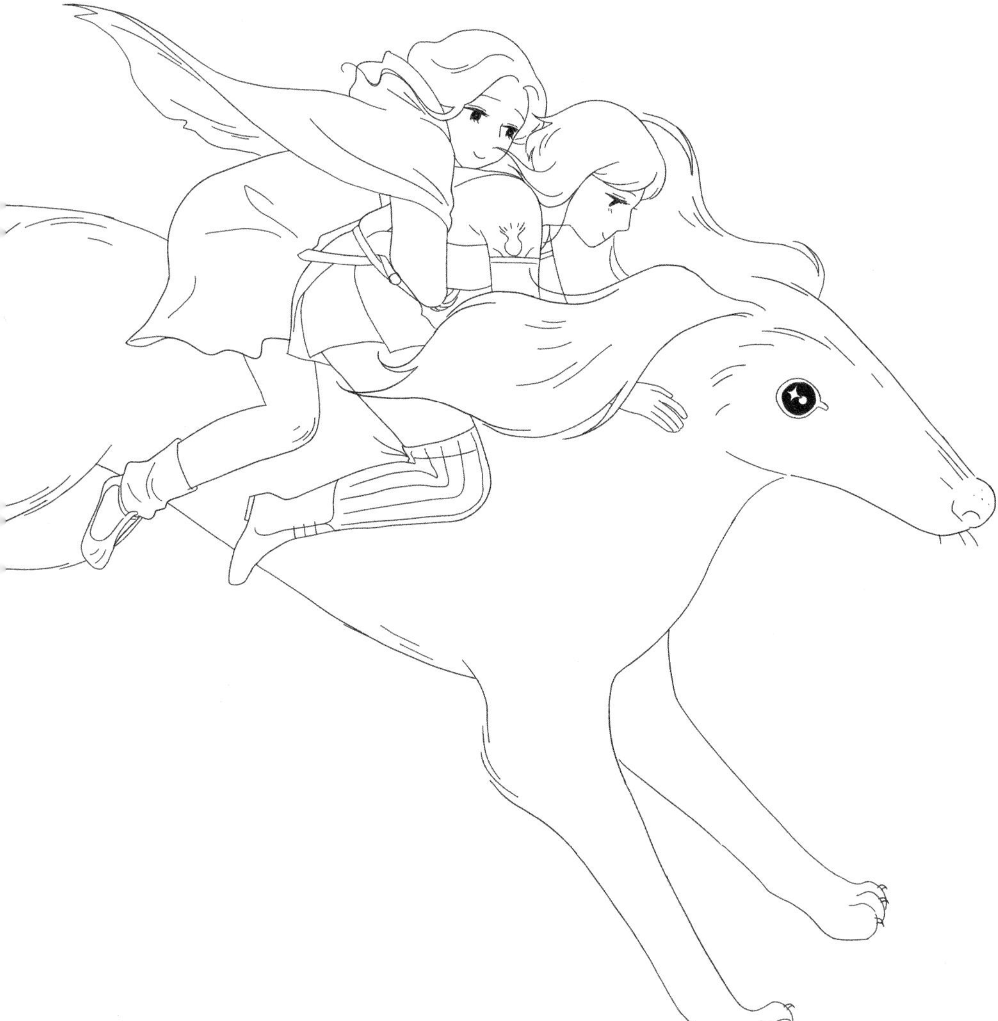

acknowledgments

Heartfelt appreciation for my understanding spouse, my family, and my friends. I couldn't make books without your care and support. I love you.

author's note

The Greatest Thing is a fictional story inspired by some experiences I had in high school. Characters like Oscar and April aren't exact replicas of my friends from that time but rather new creations that encapsulate meaningful impressions left on me by people I loved as a teenager.

But Winifred is just me, as much as my flawed memories allow. Her feelings and successes and mistakes are all things I went through when I was fifteen myself. This is my story as much as it is hers.

This book is my gift to the young me, to Win, and to anyone like her. I hope that if you feel alone, this story can be there for you but also that you find glimmers of hope in your own life. You deserve happiness. It just might take some time and effort to get there sometimes. And you're never as alone as you think you are.

resources

If you ever feel hopeless or you notice someone else is struggling, please seek help. Talk to your friends, confide in an adult you trust, and reach out to organizations who understand your situation.

The Trevor Project, thetrevorproject.org
>Trevor offers trained counselors and peer support for LGBTQIA2S+ youths in the form of a telephone hotline, texting and chat options, and a specialized social network. Their website features a robust assortment of resources for all sorts of related issues, including questions you may have about mental health and managing life at school.

National Suicide Prevention Lifeline, suicidepreventionlifeline.org
>NSPL provides a confidential telephone hotline and online text chat to support people who are in distress or who need resources to help others. They offer Spanish-language and d/Deaf-accessible options.

National Eating Disorders Association, nationaleatingdisorders.org
>NEDA includes a support hotline, text chat, online text chat, and listing of resources to help people find treatment for eating disorders.

A quick internet search for your region plus keywords relating to your problems can help you find local support groups and organizations who may be able to offer more specialized, face-to-face assistance.

But it's also important to know that if you or someone you know is ever in serious distress and needs urgent help, you should call 911 or seek other emergency/crisis services right away.

Take care. You are loved.

my zines

My guidance counselor made good on his promise to motivate me with comics. I still wanted to graduate early, but I had floundered in chemistry and dropped it to save my GPA, which meant I needed to make up an entire year in science. My counselor found me a spot in an experimental class, where a teacher was helping struggling students find passion in science with interest-based projects. They even agreed to let me double up for an entire year of credit in one semester.

Burnouts played with fire, cheerleaders learned about exercise biology, and then there was me. My teacher introduced me to the woman who ran the printing press for the school district, and she spent the semester teaching me how offset lithography works. I wrote and drew comics in my independent study in art, then in science class I made big metal printing plates for my zine and ran them through the press. My local comic shop, Casablanca Comics, invited me to sell the final product. It meant everything to me that people took me seriously as a cartoonist, and I continued making comics afterward, turning back to photocopying after class ended.

I was able to finish high school a semester early but still stopped by every other Friday until graduation to help edit the literary magazine. I spent that spring working weekends to save toward college and spending weekdays developing my drawing and writing skills. I got to treat my passion like it was my job for those few months, and that set me up to become the author I am today. Here's a peek at the zine I made for that class!

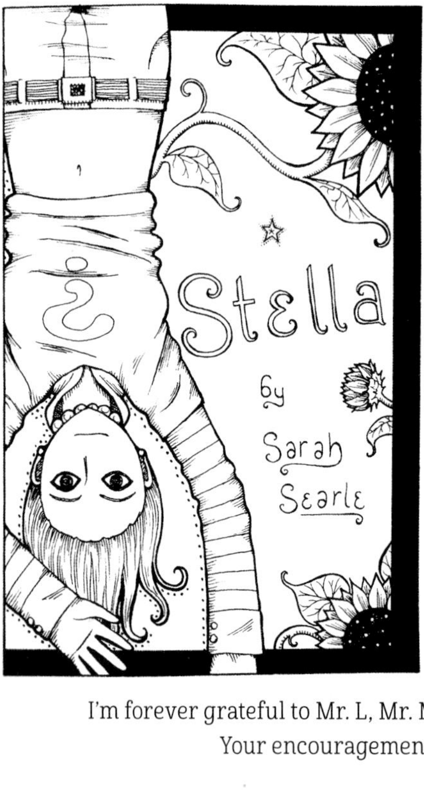
Stella
by
Sarah
Searle

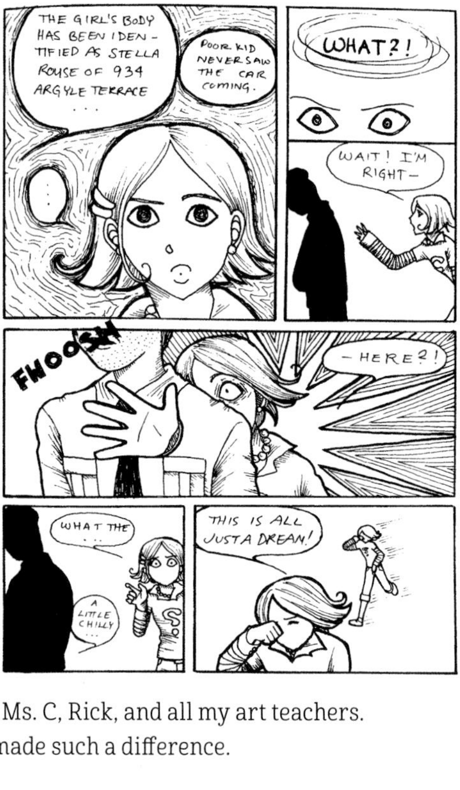
THE GIRL'S BODY HAS BEEN IDEN-TIFIED AS STELLA ROUSE OF 934 ARGYLE TERRACE ...
POOR KID NEVER SAW THE CAR COMING.
WHAT?!
WAIT! I'M RIGHT—
FWOOSH
—HERE?!
WHAT THE ...
A LITTLE CHILLY ...
THIS IS ALL JUST A DREAM!

I'm forever grateful to Mr. L, Mr. M, Ms. C, Rick, and all my art teachers.
Your encouragement made such a difference.